Poems and Short Stories

THE COMPLETE WORKS OF SANGHARAKSHITA include all his previously published work, as well as talks, seminars, and writings published here for the first time. The collection represents the definitive edition of his life's work as Buddhist writer and teacher. For further details, including the contents of each volume, please turn to the 'Guide' on pp.635–43.

FOUNDATION

1 A Survey of Buddhism / The Buddha's Noble Eightfold Path
2 The Three Jewels I
3 The Three Jewels II
4 The Bodhisattva Ideal
5 The Purpose and Practice of Buddhist Meditation
6 The Essential Sangharakshita

INDIA

7   Crossing the Stream: India Writings I
8   Beating the Dharma Drum: India Writings II
9   Dr Ambedkar and the Revival of Buddhism I
10 Dr Ambedkar and the Revival of Buddhism II

THE WEST

11 A New Buddhist Movement I
12 A New Buddhist Movement II
13 Eastern and Western Traditions

COMMENTARY

14 The Eternal Legacy / Wisdom Beyond Words
15 Pāli Canon Teachings and Translations
16 Mahāyāna Myths and Stories
17 Wisdom Teachings of the Mahāyāna
18 Milarepa and the Art of Discipleship I
19 Milarepa and the Art of Discipleship II

MEMOIRS

20 The Rainbow Road from Tooting Broadway to Kalimpong
21 Facing Mount Kanchenjunga
22 In the Sign of the Golden Wheel
23 Moving Against the Stream
24 Through Buddhist Eyes

POETRY AND THE ARTS

25 Poems and Short Stories
26 Aphorisms and the Arts
27 Concordance and Appendices

COMPLETE WORKS 25 **POETRY AND THE ARTS**

Sangharakshita
Poems and Short Stories

EDITED BY VIDYADEVI

Windhorse Publications
17e Sturton Street
Cambridge
CB1 2SN
UK

info@windhorsepublications.com
www.windhorsepublications.com

© Sangharakshita, 2018
First published in 2020.

The right of Sangharakshita to be identified as the author of this work has been asserted by him in accordance with the Copyright, Designs and Patents Act 1988.

Cover design by Dhammarati
Cover image: Front and back flap: *The Starry Night*, September 1889, Vincent van Gogh, Creative Commons.

Typesetting and layout by Tarajyoti
Printed by Bell & Bain Ltd, Glasgow

British Library Cataloguing in Publication Data:
A catalogue record for this book is available from the British Library.

ISBN 978-1-911407-46-1 (hardback)
ISBN 978-1-911407-47-8 (paperback)

CONTENTS

Editor's Preface   xxi
Instead of a Foreword, Padmavajra   xxiv
A Guide for the New Reader of Sangharakshita's Poetry,
    Vishvantara   xxxii
The Literary Influences on Sangharakshita's Poetry,
    Vishvapani   xliv

POEMS ARE STRANGE THINGS   1

1   Standing on Holy Ground   3
2   Footprints of Delight   22
3   The Whole World was a Poem   35

THE POETRY INTERVIEWS: SANGHARAKSHITA
IN CONVERSATION WITH SADDHANANDI   37

Introduction   39
1   Meditation   41
2   An Apology   50
3   The Family Reunion   60
4   The Root Speaks   71
5   Advent   79
6   The Mask   88

7 Love and Duty   97
8 The Bodhisattva's Reply   111
9 'In the Woods are Many More'   130
10 Four Gifts   138

POEMS   149

PART I: SHORTER POEMS   153

London in Wartime   155
Ruba'i   156
The Rain of Dharma   156
The River   157
Before an Image of the Buddha   158
The Ever-Beating Heart   159
Dāna Pāramī   160
Systole and Diastole   162
Lines   163
'Water From the Thawed-Out Snow…'   164
To Chenrezi   164
The Taoist Teacher   165
To a Political Friend   166
Music at Night   167
Meditation   167
The Moon of Beauty   168
The Wheel of Dharma   169
The Wandering Singer   170
The Clouded Dragon   172
Before an Image of the Buddha   173
The Parable of the Plough   174
'Above Me Broods…'   175
Night Thoughts   176
Rain   177
The Four Sights   178
Aspiration   181
Sonnet   181
The Sun-Path   182
Himalayan Sages   183

Wesak Joy   184
Advent   184
Secret Wings   185
The Tramp   186
Sri Pada   187
Wesak Thoughts   188
The Poet's Reply   192
The Word of the Buddha   193
'Tired of the Crimson Curtain...'   194
Peace   195
To the Recumbent Buddha   196
The Citadel   197
The Face of Silence   198
The Wounded Swan   200
The Lord of Compassion   202
Truth, Love, Life and Man   203
The Message of the Bowl   204
The White Calf   206
Tendai   207
The Lotus of Compassion   208
Buddhaṃ Saraṇaṃ Gacchāmi   209
The Birthplace of Compassion   210
The Only Way   210
On the Brink   211
Rhymed Tanka   211
Village India   212
The Alms of Compassion   213
The Fragrance of Compassion   214
Invocation   214
The Unseen Flower   215
The Lamp of Compassion   215
Messengers From Tibet   216
Bamboos   217
Rhymed Haiku   217
Mountains   218
'White Mist Drifts Down the Valley Dim...'   218
Stanzas   219
The Gardener   219

Kanchenjunga   219
Rhymed Haiku   219
The Bodhisattva   220
Life's Furnace   221
Frustration   221
Transience   221
Inaccessible   222
'The Ashes of all my Heartaches…'   222
Love's Austerity   223
'It is not Love that Seeks to Bind…'   223
The Evening Walk   224
Bamboo Orchids   224
Goldfish   225
The Secret   226
'Many Were the Friends…'   226
Yashodhara   228
Quatrain   228
The Root Speaks   229
Longing   229
'Forgive Me if I Have Stained…'   230
The Heart's No   230
Lines   231
Song   231
Lumbini   232
Plato's Reply   232
Animist   233
Maitreya   233
Rhymed Haiku   234
Rhymed Haiku   234
Rhymed Haiku   234
Rhymed Haiku   234
Rhymed Haiku   234
Buffaloes Being Driven to Market   235
The Charcoal-Burners   236
Tibetan Trumpets   237
No Word   237
'Up and Down the Gravel Path…'   238
Quatrain   238

Hieroglyphics   239
'I Think There Lives More Wisdom...'   239
Summer Afternoon   240
The Poet's Eye   240
Man's Way   240
'In the Woods are Many More'   241
Haiku   242
Haiku   242
The Survivor   242
Lines   242
Manifesto   243
Awakening   243
A Rainy Day in the Mountains   244
Reciprocity   245
The Abominable Snowman   246
Transformation   248
Argosies   249
Taking Refuge in the Buddha   250
The Tree of Wisdom   252
The Modern Bard   254
Winter in the Hills   255
Looking at the Moon on a Frosty Night   255
The Conquest of Māra   256
The Pioneer   256
Sonnet   257
Sonnet   258
Epitaph on Krishna, Princess Irene's Squirrel   258
On a Political Procession   258
Madrigal   259
Certainties   259
The Bodhisattva's Reply   260
Calcutta   262
Immensities   262
Nagarjunikonda   263
The Vase of Moonlight   264
The Stream of Stars   264
Nocturne   265
Joy in Flight   266

The Great Work 267
Lines 268
Elusive Beauty 269
Epigram 270
Stanzas 270
A Crumb From the Symposium 270
Kalinga 271
Defiance 271
The Quest 272
Quatrain 272
Sonnet 273
Rhymed Haiku 273
Possibilities 274
Nālandā Revisited 274
Quatrain 274
To Mañjuśrī 275
Hope 275
The Voice of Silence 276
Memory 276
Sonnet 277
Sonnet 277
Sonnet 278
Quatrain 278
Stanzas 278
The Cult of the Young Hero 279
Life and Death 280
Triolet 281
Quatrain 281
Quatrain 281
Couplet 281
A Life 282
Lepcha Song 283
Visiting the Taj Mahal at the Time of the Suez Canal Crisis and Seeing the Tombs of the Emperor Shah Jahan and Mumtaz Mahal 283
Stanzas 284
Spring – Winter 284
Study in Blue and White 284

Stanzas   285
Quatrains   285
Sappho   285
'My Soul Between the Feeling and the Thought…'   286
The Sangha   286
The Scholars   286
Quatrain   287
Quatrain   287
To ———   287
Quatrain   287
Stanzas   288
Epitaph on a 'Poem'   288
Couplet Haiku   289
In Praise of Water   289
Return Journey   290
Lines   290
Meditation On a Flame   291
The Young Hills   292
The Guardian Wall   293
Rhymed Haiku   294
Haiku   294
Quatrain   294
Siddhārtha's Dream   295
The Three Marks   295
The Buddha   296
Tibetan Refugee   297
To Shrimati Sophia Wadia in Honour of her Sixtieth Birthday   298
Three Couplet Haiku   300
Points of View   300
The People   301
Planting the Bodhi Tree   302
Spring   302
Waiting in the Car   303
Couplet Haiku   303
Stanzas   304
The Crystal Rosary   304
Poems For Four Friends   305

Ten Vignettes   306
After Meditation   307
'From the Ever-Faithful Present...'   308
The Martyrdom of Saint Sebastian   308
'I Want to Break Out...'   309
The Mask   309
Chinese Poems   310
Orpheus in the Underworld   312
St Jerome in the Desert   312
New   313
For the Record   314
Wish   315
Petals   316
Shells   317
Mother   318
Fourth Metamorphosis   319
Variations on a Mersey Sound I   320
Variations on a Mersey Sound II   321
Haiku   323
The Time Has Come...   323
Life is King   324
Dream   324
Chairlift   325
Mirrors   326
The Great Reader   327
Scapegoat   328
At the Barber's   329
In the New Forest   329
Criminals   330
Sangharakshita's Verses of Acknowledgement   331
Easter Retreat   333
The Ballad of Journeyman Death   334
Four Gifts   335
Sequence in a Strange Land   336
Song of the Windhorse   338
Homage to William Blake   340
May   341
I. M., J. and K.   342

'Every Day is a Good Day'   342
The Sunflower's Farewell   343
Autumn Vignette   343
Padmaloka   344
The Gods   345
Lines Written for the Dedication of the Shrine and the
    Opening of the London Buddhist Centre   346
The Priest's Dream   347
Too Late   347
The Sirens   348
Before Dawn   348
Hope   349
After Reading the Vimalakīrti-Nirdeśa   349
Sonnet   349
Alexandrines Perhaps   350
The Scapegoat   350
Verses   351
Haiku   352
Resurrection   352
Greenstone   353
Epigram   353
The Realms of Existence as Depicted in the Tibetan
    Wheel of Life   354
Lovelace Revisited   357
Snow-White Revisited   358
After Rilke   359
The Stricken Giant   359
'Blake Walked Among the Stones of Fire…'   360
The Dream   361
Lines Composed on Retreat During a Period of Silence   361
Reality Telegrams   362
St Francis and the Birds   366
Tuscany 1983   367
The Wondering Heart   368
Lines to Jayapushpa on her Return to Malaysia   369
Lines Composed on Acquiring 'The Works of Samuel Johnson,
    LL.D.', in Eleven Volumes, MDCCLXXXVII   370
Three Rubáiyát   372

A Wish 373
Yemen Revisited 373
Bhájá, 1983 374
Epigram on Molly the Medium 374
Poems on Paintings from the 'Genius of Venice' Exhibition
    at the Royal Academy 375
Minerva's Rebuke to Jean Cocteau 378
Three Epitaphs 379
The Golden Flower 379
Eight Tuscan Haiku 380
After Abū Sa'īd 381
The Ballad of the Return Journey 382
I. M., Tarashri 383
Neighbours 384
The People of Bethnal Green 385
Paradise Lost 386
The Oak and the Ivy 387
Betrayal 388
There is a Land More Lovely 389
Kalimpong 389
'A Man Was Walking Behind Me...' 390
'The Past is in the Mind...' 390
An Old Story 390
The Great Things of Guhyaloka 391
The Guru of Dharsendo 392
My Secret Garden 393
Time and Eternity 393
For P—— On Solitary Retreat 394
Birds and Their Gods 395
Mucalinda 398
Diptych 399
The Gods 400
Work and Play 400
Contraries 400
The Neoplatonists 401
My Pearl 401
People Like Things Labelled 402
Yesterday's Blossoms 402

The Teacher of Gods and Men   402
Crystal Ball   403
My Life   403
Four Haiku   403
Remembering the Poetry Reading   404
Ex Libris   404
Zen   404
London Bridge   404
On a Certain Author   405
To P—— in Prague   405
'Surely King Mark was Mad…'   406
The Poetry of Friendship   407
The Call of the Forest   408
The Angel in the House   410
Three Plumes   411
The Minor Poets   412
In Memory of Allen Ginsberg   413
Transmission   414
The Poet   414
The Dance of Death   415
After Visiting New Zealand   415
Revenge   416
Frozen Tulips   416
White Tārā   417
Splendor Solis   418
Padmasambhava   419
Letter to Ānanda   420
Donne's Bell   422
Revised Version   423
Epigrams   423
Guhyaloka: July 1998   424
Mother Goose Revisited   426
To C—   427
The Pilgrim   428
Lama Govinda in Capri   429
Dancing Round the Maypole   430
Then and Now   431
Queens Past and Present   432

East is East   432
Poet and Muse   433
The Double Root   433
The Warning Voice   434
Guhyaloka, September 1999   435
Remembering Arthadarshin   435
The Great Burning   436
The Listener   436
The Economic Argument   437
Justice and Pity   437
Three Arthurian Poems   438
The Six Elements Speak   440
In Krakow   442
To My Teacher, Chattrul Sangye Dorje   443
The Silver Spoon   444
To Michal, with a Photograph   444
I Am Sitting in the Late Afternoon Sunshine...   444
Epigrams   445
Haiku   446
An Apology   447
Written After Hearing a Radio Programme on Dementia   447
Mr Wireless   448
The Family Reunion   449
The Wind   450
The Brahmas and the Sages   451
The Twin Towers   452
The Beguiling of Merlin   452
To My Friend Paramartha   453
To Deji   453
Couplet   453
To Paramartha in London   454
A Fantasy   454
The Holiday   455
The Two Risks   456
The Bluebell Wood   456
Say Padmaloka   457
The Cosmic Dreamer   458

Shiva and the Love God   458
Salutation to the Lady From the Land of Snows   459
Up and Down the Gravel Path: an Update   460

PART II: LONGER POEMS   461

The Awakening of the Heart   463
Introduction to 'The Veil of Stars'   477
Argument Prefixed to 'The Veil of Stars'   481
The Veil of Stars   483
On Glastonbury Tor   499
The Caves of Bhájá   505
Hercules and the Birds   512

SHORT STORIES   521

Publication History   523
The Two Roses   524
The White Lotus   533
The Parable of the Talking Buddha   540
The Artist's Dream   544
The Antique Dealer   554
The Cave   569

Notes   587
Index of First Lines   597
Index of Subjects, Themes, and References   605
Index of Titles   630

A Guide to the *Complete Works* of Sangharakshita   635

EDITOR'S PREFACE

Welcome to this collection of Sangharakshita's poetry and short stories. Once upon a time, in a talk called 'My Relation to the Order', he compared his poems to a famously neglected fairytale character:

> At this point I would like to put in a good word for the Cinderella of my writings, that is, my poetry. Not that I expect you all to like my poetry. I am well aware that it can be characterized as traditional, neo-Georgian, and academic – though even as unacademic a person as Allen Ginsberg once assured me that in his view 'academic', as applied to poetry, was by no means a term of disparagement. But regardless of how my poetry is to be characterized – even regardless of whether it is really poetry – like all my writings the poems collected in *The Enchanted Heart* and *Conquering New Worlds* represent a communication by means of the written word, and particularly a communication to Order members. I would therefore like you to read my poetry, even to read it again and again. In my poetry, too, there is a great deal of me, perhaps more than there is in some of my prose writings, at least in certain respects. When you read my poetry you are not only very much in contact with me but in contact with me in a special kind of way.[1]

At the time I'm writing this, less than six months after Sangharakshita's death, Cinderella seems at last to have come to the ball. My sense is that his poetry has become more important to many people in the Triratna sangha, perhaps seeking contact with him in the 'special kind of way' that his poetry offers, as he suggested in that long-ago talk. It is in this atmosphere that this volume is being prepared for publication.

Sangharakshita gave his own modest assessment of his poetry in the preface of the 1978 collection *The Enchanted Heart*, and again in his *Complete Poems* which appeared in 1995:

> I have written poetry since I was eleven or twelve. Throughout my teens and well into my twenties, I wrote an enormous quantity of it, most of which has not survived. The poems appearing in this collection are selected from my published and unpublished output during the years 1941–1994, and represent all I would wish to preserve. Not that they are all necessarily worth preserving as poetry. Many of them, if not the majority, have only a biographical – even a sentimental – interest. They give expression to passing moods and fancies as well as to deeper experiences and insights. They also reflect my response to my surroundings. As such they constitute a sort of spiritual autobiography, sketchy indeed, but perhaps revealing, or at least suggesting, aspects of my life that would not otherwise be known. Some of my friends, I believe, may find an autobiography of this sort of greater interest than a more formal account. They may also enjoy, as poetry, those few poems which may be considered to rank as such. For the sake of these friends – old and new, Eastern and Western – I am bringing out this collection, and to them I affectionately dedicate it.

He wrote many more poems in the years that followed, some of which were published in *The Call of the Forest* and *A Moseley Miscellany*, and also included a few early poems not in any previous collection in *Early Writings*. In this *Complete Works* edition we have included all of these, and added a few more previously unpublished poems from the period 1944 to 1994 to add to the selection Sangharakshita himself made, on the basis that they too reveal, or at least suggest, aspects of his life that would not otherwise be known. To introduce the poems we have included the perspectives on them of three different readers: Padmavajra, who gives a very personal response; Vishvantara, who (with the help of Subhadramati) offers a reader's guide; and Vishvapani, who explores the literary influences on Sangharakshita's poetry. Many thanks to all of them for providing these three very different ways of approaching the poems.

The introductory essays are followed by some of Sangharakshita's own reflections on his poems. Quite late on in his years of public speaking he discovered that reflecting on his own poems produced new insights; this led to the talks 'Standing on Holy Ground' and 'Footprints of Delight', both included here in edited form. And at the very end of his life, he recorded a series of intimate conversations with Saddhanandi, chair of Adhisthana,[2] about ten of his poems; the edited transcripts of those conversations are also included here.

Then, at last, we come to the poems themselves, presented in chronological order, and with an index of subjects and themes as well as indexes of first lines and titles; and finally there's a sequence of short stories. Sangharakshita's occasional experiments with this form spanned the years from the early 1950s to the early 1990s, and also, in their own way, say things that could not have been put any other way.

Vidyadevi
Herefordshire
2019

INSTEAD OF A FOREWORD
by Padmavajra

Padmaloka
25 March 2019

Dear Bhante,

    It might seem strange that I am writing to you, given that back in November I participated in your funeral rites. It might seem strange as well to the other people who are reading this.

    I am writing to you because I am in some difficulty. Some months ago, Vidyadevi asked me if I would write a foreword to your *Complete Poems and Short Stories*. I have found it hard to write, making a number of false starts. Something is not right and I cannot connect with what I am writing. The writing is stilted – a poor attempt at formality which I do not find convincing.

    So instead, here I am, composing a letter to you about trying to write a foreword to your *Complete Poems*. I think if I write to you, you may in some way be able to help me. Addressing you somehow makes the writing easier, and I think I know why that might be.

    The truth is that reading your poetry is something very personal for me. When I read your poems I feel closer to you. I am not interested in whether your poetry is good or bad, or about the many styles in which you have written, and I know nothing about metre or rhyme schemes. I read your poetry because it tells me more about you.

    My first real encounter with your poetry was in Pune, India, where

I was living and doing what I could to help Lokamitra to establish the Order there. Indeed, I was there when you returned to give those wonderfully stirring lectures and conduct the first ordinations in India.

At some point during my stay, in 1978, there arrived the first edition of your collected poems, entitled *The Enchanted Heart – Poems 1946–1976*. It was a cyclostyled book in A4 format with a simple but beautiful cover painted by Aloka. Ashvajit had lovingly typed and duplicated the 168 pages. The first printing ran to two hundred copies. I have one of them now on my desk and it brings back memories of reading and rereading your poems during those days in India.

My memories tell me that much of my reading of *The Enchanted Heart* took place at night, either in my tiny bedroom in our small bungalow in Pune, or on retreat in some distant 'Inspection Bungalow' in the Maharashtra countryside. I would lie under my mosquito net reading your poems, wondering what had moved you to write them, what had enchanted your heart so.

Sometimes that was obvious to me because many of the poems described sights that I was seeing myself. I too had experienced the monsoon rain. I too had seen, almost daily, those melancholy buffaloes:

> With long-lashed eyes, and massive horns
> Low-curving from each patient head,
> They shuffle sadly up the road,
> Dusty, and lowing to be fed.

Reading lines like that helped me move closer to what I was seeing. It evoked a greater sympathy for a world that I was struggling to comprehend, because – as you well know – I was overwhelmed with difficulties during my first months in India.

There were also poems about people you had seen and met there. One in particular brought me closer to the people I was getting to know, the devoted Buddhist followers of Baba Saheb Ambedkar. The word pictures of 'The Bodhisattva's Reply' have stayed with me since the day I first read them, describing those

> Whose lives spring up between
> Custom and circumstance

> As weeds between wet stones,
> Whose lives corruptly flower
> Warped from the beautiful, …

I'm haunted by your description of those lives: that woman; this boy; the dull-eyed men; those dim shadows, forced to perform degrading acts and do terrible things; those wasted lives tossed into the gutter and trampled on. And the constant question to the anonymous bodhisattva:

> What will you say to them?

I wondered if you were addressing that question not just to the bodhisattva, but to yourself, in your hermitage in Kalimpong, and hearing an answer: that you should not say anything but just give yourself to them fully and completely.

Other poems of the late 1940s and early 1950s had me wondering about the inner experience that prompted them. I love 'Advent', which I keep returning to, describing, surely, a woman alone in a house, cleaning and preparing and waiting with intense, eventually hopeless, longing for the Stranger. At last:

> As the clock struck twelve I heard nothing
> But *felt* He had come and stayed
> Waiting outside. And I listened –
> And I was afraid.

Years later, I wondered if this poem was in the tradition of *viraha-bhakti*, the anguished longing devotion which is so much a feature of Indian religious traditions. And there are others among your 'Indian' poems that seem to evoke the same mood of intense longing and devotion. I was so glad that there was 'Bhante the *bhakta*', for obvious reasons, given my own temperament, although 'Advent' does contain a warning for me. I might long intensely for the divine, but when it comes?…

Another very early poem, 'The Unseen Flower', seemed to express, in plain and simple language, a clear and decisive insight into the very nature of things, describing the completely unselfconscious nature of Compassion, springing

Up in the emptiness which is when you yourself are not there
So that you do not know anything about it.

And then describing the scent of a mysterious unseen flower blooming

in the Heart of the Void.

But of all the poems that I read in India, the one that I kept returning to was the long poem written between 1950 and 1953 entitled 'The Veil of Stars'. In its 119 stanzas, to my intense delight I discovered Bhante the lover, as the poem traces the arc of love from its mysterious, amazed awakening to its glorious, visionary fulfilment.

The coming of love is mysterious as the flight of a bird from
    unknown lands,
Its going mysterious as the unseen tumult of the wind blowing we
    know not whither.

I can still feel the thrill and enchantment of reading that first stanza all those years ago, and the feelings became stronger as you charted the journey:

Desire for anyone flowers into love for someone
And at last bears fruit as compassion for everyone.

You took your reader on that journey not through concepts and analysis, but through vivid images of the world around you: the mountains and valleys around Kalimpong; cherry blossoms and bamboos; sunsets and full moons; glow-worms and stars. Reading and re-reading 'The Veil of Stars' (as well as other poems written in the same period) I had a sense of the intensity of your life and spiritual practice at this time. Was it, Bhante, like living in a great furnace in which all your life and studies were being smelted, or an alchemist's alembic in which your raw encounter with overwhelming beauty and love was at last transformed into the vision of the Beloved in all beings and in all things? And who was that Beloved – someone you knew, or the Bodhisattva? And at the last, after the great transformation, does that distinction even apply?

I know that even from the inmost depths of heaven I shall see your
face shining out upon me above the utmost beauty of the stars.

The secret of love is love.

Many years after I first read 'The Veil of Stars' I asked you what, or indeed who, had inspired the poem. Your reply was, at the time, a disappointment. Instead of saying anything about the circumstances, you talked about its style, saying that, inspired by Rabindranath Tagore's 'Stray Birds', you had found yourself writing down short poems which turned into a kind of story. You said nothing about who was involved, or the intensity of lived experiences. Later, I realized that all the intensity was expressed in the poetry itself and could not be said in any other way. I seem to recall you even telling me that on one occasion.

The Enchanted Heart did not only contain poems written in India; there were also poems written as you began your encounter with the Britain of the nineteen sixties and seventies. I loved the new voice of those poems, sometimes a very plain, almost documentary voice, nowhere more poignantly than in your poems about Terry Delamare. In the poem to Chögyam Trungpa, that plain voice described a movement to a new kind of communication:

> The time has come
> For us to hang up the gorgeous costumes in the greenroom
>   cupboard
> To leave the brilliantly lit stage
> The applause
> And to go home
> Through deserted streets
> To a quiet room
> Up three flights of stairs
> And to someone perhaps
> With whom we can be
> Ourselves

I also loved the ecstatic voice that entered your poetry at this time. You seem a man possessed, as if the Dharma has brought you to an energy that unites heaven and earth: earth-myth, local myth marrying cosmic transcendent vision. It is nowhere more vibrant than in 'On Glastonbury Tor', a true account of a pilgrimage you made there with a group of friends in 1969. How the opening lines drew me in! –

> Dragons were slain here
> Ages ago. Dragons' blood
> Soaked into the earth, stained
> White chalk miles deep.

The poem evoked the 'unlidded cauldron, the Tor' still boiling over. You heard voices from the past, saw the visions of 'Arthur Merlin, Cup Lance' in the white mist. 'Heard the Merlinvoice through the strong young body'. You challenged us (yourself too?) to 'accept incomprehension, accept defeat, face descent into Hell without hope of resurrection on the third day'. And you longed to lie down in the dark, in the depths of the sea with your love, to 'drift like red weed in green water'.

And at the last? Language stretched to its limit, the Tor 'swimming in space, cosmic dimensionless.'…

In your poetry I have discovered not only Bhante the devotee and Bhante the lover, but also Bhante the ecstatic. And there are so many more Bhantes to find in your poetry, too many to list in this letter. Perhaps you may even be disappointed that I'm leaving out some of the many other expressions of your heart? Perhaps the voices that I love are ones you left behind long ago. I remember asking you once to read some extracts from 'The Veil of Stars', but you declined, telling me: 'I don't have those feelings any more, and I am not an actor.'

Over the years more of your poetry has appeared in *Complete Poems* and *The Call of the Forest*, and you've written more since then, all of which will appear in the volume for which this is not quite a foreword. There are poems for your dear and close friends, and one to your teacher Chattrul Sangye Dorje. Once I wrote to you to say that I was reciting your short invocation to Padmasambhava, and you replied: 'What you said about my poem 'Padmasambava' made me turn to it after many years. In fact I asked Mahamati to read it to me, and afterwards I repeated it to myself a number of times. It struck me that the poem was like a little *sadhana*. I wonder what you will make of this thought.'

There is so much more to say about your poetry, but I fear that this letter is just getting longer and longer and I am no nearer to writing the foreword that I promised to write. I haven't even begun to think about what I might say about the short stories. I certainly recall reading 'The Artist's Dream' a number of times, the story of the old painter in Renaissance Italy painting a fresco of a dream of heaven, who attracts a community of young men to help with the work, only for the work to become disrupted by the usual worldly desires and attachments, which cause the unnamed artist so many problems. And yet he continues with the work, so determined is he to realize his dream-vision in painting. Many leave and he is left with only a few devoted young men to assist him. All he wants to do is to put everything in place so that his assistants can carry on with the great work: to fully realize his great dream vision of heaven. You wrote that story in 1972, and here we are many years later, absorbing your death and doing what we can to realize your vision in this difficult world. I wonder how we will fare.

I miss you, Bhante. Some people say your presence is stronger than ever. I know what they mean, but all the same I miss you. I miss just knowing that you were in your rooms at Adhisthana and that I could go and see you. I have even felt some anguish at this, have wept hot tears. I think of those lines of yours that tell how the heart feels:

> I do not care at all
> About writing any more poems.
> Enough if I can say
> How the heart bleeds and bleeds.

And I think back to that cold November day when you finally left us. Did you know that you left us with poetry? After your brightly coloured coffin was lowered into the earth, I read aloud your poem 'The Six Elements Speak', in which each element says its goodbye to us. I knew that I had to read with 'flavourless speech'. Later people told me that it was as if *you* were saying goodbye:

> Earth dissolves into Water,
> Water dissolves into Fire,
> Fire dissolves into Air,

Air dissolves into Space,
Space dissolves into Consciousness,
Consciousness dissolves into – ?
HŪM.

You left us in the vast mystery. But before I fall entranced into the vastness, I really must get down to writing that foreword. Or perhaps, after all, I have already written it, in the only way I could.

Much love,
Padmavajra

A GUIDE FOR THE NEW READER OF SANGHARAKSHITA'S POETRY
by Vishvantara

A few years after the volume of Sangharakshita's *Complete Poems* was published in 1994, Subhadramati and I, who had thoroughly enjoyed reading them, decided to hold an event at the London Buddhist Centre during which we would read the entire volume aloud for twelve hours at a stretch. So there we were, in the small shrine-room at the Centre, sitting opposite each other beside the image of the Buddha, with helpers bringing us lunch and dinner in covered dishes left outside the room. As we carefully and mindfully made our way through the book, cover to cover, taking turns to read aloud and following the poems' many moods, the hours flew by like minutes. Friends occasionally joined us for a while, coming and going quietly. At the end of the twelve hours we were partway through our second reading of the volume. Strangely, we did not feel tired but energized and refreshed. We had been deeply immersed in these poems, and it was as though we had imbibed something about their author which could not have been communicated to us in any other way.

Many years later, years during which we often talked about the poems we loved, we shared that love with a wider audience in a different setting: an Order gathering at Adhisthana. Here, in the company of many Order members, on 26 August 2018 – the August full-moon night and Bhante Sangharakshita's ninety-third birthday – we had a conversation about and read a selection of the poems, interspersed by Vandanajyoti's mesmerizing music, as she sang and played the tambura. We selected poems to illustrate different facets of Bhante as he appeared to us: the philosopher-monk, the lover of beauty and art, the devotee, the rebel. We read each poem aloud twice, then talked with each other about its form and meaning. Once again hours flew by like minutes, and we felt a mounting sense of meditative absorption and positive energy. As some people drifted away (it was getting rather late) and others stayed, we finished the evening with 108 White Tārā mantras for Bhante. We could have gone on and on, whether anyone stayed with us or not.

There are many reasons to recommend dipping into this collection of the poetry of Sangharakshita or, for an even more rewarding adventure, taking the plunge and reading the whole collection, as we did. Each individual poem could be a reason in itself, of course, as no two are quite alike and the range of content, tone, and style is broad and varied. Nevertheless, this 'Guide for the Reader' offers a few suggestions, pointing to a few individual poems along the way.

The first reason to read these poems is for their human interest. Bhante more than once hinted that in his poems we encounter the inner man more vividly even than in his memoirs. The memoirs are meticulous and lively accounts of what happened where and when; the poems give their own, different account, not *about* events so much as responsive to them. To read the poems is to encounter the inspirations and challenges of a passionate soul intent on discovering, penetrating, and realizing its spiritual imperatives. The poetic œuvre combines to make up what the poet himself termed a 'spiritual autobiography', and that autobiography is of a highly unusual person, one who literally tore up his passport in his twenties to go wandering in India, and many years later still yearned to

> Go tramping the black heather all day ...
> And at night, in hayloft or under hedge, find
> A companion suited to my mind.
>
> (I Want to Break Out)

His passionate soul found expression in a talk given in 1999, 'Standing on Holy Ground' [which appears in this volume pages 3 to 21], during which he quoted this couplet from his poem 'The Scholars' (1957):

> Off with your shoes! 'Tis holy ground! Depart!
> Buddhism's in the life and in the heart!

These lines ('I must have been somewhat annoyed when I wrote them,' he said many years later) were addressed to any pedant who would answer a sincere seeker's question 'What is Buddhism?' with reference to 'my latest article', to mere scholasticism. Sangharakshita said about the couplet:

> But, what is this holy ground? It is the human soul. I'm not using the word 'soul' in any strict theological sense. I'm using it for that deeper, more essential part of ourselves that feels and suffers and aspires. I could also use the word 'heart'; the poet John Keats, you may remember, speaks of 'the holiness of the heart's affections'.

Sangharakshita's poems lay bare a soul that was not afraid to feel, suffer, or aspire, and a heart whose affections teach us something about holiness, despite the fact that no poem was written with the self-conscious motivation of expressing a deliberate, formal teaching. Keats' observation that 'Beauty is truth, truth beauty' is celebrated in these pages, which contain poems of uplift and the joyful embrace of ideals, although they were written in an era when poetry tended to disparage, not celebrate, ideals such as these.

For the poet's feeling we might turn to countless poems, from the joy of the early 'Lines':

> From the unlocked cage of my heart
> White doves of love go winging,
> Wild larks of song rise singing,
> The ice of my heart is broken, broken,
> Joy's fountain leaps in the air;
> And all the while no word was spoken:
> I only looked at something fair.

to the tranquillity of 'Meditation':

> All the spirit's storm and stress
> Is stilled into a nothingness,
> And healing powers descend and bless.

From the restlessness, the chutzpah, the spiritual urgency of 'I Want to Break Out':

> I want to break through,
> Shatter time and space,
> Cut up the Void with a knife,
> Pitch the stars from their place,

to the homeliness of the acceptance of difficult feeling:

> These gods and goddesses that men have framed,
> They help not much, for in the end we come
> Back to an empty heart, a brain that aches,
> And our two hands before us on our knees.
>
> (Lines)

from the ecstatic warmth of close friendship:

> Delight in friendship, hitherto
> Unknown, whose upward flight
> Can bear the soul to realms beyond
> This sorry human plight
> And give it there a glimpse at least
> Of treasures infinite,…
>
> (To My Friend Paramartha)

to the torments of love that tear through the early poem 'The Veil of Stars':

> Bitter as death is it to me that you should clasp your hands
>   together in reverence before me,
> When I am longing for you to take my hands in your own with love.

From the peace of a retreat's pilgrimage into silence:

> Eternal Finger on the lip
> Of Being, make us truly blest.
> O give us from the ceaseless noise
> Of our own lives a little rest.

to the very different atmosphere of another pilgrimage:

> Night. Night. Night. Night. Night.
> Within the tower within the funnel the grey
> Space troglodytes we sat, refugees
> From civilization from the world from
> Ourselves perhaps, sat
> On damp earth amid cold stone....
>
> (On Glastonbury Tor)

From a deep personal experience of interconnectedness:

> Then, as the dawn's first rays did fall
> Bright through the open doorway wide,
> Turning my head, I saw a small
> White calf still sleeping at my side.
>
> Nestling upon the same soft straw
> As I, with head to hoof, he lay,
> So peacefully that one who saw
> Could hardly keep the tears away.
>
> To me that small life did impart
> A kind of aching tenderness,
> Such as may fill a mother's heart
> To see her infant's helplessness.
>
> And in the deepest depths of me
> I felt that I had understood
> In one clear flash the mystery
> Of universal brotherhood.
>
> (The White Calf)

to the imagining of a murderous mind-state completely at odds with the poet's own:

> In shadow of the castle wall
> I wait to see the sun uprise,
> My hand upon my knife, a mist
> Of blood, red blood, before my eyes.

(Revenge)

Two poems that stand out for their evocation of the poet's suffering are 'The Wondering Heart':

> What can it do, when friends avert
> Their eyes, or choose to dwell apart?
> What can it do when looks grow cold
> That once with love shone bright as gold,
> What can it do, the wounded heart?

and 'Guhyaloka : July 1998':

> I communicate in silence
> With the giant shapes of stone –
> Grey, ancient forms that tell me,
> In the stillness, 'Time will cure.
> Meanwhile, be calm, be silent;
> The secret is: Endure.'

And for aspiration, what can match the passion and fervour of 'Taking Refuge in the Buddha', with its sweep, its panoply of circumstances, contexts, places, and mind-states from which the poet turns away – from art, from politics, from the scholarship of the academicians, from the hieratic formalism of all the great religions including even Buddhism itself – to take his place at the feet of the Buddha?

> Not in Nirvāṇa's stillness;
> Not in Saṃsāra's flow;
> Not in the heavens above us;
> Not in the hells below;

> Not in thought or word or action;
> Not where mind and object meet;
>   – With Wisdom and Compassion
> My place is at Thy Feet.

Not all the poems mirror the feeling, suffering, aspiring soul quite so obviously. Others are more mysterious in their effect – a combination of the allusiveness and elusiveness of language which points towards something while refusing a direct moral conclusion. The poem 'In the Woods are Many More' ends:

> My eyes by chance fell on a shelf of books, –
> The Buddha's Teachings, – and thereafter glanced
> Up to the Buddha's image as He smiled
> Above them from the alcove. Strange it was
> That, as my eyes from book to image passed,
> Dwelling an instant on that calm, pure Face,
> There, with the frail cold blossoms in my hands,
> The words that man spoke at my door should ring
> Through my stilled heart again and yet again
> Like music – 'In the woods are many more....'

We are not told the secret of the significance of those words 'In the woods are many more' to the poet; they become wordless music. There's an echo of the *Siṃsapā Sutta*, in which the Buddha compared what he knew to the number of leaves in the forest, and all the teachings we need to know for our liberation to the handful of leaves he held,[3] but even this doesn't account for the strangeness of the repetition of the orchid gatherer's words about the 'Wild orchids which no eye has ever seen / Save ours'.

There are poems that belong in the mysterious realm of dreams and visions, even daydreams, but this one dispels dreams like dust, drawing its strength from a quiet economy of imagery and language:

> The ashes of all my heartaches,
> The dust of a hundred dreams,
> Are swept away in an instant
> When forth one white peak gleams.

> After long storm and struggle,
> My heart with quietness fills
> At the curve of this jade-green river,
> The sweep of these dark blue hills.

Thought can be as passionate as feeling ever was, and sometimes they can't be separated. One sonnet begins as cool argument and ends in impassioned imagery:

> Reading some books, you'd think the Buddha-Way,
> As though macadamized, ran smooth and white,
> Straight as an arrow, bill-boards left and right,
> And that the yellow buses, thrice a day,
> Whirled past the milestones, whose smug faces say,
> 'Nirvāṇa 15 miles.... By 10 tonight
> You'll all be there, good people, and alight
> Outside the Peace Hotel, where you're to stay.'

Here the language runs as straightforwardly easy and clear as the language of the books it describes. The two key descriptors in the first eight lines of the sonnet, the octet, are the alliterative adjectives 'smooth' and 'smug'. But a different picture is painted in the final six lines, the sestet:

> But those who read their own hearts, inly wise,
> Know that the Way's a hacked path, roughly made
> Through densest jungle, deep in the Unknown....
> And that, though burn a thousand baleful eyes
> Like death-lamps round, serene and unafraid,
> Man through the hideous dark must plunge alone.

This is not poetic exaggeration. Sangharakshita said that he thought carefully about every word he wrote and whether it was the most suitable, the most accurate, the most suggestive, for the job he wanted it to do. Hacking a path through an unexplored jungle as an image for the spiritual life may be far from that of the 'serene and unafraid' smiling meditator in lotus position of the popular imagination, but it truly suggests the visceral fear of the surrounding darkness and the sheer effort of battling against the unruly vegetation of the jungle of unhelpful habitual behaviours.

This sonnet gives us an example of the poet's sometimes archaic diction – 'thrice' and 'inly' – and archaic syntax, the inversion very common in his work, in lines like

>...though burn a thousand baleful eyes
>Like death-lamps round,...

The full rhymes and metrical rhythms may also sound old-fashioned to our ears, accustomed as we are to metrically free and unrhymed verse that follows the rhythms of modern speech. Sangharakshita himself experimented with this style sometimes. His love of reading poetry encompassed the whole genre, from his beloved Shelley, discovered in youth, to the work of Thom Gunn, read with interest in his nineties. But having absorbed pre-twentieth-century metrics and rhyme schemes when he was young, they became the natural, instinctive rhythms of his inspiration to express deep feeling and meditative thought in his own poems.

And sometimes there came – as naturally as breathing to one steeped in poetry – an accomplished piece of writing, with a word-count as brief as its implication is extensive:

>Seeing this world, this hapless world,
>With all its store of woes,
>Compassion in the Buddha-Heart
>Burst open like a rose.
>
>And from that flower, that wondrous flower,
>There came at once to birth
>A breath whose perfume even now
>With fragrance fills the earth.
>
>(The Fragrance of Compassion)

The repetition of 'world' and 'flower' in the first line of each stanza may be old-fashioned, but it works, the repetition opening up the thought by adding the opposing descriptors 'hapless' and 'wondrous', and the gentle rhythms are music to the ear.

Sometimes it does not take much effort to write a poem and it arrives, just needing to be caught in the net of words and almost transcribed directly from the Muse, as this late poem must have been:

> A wind was in my sails. It blew
> Stronger and fiercer hour by hour.
> I did not know from whence it came,
> Or why. I only knew its power.
>
> Sometimes it dashed me on the rocks,
> Sometimes it spun me round and round.
> Sometimes I laughed aloud for joy,
> Sometimes I felt a peace profound.
>
> It drove me on, that manic wind,
> When I was young. It drives me still
> Now I am old. It lives in me,
> Its breath my breath, its will my will.
>
> (The Wind)

This wind seems to be a supra-personal force, what Sangharakshita calls in 'Himalayan Sages' the 'electric urge to thrust beyond the "I"'. He called the arising of the *bodhicitta* – the cosmic flowering of that urge to Enlightenment in the highest service of all that lives – 'the most important event that can occur in the life of a human being',[4] so it is not surprising that it suffuses much of his best-loved poetry, by implication ('The Lotus of Compassion'), by storytelling ('The Bodhisattva's Reply'), or by direct reference:

> The quick sap rises in the dry stalk;
> On naked boughs the furled green buds appear;
> Returning swallows beat about
> The clay-built house they left last year.
> Earth smiles, and like an almond-tree
> The Bodhichitta flowers in me.
>
> (Spring)

An image more often associated with the *bodhicitta* is the full moon in all its majesty, mystery, radiance, beauty, and power. The moon, whether full, new, or something in between, makes its appearance in so many of Sangharakshita's poems that they are drenched in moonlight. For example, there's 'The Vase of Moonlight':

> Your beauty, in repose, is like a vase
> Of jasper or white jade with moonlight filled;
> Your smiling is as though the moonlight spilled;
> Your laugh, its shivering into a thousand stars.

And a later poem:

> Visitors all day!
> Morning mist, afternoon flowers –
> And now the full moon.

In a very late poem, 'An Apology', he would say that mankind owes the moon an apology for 'rudely invading her sacred space'.

Sangharakshita once wrote a poem called 'The Call of the Forest'. To read his poems from cover to cover is to enter into and surrender to the world of his language and lose oneself in the atmosphere of a forest as ancient, mysterious, and compelling as the one he evoked:

> The whisper's a dream-whisper,
> For 'forest' is a dream
> Of days when Man through Nature
> Had sense of a Supreme.
> The whisper's a dream-whisper
> Of a time when he could feel
> In the pressure of the actual
> The touch of the Ideal.
>
> The whisper's a dream-whisper,
> But dreams are of the Soul
> And Soul itself a forest
> Beyond the mind's control.
> The whisper's a Soul-whisper,

That like a muffled drum
Calls, 'From your mind-built Cities,
O Man, to Freedom come!'

THE LITERARY INFLUENCES ON SANGHARAKSHITA'S POETRY
by Vishvapani

In Sangharakshita's preface to his *Complete Poems 1941–1994* he remarks that many of the poems he included are worth preserving for their autobiographical merit, but not 'as poetry', distinguishing them from 'those few poems which may be considered to rank as such'. It is natural then to wonder what counts as 'poetry' in Sangharakshita's terms, and which of his poems qualify. One way to explore this is to approach Sangharakshita as a reader as well as a writer of poetry, and consider his poems in relation to the tradition of English poetry which he loved so deeply.

That love started early. He absorbed ballads and nonsense verse as a child, and as a teenager his reading ranged widely, but the intensity of his reading is even more striking than its breadth. He describes poetry's overwhelming impact on him in his memoir *The Rainbow Road*, but his most eloquent account is in the long poem, 'The Awakening of the Heart' (1949):

> Thus oft upon a Summer morn
> On our close-cropped suburban lawn
> Beneath a plum-tree's shadowing spray
> For hours entranced I sat or lay,
> On chair or rug, with cushioned head,
> And converse held with poets dead;
> Till, heat-oppressed, I sank at noon

Into a kind of waking swoon,
Wherein the sense of what I'd read,
And consciousness of heat o'erhead,
And coolness of the leafy shade,
In which, with hot lids closed, I stayed,...

[These] Blent with my trance, and did express
For one brief hour of timelessness
Its mood of utter blessedness.

By this account, poetry introduced Sangharakshita to a 'lush wonderland', a blessed realm to which the poets welcomed him. This experience is both aesthetic and spiritual, and resonates with a Buddhist sensibility that is also growing in him. The combination of emotional innocence, aesthetic reverie, and 'blessedness' owes much to Wordsworth, but perhaps the youth reading beneath a plum tree while his father tends the roses also recalls the young Gautama absorbed in *samādhi* beneath a rose-apple tree as his father ploughs a field.[5] These mingled references recur in many of his poems.

From the outset Sangharakshita's reading prompted his writing. The first poem he wrote, aged eleven or twelve, was about a lark, and was composed in the style of Shelley's 'Ode to a Skylark'.[6] In *The Rainbow Road from Tooting Broadway to Kalimpong* he describes the 'apocalypse of Miltonic sublimity' he experienced a couple of years later on reading *Paradise Lost*, which 'made of me, from that day onwards, if not a poet yet at least a modest practitioner of the art of verse'.[7] Aged eighteen and conscripted into the army, he spent his free afternoons reading poetry in a teashop in Leatherhead where 'an unusually felicitous line went through me like a spear. Sometimes, closing the book, I would fall into a muse and try to shape the rhythms and the images that were ringing in my head into verses of my own.'[8]

Tracing how Sangharakshita's own poems were influenced by the poetry he absorbed requires us to distinguish the various levels on which literary influence occurs. The range of Sangharakshita's reading is too wide and my own, alas, too narrow for a full account, but I hope at least to distinguish its main lines. Then I will identify three distinct phases in Sangharakshita's poetry; and finally I offer a close reading of his 1978 poem 'Padmaloka'.

One kind of literary influence relates to a poem's form or subject matter. Among Sangharakshita's output we find many sonnets, haiku, ballads, alexandrines. and so on. A good number of the poems are comments on poems or poets, including Herrick, Blake, Milton, and Yeats, while a number of later poems are literary exercises, modelled on famous originals by Lovelace, Rilke, Samuel Johnson, Thomas Hardy, and others.

A further level of literary influence is the impact – sometimes inspiring and sometimes overpowering – of the poetic tradition on a writer who struggles to discover his or her own voice. Sangharakshita reflects in an interview with Vidyadevi that 'It's difficult to be a modern poet in English – in some ways the rich heritage is a bit burdensome, and you can't compete with it.' He is by no means the only poet to experience this burden, and one way to read a poet is to trace how he or she discovers their distinctive contribution despite its weight. When Sangharakshita writes of 'those few poems which may be considered to rank as such', I think he means that they are able to stand alongside strong precursors without being entirely overshadowed.

The first phase of Sangharakshita's poetry is what I shall call his Indian poetry, largely written in his twenties and reaching a highpoint with 'The Veil of Stars' (1954), after which he wrote much less. The next distinct phase is what I shall call post-Vihara poetry, written on his return to the West and his departure from the Hampstead Buddhist Vihara in 1967. From the early 1970s onwards his poetry reverts to a more formal style, akin to the Indian period but, with some exceptions, lacking its intensity. I call this 'the Long Tail'.

INDIAN POETRY

Leaving aside the poetry he wrote in his teens, most of which has not survived, the bulk of Sangharakshita's poetic output was written by the time he was thirty (i.e. before 1955). In this work the poetry he absorbed in his first, overwhelming immersion is still a strong influence, the rhythms ringing in his mind, the images shaping his consciousness and infusing his writing. The imprint of Wordsworth, Coleridge, and Blake is widely evident; Keats is a lesser influence, but Keats' nineteenth-century heirs, including Tennyson, Swinburne, and both Rossettis, are important presences; and in the generation that followed them and preceded Sangharakshita's youth he was close to Housman, Kipling, and especially Yeats.

'Song' (1951) illustrates the influence of a literary model on Sangharakshita's poetry. It is a pastiche of Yeats' short lyric 'He Wishes For the Cloths of Heaven' with its famous ending:

> I have spread my dreams under your feet;
> Tread softly because you tread on my dreams.

Sangharakshita's echo is deliberate:

> But tread most softly when
> You have to do with men
> Of simple parts;
> For, if truth were said,
> All unawares you tread
> Upon their hearts.

The poem's effect requires the reader to understand that Sangharakshita is reversing Yeats' appeal to his lover for gentle treatment with the moral reflection that strength brings the capacity to hurt 'men of simple parts'. The later poem, therefore, cannot be read independently of its predecessor. There the parallel ends, however, and Sangharakshita's modest lyric cannot withstand further comparison with Yeats' masterly lines.

If there is a single precursor who most strongly influences Sangharakshita's Indian poetry it must be Shelley. As an adolescent he read and reread Shelley's long poems 'Adonais', 'Prometheus Unbound', and 'Epipsychidion', and felt a distinctive affinity with Shelley's outlook. Even in the mid-1950s, as he recalls in his memoir of the period, when he studied some of Shelley's shorter poems with his friend and student Sachin, 'We were both sometimes left, at the end of the session, in a mood bordering on the ecstatic.'[9] He later acknowledged that other poets might be greater than Shelley, but in a series of interviews with Vidyadevi about his favourite poetry he recognized how much Shelley had meant to him, especially in his youth. 'Shelley has been for me a source of great inspiration, that Neoplatonic element of upward aspiration, and I think his poems are among the greatest treasures of English literature.'[10] Towards the end of his life he commented that upward aspiration was an important element in his personality and that he 'had an affinity with Buddhism inasmuch as the path taught by the Buddha led to higher and ever higher states of being and consciousness'.[11] As a youth his intuitive sense of spiritual life was very strong, and Shelley's poetry powerfully articulated both his intuitions and the idealism they stimulated, even before he formulated it in Buddhist terms.

'Argosies' (1951) is a short blank verse meditation centred on the image of a boy sailing a boat on a pond, which becomes a metaphor for spiritual life. The opening lines are a Pre-Raphaelite echo of Ophelia's death in *Hamlet*:

> A solitary boy would sail his boat
> All day in a green pool, where willows wept
> Over the stony verge, and sadly trailed
> Their slim green leaves along the water's face.

The central image is familiar from biographies of Shelley, who sailed paper boats in his childhood, and his poetry is filled with images, often connected to swans and the soul. Sangharakshita particularly loved Shelley's 'Prometheus Unbound', and the connection to 'Argosies' is Asia's famous 'Song' at the end of Act III:

> My soul is an enchanted boat,
> Which, like a sleeping swan, doth float
> Upon the silver waves of thy sweet singing;
> And thine doth like an angel sit
> Beside a helm conducting it,
> Whilst all the winds with melody are ringing.

Compare this with 'Argosies':

> Oh how like a white swan it seemed to cut
> Through the clear water, tilting as the breeze
> Leaned on the silver sails, until it dipped, –
> So gracefully, – one white wing in the waves!

The same images recur in 'A Stream of Stars', one of Sangharakshita's strongest lyrics from this period, in which the echo of 'Asia's Song' is even clearer and now combines with the dead leaves of Shelley's 'Ode to the West Wind':

> No more on my soul's current float
> Dead leaves from wind-dishevelled trees;
> But swanlike, many a shining boat
> Bends low before the heavenly breeze.

W. B. Yeats' poem 'Nineteen Hundred and Nineteen', referring specifically to Shelley, explains the image's significance:

> Some moralist or mythological poet
> Compares the solitary soul to a swan.

The conclusion of 'Argosies' agrees that the swan represents the soul, but also makes the memory an intimation of later experience:

> Was to his infant soul obscurely given,
> Beneath the brown shade of the willow trees,
> Foreknowledge of those argosies which now
> Loom white-winged o'er him from the deeps of life?

It is surely curious that Sangharakshita's personal recollection should find expression in images strongly shaped by a precursor poet. In this period Sangharakshita was entering a 'world of mysteries and magnitudes', as he says in the stirring fragment 'Immensities' (1947), and in seeking a language for experiences that emerged 'from the deeps of life' he turned to images learned from Shelley – not just boats and swans, but mountains, clouds, sunsets, and much else – which had already seared themselves into his imagination.

The highpoint of Sangharakshita's Indian poetry is 'The Veil of Stars', composed between 1951 and 1954. Its story could make a novel: the lover (presumably the young Bhikshu Sangharakshita) falls in love, and his emotions hurtle between joy and despair. Sangharakshita chose not to fully describe the story in his memoirs, despite their novelistic qualities. This may be attributable to an understandable reticence, but perhaps he wanted to do something else with the experience: 'The Veil of Stars' is interested in crystallizing his experience rather than elaborating on it. The aphoristic form is taken from Rabindranath Tagore and, as Lama Govinda says in his Introduction, each of its short sections 'forms a complete unit in itself, though in the way they are strung together they reveal a still deeper meaning'.[12]

'The Veil of Stars' uses the same range of images that we find in Sangharakshita's shorter poems of this period, and even its novelties have sources in Shelley. The glow-worms that Sangharakshita rather oddly invokes as worldly counterparts to the heavenly stars are also present in Shelley's 'The Cloud', 'The Witch of Atlas', and other poems. But the strongest link is the theme of the sublimating of erotic love. It's an ancient subject, most strongly associated with Plato, Dante, and the courtly love tradition, but if we seek an explicit link I would suggest Shelley's 'Defence of Poetry'. Sangharakshita often quoted the famous section on imaginative sympathy that starts 'The great secret of morals is love', but Shelley also makes the connection to courtly love:

> The Provençal Trouveurs, or inventors, preceded Petrarch, whose verses are as spells, which unseal the inmost enchanted fountains of the delight which is in the grief of love. It is impossible to feel them without becoming a portion of that beauty which we contemplate.[13]

In a similar spirit, Sangharakshita explains in the Argument that prefaces 'The Veil of Stars' that his protagonist 'joyfully embraces the pain of Love ... gradually learns of a higher love [and] rises to spiritual illumination, understanding the true nature of Love, and realizing that his own love, like all other things in the universe, is in turn reflected in the heart of Reality'. This recapitulates the journey of the courtly lover, but the poem attempts to move beyond the western poetic trope of love by adding something that is both Eastern and Buddhist:

> When the sun of passion has gone down dazzlingly behind the
>   Western horizon of my heart,
> The moon of love will arise starrily behind the Eastern horizon of
>   my soul. (XCIV)

Sangharakshita's writing changed after the mid-1950s, when he was about thirty. For several years he produced very little new poetry, and one reason must be that he started to write his enduring prose works, including *The Religion of Art* and *A Survey of Buddhism*. He changed from a poet who wrote essays to a prose writer who sometimes wrote poems; but the influence of poetry persists in the high style of the prose he was writing and its copious references to Romantic poetry. Even in the 1950s, this style was anachronistic, and in the following years Sangharakshita's prose gradually changed, and in my view improved. The rhetoric of *A Survey* made way for clarity and concision in writing that is illuminated by literary references but not determined by them. While the cadences of poetry never left Sangharakshita as a reader and auditor, I suggest that, as a writer, he needed to distance himself from them.

This changing style also meant an altered relation to the poetic tradition. According to 'The Awakening of the Heart' Sangharakshita left the enchanted 'summer meadow' of poetry when a bomb fell on his house, and thereafter trod 'experience' flint-strewn path' with a new awareness of death and suffering. The emotions and cadences of 'The Awakening of the Heart' show that poetry remained powerfully alive in Sangharakshita's experience, but its source, according to the poem, now lay within the poet himself. However we judge that, the poem points us towards a strain of ambivalence towards a poetic vocation that deepened over the years. The shift from poetry to prose in the mid-1950s took this a step further, but on his return to the West, and especially after his departure from the Hampstead Buddhist Vihara in 1967, it produced a new approach to poetry itself.

POST-VIHARA POEMS

An outsider in British society, largely *persona non grata* in the established Buddhist world, and separated from established Buddhist traditions by his non-denominational stance, Sangharakshita gravitated towards the London counter-culture, and found that his outlook overlapped with that of young people who idealistically rejected societal norms. Sangharakshita continued to see himself as a reformer of Buddhism in the light of his particular vision of the Dharma but he also came to see himself as a cultural translator who needed to draw on Buddhism's unconditioned depths: 'bringing up ... what one has experienced ... in the depths of one's own being'.[14]

Sangharakshita's poetry also changed, and between 1967 and 1971 he wrote a series of poems that differed radically from what he had produced before or what he was to produce later. The most substantial of these is 'On Glastonbury Tor' (1969), but the signature poem is 'New':

> I should like to speak
> With a new voice, speak
> Like Adam in the Garden, speak
> Like the Rishis of old, announcing
> In strong jubilant voices the Sun
> Moon Stars Dawn Winds Fire
> Storm and above all the god-given
> Intoxicating ecstatic
> Soma, speak
> Like divine men celebrating
> The divine cosmos with divine names.
> I should like to speak
> With a new voice, telling
> The new things that I know, chanting
> In incomparable rhythms
> New things to new men, singing
> The new horizon, the new vision
> The new dawn, the new day.
> I should like to use
> New words, use
> Words pristine, primeval, words
> Pure and bright as snow-crystals, words
> Resonant, expressive, creative,
> Such as, breathed to music, built Ilion.
> (The old words
> Are too tired soiled stale lifeless.)
> New words
> Come to me from the stars
> From your eyes from
> Space
> New words vibrant, radiant, able to utter
> The new me, able

> To build for new
> Men a new world.

The newness Sangharakshita desires is not so much a matter of innovation as a return to a primordial freshness, before history, culture, and religion, that connects him to the elements through a timeless, shamanic vision and coalesces with his search for radical ways to re-express Buddhist teachings. But the 'new voice' with which he wishes to speak also repudiates his old ways of expressing himself and, as this is a poem, that means his former poetic style. Rhymes, stanzas, and regular iambics give way to informal versification and freer rhythms that mingle conversational speech with incantation, and the old words that now seem 'tired soiled stale lifeless' must include those of the old poets.

The aspiration is clear, but it cannot evade a number of ironies. 'New' opens with tropes of origination invoking the Biblical Adam and the Vedic Rishis, and the word turns out, imaginatively speaking, to mean something even older than 'old'. Despite Sangharakshita's desire for new words, he cannot avoid using English and the history this brings. His rather unconvincing solution in 'On Glastonbury Tor' comes via the mysterious figure (or perhaps it is simply a young man in the grip of hallucinogens) who declaims '*Anarakatiya mabana / Katanama ragaliyapava*' in a 'hieratic infallible ... daimoniacal voice'.

A further irony is that in his desire to step out of history Sangharakshita was, for perhaps the only time in his life, articulating the views of a wider culture – the 1960s counterculture – and these poems are unmistakably products of their time. His alternative to the old poetry adopts the idiom that many others were using and had already been thoroughly explored by his friend Allen Ginsberg, whose own 'innovations' in fact owed much to Walt Whitman and the American poetic tradition. Sangharakshita's concluding plea for 'New words' that can 'build for new/Men a new world' repeats Nietzsche's trope of cultural rejuvenation. For all its breathless intensity, having abandoned the old poetic resources, 'New' relies chiefly on assertion and repetition.

I point out these ironies not to dismiss the poetry Sangharakshita wrote in this period but to locate it in his changing relationship to the poetic tradition. Perhaps the most telling commentary on 'New' is a passage in Harold Bloom's *Yeats*, which was published in 1970:

> The ephebe [aspiring poet] cannot be Adam early in the morning. There have been too many Adams and they have named everything. The burden of unmaking prompts the true wars fought under the banner of poetic influence, wars waged by the perversity of spirit against the wealth accumulated by the spirit, the wealth of tradition.
>
> (Harold Bloom, *Yeats*, Oxford University Press, New York 1970, p. 4.)

'New' could not be a final destination for Sangharakshita. Fiery radicalism was one part of his temperament, but another was a love of continuity that accepted the ascendency of tradition. It is no surprise that his post-Vihara period only lasted for a few years, and that his poetry changed again in the early 1970s as his poetic output entered a prolonged third stage.

'PADMALOKA' AND THE LONG TAIL

I would say that most of what Sangharakshita produced from 1973 to his death lacks the musicality of his early writing, even when it expresses 'passing moods and fancies as well as deeper experiences and insights' (as he said in his Preface to *Complete Poems* published in 1995). However, there are notable exceptions across the decades: poems to which Sangharakshita gave his concerted attention that converse with his poetic precursors and occasionally find a maturity of expression beyond anything he achieved as a young man. My favourite is 'Padmaloka', which takes its title from the large house in Norfolk where he moved in 1976. The poem was written three years later and published in the 1990 collection *Hercules and the Birds*.

Sangharakshita loved poems about autumn, a substantial genre that traditionally connects the decline of the year with the individual's progress towards death. He numbered several autumn poems among his favourites, including D. H. Lawrence's 'The Ship of Death', whose attitude to dying is close to Sangharakshita's own:

> And it is time to go, to bid farewell
> to one's own self, and find an exit
> from the fallen self.

'Padmaloka' is Sangharakshita's own beautiful contribution to the genre, and a deeply-felt meditation, written at the age of 53, on his own mortality. He was to live for another forty years, but he died at the height of autumn, on 30 October 2018, and when I saw the golden-leaved trees framing the sky at his funeral, the poem seemed more fitting than ever.

'Padmaloka' comprises six sestets, composed on the model of the sestet of a Shakespearean sonnet with an alternately rhymed quatrain followed by a closing couplet. The mood is reflective and elegiac and the pace is slow. Ending a stanza with a couplet brings a sense of closure that breaks up the poem's flow, and Sangharakshita extends this by ending each line of the couplet with a feminine rhyme (meaning that an extra beat ends the line with an unstressed syllable). The effect is of a dying fall, as if the stanza were ending not so much with a conclusion as with an exhalation.

> Three Summers and three Autumns have I seen,
> And two white Winters, in this quiet spot,
> And now the gold shines out among the green,
> And reddest roses are remembered not.
> For the third time are Winter's icy fingers
> Stretched out – and yet the latest sunflower lingers.

Sangharakshita starts by measuring his time at Padmaloka by the seasons in the manner of a favourite poem of his, Yeats' 'Wild Swans at Coole', written in a similar form (though with shorter lines) and a comparably reflective mood. The second stanza of 'The Wild Swans at Coole' starts by reckoning the years, as Sangharakshita does – 'The nineteenth autumn has come upon me/since first I made my count' – and in both cases the noting of the passage of time commences a greater reckoning. At the outset, 'Padmaloka' describes early autumn when 'the gold shines out among the green', though by its close it speaks of the time when 'the Autumn ends'. The poem itself therefore marks the passage of time on the model of Keats' 'To Autumn', which starts in the 'season of mists and mellow fruitfulness' and ends with stubble plains and 'full grown lambs'. Red roses are a traditional image not just of summer but of romantic love, and perhaps the decline of the year mirrors Sangharakshita's own waning physical energy as 'winter's icy fingers' (a phrase adapted from Shakespeare's 'King John')[15] reach towards the poet as well as nature.

The sunflower of the final line lingers unassumingly, but it gains significance when set beside 'The Sunflower's Farewell', which followed 'Padmaloka' in *Hercules and the Birds* and also looks forward from an autumn scene towards the poet's death. Sangharakshita's sunflowers cannot be ignorant of the sunflower of William Blake (a poet Sangharakshita studied deeply in this period), which seeks after transcendence:

> Ah Sun-flower! weary of time,
> Who countest the steps of the Sun:
> Seeking after that sweet golden clime
> Where the traveller's journey is done.
>
> ('Ah! Sun-flower', *Songs of Experience*)

'Ah! Sun-flower' had a famously transformative effect on Allen Ginsberg and prompted his 'Sunflower Sutra', in which the fading plant is an image for forgotten human potential. Disputing both Blake and Ginsberg, for Sangharakshita the sunflower's decay signifies completion and an autumnal acceptance of impermanence: 'Its seed is ready and its work is done.'

> Three Summers and three Autumns! In that time
> I have made friends with walnut and with oak,
> Have clasped the trunks of holly and of lime,
> And cómmuned with them, though no words we spoke.
> Watching black ants among the roots of grasses
> I heard the wind sigh how our pleasure passes.

The celebration of trees in the second stanza invokes not just Sangharakshita's love of the natural world, but the tradition of poetry directed towards trees from Ovid onwards. The reflection on the transience of pleasure in the concluding line may recall Burns' 'But pleasures are like poppies spread/You seize the flower, its bloom is shed' ('Tam O'Shanter', another of Sangharakshita's favourites); but it is also a Buddhist reflection, and a closer antecedent may be Edwin Arnold's *Light of Asia*:

> What pleasure hast thou of thy changeless bliss?
> Nay, if love lasted, there were joy in this;
> But life's way is the wind's way, all these things
> Are but brief voices breathed on shifting strings.[16]

The third stanza looks ahead to winter, counterpoising the prospect of death with the deep-rooted trees:

> Russet and gold, the drifts of leaves are deep,
> And the third Winter deep will be the snow;
> But the trees mourn not, though no sap may leap,
> For deeper still the gnarled roots thrust below.
> In this quiet spot, girt by the reeds and rushes,
> The soul roots deeper, and the spirit hushes.

The roots introduce the thought that winter will not be an end, a reflection that roots the soul and hushes the spirit, permitting the poem to move from water and death to spring and rebirth:

> Summer and Autumn, on the margined pond,
> The waterlily's leaves are broad and green,
> Soon to be yellowed, with the shrubs beyond,
> And underneath a film of ice be seen.
> But come first Spring, among her budding daughters
> Red blooms the lily on the sunlit waters.

With a third repetition of 'Summer and Autumn', the stanzas echo one another; the whole poem is a musical composition of balancing cadences. The verses also echo other poems: Shelley's 'Cloud' declares 'I am the daughter of Earth and Water', while 'sunlit waters' appear in Whitman's 'Crossing Brooklyn Ferry'. We cannot say whether these are deliberate references or simply similar occurrences in the great ocean of poetic phrasings; but I think we can say that Sangharakshita's poetry resonates most fully when it is close to that ocean.

Literally, the lily in the final line is the waterlily in the pond at Padmaloka; but metaphorically the lily is a traditional symbol of purity, perhaps in contrast to the red rose, and of the innocence that follows death (giving us the lily's association with funerals). The strongest association, though, is between the waterlily and the lotus. 'Padmaloka' means 'the place of the lotus', and the name evokes Sukhāvatī, the Pure Land of Amitābha, the red Buddha of infinite light, whose emblem is the lotus, according to the *Sukhāvatī-vyūha Sūtras*.

Before the poem turns to what comes after death, it meditates on impermanence in the fifth stanza: a Keatsian adagio of melancholy beauty:

Dreaming and thinking as the Autumn ends,
I like the swallow must prepare for flight,
Must leave deep-rooted here my ancient friends
And go where night is day, and day is night.
Brief though my stay, I shall be thinking ever
Of this quiet spot, beside the sluggish river.

Thinking and dreaming, in this quiet spot,
Summer and Winter, I shall end my days,
Till like the rose I am remembered not,
And life has vanished with the sunset-rays.
Then, among silver lakes and golden mountains,
The new-born lotus smiles beside the crystal fountains.

Shelley's 'Adonais' also rhymes 'mountains' and 'fountains'; and in verse 15 Shelley says of the dead Keats:

... the pure spirit shall flow
Back to the burning fountain whence it came.

But Sangharakshita subsumes Shelley's imagery within the Buddhist image of a Pure Land filled with lotuses, jewels, silver lakes, and golden mountains. In the *Sukhāvatī-vyūha Sūtras* Amitābha sits on a lotus in the midst of a terraced pond and the newly dead enter into lotus buds which unfold when the occupants have been purified. Death, or perhaps the accommodation with dying which the poem enacts, will be Sangharakshita's form of purification; and his destiny will be a return to the imaginal realm of spiritual vision he had so long cherished. Shelley helped him form his sense of what that meant, but the Pure Land

Sangharakshita envisages adds a new dimension. He remarks in *Milarepa and the Art of Discipleship* (a commentary on Milarepa's songs based on seminars given in 1980):

> My own experience is that, even after reading the classics of Western literature or listening to the Western musical repertoire, if I then immerse myself in a Mahāyāna *sūtra*, the atmosphere is totally different and goes completely beyond even the best of Western culture.... It is not just that there's some difference. It leaves it completely behind. My real inspiration definitely comes from such sources.'[17]

After death, 'the soul of Adonais like a star,/ Beacons from the abode where the Eternal are', but Sangharakshita's destination is more clearly imagined. He is no longer a wonderstruck youth, grappling with incomprehensible spiritual intimations, but a mature Buddhist whose thought-world has been recast by the Dharma. Shelley would have recognized the idealism of 'Padmaloka', but (at least by the testimony of his last major poem, 'The Triumph of Life') Sangharakshita's reflective acceptance of death and confidence in what lay beyond it would have been alien to him.

'Padmaloka' is a rare highpoint in Sangharakshita's later poetry, much of which versifies more prosaic reflections, and he offers a telling comment on his lowered horizons in 'The Minor Poets' (2000):

> Shakespeare, Milton, Wordsworth, Coleridge
> Are godlike spirits; we are men,
> And cannot always brook their splendour –
> The Minor Poets please us then.

Those who are 'merely pickers up of pence' (as he witheringly calls literary critics in the 1979 poem 'Alexandrines Perhaps') are in no position to criticize the modest achievements of his later poetry. But the sentiment of 'The Minor Poets' is far from that of the young Sangharakshita, who was so compellingly inspired to attempt to transform that splendour into his own compositions.

Sangharakshita remained a lover of poetry even when his principal creative outlets were his memoirs, his Dharma books, and the Buddhist movement he founded. In quantity alone, his prose vastly outweighs his verse, and his oral Dharma teaching outweighs his written work. But a stanza of a 1991 poem, 'The Great Things of Guhyaloka', modelled on Thomas Hardy's 'Great Things', attests to his love of the poets, which persisted when gas lamps were no more and night-long rhapsodizing was a distant memory:

> Poetry is a great thing,
> A great thing to me,
> With gas lamp lit and sonnets fit
> For night-long rhapsody;
> And sleeping till the blackbird
> Trills sweet within the tree:
> O poetry is a great thing,
> A great thing to me.

POEMS ARE STRANGE THINGS
Sangharakshita's close reading of a few of his poems

I
STANDING ON HOLY GROUND

A talk given at the Birmingham Buddhist Centre in 1999

A couple of years ago I happened to find myself in Berlin for a few days, meeting people and doing a bit of sightseeing, and inevitably before very long someone asked me if I would mind giving a talk. For some reason I didn't want to give a full-blown lecture, and I didn't exactly want to give a poetry reading, because even though so many people in Germany speak excellent English it didn't seem fair to inflict a reading of English poetry on them, especially not mine. So I decided that I would try a little experiment. I thought I would do something that I hadn't ever done before and just see whether people took to it or not. I didn't intend reading my own poetry but in a way that's what I ended up doing: not lots of poems but just one, which I explained line by line at some length.

The poem I chose to read and comment upon was 'Meditation', the one that begins 'Here perpetual incense burns'. I read this poem and explained it line by line (I had a very good translator in Anomarati) and I believe we really did go into that poem. The response was very positive, and I concluded that my little experiment had been quite successful.[18] In fact, I was quite surprised at how successful it had been. Not only that. As I explained the poem line by line, I was surprised to find how much there was to explain. Even though I myself had written the poem, I was surprised how much there was in it. I think I can say that, by way of commenting on that poem, I managed to draw out practically the whole of Buddhism. I hadn't expected to do that, and it made me realize that the poet or the artist is not always fully conscious of exactly what he is doing or saying. That is no doubt why Plato in the *Phaedrus* speaks of poetic inspiration as a kind of madness, a madness that comes from the Muses.[19] It doesn't come from you, not you in your ordinary everyday selfhood. When I wrote that poem, I didn't consciously or deliberately try to put all of Buddhism into it. I wasn't trying to write about Buddhism at all. It was a poem about meditation, based, I suppose, on my own experience of meditation at that time. But although I hadn't tried to put any Buddhism into it, nevertheless if one looked closely enough, there was quite a lot of Buddhism there.

Last year I had a similar experience. I get a lot of letters, as well as cards and little presents and photographs, and from time to time people also send me their MA and their PhD theses. One of them, I remember, was on some obscure branch of chemistry. I looked at it – I can't say that I read it, and I don't think I could have understood it even if I had – but I think it is very nice that people think of me in this way, that they send even their thesis on some obscure branch of chemistry. On this occasion, a young man in Finland sent me a copy of his MA thesis on one of my own poems, 'Hercules and the Birds'. The thesis was written in Finnish, which at first was rather frustrating. Here was this fat little volume, this tantalizing thesis, which I knew was on my own poem, and I couldn't understand a word of it. Fortunately, Sridevi came to my rescue and very kindly sent me a summary of the thesis in English, and when I read the summary, I was astonished, because the young man who wrote it had seen in my poem all sorts of things that I had not consciously put there, though I had to admit that those things definitely were there. Remembering my Plato, I couldn't help wondering whether I was mad when I wrote 'Hercules and the Birds' or when I wrote 'Meditation'. Did they come from the Muses? Or perhaps I was just a little bit mad at the time; I hope so. But mad or not, this evening I am going to repeat the Berlin experiment. I am going to explain one of my poems. I wrote this one in Kalimpong in 1957, and it is relatively short. It is called 'The Scholars'.

> Asked 'What is Buddhism?', off they go,
> Consult the dictionaries, row on row,
> Sanskrit, Tibetan, Pāli – German too,
> As though it was the only thing to do,
> Until we wish in all sincerity,

A second Burning of the Books could be.
Have they no other word for sick souls full
Of doubt than 'Read my latest article'?
Off with your shoes! 'Tis holy ground! Depart!
Buddhism's in the life and in the heart.

I can't remember the exact circumstances in which I wrote this poem, but 1957, the year in which I wrote it, was the 2,500th anniversary of the Buddha's *parinirvāṇa*, and it was being celebrated all over the Buddhist world. In India there were all sorts of celebrations, and I myself participated in some of them, as described in my memoirs. In that year, many books on Buddhism were published. They were of varying quality, and quite a number of them, I'm afraid, were rather dry. Not only that; they very often showed a complete lack of any real understanding of the Dharma. I must have read at least some of these books, and I think some of them must have rather annoyed me, hence the poem. I must have written it in a mood of some annoyance. But before I go on to look at it line by line, I want to say a few words about the title, 'The Scholars'.

In his famous dictionary, Dr Johnson distinguishes four meanings of the term 'scholar'. 1: the scholar is 'one who learns from a master'; a scholar is a disciple. 2: a scholar is 'a man of letters'. 3: a scholar is 'a pedant, a man of books'. And 4: a scholar is 'one who has had a lettered education'. According to the *Concise Oxford Dictionary*, the primary meaning of the word is 'a learned person, especially in language, literature etc., an academic'. In the poem I am speaking of a certain type of scholar, corresponding more or less to Dr Johnson's pedant or man of books, and of course I am speaking of a certain type of Buddhist scholar, or rather a certain sort of scholar of Buddhism, that is to say, someone who is learned in the history, the doctrine, the development, the archaeology, and so on of Buddhism, who knows the canonical languages and literature of Buddhism, in Pāli, Sanskrit, Chinese, Tibetan, and so on, and who holds perhaps a teaching post in a university. In other words, I am speaking of someone who is an academic in the field of Buddhism. Of course, such a person might not regard himself as a Buddhist – he might even be somewhat hostile to Buddhism – but nonetheless you might find him teaching Buddhism at university level. You might find him writing books and articles on the subject, and he might even be regarded as an authority on Buddhism. It is with scholars of this type that my poem is concerned. That is to say, it is concerned with those who know a lot about Buddhism intellectually but who have little or no experience of it and don't try to practise it, or even think of trying to practise it.

But it is time we proceeded to the poem itself. The first line envisages a situation in which someone has heard about Buddhism and they want to find out more about it, so they start looking for someone to ask, an authority. As we usually do in all sorts of fields of life, they turn to the specialists, the scholars, the academics and ask them, perhaps not directly, but through their books, 'What is Buddhism?'

In 1957, when the poem was written, there were comparatively few books on Buddhism available, and comparatively few translations of *sūtras*, especially Mahāyāna *sūtras*. Whenever a new translation of a Mahāyāna *sūtra* came out we were very excited, it was a real gift. They weren't readily available, there were very few of them, and we valued those early translations, imperfect though they were, very highly. They were mostly the work of scholars who were not Buddhists, but we had no alternative, on many occasions, but to turn to the scholars, especially if we were living in the west.

Now it mustn't be thought that I am just criticizing those early scholars. They did their best and we should be grateful to them, both for their translations and for their writings, through which at least something of the Dharma usually managed to shine. But on what were those writings based? When the scholars in the poem are asked, 'What is Buddhism?', what do they do? They go and consult the dictionaries: the dictionaries of the languages in which the Buddhist scriptures are written, and the dictionaries of modern European languages. Not only that – they consult them as though it were the only thing to do. So what does that all mean? I'll have to go into it a little.

But first of all, a few words about consulting dictionaries. I don't want to give the impression that I think it's wrong to consult dictionaries. I think in fact that we should consult them very much more than most of us do. Most of us, it has to be admitted, speak and write very badly. We have a poor command of our own language, and we therefore can't communicate our thoughts and feelings to others effectively, and in this way all sorts of misunderstandings between people arise. Fairly often we've only a vague idea of the meaning of the words we use and sometimes we confuse words that sound alike, like 'militate' and 'mitigate', or 'affect' and 'effect'. We need to take more care. We should be proud of our mother tongue, whatever it happens to be, and we should do our best to speak it and write it correctly, effectively, and as beautifully as possible.

The total number of words in the English language is said to be somewhere between 400,000 and 600,000, but most of us use only a couple of thousand words; some people, it's said, use only a few hundred. We overwork certain words, like 'nice': 'have a nice day', 'a nice book', 'a nice meal', 'a nice film', 'a nice meditation' – almost anything can be nice. Another is 'fantastic'; this is a word that young people are very fond of using. And then there's 'devastated'. Every day I hear on the radio or read in the paper about people being devastated. Someone loses his job, he's devastated; his football team doesn't win the match, he's devastated; his father dies, he's devastated – and that strong word loses its power because it's overused. We therefore need to consult the dictionary much more than we do. That will help to clarify and refine our use of words and we will be able to express ourselves better and communicate better, whether in speech or in writing. It will also help us to think more clearly. Personally, I consult the dictionary quite a lot. In fact, when I am writing, whether I am writing memoirs or even a letter, I habitually consult three dictionaries, just to make sure, because they don't always have quite the same definitions or explanations of words. I consult *Collins*, I consult the *Concise Oxford*, and I consult my dear old friend Dr Johnson's *Dictionary*, a facsimile copy of which a kind friend presented me with quite a few years ago. And for emergencies, when *Collins*, *Concise Oxford* and even Dr Johnson aren't of any help, there is the great thirteen-volume *Oxford Dictionary* to fall back on. I also consult the *Thesaurus*.

When I am writing I ask myself the meanings of the words I'm using. First thoughts are by no means always the best; any practising poet or writer can tell you that. So I ask myself, 'Does this word I am thinking of using convey the precise shade of meaning, of thought, of suggestion, of resonance that I want to communicate?' I ask myself this question with regard to almost every important word I set down on paper, especially if I am writing something like my memoirs. Then of course there is the question of spelling, punctuation, syntax, and grammar; I am not going to go into all that, otherwise this talk will sound too much like a lesson. But we need to consult the dictionary.

The dictionary, we may say, is the writer's best friend – that is, his best friend as a writer. And the dictionary is also the reader's best friend as a reader. In your reading, if you come across a word you don't quite understand, look it up, or make a note to look it up later on, otherwise you may miss something of the author's meaning, miss a subtlety that may be quite important.

But it's time we got back to the scholars and their use of the dictionaries.

> Asked 'What is Buddhism?' off they go,
> Consult the dictionaries, row on row,
> Sanskrit, Tibetan, Pāli – German too,
> As though it was the only thing to do,

What do I mean by saying that they consult the dictionaries? The Buddha's teachings, that is to say the Dharma, is found in the Buddhist scriptures, and those scriptures consist of words. The mere scholar thinks that if he's understood the words in which the teachings find expression he's understood that teaching itself, so he consults the dictionaries in order to find out the meaning of the words and thus the meaning of Buddhism. Not only that; he consults the dictionaries as though it were the only thing to do. In other words, within the context of the poem, 'scholars' are people who think you've understood Buddhism when you've understood the words that Buddhism uses, especially the words of the scriptures. A scholar in this sense is one who believes you can know what Buddhism is without practising it, without experiencing it, and without contact with others who also are practising it.

Of course, I am not saying that consulting dictionaries is of no help at all in our attempt to understand Buddhism; that would be to go to the opposite extreme. What I am saying is that consulting dictionaries and understanding the words in which the Dharma finds expression is by no means enough. The words by themselves are not the Dharma. This is perhaps why in the *Laṅkāvatāra Sūtra* the Buddha is represented as saying that from the night of his Enlightenment to the night of his *parinirvāṇa*, he has not uttered one single word.[20]

So the first four lines of the poem describe what scholars, mere scholars, do when asked 'What is Buddhism?' They consult the dictionaries, they write books and articles based simply on knowledge of the words of the scriptures. But how do we feel when we get that sort of answer to our question, an answer just based upon words? Well, we feel frustrated. Sometimes we feel very frustrated indeed. We asked a serious question. Perhaps we really did want to know what Buddhism is. I have met people who were put off Buddhism by the kind of books they had read. The books were just too dry, too scholarly, too abstract, too academic, and they concluded that Buddhism was not for them. This is much less likely to happen nowadays. Nowadays there are a lot of good books on Buddhism written by scholars who are also practising Buddhists. But at the time I wrote my poem, quite a lot of the books on Buddhism that were available were very dry, so naturally people sometimes felt frustrated. In the biblical phrase, they had asked for bread and been given a stone.

I remember a sad case of this sort of thing. It happened soon after the mass conversion to Buddhism of Dr Ambedkar's followers. I had a good friend who was himself a follower of Dr Ambedkar. He was about my own age or a little older, a little, skinny man, a bit fiery, and he happened to be a lecturer in Pāli in a college in Bombay. After the mass conversion, he thought we should start up classes on Buddhism in the college where he was teaching. Perhaps I should also mention, to throw a little light onto the type of person he was, that some years later he got it into his head that he should do just what the Buddha did, so he decided he'd get married, he'd have one son and then he'd leave his wife and son and become a *bhikkhu*. He was a very determined person and, believe it or not, that is exactly what he did. He did get married, he did have one son (I suppose he thought it lucky the child wasn't a daughter) and a little while later he went forth and became a *bhikkhu*.

Anyway, we got together a Buddhism class. I was supposed to give a little talk on Buddhism in the first part and he was going to teach Pāli grammar during the second half. About 30 or 40 people came along to begin with, and we had to start at 8 o'clock because they were mostly mill workers and didn't finish work until then. They had converted to Buddhism as part of Dr Ambedkar's programme of mass conversion, but they didn't know anything about Buddhism, and some of them hardly knew how and why they'd been converted. They really did want to know about Buddhism, though, although many of them could not read or write. So I would give my little talk and then my friend the professor would start giving his lesson in Pāli grammar, and he used to go on and on and on. After a few weeks my Dharma talk got squeezed out completely. The Buddhist scriptures are written in Pāli, so the professor thought (he was a Theravādin) that if you want to learn Buddhism you've got to read the scriptures, if you want to read the scriptures, you've got to know Pāli, and if you want to know Pāli, you've got to do the grammar. So there he was, night after night, hammering away at Pāli grammar, making those poor tired men, after a full day's work, recite all those declensions and conjugations and get them all by heart. He drilled them like anything, and afterwards he'd say to me 'Ah, Sangharakshita, I love teaching Pāli grammar.' But the result was that after a few weeks nobody came any more.

This illustrates the sort of thing I'm talking about. These people wanted bread, but my friend, with the best of intentions, only gave them a stone. At that stage he was just a scholar – a very good one, he knew his Pāli grammar back to front, he was ablaze with enthusiasm when he was doing all that declining and conjugating – but he lost all those students who might have imbibed something of the Dharma. They must have felt quite puzzled as to what was going on, they must have felt frustrated, even angry. If they did, I wouldn't blame them. So that's the sort of situation that I envisage in the next lines of the poem:

> Until we wish, in all sincerity,
> A second Burning of the Books could be.
> Have they no other word for sick souls full
> Of doubt than 'Read my latest article'?

The scholarly, abstract books haven't answered our questions, they haven't told us what Buddhism really is, so we throw them aside, get rid of them, or we don't come to the Pāli grammar class any more. We may even want to burn those books. That's putting it rather strongly, but if we are deeply disappointed we do feel strongly. I forget which particular burning of the books I had in mind. It may have been the burning of the books that took place in China in 213 BCE, under Qin Shi Huang, or that which took place in India in 1197 CE when Muslim invaders sacked the great monastic university of Nālandā and burned down its great library with all those treasures of Buddhist literature, *sūtras* and *śāstras* and other works in palm leaf manuscripts. The library at Nālandā is said to have burned for six whole months, and hundreds of thousands of valuable works must have been lost. For the purpose of the poem it doesn't matter which particular burning of the books I had in mind. In any case, nowadays we're faced by a rather different problem. We're not frustrated because we get a stone instead of bread; we get too much bread. That is to say, there are too many good books on Buddhism available: some of them may be quite scholarly, but they are based on a certain amount of spiritual experience. Also, there are too many reliable translations, too many in the sense that there are more of them than we have time to read. So let me make a few suggestions as to what to do if you find yourself in this position.

First suggestion: read, if you possibly can, books written by Buddhists, books in which scholarship is subordinated to understanding and practice and experience of the Dharma.

Second suggestion: read books that concentrate on the basic Buddhist teachings, on the Four Noble Truths, the Noble Eightfold Path, conditioned co-production, the bodhisattva ideal, and so on. Don't bother with material dealing with obscure schools and teachings.

Third suggestion: read Buddhist scriptures. One gets the impression that some Buddhists read almost anything except the Buddhist scriptures. Read the Pāli canonical texts – the *Dīgha Nikāya*, the *Majjhima Nikāya*, the *Dhammapada*, the *Sutta Nipāta*, the *Udāna* – and the great Mahāyāna *sūtras*. The Pāli texts will give you a vivid idea of the Buddha as a historical personality living in India in about 500BCE, and the kind of conditions under which he lived and worked and taught and associated with his disciples. The Mahāyāna *sūtras*, some of them at least, will give you a vivid impression of the grand, as it were archetypal, background of Buddhism. The Mahāyāna *sūtras* are full of inspiring, archetypal imagery. They transport one to other worlds, worlds full of light and colour and music and beauty, far transcending the world in which we live, but of which nonetheless our world, at its best, in the person of some individuals, can be at least a distant reflection. We shouldn't even just read the scriptures by ourselves or to ourselves. We should sometimes at least read them aloud, perhaps in a ritual context so that the reading of the scriptures becomes a spiritual exercise in itself.

Fourth suggestion: select, even specialize. I think this is particularly important, especially from a practical point of view. Some of us read far too much, which sometimes means we read hastily and superficially. And when I say some of us read far too much, I'm afraid I have to include myself in this category. But, fortunately, some years ago I had a lucky escape. I spent fourteen whole years in Kalimpong and I didn't have access to many books, even books on Buddhism. For one thing, I didn't have the money to buy them. If I spent two rupees on a book, that was quite a big item of expenditure. And in the area in which I lived there was no public library. But somehow I managed to build up a small collection of books, mainly on Buddhism, perhaps a hundred volumes, and those hundred volumes are the nucleus of the present Order library.[21] Most of these volumes I read again and again. I got to know them thoroughly, both books about Buddhism and translations of the Buddhist scriptures, and this is what I suggest you try to do. Build up a small collection of Buddhist literature of your own. It doesn't have to be one hundred volumes. It need be only ten or twelve. But whatever the number, get to know them thoroughly. Read them again and again. Discuss them with your friends. Don't always go running after something new, the latest publication or the latest theories about Buddhism.

So these are my suggestions. There's another quite important aspect to the whole question and that is the aspect of spiritual temperament. I want to go into that just a little. In Buddhism traditionally there are several classifications according to temperament. This evening I'm concerned with only one of them, one that will be familiar to many of you, especially if you've studied chapter 15 of my book *The Three Jewels*. According to this classification, people are of three spiritual types: the faith follower, the doctrine follower, and the body witness. The faith follower is the devotional type of person, the type of person who experiences strong feelings of love and devotion towards the ideal, especially perhaps as embodied in the figure of the Buddha, the archetypal Buddhas and bodhisattvas, the great teachers, and so on. A person of this type is very fond of puja and chanting and perhaps religious music, and he or she likes to go on pilgrimage. Just recently, I've had quite a few postcards from people who are on pilgrimage to the Buddhist holy places in India, and they seem to be having a very good time in the very best sense. Several of them have written to the effect that seeing the places where the Buddha lived and taught has made the Buddha and his teaching very much more alive for them than before. It's people of this kind of devotional temperament who love to go on pilgrimage and make their knowledge of the Buddha and his life more vivid in this way. The faith follower also seems to feel the need for personal contact with the teacher – not just reading the teacher's books, but having personal contact with the teacher whenever possible. The faith follower also likes to serve fellow disciples, thinking that to serve the teacher's disciples is in a way to serve the teacher himself.

The doctrine follower is a more intellectual type of person. In modern times 'intellectual' sometimes assumes a negative connotation, but here I'm using the word in an entirely positive sense. The doctrine follower feels a strong need to understand the Dharma. For him or her it is not enough to love and serve the Dharma; he or she wants to *understand* it. So the doctrine follower is fond of studying the *sūtras* and *śāstras*, poring over them line by line, and of course consulting the dictionary. The doctrine follower is interested in Buddhist philosophy, and wants to know all about the Madhyamaka and the Abhidharma, and the Yogācāra, and all the subtle shades of difference between them and their various subschools and sub-subschools. He or she enjoys discussions about Buddhist metaphysics and Buddhist epistemology and all that sort of thing with other intellectually inclined people. As a doctrine follower you don't perhaps experience much in the way of devotional feeling. You may respect your teacher but you don't feel as great a need of contact as the faith follower does. You're quite happy to get your knowledge mainly from books.

The body witness is the meditator or yogin. I say a bit more about this in *The Three Jewels* but it's a little complicated, so here I'll just refer to the body witness. This is the person of contemplative temperament, the person who is primarily interested in his or her own inner experience. If you are a 'body witness' you are not especially interested in ideas, or books, or ritual. You have no wish to study Buddhist philosophy and very often you enjoy silence and living alone, preferably in the midst of nature. You may have a strong feeling for your teacher, especially at the beginning of your spiritual career, because if you specialize in meditation, personal guidance is usually necessary.

So, these are the three temperaments: the faith follower, the doctrine follower, and the body witness. It would appear that in the Buddhist tradition, the differences between these three kinds of spiritual temperament hold good on both sides of Stream Entry, though the tradition is not altogether clear on this point. It would also seem that under certain conditions it's possible to switch from one kind of temperament to another, but I won't go into that now. At present I'm concerned with one important practical question, which is: Is studying the Dharma, is reading Buddhist literature, necessary to the same extent for people of all three temperaments? Well, apparently not. It would seem that there is a great deal of difference between people's needs in this respect. The Dharma follower, the doctrine follower, of course does study and think quite a lot, reading many books, and perhaps writing books too. The faith follower studies and thinks much less, and reads perhaps just a few favourite books, often of a devotional nature. And the body witness may study hardly at all. Once they get really deeply into meditation, they may not read a book from one year to the next.

Here perhaps a word of warning is necessary. One should not rationalize one's failure to study. One shouldn't say, 'I'm a faith follower' or 'I'm a body witness' as a way of excusing one's laziness with regards to study. If one is really a faith follower one will not show it just by not studying; one will show it by being very devoted. And in the case of the body witness, one will not show one is a natural meditator just by not studying; one will show it by meditating whenever one gets the opportunity.

Here another important question arises, perhaps even more important than the previous one. Do people of these three kinds of temperaments – the devotional, the intellectual, the meditative – make the same spiritual progress, assuming that they make the same kind of effort under roughly the same conditions? I'm going to answer this question with the help of another threefold classification: the three kinds of *prajñā*, or wisdom. First of all there is the wisdom that comes by hearing the Dharma or, in modern times, by reading the Dharma in the form of the *sūtras*. Secondly, there's the wisdom that comes by reflecting on the Dharma, that is to say, reflecting on what one has read so that one understands it. And thirdly, there's the wisdom that comes by meditating on the Dharma that one has read about and reflected on. These three are usually understood to represent three different degrees of wisdom. In the first, the wisdom based on hearing, one simply knows about the Dharma, one accumulates information about the Dharma. In the second, through reflection, one understands what one has informed oneself about. And in the third, through meditation, one realizes it, one comes to understand what one has informed oneself about and reflected on.

The first two wisdoms are mundane; only the third, the *bhāvanā mayī prajñā*, is transcendental, only the third leads directly to Enlightenment. That's the usual explanation. But there's another way of understanding these three *prajñās*. Here the difference is not in the wisdom itself, but in the approach to that wisdom. According to this way of understanding it, there is only one transcendental wisdom, but there are three different ways in which it can be approached and realized. It can be approached and realized through intense faith and devotion; after all, the Buddha says in the *Sutta Nipāta*, 'by faith the flood is crossed'[22] – that is to say, the flood of mundane existence. That same transcendental wisdom can equally be approached and realized through intense and prolonged philosophical reflection. And of course it can be approached and realized through intense meditation. The first is the approach of the faith follower, the second is the approach of the doctrine follower, and the third is the approach of the body witness.

I could say quite a bit more about this correlation, but I've already strayed quite far enough away from the scholars, so we will have to retrace our steps a little. We got on to the question of the three wisdoms as a result of discussing the three temperaments. We saw that not all practising Buddhists are equally interested in Dharma study. Before that, I gave four suggestions for Dharma study, for those who might feel overwhelmed by the sheer quantity of Buddhist literature now available and who are wondering how to resolve that issue. If those suggestions of mine are followed, perhaps we won't feel frustrated and won't be tempted to give up study altogether, and we will certainly not wish for a second burning of the books.

So we come to the next two lines of the poem:

Have they no other word for sick souls full
Of doubt than 'Read my latest article'?

'They' are the scholars, but who are the 'sick souls full of doubt'? They are, in the poem, those who ask the scholars 'What is Buddhism?' Perhaps we ourselves were among those 'sick souls full of doubt' once upon a time. But what do the scholars say when they are asked 'What is Buddhism?' They just say 'Read my latest article.' Read the results of the latest scholarly research into Buddhism, maybe about the dates of the Buddha's life or whether a particular text was really the word of the Buddha or not. They are usually unable to say very much more than that. We ask for bread and we're given a stone.

As I mentioned at the beginning, I must have been rather annoyed when I wrote this poem, and you may have noticed that as it proceeds there is a mounting sense of indignation, which reaches a climax in these two lines. So in the poem (I don't feel indignant now), what makes me indignant? In the poem people are not asking, 'What is Buddhism?' just for fun. The question is not theoretical. They desperately want an answer that will give meaning to their lives, because they are psychologically and spiritually sick. They suffer, they're full of doubts, they ask themselves: 'What is the purpose of life? Does life have a meaning at all? Why am I here? What am I supposed to be doing? Is death the end or not? Is there something more than this ordinary life, this humdrum routine?' Perhaps they've heard somehow that there is an answer to such questions in Buddhism, so they ask 'What is Buddhism?' and unfortunately they often ask the wrong people; they ask the mere scholars, not perhaps directly but through their books, though this is less likely to happen nowadays than it was in the past. And the scholars give them an answer that is no answer; in effect the scholars fob them off. It's this that makes me indignant in the poem. I'm indignant that scholars should be so blind to people's real needs, so insensitive, so indifferent, sometimes so complacent, thinking that they are the great authorities on Buddhism. Sometimes they even smile at the idea of actually practising it.

Of course, it's not just some scholars of Buddhism who are at fault in this kind of way. There are pundits, know-alls, in every walk of life, especially perhaps in the media – people who don't realize the extent to which many ordinary people are looking for an answer to the real problems of life. Such people are unsympathetic when ordinary people try to work out a solution to the problems of life for themselves. A few weeks ago there was a rather disgraceful example of this kind of attitude. It involved someone called Glenn Hoddle, who expressed his views on reincarnation. I must admit that I hadn't heard of him before, but I gathered from various sources that he was quite an important person.[23] Anyway, it seems he expressed some views on the subject of reincarnation, and the pundits of the media came down on the poor man like the proverbial ton of bricks. His views were denounced as preposterous, offensive, insulting, idiotic, and so on, and the very idea of reincarnation was described as bizarre and ridiculous. Admittedly

Glenn Hoddle's views on reincarnation were a bit muddled and they didn't quite agree with Buddhist teaching on the subject, but the poor man was only trying to make sense of life for himself, he was only trying, in his own way, to work out a philosophy. His critics didn't appreciate that, however, and his views eventually cost him his job. He had the wrong theological opinions. So much for our tolerant, liberal society. So once again, I couldn't help feeling rather indignant.

This brings me to the last line of the poem but one:

Off with your shoes! 'Tis holy ground! Depart!

The first four lines of the poem envisage a situation in which the scholars are asked 'What is Buddhism?' and in which they simply go and consult their dictionaries. The next two lines describe our reaction to their response. We feel disappointed, frustrated, even angry. In the next lines I ask if the scholars really can do no more than advise us to read their latest paper on Buddhism. The question is, of course, rhetorical. I'm really saying, 'They can't help us at all.' So in the next line I address the scholars directly and say 'Off with your shoes! 'Tis holy ground! Depart!' But what is this holy ground? It is the human soul. I'm not using the word 'soul' in any strict theological sense. I'm using it to stand for that deeper, more essential part of ourselves that feels and suffers and aspires. I could also use the word 'heart'; the poet John Keats, you may remember, speaks of 'the holiness of the heart's affections'.[24] So when I say to the scholars 'Off with your shoes!' what I mean is, show some respect for people's feelings, especially their deeper feelings. Take their questions seriously, even if they can't express themselves very well, even if they are a bit muddled in their thinking. This applies not only to scholars in the field of Buddhism but to the pundits and know-alls of the media as well, and it applies to us. We may disagree with people's views but we shouldn't abuse people on account of their views, and we shouldn't ever describe the views themselves as offensive or insulting or bizarre; these are purely subjective judgements and tell us nothing about the validity or invalidity of the views themselves.

I haven't quite finished with that line. The last word is 'Depart!' If the scholars are in fact incapable of showing respect for people's feelings, if they're oblivious to them, the best thing they can do is to remove themselves from the scene altogether. If they can't tell us what

Buddhism is, they have nothing at all to do with Buddhism in the real sense, so the best thing they can do is simply to disappear.

In the East, Buddhists and Hindus take off their shoes when entering a temple or a monastery, but I wasn't thinking of that when I wrote this line. Don't those words have a slightly familiar ring? Haven't you heard them somewhere before? Well, you probably have, because they come from the Bible, from the book of Exodus in the Old Testament:

> Now Moses kept the flock of Jethro his father-in-law, the priest of Midian: and he led the flock to the backside of the desert and came to the mountain of God, even to Horeb. And the angel of the Lord appeared unto him in a flame of fire out of the midst of a bush and he looked, and behold, the bush burned with fire and the bush was not consumed. And Moses said, I will now turn aside and see this great sight, why the bush is not burnt. And when the Lord saw that he turned aside to see, God called unto him out of the midst of the bush, and said, Moses, Moses, and he said, Here am I. And he said, Draw not nigh hither: put off thy shoes from off thy feet, for the place whereon thou standest is holy ground.[25]

What is an image from the Bible doing in a poem about Buddhism? As I mentioned, I wrote the poem in 1957, when I was living in Kalimpong. I'd been a Buddhist for twelve years. But though I was living in India, I was a western Buddhist, and it was as a western Buddhist that I wrote the poem. But what is a western Buddhist? I've dealt with this question before in other lectures. Very briefly, in those other lectures I said that a western Buddhist is one who seeks to practise the Dharma under the conditions of modern western civilization – that is to say, a civilization that is predominantly industrialized, urbanized, and secularized. But that is by no means the whole story. A western Buddhist is also one who, as a westerner, has a western cultural heritage; and that heritage is a very rich one. It includes the legacy of classical Greece and of ancient Rome. It includes the Renaissance, the eighteenth-century Enlightenment, the Romantic movement, and very much more. It includes countless masterpieces of art, literature, music, architecture, and so on. As western Buddhists we cannot ignore that great heritage, and we certainly cannot repudiate it. There is so much that is inspiring and uplifting in it. There is so much in it that stimulates our imagination and deepens our understanding.

But what of Christianity? Where does that fit in? Surely that too is part of our heritage, even as western Buddhists? Here it is important to make a distinction between Christianity as a religion and Christianity as a culture, or more precisely between Christianity as a doctrinal, not to say dogmatic, system and Christianity as a body of cultural expressions of various kinds. Christianity as a religion is definitely not part of the heritage of the western Buddhist. We should be very clear about this. Christianity is theistic, Buddhism is non-theistic, and the two are quite incompatible. And there are other fundamental differences; I need not go into those now. But Christianity as a culture may, however, be part of the cultural heritage of the western Buddhist.

Let me give you an example from my own experience. When I was very young I read Homer's *Iliad* and I was fascinated by the story, by the characters, and especially, for some reason or other, by the gods and goddesses who appear in the story: Zeus, Hera, Pallas Athene, Aphrodite, Ares. I thoroughly enjoyed reading the great poem, and I've read it many times since. It has become part of my personal cultural heritage. But I've never believed in the literal existence of the gods and goddesses of the *Iliad*. I've never worshipped them as an ancient Greek or Roman might have done. The *Iliad* is part of my cultural heritage; it's not part of my religious heritage. Similarly, two or three years later, when I was still quite young, I read Milton's *Paradise Lost*, that great epic. I was fascinated by this too, by the story and by the characters: God, the Messiah, Satan, Adam and Eve, Sin and Death. But I did not believe in the literal truth of the story of *Paradise Lost* in the way that many Christians still do, and I certainly did not believe in the literal existence of the different characters. For me, God was as real or as unreal as Zeus or Apollo or Aphrodite. *Paradise Lost* is part of my cultural heritage, not part of my religious heritage, so in that way Christianity is part of my cultural heritage as a western Buddhist. The Bible, especially in the Authorized Version, is part of my cultural heritage. If I read it, I don't read it as the word of God, I read it as literature. I read the Old Testament, if I read it at all, as ancient Hebrew literature, just as I read the *Iliad* and the *Odyssey* as ancient Greek literature.

Not only that; my cultural heritage is part of me. It enters into what I write, it enters into my poetry. This is not of course to make any great claims for my poetry! Earlier I referred to my poem 'Hercules and the Birds', the one on which the Finnish student wrote his thesis. Hercules is an ancient Greek hero, a demigod who eventually becomes a god; he was worshipped throughout the Graeco-Roman world for many centuries. But though I wrote that poem about Hercules, I don't believe literally in his existence as a god and I certainly don't worship him. In my poem I simply make use of the image of Hercules because it enables me to express something that I want to say. It is the same with the image from the Book of Exodus that I use in 'The Scholars'. It helps me to express something. The Bible as literature and its images and characters are part of my cultural heritage, part of my language, so to speak, so that they enter into my poetry quite naturally. There's no need for western Buddhists to be afraid of Christianity. Much as we may reject it as a religion, there's no need for us to reject it as a culture.

This brings me to the last line of the poem:

Buddhism's in the life and in the heart.

You'll notice that I distinguish between 'life' and 'heart'. The heart is the principle of vitality; it is the seat, metaphorically, of the emotions, especially of our deeper emotions. And life is the expression of that principle, the principle of vitality, in action. So in what way is Buddhism in the heart? When is Buddhism in the heart? Buddhism is in the heart when we go for Refuge. And when is Buddhism in the life? Buddhism is in the life when our Going for Refuge finds expression in the day-to-day observance of the five or the ten precepts, when it finds expression in an ethical lifestyle, in spiritual friendship, and so on. There's a lot that I could say about all of this, but I'm not going to do so, because we've reached ground, holy ground, that will be familiar to all of you.

I will conclude with just a few reminders. Let us remember that mere scholars are not authorities on Buddhism. Let us remember to consult the dictionary. Let us remember my four suggestions for the study of the Dharma. Let us remember that people are of different temperaments and approach the Dharma in different ways. Let us remember not to be dismissive of people's attempts to make sense of life, however clumsy those attempts may appear to be. Let us remember that as western Buddhists we have a western cultural heritage. And above all, let us remember that Buddhism is not just in books, not just in words. Buddhism is in the life and in the heart.

2
FOOTPRINTS OF DELIGHT

When we are young we tend to look to the future, to anticipate what is yet to come, but when we are old we're more inclined to look back to the past, to past experiences, past friendships, past contacts of every kind. Ultimately, of course, as Buddhists we have to look beyond both the past and the future. In fact we have to look even beyond the present, beyond the present moment. As the Buddha says in the *Dhammapada*,

> Give up what is before in time, give up what is after, give up what is in between. Cross to the further shore of existence and with mind wholly released you will undergo birth and decay no more.[26]

Well, I have to admit that I am now quite old. I've recently celebrated my seventy-fifth birthday, so it's only natural that I should be looking more to the past than to the future. There seems to be much more of past than there probably will be of future. So I look back at my life. Sometimes I look back at it when I wake up in the night and can't get back to sleep for a little while, sometimes I think about it as a result of something I've read, and of course I think about it when I'm writing my memoirs, as I'm doing just at present. At present I'm dealing with that very crucial period that led up to the founding of the FWBO in 1967, which really is quite a long time ago.[27]

So in these various ways, I look back from time to time on my life as a whole. Sometimes one can see an overall pattern – well, perhaps pattern is not quite the word – an overall direction of which one wasn't aware at the time. As I look back on my life – the things I've done, the things I've thought, the people I've met, my contact with my teachers, my contact with Kashyapji, with my Tibetan lama teachers in Kalimpong, and with Yogi Chen – all sorts of ideas, associations, and feelings float into my mind. And at these moments of reflection, I also look back on my writings. My writings are quite important to me, even quite precious to me. They're rather like my children, one might say. Some of them are quite old by this time, while others are much younger. Some, of course, are favourite children, and others are not quite such favourites. I feel a little sad, even a little disappointed, when some of my favourite children appear to be a little neglected by others, and sometimes I gently draw attention to that fact in the hope that in the future, perhaps after I've passed away, they will be given a little more attention than they have hitherto received. I won't mention any names or titles, but some of you probably know to which children of mine I'm referring.

As I look back at my writings, I remember the conditions under which I wrote them, and what an effort they were to write in some cases, though others came easily from my pen. And among my writings my poems are quite important to me, quite precious to me, so sometimes I look back at them. I have to admit that I remember very few of my own poems. I don't know why that is. After writing them, I've read them often enough, but there's probably only one poem that I could recite straight off without thinking too much about it. I won't tell you which poem that is! It's not necessarily a favourite one of mine, but somehow or other it has stuck, and I can repeat it whenever called upon to do so. When I look back to my poems and reflect upon them, quite often I understand them better now than I did at the time I wrote them. Poems are strange things. Sometimes one doesn't know quite where they've come from. They just emerge. You can decide to sit down and write a book, but you can't decide to sit down and write a poem, or at least I can't. My poems simply emerge, and I don't always know where they've emerged from. Some people have been a little surprised by some of the poems contained in my most recent little collection, *The Call of the Forest*. One or two people thought that some the poems weren't very, well, Buddhistic, especially the one called 'Revenge'. But I didn't think, 'Well, it's about time, just to show how human I am, to write a poem about revenge.' In the silent hours of the night this little poem started emerging, and I wrote it down verse by verse. I don't know why I wrote it. Probably in a sense I didn't write it. I can't say exactly where it came from. It must have come from some unsuspected corner of my psyche. I can't disclaim it. It's one of my children, although it may not be a very good child, so to speak, not a child of which one can be particularly proud.

As I look back and think about my poems I can sometimes see much more meaning in them than I realized was present in them at the time I wrote them, and it's one of these poems that I'm going to consider now. I wrote this poem more than fifty years ago, in India when I was still living as a freelance wandering ascetic.

SRI PADA

I saw His shining footprints
Gleaming in the grass like dew;
The flowers, where they had fallen,
Sweeter and fairer grew:
They led into the distant hills,
Those hills all misty-blue.

I will follow, I will follow,
'Neath the Spring Moon full and bright,
Through field and copse and hollow,
Those footprints of delight,
And walk upon those distant hills
One dawn all golden-white.

'Tis many an age of darkness
Since the days my Lord did pass
Leaving His dewy footprints
Like pearls upon the grass,
And rank weeds have o'ergrown them,
And thorns obscured, alas!

Yet will I follow boldly,
Using the hunter's art,
Until one day I find Him,

From all things else apart,
Sitting beside the Pool of Peace
In the blue hills of my heart.

Now, I'm not saying that this is one of my best poems. In fact, I'm quite sure that it isn't. I'm not even saying that it's a particularly good poem. Nonetheless, there seems to be rather more to it than I realized when I wrote it all those years ago, and I'm going to try to bring out something of what I've seen in it more recently.

To begin with, it's obviously about footprints: shining footprints, footprints of delight, dewy footprints. But whose footprints are they? The poem doesn't say very clearly. When I started reflecting on the poem, I realized that it was autobiographical. I realized that the 'I' of the poem really was me, Sangharakshita. It didn't simply represent a sort of poetic persona. It was a record of my own personal experience. So what was the nature of that experience? I'll have to go back a little way to explain that.

When I was very young I became a great reader, and I'm probably a great reader still. In my younger days, even in my pre-teen years, I read everything that I could get hold of, and I was particularly fond of poetry. In fact, I had a positive passion for poetry, especially as I entered upon my teen years. I can remember very clearly what I read and the circumstances under which I read it. I can remember reading Shakespeare's plays and poems, especially *Venus and Adonis*. I can remember reading all of Milton's work, and Keats, Shelley, Rossetti. I didn't confine myself to the English poets. I also read translations of Dante and Goethe, Heine and Baudelaire. Some of the poetry I read affected me very deeply indeed. In fact it wouldn't be an exaggeration to say that sometimes reading these poets I was thrown into a sort of ecstasy, a sort of rapture. As far as I remember, the poetry that affected me most strongly was that of Shelley. It's said that Shelley affects all adolescents who get round to reading him, and I was certainly an adolescent when I read him. I especially remember reading 'Adonais' and certain parts of 'Prometheus Unbound', especially that wonderful dialogue between the moon and the earth. So in those pre-teen and teen years I read a great deal of poetry, and was thrown again and again into a sort of ecstatic state while I was reading it. But one day a new thought struck me. So far, I had been reading western poets – English, French,

German, Italian. But one day a thought struck me like a thunderbolt: 'Why should I confine myself to the poetry of the West? What about Eastern poetry? So I looked around – by this time I was in my middle teens – for translations of Eastern poetry. I read translations of Persian poetry, and Chinese poetry, and Sanskrit poetry. I remember reading among the Persian poets, especially Hafez. I read Li Bai, especially Arthur Waley's beautiful translations, and I read translations from the Sanskrit of Kālidāsa, and in this way I was introduced to the literature of the East.

Now the literature of the East is very often a religious literature. In the case of Persian literature the religion is Sufistic and in the East, in Chinese literature, Japanese literature, a Buddhistic note is struck. In the case of Sanskrit literature there's the element of Hinduism. In fact, in the literature of the East, it's sometimes difficult to tell where literature in the narrow sense ends and religion begins. So eventually, to cut a long story short, I came across the Buddhist scriptures, and in particular the *Diamond Sūtra* and the *Sūtra of Wei Lang*, or Huineng, as his name is also pronounced. And these two scriptures affected me very deeply. They too threw me into a sort of ecstasy, but not just in the purely emotional sense. There was an element of insight there too. I'm not saying that there wasn't an element of insight in any of the poetry I read, but the insight that arose as a result of reading the *Diamond Sūtra* and the *Sūtra of Wei Lang* was of an entirely different order. To a certain extent, indeed, the reading of those two scriptures changed my life, or perhaps I should say the reading of them revealed to me the true direction of my life. The rest of the story is probably known to you, at least in outline, so I won't say anything more of an autobiographical nature.

But what had happened? What had happened was that one thing had led to another. Reading had led me to poetry. Poetry had led me to Eastern poetry. Eastern poetry had led me to Eastern literature in the broader sense, and Eastern literature had led me to the Buddhist scriptures. Thus I'd been following a sort of track, a series of footprints. And this is what the first verse of my poem is all about. The experience of poetry, the experience of the arts, belongs to the same sequence of experiences as our experience of the Dharma. Or, to put the matter in a nutshell, art and religion have something in common. There is an area where the two overlap, and I dealt with this area in my essay *The*

Religion of Art.[28] But though the footprints of which I've spoken form a series, they're not all equally distinct. Some of the early ones are quite faint. Some of them, in fact, are so faint that we can hardly make them out. Nonetheless, the faint ones lead us to the more distinct ones. Poetry, in a way, led me to the Dharma, led me, one might say, to the Buddha.

So the footprints, even the faint ones, are the Buddha's. And where do they lead? They lead into the 'distant hills', the hills that as yet for most of us are still very far distant. One can even go further and say that they lead not just into the hills but into the mountains. They lead us into higher realms of experience, realms that, like the mountains themselves, are as yet very far distant. The poem is called 'Sri Pada', and Sri Pada means 'holy footprint' – that is to say, the footprint of the Buddha. In Sri Lanka there is a mountain called Adam's Peak. It's more than 7,000 feet high, and its summit is conical. In the top of the cone there is a flat, oblong platform, and in the middle of the platform there is a huge footprint which Sinhalese Buddhists believe to be the footprint of the Buddha. They believe that the Buddha did once – in fact three times – visit Sri Lanka, and they call that footprint, right at the very summit of Adam's Peak, the Sri Pada, the holy footprint. And above that holy footprint, there is only the sky, the void. One can't go any further. One could say that the Sri Pada represents the last footprint in the whole series, and with that last footprint we come to the end of the track, the end of the trail.

So let me repeat just that first verse, and as you read it, try to bear in mind, or try to see, some of the significance that I myself have started to see in the poem, in this first verse especially.

> I saw His shining footprints
> Gleaming in the grass like dew;
> The flowers, where they had fallen,
> Sweeter and fairer grew:
> They led into the distant hills,
> Those hills all misty-blue.

Before we go on to the next verse, just a word about the flowers. I say in the poem that wherever his footsteps had fallen, the flowers grew 'sweeter and fairer'. Now what does this mean? Well, there is a meaning, and I hope it's not too far-fetched. Though I didn't realize it at the time, I think the flowers represent culture, culture in the highest and best sense. Wherever the Buddha leaves his footprints, wherever the Dharma leaves its mark, there is an efflorescence of culture, an efflorescence of literature and the fine arts. We certainly see this in the history of Buddhism in the East. We see it in India, the original home of Buddhism. We see it in Nepal, in Tibet, in central Asia. We see it above all in some ways in the literature and the arts of China and of Japan. We see this not only in the history of Buddhism of the East. We also begin to see it in Buddhism in the West. We see a little of it even in our own movement, in the paintings that are produced, the music that is being written and sung, the poetry that is being written.

So let's go on to the second verse:

I will follow, I will follow,
'Neath the Spring Moon full and bright,
Through field and copse and hollow,
Those footprints of delight,
And walk upon those distant hills
One dawn all golden-white.

In the first line, 'I will follow, I will follow' – that is to say, I will follow those footprints wherever they lead. We don't always realize when we start following the footprints just where they will lead us. We go along perhaps to a meditation class at the Buddhist centre in all innocence. We don't know where it is going to lead. But if we look back fifteen or twenty years later, we can see very well in retrospect just what we were letting ourselves in for, even though we couldn't know it at the time. So it's not enough simply to admire those shining footprints. It's not enough to admire the flowers that have sprung up where those footprints have fallen. In other words, aestheticism is not enough. It's not enough to feel a sort of aesthetic or pseudo-aesthetic appreciation of the beauty of those footprints.

Years ago, in the very early days of the FWBO, people used to be very fond of reading the *Songs of Milarepa*. They loved the idea of Milarepa sitting there in the snows and meditating day and night, and they loved those wonderful songs and all that poetic imagery. So they'd sit in their armchairs reading the *Songs of Milarepa*, every now and then reaching out to take a chocolate from a box. That's the sort of thing I've got in mind. We can read and enjoy books on Buddhism, we can read and enjoy the scriptures, but only too often it's just a sort of aesthetic appreciation, it's not a real acceptance of their significance. We have actually to follow those footprints and go wherever they lead, not just stand there looking down at them and thinking, 'What beautiful footprints!' We have in other words to commit ourselves to following the path shown by the Buddha. You'll probably have noticed that in that first line 'I will follow' is repeated not once but twice. I think if the exigencies of metre and rhyme had permitted, I would have repeated it three times, for obvious reasons. But the repetition – 'I will follow, I will follow' – expresses a sense of the urgency and determination of the commitment involved. It's equivalent to saying *Buddhaṃ saraṇaṃ gacchāmi*. It's equivalent to Going for Refuge to the Buddha, equivalent to effective and eventually real Going for Refuge.

There are other points to notice in this verse. I say, for instance, that I will follow those shining footprints 'Neath the Spring Moon full and bright'. The full moon here symbolizes the ideal of human Enlightenment. It symbolizes our as yet unrealized potential, the potential that will be actualized when we reach the end of the trail, when we reach that last footprint and gaze up, or soar up, into the blue and become ourselves Enlightened. I'm not sure why I spoke in the poem of the spring full moon – possibly because spring is associated with new life, with the rebirth of nature, and when we start following the Buddha's footprints, when we go for Refuge to him, we begin a new life, we are spiritually reborn.

The poem goes on to say that I will follow those footprints of delight 'Through field and copse and hollow'. What does this mean? It means that we will follow the path shown by the Buddha through all the vicissitudes of life, in youth and in age, regardless of changes in our external circumstances, in our fortunes, regardless of our lifestyle, in health and in sickness, in happiness and in sorrow, in life and in death. In other words, we will follow that path to the end. We'll follow it up into those distant hills, up the mountainside, to the top of Adam's Peak.

Just notice the adjective that I attach to the footprints in this verse. They're not just shining footprints; they're also footprints of delight. The two epithets are of course connected. What is bright and shining gives delight. Beautiful colours give delight, whether in nature or in art. One of the Pāli and Sanskrit words for delight is *rati*, and thus the

Dhammapada says, *sabbaṃ ratiṃ dhammaratī jināti*: 'Delight in the Dharma surpasses all delights.'[29] We delight in the Dharma when we study, understand, and practise it. The Buddha's footprints are footprints of delight when we actually follow them. This doesn't mean that we will always have an easy time. There will sometimes be difficulties. But to the extent that we practise the Dharma, even in the midst of those difficulties we will experience delight.

> 'Tis many an age of darkness
> Since the days my Lord did pass
> Leaving His dewy footprints
> Like pearls upon the grass,
> And rank weeds have o'ergrown them,
> And thorns obscured, alas!

So far the Buddha of the poem has been a legendary Buddha, a mythical Buddha, perhaps even a metaphorical Buddha. But with this third verse we come to the historical Buddha, Śākyamuni. The Buddha lived a long time ago, 2,500 years ago, and since then humanity has passed through some very dark times. With its two catastrophic world wars, the twentieth century could be regarded as an age of darkness, despite our vastly improved technology and our higher standard of living, at least higher for a very large proportion of the inhabitants of the earth. Notice also in these lines a change from the rather anonymous personal pronoun of verse 1 to the more intimate and familiar 'my Lord'. The Buddha, the Lord, did leave footprints, and we can still see something of those footprints even in this present age of darkness. They are to be found in his teachings as recorded in the Buddhist scriptures. The title of the *Dhammapada* could in fact be translated as 'footprints of the Dhamma'. This verse of the poem describes the Buddha's footprints as dewy. They're dewy because they are fresh, because they're alive. The Dharma is fresh, is alive. Reading the *Dhammapada*, for instance, you feel as though those verses were spoken not 2,500 years ago, but yesterday. They're so fresh, so appropriate, so relevant. I became especially aware of this the year before last when I was staying for a month at Guhyaloka and completing my own translation of the *Dhammapada*. I was quite immersed in the *Dhammapada* for all those weeks, and I realized again and again, with almost every verse, how fresh, how appropriate, how relevant it was. This is one of the reasons why the Dharma is termed *akāliko*, timeless. It's always appropriate, always relevant to our human condition. When I say that the Buddha's footprints are dewy, it's just a poetic way of saying that the Buddha's teaching is timeless. And then again this third verse describes the Buddha's footprints as being like pearls. That's rather extravagant, perhaps, but poetry is like that. They're like pearls because the Dharma is precious. The Three Jewels are precious. That's why they're called jewels. They're precious because they give meaning to our lives, because they're what, as Buddhists, we most highly value in the world. They are what, ultimately, we live for.

So, the Buddha's footprints are gleaming. They're footprints of delight. They're dewy footprints. They're like pearls. In other words, they are attractive. The Buddha's footprints are supremely attractive. The Dharma is supremely attractive, and the Buddha is supremely attractive. This reminds me of a passage in the *Śuraṅgama Sūtra* in which the Buddha asks Ānanda what it was that had led him to follow the Buddhist way of life, giving up all worldly pleasures. Ānanda replies in effect – it's rather a long reply – that he had been impressed by the beauty of the Buddha as expressed by his thirty-two marks.[30] Now, we don't usually think in terms of the beauty of the Buddha; we're more inclined to think in terms of the truth of his teaching. We might think that a Buddha image is beautiful, but when we think of the Buddha himself, Śākyamuni, it's not usually of his beauty that we think, despite the presence in the Buddhist scriptures of quite a number of passages which refer to it. But Ānanda goes on to say, 'These thirty-two marks appeared to me so fine, as tender and brilliant and transparent as crystal.' In other words, Ānanda was attracted by the Buddha, attracted by the Dharma, rather than repelled and disgusted by the world. This was very much my own feeling too, and I think that this poem of mine, 'Sri Pada', gives expression to the approach that consists in being attracted by the Dharma, attracted by the Buddha, rather than repelled and disgusted by the world. Of course, the two are not mutually exclusive. More often than not it's a question of relative proportion between the two.

But let us get back to verse 3. The Buddha, Śākyamuni, has left his footprints in the form of the Dharma, but those footprints have been overgrown by weeds and obscured by thorns. So what are the weeds? The weeds, we may say, are all the customs, practices, and beliefs that in many parts of the Buddhist world have grown up around the Dharma but have no essential connection with it. In this verse I describe the weeds as rank. 'Rank' means primarily too luxuriant. There's perhaps no harm in having a few weeds. One mustn't be too rigid, one mustn't be too strict. This is something one hears nowadays. One must allow a few little weeds, so long as they don't get too much in the way of the path. They shouldn't be allowed to overgrow the flowers, and they certainly shouldn't be allowed to overgrow the Buddha's footprints.

But what about the thorns? The thorns are all those elements, historical and otherwise, that oppose and are hostile to the Dharma. The extreme form of that opposition, the sharpest thorn, is persecution, such as the persecution of Buddhism by the Muslim invaders in India in the twelfth and thirteenth centuries, but we mustn't forget the destruction happening in our own day. Even in today's newspaper I read a rather sad little paragraph to the effect that in Afghanistan the government have given orders for the destruction of all images, which of course means predominantly Buddhist images, of which Afghanistan has quite a number in its museums and private collections. It wasn't human beings being attacked, but 'only' images, but once you start destroying images, you may be tempted to destroy human beings too, and this in fact has happened in other countries where Buddhism is being destroyed in our own day.

We must also bear in mind that the weeds and the thorns also grow in our own hearts. In our hearts the weeds are the different forms of craving, the thorns are the different forms of hatred and aversion, and the soil from which they grow is the soil of ignorance. But that's not all we find in our hearts. I've spoken of the Buddha's footprints as being found in poetry and in art, even though comparatively faintly. I've spoken of those footprints being found in the Buddhist scriptures. But one could also say, though the poem doesn't say this, that those footprints are found in our own hearts. That well-known Chinese Buddhist text *The Awakening of Faith in the Mahāyāna* speaks of the Enlightened mind leaving a subtle trace of itself, which is sometimes compared with a perfume, in the unenlightened mind.[31] One could say that the Enlightened mind leaves an imprint, a footprint even, in the unenlightened mind. So our task is to clear away and even to uproot the weeds of craving and thorns of hatred. We clear them away by means of *śamatha* and we uproot them by means of *vipaśyanā*, by means of *prajñā*. And having cleared away and uprooted the weeds and the thorns, we can see the footprints clearly and can begin really to follow them.

> Yet will I follow boldly,
> Using the hunter's art,
> Until one day I find Him,
> From all things else apart,
> Sitting beside the Pool of Peace
> In the blue hills of my heart.

The third verse dealt with difficulties, the footprints of the Buddha as being overgrown by weeds and obscured by thorns. But in the fourth verse I resolve to follow them nonetheless, and to go on following them. I say in the first place that I will follow boldly, and secondly that I will follow them 'using the hunter's art'. To follow boldly means to follow courageously, fearlessly. It means to follow with confidence in what one is doing. It's of no use to follow half-heartedly. That way we shall get nowhere. Sometimes we may feel downhearted, or disappointed with ourselves. At such times we need, and should take advantage of, the help of our spiritual friends. I'm sure every one of you understands that very well, so I'll say no more about it. But what is meant by 'using the hunter's art'? In some ways it's not a very Buddhistic metaphor, but we won't go into that. The hunter's art is his skill in tracking. He can see the footprints of the deer or whatever animal he is following even when they are very faint, or quite scattered or discontinuous. In the same way, we must be on the lookout for the Buddha's footprints, even though they may be overgrown or obscured. We must keep our eyes open. We must be prepared to see the footprints of the Buddha in quite unlikely places.

I say in the poem, 'Yet will I follow boldly, using the hunter's art, until one day I find Him....' Find who? The Buddha. And where will I find him? Ultimately, I will find him in my own heart. I will find him 'from all things else apart'. This suggests the transcendental nature of Buddhahood – apart from all things, apart from everything mundane, even the subtlest mundane experience. But Buddhahood is both immanent and transcendent. It is beyond all dualities. This verse also says that at the end of my quest I shall find the Buddha sitting beside the pool of peace. This pool of peace is *samādhi*. It's the purified mind, the purified *citta*. It's there, if anywhere, that we will find the Buddha.

So much, then, for the fourth and last verse of my poem. You may have noticed a couple of things about the poem as a whole. First, it's a very visual poem. Perhaps the artists among you will have noticed this. It's full of visual images: shining footprints, misty blue hills, the full moon, and so on – the whole poetic paraphernalia. And secondly, in the poem I'm on my own. Did you notice that? I'm following the Buddha's footprints alone. In fact, I stumbled upon them alone. No one drew my attention to them or pointed them out to me. And of course it's not easy to follow the spiritual path on one's own. One needs the help of spiritual friends. One needs the sangha. The spiritual life is a bit like mountaineering. It's quite dangerous to climb alone. You're much safer if you climb as a member of a team, especially if you're all roped together. Don't overdo this image! I'm very well aware that some people are a bit sensitive to any suggestion of being roped to anybody else. But take the image for what it's worth. If you're all roped together, even if you fall, you won't fall very far. Your team-mates will hold you and pull you up again. Whereas in my early days as a Buddhist I was very much on my own, you are all fortunate in belonging to a sangha, and your progress up that metaphorical mountainside should therefore be all the faster. I won't say you should be racing up, but you should be making quite steady progress.

3
THE WHOLE WORLD WAS A POEM[32]

Whether because of the more relaxed routine that I was still following, or on account of the peace and silence with which the retreat was increasingly pervading the house, I felt my more 'creative' energies beginning to rise to the surface, displacing – to some extent – the 'executive' energies. Indeed, as the retreat, and the year 1979, started coming to an end, and as the Christmas season stole upon us, I found myself in a more strongly, and more exclusively, 'poetic' mood than I had known for quite a number of years.

It is difficult to describe this mood, which lasted for several weeks. First of all came a period of 'silence', both internal and external, during which there were no objective demands made upon me and no 'needs' to meet. This meant that I could allow the responses that usually arise in connection with such demands and needs to die down, so that whatever mental processes then went on were, on the whole, self-originating. Next, out of the silence, which was also a kind of creative rest, there arose a certain rhythm, or a poem without words – a poem that went on and on, without interruption. This rhythm, or wordless poem, seemed to blend with whatever I saw, or rather, with whatever it was to which I directed my attention, or on which I allowed my mind to dwell. It could blend with it because, whether it was a natural object like a tree, a realm of existence, or a figure from ancient Egyptian mythology, its rhythm was the same as the rhythm that had arisen out of my own silence, my own creative rest. As they blended, the two rhythms gave birth to words, words that were descriptive of the particular object on which I had allowed my mind to dwell and which formed, in some cases, complete poems, in others, only fragments of poems – perhaps a line or a couplet. At one stage it was as though the rhythm that arose within me was the same as, or at least in accordance with, the rhythm that arose within the depths of external nature and found expression in trees, flowers, houses, and human beings – in the whole objective order of existence. Whatever I allowed my mind to rest on became a poem, just as whatever Midas touched turned to gold. The whole world was material for poetry. In fact, the whole world was a poem. It was a poem, to the extent that the 'observer' was a poet.

I recollected that, when I was in my teens, I used to remain in this kind of 'poetic' state for months on end: it was my normal state. In that state, it was far easier for me to write poetry than not write it, and I wrote hundreds of poems. (The nature of the process, of course, tells us nothing about the value of the end result, i.e. the poem, considered from a purely 'artistic' point of view.) On this occasion, even, I managed to produce a couple of dozen poems, more than I had written in the previous half dozen years, though not all of them were as easy to produce as the account I have given might suggest. At any rate, a handful of poems I did produce, among them six sonnets on the six realms of sentient existence – one sonnet for each realm [see pages 354–6]. Reflecting on the whole episode afterwards, I came to the conclusion that the 'poetic' state of mind is, as I had sometimes felt before, a state in which the subject assimilates the object in such a way that the duality between them is to some extent mitigated and that this mitigated duality finds expression in the 'poem', or work of art generally, which is both subject and object, or in which the subject–object duality finds expression on a higher, more refined level. Poetry is thus the mediator between the 'real' and the 'Ideal', the mundane and the Transcendental: it is the angel; it is the *deva*; it is the archetype.

THE POETRY INTERVIEWS
Sangharakshita in conversation with Saddhanandi

INTRODUCTION

To celebrate Sangharakshita's ninetieth birthday in 2015, he and I recorded a series of nine conversations about each decade of his life, focusing on some of the personal possessions that prompted his memories of those times. Following the success of those interviews, he and I talked about what we might do next, and he was keen to be interviewed about some of his poems. I could see the possibilities: as well as touching on the poems themselves, our conversations might bring to mind his reflections on the times the poems were written. I chose which poems to include in consultation with a few people who were very familiar with them, as well as Bhante himself, and we started the interviews.

It was much harder to talk about the poems than I had anticipated, mainly because Bhante followed his intuition so strongly when writing poetry that it was hard to draw out his thoughts on the details or his motivations. It was like asking an abstract painter why they had used a particular colour; the rationale wasn't totally explainable. But there were moments when Bhante's inner life seemed to unfold in front of me, as in our conversation about the poem 'The Family Reunion', which describes members of his family, and his reflections on the process of growth in the poems 'Advent' and 'The Root Speaks'. I also remember an acute experience during our conversation about the last verse of 'The Bodhisattva's Reply'. I realized I didn't have the depth of understanding to direct the conversation, and whilst grappling with the topic I think I missed the opportunity to ask the right question: a question that could have led to a deeper understanding of Bhante's perspective on the last verse of the poem, especially the lines:

or

Till I have become like them
A seed between wet stones
Of custom and circumstance.

Throughout our conversations, which took place in 2016 and 2017, it became very clear how knowledgeable Bhante was in the areas of politics, literature, poetry, culture, current affairs – all sorts of things. When we were talking about 'The Bodhisattva's Reply', he talked about things he'd read or heard that week about what was happening in India at that time, and he often quoted the poetry of others whose work addressed the same topics as his own.

Towards the end of the series, I was struck by the quality of service in Bhante's engagement with the interviews. I was aware that I was meeting someone who had been serving the Dharma for more than seventy years, and he was now near the end of his life of service, while he was meeting me part way through *my* life of service. In a way it was like a living out of lineage.

Saddhanandi
Adhisthana
February 2019

I
MEDITATION

Here perpetual incense burns;
The heart to meditation turns,
And all delights and passions spurns.

A thousand brilliant hues arise,
More lovely than the evening skies,
And pictures paint before our eyes.

All the spirit's storm and stress
Is stilled into a nothingness,
And healing powers descend and bless.

Refreshed, we rise and turn again
To mingle with this world of pain,
As on roses falls the rain.

SADDHANANDI: Do you remember writing this poem?

SANGHARAKSHITA: I remember writing it very well. It's one of those poems that came to me very smoothly, as it were – I didn't have to work on it – and I remember exactly where I wrote it. I was on a sort of solitary retreat in India, staying in a small ashram. I had been there for a few days with other people, but they'd all left, so I was there on my own, meditating and doing a little study, and the poem just came to me.[33] Though I wasn't conscious of it at the time, afterwards I reflected that the different verses of the poem represent different stages of meditation, or even different stages in the spiritual life itself.

SADDHANANDI: Maybe you could say a bit about those stages. For instance, it starts with the line 'Here perpetual incense burns'.

SANGHARAKSHITA: That as it were sets the stage. One is going to meditate. But why is one meditating? The lighting of the stick of incense to my mind represents faith. The smoke of the incense goes upwards, just as in the spiritual life one is going, hopefully, from a lower to a higher stage. So that line seems to make a setting, an environment, for the meditation. 'Here *perpetual* incense burns.' I say perpetual because it's something that you have to keep maintaining. You don't just have it for a while and then lose it – no, you have to continue to have faith in what you're doing, faith in the meditation. So, on account of that, 'the heart to meditation turns'. There's a turning of the heart away from the things of the world to something more spiritual. Then the next line represents the negative side of that: 'And all delights and passions spurns.' One is leaving behind, or trying to leave behind, all worldly thoughts and passions, and to enter upon a higher meditative state.

SADDHANANDI: So then the next section of the poem:

> A thousand brilliant hues arise,
> More lovely than the evening skies,
> And pictures paint before our eyes.

SANGHARAKSHITA: This is a reminiscence of my own experience very much earlier, when I started meditating seriously, and I did see quite literally, as I closed my eyes, a beautiful panorama, almost like a sunset. I think it represents an ascent into a world that is not just more spiritual but more colourful. So for me that line represents the early stages of spiritual experience. And then 'And pictures paint before our eyes' to my mind, reflecting on the poem later, stands for our visualizations, the picture of the Buddha or Bodhisattva that we paint, as it were, in our mind's eye, and on which we meditate, and to which we're devoted. So that line represents the stage of *sādhana* practice. Of course in those early days I wasn't doing any practice of that kind.

SADDHANANDI: In the next section,

> All the spirit's storm and stress
> Is stilled into a nothingness,

SANGHARAKSHITA: Spiritual death. Nothingness, nothing of a worldly nature, nothing conditioned, no self. Spiritual death.

SADDHANANDI:

> And healing powers descend and bless.

SANGHARAKSHITA: That's the condition for the descent of those healing powers from a higher source. Once you have as it were negated or seen through your self, healing powers descend and they bless you. That's the spiritual rebirth.

SADDHANANDI:

> Refreshed, we rise and turn again
> To mingle with this world of pain,
> As on roses falls the rain.

SANGHARAKSHITA: This is the bodhisattva ideal. As I said, when I wrote the poem I wasn't consciously thinking all this. It just came. But afterwards, when I reflected on it, I could see that this was what it was about: the stages of progress in meditation and in one's spiritual life more broadly.

SADDHANANDI: It's interesting that the bodhisattva ideal, that more altruistic dimension of our spiritual life, comes in at the end of a poem on meditation. It starts with the quality of withdrawal and ends with the quality of service, or engagement with this world of pain. Have those two aspects of spiritual life always been very alive for you?

SANGHARAKSHITA: I suppose they have. In the earlier part of my life I was more concerned with the inner experience, with meditation and study, but then I came into contact with the movement of mass conversion to Buddhism by the so-called 'ex-Untouchables', the Dalits, and that meant that there was another very important aspect in my life, that of service to these people who had embraced Buddhism and who wanted to know about it and learn about it.

SADDHANANDI: How important is meditation in the spiritual life?

SANGHARAKSHITA: One has to ask oneself what one means by meditation. The word can be used quite loosely, but for me it's always been the traditional *samatha-vipaśyanā*, on the basis of the observance of the *śīlas*, and leading ultimately to spiritual freedom. I've used the word *vipaśyanā* but nowadays people tend to translate it as 'insight', which has a rather intellectual connotation. An earlier translation was 'clear vision', so rather than *samatha* and *vipaśyanā* you had 'calm' and 'clear vision': calm, and then on the basis of the calm, clear vision into the nature of human life, the nature of existence.

SADDHANANDI: Did you respond naturally to meditation or was it a struggle?

SANGHARAKSHITA: Well, sometimes it's the one and sometimes the other. So much is dependent on external conditions, quite apart from what is going on in one's own psyche. Sometimes people are described as natural meditators, but I don't think meditation, certainly not meditation of any degree, is easy for anyone to begin with, though in India I knew people who couldn't read but who seemed to slip into meditation much more easily than some of those who know quite a lot about the Dharma. I'm remembering one woman who was brought to see me when I was travelling around. I was on a railway station platform with a *bhikkhu* friend and this woman was brought to me and I was told, 'She's always meditating. She's always getting into *samādhi*.' My friend and I asked her various questions to which she replied very straightforwardly and simply, and it was clear that she was experiencing *dhyāna* states. I asked her, 'What did you do to get into this state?' and she smiled and said, 'I was repeating *oṃ maṇi padme hūṃ*.' I asked her, 'Do you know what that means?' and she said, 'No, but it's at the end of one of Baba Saheb's books, so that's what I repeat.' (By Baba Saheb she meant Dr Ambedkar.) She clearly was experiencing states of *dhyāna*, there's no doubt about that. She considered herself Buddhist, she'd been converted, but she didn't know anything about Buddhism in a technical sense. So yes, there are perhaps a few people who find meditation a natural thing, but they're comparatively rare. Usually at least for part of the time one has to struggle and make an effort and overcome obstacles and so on.

SADDHANANDI: Have you had periods in your own practice of meditation when it's been a struggle, when you've had to work with difficult conditions?

SANGHARAKSHITA: I've been fortunate on the whole. I didn't take up serious meditation when I was in the army because conditions weren't conducive, but later, when conditions were more conducive, the things I had to struggle with most obviously were connected with my own mind. The struggle was an inner one.

SADDHANANDI: I've got a few quotes from the diary you kept in the 1950s, and I'd like to ask you about them. To start with, here are some statements from 1953 – all very succinct, in your particular style. 'January 12th, Monday. Experienced a feeling of great peace and coolness. Understood the illusoriness of individuality.' Can you say something about that experience, and the meditation practices that you were doing at the time?

SANGHARAKSHITA: I can't remember writing those words, and I can't remember those experiences, but I notice the word 'coolness', which suggests going away from the feverishness of things, the feverishness of one's mental activity. As this was 1953, I must have been practising the mindfulness of breathing, the *ānāpanasati*. That was the first kind of meditation I did, and I gained a lot from it in various ways.

SADDHANANDI: Was your practice of the *ānāpanasati* according to the same structure we use in Triratna these days – watching the breath, counting the breaths, all of that?

SANGHARAKSHITA: Yes, it was the same practice that I introduced into the Movement many years later, and which I also taught to a few people in India. It's a very basic, straightforward practice.

SADDHANANDI: Also in your diary at this time you say: 'Thought very deeply about the nature of art.' And then, the next day: 'Glimpsed a whole world of new truths, but found it difficult to put them into any sort of order.' There were quite a few threads of reflection going on at this time, it seems.

SANGHARAKSHITA: They're similar to reflections that have come to me from time to time over the years about the nature of beauty, about the relationship of beauty to the spiritual path, about the Platonic and Neoplatonic conception of beauty as something spiritual, and about my sense that there is a path of cultivation of beautiful states of mind.

SADDHANANDI: There seems to be a connection between meditation, reflection, and writing poetry.

SANGHARAKSHITA: Yes. I have written a good deal of poetry, and it's been of two kinds: poems that I have to work on, and those that come to me much more spontaneously, and which I just scribble down as fast as I can. The poem 'Meditation' is one of the latter.

SADDHANANDI: In your diary for 1955, you wrote, 'Deep concentration and some development of *vipassanā*.' And then a couple of days later: 'Deep concentration and faint *vipassanā*.' These extracts suggest that your sense of *vipassanā* is something that you've developed over time.

SANGHARAKSHITA: Yes, *vipassanā* or clear vision is something that you can develop. Sometimes it's relatively superficial, and at other times it's more profound, and therefore has a more far-reaching influence upon one and changes one to a greater extent.

SADDHANANDI: I wonder if it's a little like writing poetry, in the sense that sometimes it arises spontaneously and has a kind of natural process of its own, and sometimes you're working at it over a period of time.

SANGHARAKSHITA: Yes. If one's working on developing clear insight, sometimes there's a sort of after-effect, and a deeper insight arises which you hadn't experienced at the time you were making the effort. It's like an inspiration or even a revelation, something that you haven't grasped before.

SADDHANANDI: Another diary extract says, 'Felt a change of consciousness.' All of us, I'm sure, have experienced a change of consciousness. How does that manifest for you?

SANGHARAKSHITA: I think that if there is a genuine change of consciousness for the better, and if it is permanent or relatively permanent, it must express itself in one's whole life and in everything that one does.

SADDHANANDI: There's also the area of devotion, which comes out a little bit in your poem, and comes out very strongly in the diary extracts in your memoir *In the Sign of the Golden Wheel*. You had a lot of devotional responses, particularly to the Buddha and to Avalokiteśvara. Does that kind of clarity, that clear seeing, to use your phrase, sometimes manifest as faith and devotion?

SANGHARAKSHITA: Well, faith, *śraddhā*, is one of the five spiritual faculties, and is therefore an integral part of the spiritual life, and that aspect of my spiritual life and feeling has found expression in quite a few of my poems, especially some of the earlier ones. I think some of them are among my more popular poems within our movement, because people feel that devotion to the Buddha, or to a bodhisattva, and therefore some of these poems resonate with them and with their experience.

SADDHANANDI: In your memoir *In the Sign of the Golden Wheel* there's a diary extract as follows: '12 February: Good concentration. Sense of positive peace descending. Asked "What should I do?" Awareness of answer came at once: Nothing. Experience of emptiness and stillness. Self reduced to an absolute pinpoint. This state lasted for some time.

Awareness that whatever works you may have to do later on, in the midst of them you will have to maintain this state of mind.'

SANGHARAKSHITA: That's interesting. I don't remember writing that, but there it is – that was my experience at the time, and of course it connects with the poem. 'Stilled into a nothingness' and then 'Healing powers descend and bless'. I'd forgotten those diary entries.

SADDHANANDI: That extract stood out for me because it gave a sense of how we take the quality of meditation we have out into the world – and that brings us back to the poem, as you say. So we've got that concluding statement:

> Refreshed, we rise and turn again
> To mingle with this world of pain,
> As on roses falls the rain.

SANGHARAKSHITA: Of course, we're not all like roses, and roses have thorns, some of them, but the idea is clear that there's a close relationship between your deeper inner experience and what you do with your life, and your relationships with other people.

SADDHANANDI: Is there anything else you'd like to say about meditation or about this poem?

SANGHARAKSHITA: I find it interesting to go back to the poem. In fact, this is not the first time that I've talked about it. I gave a talk about it at the Buddhist centre in Berlin some years ago. It was then that I saw more clearly the way in which it describes the different stages in the spiritual life: being inspired by faith, turning away from worldly activities and mundane mental states to concentrate on something higher, actually experiencing that, even to the point of self-negation, and then coming back into the world refreshed by that experience, so that one can live more for the benefit of other people than just for one's own.

SADDHANANDI: I believe you once said that you think you might be remembered more for your poetry than for anything else.

SANGHARAKSHITA: I've enjoyed writing my poems. I've enjoyed receiving those that came spontaneously, and I've enjoyed working on those that didn't come so spontaneously, but how good they are, I can't say. I doubt if I'd be remembered only for them, but I know that people within Triratna do value and appreciate many of the poems, and even use them in their devotional life, so I think some of them will survive, at least within Triratna. I hope so, anyway, because there is quite a bit of me in them. I suggest that if some of them seem hard to understand, people should take a closer look at those poems and try to see what I'm getting at. Some of them are a bit obscure, I know.

2
AN APOLOGY

We live in the Age of Apologies. Here is an apology that is much more meaningful than many being made today.

Mankind owes a profound apology:
To the Birds, for having polluted the air through which they fly,
To the Ape and the Tiger, for having destroyed the forests in which they live,
To the Deer and the Bison, for ruthlessly hunting them almost to extinction,
To the Rivers and Streams, for poisoning them with chemicals,
To the Earth itself, for greedily pillaging its riches of silver and gold,
To the Ocean, for slaughtering the greatest of her children, the Whale, 'for scientific purposes',
To the Mountain Peaks, for defiling their virgin snows with our trash,
To the Moon, for rudely invading her sacred space,
To the Stars, for obscuring their brightness with the smoke of our cities,
To the Sun, for not gratefully acknowledging our dependence on his bounty,
To the truly great Men and Women of the past, for not honouring their memory as we should and for not walking in their footsteps.

SADDHANANDI: Can you remember what stimulated you to write this prose poem?

SANGHARAKSHITA: I must have been living at Madhyamaloka, and I must have been stimulated by a news item about the Japanese whaling industry and how they got around the internationally agreed restrictions, which included a clause allowing whaling 'for scientific purposes'. So here they were, killing dozens and eventually hundreds of whales allegedly for scientific purposes. I didn't know whether the Japanese were particularly fond of whale meat or whether they were just being bloody-minded, but that's what sparked off the prose poem.

SADDHANANDI: You start with this statement: 'We live in an age of apologies. Here is an apology that is much more meaningful than many being made today.' What are you getting at there?

SANGHARAKSHITA: If one does something wrong, obviously one should apologise. But what I was getting at, as far as I remember, was the fact that you shouldn't apologise just because other people, rightly or wrongly, think that you've done something wrong. An apology should come from the heart. I say we should *profoundly* apologise to the rest of the world. The apology must be deep, it must come from the heart. It shouldn't just be a formal apology. We should really feel that we, the human race, have done and are still doing real harm to this planet and its other inhabitants. It's not as if it was a hundred years ago. We're still doing it, more and more.

SADDHANANDI: Can you apologise when you're still doing something?

SANGHARAKSHITA: Not altogether sincerely, no.

SADDHANANDI: And is an apology enough?

SANGHARAKSHITA: No, in some cases there must be reparation. There must be a change of heart, a change of direction.

SADDHANANDI: The first section of the poem is about the animals.

To the Birds, for having polluted the air through which they fly,
To the Ape and the Tiger, for having destroyed the forests in
  which they live,
To the Deer and the Bison, for having ruthlessly hunted them
  almost to extinction.

SANGHARAKSHITA: We hear almost every day news of vast areas of forest being cut down. I'm thinking of Brazil and some parts of Africa, where there's an incredible haste to cut down the forest for the sake of its wood and other products. Of course that means loss of habitat for a variety of wild creatures.

SADDHANANDI: Do you relate to animals?

SANGHARAKSHITA: Yes, I think I always have, especially wild animals, though domestic ones as well. I remember that when I was very small my father took me to see a film called *Africa Speaks*, about the wildlife of Africa. What struck me especially was how much of it there was: great herds of zebra, hundreds and hundreds of giraffes, and lions eating their prey. This really impressed me, and I've been a great lover of the wildlife of the world ever since.

SADDHANANDI: I hear that you have a great love of donkeys.

SANGHARAKSHITA: Yes, I feel very sorry for donkeys, the way they're mistreated and misused in some countries.

SADDHANANDI: I think a donkey charity is one of the charities that you support?

SANGHARAKSHITA: That's right. Some people of course think you should support children, not animals, but one selects one's own charities. I remember that once when I was in India I was travelling by train and got talking to an elderly man who asked me what I was doing. I referred to my work among the ex-Untouchables, the Dalits. 'Oh no,' he said. 'You should be working for lepers, as I am doing. That's much more important.' But we select our charities according to our own feeling, and the selection is not always logical. It doesn't have to be.

SADDHANANDI: So then we've got a section of the poem about the environment.

> To the Rivers and Streams, for poisoning them with chemicals,
> To the Earth itself, for greedily pillaging its riches of silver and gold,
> To the Ocean, for slaughtering the greatest of her children, the
>   Whale, 'for scientific purposes'.

SANGHARAKSHITA: I've been reading a bit of history recently and I read that in the nineteenth century the River Thames in London stank so badly in the summertime, because it was polluted, that people couldn't bear to be anywhere near it and moved out into the country if they could. But now there are fish in the Thames, because of all the anti-pollution measures that have been taken in the last hundred years. That shows that some of the damage is reversible.

SADDHANANDI: We need to make a lot of effort, don't we? We need to start doing that, making a change.

SANGHARAKSHITA: With the oceans, it's not just a matter of killing whales, it's a question of polluting them with plastic, which in some areas is becoming a serious problem. There's the famous case of the plastic bag, which some stores are now charging for, so that people won't throw so many of them away. We need such measures. Otherwise, if we're not careful, there'll be more landfill than habitable land.

SADDHANANDI: The whale – the animal that sparked you off to write this poem – is quite a mythic animal, isn't it, coming up from the depths?

SANGHARAKSHITA: In the novel *Moby Dick* there's a passage in which the narrator, when the sea is calm, looks over the side of the vessel and sees deep down whole families of whales, young and old, mothers and fathers and children, all peacefully grazing.[34] Of course, nowadays they're dramatically disturbed by human beings, and they don't just shoot them with a harpoon as they did a hundred years ago. They've got much more dangerous weapons. It's the same with the bison. When I was in the States I was taken to a reserve to see them. There was wonderfully lush grass full of wild flowers and the bison, young and old, were just very peacefully grazing there. There used to be millions of them. Now there's just a few thousand, and they're protected to some extent. Their loss is a great shame, and one can't help feeling that.

SADDHANANDI: These are very large creatures, but we've also got concerns about smaller life – about the bees, for instance.

SANGHARAKSHITA: The bees, yes, and from small to great, the elephant. The elephant is being poached in some African countries for the sake of its ivory. The demand comes from China, and the elephant hunters and their middlemen make huge amounts of money selling this illegal ivory. I heard recently that they aren't using guns any more to kill the elephants. They kill them with darts carrying a deadly poison, shooting these darts into the tenderest parts of the elephants so that the poison will get through into the blood and spread quickly. It's a horrible story. But if human beings can treat one another so badly, perhaps it's not surprising that they treat animals badly too. One's only got to read a bit of history to be really horrified by what human beings are capable of doing to one another.

SADDHANANDI:

> To the Mountain Peaks, for defiling their virgin snows with our trash,
> To the Moon, for rudely invading her sacred space.

The poem then moves into a different phase, taking us to slightly different places.

SANGHARAKSHITA: I'm taking a more cosmic view. In a way it's an aesthetic view. It's not just that we're doing things which in the long run will go against us. It seems as though we've lost our imagination. We don't appreciate any more the beauty of the untrodden snows. We don't appreciate the moon as an object of wonder. We just think of it as a place where someone landed on a certain date and 'conquered' it. We've lost that mythic outlook, and I think probably we've lost our *feeling* for the natural world.

SADDHANANDI: You described it earlier as a non-utilitarian sensitivity.

SANGHARAKSHITA: Yes, an imaginative sympathy.

SADDHANANDI: Places like mountain peaks would have been visionary places in the past.

SANGHARAKSHITA: Yes, places where the gods lived. Even in my own time, when I lived in Kalimpong, the Sikkimese government – Sikkim being a Buddhist area – didn't allow expeditions to go up to Kanchenjunga from Sikkim. There was a god of Kanchenjunga....

SADDHANANDI: That kept it a sacred space. But we don't have sacred spaces any more, do we? They've all been defiled, as you say.

SANGHARAKSHITA: I think there are still *some* places where some people still have some feeling of reverence or awe. I felt this in Delphi when I went there some years ago.[35] It helped that the little township of Delphi was hidden away round the corner, so you couldn't see any house or building apart from the ruins of the ancient ones. The moment you stepped round the corner there were all the souvenir stalls and the hotels, but ancient Delphi itself was relatively unspoiled. The early Christians did spoil it as best they could, but a lot was left.

I notice that in this section of the poem I'm using very religious terminology: 'virgin', 'sacred'. That's where the imagination comes in.

SADDHANANDI: It's interesting that you connect that to us then losing our sensitivity in an ethical way. You continue even more imaginatively:

> To the Stars, for obscuring their brightness with the smoke of our
>   cities,
> To the Sun, for not gratefully acknowledging our dependence on
>   his bounty,

SANGHARAKSHITA: I once wrote a poem about the sun, 'Splendor Solis', inspired by reading an account of the life and work of a certain teacher; he and his followers were sun-worshippers, and they had a ritual of going to the nearest high place at dawn and saluting the sun. Ancient peoples also worshipped the sun. Of course, without the warmth and light of the sun, there'd be no life on this Earth. So we need to acknowledge our debt to the sun. We can make use of it – nowadays we are making more and more use of solar panels – but our appreciation should not just be utilitarian. There's a highly imaginative element, even a spiritual element, in our relationship with the sun. The sun is a symbol. At the end of the Mañjughoṣa Stuti Sādhana we address Mañjughoṣa as 'kind sun of speech'. I remember there was a hymn I learned at school: 'Sun of my soul, Thou Saviour dear', and in the Egyptian religion there's the sun god, Ra. The sun has all sorts of mythic and religious overtones, as well as utilitarian uses.

SADDHANANDI: There's that moment in December when we have our shortest day and our longest night, and once that's acknowledged, you know that from then on it's going to get lighter again, and that does make a difference, it's quite uplifting.

SANGHARAKSHITA: Light gradually predominates over darkness. Even if we're living in the city we can be sensitive to these changes. Of course in England we're very well aware of the weather, because it's so changeable.

SADDHANANDI: This prose poem ends with the final line:

> To the truly great Men and Women of the past, for not honouring their memory as we should and for not walking in their footsteps.

Tell me something about this last statement.

SANGHARAKSHITA: Well, in a sense, man is the highest product of nature. If you look at the evolutionary series, eventually along comes man – man of course means man and woman – as it were the highest product of life on Earth. And among these human beings there are some men and women who represent a higher point of development than the average, physically, aesthetically, spiritually – so we should look up to them and admire them, not try to denigrate them. These men and women are truly great, not just big and important. People like Stalin or Hitler may loom large in history because of the scale of the damage they did, but they were very small men, morally speaking.

But we must look up to the great spiritual figures, the great artists, the great musicians, the great painters.

SADDHANANDI: So they're truly great because of their connection with values?

SANGHARAKSHITA: Yes. I remember in this connection the first line of a poem that impressed me very much once upon a time and still does. It's by Stephen Spender, and it starts, 'I think continually of those who were truly great'. The last two lines of the poem are 'Born of the sun, they travelled a short while toward the sun, and left the vivid air signed with their honour.' It's one of his finest poems, describing those who were truly great men and women.[36]

SADDHANANDI: In what way would we honour their memory?

SANGHARAKSHITA: We do have anniversaries of certain great people. We honour their memories first of all by remembering them and appreciating the way in which they were great, and then within our own sphere trying to follow in their footsteps. That's what we're doing as Buddhists in relation to the Buddha himself and other great Buddhist teachers. The opposite of this is the unfortunate tendency to denigrate, not just not recognizing true greatness but being sarcastic and spiteful and cynical about it. You don't believe in certain values yourself, so you can't believe that anyone else really believes in them, and seek to undermine any respect anyone else has for those values as embodied in great people.

SADDHANANDI: We're directed by the media to pay attention to people who are famous rather than truly great.

SANGHARAKSHITA: Well, I'm an old fogey. Every few days I hear on the radio of the death of someone who's wonderfully famous all over the world, and I've never heard of them, and perhaps they'll be forgotten in a few years' time. Who are the modern heroes, leaving aside the politicians, both the straight and the crooked? There are the footballers, and the celebrities of stage and screen – they seem to receive great admiration.

But we must be careful that we don't end up being moaning Minnies. We have to try to think what can we do to help save the planet from mankind. There's not very much that we as individuals can do, but at least we can do something. For instance, in our own movement, most people are vegetarian. That helps. You're not eating meat, so meat is not being produced for you, at least. That means land that would have been used for raising livestock is probably now used for producing cereals. That's just a small example. And we can treat animals kindly when we come into contact with them.

SADDHANANDI: Presumably as Order members we should be trying to simplify our lives and have less impact on the world generally.

SANGHARAKSHITA: We should try to have as much influence as possible, and we should be looking out for ways of doing that. Of course, in India our work is concerned with human beings in a much more basic way than in the West. In some areas we are supplying not just the Dharma but basic things for living – as well as hope, in the case of those who were brought up as Dalits in very unsatisfactory surroundings. And we set an example by treating one another well. Human beings don't always treat one another well, even neighbours don't always treat one another well, and of course people go to war. As an Order we can provide an example of how human beings can get on well together if they're inspired by a common vision – in our case the Dharma. That's a great contribution in itself. All the things we've been talking about are aspects of violence – violence towards our surroundings and other beings, as well as human beings. In the case of some of the forests being devastated, it's not only the animals being driven out, it's very often tribal people. Their habitat and way of life is being destroyed, not just that of the animals.

SADDHANANDI: You care about all this, don't you, Bhante?

SANGHARAKSHITA: Yes. As Buddhists we should care. Of course, one naturally has more feeling for some things, some beings, than others, but we need to do our best individually and also collectively as an Order, and at least raise our voices against the things that are going on in the world that are harmful not only for the world but for the perpetrators of the harm – that is to say, we human beings. But despite all this, we shouldn't feel despondent. What mankind has done, mankind can even now, I think, put into reverse and remedy. We can change direction. We shouldn't lose heart, and even if we can't do anything else, we can at least raise our voices in protest against this or that abuse of the natural world. As Buddhists we stand for peace among human beings, harmony among human beings, and as an Order we try to set an example of that.

3
THE FAMILY REUNION

Full twenty years I stayed away.
My father grew thin; my mother grey;
And my young sister went astray.

Now, I see them in my dreams;
A mystic light about them gleams.
They have become my Muse's themes.

My mother and I in an orchard strolled.
Her looks were neither young nor old,
And she was wearing a gown of gold.

Apple blossom was overhead;
Sunlight on the green grass was shed.
At peace we walked, and no word was said.

In front of his cottage my father stood;
Before him a stream, behind him a wood.
He has lived his life as a true man should.

Black his hair as the fur of mole;
He beckoned me in to share a bowl,
And I saw that his withered arm was whole.

My sister had lived with a gypsy man
In a gaily painted caravan
Drawn by a horse. So the story ran.

Now she was dancing the 'Dying Swan'.
Snow white the plumage that she had on,
And joy from her every movement shone.

SADDHANANDI: Do you remember writing this poem? Is it something that came to you spontaneously, or did you work on it over a period of time?

SANGHARAKSHITA: It came to me pretty spontaneously.

SADDHANANDI: It seems to be a combination of fact and something else, the Muse's themes, as you say, or a dream. Can you tell us something about the meaning of the poem for you?

SANGHARAKSHITA: Well, there's a basis of fact, but there's also the dream element, though the dream is also fact. I've not invented those dreams. I actually did dream about my mother and my father, and I've described those dreams in the poem. In the case of my sister there wasn't a dream, so what I've written about her at the end is based on recollections of our childhood. When she was in her early teens she was very keen on dancing. She went to a dance school, and she used to practise Pavlova's famous dance *The Dying Swan* at home. My father and I used to tease her about it; we'd say she was doing the dying duck! So that verse is based on that memory, invested with a sort of poetic glamour. By the way, when it comes to the title of the poem, I must acknowledge a debt. 'The Family Reunion' is also the title of a play by T. S. Eliot.

SADDHANANDI: Let's look at the poem in a bit more detail. Here's the first verse:

Full twenty years I stayed away.
My father grew thin; my mother grey;
And my young sister went astray.

How was it for you to stay away for twenty years? Did you have any contact with or news of your family during that time?

SANGHARAKSHITA: Well, the twenty years passed very quickly. Of course, I was young then, and when you're young the time does seem to pass quickly. I had some communication with my parents and my sister at the beginning of that time and also towards the end, so I wasn't completely out of contact with them, though we didn't meet physically. When I was in Sri Lanka I wrote to my parents saying that I was thinking of becoming a monk and staying on in India indefinitely. My father wrote back and said that my life was my own and I was free to do with it what I wished, and my mother wrote and said, 'That's all right, but I hope you'll be able to see me from time to time.' I can't remember whether I told my sister anything, but I remember getting a letter from her saying that she was going to have a child, which came as a bit of a surprise. So we were in contact to an extent.

SADDHANANDI: This first verse describes the kind of very clear observation of people which we sometimes have when we haven't seen them for a long time. Do you remember the experience of meeting your family members after twenty years?

SANGHARAKSHITA: Oh yes, I remember it very clearly. I remember seeing how they'd changed in appearance, which was only natural. In their eyes I must have seemed even more changed, because I left when I was 19 and I came back when I was 39, so I must have looked quite a bit older. But neither of my parents expressed any surprise. They both took my first visit in a very matter of fact way. My mother was living on her own then, her second husband having died, and my father was living with his second wife, who I had known as an aunt and therefore knew quite well already. It was as though I'd only been away for a few months. They certainly didn't overwhelm me with demonstrations of affection. The family just wasn't like that. After all, it was an English family.

SADDHANANDI: Was that a relief for you, or was it a bit disappointing?

SANGHARAKSHITA: It seemed quite in order. I wasn't expecting anyone to weep with joy. I'd been away and they'd been getting on with their own lives. Their lives didn't stop after I went away – far from it.

SADDHANANDI: What are your thoughts now on family within a spiritual life? Is there anything you could say about that?

SANGHARAKSHITA: Well, there's quite a lot that one could say, and some of it would perhaps be a bit controversial. If you're an Order member, you're taking your spiritual life, your living of the Dharma, very seriously, and you have to consider the extent to which a family of one kind or other may impinge upon that life. Obviously one should not commit oneself to the Three Jewels as an Order member without a lot of serious thought, and if you add to your personal responsibilities, whether as an Order member or not, by taking on a family, again you need to think very seriously and consult your spiritual friends, because it will make a difference. We shouldn't rush into any important change in our lives without due consideration and without consulting our spiritual friends. It's not a question of 'It's my life, it doesn't concern other people.' If you're an Order member, in a sense your life isn't your own. You've committed yourself to the Buddha, the Dharma, and the Sangha, so you're not leading any longer, if you did lead originally, a purely self-centred life, and you don't think simply in terms of what you as an individual would like to do. You take into account the fact that you are a member of an Order. When you become an Order member it's goodbye to individuality in the negative modern sense.

SADDHANANDI: Has that quality of individuality in a negative sense become stronger, do you think, either in the Order or in society generally?

SANGHARAKSHITA: I think it's become stronger in society, partly because there's a greater emphasis on one's rights and a decreasing emphasis on duties. I wrote about this more than half a century ago, and I think what I wrote then still holds good.

SADDHANANDI: The second verse:

And now I see them in my dreams.
A mystic light about them gleams.
They have become my Muse's themes.

Do you often dream about your family, or about other people?

SANGHARAKSHITA: It varies from time to time, but I do have quite a lot of dreams, and some of them are quite significant. In the course of the last decade, both while I was living at Madhyamaloka and while I've been living here at Adhisthana, I've had quite a few dreams about members of my family, mostly about my mother. I've also had many dreams about Tooting Broadway, where I lived in my early days. In quite a few dreams I'm waiting at the bus stop for the bus that goes to Tooting Broadway, or I'm on the underground platform waiting for the tube train that will take me there. I had a whole series of dreams of that kind for a while. I haven't had them for some time now. In fact I don't think I've even had dreams about my mother for some time. I've also had dreams about friends, and dreams about my teachers. I especially remember that when I made the announcement about handing on my responsibilities as head of the Order to a group of senior Order members, during the preceding week I had dreams about all of my teachers, and dreams about most of them many times over, and I took that to mean that the steps I was taking to hand on my responsibility had their blessing.

SADDHANANDI: Do you have any thoughts about the significance of dreams generally?

SANGHARAKSHITA: I think one very often has to take dreams at face value. For instance, I took those repeated dreams about my teachers as meaning that the step I was taking had their blessing. I think that was pretty obvious, and I didn't try to interpret it in some abstract, abstruse, or esoteric way. Some dreams may require a certain amount of interpretation, but I think we can go too far into that. What's important is the feeling quality of a dream, whether it's a feeling of joy or terror or whatever, and sometimes if you can recreate the feeling it gave you when you woke up, you can work your way back to the dream itself. I have many dreams in which I'm in the midst of monks as another monk and in Buddhist temples. I also have dreams of being in Buddhist 'churches' and sort of changing them into something else. I've had quite a rich dream life, but I've not allowed it to become too central in my life. I find my dreams interesting, but I don't often take them as being much more than that.

SADDHANANDI: You say, 'They have become my Muse's themes.' What does it mean to have a Muse?

SANGHARAKSHITA: We've inherited the Muses from ancient Greek mythology, but references to the Muse have become rather stereotyped. I don't think many modern poets would invoke the Muse, but some may think in terms of getting inspiration from some other source, which can be thought of as a Muse, a goddess, even, who inspires you, who almost puts the words into your mouth. In this poem I'm just saying in an old-fashioned poetic way that I write poems about my parents and my sister. But for me the Muse is not just a hackneyed old expression. It does mean something a bit more than that, as perhaps it does for some other modern poets.

SADDHANANDI: Is there anything about the family that lends itself to being a Muse? Is there a quality that goes with memories of the family that calls out a slightly more poetic side of us?

SANGHARAKSHITA: It's well known that a lot goes on within the family that doesn't always come to the surface. Sometimes the family itself is a bit of a myth, and the myth doesn't always correspond to reality. Nowadays we talk about the dysfunctional family, but I suspect that the dysfunctional family doesn't regard itself as dysfunctional, but probably thinks of itself as a normal happy family. I was made aware of that in the case of my friend Terry Delamere, who committed suicide. At one point he tried writing to his parents and explaining that he had been very unhappy as a child, and they reacted by saying it was impossible. He had had everything he needed. He was well fed and well clothed. How could he possibly have been unhappy? They clung to the myth of the happy family regardless. But to him it hadn't been a happy family.[37]

SADDHANANDI: On to the third and fourth verses:

My mother and I in an orchard strolled.
Her looks were neither young nor old,
And she was wearing a gown of gold.

Apple blossom was overhead;
Sunlight on the green grass was shed.
At peace we walked, and no word was said.

SANGHARAKSHITA: That's a pretty literal transcription of the dream. The gown of gold may have been a slight elaboration, but all the rest was exactly as the verse says. 'Her looks were neither young nor old'; she was just my mother – my mother in as it were her essence.

SADDHANANDI: There's a quality of nobility and ease around this image of your mother. My sense is that the verses are describing a wordless moment, as though something's happening between you without the need of speech. Was that a reality in your relationship with your mum?

SANGHARAKSHITA: I can't remember us having much in the way of serious conversation as adults, but I think we did understand each other pretty well. I think perhaps I was close to my mother in a way my sister wasn't. My sister was close to my father in a way perhaps I wasn't as an adult, though later on in her life there was a big disagreement between them. I think there was a degree of empathy between myself and my mother, but I think that is natural between mother and son. If it isn't there, there's something wrong with the relationship. I think I could see my mother's point of view. In my teens I could understand, for instance, why my mother left my father. I could see that her temperament was in some ways very different from my father's, and her needs were different, so although it was a big blow, it didn't surprise me too much when she left him, because she had interests and needs which he didn't have. In that sense I did have empathy with my mother. I could see things, even at that time, from her point of view.

SADDHANANDI: Were you more similar to your mother or to your father?

SANGHARAKSHITA: In features I'm more like my mother. She had a big nose, and I've got a pretty big nose too, as did my sister. And my mother was a worrier, and I'm a worrier too. My father was much more relaxed. He was very conscientious, but he wasn't a worrier. My sister was very much like that too. After I came back, my mother said to me one day, 'Your sister gave me a lot of trouble.' I didn't enquire into the details – I knew some of them anyway – but there was a difference of temperament. I took more after my mother than my father, and I think I've got my mother's physical constitution. She was very rarely ill, and of course she died at 92, and here I am at 90, whereas my father died at 71.

SADDHANANDI: Well, let's come on to your father then. I'll read the verses about him:

> In front of his cottage my father stood;
> Before him a stream, behind him a wood.
> He has lived his life as a true man should.
>
> Black his hair as the fur of mole;
> He beckoned me in to share a bowl,
> And I saw that his withered arm was whole.

Earlier in the poem you mentioned that your father had grown thin while you'd been away for twenty years, so the image is of someone who's a bit undernourished, or a bit pinched. But these verses have got a sense of integrity, of healing. Is that a process you saw in your father?

SANGHARAKSHITA: I may have seen the archetype of my father, in the same way as I dreamed of the archetype of my mother, not my mother in any particular period in my life. In the case of that dream about my mother, the dream is highly idealized. I can't remember in real life ever walking with her in an orchard, but that was how I dreamt it. My mother didn't like the countryside particularly. She got bored. My father loved the countryside, and I've given him in the dream-picture a rural background – the wood behind and a stream in front. It was one of the misfortunes of his life that he had to spend most of it living in London. My mother loved the city. She loved shops and cinema and the restaurants, but my father never went shopping with my mother, he went only to very selected films, and he didn't like going out to restaurants. In these verses I see my father in a more ideal way. His hair is black, he's not an old man with white hair any more, but he still likes a drink. Neither my mother nor my father drank very much, and towards the end of her life my mother didn't drink at all. My father liked a drink and he had a very strong head and could usually outdrink his friends. If he went out drinking with a party of his friends, he'd always see all of them home first, because he was the one who was the most sober. In the poem he invites me in 'to share a bowl'. And he's not blemished as he was in real life. His withered arm, the arm that had been badly damaged by shrapnel during the First World War, has healed, it is whole. So again the poem shows us my father as he was in his essence, so to speak.

SADDHANANDI: So your father really did have a withered arm.

SANGHARAKSHITA: Yes. I've called it withered, which is probably not quite an accurate description, but all the fingers of his right hand were twisted back, he couldn't open them, and the right arm was not much more than skin and bone, and not much use to him. He had to use his left hand a lot. But he was always very cheerful. He was cheerful by nature. He never got downcast. I well remember him whistling a cheerful whistle when he got up in the morning and at other times.

SADDHANANDI: Was he injured at quite a young age?

SANGHARAKSHITA: Yes. Recently I've written a little about him as a young man from things he told me. He must have been 16 or 17. He volunteered for the army giving a false age, as a lot of young men did at the time of the First World War.

 When I say that my father 'lived his life as a true man should', that's my tribute to him. He was a true man. He was very honest and upright, straightforward, friendly. He wasn't given to worrying unnecessarily, loved the countryside, wasn't much in sympathy with modern city life, and had a strong sense of duty. So the picture I have of my father is a very positive one, and when I was very young especially, I was very close to him. When I was very young my greatest joy was to spend time with my father, because he used to talk to me and explain things and tell me the names of things, whereas my relationship with my mother was rather different from that. I've sometimes thought that in my memoirs I've not really done justice either to my father or to my mother. I'm sure that I was very fortunate in having such parents, even though they did separate in my late teens, and I had a very happy childhood, especially early childhood, despite the fact that for two years I was confined to bed. I always remember my parents with gratitude. I think I can say that I remember them every day, and I'm grateful to them for giving me that happy and secure childhood.

SADDHANANDI: Well, let's look now at the verses about your sister:

> My sister had lived with a gypsy man
> In a gaily painted caravan
> Drawn by a horse. So the story ran.
>
> Now she was dancing the 'Dying Swan'.
> Snow white the plumage that she had on,
> And joy from her every movement shone.

SADDHANANDI: Earlier in the poem you have the line 'My young sister went astray'. Was that true? And did she go on to live in a gypsy caravan?

SANGHARAKSHITA: I don't know how long she lived in a gypsy caravan, I was never told that. She was married twice. Her first husband died and I think her second husband, whom I met, was the brother of her previous husband. But there was a lot about Joan's activities while I was away that no one ever talked about and that she herself never mentioned to me. At the time I returned to England, she was living with her husband in a caravan; it seemed that, like my father, she didn't like living in the city. Apparently she'd been living in a caravan, gypsy or otherwise, for some time, and once or twice I visited her when she was living in the caravan with her husband and her youngest child, who was born soon after I got back from India. She came and visited me with her daughter at Padmaloka, and she really enjoyed walking about on the grass there in her bare feet, and wished she could live in a place like that. Joan died some years ago and the woman minister who conducted the funeral service gave a little talk about her which was quite an eye-opener, because some of us learned things about her that we had simply not known before. My niece Kay, who was born just after I returned from India, had told the minister things that Joan had told her, including the fact that at some stage early in her life Joan had been a Windmill girl; she'd been, that is to say, in the chorus line at the Windmill Theatre in Soho. None of us, apart from her daughter, had heard about that before.

SADDHANANDI: So she did take up dancing. It seems a very happy last verse. Although she's dancing *The Dying Swan*, it's a very beautiful dance.

SANGHARAKSHITA: I think she was of a happy disposition. She didn't worry. Perhaps she didn't worry about things she ought to have worried about. I gather that in the case of her earlier children, she wasn't a particularly good mother, though she was a doting mother as far as her last child was concerned. So yes, although the verse about *The Dying Swan* is from my own imagination, that was what my sister was really like – she was happy and joyful and dancing: 'And joy from her every movement shone'. She didn't easily get upset. Sometimes her husband and my mother didn't get on very well, and they even quarrelled, and my sister would just take no notice. She'd carry on reading a book. She just didn't get involved. I heard about these things afterwards from my mother. Her husband outlived her for many years. He lived on well into his nineties.

4
THE ROOT SPEAKS

Mock me not, O Rose, that I am hidden
Here in the black soil. The sap descends
In Autumn with the long tale of thy Summer beauty
And I know all thy ways. Oh mock me not
That my roots are hidden in the earth, that I love the earth
With its moist smell of rotting leaves and its decayedness.
Mock me not that my friends are all children of uncleanness
And my loves the daughters of earth. I have heard report
Of your pure white beauty bediamonded with drops of dew,
And of how you stand stately and aloof among your leaves and thorns.
The stars are all on fire for you,
And the moon maddened by your beauty.
Oh mock me not that I am ugly and twisted and black.
I am out of your sight. Why should you mock me?
But tell me, Whence comes the sap that invigorates your veins,
And the beauty that blushes in every petal?
Does it not come with the ascending sap in Spring?
Comes it not through these roots, from this dank black soil,
From these rotting leaves, this decayedness, this uncleanness –
Out of urine and ordure? So mock me not,
O Rose, nor be ashamed of your father the Root
Before the faces of your friends, the Stars.

SADDHANANDI: Do you remember when you wrote this poem, Bhante?

SANGHARAKSHITA: I don't, but I checked when it was written, and apparently I wrote it at the beginning of 1951, which really surprised me. I have no recollection of why I wrote it or even what it means. Obviously it's my poem, I wrote it, I'm responsible for it, and I should know what it means, but I don't.

SADDHANANDI: Well, it's a very interesting poem, and it seems to be describing a communication between two aspects of a single plant. Does that sense come back to you now, this idea of two things in communication?

SANGHARAKSHITA: Yes, I can certainly see that. I can see the connection between the root on the one hand and the beautiful rose on the other, and of course they're both parts of the same plant. There's a conversation going on between them, even though the rose doesn't speak. Only the root speaks, but there's a dialogue nonetheless between the two, some tension even between the two. It's as though the root isn't happy with the relationship, and of course the rose has been described as aloof. We're not told, but perhaps the root is male and the rose is female.

SADDHANANDI: Is this dynamic familiar to you in the sense of an aspect of yourself that's more hidden or more at the root, and a flower, or something reaching for the stars?

SANGHARAKSHITA: That may well be, but the root describes himself in very negative terms. Why should he be feeling so negative about himself? He's ugly, he's twisted, he's black, and clearly he's not very happy about that. But he's also not very happy that the rose should be mocking him. After all, she has sprung forth, as it were, from him. Something almost sociological occurs to me. Modern novels and biographies often describe a generational split between parents and children. Perhaps a child is very clever, passes examinations, gets to university, but the further they go, the more remote they become from their roots. Maybe they come from a very working-class family. A certain estrangement happens. You might imagine a father saying to a rather uppity child who's won all sorts of prizes at university, 'Don't forget that it was my money that originally paid for all this, so don't look down on your father.' There's that sort of sociological slant that could be given to the poem, though that's not what I had in mind at the time of writing, I'm sure of that. But then who is the root, what is the root? Who is the flower, what is the flower?

SADDHANANDI: There's certainly a causal relationship between the two, isn't there?

SANGHARAKSHITA: Evidently. The root is the root of the stem from which the beautiful rose blooms. I'm also reminded a bit of the so-called decadent literature of the end of the nineteenth century, thinking of the poet Baudelaire and his collection of verses called *Les Fleurs du Mal*, 'The Flowers of Evil'. It's as though the flowers of the poems have sprung from something evil in himself, social circumstances and so on. He's the poet of the city. Perhaps there are unpleasant aspects to city life, but poetry springs from them, flowers spring from them. So this is another possible connection. In my teens I was very fond of Baudelaire, though I could only read him in translation.

SADDHANANDI: When we were talking about this a couple of weeks ago, you mentioned the Zen saying: 'The bigger the heap of clay, the bigger the Buddha.' It's like when you're creating a statue of the Buddha you need a lot of clay, and you used that as a metaphor for working with the heap of defilements. Can you say anything about that?

SANGHARAKSHITA: The little proverb goes on to say, 'Just as the more the clay, the bigger the Buddha, in the same way, the more the defilements, the greater the Enlightenment.' I don't think you can equate them in that way, but it's true that out of our present being we have to create something that goes beyond what we are. It's we who have to create that. And there is a sort of puzzle, because traditionally in Buddhism we distinguish what is conditioned from what is unconditioned, and we who are conditioned have to achieve the Unconditioned, but no transformation of the conditioned can possibly be the Unconditioned. There has to be a sort of leap, almost, as in fact some Buddhist traditions maintain. So there's the problem of how does the beautiful flower of Enlightenment come from the black root of our *kleśas*? In a sense it doesn't come from them. In a way the simile fails, it's not complete, it cannot carry the full weight of the meaning. In some ways the rose – to carry the association – has to bloom in mid-air, without any root. But on the other hand there has to be a root. There has to be something in us that we are trying to transform, that we hope will become a beautiful white rose in the end.

When we become a little more advanced in our spiritual life, we shouldn't look back on our early spiritual efforts with a lack of appreciation. We may have done silly things, thinking that they were the right things to do, but we shouldn't look down on them. We were doing our best according to our understanding at that time, even though we may have been pursuing a wrong track. Maybe there's a dynamic of that sort going on in the poem, as if to say, 'Don't be too proud of your achievements now. Don't forget they had very humble beginnings.'

SADDHANANDI: And don't get cut off from your roots.

SANGHARAKSHITA: Yes indeed. Don't stop doing your mindfulness of breathing and your *mettā bhāvanā* because you're now so preoccupied with all sorts of interesting Tantric things.

SADDHANANDI: There's this phrase we use in meditation sometimes: 'You need to start where you are' or 'You need to know where you're at'. Does that mean anything to you?

SANGHARAKSHITA: Well, it's obvious. Where else can you start? But it also means knowing yourself. It's very difficult, at the beginning of your spiritual life especially, to know yourself and to know what you need to do at that particular stage. This is where the counsel of wise friends helps, and this is why we have teachers and don't go it alone.

SADDHANANDI: There's this modern phrase 'spiritual bypassing'. When we talked about the poem earlier, you said it's not about that, but could you say something about spiritual bypassing?

SANGHARAKSHITA: I've only recently heard the term and I don't really know in what sense people use it, but I suppose it means being so occupied with beautiful spiritual ideas that you forget what you really are like, forget what you have to do in order to achieve and realize those beautiful spiritual ideas. You might, for instance, have a bad temper but not fully recognize the extent to which it gets in the way of your spiritual life. Sometimes you need a friend to point it out. I can understand that the term spiritual bypassing makes some sort of sense, but I hope it's not one of those glib terms that people use without thinking about it. Some people may use the term because they are essentially more interested in psychology than spiritual practice and thus find it useful to label spiritual practice as 'spiritual bypassing'.

SADDHANANDI: So there are dangers on both sides.

SANGHARAKSHITA: Yes. Using the term spiritual bypassing may suggest something very clever, something very superior that you've seen but other people don't see, so you wag your finger and say, 'Aha! You mustn't be guilty of spiritual bypassing!'

SADDHANANDI: We do have to recognize that we have tendencies, *kleśas*, defilements that need to be worked with. In the Sevenfold Puja we use the word evil – the evil that I have heaped up – which is quite a strong term.

SANGHARAKSHITA: It's quite a strong term because *kleśas* are very nasty things. I've heard recently that some people don't like to say that there's evil in them, but I think we shouldn't be afraid to say that. As I said, *kleśas* are very nasty things, and they go right down deep. Perhaps we wouldn't be here in this world if there weren't *kleśas* – in our past lives, from a Buddhist point of view – that have precipitated us into this life. Also, we don't know what we may be capable of in certain circumstances. Would we always do the right thing under pressure? We don't know. Very often people who commit murder are not the sort of people who have been in the habit of committing murder. It's something they do in the heat of the moment and regret for the rest of their lives. That potentiality was there, and it's there in all of us. There's evil there. It hasn't been acted upon, but the potentiality is there. So we shouldn't be afraid to recite 'the evil that I have heaped up'. We may have done, and may do, evil through our ignorance and foolishness, and we need to recognize that. We know from our own experience that it's possible to suddenly become angry in a way that might surprise people. There's a story in the Pāli scriptures about a maidservant called Kāli. She was a very good maidservant and her mistress was pleased with her, and the mistress had the reputation of being very good-tempered. But one day Kāli thought, 'I always behave properly. No wonder she's good-tempered. But supposing I were to behave in some other way. What would she be like then?' So quite deliberately Kāli started making mistakes, and her mistress became quite upset and ill-tempered. At some point she even struck Kāli in her anger. And Kāli said, 'Where is the good-tempered one now? She was quite good-tempered as long as I was a good servant, but when I changed she showed her true colours.'[38] We never really know ourselves until we're tested by circumstances. I know that some Order members have recently been tested very much by circumstances, and usually they've responded very well and very positively, but they've been tested. Sometimes one doesn't know within oneself what one is capable of, for good or ill, until a testing from circumstances comes.

SADDHANANDI: This highlights the danger of having a comfortable life. We have created a life for ourselves where we can maintain ourselves very well.

SANGHARAKSHITA: Yes. There's another modern expression I've heard recently: not straying beyond your comfort zone. We should be very careful that we don't create a little comfort zone for ourselves and resist anything that would move us beyond it. There's nothing bad about comfort, but it can be very seductive. When I was in India, I had a few friends who were Thai Buddhist monks and I noticed that they liked this word comfortable. They used to say, 'You should come to Thailand. You will be very comfortable there.' I used to say, 'But I don't want to be comfortable!' They'd say, 'People will give you so many things there. They'll give you watches and TV sets', and I'd protest that I didn't want any of those things. We don't want to be comfortable Buddhists. In the East, the monastic life can be a very comfortable life. Everything is provided for you. You don't have to work, of course. Indeed, you're not supposed to work, according to the Vinaya, at least not in gainful employment. It's very easy to settle down in that monastic routine, where you're waited upon by the laity, and you feel very good in yourself on account of that. This isn't how it was in the Buddha's day, but it has become like that in some Buddhist countries.

SADDHANANDI: The modern life can be a very comfortable life too.

SANGHARAKSHITA: People try to make themselves as comfortable as possible, and in a way that's not a bad thing. We mustn't be masochists. We mustn't give ourselves an unnecessarily hard time. But we certainly shouldn't give ourselves a soft time, an easy time, especially as Order members.

SADDHANANDI: It's not easy to know how to create an edge in our lives without its being just artificial.

SANGHARAKSHITA: It has to be in response to a natural demand. We've wandered quite a long way from the poem, but it has been interesting. In the spiritual life one thing always leads to another. One can't shut off any particular part of it, so if one starts talking about one aspect of the spiritual life, sooner or later one will be talking about another.

SADDHANANDI: The poem is about a flower, an organic being. Sometimes the spiritual life can seem quite mechanistic: if you do this, that happens. We talk a lot about causality. What is the spiritual life in a general way?

SANGHARAKSHITA: There is that mechanical aspect, and we can create almost a spiritual routine for ourselves, but sooner or later reality in the form of external circumstances breaks in. Maybe your parents die or you come to know that you're suffering from an incurable disease. Reality will intervene. Something will happen in your life to upset you in your comfortable circumstances. It's bound to happen sooner or later, even if it's only at the time of death. That will certainly intervene in a very dramatic way.

But I'm interested in the imagery of the poem. What about those stars? What's that all about?

SADDHANANDI: You tell me!

SANGHARAKSHITA: I don't know! Why is the rose friendly with those stars? The rose is down here on earth and the stars are up in the sky, but the rose seems to have stars for friends. I don't know what I meant when I wrote it, but I wonder whether the stars stand for our higher spiritual achievements or aspirations. Different poets use stars in different ways. For Blake, for instance, stars sometimes seem to represent something rather negative, as far as I remember, unreal aspirations, but I don't think they represent that in this poem. There's three levels: root, flower, stars. It's a sort of hierarchy.

SADDHANANDI: Do you have a particular connection with the word 'stars', or the image of stars?

SANGHARAKSHITA: I think whenever I refer to stars in my poetry, it has a very positive significance. I think it represents our spiritual ideals, roughly speaking. But between the root and the rose there's a continuity of development. There's no continuity between the rose and the stars. There's a gulf, as it were. The stars are way up in the sky. The rose and the stars may be friends, or perhaps the root is being a bit sarcastic. It's difficult to tell. I don't know what I intended. But the root certainly doesn't like being mocked. Perhaps the rose isn't really mocking it, but that's how the poor old root feels. There are people who feel looked down upon by others, and perhaps that's introjected and they start looking down on themselves, not valuing themselves as they should. So perhaps we've all got these different aspects: we're root and we're flower and we're star.

We've talked a lot about the poem, but I feel that there's a lot we haven't explored. I don't think we've really got to the bottom of what it means. We're no wiser than before! But nonetheless, I've enjoyed the exploration and I've enjoyed our conversation as we've tried to make sense of this rather odd poem.

5
ADVENT

I listened all day for the knock of the Stranger,
And I often looked out from the door.
The table was scrubbed, the brass shining,
And well swept the floor.

The shadows grew longer and longer,
In the grate the fire flickered and died.
'It's too late. He never will come now'
I said, and sighed.

I sat there musing and musing,
The spinning-wheel still at my side.
The moonlight came in through the window
White like a bride.

As the clock struck twelve I heard nothing
But *felt* He had come and stayed
Waiting outside. And I listened –
And I was afraid.

SADDHANANDI: Do you remember writing this poem? Would you have written it when you were in India?

SANGHARAKSHITA: Oh dear. I can't remember, but I'm pretty sure I wrote it in India.

SADDHANANDI: I imagine the imagery is very different from your life in India.

SANGHARAKSHITA: Yes, but it was all there at the back of my mind. I don't remember writing it at all, but I do remember the poem. What struck me as you read it was that the speaker in the poem speaks of the stranger, and yet she seems to know who he is. There's knowledge, and there's non-knowledge. That's part of the feeling of the poem. And there is fear. The last word of the poem is 'afraid'. On the other hand there's a sort of confidence in what is expected.

SADDHANANDI: So who is the stranger?

SANGHARAKSHITA: That's very difficult to say. It's probably easier to say who the speaker is. That might give us a few clues. There's an interior, a room, and it seems to be a very simple room, even a humble room. 'The table was scrubbed.' Well, what sort of table do you scrub? You don't scrub a table of polished mahogany. You scrub a bare wooden table. That suggests simplicity of lifestyle. And the floor is well swept. Whoever is speaking is a good housewife. There's an echo, I think, of the devotional poetry of George Herbert, who speaks of the soul preparing itself, purifying itself, putting itself in order. There's a line in one of his poems which goes, 'Who sweeps a room as for Thy laws makes that and the action fine.' So in this poem we've got the sweeping of the floor, the making of everything clean and prepared and ready for the reception of an important guest. But who is that guest? He or she is only called the stranger.

SADDHANANDI: As the poem is written down, the Stranger begins with a capital S.

SANGHARAKSHITA: Yes. So it's not just any old stranger. It's *the* Stranger, something almost archetypal, something coming from another dimension, which is wanted but also feared. And then also there's this imagery of the moonlight and 'white like a bride'. Why that particular imagery? If one thinks of a bride and a white wedding dress, one thinks of marriage, union. So maybe there's a question of union between the person, presumably a woman, who is speaking, and the stranger at the door. The fact that the speaker is a woman is confirmed by the presence of the spinning wheel: 'The spinning-wheel still at my side'. She's stopped working on her spinning-wheel, stopped spinning wool. She's just waiting with expectancy. There's concentration and suspense, and a tremor of fear.

Going back to this theme of marriage and union, in the old days, in respectable families a young woman never knew what was going to happen on the wedding night. This comes out in quite a few novels of the period. For the young woman, getting married is what she wants, but there's something in marriage that she doesn't yet know anything about. There's a short story by the French writer Maupassant in which the father warns the daughter just before she gets married, 'There are some things we haven't told you, we've tried to shield you from, but I have to tell you that there's a brutal side to marriage.' And the poor girl does find that out. So there is something that's desired, but it's also feared. Of course, that sort of situation hardly arises today, certainly not in the West, but that was the situation, certainly in this country, in Victorian times. So there's this associated imagery of marriage, the wedding, something that is wanted, desired, but of which one is a little afraid at the same time because it's unknown, it's strange.

SADDHANANDI: Have you had an experience like that in your own life?

SANGHARAKSHITA: It can happen in meditation. It's as though the ego is being nibbled away at, it's disintegrating. You want that, but there's a part of you also that's afraid of it happening. Another association that comes to me, which you may think relevant or not, is with taking LSD. I took it twice, years ago. The first time I took it – I was with a good friend – I had no idea what sort of experience I might have, or if I might have an experience at all. After you take the pill, you're waiting for something, you're supposed to be getting some great experience, but you don't know what. That's a bit like waiting for the knock of the stranger. I've talked about that sort of nibbling away in relation to my first experience of LSD. I felt that little fishes were nibbling at my brain! I thought I would keep a record of my LSD experience, so I had a sheet of paper and pen all ready. As the LSD started taking effect, I wrote down, 'Little fishes nibbling at my brain', and then I started laughing, and after that I couldn't write anything else.

SADDHANANDI: Did anything else happen while you were on LSD?

SANGHARAKSHITA: It's very difficult to say. One is in such a different dimension that it's not easy to describe it in terms of another dimension, so I've written very little about that experience. But one of the things I have written is that I had a sense of a vast cosmos, a primeval ocean at the beginning of things, even before Time, and a light shining on that ocean. And the words came to me in the LSD experience: 'First light on first water'. But we're getting a bit far away from the poem! One thing leads to another. It's not completely disconnected, because in the case of the LSD experience, I wanted to try it, but at the same time it was something very unfamiliar. I didn't know what was going to happen. But I wanted it – not just for my own sake. I had a friend staying with me at the time and he'd had seven or eight LSD trips and they'd all been bad ones. He was very concerned to have a good one, and he felt that with me he'd have a good trip, which in fact he did.

SADDHANANDI: Going back to the poem, you've got images of a very ordinary life, a very ordinary house, and this slightly magical, mysterious other that's come into the situation. So you've got these two things going on at the same time.

SANGHARAKSHITA: You could say, if you want to look at it in a Neoplatonic way, that the woman or the speaker is Soul, and the Stranger is Spirit. When I say Spirit I'm using the word in the Neoplatonic sense, something approaching the Transcendental. So we could say that the poem represents what we have to do on the mundane level, the conditioned level, in order to be ready to receive what we may call a more transcendental experience. But the mundane is the mundane, and the Transcendental is the Transcendental. And the mundane fears the Transcendental, because in a sense the Transcendental obliterates the mundane. You die. There's a phrase by a Christian mystic that I sometimes quote: 'Reason dies in giving birth to ecstasy.'[39]

SADDHANANDI: You make it sound very 'other', like something other is going to happen.

SANGHARAKSHITA: Yes, but that other is what you want. Your whole spiritual life is a preparation for the experience of that other, which is going to annihilate your ego, you might say. In a way you want that. The ego wants to be annihilated. It's so uncomfortable with itself, it doesn't like itself any more. It wants to open up to something higher.

SADDHANANDI: So is the spiritual life a lot about preparation?

SANGHARAKSHITA: I think it's about preparation all the way. You go on preparing up to the last minute. I don't think you can sit back and say, 'I've done the preparation,' – the preparation is going on the whole time.

SADDHANANDI: Do you think we understand that as well as we need to?

SANGHARAKSHITA: Perhaps not. There's a saying attributed to Gandhi: 'The end is the extreme of means.'[40] I can see the sense of that. In this context you could say that the preparation is the goal. You can't separate the two. It's not that you prepare and then you stop preparing and get some sort of result or fruit. No, in the preparation itself you experience the end.

SADDHANANDI: It makes me think of a quote that I was very inspired by when I was a young Mitra: 'The goal of the spiritual life is to be always on the path.'

SANGHARAKSHITA: That's another way of saying that the path is the goal. In a sense path is one thing and goal is another, but one should beware of making too hard and fast a distinction between the two.

SADDHANANDI: We're often quite goal-orientated, aren't we? Maybe more and more in this world, where outcome seems to be very desirable.

SANGHARAKSHITA: Another quote comes to my mind, from Matthew Arnold: 'We want all pleasant ends, but will use no harsh means.'[41] In other words, we want to get things on easy terms. We don't really want to put in the necessary work – that is, if the work is a bit demanding or even painful.

SADDHANANDI: Did you have periods in your own life when you felt you had to put in a lot of spiritual work?

SANGHARAKSHITA: There's always spiritual work to do, and it comes up in different contexts and from different angles, depending on what you are doing at that particular time – whether you're meditating or giving lectures or talking with people or just being quiet by yourself. There is always something you can do, spiritually speaking.

SADDHANANDI: Do you articulate that to yourself? For instance, in the last couple of years have you had a sense of your own spiritual project?

SANGHARAKSHITA: For many years my own spiritual project has been inseparable from that of the Movement. But now that I'm so to speak retired, I've got plenty of spare time, and I do look back over my life. That is pleasing, it's instructive, it's sometimes eye-opening. The poem speaks of 'musing and musing'. Musing is an interesting word. It's not exactly reflecting. It's not thinking. It's a sort of contemplative reflecting. You let the spinning-wheel stop, it's not turning over and over any more. In a way your mind is at rest.

SADDHANANDI: It reminds me of a softer approach to reflection. You're allowing things to turn over in your mind, but it's not that you're trying to get somewhere.

SANGHARAKSHITA: Yes, you're turning things over in your mind and just looking at them in a gentle way. To generalize, the poem seems to be about preparation, receptivity, openness to some higher or further experience which you don't know a lot about but which you need to be open to. There's trust, but there's also fear. You're not afraid of the stranger in the ordinary sense, but when you think that he's coming for *you*, that he's not going to be a stranger for ever, there's that little tremor of uncertainty or fear, like that of the old-fashioned bride on her wedding night.

SADDHANANDI: And why did the stranger come, but stay waiting outside?

SANGHARAKSHITA: He was waiting for you to complete your preparations, I suppose – waiting for some initiative on your part, even. It's not that you have to be completely passive. Perhaps you have to make a move. Perhaps you have to open the door, not wait for him to knock. If you know he's there, why shouldn't you just go and open the door? That suggests that preparation and waiting is not an entirely passive thing, leaving the initiative to the stranger. He's there, he's waiting for you, he's outside. Maybe he wants you to open the door, or to go out into the garden and meet him there.

SADDHANANDI: It's all very metaphorical, isn't it?

SANGHARAKSHITA: Yes. She goes on waiting a long time, and then she gives up. '"He never will come now," I said, and sighed.' But the poem doesn't actually say that the stranger is there. 'But *felt* he had come'. It's a bit contradictory. During the day she's been going to the door and looking out for him, but now, even though she feels he's there, she doesn't go and open the door. There's a conflict going on. She wants to meet him, but she's afraid too, so when he does come, or when she thinks he's there, she doesn't do anything about it.

SADDHANANDI: So here you are as a man writing a poem from a woman's point of view. I know it's not a woman as in an ordinary woman, it's all archetypal, but do you want to say anything in relation to that?

SANGHARAKSHITA: In terms of traditional imagery, Soul is usually regarded as feminine and Spirit as masculine, and perhaps in the poem there's an interplay between the two, the Soul inside the room, having prepared itself for the reception of the Stranger, and the Stranger, the Spirit, perhaps outside waiting for the Soul to make a movement towards it. That's a little Neoplatonic, one might say.

SADDHANANDI: That makes me think of your description of yourself as Sangharakshita I and Sangharakshita II.

SANGHARAKSHITA: I think I'd probably change that now and say Sangharakshita I, Sangharakshita II, Sangharakshita III, Sangharakshita IV, and so on.... But at the time I wrote about that, or thought about that, yes, there were Sangharakshita I and Sangharakshita II – at least that was how some people saw me. Some appreciated Sangharakshita I but didn't like Sangharakshita II and vice versa.

SADDHANANDI: And did the Soul belong to one of those particular personalities?

SANGHARAKSHITA: Mm. Yes, I think the Soul belonged to Sangharakshita II. On the other hand, one must say that the Sangharakshita I that was seen by others was not the same as the Sangharakshita I that was seen by me. For instance, when that monk in Ceylon thought I should stop writing those foolish poems and write something more intellectual, he didn't realize that those poems were an expression of my spiritual life. They weren't separated from my practice of the Dharma, but he didn't see that. And the young woman who wrote admiring the poetry but not liking the dry, intellectual articles didn't realize that for me those articles were not dry or intellectual, but my effort to understand the Dharma. So they both misunderstood me in their different ways. The Sangharakshita I and the Sangharakshita II that they each saw were different from the Sangharakshitas I and II that I saw and experienced.[42]

SADDHANANDI: And for the Spirit to be really vital and for the Soul to really have soul, they need to be in communication.

SANGHARAKSHITA: Yes. Perhaps one could say that that poem was about preparation for an important communication that has not yet taken place between the speaker and the stranger. The speaker is not identified except that she seems to be female, and the stranger is evidently male. The title 'Advent', which means 'the coming', has Christian associations, but those aren't very strong in the poem, despite the possible influence of George Herbert in the description of the interior. But one could say that the scrubbing of the table and the sweeping of the floor have something to do with ethical preparation, purification, cleanliness. The woman who is speaking wants the stranger to find everything in good order. Using another kind of symbolism, he's perhaps the guest. As I've mentioned in some of my lectures, in Indian tradition you welcome the guest in a very elaborate way, and that's ritualized in Buddhist puja. So the Buddha can represent the guest. He doesn't belong to your home, he comes from outside, even from some other dimension, some other world. So the guest is a bit like the stranger. They both represent a sort of irruption from another dimension, a higher dimension, into your ordinary life.

SADDHANANDI: I think you mentioned before that the stranger sometimes crops up in Gnosticism as well.

SANGHARAKSHITA: Yes, Gnosticism says that we ourselves are strangers here. We have come from some other world, and we've forgotten that, but we have to remember and find our way back to that higher world. My old friend Clare Cameron published a volume of poems called *A Stranger Here*, and that's how she felt – that she was a stranger in this world and in this life.

It's not easy to summarize what the poem means, or stands for, but there is a sort of dialogue between two people, one of whom speaks and the other is silent, but they're both there. One of them is waiting for something to happen, and perhaps the other is also waiting for something to happen.

6
THE MASK

For seven years a mask I wore,
Secure behind, and firm before;
A mask acceptable and neat,
As folk accustomed are to meet.
It went to school, it went to college,
A mask it was of wit and knowledge;
Older grown, it wined and dined,
Was mask superior, mask refined,
Mask prominent, mask most renowned,
Mask with a hundred masks around.
One day, it felt so hot and tight,
I took it off to say goodnight,
Shake hands, – I think I tried to smile
('Twas only for a little while).
They shrieked aloud with rage and pain
Until I put it on again.

SADDHANANDI: It's quite a witty poem, isn't it?

SANGHARAKSHITA: Yes. I don't usually write witty poems, but that is one of them.

SADDHANANDI: What's it generally about?

SANGHARAKSHITA: Concealment – perhaps the necessity or mutuality of concealment? The fact that people find it so difficult to be open with other people that they very rarely represent their true selves, but that in the long term it's a relief to get rid of what I've called here the mask.

SADDHANANDI: Was this poem stimulated by a particular experience, or was it just a general experience in your life?

SANGHARAKSHITA: It was written very early in the history of the FWBO, but it may have some connection with an earlier experience, going back to my days at the Hampstead Buddhist Vihara. At that time I realized there was a lot of gossip going on about me and my friend Terry Delamere and the nature of our relationship. I thought I needed to talk to someone about that, someone who was not directly connected with the Hampstead Vihara. There was someone I had met in Bombay whom I happened to meet again in this country, and I decided to try to talk a bit about it with him. I started talking, but immediately he stopped me and said, 'Look at that tree. Aren't the leaves a lovely colour?' It was as though he was saying, 'Don't tell me. I don't want to know. I don't want you to confide in me.' This struck me at the time, and I may have remembered that when I wrote the poem.

SADDHANANDI: You've got this idea of concealment and wearing a mask. That's a state that a lot of us live in a lot of the time, isn't it?

SANGHARAKSHITA: Well, to an extent it's necessary, because you can't tell everybody everything on the spot. To an extent, not only concealment but reserve is not just necessary, but very often unavoidable. When the situation becomes serious is when we have to wear a mask with everybody, when we have no friend with whom we can take off the mask and as it were be ourselves. That's the crux: not that we have to wear the mask in certain situations, but that there's no situation in which we can take it off, so that our mask not only grows hot and tight, but becomes inseparable from our face. We may even start thinking that it *is* our face, that that is what we are, suppressing any knowledge we might have about what we're like without the mask. We may come to identify with the mask, and other people may come to identify us with it. That's especially the case when we have some kind of position. This comes to my mind just now because recently there's been news about Pope John Paul II. A cache of love letters written by him has come to light, and shed an entirely fresh light on his character. This correspondence carried on possibly even until he was Pope, certainly until he was a cardinal. It wasn't exactly that he was concealing it, but he certainly wasn't letting the world know about it. Well, in view of his position, what could he do? It was apparently an innocent relationship, but it was a relationship nonetheless, so he had to wear a mask. In fact, he wore the mask so successfully that very soon after his death he was canonized.

SADDHANANDI: What about wearing monastic robes? Is that a mask?

SANGHARAKSHITA: It is to an extent, certainly in the Buddhist countries of the East, because the robe tells people you're a monk, and in certain Buddhist contexts, such as the Theravādin context, it tells people who you are and how they are to behave towards you. For instance, if you are a woman, you certainly mustn't shake hands with a monk or touch him in any way. So in a way the robe is a mask, but the purpose of the mask is clear.

SADDHANANDI: You went through a period yourself of wearing robes but then growing your hair long. That must have been a confusion of masks, a confusion of identity. Did that stir up anything?

SANGHARAKSHITA: In some other people it did. They became quite confused and in some cases quite indignant. But I was sending a signal. When I wore my robes I was sending a signal that I was a monk at least to some extent, and when I let my hair grow long, I was sending a signal that I was a layman to some extent. Wearing robes showed that I was not a layman, and growing my hair long showed that I was not a monk.

I was working towards saying that I was neither the one nor the other. I think it would have been very difficult for me to make an immediate transition from being a monk to being as it were a layman. I was starting a new Buddhist Order in which members were neither monk nor lay, so I was anticipating that, in a way, or proclaiming it. And I was criticized by some people who didn't realize what I was getting at.

SADDHANANDI: On this subject, what does an Order member wearing their *kesa* mean?

SANGHARAKSHITA: Well, someone once said an Order member should wear his or her *kesa* with pride. It's not a mask, it's a means of communication. It means that you're not just a Buddhist, but an ordained Buddhist, committed to practising the Buddha's teaching. A *kesa* should never be a mask but a way of communicating something.

SADDHANANDI: I think that when I first began to meditate, that was when I began to see a bit beyond my mask, or go underneath that, or understand that I was more than just the sociable person that I looked like from the front. Meditation does seem to be somewhere we can break that down a bit, become more authentic.

SANGHARAKSHITA: Well, one of the things we try to do with the help of meditation is see things more clearly, including seeing ourselves more clearly. And we need time to do that. We need time for reflection, and of course for meditation. The kind of meditation in which we try to see ourselves more clearly is the more discursive kind, where we're concentrated, but there is some thought, some reflection, going on, and in this case the thought or the reflection is about ourselves, trying to see who and what we really are, behind whatever mask we wear.

SADDHANANDI: Have you always found it easy to be quite naturally authentic, or have you had to take time to reconnect with yourself to be authentic? I'm aware that you are busy, and you've had a very public life.

SANGHARAKSHITA: Not all the time. In India I had a quite public life, in that I was eventually ordained as a Buddhist monk and people saw me in that way. This reminds me, in connection with my Tibetan teachers, that it's not the Tibetan custom to refer to people who you respect by name. You refer to them by title. For instance, I never knew what Dhardo Rimpoche's personal name was. He was always the Dhardo Rimpoche, the Precious One of Dhardo, Dhardo being the place where he came from. In the same way, people talk about the Dalai Lama or the Karmapa. Dalai Lama is a title, not a personal name. He has a proper name, but no Tibetan would ever think of using that. So you might say that in a sense people are dealing only with masks, in the Tibetan context. They wouldn't expect to relate to the man behind the mask. They would see the man as the mask and the mask as the man. And it can be like that with other titles – you're more conscious of the title than the person having the title.

SADDHANANDI: I suppose in those instances we're functioning more on an archetypal level in relation to other people. The Dalai Lama is quite a significant symbol for a lot of people.

SANGHARAKSHITA: Yes. They wouldn't be thinking in terms of getting to know him as a person, even if they did have that category in their vocabulary. On this sort of subject, I'd mention Chögyam Trungpa and Akong Rimpoche, who set up the Tibetan Buddhist centre Samye Ling. Akong Rimpoche was rather conservative, and he was rather concerned about some of the things that Trungpa was doing that weren't very monk-like, so there was that difference of opinion between them. I'm told that on one occasion Akong said, 'Look. I don't mind what you do. Do as you like. But you have to do it in private, not in public.' Trungpa didn't agree with that, so the two of them parted, and that's why Akong remained at Samye Ling and Trungpa went off to the United States. I've written a little poem about that, dedicated to Trungpa.[43]

SADDHANANDI: Have you had to do things in your life to help you step back from the public eye so much? You seem quite good at keeping a balance between your personal life – your poetry and being with friends – and then going out and giving talks.

SANGHARAKSHITA: I haven't found it difficult to keep up a personal life, mainly with the help of books, especially poetry and writing poetry, and also having at least one or two very close friends.

SADDHANANDI: In your book *A Moseley Miscellany* you say that Allen Ginsberg the poet was a man without masks.

SANGHARAKSHITA: Yes, I did feel that about him. I don't think he was born without a mask. I think he grew up with a mask, especially with regard to his sexual feelings, but he must have worked on himself, because by the time I knew him, he was a very open person. There was that story about him taking off all his clothes at a poetry meeting in California. When we met on one occasion, I asked him whether he really did that, and he said he did. When I asked about the circumstances, he said, 'Well, there'd been this poetry reading and people started asking me questions, and I said something about the naked truth. Someone asked 'What is the naked truth?' so I just took off all my clothes and said, 'That's the naked truth!' That was very characteristic of Ginsberg, and I suppose one could do that sort of thing in California at that time. I doubt if he could have done it at the Albert Hall in stuffy old England.[44]

SADDHANANDI: He was quite strident about being a man without masks in that respect, wasn't he?

SANGHARAKSHITA: I think he was, partly because he'd had to struggle to live without a mask. I've mentioned before what he said to me when we met in Kalimpong. I'd never met him before – I may not even have heard of him before – and he mentioned that he was travelling on his own. He had been travelling with someone but he'd left that person in Calcutta. He said, 'I left Peter in Calcutta. Peter's my wife.' I thought, 'Peter? That's a male name, but maybe women do have those these days.' But from what he said later on I gathered that Peter was a man. So that was an example of Ginsberg wanting to be quite open from the very beginning, not wanting me to be under any misapprehension about the nature of his relationship with Peter – it was of course Peter Orlovsky.[45] He was a good example of a man who lived without a mask, or at least did his best to do so.

SADDHANANDI: We use this phrase sometimes that we're trying to be ourselves, or trying to become more and more ourselves.

SANGHARAKSHITA: That phrase is rather tricky. It depends what sort of self you have. Perhaps it's a self that you shouldn't try to be. You ought to try to be something else. Of course, you have to start with where you are and what you are at a particular moment, but I think to say that one should always try to be oneself sometimes gives leeway for some people to be quite unpleasant. So we should examine our usage of that expression. Sometimes it's better that we shouldn't be ourselves.

SADDHANANDI: As an Order member, you want to be authentic and live up to your ideals, but sometimes this can seem a bit like you're wearing a mask. You're trying to do your best. Maybe it's just a case of being honest with yourself and with others about what's really going on. At the same time you've got to have standards....

SANGHARAKSHITA: I think it's well understood within our movement that Order members are not perfect. I doubt very much whether anyone, even a new Mitra, however dewy-eyed, thinks that Order members are perfect. It's only too obvious that they're not. I don't think Order members need to be concerned about that, but simply do their best to live up to the ideal that they've committed themselves to.

SADDHANANDI: What about these communication exercises that you introduced to us a long time ago. They're something about living with a mask, aren't they?

SANGHARAKSHITA: They are, perhaps especially the first one, when you're just looking at the other person, or you're looking at each other, trying to read the other person from their facial expressions. That makes some people feel a bit uncomfortable, and sometimes they start giggling, because they're not used to being looked at in a friendly, non-hostile manner. You're just looking at someone else's face, almost as if you were looking at an apple or an orange, and noting what their face is like, the wrinkles, the expression. You are looking at the other person and the other person is looking at you, and you are trying to see one another without masks. But you have really to look. Don't stare. Just look.

SADDHANANDI: Did you notice those exercises having an effect on the people that you had around you?

SANGHARAKSHITA: Yes, when I was leading those exercises I found that they certainly had an effect of opening people up, and people became more communicative among themselves, not just with the person they were looking at but generally speaking. They were able to communicate more freely than they could before.[46]

SADDHANANDI: Are there any particular things we do in the Order or in the Movement that help us live more freely, without a mask?

SANGHARAKSHITA: I think the practice of confession within the context of one's chapter is very important, and it does help us to live without a mask, at least when we are with our friends in the Order. For Order members the chapter should be a place where, if nowhere else, you can be without a mask, and be able to talk freely about yourself, and confess what you have done that you should not have done. Confession is the key. It's the working ground. There's always something to confess, I'm sure. There may not be any major sin, but there are always little shortcomings or inadvertencies or lapses of mindfulness. I would stress the importance of the chapter as a venue within which one can be completely open. It's a very precious situation, and we should make sure that we make use of it.

In the poem, there's also the point that it's painful sometimes for other people when one takes off the mask. They don't want to see you without your mask. They've become accustomed to it, they like it, in fact they think that the mask is you, and they don't like to think that they've been deceived all this time, so they react: 'Please put on your mask. We feel so uncomfortable with you when you're not wearing it.' They feel as though you've taken off your clothes, like Ginsberg did. Taking off your mask can be a revolutionary activity, and to be without a mask can represent a very considerable degree of spiritual attainment.

SADDHANANDI: Because it takes self-knowledge and courage?

SANGHARAKSHITA: Yes – and disregard of other people's opinions, when they need to be disregarded. In other words, it's the true individual who is able to live without a mask, or to live making the effort to live without a mask.

SADDHANANDI: I remember reading in one of your books that there's so much projection in communication that you're surprised communication can take place at all, because it's just masks communicating with other masks, I suppose.

SANGHARAKSHITA: Yes, isn't that what happens in society? – 'Mask with a hundred masks around', communicating, if one can use that term, with other masks. Of course, that is not real communication. It happens very often at ordinary social gatherings. You talk about the weather, about the job, about the wife. It's one mask talking to another, and this can be terribly boring to someone who's got a bit tired of their mask and would like to take it off.

7
LOVE AND DUTY

SADDHANANDI: I thought I'd read all three poems and then we'll talk about the one in the middle. They're three Arthurian poems, from *A Moseley Miscellany*.

I
THE WHITE HAWTHORN
A Recollection of Burne-Jones' 'The Beguiling of Merlin'[47]

If it could speak, the white hawthorn,
What would it say?
Merlin and wily Vivian
Wandered this way.

If it could speak, the white hawthorn,
What could it tell?
Vivian wrested from Merlin
A mighty spell.

If it could speak, the white hawthorn,
What then the sound?
With the spell Vivian pent Merlin
Far under ground.

If it could speak, the white hawthorn,
What were the sighs?
Female beauty can overbear
Even the wise.

II
LOVE AND DUTY

Guinevere loved the King
Much less than she esteemed,
And so of gallant Lancelot
She dreamed and dreamed and dreamed.

One day the dream became so deep
That it was dream no more,
And she and gallant Lancelot
Stood on a lonely shore,

And standing on that lonely shore
They heard a dreadful sound,
A sound as of the Crack of Doom,
As split the Table Round;

And thus the lawless passion
Of Arthur's guilty queen
Broke up the goodliest fellowship
That e'er on earth was seen.

Let love and duty coincide,
Lest both of them be hurled
To ruin, and the Crack of Doom
Be heard around the world.

III
THE CELL OF GLASS

Merlin, in his cell of glass
Imprisoned, sees the centuries pass;
Sees the nations come and go
Like clouds in Autumn, fast or slow;
Sees cities rise and cities fall
Like flowers in Springtime, one and all.
Grieved or rejoicing, inly wracked,
He sees, and sees – but cannot act.

So we've got these three poems about the myth of King Arthur.

SANGHARAKSHITA: It's a legend rather than a myth, I would say. Well, it's a whole complex of legends which survive in various languages. In England we know them best through Malory's *Mort d'Arthur* and Tennyson's *The Idylls of the King*. I think in writing these poems I was thinking more of Tennyson than of Malory. Some of the Pre-Raphaelites illustrated some of the poems of Tennyson which dealt with the Arthurian legends, as in the case of the poem about the beguiling of Merlin. It's a very rich source from which to draw.

SADDHANANDI: Has it stimulated your imagination over the years?

SANGHARAKSHITA: I think it has. It's found poetic expression only relatively recently and to a limited extent, but I've always been aware of that Arthurian background, perhaps more through nineteenth-century art, especially that of the Pre-Raphaelites, than through literature.

SADDHANANDI: Does this legend carry particular significance for you, in your life or in Triratna?

SANGHARAKSHITA: Well, the legend of the Round Table has an evident connection with our own Order, in the sense that the Round Table was an association of knights who served the king, and who observed certain rules, a certain ideal, and went forth on various adventures. In my mind, or at least the back of my mind, there's that association between the knights of the Round Table and our own Order. Of course, that's putting it rather crudely; it's subtler and richer than that. I don't know if any of our Order members are inspired by the Arthurian legends. Many of them, those in India for example, are probably not aware of the legends, and have maybe not heard of King Arthur, but for me personally there is that connection.

SADDHANANDI: Do you think it's important that all of us have some sort of legend or myth as part of our lives?

SANGHARAKSHITA: That whole legendary aspect, or mythic aspect, to our experience is very, very important. We'd be very poor without it. But it can come from various sources. Not so long ago, maybe even now, quite a few of our friends drew inspiration, or imaginative sustenance, from *The Lord of the Rings*, and sometimes developed those stories in their own way. I myself was fascinated by the ents and the elves. I wasn't so keen on the hobbits, I must say. They seemed to me rather greedy little creatures with their six meals a day. That didn't appeal to me at all.

SADDHANANDI: What did the elves have that the hobbits didn't?

SANGHARAKSHITA: They were a bit other-worldly, a bit like angels, in a way, beings of another kind – perhaps somewhat superior to human beings. In the legend of King Arthur there's Merlin. Merlin represents a sort of magical element. He's a wizard, but he's a good wizard. He's not infallible, he has his weaker side, but nonetheless for years and years he is Arthur's advisor.

SADDHANANDI: It must be very interesting to have a wizard as your advisor! That sounds very handy. So do you remember writing these poems?

SANGHARAKSHITA: As for 'Love and Duty', I can remember it coming. I can't really say that I wrote it. I didn't deliberately compose it. I certainly didn't think, 'Here are all these beautiful Arthurian legends, let me write something about them.' Quite unaccountably those first three verses came to me, one after the other, and the fourth one came the day after. I have had that sort of experience before – a poem just coming – and I think it's not unusual for people who write poetry. The fact that a poem just comes doesn't mean that it's necessarily any good, but I think 'Love and Duty' is one of my better poems, if I may say so. I think the other two were written more in the usual way, as it were. In the case of 'The White Hawthorn' my inspiration came from Burne-Jones' painting. I was at that time looking through an album of his paintings, so the image was very much in my mind. 'If it could speak, the white hawthorn,...' – then the rest of the poem came. I had to work on it a little. And it was the same with the Merlin poem. But I didn't have to work on 'Love and Duty' at all. It just came. It must have come from somewhere very deep within myself that needed to find expression at that particular time. As I said, I think it's one of my better poems, and perhaps one of my more significant ones.

SADDHANANDI: A moment of inspiration.

SANGHARAKSHITA: Yes.

SADDHANANDI: Did this happen at a time when your eyesight allowed you to write it down yourself or were you having to dictate it?

SANGHARAKSHITA: As far as I remember I wrote it down myself.

SADDHANANDI: And did the three poems come at different times or more or less the same time?

SANGHARAKSHITA: I think more or less the same time. In a sense they form a natural group, like a triptych, with a main panel in the middle and two side panels. 'Love and Duty' is the central poem and it's flanked by those two other shorter poems.

SADDHANANDI: So let's look in particular at 'Love and Duty'. Perhaps we could look at each verse and see what we can draw out from it.
First verse:

Guinevere loved the King
Much less than she esteemed,
And so of gallant Lancelot
She dreamed and dreamed and dreamed.

SANGHARAKSHITA: In a way it's a dilemma, taking the surface meaning. Arthur is an elderly man, certainly as described in Tennyson, and Guinevere is a young woman who has been married to the king in an arranged marriage. She may think very highly of him, she may look up to him, but she may not love him, and her fancy is captivated by a younger, much more handsome man. There is an account – I don't think it's in Tennyson – of how Lancelot was sent on behalf of King Arthur to bring Guinevere to him, after their forthcoming marriage had been announced. Guinevere hasn't seen King Arthur or Lancelot before, and when she looks out from her tower and sees Lancelot coming along the road, she thinks it's the king come himself to escort her and she falls in love with Lancelot. In another Arthurian poem, one by William Morris called 'The Defence of Guinevere', she defends herself, which is another angle on the story. Eventually she realizes that Lancelot has only come to fetch her, he's not the king, but she's fallen in love with him. She's pledged to Arthur, though, and she has to go and be married to him. She sees him as a very worthy man deserving of her respect, she admires him, she esteems him, but she doesn't love him. Her heart is set on Lancelot.

This to my mind represents a situation where in principle we're devoted to an ideal, something we recognize as higher, but at the same time we are drawn to and attracted by something very different, even though we recognize that it isn't so lofty, it isn't so much of an ideal as what we've committed ourselves to. People involved in spiritual life, including Buddhist spiritual life, can very easily find themselves in that sort of situation. You look up to the Dharma, that's what you're committed to, but you've got some other interest and perhaps that's where your heart is. It's a question of bringing the energy that's invested in that other interest into harmony with your spiritual ideal, and if possible to integrate them. I think that's basically what that first verse is about.

I've noticed sometimes that when people have come to see me, we've talked about the Dharma, but the person doesn't seem very much enthused by it. It's clear that they're committed to it, but the conversation flags. But if I happen to touch on something that that person is really interested in, at once they become more enthusiastic and they speak more emotionally. The subject can be something quite innocent. I remember once it was someone's interest in photography, and that was clearly where his heart was, not with the Dharma, even though he was sincerely committed to the Dharma. He was like Guinevere in relation to King Arthur.

SADDHANANDI: Why is it so important to bring our heart into the Dharma?

SANGHARAKSHITA: Well, we *are* our heart. There's a verse in the Bible: 'Where your treasure is, there will your heart be also.'[48] Your heart will be with whatever you really value, and sometimes people are not wholly devoted to the Dharma because they value something else more. Ideally as an Order member you're trying to bring your life, your emotions, into harmony with the Dharma.

SADDHANANDI: And how do we go about doing that?

SANGHARAKSHITA: Well, first of all you have to be aware, you have to have a degree of self-knowledge. And you have to interact with your spiritual friends, and to ask them what they think, and to listen to them and follow their advice.

SADDHANANDI: It's quite a project, isn't it?

SANGHARAKSHITA: It is. Well, in the case of an Order member it's not *a* project, it's *the* project.

SADDHANANDI: Did you have to work through those sorts of things yourself? Your heart was obviously in the Dharma most of the time, but were there times when your heart was somewhere else, say with your poetry?

SANGHARAKSHITA: Well, I've written about the two Sangharakshitas, and that's another way of expressing the same problem. In the legend, according to Tennyson, Guinevere eventually recognizes that Arthur is a greater man than Lancelot and therefore more deserving of her love.

SADDHANANDI: But sometimes we know that something's more deserving of our love, but that doesn't necessarily mean that we love it more, does it?

SANGHARAKSHITA: No, it doesn't.

SADDHANANDI: Let's look at verses 2 and 3:

> One day the dream became so deep
> That it was dream no more,
> And she and gallant Lancelot
> Stood on a lonely shore,
>
> And standing on that lonely shore
> They heard a dreadful sound,
> A sound as of the Crack of Doom,
> As split the Table Round;

SANGHARAKSHITA: Adultery isolates.

SADDHANANDI: That's the lonely shore.

SANGHARAKSHITA: Yes. I'm reminded of Tolstoy's *Anna Karenina*. Once she's run away from her husband with her lover, she has no social context. They're on their own. They have to go off, maybe to Italy or somewhere where they're not known, but there they still have no social context. Adultery cuts you off from everybody; in some ways, even from the person with whom you commit the adultery.

SADDHANANDI: Well, you've invested so much in just being with them, haven't you? It reminds me of something you say: 'Be careful what you wish for.' You don't realize what the implications are going to be.

SANGHARAKSHITA: 'The dream became so deep that it was a dream no more'. They were acting out.

SADDHANANDI: Is that really the nature of mind: that as we dwell on something, as we think about something a lot, we make it come into being?

SANGHARAKSHITA: Yes. Not only if we dream about it a lot, but if we talk about it with other people. That can be a positive thing. If we are really keen on getting something done, we're more likely to get it done – if we need the help of other people – by talking to other people about it. Sooner or later, depending on circumstances, it will come into existence.

As we see in verse 3, their action has social consequences. You shouldn't think that what just the two of you do doesn't affect other people. In the Tennysonian version of the legend, the fact that Guinevere and Lancelot have committed adultery sets a very bad example, and some of the knights start being unfaithful to their mistresses. One of the ideals of the knights of the Round Table was to be faithful in love, to serve your mistress in various ways for maybe a year, maybe longer, until you were considered worthy of her hand. In that context adultery was a very dreadful thing, and eventually the ideal on which the Round Table was founded was shattered. That's important. The actions of individuals, of two people in that sort of relationship, have social effects in your immediate circle. So you shouldn't just follow your blind impulses and think about what's good for you, what you want. You have to think about what is good for everybody, especially those with whom you are in personal contact. Of course, in modern times, at least in the West, we don't think in that sort of way very often. It's *me*, what *I* want. In other words, it's extreme individualism.

SADDHANANDI: It's very hard to take other people into account when our own passions are involved very strongly.

SANGHARAKSHITA: In Guinevere's case, taking it all literally, it must have been quite a struggle. Here she is, married to Arthur. She's a queen. She has something to live up to. People respect her. She respects Arthur, she esteems him, but her heart is elsewhere. She must have gone through many a lonely night struggling with it all. But then her feeling, her passion, is too much for her, so one day the dream 'became so deep that it was dream no more'.

SADDHANANDI: I assume Lancelot was going through a similar experience, given that he was a friend of Arthur.

SANGHARAKSHITA: Yes, and he knew how Arthur trusted him. In one version Arthur had sent him to bring Guinevere to him, to escort her, and here he was, betraying him – committing adultery, but it was almost worse than that. He was betraying his lord, his sovereign, to whom he looked up so much. In Tennyson's version Lancelot and Guinevere both expiate their 'crime', their wrongful behaviour. Lancelot ends up as a holy hermit and Guinevere as the abbess of a nunnery. There's so much in the legend, and even, if I may say so, in the poem.

SADDHANANDI: The poem doesn't come down very favourably on the side of romantic love. Is there any benefit of that kind of love?

SANGHARAKSHITA: It varies from one person to another, and some people seem to be more prone to it than others. Usually when one thinks of romantic love like the love that is celebrated by the troubadours, one thinks of it as something non-sexual, but of course that wouldn't be the case nowadays. I think nowadays one would consider the sexual element to be essential to romantic love. The troubadours sang the praises of their mistress, but she was usually some highborn lady with whom they could not possibly have that sort of personal connection, so the love was – for want of a better term – spiritual. The English romantic poets had that sort of idea of romantic love too, but it's not the modern way of looking at it. In fact, I doubt whether people would often use the expression 'romantic love'. They just say 'love' and take the romance, and the sexuality, for granted.

SADDHANANDI: Being in love, or having that strong relationship with another person, can draw us out, can't it? We've got a very close companion in our life, with whom we can perhaps talk very openly about things.

SANGHARAKSHITA: That brings in the question of friendship, and whether romantic love is the same thing as friendship. Sometimes people have talked of romantic friendship, especially in the Victorian period and earlier, but it's perhaps rather a questionable genre. There's a whole gamut, from a very highly spiritual love, like Dante's for Beatrice, to a very down-to-earth love at the other end of the spectrum, and all sorts of shades and variations in between. Emotion is such an important part of our lives, especially our emotions towards people with whom we're closely connected – our parents, our siblings, wives, husbands, girlfriends, boyfriends, lovers.

SADDHANANDI: So their love has 'split the Table Round'.

SANGHARAKSHITA: Yes. In other words, an individualistic relationship has had very negative social consequences.

SADDHANANDI: And the 'Table Round' is an image for that kind of fellowship between people?

SANGHARAKSHITA: Yes. It's significant that it's round. Roundness is a symbol of wholeness and completeness, and also there's no one at the head of the table. No one has any special position, apart from King Arthur. All the knights are on an equal footing among themselves. Their devotion to the king and to a common ideal makes them brothers. It's just like that in the case of our own movement. We're members of the same sangha because we practise the same Dharma, and that Dharma is Dharma because it comes from the Buddha's Enlightenment. No sangha without Dharma, and no Dharma without Buddha.

SADDHANANDI: I think you once said that in the spiritual community you can have a teacher, but you can't have a leader, which suggests that there's no one sitting at the head of the table.

SANGHARAKSHITA: In the early days of the movement there was quite a bit of talk about who would succeed me as the head of the Order. And of course I *was* the head of the Order. It couldn't be otherwise because I founded it, with the help of others. I thought about it quite a lot, and I didn't like the idea of a leader. Don't forget, I lived through the war, and I heard a lot about the *Führer* and the *Duce*, and all those terms acquired all sorts of sinister connotations. Also, I looked back to the Buddha's sangha. The Buddha said on one occasion: 'If anyone thinks he leads the sangha, let him declare it.'[49] Clearly the Buddha didn't think that anyone should lead the sangha. In those days the sangha consisted mainly of very highly developed people, even *arhants*. They would not be likely to disagree among themselves. There was one occasion when they all spontaneously gathered together in the same place on the same day. They didn't need any email to inform them; they just knew they had to be there. There was that sort of spontaneous unity. I eventually concluded that I didn't want to hand on the headship of the Order to any individual, but to a group of senior Order members, and that's how we come to have the College of Public Preceptors. I hope it'll work. Of course, I'm still around. I hope it will work without me. I'm not part of it. It's quite separate from me in a sense, independent of me.

SADDHANANDI: And is that the Round Table from which we need to take leadership?

SANGHARAKSHITA: The leadership, if one uses that term, is collective. The College of Public Preceptors exercises leadership in the true sense of spiritual leadership.

SADDHANANDI: I'll read the next verse:

> And thus the lawless passion
> Of Arthur's guilty queen
> Broke up the goodliest fellowship
> That e'er on earth was seen.

SANGHARAKSHITA: Individualism is destructive of spiritual fellowship. If everybody goes their own way, there can't be any spiritual community. That's why the sangha has to be based on a common understanding of the Dharma. If you all have your different understandings and different interpretations and go your own way regardless of what others think, there's no sangha. There's no Order. There's no Round Table.

SADDHANANDI: Sometimes you've got individuals with their own individual creativity following a particular path, and then you've got the values around creating the collective or the sangha. Those two things might be not in competition exactly, but …

SANGHARAKSHITA: There will often be tension between them, because you as an individual, to use that term, may want to do something that does not altogether meet with the approval of at least some of your fellow Order members. It's important that there should be discussion if that sort of situation arises. There needs to be a body exercising some sort of leadership. So there is that tension, but ideally it should be a creative tension that is resolved through discussion. In the present situation, I think it unlikely that any Order member is going to be doing things that are so unspeakably crazy that it'll create a problem.

SADDHANANDI: We need to invest in the sangha, but also we need to create a sangha that's a creative sangha.

SANGHARAKSHITA: That means constant reference to the Dharma, and to the application of the Dharma and putting the Dharma into practice. And that of course means agreeing upon what the Dharma is. In our case, it's the Dharma in the presentation that I have given it. Again I say no sangha without the Dharma, and no Dharma without the Buddha.

SADDHANANDI: How is your presentation of the Dharma going to be developed?

SANGHARAKSHITA: It depends what one means by 'developed'. It will be maintained if people understand that presentation and base their spiritual lives upon it. It's pretty broad – I hope not too broad.

SADDHANANDI: Do you have a concern about that sometimes?

SANGHARAKSHITA: I have emphasized recently that it's important that the College of Public Preceptors should speak with one voice.

SADDHANANDI: I wonder if that's an aim that they can achieve?

SANGHARAKSHITA: Well, certainly with respect to basic or fundamental principles they have to speak with one voice; otherwise there will be division, with different people going their own way. This is one of the things that I know is currently being thrashed out.

SADDHANANDI: So, the final verse:

> Let love and duty coincide,
> Lest both of them be hurled
> To ruin, and the Crack of Doom
> Be heard around the world.

SANGHARAKSHITA: In the terms of the first verse, what you esteem and what you love should be the same, ideally. If you love something that you can't esteem, you're in trouble. And if you esteem something that you can't love, you're also in trouble.

SADDHANANDI: Is it a different kind of trouble?

SANGHARAKSHITA: Well, you're in a state of non-integration. If you are to develop spiritually, or even as a reasonably developed human being, the two sides need to come together. There can't be too much division of loyalties in your life.

SADDHANANDI: But if you're too dutiful, don't you end up with rather an odd life?

SANGHARAKSHITA: Tennyson has gone into that in his long poem 'The Palace of Art', which I've written about in *The Religion of Art*. 'Glorious devil, large of heart and brain, that did love beauty only.' There isn't an ethical element in his life, and towards the end of the poem he realizes that this needs attention, and he tries to connect with other people instead of living in his ivory tower. But it's not easy, because sometimes the artist, the poet, or the painter has to devote himself so wholeheartedly to his art that he could seem to sacrifice other interests. I was reminded of that when I read a biography of Paul Scott, who wrote the *Raj Quartet*. It cost him a lot psychologically: he had to shut himself up on his own, and he neglected his family, which morally speaking he should not have done, but he was so immersed in the production of his masterpiece that he couldn't help it. One can see how this sort of situation can arise, though perhaps the position of the artist is a rather special one. But it isn't just a simple question of keeping up a nice balance. Also, one has one's phases. Everyone has. Sometimes you go this way, sometimes you go that way, but in the end you hope to achieve a balance and an integration. Sometimes I was Sangharakshita I, sometimes I was Sangharakshita II. Sometimes I was Sangharakshita III or IV. I hope that in the end, at my age they have come into some sort of harmony or resolution.

8
THE BODHISATTVA'S REPLY

What will you say to those
Whose lives spring up between
Custom and circumstance
As weeds between wet stones,
Whose lives corruptly flower
Warped from the beautiful,
Refuse and sediment
Their means of sustenance –
What will you say to them?

That woman, night after night,
Must sell her body for bread;
This boy with the well-oiled hair
And the innocence dead in his face
Must lubricate the obscene
Bodies of gross old men;
And both must be merry all day,
For thinking would make them mad –
What will you say to them?

Those dull-eyed men must tend
Machines till they become
Machines, or till they are

Cogs in the giant wheel
Of industry, producing
The clothes that they cannot wear
And the cellophaned luxury goods
They can never hope to buy –
What will you say to them?

Or these dim shadows which
Through the pale gold tropic dawn
From the outcaste village flit
Balancing on their heads
Baskets to bear away
Garbage and excrement,
Hugging the wall for fear
Of the scorn of their fellow men –
What will you say to them?

And wasted lives that litter
The streets of modern cities,
Souls like butt-ends tossed
In the gutter and trampled on,
Human refuse dumped
At the crossroads where civilization
And civilization meet
To breed the unbeautiful –
What will you say to them?

'I shall say nothing, but only
Fold in Compassion's arms
Their frailty till it becomes
Strong with my strength, their limbs
Bright with my beauty, their souls
With my wisdom luminous, or
Till I have become like them
A seed between wet stones
Of custom and circumstance.'

SADDHANANDI: This is quite a strong poem of yours.

SANGHARAKSHITA: Yes, I think it's one of my strongest poems. You could call it a poem of social protest. But one thought does occur to me. As Buddhists we have a good idea what is meant by bodhisattva, but if someone who wasn't a Buddhist was to read this poem, it might not mean very much in the sense that they might not know who a bodhisattva was. So maybe we should say a bit about the bodhisattva. As you know, the word literally means 'bodhi-being'. It means someone who has consciously devoted their life and work to helping others out of compassion – helping them not just in a spiritual way, by teaching them the Dharma, but also in all sorts of practical, even material ways. That is the bodhisattva ideal, and through the ages many Buddhists have been inspired by that ideal and have sought to act in accordance with it.

SADDHANANDI: The whole poem is a conversation between somebody who is seeing a lot of things that are going on around them and asking the bodhisattva, 'What are you going to do about them?', and then the bodhisattva's eventual reply.

SANGHARAKSHITA: Yes. I hear those voices on the radio all the time. What are you going to do about this? What are you going to do about that? Usually there's at least a hundred things that need to have something done about them. It's not always defined what that something is, but that cry or that call is there.

SADDHANANDI: Perhaps it's also the sort of conversation we all have internally. We see something and question, 'What am I going to do about that? In what way does the spiritual life help that?'

SANGHARAKSHITA: Also, in a broader sense, what am I to do with my life? Am I to spend it just looking after me, or am I going to contribute something to my society, to my community, to my friends? The poem poses a very big question, both directly and indirectly. What are we to do with our lives? What are we to do with our time? What are we to do with our resources? What's the best use that could be made of them? What's the best use that could be made of us?

SADDHANANDI: There's a quote from Dhardo Rimpoche: 'If you don't know what to do, then do something to help other people.'

SANGHARAKSHITA: *Dāna* is the first step. There's *dāna*, then there's *śīla*, then there's *samādhi*, then there's *prajñā*, then there's *vimutti*. *Dāna* comes first. If you can't give, you're scarcely a Buddhist at all. At least you can do that. It doesn't have to be money. You can give someone a smile, and that smile may brighten their day.

SADDHANANDI: So this is the bodhisattva's reply to those kinds of questions, isn't it?

SANGHARAKSHITA: Yes. You notice that there are lots of questions but the reply is very succinct. Bodhisattvas don't waste words.

SADDHANANDI: Do you remember writing this poem?

SANGHARAKSHITA: No, I don't. Of course that's true of many of my poems. But I was surprised to find how long ago I wrote it. It was early on in my stay in Kalimpong, long before I had any contact with the ex-Untouchable Buddhists. At that time they hadn't converted to Buddhism anyway. There weren't those sorts of problems in Kalimpong, so it must have been a memory of what I'd seen in other parts of India.
[Editor's note: Although when he was talking with Saddhanandi, Sangharakshita couldn't remember writing the poem, in his memoir *In the Sign of the Golden Wheel*, describing the events of 1953, he describes how it was inspired by his meeting in Kalimpong a young Hindi teacher called Dinesh:

> [He was an Untouchable, or rather, untouchability having been officially outlawed, an ex-Untouchable. A native of the then Madhya Pradesh, he had been born into a very poor family (Untouchables were poor almost by definition), had received only a limited amount of education, had worked for Anand-ji when the latter was general secretary of the Association for the Advancement of the National Language, and had become a qualified teacher of Hindi. At one stage he had spent a couple of years in Bombay, that deceitful Mecca of the rural poor, making

his living as an itinerant massage boy and in any other way that was offered. It was as a result of hearing, in the course of that autumn (1953), about Dinesh's experiences that I wrote the poem 'The Bodhisattva's Reply', with its vignettes of the prostitute and the massage boy, the exploited, robotic factory workers, and the despised early morning scavengers from the outcaste village. The story of Dinesh's life had, in fact, moved me deeply, and given me a better understanding of the plight of India's ex-Untouchables who, despite legislation, were still being treated with inhuman cruelty by their Caste Hindu compatriots and co-religionists. Three years later that understanding, for all its limitations, was to stand me in good stead when I came in contact with the newly converted ex-Untouchable Buddhists of Bombay and Nagpur and started working among them.][50]

SADDHANANDI: Do you remember India shocking you at all? Do you remember your first experiences of India?

SANGHARAKSHITA: I remember it very well. I'd landed with my army unit in Bombay and we were on the train to Delhi. We were waiting to leave the station, and looking out of the window. And there we saw beggars, crippled beggars, children with babies, all demanding 'Baksheesh, baksheesh'. It was a horrifying sight. We'd not seen anything like that in our lives before. It was a real shock. So that was my first impression. People will say that there are many other sides to Indian life, and that's true, but beggary and Untouchability are still problems, even so many years after Independence. Later on, during my wanderings in South India with my friend Buddharakshita, I saw many examples not only of Untouchability but invisibility. Some castes were so low that they had to keep out of the way of everybody else, because even the sight of them would be polluting. I've written a bit about this in my memoirs.

SADDHANANDI: And do you remember having that internal question: 'What should I be doing with this amount of suffering? How should I be responding?'

SANGHARAKSHITA: I must say that I didn't feel like that very early on. In those days I was much more concerned with my own spiritual life;

my broader interest in what might be called the social implications of Buddhism struck me only later in life. In any case I felt that one has to develop a certain degree of spirituality, for want of a better term, before one can try helping others. That's not altogether true, because one can give quite a bit of help to others without being very spiritual oneself at all, but you see what I mean.

SADDHANANDI: What is the nature of spirituality that we've got to develop in order to help others?

SANGHARAKSHITA: From a Buddhist point of view, caring for others, acting with compassion, is an essential part of one's own spiritual life. For instance, I've pointed out from time to time that even if you just want to observe the five fundamental ethical precepts, they all involve other people or other beings. There is non-violence, but you undertake to abstain from violence towards whom? Other people, even animals. If you take the precept of speaking the truth, you don't just speak the truth into the air. You speak it, or don't speak it, to other people. There cannot be a spiritual life which has no contact at all with other living beings.

SADDHANANDI: So let's look at the first verse:

> What will you say to those
> Whose lives spring up between
> Custom and circumstance
> As weeds between wet stones,
> Whose lives corruptly flower
> Warped from the beautiful,
> Refuse and sediment
> Their means of sustenance –
> What will you say to them?

SANGHARAKSHITA: There's quite a lot in that opening verse. Those whose lives spring up between custom and circumstance are those whose lives are circumscribed, who have no freedom of action. Their lives are determined by external conditions. I've recently been quite concerned with this idea of freedom, because I've been doing a bit of study of the existentialists, for whom the whole idea of freedom is quite fundamental. So here I envisage a situation where people are cramped by their surroundings, limited in all sorts of ways, so they can't really live as human beings, and I give various examples of how their lives are constrained.

SADDHANANDI: What are these words 'custom and circumstance' describing in particular?

SANGHARAKSHITA: Well, if I think of India I think of the caste system, and of economic circumstances, but of course those words apply universally, not just to India.

SADDHANANDI: So their lives spring up 'as weeds between wet stones'. They 'corruptly flower, warped from the beautiful'.

SANGHARAKSHITA: I rather like those phrases. There's a flowering, but if you're a weed, it's the flowering of a weed, it's not particularly beautiful. Of course, some people say that weeds are beautiful, but this is from a different point of view. And the wet stones represent custom and circumstance. I have in my mind an image of two big stones, and some poor little weed growing up between them, unable to expand itself. It produces a bit of a flower, but it's not much to look at. The lives of the sort of people I'm thinking of are a bit like that. The phrase 'corruptly flower' seems to have an echo of Baudelaire's work *Les Fleurs du Mal*, 'The Flowers of Evil'. Even evil produces flowers, but they're corrupt.

SADDHANANDI: Is there evil in Buddhism?

SANGHARAKSHITA: It depends how you translate various Pāli and Sanskrit words. I have heard that there are some people in our movement who don't like the word 'evil', but that may be because they haven't fully faced up to what they themselves might be capable of given a change in circumstances. Evil is a very strong word. There's physical evil, like physical suffering, and the suffering of illness. There's the suffering of separation from people we love. These are as it were objective evils. But then there's moral evil. And the great moral evil in simple terms is selfishness, self-centredness, egoism, pride, conceit. That's moral evil: the wish to harm others, even; cruelty. There are plenty of examples of that in our own day, if we look around the world. I think we shouldn't be afraid to use the word evil when it's appropriate.

SADDHANANDI: The verse carries on: 'warped from the beautiful'. And then it says, 'Refuse and sediment their means of sustenance'.

SANGHARAKSHITA: 'Warped from the beautiful'. Well, you know what warping is. If you have a piece of unseasoned wood and expose it to the air, it warps, it twists. So that sort of constrained life doesn't just limit you; it distorts you, it distorts your personality and warps you from the beautiful. Had you been in different circumstances you could have grown up beautiful in every way. But since you're a weed between wet stones you can't grow up beautiful. There is some beauty there, because you're human after all, but it's warped, it's twisted.

SADDHANANDI: The verse ends with a question that gets repeated: 'What will you say to them?'

SANGHARAKSHITA: Yes, it's like a chorus.

SADDHANANDI: Going on to the second verse:

> That woman, night after night,
> Must sell her body for bread;
> This boy with the well-oiled hair
> And the innocence dead in his face
> Must lubricate the obscene
> Bodies of gross old men;
> And both must be merry all day,
> For thinking would make them mad –
> What will you say to them?

SANGHARAKSHITA: This highlights a great social evil, which I was certainly conscious of during the time that I was in India. Of course it exists in every country, practically. It's a very extreme example of being forced to do something you don't want to do, or would prefer not to do under any circumstances, but the economic pressure is such that there's no way out.

SADDHANANDI: Was prostitution in India very visible when you were travelling around?

SANGHARAKSHITA: It wasn't very visible, but one knew about it, one heard about it, one read about it from time to time. There were articles in the papers about it. In some countries it is rather more open. Here I'm speaking of prostitution as the result of the force of economic circumstances. I know that there are feminists who take the view that a woman's body belongs to her and she's free to do with it what she wishes, but that's a different point altogether. Here I'm concerned with women who become prostitutes out of sheer economic necessity, or who are trapped into prostitution in some way. I came across that when I was in India because one of my students started a course in social sciences at a Bombay university, and he said he came across quite a number of Nepalese girls who were prostitutes. He was rather surprised, but then he found out what happened. He said the Nepalese girls were usually quite light-coloured, so that was an attraction in itself, and what often happened was that a Nepalese girl who found herself being a prostitute in Bombay might write to a friend in Nepal and say, 'Look, I've got a lovely job and I'm very happy with it. Why don't you come and join me?' And then the innocent girl goes there and finds that the job she's been promised is that, and she can't retreat. She might even literally be imprisoned by the people who are running that racket.

SADDHANANDI: You told me about an incident in India when you found yourself teaching prostitutes.

SANGHARAKSHITA: Yes indeed. This was in an area called Kamathipura, which is a district of Mumbai, and I was invited to speak to them. Many of them would have been from the Dalit community, and they'd become Buddhist with the rest of their community. So here I was, with my translator, one evening in Kamathipura, and I did what I usually did when I came to any new place, or met a new group of New Buddhists. I explained what was meant by Going for Refuge to the Buddha, who the Buddha was, what Buddhahood meant. Then there was Going for Refuge to the Dharma and the Sangha, I explained all that. And then I came to the precepts – non-violence, non-stealing. But when I came to the third precept, I said, 'Well, I can't say very much about that. You'll just have to do the best you can.' And they laughed. There they all were, these several hundred women, and you couldn't tell just by looking at them what they did. They were dressed in colourful saris, and each had the edge of her sari over her head in a modest sort of way. So many of them! But they were women, they were human beings. They didn't look different from anybody else, but there they were, living that sort of life.

SADDHANANDI: You had a lot of sympathy for them, Bhante.

SANGHARAKSHITA: Yes indeed.

SADDHANANDI: In the poem you're not just talking about women, but boys as well.

SANGHARAKSHITA: Yes, that too happens in India as well as elsewhere.

SADDHANANDI: This line 'And the innocence dead in his face'.

SANGHARAKSHITA: If you've become involved in something that is against your moral sense, you lose whatever innocence you had.

SADDHANANDI: What is precious about innocence? What does that mean?

SANGHARAKSHITA: Well, there are two sorts of innocence. There's the innocence of ignorance, which is not necessarily a good thing. But there's also the innocence of a person who is naturally good, who doesn't have to make too much effort to be good. One knows people who are well known to be like that, both men and women.

SADDHANANDI: And then you say, 'Both must be merry all day, for thinking would make them mad.'

SANGHARAKSHITA: Yes. If you're in a situation that you've been pressured into, and that you don't want to be in, that's a very terrible thing to have to face, especially if you feel that you're doing something that is wrong. You can't bear to think about it. You just have to pretend it's all right, even pretend to be merry, forget your sorrows, maybe even take to drink or drugs. Those things are also bound up with that way of life, or that way of death, as one might say.

SADDHANANDI: So then we have again the question, 'What will you say to them?' We're going to hear later what the bodhisattva says. Next verse:

> Those dull-eyed men must tend
> Machines till they become
> Machines, or till they are
> Cogs in the giant wheel
> Of industry, producing
> The clothes that they cannot wear
> And the cellophaned luxury goods
> They can never hope to buy –
> What will you say to them?

SANGHARAKSHITA: This is about victims of industrialization, and it applies not only to India and Bangladesh, but to other countries too, where it may be more sophisticated. Some years ago, quite by accident, I got hold of a copy of Engels' *The Condition of the Working Class in England*. He wrote it in 1845, and it was a terrible story. He had all sorts of facts and figures for what it was like for people who had been caught up in that industrial system in the Victorian period. It was a horrific picture. I'd never realized just how bad conditions were for people working in factories at that time. They worked twelve hours a day, and small children worked in factories and worked all day too. Their living conditions were appalling, and slums sprang up in many of our major cities. Engels was a Communist, and what he wrote was what he had found, his own observation, looking around and inspecting things.

SADDHANANDI: There were some factory owners, like the Cadbury family, who built new houses for people.

SANGHARAKSHITA: Yes, there were exceptions. Not all mill owners were so neglectful of their workers. Not long after 1845, there were the Pre-Raphaelites painting their beautiful pictures of the Arthurian legends.

That was in part a protest against the ugliness of their surroundings in Victorian industrial England.

SADDHANANDI: Today we're often very naive about how our luxury goods are made.

SANGHARAKSHITA: They're not luxury goods any more, they're things we take for granted. It's the throw-away society. You don't mend a pair of socks when you get a hole in them, you throw them away and buy a new pair. That's the way the industrial system works.

SADDHANANDI: Sometimes with computers, or televisions, or electrical equipment, it's often cheaper to buy a new one than to get it mended. We have a naivety about how those items are created. We sometimes think it's made in a factory, but actually it's made by people living like machines.

SANGHARAKSHITA: A few years ago there was a terrible scandal in Bangladesh. Several hundred people were burned to death when the building in which they were working caught fire. The owner of that building fled to the border to try to get to India and escape justice, but he was caught. I don't know what happened to him, but if he had friends in high places, it's possible that he might have gone unpunished.

SADDHANANDI: And I know that that factory was connected to quite famous chains of department stores in Britain.

SANGHARAKSHITA: That sort of work dehumanizes you. Your eyes become dull. They don't light up. You're not happy, not content. You just have to work. This is no longer the case so much in this country – certainly children don't have to work long hours in factories – but it is true in many other parts of the world. Nowadays we're more likely to be slaving away in an office, in relative comfort.

SADDHANANDI: I remember once when I was travelling in a particular country where donkeys were used a lot, there was a woman leading a donkey, and I realized that the donkey and the woman had the same expression.

SANGHARAKSHITA: Oh dear.

SADDHANANDI: It's that dullness, isn't it, of very boring work. These people are 'producing the clothes that they cannot wear and the cellophaned luxury goods they can never hope to buy'.

SANGHARAKSHITA: You get that division between those who work and produce and those who consume.

SADDHANANDI: Moving on to the next verse:

> Or these dim shadows which
> Through the pale gold tropic dawn
> From the outcaste village flit
> Balancing on their heads
> Baskets to bear away
> Garbage and excrement,
> Hugging the wall for fear
> Of the scorn of their fellow men –
> What will you say to them?

SANGHARAKSHITA: You see the contrast. There's the beautiful natural scene – dawn in any part of the world can be really beautiful – but it's the backdrop of this scavenging work. I came to know quite a bit about that once I started making more contact with the followers of Dr Ambedkar – people, women especially, carrying away baskets full of garbage and excrement.

SADDHANANDI: So Dr Ambedkar was trying to address this.

SANGHARAKSHITA: There was a programme on the radio just very recently in a series called *Incarnations*, consisting of little sketches of fifty Indians who have contributed to India's history. Ambedkar was one of them. The programme was very well done, considering it was just fifteen minutes long, but nothing was said about his conversion to Buddhism or that of his followers. I thought that very significant. Of course, Ambedkar himself was born into an Untouchable family, but luckily his father had been educated a little when he was in the army, so his father encouraged him, and Ambedkar was a brilliant boy and eventually became a very highly qualified man, studied in the States and in England at the London School of Economics, and went back to India determined to do something to raise the position of the people from whom he sprang. He found it very difficult and encountered a lot of resistance from the higher caste people, who of course were Hindus, and in the end he came to the conclusion that there was no hope for the Untouchables, his followers, if they remained Hindu, so he proposed the radical solution of conversion to Buddhism. He considered Marxism, but rejected it, feeling that human beings needed a religious or spiritual basis to their lives, that that was the basis of everything. So he embraced Buddhism publicly, along with 400,000 of his followers. The conversion movement spread, and I became involved with that, especially after his death. Through my New Buddhist friends, I learned quite a lot about how they'd been forced to live, what their difficulties had been, and sometimes I experienced it myself. I remember once on one of my lecture tours, I had lunch at the home of one of the Dalits, as they came to be called later. There was a glass of water with my food, and I saw there was a lot of sediment in it. My host explained that they had to take water from the river because the Hindus wouldn't allow them to touch the well. The Dalits were in the minority in the village, so they couldn't do much about it. That's just a simple example. They usually had separate quarters, a sort of sub-village of their own on the outskirts of the village, and there are so many stories about how they were treated. Well, one still gets these stories in the newspapers in India, and occasionally those stories reach the West.

SADDHANANDI: When you continued the work of Dr Ambedkar, were you serving him? Were you serving spiritual values, or political values? What were you doing?

SANGHARAKSHITA: I felt I was serving the Buddha, that this was what the Buddha would have wanted me to do. Ambedkar had converted to Buddhism partly because he believed that society needed to have a bedrock of religion, but it had to be a religion that promoted human values, not a religion that denies those values, as Hinduism did. I certainly didn't see myself as just a sort of social worker – no, I was doing the Buddha's work, because those people had gone for Refuge to the Buddha, Dharma, and Sangha, and I saw my duty as helping them to understand what that meant.

SADDHANANDI: In a sense Dr Ambedkar was leading a political movement which he saw needed to have spiritual values. Are we a spiritual movement that should be having much more political engagement?

SANGHARAKSHITA: Within the Triratna Buddhist Order we don't all have the same view in this respect. Some are genuinely devoted to their spiritual practice, and maybe they have full-time jobs and they have families, so they may have sympathy for what we're doing in India, but they don't have any strong feeling to take part in that. But there are some Order members with more of a social conscience, one might say, and they are more aware of the problems we're having to face nowadays, not only in India but in the world as a whole. I have sometimes said that I probably would not have become socially involved in any way as part of my Buddhist life if I'd not been in contact with the ex-Untouchable Buddhists. That was a particular situation, as we see from the poem, but it's a situation that in different ways exists in most countries.

SADDHANANDI: Did you get involved in that work because of your connection with Dr Ambedkar? You'd made a few connections with him, you'd met with him.

SANGHARAKSHITA: That was useful, because it gave me a certain credit in the eyes of his followers. Dr Ambedkar I know had spoken about me and my work in very positive terms. It also helped that I was English. That surprises some people, but I always say that being English helped in two ways. I used to say to people, 'You're New Buddhists, you were not born Buddhist. I'm also a New Buddhist, I was not born a Buddhist. I've chosen to be a Buddhist, just as you have. And also, I'm not part of the caste system. I've got nothing to do with that.' They felt they could trust me because I was one of them, in a sense.

SADDHANANDI: You said to me the other day, 'Look. Spiritual values have to be given concrete expression, which sometimes involves politics. If you want the law to be changed to express those ideals, you have to engage with politics.'

SANGHARAKSHITA: Yes, the assumption being that you live in a democratic society where action on your part, together with other people, can change things, and change things non-violently.

SADDHANANDI: Let's move onto the next verse:

> And wasted lives that litter
> The streets of modern cities,
> Souls like butt-ends tossed
> In the gutter and trampled on,
> Human refuse dumped
> At the crossroads where civilization
> And civilization meet
> To breed the unbeautiful –
> What will you say to them?

SANGHARAKSHITA: This paints a vivid picture, doesn't it, of what happens in the big cities – every big city in the world, including cities in this country. It shows us how human beings come to be treated.

SADDHANANDI: We're at 'the crossroads where civilization and civilization meet'.

SANGHARAKSHITA: Well, you've got these big cities, with all that wealth of culture and amenities, but there's a price to pay. People are attracted to the big cities in the hope of finding work, and they come from different countries, or different parts of the same country, and from other cultures and civilizations even. But sometimes the meeting of these two different elements has tragic human consequences. People end up on the streets, begging.

SADDHANANDI: 'Like butt-ends'.

SANGHARAKSHITA: Yes. Society has no use for them, or maybe society has used them and then thrown them away. In a country like England it doesn't happen to such a great extent as in some other places, but it happens here too, and we can't be complacent.

SADDHANANDI: OK, so then we come to the final verse, which is the bodhisattva's reply:

'I shall say nothing, but only
Fold in Compassion's arms
Their frailty till it becomes
Strong with my strength, their limbs
Bright with my beauty, their souls
With my wisdom luminous, or
Till I have become like them
A seed between wet stones
Of custom and circumstance.'

SANGHARAKSHITA: The bodhisattva has no five-year plan. He says he won't say anything, but that doesn't mean he won't do anything, although he might not do what you might have expected him to do. After all, the bodhisattva is a bodhisattva. He doesn't think in the way that other people who are not bodhisattvas think. He's saying, 'You're asking me these questions, but don't think that I shall answer them on your terms. I shall answer them on my terms, the terms of the Dharma.' And then what does he go on to say?

SADDHANANDI: 'But only fold in Compassion's arms their frailty until it becomes strong with my strength'

SANGHARAKSHITA: Yes. He will identify himself with them. He won't have the attitude of standing above them and doing things for them. He will identify with them and try to share with them, to the extent that he can, whatever he himself has gained spiritually. But if that doesn't work, if he can't do that, what will he do, or not do?

SADDHANANDI: He says, 'Or, till I have become like them a seed between wet stones of custom and circumstance.'

SANGHARAKSHITA: He says that if he can't do anything else, if circumstances don't permit, he'll just identify himself with the people about whom he has been asked. This could be understood in various ways. Like the other verses, I think this one came to me. I didn't think it out and say, 'This is how the bodhisattva would reply.' But if a bodhisattva is literally reborn as one of the people he has been asked about, he is still a bodhisattva. He still has his bodhisattva nature, and that will have its effect on that community and those individuals among whom he will be reborn. That's one way of explaining that passage. Otherwise, it's not so much that the bodhisattva should do anything in particular. It's important that the bodhisattva *is*. If he just *is* a bodhisattva, even without doing anything, people will pick up on that and it will influence them, it will affect them. That's a very big thing.

SADDHANANDI: You say that with a lot of confidence, Bhante. Have you seen that happening?

SANGHARAKSHITA: In the course of my life, including my life among the ex-Untouchables, I have met some very good people who have influenced others through the force of their personality, to use that term. Even if we're not bodhisattvas, we shouldn't underestimate the effect of personal influence. Quite a long time ago someone came to see me after having been on one of our big winter retreats. I must have asked him how it had affected him, and he said, 'It was a wonderful retreat, with wonderful meditations. We listened to talks on the Dharma and we talked with one another, and there was such a friendly atmosphere. But the thing that impressed me most was the team that was running the retreat. I've never before seen a team of people working together so harmoniously.' That really struck him – not just the activity of one person, but of a group of people. Perhaps he worked in an office – there are all sorts of tensions and jealousies in office life, as I saw myself when I was working at County Hall. But he saw these Order members working together so harmoniously, in a way he'd never seen before, and that affected him very deeply, to the extent that that was what he took away above all from that retreat.

SADDHANANDI: Does that make you think that we should be exemplifying teamwork more than we do?

SANGHARAKSHITA: Yes indeed. It's not just the individual influence, it's also the influence of a team.

SADDHANANDI: What do we need to do to have that kind of positive influence?

SANGHARAKSHITA: We have to practise the Dharma. One of our Mitras has been elected as a Member of Parliament, and she will be in a position to have some influence. One individual Member of Parliament doesn't have an enormous amount of influence, but they have some. In fact, this particular person told me that she met with the Prime Minister and made it clear to him that even though he didn't want to ban foxhunting, she did.

SADDHANANDI: So it's maintaining our spiritual ideals in whatever circumstances we find ourselves in.

SANGHARAKSHITA: Yes. There's often so much pressure on us to move a little bit away from practising those ideals. There's quite a lot in this poem, thinking about it as a whole

SADDHANANDI: There is. It's a whole world being witnessed. Is there anything else you want to say about it?

SANGHARAKSHITA: Well, there's a bit more about Dr Ambedkar. Our Indian Buddhist friends like to think of him as a bodhisattva, and certainly there's something in 'The Bodhisattva's Reply' that could be applied to him, because the bodhisattva says he will give them his strength, and this is what Ambedkar did, because he was the man who had the vision. Perhaps none of them would have found their way to the Dharma without his example, his exhortation, his understanding of the situation. That shows, among other things, the importance of the individual. One person – one man or one woman – can do so much. Not everybody is as gifted as Ambedkar was, but nonetheless one person can do quite a lot, influence quite a lot of other people.

9
'IN THE WOODS ARE MANY MORE'

Selling wild orchids at my door one day
A man said, 'In the woods are many more....
Deep in the gloom, high on the thickset trees,
Wild orchids hang like clouds of butterflies,
Golden and white, spotted with red and black,
As huge as birds, or tiny as a bee,
Wild orchids which no eye has ever seen
Save ours, who wander in these rich green glooms
All day throughout the year.' I bought his sprays,
Paid him, and bore them in; and as I went
My eyes by chance fell on a shelf of books, –
The Buddha's Teachings, – and thereafter glanced
Up to the Buddha's image as He smiled
Above them from the alcove. Strange it was
That, as my eyes from book to image passed,
Dwelling an instant on that calm, pure Face,
There with the frail cold blossoms in my hands,
The words that man spoke at my door should ring
Through my stilled heart again and yet again
Like music – 'In the woods are many more....'

SADDHANANDI: Do you remember where you were when you wrote this poem?

SANGHARAKSHITA: I was definitely in Kalimpong. It must have been in the early 1950s. Quite near Kalimpong, this little town in the eastern Himalayas, there's lots of forest, and lots of very big trees. Orchids tend to grow on branches which have rotted, which means it's not easy to get at them. Someone has to climb up, and the local people do that and sell the orchids as best they can. They're usually bought by tourists because local people are so used to them – there are so many of them – that they don't value them at all.

SADDHANANDI: What kind of life were you leading at this time?

SANGHARAKSHITA: I can't remember very clearly, but I must have been doing quite a bit of teaching. I was meditating. I was meeting Tibetan lamas. And I was writing. I had probably started work on the lectures that became *A Survey of Buddhism*. So I had quite a rich life at that time.

SADDHANANDI: Was this during the time that you lived in the vihara that you founded?

SANGHARAKSHITA: No, because it was written early in my life in Kalimpong. I can't remember where I was living at the time. I moved several times before I acquired the Triyana Vardhana Vihara and settled there. But definitely it's a Kalimpong poem.

SADDHANANDI: Give us an idea of what this poem's describing. You're in your own world, so to speak, and then you get an interruption from this man selling orchids, and it sparks something off in you.

SANGHARAKSHITA: It reminded me of an episode in the Pāli scriptures. The Buddha is with a number of his disciples, and apparently they are in some woodland, there are trees around, *siṃsapā* trees. The story goes that the Buddha stooped down and gathered up a handful of *siṃsapā* leaves, and he asked his disciples, 'Which is greater, the number of *siṃsapā* leaves in the whole forest, or those in my hand?' The disciples naturally said, 'The number in the forest is far, far greater.' And the

Buddha said, 'Even so, the amount I have not disclosed to you is far, far more than what I have disclosed to you. I've disclosed to you just what you need for your spiritual development.'[51]

SADDHANANDI: So there are many more teachings.

SANGHARAKSHITA: Yes. Another way to think about it is that he's excluding mere speculation about things that have no significance for the spiritual life. So that's the association I made in the poem. And of course I'm referring to my own shelf of Dharma books, with the image of the Buddha placed above them.

SADDHANANDI: How did you acquire Dharma books at that time? There can't have been many books that were translated into English then.

SANGHARAKSHITA: For one thing, I had memories of the Dharma books I had read when I was back in England. The Buddhist Society, of which I was a member, had quite a good Buddhist library for those days, and I made good use of it. That comes out in some of my early writings. Then, as I travelled around India in the earlier days, I kept a notebook and if anything struck me I copied it out in my notebook, so I didn't have to carry a lot of books around with me. And then I lived for a year with Bhikkhu Jagdish Kashyap, studying Pāli, and I used to use his university library ticket, and I did a lot of reading, especially about Buddhism.

SADDHANANDI: Among the collection of your books that form the library at Adhisthana, there's a bookcase of a hundred books that came back with you from India. Tell us a bit about their history. Did you gradually buy them? Did you write to publishers and ask them to send you books? How did you get hold of them?

SANGHARAKSHITA: From time to time, especially after I started editing the *Maha Bodhi* journal, I used to go down to Calcutta, where there were some excellent bookshops. There were also two quite good English bookshops in Darjeeling, one called the Oxford and the other called the Cambridge. The Oxford in particular stocked those books about Tibetan Buddhism that were available at the time. And I had a friend, Marco Pallis, whom I had known when he lived in Kalimpong, and when

I started writing the *Survey*, I wrote to him and asked him to send me various books. He sent me quite a few, and that's how my little library developed.

SADDHANANDI: How did you get money to buy those books?

SANGHARAKSHITA: I used to write articles for journals, even for newspapers sometimes, and got paid for some of those, and I got *dāna* from people. I never really bothered about money. It came, and though sometimes I might go for a couple of weeks without any cash I could always get credit in the bazaar.

SADDHANANDI: They knew you, they knew you were trustworthy.

SANGHARAKSHITA: Of course, we don't need many books. Even though the Buddha says that there are just a few *siṃsapā* leaves in his hand, from our point of view that's plenty, and there's no need for us to go looking in strange byways, so to speak. All we need is in those few *siṃsapā* leaves, the basic teachings: the Noble Eightfold Path, the Four Noble Truths, the *pāramitās*, the *Satipaṭṭhāna Sutta* and so on. In just a few teachings there is so much. That's why I said, years ago, we should have more and more of less and less. You can take a few verses of the *Dhammapada* and spend the rest of your life studying them and practising the teachings they contain. Even though the teachings are familiar to us, they are also a mystery. They can't be understood by the intellect. We have to understand them by putting them into practice, and as we put them into practice we find a greater and greater depth of significance in them. We should never think that we've understood it all, even when the teaching is quite simple. There are still depths that we have not fathomed. And one might say that life is like that. Everything is unfathomable if you study it. You can always go further. I'm thinking especially of modern discoveries in nuclear physics, discoveries about the nature of the universe. It's all so mysterious. And people are mysterious. It's not easy to understand people in depth. You have to be close friends with them for a long time, and even live with them. So in the woods are many more, with regard to the Buddha's teaching, and with regard to the universe, and to people we know. There's always more to know, more to understand.

SADDHANANDI: Did this incident, this man turning up and saying 'In the woods are many more', actually happen?

SANGHARAKSHITA: Certainly a man did turn up, and he had for sale orchids that he'd gathered. I was very happy to take them – they were very beautiful – and I paid him, of course. I hadn't commissioned him to pick the orchids. You could do that, and there were two options for payment. You could pay two rupees for the basketful, and if he injured himself collecting them for you, or even died, you would have to pay his family a hundred rupees. If you didn't want to take that on, he would charge you five rupees. The orchids I bought were very big: yellow and white, with waxy, smooth petals.

SADDHANANDI: It was a very exotic life you led, wasn't it?

SANGHARAKSHITA: Kalimpong was a remarkable place. There were Nepalese living there, and Lepchas, and Tibetans of course, Tibetan lamas, all sorts of tribes. There were some educated, English-speaking people, and missionaries. Most people were a mixture of Hindu and Buddhist. So yes, it was a very exotic place.

SADDHANANDI: Did you miss it when you came back to England?

SANGHARAKSHITA: I can't say that I missed it in the sense of longing to be back there. It was a fourteen-year-long stage of my life and it was quite important, but after I'd settled back in England I had things to do, and there was no time for nostalgia or looking back. But I'm very glad that I had those fourteen years in Kalimpong, seven of them in my own vihara. I have very positive memories of my teachers there, and my friends, and my students.

SADDHANANDI: So you were leading your life, living wherever you were living in Kalimpong, and this man came and interrupted you, and that sparked off a reflection about the Dharma and the Buddha. The interruption seems to have deepened your musings rather than interrupted them.

SANGHARAKSHITA: When the man came to my door with the orchids

I don't think he interrupted me in anything. But later – I don't know whether it was later that day or the next week – when I was writing the poem, I was interrupted by some visitor, just as Coleridge famously was when he was working on his poem about Kubla Khan, and that broke the thread of my concentration. Explaining what had happened, Coleridge said that he was interrupted by a person from Porlock, and that's become a stock phrase. When you're interrupted in the midst of some creative activity, along comes the person from Porlock – Porlock being a town near where Coleridge was living. Scholars give all sorts of explanations about that. Some say that it was Coleridge's excuse because he hadn't been able to finish the poem. He was a taker of opium and that put him into strange states sometimes. But anyway, I too had a 'person from Porlock' experience.

SADDHANANDI: But you did manage to finish the poem.

SANGHARAKSHITA: I did, but there was a sort of join in the middle which I felt didn't quite work. I don't know if it's evident or not, but that was my feeling.

SADDHANANDI: It doesn't seem to be evident, though it naturally seems to be a poem of two halves. There's the incident of the man coming with the orchids, and then there are your reflections after he's departed. I was very struck by the last few lines of the poem, where you say:

> Strange it was
> That as my eyes from book to image passed,
> Dwelling an instant on that calm, pure Face,
> There with the frail cold blossoms in my hands,
> The words that man spoke at my door should ring
> Through my stilled heart again and yet again
> Like music – 'In the woods are many more....'

It's a striking comparison between the frail cold blossoms, which have been picked, so although they're still bright, they're dying, and the Buddha's calm, pure face, as though there's impermanence, and then there's the Buddha's teaching, which is eternal. It's quite a mysterious poem, pointing us in a direction we don't entirely understand. 'In the woods are many more.'

SANGHARAKSHITA: Yes. Our experience is limited. There are greater possibilities, there's always more for us to understand and experience. That's especially the case with the Dharma, and with the scriptures. There's so much that we come to understand perhaps after many years of study and reflection and meditation.

SADDHANANDI: Sometimes when you're practising the Dharma you feel you *have* understood something. I can feel I've got somewhere, I'm understanding it, and I think, 'Oh, now it's clearer to me. Now I feel nearer to Enlightenment.' Is that a positive thought to have?

SANGHARAKSHITA: Well, one shouldn't take oneself too literally. Generally, if you think you're near to Enlightenment, you're far from it, and if you think you're far from it, you're near to it.

SADDHANANDI: Say a bit more about that.

SANGHARAKSHITA: If you think you're near Enlightenment, you've probably got a very superficial idea of Enlightenment, and you probably haven't really understood it. But if you feel that you're far from it, it means that you have some inkling of its greatness. That's in a way a safer attitude, provided that's what you really deeply feel. Sometimes in an optimistic mood we may feel, 'Oh, I've only got to dig a little deeper under all those *kleśas* and there it is, the Buddha nature', but that can be a very superficial understanding. But if you think, 'Enlightenment is something so tremendous, so magnificent, that we can get no more than a glimpse of it,' that's more realistic.

SADDHANANDI: Is Enlightenment something we're aiming for in this lifetime, Bhante?

SANGHARAKSHITA: We're aiming for it in every lifetime, one might say. One does have it as one's ultimate ideal, and without that goal it would be difficult to harness all one's energies to practising the path. We have to have that conviction that we have that potential and we could realize it, even though it's so far removed from our present experience.

Another thought that occurs to me about the poem is that the man is represented as saying, 'Which no eye has ever seen save ours'. He's in the midst of the forest so he can see the orchids, whereas I'm not in the forest. In the same way there are metaphorical forests. In one of his discourses the Buddha talks about the great ocean in which there are many mysterious beings.[52] In the same way, there are people around who have a deeper experience than we do. They are natives of the forest. They see the orchids, and we have to rely on them to experience the orchids ourselves. We can't climb up into the trees, but there are people who can. So that's another way of looking at what the man said. He was a native of the forest, he knew his way around it, and he was able to climb up and get the orchids. There are all sorts of analogies there.

SADDHANANDI: I'm reminded of that collection of poems of yours, *The Call of the Forest*. It's like hearing the call of something mysterious or separate from us.

10
FOUR GIFTS

I come to you with four gifts.
The first gift is a lotus-flower.
Do you understand?
My second gift is a golden net.
Can you recognize it?
My third gift is a shepherds' round-dance.
Do your feet know how to dance?
My fourth gift is a garden planted in a wilderness.
Could you work there?
I come to you with four gifts.
Dare you accept them?

SADDHANANDI: This is a poem that you wrote in 1975, when the Order and the Movement was still quite young.

SANGHARAKSHITA: When the Order was six years old, I thought that I should have a sabbatical. It turned out to be a six-month sabbatical, not a whole year. I think it was in connection with that that I wrote this poem, because this was the legacy that I was leaving to people as I left for my sabbatical.

SADDHANANDI: So when you're saying in the first line, 'I come to you with four gifts', you're the 'I' in that line.

SANGHARAKSHITA: And by 'you' I mean the Order members and Mitras of the FWBO. It's to them that I'm offering these gifts. But it could be understood in a wider sense as being addressed to people in general, whoever is able to accept these gifts.

SADDHANANDI: Sometimes people don't want to accept a gift.

SANGHARAKSHITA: Sometimes people feel embarrassed at having to accept a gift because they feel it places them under an obligation. 'Oh, he's sent me a Christmas card, I suppose I'll have to send him one.' Sociologists have discovered that many primitive communities have a culture of gifts, and in Buddhism we have the gift of *dāna*. *Dāna* is a free gift, whether of goods or money or services. So the poem ties in with human history and also with Buddhist tradition.

SADDHANANDI: Let's look at the first gift:

> The first gift is a lotus-flower.
> Do you understand?

SANGHARAKSHITA: Well, obviously that's full of symbolism. I could just as easily have said a rose. The symbolism of the lotus in Buddhism is well known, because the lotus is rooted in the mud, but it grows up towards the light and the sun, and it expands into a beautiful flower. I think for me at that time the gift of the lotus represented the whole process of human development. Not even just human development –

I think it could stand for the whole evolutionary process, the whole upward movement of life. It could stand for the lower evolution as well as the higher evolution, the whole unfolding of the potential of life, from the lower forms of life up into human life and right up into the life of Enlightened beings. I'd been teaching meditation, and the Dharma in general, for the benefit of the growth of individuals. So yes, I'd been giving the gift of the lotus flower. *You* are the lotus flower, as it were.

SADDHANANDI: Do we really grow like that? Are we like plants, or is that just symbolism?

SANGHARAKSHITA: Well, there's clearly an analogy. The plant needs soil, air, water, and space in which to grow. In the same way, human beings need to be rooted. They need to have the light of friendliness or compassion shining on them and giving them support. They have to be a healthy seed, because some seeds are damaged and the plant doesn't develop as it should. In our society, many human beings start off a bit damaged, by conditions or whatever, so we have to be aware of that. Not every seed is a perfect seed, but even a damaged seed is capable of development.

SADDHANANDI: You've emphasized in your path of personal development a lot of indirect methods in a way that not many Buddhist groups have, as far as I know.

SANGHARAKSHITA: Yes, I'd forgotten that expression 'indirect methods'. I used it a lot in the early days. The appreciation of the fine arts has its place here, and of course there's spiritual friendship. I regard that as being essential. You could say that spiritual friendship is the soil from which you grow and develop, and that the kindness you experience from other human beings is like the sunshine that stimulates your growth.

SADDHANANDI: We've got the ethical life as well, and the life of service. How far can these practices take us?

SANGHARAKSHITA: They can take us a very long way, especially service, I would say, because service suggests self-abnegation. You're concerned with other people, not with yourself. You're also concerned with the ideal.

You don't want to be self-serving; you want to serve the ideal. Service as part of the path of spiritual development is probably undervalued. In the traditional Buddhist world, especially the Theravāda, there's a lot of emphasis on serving the monks. I've been a monk myself, so I know what it's like to be on the receiving end. It's very pleasant. But there can be an overemphasis on that kind of service. In the case of our own movement, putting it simply, it's serving the Buddha. You serve the Buddha by serving the Dharma, and you serve the Dharma by serving the Sangha. So service is of great importance. But some people don't like to think of themselves as servants, not even of the Dharma or the Buddha, and some don't like to think of themselves as disciples, which amounts to much the same thing.

SADDHANANDI: In this first verse you say that the first gift is the lotus-flower. Then you ask, 'Do you understand?'

SANGHARAKSHITA: Yes. So who am I addressing, with that indefinite 'you'? I think I'm addressing people who are coming along to FWBO, now Triratna, classes. Do you understand what it's all about? It's not just amusement. It's not just entertainment. It's about your personal development. You don't come to one of our centres just to socialize. You come to do serious things. You come to learn to meditate, to understand the Dharma, and that is ultimately in the interest of your personal development. Do you understand this? Not everybody does at first. Some people like the people at the centre and want to see more of them. They think more in terms of friendship in the ordinary sense, and a bit of social life. But that isn't what it's all about. It's about personal development in the very best and most positive sense.

SADDHANANDI: What do you think is the main thing we have to develop in ourselves?

SANGHARAKSHITA: There are some things that benefit everybody, or nearly everybody, like meditation: the mindfulness of breathing, the *mettā bhāvanā*. They aren't concerned with differences in temperament or education or anything else. Anybody can learn to meditate in those simple ways, and that's why all our centres teach these practices and have done so from the beginning.

SADDHANANDI: But is there one thing that we as individuals need to develop in ourselves when we start? I wonder if there's something that you think over and over again, 'Oh, it's this problem again.'

SANGHARAKSHITA: There's a need for self-confidence. I know that some people come to our centres in a rather battered state, with low self-esteem, low self-confidence. That has to be built, perhaps on a purely psychological level, before they can begin to practise the Dharma seriously. You need confidence that if you put in the necessary effort there will be results. You will grow, you will develop, and other people will notice that.

SADDHANANDI: And then there's the second gift:

> My second gift is a golden net.
> Can you recognize it?

This golden net is very interesting as a symbol. Nets catch us, don't they? They trap us, in a way. But what did you have in mind when you used this image?

SANGHARAKSHITA: I can't remember, to be frank. You'll have to help me by referring to the talk I gave later.

SADDHANANDI: Well, later on, in your talks on 'Buddhism for Today – and Tomorrow', you talked about this as a philosophy or a vision of existence.

SANGHARAKSHITA: Perhaps what I had in mind was that all the different bits of a net are interconnected. It's like that with the Dharma. You catch hold of one bit of the Dharma and all the other bits follow. For instance, take *śīla*, ethics. You practise the precepts. Even if you just do that, that purifies the mind and you move into meditation. And if you meditate, eventually you discover that there are two kinds of meditation – what we call *samatha bhāvanā* and *vipaśyanā bhāvanā*. And *vipaśyanā* gives you an insight into the whole nature, the whole structure, of reality, relative and absolute. That's wisdom. So the golden net is the interconnectedness of every aspect of the Buddha's teaching. That's why, also, if you meddle with one bit, you meddle with it all. For instance, if you try to teach mindfulness without the context of the Dharma, sooner or later you're not teaching mindfulness at all, you're teaching something else, because you've tried to snip off a bit of the golden net, but you can't really do that. The different parts of the net all hold together, they all support one another.

SADDHANANDI: So this golden net is about a vision of the Dharma, a vision of existence.

SANGHARAKSHITA: Yes. I suppose I called it golden because gold is rich and precious and beautiful, and that's what the Dharma is like too. It's not just some grey system of philosophy. It's beautiful, and the interconnection of its parts is beautiful, golden. Gold inspires; if we look at something golden, we feel happy and pleased. So that's the golden net, the whole system of the Dharma. It's all its interconnected teachings: ethics, meditation, what might be described as the more philosophical nature of the Dharma, it's all there in that golden net. So accept the whole thing. Don't try to snip off a bit and just concentrate on that. Work your way round every part of that golden net. You could also say that a net is something that you hold. This golden net, if we take the metaphor a bit literally, has to be supported by a number of people. It's practising Buddhists who maintain the integrity, the wholeness and completeness of that net.

And who or what are you trying to catch? Well, you could say that it's Māra. Not so long ago I was going through the *Śūraṅgama Samādhi Sūtra*, and Māra enters into the *sūtra* as a character. And he's so cunning, so deceitful, and so wicked, so difficult to deal with. So yes, he has to be caught and immobilized. Māra stands for all that is negative in our lives, in our personal experience, what the Pāli scriptures call Māra Pāpiyan, Māra the evil one, and he's very, very cunning. Sometimes he even fabricates something like a net himself, though it's not particularly golden.

SADDHANANDI: I was struck by this golden net as being like a kind of vision, and we're trying to recognize it. I'm wondering whether we as individuals have enough vision. Maybe you can never have enough vision, but I've been quite struck sometimes by the lack of confidence we have sometimes because we haven't had a strong enough vision, something that will really see us through the spiritual life.

SANGHARAKSHITA: We have to acquaint ourselves sometimes with other people's vision. Some people get it from reading about and reflecting on the life of the Buddha or some other great Buddhist teacher, or on what – for want of a better term – we call Buddhist philosophy, and find that very inspiring. But we do need a vision. I can't help quoting from the Bible: 'Where there is no vision the people perish.'[53]

SADDHANANDI: Sometimes when we're thinking about people's readiness for ordination, the question arises, do they have a glimpse of the Transcendental? I've often wondered what is meant by that.

SANGHARAKSHITA: I use the term Transcendental as a synonym for what is *lokuttara*, what is beyond the world. It means something that is beyond our thought, beyond our imagination, but as it were there. We can think of it as Enlightenment, supreme wisdom, and so on. But we shouldn't be too literal about that glimpse, because you can have a theoretical understanding that there is something beyond without having a real glimpse of it. A real glimpse would amount to genuine insight, and perhaps that's a bit too much to ask of someone who is preparing for ordination. To have a real glimpse of the Transcendental suggests quite an advanced level of experience. But there needs to be at least a theoretical acknowledgement that there is something that is beyond.

SADDHANANDI: Maybe you need a glimpse of how that vision can have an impact on your life, going back to the lotus flower.

SANGHARAKSHITA: Yes, you could at least have a theoretical understanding, so that devotion to that which is beyond doesn't leave you unaffected. If you have even a glimpse of it, a true glimpse, that can radically affect your whole life. But perhaps a glimpse of a glimpse is enough!

SADDHANANDI: And then there's the third gift:

> My third gift is a shepherds' round-dance.
> Do your feet know how to dance?

SANGHARAKSHITA: I think perhaps I had Nietzsche in mind here: Zarathustra. But apart from Nietzsche, what is the shepherds' round-dance?

SADDHANANDI: Well, I think it's the Order. It's about people dancing together. It's quite interesting, thinking of what we're trying to create between us as an Order as a dance.

SANGHARAKSHITA: I think dance is an important symbol because it suggests something we enjoy. I'm not quite sure what a round-dance is, but it's clearly something that a lot of people do together. It's not just a you and me sort of thing. The mention of shepherds suggests something idyllic, Arcadian, and that links with the garden which is the fourth gift, because once you've done your day's work you can enjoy yourself, or the work itself is pleasurable. Very often you can ask a gardener what he's going to do when the day's work is over, and he might say, 'Well, just go to bed and rest, and look forward to getting up in the morning and doing some more gardening.' It's something enjoyable. I think enjoyment is the key note.

SADDHANANDI: A group of people can become more accomplished in their dance. This is certainly true in the case of literal dancing; you see a company of dancers and they get more and more accomplished through working together, not just as individual solo artists.

SANGHARAKSHITA: I think a round-dance is something that returns to itself. It goes through certain motions again and again, perhaps with other people joining in. The dance goes on but the people dancing change. In some dances you change partners, and if you have different partners in the dance, that widens your experience. If you're paired off with someone, you may be better than them or they may be better than you, and in either case you learn something, maybe about the person with whom you're dancing. Also, one has to pay attention to the music of the dance. Some dance music is very raucous, from the Dharmic point of view, and difficult to dance to. Other music is more refined, more beautiful, and you learn to dance to that. The line is not 'Do you know how to dance?' but 'Do your *feet* know how to dance?' It's as though the dancing must be instinctive, a natural thing.

SADDHANANDI: The fourth gift:

> My fourth gift is a garden planted in a wilderness.
> Could you work there?

There's a lot of symbolism in this, isn't there? The wilderness is an uncultivated area, and then you're planting a garden there, so you're cultivating an area within an uncultivated area.

SANGHARAKSHITA: I suppose it's the wilderness of the world. It's *saṃsāra*, our ordinary social life, domestic life, work life and so on – family life. I hope people don't mind me including family life in the wilderness. From the Buddhist point of view it's something from which you go forth, whether literally or metaphorically. So yes, the wilderness is the world. I think nowadays we're very much aware of this world as a wilderness from all the news reports we get of things happening in this or that part of the world, and within it we're trying to create a garden, something beautiful and inspiring. In the different religions of the world the symbol is used – in the Bible we get the Garden of Eden – and there's also the simile of the oasis: water, which is essential to life, in the midst of the dry, burning desert. If you're not able to get to that oasis in time, you could die. T. S. Eliot saw modern life as a wasteland, and within that wasteland we're trying to create a garden, something beautiful and enriching.

SADDHANANDI: So the question about this garden is, can we work there?

SANGHARAKSHITA: Well, this garden is in the process of creation. We started off with a few seeds and a little patch, and we planted those seeds, but gardeners are needed. Rather than waiting for it to be completed by others, could you be one of those who helps to bring that beautiful garden into existence? In other words, in a spiritual movement like Triratna, you don't just go along to the centre or other activities and passively take things in. It's part of the growing process to help out. That's why when I drew up those criteria for Mitraship, along with doing a daily meditation practice, practising ethics, committing yourself to this particular sangha, and getting to know Order members, there was helping out at the local centre. That way, from very early on you become involved with the life of that community in quite an active way. You become a fellow gardener.

SADDHANANDI: You have to be dissatisfied with the world, or dissatisfied with the wilderness, don't you?

SANGHARAKSHITA: You have to see that the wilderness is a wilderness. It's normal to avert your eyes from the unpleasant aspects of the wilderness and try to make yourself comfortable within it, but from a spiritual point of view that's fatal.

SADDHANANDI: The poem ends with 'Dare you accept them?'

SANGHARAKSHITA: The four gifts are a challenge. I'm not only giving them but challenging people to accept them. That's not easy. You don't just accept gifts of this sort and put them aside. Accepting them has implications. It makes a demand upon you.

These are the implications of the four gifts: Do you understand that you're an individual who can grow and develop? Do you see that the Dharma, the different aspects of the Buddha's teaching, are all interconnected? Do you see that involvement with the Dharma is something you can enjoy? And fourthly, do you see that the movement is like a garden where we cultivate ourselves and help others to cultivate themselves, and where we need to work on the garden which means also working on ourselves? That's the challenge I threw to our little movement when I had my semi-sabbatical all those years ago, and there were people who did respond to that challenge. Otherwise, at the end of that six months I would have come back and found that everything had collapsed. But during those six months things continued to grow and develop without me, which was very reassuring. I think it wasn't just that I needed a break, though that may have been part of it. I wanted to finish writing what became *The Rainbow Road*, and I also wanted to give the people who had been coming along for five or six years the experience of having to run things themselves, not just leaving it all to me.

SADDHANANDI: And has the Movement taken up the challenge, Bhante? Here we are, so many decades on.

SANGHARAKSHITA: Yes, there were some people who took up that challenge very seriously. Otherwise we would not be here this morning talking about these four gifts.

SADDHANANDI: And now, although in the poem you say, 'I come to you with four gifts', it's not so much you, but us. We're coming to other people with these four gifts.

SANGHARAKSHITA: Yes, the four gifts are being passed on. We don't create that garden just so that we can play in it ourselves, but so other people can come and enjoy it too, and eventually also work there.

POEMS

I stayed alone
Thinking over every tone
Which, though silent to the ear,
The enchanted heart could hear.

Percy Bysshe Shelley
From 'Lines Written in the Bay of Lerici'

PART I
SHORTER POEMS

LONDON IN WARTIME 1941

Athens, the olive and grey eyes,
And Rome, the martyred whore;
Paris, Berlin and Amsterdam,
Madrid, a hundred more:

This city makes their glories fade,
Her splendour makes them dumb –
London, on whose majestic brow
All the ends of the world are come.

1944 RUBA'I

Love springs into the Bodhisattva's eyes
As sweetly as the flowers of morning rise;
Like them, his thoughts leap up towards the sun;
He leaves the earth and yearns to kiss the skies.

THE RAIN OF DHARMA

Fall, Rain, upon the dry and thirsty land:
The trees will weave fresh garments on the earth,
And all be gardens where before was sand –
This is the second birth.

Fall, Dharma, on our dry and thirsty souls,
And we will weave fresh robes of living truth,
Which now are ragged and are full of holes;
For thou hast ruth.

Then, as the earth sits smiling in the sun,
After long day of heavy showers has ceased,
So shall we sit beneath thee, Glorious One,
From pain released.

THE RIVER

O limpid river in the evening air,
Trembling along the confines of a wood,
The dark blue swallows darting here and there,
Bright as the glance of perfect Buddhahood!

Deep peace is in thy waters, holy stream.
The pebbles of thy bottom and the sand
Are fragments of a broken shard of dream
Infinities of Buddhas understand.

Each pebble, and each ripple of thy wave,
Each bird and flower, the mighty girth of trees
Which hem thy banks, the Buddha came to save –
His own Enlightenment attains through these.

The little flower with her face of light,
The swallows, born of midnight and the snow,
The burgeoning trees, exfoliating might –
These are what Bodhisattvas seek to know….

Yearning to save – a blossom of compassion –
Wiping the tear from every sufferer's eye,
He springs up strangely from the soil of passion,
Golden and lovely like the evening sky….

Nirvāṇa's night now slowly is descending,
The stars uncover their diminished heads
And shine in radiance, from Heaven's windows bending,
Invite him in to their eternal beds.

No, not for him are any means of pleasure.
Only the limpid water now remains –
Its birds and flowers, and its pebbly treasure,
Its rocky bottom and its golden grains.

1946 BEFORE AN IMAGE OF THE BUDDHA

O great golden image!
I am here humbly kneeling before Thee.
My prayers, my supplications, my petitions
Rhythmically mingle with the incense
And ascend to Thee.
I hear afar off
The noise of mine ancestors
Calling me back.
'Why does he go after strange gods?'
Thus they demand.
When my face in the mirror is strange to me,
And the face of my mother in the morning;
And strange to the babe the breast that feeds it;
When the sky seems strange to the earth,
And the stars to the sky at night;
When man seems strange to woman,
And love to sorrow strange –
Then only wilt Thou appear strange to me,
O great golden image.
I go not after strange gods,
But after mine own heart.
Thou hast a million abodes,
In a million worlds.
I have but one only –
At Thy feet.
I am here humbly kneeling before Thee,
Gazing on Thy face;
Like an enamoured nightingale
At the maiden moon.
The nightingale sings songs to her love,
But I am silent.
I have no word to say.
Sooner wilt Thou rise up from Thy place
On the Lotus-throne
And go away,
Than I will.

It is almost as though I were the statue,
And that Thou, O Image, wert sitting there before me,
Steadfastly meditating upon me.

THE EVER-BEATING HEART

I do not want to see this world of Thine,
O Lord, with vision merely mine.
Teach me to look, like all-surrounding air,
On everything from everywhere.
Oh let my vision through Thy creatures pass
As though through panes of glass
And see Thy Light. May I behold Thy Face
Though hid by veils of Time and Space.
Let me now only from a distance see,
But intimately feel, that I am Thee;
And feel the world, in every single part,
Hath Thee within for ever-beating heart.

DĀNA PĀRAMĪ

When the pearls of morning
Globed milkily the spray
From which the red hibiscus
Shed perfume on the way,
One walked with godlike bearing
Though more than god was He –
Lord Buddha in the morning
Went forth for charity.

Behind Him paced another
Like the moon behind the sun.
Love followed after Wisdom,
And yet the two are one.
Like a golden shadow
Less bright than the Adored,
Came Ānanda the Lovely,
The cousin of Our Lord.

When going forth together
The trees flushed darker green;
In all the pleasant meadows
Far brighter flowers were seen.
The Ganges rippled purely,
They stooped and drank their fill;
But the faces she reflected
Were sweeter, purer still.

How gladly came the women,
The youths and children, too,
To feed the noble Strangers
With food more fresh than dew.
In silence they receive it,
The silence of their kind,
Then go away together –
Yet leave their love behind.

How happy was the morning,
How happy was the day,
When two such noble Bhikkhus
Walked down the perfumed way.
Happy were the people,
And all the kin also
Of those who gladly gave them
And smiling saw them go.

SYSTOLE AND DIASTOLE[54]

Whén the latency of thought
   Has winged itself with power to be
And flashes from its former naught
   Into actuality,
The consciousness of man expands like light,
Conquering new worlds from nescience and night.

Oh from the rearward of my mind's abyss
Let me bring forth the monstrous thought of bliss!
This is the mother-root of all creation –
Projection, maintenance and consummation.
Spring is the source of each green-thrusting thing,
And Summer's source: this is the source of Spring.
This is the breath, for better or for worse,
In the huge body of the universe,
Impelling it to motions vague and vast,
Of which, as none was first, shall none be last.
Love's rose unfolds its petals but for this,
Winnowing the circumambient air of bliss.
Even the lily white of chastity
Springs from this hidden root to breathe and be
On the bright brink of immortality.
Even the saint, in sunwardness of soul
Soaring and singing as he sights the goal,
Fledged the far winging of his eagle thought
In this rich mother-nest which all forth-brought.
But when the thought sinks in
   As waters from a fountain rise and fall,
Ending where they did begin,
   Or as the rain from clouds purpúreal
Falls on the fields which once as dew it pearled,
Thought's refluent flood falls back from all the beaches of the world,
Leaving them dry and bare.
Retreating o'er itself into the deep
Wherefrom its youthful waves did erstwhile leap
Into the broad bright air,

It falls into itself from everywhere.
From every object of the mind
Whose borrowed light has power to blind,
From God's existence and its own
As easily as from a stone,
The outward thought, now taught by pain,
Runs back into the natal brain,
And draws into a point vibrating
With energy for more creating.
But even this is hushed and stilled
If so the almighty mind has willed;
Even this shall disappear
Like a ripple in a mere.
Ah, how calm the lake tonight!
The trees how still! the moon how bright!
And moonlight over all with infinite delight!

LINES

From the unlocked cage of my heart
White doves of love go winging,
Wild larks of song rise singing,
The ice of my heart is broken, broken,
Joy's fountain leaps in the air;
And all the while no word was spoken:
I only looked at something fair.

'WATER FROM THE THAWED-OUT SNOW…'

Water from the thawed-out snow
Trickles to streamlets far below;
Joining with rivers strong and free
It pours at last into the sea.

It loitered not among the sedges,
Nor hung in rainbows over ledges;
It kissed the pebbles as it went,
And yet to go it was content.

Oh keep like water in its flow
The pristine purity of snow;
With deeper currents, swifter streams,
Descending through our land of dreams.

Loiter in no stagnant pool,
Though mossy banks are green and cool;
Sport not long with flags and flowers,
Or swallows in the willow-bowers.

The sea our goal, the snow our source –
Such is our appointed course,
Flowing with sunbeam-spangled motion
Calmly to the moonlit ocean.

TO CHENREZI

Lord, from my shadows do I flee
Into Thy lovely light:
To sin's black dross that beauty seems
A furnace fierce and bright;
But its cool light shines on virtue
Like the moon on flowers by night.

Thou smilest, gentle, on those saints
Who tread the Noble Way;
But fierce and furious dost Thou scowl
On fools who walk astray;
These, with a lotus, do You bless,
These, with a sword, You slay.

Teach me to see beyond, Lord,
Thine aspects sweet or stern;
Let my soul not fear destruction,
Nor yet for blessings yearn:
May I leave behind all names and forms
When to Thy light I turn.

THE TAOIST TEACHER

I did not seek, and so I found;
I travelled rooted to the ground.
Words that in jest I uttered here
Were wisdom in the heavenly sphere.

The Secret of the Universe,
Disputed oft in prose and verse,
I never bothered much about –
And that was how I found it out.

All men's questions and replies
Are sometimes foolish, sometimes wise.
I never asked or answered aught –
And that way I both learned and taught.

If you wish to learn of me
Forget all this immediately;
Forget there's such a thing to do –
And then perchance I'll wink at you.

TO A POLITICAL FRIEND

Thine is the outward action,
Mine is the peace within;
You forge the chains of faction,
I strive to wear them thin.

Through no dissensions narrow
Did you thus dearly go
With the swiftness of an arrow
From the stillness of this bow.

When your hot blood is abating
And anxious thoughts begin
You will feel me meditating,
And peace shall fold us in.

When the limit of your action
And the limit of my peace
Are joined by strong attraction
Our separate selves shall cease.

MUSIC AT NIGHT 1947

The noise of day is hushed at last,
A cool wind softly blows,
And nightingales make beautiful
The silence of the rose.

Stilled is the storm of passion,
And anxious thoughts depart.
Sweet voices do but make more deep
The silence of my heart.

MEDITATION

Here perpetual incense burns;
The heart to meditation turns,
And all delights and passions spurns.

A thousand brilliant hues arise,
More lovely than the evening skies,
And pictures paint before our eyes.

All the spirit's storm and stress
Is stilled into a nothingness,
And healing powers descend and bless.

Refreshed, we rise and turn again
To mingle with this world of pain,
As on roses falls the rain.

THE MOON OF BEAUTY

When Truth and Good like phantoms fade
Into the reddening West,
My Moon of Beauty rises soft
To soothe an aching breast.

When Reason's lamp grows dim and faint,
And Aspiration's wing
Beats feebly on the starless dark,
I take my pipe and sing.

For Beauty, whether seen or heard –
When Truth nor Goodness can –
May woo the weary heart from tears
And soothe the grief of man.

THE WHEEL OF DHARMA

Roll forth, O Conquering Wheel,
And cross both land and sea;
Love is more strong than steel,
And hate must yield to thee.
Roll forth on thy victorious course,
And set the nations free from force.

Before thy sun-like sweep
The hosts of Māra fly
Like wan stars to the deep
When Dawn impearls the sky.
Thy splendour spreads from zone to zone –
Roll forth, and make the earth thy own.

Conquer the hearts of men
With love intense, profound;
And penetrate that den
Of darkness underground,
Where, in the midst of shadows deep,
Lust and hate and folly sleep.

Ascend into the sky
And like the sun at noon
Shed radiance from on high –
Thy love's unstinted boon.
When thou hast set the people free
The universe will worship thee.

THE WANDERING SINGER

It was the season after rain:
Our feet were cold upon the floor;
A chill wind breathed against the pane;
White mist crept through the door.
With shawls drawn round our shoulders, we
Conned books of deep divinity,
And saints' and sages' subtle lore
Passed our studious eyes before.

We scarce marked, through the cold blue glass,
The flickering stars all frosty white,
Or mountain-muffling cloudlets pass
Across the face of night;
Nor heard, or hearing did not heed,
The faint sound of a far off reed,
Through rising mist and drizzling rain
Sobbing like a soul in pain.

The dust of books was blown away
By breaths of new, yet ancient, song;
A pipe shrilled at the close of day
To voice both sweet and strong.
What though the harlot at our door
Little knows of sages' lore!
Her song, so artless and so wild,
Voices a wisdom undefiled.

Piping and singing fade away,
And melts the mist upon the hills;
Bright in the silver moonlight play
The river's thousand rills.
Now from the mist-admitting door
We watch two shadows flitting o'er
The neighbour ridge and, listening, hear
Both pipe and song again rise clear.

Before some other hut she sings,
Base scion of an ancient art,
Whose voice has power to pluck those strings
That tremble in the heart.
Though sings she at some distant door
My heart shall hearken as before,
And race-deep memories rise to greet
That world-old song so wild and sweet.

THE CLOUDED DRAGON

Behold the Clouded Dragon –
Imperial, gold, benign,
Clad in thunder, eyed with lightning,
Rushing madly, scales ashine,
Down to Earth and up to Heaven
With energy divine –
Soaring, plunging, rolling, twisting
With force all furious-fine.

Behold the Clouded Dragon
As he breasteth, strong and free,
The immensities of Heaven
And the tumult of the sea:
Then draws his clouds around him,
And his cloudlets quietly,
As into mist and pelting rain
He melts mysteriously.

Behold the Clouded Dragon
As a symbol, as a sign,
Of the Sage whose thoughts are thunders,
Whose intuitions shine
Like lightnings in the dark blue sky,
Blinding to mortal eyne;
While he feels the Central Silence
In the storm of the divine.

Behold the Clouded Dragon,
This Sage who smiles at thee;
Follow his furious footsteps,
Win his tranquillity.
His thoughts he draws around him,
For his True Form, fierce and free,
Half hidden by his wisdom,
No man may ever see.

BEFORE AN IMAGE OF THE BUDDHA

What thoughts are present to Thy mind
In that Beyondless State, refined
Through ceaseless discipline and pain
From the crude stuff of flesh and brain;
Or is no thought presént to Thee
At all, in that Infinity?
Looking, in this lonely place,
On Thy silent, sculptured face,
In whose proximity do cease
All unquiet thoughts, and melt in peace,
I struggle, with my little wit,
To fathom out, whilst here I sit,
The calm which beautifieth it
As full moon, on a summer's night,
Silvers still waters with her light.
Thy Sea of Peace is too profound
For plummet of our thought to sound;
Yet, from smooth brow and half-closed eyes,
And silent lips, void of replies,
From coolness and tranquillity
Made palpable to us in Thee,
Our groping minds may somehow guess
That Plenitude yet Emptiness,
That state of passionless Delight,
Mastered by Thee on Wesak Night;
May see, and for a moment sense,
Love, which is Wisdom's effluence,
And feel our being's tiniest part
Beat with the beating of Thy Heart –
Feel too, like Thee, each tear of woe
Fall on our hearts like fire on snow.
O may we, contemplating Thee,
Be lost in that Immensity
Of Peace and Bliss which now Thou art,
And realize the Buddha-Heart!

THE PARABLE OF THE PLOUGH

Where green and purple strips of earth
Stretched to far hills of misty blue,
He walked with slow and solemn step
That sanctified the flowers and dew.

The sun shone fiercely white above
And darted down its quivering flame,
As through the new-ploughed fields the Lord
Of Wisdom and Compassion came.

Two milk-white oxen drew the plough
With meek, bowed heads that seemed to hear
The sighful rustle of the palms
And the dry clods breaking in their rear.

The peasant drove the ploughshare deep
Which two strong hands did strictly guide.
Lo, as he turned his docile team,
The silent Lord was at his side.

He knelt with joined, uplifted palms;
His eyes with tears of joy were dim.
And while he knelt, his oxen seemed
To bow their patient heads with him.

The Lord in mercy sweetly spake –
No hour for high discourses now;
He spoke of simple, homely things,
And parabled upon the plough.

By that so gracious accent, all
The humble ways of field and fold –
Ploughing, sowing, reaping, threshing –
Were touched as though with rays of gold.

Yea, as the Lord discoursed to him,
The hardy peasant quickly saw
In lives of clod, flower, beast and man,
The workings of a common law.

Three milk-white blooms the peasant plucked
And with them touched the Blessed Feet.
'I take my refuge, Lord, in Thee,
Thy Doctrine, and Thine Order meet'.

The Lord stepped o'er the thread-thin stream
And went His calm and solemn way.
The ploughman, joyful, gripped his plough,
And plied a whip of song that day.

'ABOVE ME BROODS…'

Above me broods
A world of mysteries and magnitudes.
I see, I hear,
More than what strikes the eye or meets the ear.

Within me sleep
Potencies deep, unfathomably deep,
Which, when awake,
The bonds of life, death, time and space will break.

Infinity
Above me like the blue sky do I see.
Below, in me,
Lies the reflection of infinity.

NIGHT THOUGHTS[55]

Across the vastness of the sky
White continents of cloud are spread;
From bank to bank the moon doth ply
Her silver traffic overhead.

Below me, is a single world;
Above, ten thousand million are.
The moon her silver sail has furled
To anchor near the Morning Star.

Each world a million million lives
Contains, yet all with all are one –
The humblest flower of grass that thrives
Is sister to the regnant sun.

Yet must my heart recoil from these
As the burnt hand jerketh from the fire,
And seek within, to find without,
Peace, and cessation of desire.

The moon tonight is bright and new,
Her sail is trimmed to journey far –
The realm of thought I travel to
Is worlds beyond the Morning Star.

Lo, on a starry foaming borne,
Fast paling now, no longer bright,
She strikes the fiery Rock of Dawn
And founders in a sea of light.

That Moon for which I journey far
Shall never wax, wane, or be spent,
And anchors near no Morning Star –
The Full Moon of Enlightenment.

RAIN

How sweet it is, how sweet again
To hear and see and smell the rain!
The birds take shelter in the trees
And sway with the bough that sways with the breeze
As the big drops fall from the silver sky
On the fields of rice that all withered lie.

The peasant shelters, with smiles of relief,
Beneath the broad green plantain leaf.
Sweet to that son of toil to see
The fair rain falling fresh and free;
While on his body, bright with sweat,
The soft cool breeze blows sweeter yet.

The channels fill, then overflow,
As the sweet rain slants to the earth below.
Each blade of grass is bright with gems;
Each grove of palms wears diadems.
The crimson streaks of the western sky
In the glassy fields reflected lie.

Praise to the rain, that falleth fine
On field and tree, on flower and vine:
Praise to the labourers in the sun,
Who rest not till the day is done:
Praise to our patient Mother Earth,
Who gave to us our common birth.

1948 THE FOUR SIGHTS

1. YASHODHARA

Lord of the black locks, lord of thy handmaid,
Lord of the clouded but beautiful brow,
Lord of all music, lord of all laughter,
Why dost thou ponder so mournfully now?

Say, has some new blossom-shaft of the love god
Wounded the heart that once beat but for me,
Or, dost thou think that the white flame within me
Burneth for one more beloved than thee?

Here in these gardens where fountains are falling,
With the green grass beneath, and the blue sky above,
Where we hover like bees round the blossom of beauty,
No sorrows may come but the sorrows of love.

Lift up thy sad eyes, and see in the heavens
The moon in her beauty, the stars with their light.
Now, while the soft wind blows heavy with perfume,
Dost thou not think of the pleasures of night?

Oh why dost thou stir not, why dost thou speak not,
Why do thy mute lips vouchsafe no reply?
Though heavy as death be the sorrow that bows thee,
Yea, thy beloved must share it or die.

2. SIDDHĀRTHA

Pity may move me, though passion may never,
To open the source of my sorrow to thee,
Folding back petal on petal of pining,
As the flower shows its heart at the hest of the bee.

Our love which, as jasmine, grew fragrant at nightfall,
When sweet-voiced musicians were tuning the string,
Had a cool palace roof for the heat of the Summer,
A palace for Winter, a palace for Spring.

With wreaths of blue lotus our black locks adorning,
With garments of muslin and garlands of rose,
Day after day in the gay painted chamber,
In the season of flowers, in the season of snows;

Month after month in the green parks of pleasaunce,
At morning the orchards, at evening the bowers,
No joy was unknown there, no pleasure untasted,
When lamplight and starlight and moonlight were ours.

But now, the delights of the couch and the garden,
The collar of turquoise, the chaplet of pearls,
The hymns of the poet, the hope of a kingdom,
The stripling musicians, the chorus of girls,

Even thy moon-apple breasts, my beloved,
Thy swan-like demeanour, thy sweetness in talk,
Thy kohl and thy carmine, delight me no longer,
Like blossoms which wither when cropped from the stalk.

For of late as I raced through the streets of the city,
With flying white horses all hurrying-hoar,
Three sights did I see – things common as kisses –
But it seemed I had never beheld them before.

The first sight I saw was a grey-bearded grandsire,
Withered and weak who was blooming and strong,
His slow, painful steps on a bamboo supporting,
Creeping and wheezing and mumbling along.

The second a man who lay wasted with fever,
Burning yet freezing, fighting for breath,
Twitching and trembling, his features distorted,
As fearful and frantic he wrestled with death.

The third sight I saw as I whirled through the city,
With stiff, lifeless hands, its blank face upturned,
Borne on a bedstead, by mourners surrounded,
Was a grim, silent corpse on its way to be burned.

Then, as the silver-white beauty of morning
Springs from the mountains and dapples the skies,
Chasing the goblins and ghosts with its arrows,
A fourth sight, beloved, confronted my eyes.

Lord of his senses, lord of his thinking,
Humble yet mighty, lowly but high,
A monk in pure beauty outshining the many
As the full moon the host of the stars in the sky.

These three sights of sorrow have soberly shown me,
Pitiless-plain as the midsummer sky,
That in spite of their youth and their beauty of body
All men must wither and sicken and die.

This is the source of the sorrow that bows me,
Making me weary of music and flowers,
Making my heart in its anguish not heeding
The call of the orchards, the bliss of the bowers.

The fourth sight I saw by the roadside has taught me,
Simple-sublime as the mountains of snow,
That forth from my house to the fear-haunted forest
To solve these dark riddles of life I must go.

And I know not of months, weeks or days now the number
The flag of a prince shall for me be unfurled,
Ere I go forth to seek for a way to the Deathless
With heart of compassion, the hope of the world.

ASPIRATION

The dim sun sinks to rest
In a west of watery gold.
The young stars climb the sky
And there like flowers unfold,
In the forest vast of night,
Petals of purest light.

So may my heart unfold,
When the suns of the world have set,
In the forest vast of the Void,
Wisdom with Mercy met
In that tranquil, silent hour,
Like a flower and the scent of a flower.

SONNET

Aloft the many-petalled lotus rears
From sunlit water its pure beauty white;
And shining presences adore the sight
Of Him Who sits upon it, free from fears;
For, having tasted the sharp salt of tears,
Back to the bitter springs of false delight
He tracked through transformations infinite
The lust that lures men into births and biers.

Oh to the multitude of gods and men
Do Thou reveal in every faultless part
The Law that leads to Peace most radiant –
Love beyond love, Light beyond light – and then
Sit Thou upon the lotus of my heart,
O Lord, and teach me, being ignorant.

THE SUN-PATH
Adiccapathehaṃsa yanti[56]
Dhammapada

Swanlike, upon the Sun-Path let me soar
To That which lives beyond the Threefold Veil,
Leaving this weed-choked pond for evermore
Fringed with sweet-fuming poisonous poppies pale.

I follow One Love-Winged and Wisdom-Eyed
Who first upon that Path did soar and see
The rending of the Threefold Veil, and cried
Before He passed Beyond, 'Oh follow me!'

The clear, sweet music of His Victory-Song
Rainlike from far away and long ago
Falls on their hearing and their hearts who long
Swanwise upon that Solar Path to go.

Pierced by the arrows of a million stars,
Through banks of cloud, through darkness absolute,
Through gulfs of soundlessness no music mars,
Past suns the reeling brain might ne'er compute;

Onward and upward with aspiring wing
Undaunted through a myriad worlds they press –
Now in the Realm of Beauty bosoming,
Now floating in the Vast of Nothingness.

Oh last and least of all that glorious train,
Though feeble-winged and fearful, may I be!
Let me not paddle in the Pool of Pain,
Nor ruffle to the Wind of Transiency!

Leaving the mud-flats of mortality,
With flight unwearied, faith that may not fail,
Not swerving from the Sun-Path, may I see
At last the rending of the Threefold Veil.

With crowding suns and moons left far behind,
That Bliss and Peace which now they cannot guess,
My wings, for ever folded, there shall find,
Upon the sapphire Lake of Deathlessness.

HIMALAYAN SAGES

Those who have hid themselves on heights of snow,
Face to face with the stars and the silver moon,
Shall read upon the rocks the Ancient Rune
And thus decipher secrets. They shall know –
Far from the lips of any earthly lover –
What the mists hide and what the winds discover.

And, with grave eyes of wisdom, they shall scan –
Pitting terrific wills against th' Unknown,
Wringing its secret out of every stone –
The origin and destiny of man;
Shall see a hundred thousand ages roll
Through one brief instant of the human soul.

They shall know utter peace. They shall not feel –
Immersed, upon those constellated peaks,
In that deep joy whereof no language speaks –
The bitterness and bite of brandished steel.
The tumult of the world rolls on and on:
They shall not hear or heed it. They have gone

Afar upon that path which no man knoweth
Save who can frailties and passions tread
Underfoot, leave the living and the dead
For snowy heights whereon no green grass groweth,
And, meditating there, intensify
Th' electric urge to thrust beyond the 'I'.

WESAK JOY

The swiftest, sweetest pen could ne'er indite
What joy Thou hadst upon that Wesak Night;
And though a voice such as the stars may have
Should breast all music as a swan the wave
And bear on to the utmost verge of sound,
They could not utter forth Thy joy profound.
And this I know; for now, by following Thee
With first weak steps to Perfect Purity,
I bear within my heart a mite of bliss,
And bearing, cannot even utter this.

ADVENT

I listened all day for the knock of the Stranger,
And I often looked out from the door.
The table was scrubbed, the brass shining,
And well swept the floor.

The shadows grew longer and longer,
In the grate the fire flickered and died.
'It's too late. He never will come now'
I said, and sighed.

I sat there musing and musing,
The spinning-wheel still at my side.
The moonlight came in through the window
White like a bride.

As the clock struck twelve I heard nothing
But *felt* He had come and stayed
Waiting outside. And I listened –
And I was afraid.

SECRET WINGS

We cry that we are weak although
We will not stir our secret wings;
The world is dark – because we are
Blind to the starriness of things.

We pluck our rainbow-tinted plumes
And with their heaven-born beauty try
To fledge nocturnal shafts, and then
Complain 'Alas! we cannot fly!'

We mutter 'All is dust' or else
With mocking words accost the wise:
'Show us the Sun which shines beyond
The Veil' – and then we close our eyes.

To powers above and powers beneath
In quest of Truth men sue for aid,
Who stand athwart the Light and fear
The shadow that themselves have made.

Oh cry no more that you are weak
But stir and spread your secret wings,
And say 'The world is bright, because
We glimpse the starriness of things.'

Soar with your rainbow plumes and reach
That near-far land where all are one,
Where Beauty's face is aye unveiled
And every star shall be a sun.

THE TRAMP

I will not read the scriptures
Of advertisements obscene;
I will not offer incense
To the godhead of Machine;
I will not be a pawn in
The game of politics;
I will *not* sell my birthright;
I *will* kick against the pricks.

Not in tired but sleepless cities
Where the black smoke shrouds the stars;
Not in the reeking rottenness
Of brothels and of bars;
Not in office or in workshop
Where, labouring night and day,
The sullen millions languish,
One second will I stay.

I will read the Book of Nature
That reveals the things above;
I will offer my heart's incense
To Wisdom and to Love;
I will fill my life with beauty
And with joy transfigure it;
I will rise and claim my birthright
And to Truth alone submit.

By willow-shaded waters
From village snug not far;
On slow-trailed creaking barges
Beneath the Evening Star;
In fields, by hill or valley,
Contented, night and day,
With birds and flowers and butterflies
For ever will I stay.

SRI PADA

1949

I saw His shining footprints
Gleaming in the grass like dew;
The flowers, where they had fallen,
Sweeter and fairer grew:
They led into the distant hills,
Those hills all misty-blue.

I will follow, I will follow,
'Neath the Spring Moon full and bright,
Through field and copse and hollow,
Those footprints of delight,
And walk upon those distant hills
One dawn all golden-white.

'Tis many an age of darkness
Since the days my Lord did pass
Leaving His dewy footprints
Like pearls upon the grass,
And rank weeds have o'ergrown them,
And thorns obscured, alas!

Yet will I follow boldly,
Using the hunter's art,
Until one day I find Him,
From all things else apart,
Sitting beside the Pool of Peace
In the blue hills of my heart.

WESAK THOUGHTS

Since that auspicious Full-Moon Day
Which saw Thy pangless birth,
How many bloodstained centuries
Have stormed across the earth.

Across her green and pleasant face,
More savage than the lion
How many conquerors have rolled
Their chariots of iron.

How many battles lost and won,
How many cities razed;
How many a trail with fire and sword
Through town and village blazed.

But here and there, like halcyon birds
That nest upon the flood,
Or like to azure lotuses
Blooming in pools of blood,

The Winners of the Paths and Fruits
In many an age and clime –
Throughout the islands of the East –
Have taught Thy Truth sublime.

On Ganges' silver-sanded shores
Full many a Sage hath seen
The Truths of Ill, its Cause, its Cure,
And trod the Path between.

In forest bower and mountain cave,
Remote from passions vile,
How many Saints illustrious made
The copper-coloured Isle.

The Country of the Yellow Robe
Was rich in days of old
With many a Seer more precious than
Her rubies and her gold.

On dizzying peaks, in blinding snows,
How many Dauntless Ones
Have seen the dawning of a Light
More glorious than the sun's.

In China's dragon-haunted land
The heirs of Truth and Art
Have pictured with a brush inspired
The moonlight of the heart.

And Isles that greet the rising sun
Have glimpsed upon the wing
Enlightenment more beautiful
Than cherry trees in Spring.

In these and many other lands,
Where hearts were erst on fire
With lust, Thy sons, O Lord, have known
The bliss of non-desire.

When hatred like a tidal wave
Engulfed the coral isles
Of peace, Thy sons with love have swept
It back a hundred miles.

Oh here and now how great the need
For Sage and Saint and Seer!
Oh when will Metteyya come, Oh when
Will Arahants appear?

For now upon the roofless world
The floods of sorrow pour;
Like dreadful, distant thunderclouds
Are heard the drums of war.

With leprous fingers interclasped
And blood-stiff garments sere,
From heart to heart with crimson steps
Stalk lust and hate and fear.

Tormented on his bed of pain
With many a grievous ill,
Mankind must now or never use
The Great Physician's skill.

Now with its clear, triumphant voice
Must sound, as ne'er before,
In all the quarters of the earth,
The Trumpet of the Law.

Though in this world that now must pluck
The bitterest fruits of sin,
The reign of hate will cease one day,
The reign of love begin,

Not from blue cloud or silver star
Will love be wafted then,
But from the self-same place where hate
Was born – the hearts of men.

Oh now must Ganges' silver shores,
The copper-coloured Isle,
The Country of the Yellow Robe,
Each peak and snowy pile,

With China's dragon-haunted land
And Isles that greet the sun
At morn, and other islands, see
Once more Nirvāṇa won.

In North and South, in East and West,
In house or hermitage,
The Lord's disciples ceaseless war
With Māra's hosts must wage.

With ardent hearts and tireless hands,
On Truth's foundation sure,
Vow, friends, to build upon the earth
The City of the Law.

Nerve your strong hearts and steel your wills
For conquest over pain;
Desire uproot unflinchingly
The Deathless to attain.

And then across the verdant earth,
Which erst iron chariots saw,
Will sunlike roll from East to West
The glorious Wheel of Law.

And rising in its azure track
Will beam with rich increase
The moon that men are pining for –
The Wesak Moon of peace.

THE POET'S REPLY

'With your holy vows,
Your shaven head,
And your stitched-stuff robes
Ensaffronéd,
How can you sing still?'
The people said.

They pointed fingers
Of scorn at me.
'A true ascetic
He cannot be;
For his lips are stained
With poesy.'

'Poor fools', I replied,
'These songs of mine
Are the rapturous lilt
Of the life divine;
But yours are tainted
With lust and wine.

'If a song-bird caged
Can sing merrily,
With its wings close clipped
(And such are ye),
Oh how much sweeter
'Twill sing when free!'

THE WORD OF THE BUDDHA

If thirst for truth doth like a fire
Consume thy soul in every part,
Oh quench it with the words that pour
In streams from His Himálayan heart.

From heights of Vision crowned with stars,
Cleaving the thunderous clouds of strife,
Those waters pour to fructify
The barren fields of human life.

Oh questing hearts who have not known
How rich those precious waters are,
In every azure wavelet gleams
A pearl more brightly than a star.

Forsake the fen of sickly thoughts,
Which now thy heart doth so entrance,
Where croak the frogs of doubt, where bloom
The purple flowers of ignorance,

And journeying to those green-turfed banks
Stand breathless on the moonlit beach,
And see and hear beneath the stars
The mighty river of His Speech.

Oh sun-scorched pilgrim, drink at last
Those waters pure from snow to sea –
Those jewelled waves which are to men
The Draught of Immortality.

'TIRED OF THE CRIMSON CURTAIN...'[57]

Tired of the crimson curtain,
Tired of the gilded chair,
Tired of the scented bosom,
Tired of the loosened hair,
I went into the garden
To breathe the sunlit air.

I heard the drowsy murmur
Of flower-emerging bees;
Before the holy Passion Flower
I sank on both my knees;
I talked on Art with tulips;
I fell in love with trees.

Crazed by incessant searches
In the Wilderness of Word,
Crazed by close-printed volumes
Whose dust lies aye unstirred,
I stole into a thicket
To hear a singing-bird.

Perched on a spray of roses
She poured into my ear
The sorrow of the nightingales
For Ítylus so dear,
The ecstasies of skylarks,
The lusts of chanticleer.

Maddened with thirst for being,
Maddened with circling round
In the vortex of existence,
Baffled, blinded, bound,
I cast aside three bodies
Which in three worlds are found.

Like an avalanche descended
Unbounded ecstasy;
Unending vistas opened out
Into eternity;
The Ocean of Nirvāṇa
Swallowed the droplet 'me'.

PEACE

Turn away from the world, weary pilgrim,
There is no rest for thee there;
The quietness of star-communing hills
'Twere better for thee to share;
In the silence that lies at the forest's heart
Breathes a peace beyond compare.

In glades where Spring-buds quicken
When frosts no more appal,
In fields and leafy by-lanes red
With ripened fruits of Fall,
The leaves, now green, now yellow, teach
That change must come to all.

Comes peace more cool than the moonlight is
That silvers the gliding stream,
When the stilled heart knows, in the forest depths,
The world is an empty dream,
And turns with delight to the Things That Are
From the things that merely seem.

TO THE RECUMBENT BUDDHA
Mahaparinibbana Temple, Kusinara

Thou art not dead, nor dost Thou even sleep
Here on this solemn couch of flower-strewn gold;
But lying plunged in meditation deep
Dost with a peace ineffable enfold
All who with pilgrim footsteps wend to Thee
Sick of the world, and longing to be free.

Couched on my knees before Thy figure vast,
Soothed by the stillness of this silent place,
After much striving I behold at last
The lamp-illumined beauty of Thy face,
And, trembling, feel around, below, above,
The pulsing of Thy vibrant peace and love.

Though witless ones may deem asleep or dead
One who hath shuffled off this mortal form,
O Winner of the Deathless, Thou hast said
Thou livest on for ever in Thy Norm,
And therethrough with unconquerable might
Dost guide the worlds along the path of light.

For in this low-ceiled chamber throbs a heart
Which never was, nor ever will be, still;
But must, like dew, invisibly impart
Its fruit-maturing influence, until
Men feel its pulse in every quickened vein
Strong as the Spring-tides of the moon-charmed main.

Still through this tomb-quiet temple thrills that voice,
In accents by the sensual ear unheard,
Which once the triple world did so rejoice
With its immaculate, majestic word
That taught the origin and end of pain,
And which to this sick world must teach again.

Not in this solitary cell alone,
Not in soft whispers to the faithful heart,
Not with stiff, gilded hand and lips of stone,
But loud in busy street and bustling mart
Through living, breathing lips Thy truth must be
Proclaimed with love by those who follow Thee.

Flicker the lamps. The incense, ashen-white,
Distils no more its tribute of perfume.
On Thine unblinking eyes and visage bright
I gaze with love before I quit the room.
Thy still lips whisper, soft as wind in grass,
'My son, despair not: it shall come to pass.'

THE CITADEL

Build thou upon thy spirit's mountainous height
Strongholds of Light!
Build with the square white stones of virtuous deed
Mortared with love's rich meed;
Build terraces of loftiest meditations
For watchmen's stations;
And pinnacles of wisdom higher still
Uprear with dauntless skill;
And then command Truth's banner be unfurled
Above the world.

For streaming from their Light-beleaguered coasts
Come Māra's hosts:
Hating that flaming Hand they seek to smite
Direct the Heart of Light;
And tow'rd thy mount from regions far asunder
Their chariots thunder.
Yet fear thou not! the ponderous sword of Good
Was ever unwithstood.
If thou dost guard thine own heart's citadel
All will be well.

THE FACE OF SILENCE

Before me through the evening air
With robes of saffron hue
And one lean, sunbrowned shoulder bare
And shadow long and blue

He went. I watched him till he turned
A turning of the road.
The West one golden glory burned
And all the treetops glowed.

With such a flood of beauty came
The setting sun that day
That him who walked as though in flame
Before me on the way

I quite forgot. The stars of night
Like silver doves did seem
On the bare branches to alight –
I thought that I did dream.

Then at that turning as I turned
Where he had turned before
When all the trees like torches burned,
At the tree-root I saw

Him sitting on a grassy space
Poised in some lofty swoon:
On his still form and peaceful face
Shone bright the broad full moon.

All breathlessly and silently
With awe I tiptoed near;
And yet – he looked so peacefully –
I had no sense of fear.

O'er his still features breathed a calm
I had not seen before.
It drew me as some maiden's charm
A lover to her door.

The light he saw I could not see,
And yet it seemed to glow
Upon his face more beauteously
Than sunlight on the snow.

At last I turned away, and blessed
The womb that gave him birth,
Knowing that there in truth was rest
And peace for those on earth.

THE WOUNDED SWAN

Out of the sunset with the Evening Star,
And with eve's long blue shadows falling down
Into the lotus bed which hides our bower,
Behold, my love, I come again to thee.

O wild thy shriek, O terrible thy grief,
When from the royal swan-flight reeling down,
A mass of fluttering feathers, wing-transpierced,
I fell with bloody plumage to the ground.

How gentle was the hand that smoothed my neck,
How pitiful the eyes that gazed on me,
How musical the voice that sadly said
'Alas, poor bird, what have they done to thee!'

He bore me on his breast with boundless love,
And though the evil prince who brought me down
Came proudly with his friends to claim his prize
The arms that clasped me would not let me go.

With heart pressed close to beating heart we went
Into the perfumed chambers of the king –
I with the prince's muslin round my wing,
He with the wild swan's blood upon his clothes.

And there the king in council did decree
That the poor wounded life of right belonged
Not to the cruel hand that brought it low
But to the loving one that raised it up.

Laid on a bed of azure lotuses,
Fed on delicious honey, fruits and milk,
And tended by the hands that rescued me,
My pulse of life began to throb again.

And often, as he stooped to smooth my wing,
The prince would murmur like a wind in reeds,
Pressing his tear-bright cheek against my neck,
'Alas, the grief that comes to living things!'

And often, when the moon was full and bright,
Wrapped in the purple shadows of a tree
Whose boughs spread out against the stars, the prince
Would sit and muse upon the woes of men.

Though rich the fragrant chambers where he dwelt
With softly burning lamps and blazing jewels,
I think the prince was far less happy there
Than we two are in this blue lotus bower.

For when, what time my stricken wing was healed
And all its silver plumage bright again,
I took once more the freedom of the skies,
The sad prince almost seemed to envy me.

Into the sunrise with the Morning Star
And with the mists of evening rising up
Above the pale gold clouds, I sought once more
This silver tarn set in these dark blue hills.

Bright as the heaven with stars doth seem this bed
Of azure lotuses agleam with dew,
And like a bank of moonlit clouds our nest,
And therein like the moon of Autumn thou.

Far higher than the starry arch of heaven,
And deeper than the distant emerald seas,
Far brighter than the brightest Autumn moon,
Far stronger than our love, his love for me.

Before the sunrise blushes through the East,
Before the fields are bright with morning dew,
Before the sad prince, rising from his couch,
Beholds the swan-deserted lotus bed,

O come, my love, and wing to wing with me
Flash like a silver arrow through the night,
Down from the blue hills like a shooting star
Into the prince's azure lotus pool.

There let us build again our reedy bower
And glitter in the moonlight of his love –
Love higher than the starry arch of heaven
And deeper than the distant emerald seas.

THE LORD OF COMPASSION

In the midnight of the dense ignorance of the world the flower of Thy Compassion blossomed like a great golden lotus on the unruffled surface of the waters of Thy Mind,
Whilst the Full Moon of Thine Enlightenment hung overhead in the azure heavens ablaze with stars....
The wind that bore freezingly from the bare hills and leafless forests shrill voices of grief, shrieks of pain, sobs of despair,
Returning, blew back thither warm with the infinite fragrance of the unfolding petals of the great golden lotus of Thy Love....
Though that Full Moon is no more seen gloriously bright in the azure heavens amidst a host of blazing stars, and though that wondrous blossom long since closed its dawny petals bright,
Still through the moonless, starless darkness of the midnight of the dense ignorance of the world
Is wafted, O Lord of Compassion, the exceeding sweetness of the fragrance of Thy Love.

TRUTH, LOVE, LIFE AND MAN

Truth is not truth, unless to men it is
A path that guides their winged or weary feet
Up to its heaven-high sublimities
Adazzle with the snowfall, sheet on sheet.
Unless Truth leads men from the dark, it is
Not Truth but only words, and false as sweet.

Love is not Love, unless to all it is
Free as the air, impartial as the sun,
And leaveth not, to dote on deities
Unreal, the creatures real it could have won.
Unless Love feels for all alike, it is
Not Love for any, but desire for one.

Life is not Life, unless to joy it is
A bringer of swift death, to grief a friend,
Or if it spoils not bliss with agonies,
Teaching that sweetest things have soonest end.
Unless Life teach, and we learn this, it is
Not Life but mere existence that we've kenned.

Man is not Man, unless to Truth he is
A pilgrim pledged who tries with might and main
To scale its dazzling-white divinities,
With boundless love for those who tread the plain.
Unless Man strives for Truth and loves, he is
Not Man but merely brute, and lives in vain.

THE MESSAGE OF THE BOWL

Hardly in words these lips can tell
Those noons I recollect so well,
When, after many a dusty mile
Which talk did something to beguile,
We entered, glad of coolth and breeze,
A dense green grove of mango trees,
Unslung our bowls, then bright as glass,
And after resting on soft grass
Tow'rd neighbouring village took our way –
A village all of thatch and clay;
And there, past many a straggling row
Of mud-walled cabins cramped and low,
Past tiled and timbered mansions which
Carved post and portico made rich,
Bearing our alms-bowls, quietly went
Questing the heart's enlightenment.
Yea, with the hope of winning truth,
And to curb the flame-fierce pride of youth,
We moved in silence from door to door
And begged from the poorest of the poor.
The white kine eyed us as we passed,
And wide-eyed children stared aghast,
While women pitied, as women must,
The strangers covered with heat and dust;
And old men, roused from noontide beds,
Watched and wondered and shook their heads.
Cool courtyards smeared with cowdung clean
We entered noiseless and unseen,
And there in silence stood before
The little, low, unlintelled door,
Till someone stirred within, and came
To ask our need, and grant the same.
Oh, to the poor the poor are kind,
Sharing their board with lowly mind.
If in receiving I could be
Humble as they in giving me,
Winged would I tread that path of peace

Which uphill winds to the heart's release,
And in this loathsome body find
Immaculate the Buddha-mind.
Those palaces of blue-veined stone
Where pining greatness reigned alone
Behind the jewelled ivory screen,
Where perfumed lamps of amber sheen
As though with moonlight did illume
The barren richness of the room,
Are far less precious in my sight
Than those poor huts, neglected quite,
Of paddy-thatch and sunburnt clay
Where first we begged our food that day;
Nor was my father's house more dear
Than those dark doors wherefrom did peer
The quiet-eyed women, gravely kind,
Who brought the best their hearts could find,
And gave with sweeter, gentler grace
Than ever beamed from beauty's face.
Thin, flat, round cakes of barley-bread
White from the hearth, raw onions red,
Brown country rice, hot chillies, greens,
Chutneys and achars, potherbs, beans,
All, as from door to door we passed,
Into our round-mouthed bowls they cast;
And all, together kneaded, we
Ate 'neath the dense-leaved mango tree.
Ah, and more bliss that almsfood brings
Than all the sugared cates of kings –
Epícurean banquetings!
Then did my deepest heart-thoughts feel
Knit with the poor through woe and weal,
And passionately longed to thrust
Plumed pride into that sacred dust,
And mingling there, foot-trampled, be
Levelled with holiest poverty
Which doth with love enrich the soul,
And spells the Message of the Bowl.

THE WHITE CALF

Outstretched upon the sandy ground
Beneath the trees, beneath the stars,
We watched the silver full moon round
Dapple the earth with silver bars.

After long toil and tardy ease
How sweet it was at last to lie
Silent beneath the moon-blanched trees
Feeling the stillness of the sky.

With sleep at last our lids were sealed
And all the night long we had lain,
But loud from heaven the thunder pealed
And down in torrents rushed the rain.

We scrambled up. The stars were fled,
The wind was straining at the trees
And whipping up our sandy bed
In wavelets like a stormy sea's.

Into a narrow shed of clay
With cowdunged and uneven floor
For shelter then we groped our way,
And shivering bedded in the straw.

Chill through the open doorway blew
The wind, and with the wind the rain,
While we, for more we could not do,
Huddled beside the sacks of grain.

Above, the thunder boomed and crashed,
And all without was dark and drear,
Save when the fitful lightning flashed
And showed the tumult we could hear.

At length, by weariness oppressed,
In spite of cold and wind and rain,
Sprawled on the floor with placid breast
We slumbered till 'twas day again.

Then, as the dawn's first rays did fall
Bright through the open doorway wide,
Turning my head, I saw a small
White calf still sleeping at my side.

Nestling upon the same soft straw
As I, with head to hoof, he lay,
So peacefully that one who saw
Could hardly keep the tears away.

To me that small life did impart
A kind of aching tenderness,
Such as may fill a mother's heart
To see her infant's helplessness.

And in the deepest depths of me
I felt that I had understood
In one clear flash the mystery
Of universal brotherhood.

TENDAI

How can I scorn the beggar's lot
When heart and mind have understood
The wayside dust in which he sits
Shall rise to Perfect Buddhahood?

Rather in reverence shall I fold
My hands, the beggar's lot to see.
Hail, Jewel of Enlightenment
Stitched in the hem of poverty!

THE LOTUS OF COMPASSION

The Lotus blooms tonight,
The great golden Lotus of the Lord's Compassion.
With white roots deep in the slime of this sad world,
And huge green leaves spread on the surface of the waters of the Lake of Tears,
And surrounded by myriads of silver lotus-buds,
Like white hands folded in prayer for succour from the miseries of the world,
That Lotus blooms tonight.
O leave the crowded shore where men buy and sell,
Shake off the soft detaining fingers of your friends,
And in a little boat,
At midnight, when the moon is full,
And glitters at you from the water,
Row swiftly to the quiet Heart of the Lake where the Lotus blooms,
The great golden Lotus of the Lord's Compassion;
And you will feel the sweetness ineffable of its heart-fragrance
Coming on a breeze which ripples the face of the silent waters
To meet you beneath the stars.

BUDDHAM SARAṆAM GACCHĀMI

There wends a long procession
Through the ages, up to Thee,
With dew-besprinkled blossoms
And incense endlessly.

They wend in awe and wonder
To the garden of the Birth
(Where Thou wast enlightened)
The nations of the earth.

The simple with the learnéd,
The old with young and free,
Together wending, murmur:
'I take refuge, Lord, in Thee.'

With slow, uncertain footsteps,
Through wasted years, to Thee,
With wilted, withered blossoms
I draw nearer, doubtingly.

Scarlet sins and purple sorrows
Have dyed deep my weary heart;
But now white hopes are winging
Like doves to where Thou art.

With all my imperfections,
Each day less falteringly,
I draw nearer to Thee, crying:
'I take refuge, Lord, in Thee.'[58]

1950 THE BIRTHPLACE OF COMPASSION
Buddha Gaya, 1949

Here, where the Goatherd's banyan-tree
O'ershadowed, was, to world forlorn,
The first child of Enlightenment,
Compassion, born.

Seeing men bloom like lotus flowers
With petals closed, or half apart,
Her pulses fluttered underneath
The Buddha-Heart.

And when that high and holy hour
With stars shone down upon her birth,
There opened wide a way to peace
For all on earth.

THE ONLY WAY

One need, and one need only,
All earthly things above,
This world hath now as ever –
The need of boundless love.

One way, and one way only,
There is to outward peace –
That Great Heart of Compassion
Which bids all sorrows cease.

ON THE BRINK

Here on the river-brink I sit
Where thick the tall white lily grows,
And feel the clear, cold ripples break
With icy kisses on my toes.

The willows trail their almond leaves
With one side white, and one side green,
Atop the glasswaves tremblingly,
While the shrill wind blows cold and keen.

The waves that nibble at my feet
Are touched with dull, hard glints of gold,
And the shadows of the tired sun
Stretch out more long and black and cold.

The moon, by one white star attended,
Lies on her bright back crescent-thin.
I weep beside the blackening waves
Because I failed to venture in.

RHYMED TANKA

Mountains bathed in mist
How mysteriously you stand!
But when darkness falls
Deeper on hill after hill
You grow more mysterious still.

VILLAGE INDIA

I have found you, India,
Here in the villages,
In the houses with clay walls and thatched roofs
And ricefields and wheatfields
Green at their doors....
Not in the cities
With their tramways and talkies
From the West mass-imported;
Not in the museums
Behind the long, shining
Rows of glass cases
With brickbats and potsherds;
Not in the temples
Where the smells of decayed flowers
And stale incense mingle,
And garish lights shine on the faces of stone gods,
And coconuts broken, and priests fee-demanding;
Not on the snow-peaks
With hermits in hiding,
Nor yet by the stream-side
In the gardens of poets with flowers –
But here in the villages
Which birthed the great cities,
And filled the museums
With wrought gold and jewelled work
And lingams of silver;
Which flung up the stone walls
Of temples, and scooped out
Their sanctuaries, and lit there
Innumerable rows of lamps before deities,
Splitting coconuts and scattering rice
To fatten the priests;
Which nurtured the hermit
And showed to the eyes of the poet his first sight of beauty –
Here in the villages
Which ploughed, sowed, reaped and threshed

The ricefields and wheatfields
I have found you, India,
At last, and embrace you
And feel on my shoulder
Your cool flowing tresses.

THE ALMS OF COMPASSION

In the saffron robe of yearning,
And my heart in my hand for a bowl,
I went from door to door, seeking
Alms for my soul.

Some gave me wealth and pleasure,
Some gave me knowledge and skill,
But the small round heart-bowl in my hand
They could not fill.

And as the hot sun ascended
I went with such weary feet
From door to door and from house to house
Down life's long street.

Nor had I ever found there
The alms that was life to me,
And had died, perhaps, on their doorsteps,
But suddenly

I was ware of a Jewel-Tower standing
Like a flower beside the sea,
And One with face most beautiful
Gave alms to me.

Oh when, at the end of my journey,
I stood in the dusty road
And received the great alms of Compassion
My bowl o'erflowed.

THE FRAGRANCE OF COMPASSION

Seeing this world, this hapless world,
With all its store of woes,
Compassion in the Buddha-Heart
Burst open like a rose.

And from that flower, that wondrous flower,
There came at once to birth
A breath whose perfume even now
With fragrance fills the earth.

INVOCATION

Field-freshening rain,
White night-rain lingering on in drizzles till the dawn,
Pools of bright silver making, birthing streams
In dry clay river-beds, pour down, O rain,
All day, all night, pour down pour down, O rain,
Pour down....

World-welfaring Compassion,
Void-born Compassion diamond-hard and petal-tender,
Peace to wild heartwaves bringing, birthing love
On the low couch of self, pour down, Compassion,
All day, all night, pour down pour down, Compassion,
Pour down –
Pour down like rain on this compassionless
Lost world....

Pour down, pour down, pour down....

THE UNSEEN FLOWER

Compassion is far more than emotion. It is something that springs
Up in the emptiness which is when you yourself are not there,
So that you do not know anything about it.
Nobody, in fact, knows anything about it
(If they knew it, it would not be Compassion);
But they can only smell
The scent of the unseen flower
That blooms in the Heart of the Void.

THE LAMP OF COMPASSION

My heart-wick now is charred with sin,
And dully red it glows
With greed or hate, afloat upon
The viscous oil of woes.

Oh may I set it flaming with
Compassion's golden fire,
Which feeds upon the twisted strands
Of anger and desire,

And hold its rainbowed radiance up
In wisdom's crystal vase
To light their way who from this world
Are stumbling to the stars!

MESSENGERS FROM TIBET[59]

Whence come these asses, brazen-belled,
That jingle down the dusty lane
With big brown bales of tufty wool –
A hundred in a single train?

Whence comes their master, crimson-cloaked,
Who drives them onward from the rear,
With braided and beribboned locks,
And gold- and turquoise-studded ear?

Whence comes this music, weird and wild,
Of clashing cymbals, tinkling bells,
And trumpets deep that thunder out
The sorrows of a hundred hells?

Whence come these banners, bright as gems,
Above the images unfurled
On shadowy temple walls, that seem
Like glimpses of another world?

Whence come these memories, vague as dreams,
Of peaks where snow eternal reigns,
Of boundless grassy wastes beyond –
The silent Central Asian plains?

Whence comes this yearning, sharp as life,
Strong as death's self, to mount and go
Beyond the hundred-headed hills
High up the sky-ascending snow?

Oh land of turquoise, land of gold,
Land of the whispered, mystic lore,
Land of the Buddha, land unknown,
Were you *my* land in days of yore?

Though dense the mists of birth and death
Your messengers are riding through.
How shall peace fill my heart again
Unless I journey back to you?

BAMBOOS

Among all branched things, I for beauty choose
The yellowness and slimness of bamboos,
Whose bunched leaves twinkle on a gusty day
And back and forth the clattering branches sway.

And when from frozen skies the pure snows fall
In large white flakes that softly mantle all
The loaded branches stoop without a sound
Till their green leaf-tips almost touch the ground.

Then, when they seem a kind of crystal tree
Sparkling with diamond buds and silvery
Shoots, by the snowflakes' overburdening
And their own patience freed, the lithe boughs spring

Up, and in powdery showers the white snow flies
Flung by the wind across the freezing skies,
While, as the bamboos dance in wind and rain,
Like stars the bunched leaves twinkle forth again.

Hence, among branched things I for beauty choose
The yellowness and slimness of bamboos,
Which taught me, more than what in books is writ,
That life is conquered when we yield to it.

RHYMED HAIKU

On the blue hill-side
Village fires like orange jewels
Gleam at eventide.

MOUNTAINS

Golden in laughing sunlight,
Silver in mist and rain,
I see thee, mighty mountains,
Tower heavenward from the plain,

And pray my heart unmoved by
Sweet joys or sufferings dire,
Like thee through cloud and sunlight
May upward still aspire.

'WHITE MIST DRIFTS DOWN THE VALLEY DIM…'

White mist drifts down the valley dim,
Then spreads and rises noiselessly,
And the blue hill-tops seem to swim
Like islands in a spectral sea.

Swiftly the silver edges rise
Until the white waves overflow
The shadowy hills, and with the skies
Make one vast sheet as though of snow.

One moment all the world seems white,
A pearly whiteness tinged with blue,
Till the fierce storm-gods rush and smite
That sea of massing clouds in two.

Oh when, with darkness overhead,
In two vast waves they roll apart,
A river like a silver thread
Gleams in the valley's azure heart.

STANZAS

Let my life burn like incense
Before Thy precious shrine,
Consuming, for Thy Doctrine's sake,
All thought of 'I' and 'mine';

That from its smouldering selfhood
May rise up unalloyed
The white cloud of compassion –
Pure perfume of the Void.

THE GARDENER

The gardener crops his rose-tree's hundred buds,
That when it grows
Rich with the breath of Summer, it may bear
One perfect rose.

And even so I prune my budding thoughts,
That in me should
Spring sweetly forth the single perfect bloom
Of Buddhahood.

KANCHENJUNGA

One white wave of snow
Towering against the blue
Sky, with clouds below.

RHYMED HAIKU

Below in the deep
Blue valleys the white clouds
Are lying asleep.

THE BODHISATTVA

Because I could not muse apart
In world-oblivious ecstasy,
But felt like fire-drops on my heart
The tears of all humanity,
I cast aside that source of pride
The glittering robe of selfish peace,
And donned the dress of painfulness
Until all others' pain should cease.

In house and market, shop and cell,
Wherever men in bondage be,
Yes, in the very depth of Hell,
My puissant pity sets them free.
Nor shall I cease to strive for peace
Till every trembling blade of grass
That feels with pain the sting of rain
Into Nirvāṇa's bliss shall pass.

Let me endure unending pains,
Drain to the dregs grief's bitterest cup;
While one unhappy life remains
My own I cannot render up.
Nirvāṇa's joy would only cloy
Should it to me alone befall:
Closed evermore Nirvāṇa's door
Unless I enter last of all!

LIFE'S FURNACE

As bellows roar, and red coals glow,
And softened silver slowly bends,
Deft chisels, glancing to and fro,
Are fashioning use to beauty's ends.

Life's furnace flames, shower sparks of ill,
In pain the heart doth burn and glow,
As the keen chisel of the will
Shapes final good from passing woe.

FRUSTRATION

Love finds no fulfilment,
Its bitter-sweet
Fragrance no flower – no path
Its blindly wandering feet.

Only shrivelled buds in
An empty tomb,
A vase for tears – a star
Extinguished by the gloom.

TRANSIENCE

The world is full of falling leaves,
Of wistful things that come and go –
Flights of swallows through the skies,
Footprints of starlings in the snow.

Only one day the Summer rose
Across our path her scent can fling;
Not long the Autumn lily blooms,
Not long the crocus of the Spring.

INACCESSIBLE

I saw one misty morning
An orchid on a tree,
And like a flute of silver
Its blossoms called to me.

The plaintive cry of beauty
That mid decay is born
I heard there standing breast-deep
In sparkling dews of dawn,

And longed to pluck those mauve sprays
(Too high, alas, for me!)
From the shadow-weaving branches
Of that old and moss-draped tree.

'THE ASHES OF ALL MY HEARTACHES...'

The ashes of all my heartaches,
The dust of a hundred dreams,
Are swept away in an instant
When forth one white peak gleams.

After long storm and struggle,
My heart with quietness fills
At the curve of this jade-green river,
The sweep of these dark blue hills.

LOVE'S AUSTERITY

How sweet is love's austerity,
How fiercely sweet, when it denies
My hands the bliss of touching thee,
The heaven of looking to mine eyes.

With no more sweets to seek and find
Love wanes as bright full moon above;
But this harsh abstinence shall grind
A finer point upon my love.

A point so fine, an aim so true,
Upon my passion shall there be,
That it will pierce like lightning through
The veiled heart of Reality.

'IT IS NOT LOVE THAT SEEKS TO BIND…'

It is not love that seeks to bind
Two bodies in a fierce embrace;
Nor love, true love, that dreams to find
The highest beauty in a face.

Love soars beyond the scathe of hands,
Outstrips a face, and is employed
Where it both sees and understands
A Beauty without form and void.

THE EVENING WALK

We walked where thick green bamboo groves
Point down their speary leaves,
Feeling the quietness of the hills,
The silence that is eve's.

The sun's last light, all flecked with gold,
Full on our path did lie,
And mountains piled up inky blue
Against a pale green sky.

How strange, that when night's first white star
Burned through the heavens wide,
My heart should be so lonely, though
My love walked at my side!

BAMBOO ORCHIDS

With slender rosy stem
And long green leaves thrust out
Pink orchids violet-lipped
Stand poised as though for dance
Upon the gnarled tree's fork.

So fairy-like, so frail,
With long green trailing leaves,
So like a butterfly
Each exquisite rare bloom,
We half expect to see
Them flutter and fly away.

GOLDFISH

In the dim green stillness of the pool
There is a redness as of gold
Flashing among the dark brown weeds,
Glimmer on glimmer, bright but cold,
Of the black-finned goldfish beautiful
That breathe down there where the lotus breeds.

Deep in the ocean of my soul
Flickers an anguish red as fire,
Twining among my oozy thoughts,
Glimmer on glimmer of hot desire
Leaping and sparkling beyond control
In the darkness there where the heart contorts.

As the fish that rises for grub or fly
May be laid gasping-golden on sand-strewn shore,
And glimmer no more in the dim green dawn
Of waters where lily and lotus lie,
So the fierce red love that racks me sore
May be laid on the bank of the harsh world's scorn

If up to the surface it should swim
For the grub of words or the fly of phrase
From where like the glimmer of fish in shoal
Now through the dark brown weeds it plays
With a ruby redness, a faint fierce gleam
In the dark green depths of my innermost soul.

THE SECRET

Roll on, roll on for ever,
Thou Wheel of Death and Birth –
Build up another Heaven,
Spread out another Earth,
Where men may reap the harvest
Of deeds done ill or well,
Scoop out a place of torment,
Hollow another Hell –
Lift to the heights or hurl me
Sheer down the steep abyss;
I shall not laugh for that,
I shall not weep for this.
Who knows this wondrous secret
Has naught to seek or shun:
That the pain of the Wheel of Death and Birth
And Nirvāṇa's peace are one.

'MANY WERE THE FRIENDS…'

I
Many were the friends who sought with eager hands to lay hold of me
    as I passed along the way;
But I have shaken them all off and come with lonely longing to the
    door of my Friend.
Many were the flowers that blossomed around me in the garden where
    I strayed;
But I have sought out the White Rose while it was still bright with
    morning dew.
Many were the instruments I heard playing in the symphony of life;
But I have cared to listen only to the melancholy sweetness of Thy
    flute beneath the stars.

II
When the dawn wings like a great golden bird from the East,
In the cool of early morning, beside the pine trees,
    I wait for Thee....
When the sun hangs poised like a red flamingo in the heavens,
In the quivering heat of noon, wrapped in the mauve-blue mist of the jacaranda,
I wait for Thee....
When the pale moon breasts the sky like a silver swan on a blue lake,
    In the lone garden of my dreams, beneath the wide-spreading branches of the Tree of Life,
I wait for Thee....
While youth comes and goes, while manhood waxes and wanes as the moon,
In the midst of the world's tumult, and in the deep silence of my heart,
    Through life and through death, through the birth and dissolution of millions of universes, eternally
I wait for Thee....

III
When will He come?
When will the dust of my life blossom beneath the invincible ardour of His footsteps?
When will the ashes of my heart flame beneath the all-enkindling touch of His hands?
O listen! By day the tall grass whispers to the listless trees,
    When will He come?
And all night the jasmine murmurs to the stars,
    When will He come?
But day and night I make question of the heavens and the earth,
    When will He come? When will He come? When will He come?

YASHODHARA[60]
After the Painting by W. S. Bagdatopulos

Though rained thy kisses on His hand
Beneath the soft faint light
Of golden lamps, thy Lord slept on
Through the rich violet night.

The crimson flowers that round thy bed
Were scattered heedlessly,
Lay flung, although so beautiful,
Forgotten there – like thee.

With watching and with longing tired
You slept at last upon
Your soft white breasts, and dreamed till dawn
Rose drear – and He was gone.

QUATRAIN

What a fantastic creature is the poet,
Who in his quiet secluded garden sits
Musing upon a flower, while any minute
An Atom Bomb may blow the world to bits!

THE ROOT SPEAKS   1951

Mock me not, O Rose, that I am hidden
Here in the black soil. The sap descends
In Autumn with the long tale of thy Summer beauty
And I know all thy ways. Oh mock me not
That my roots are hidden in the earth, that I love the earth
With its moist smell of rotting leaves and its decayedness.
Mock me not that my friends are all children of uncleanness
And my loves the daughters of earth. I have heard report
Of your pure white beauty bediamonded with drops of dew,
And of how you stand stately and aloof among your leaves and thorns.
The stars are all on fire for you,
And the moon maddened by your beauty.
Oh mock me not that I am ugly and twisted and black.
I am out of your sight. Why should you mock me?
But tell me, Whence comes the sap that invigorates your veins,
And the beauty that blushes in every petal?
Does it not come with the ascending sap in Spring?
Comes it not through these roots, from this dank black soil,
From these rotting leaves, this decayedness, this uncleanness –
Out of urine and ordure? So mock me not,
O Rose, nor be ashamed of your father the Root
Before the faces of your friends, the Stars.

LONGING

For the Boundless, the Unlimited, the Infinite I long.
Unfold the wings of my heart like the wings of a bird in song
At the midmost arch of the sky, in the full blue blaze of day,
When the ear can hear its note, though the eye tracks not its way.

For the height of the Beyondless, All-Transcending, do I yearn.
My heart's desire flames upward, as the red fires upward burn
From the earth's fierce fiery centre, through the cold grey crust that
    bars
Life's journey up the Milky Way, love's flight among the stars.

'FORGIVE ME IF I HAVE STAINED…'

Forgive me if I have stained
Your beauty with my desire,
Or troubled your clear serene
Light with my fury of fire.
Forgive me; let us be friends.

Forgive me if I have looked
For response that you could not give,
Or raised in the deeps of my heart
This red rose too sickly to live.
Forgive me; let us be friends.

THE HEART'S NO

Brain says, Beauty will perish,
Flake on flake, like the snow,
Leave but a pool of wan water
That you may see and know
How grey you have grown with dreaming –
But still the heart sings 'No'.

Head says, loving is folly,
And only the cold are wise,
Who have sealed up Love's mouth of music,
Put out his burning eyes,
And turned him loose in the desert –
But the heart still 'No' replies.

LINES

I questioned, in my greener age,
Whether it were best for me
To blossom Poet or burgeon Sage;
But now in riper days I see,
And with what gladness know it:
The Poet is the truest Sage,
The Sage the sweetest Poet –
The piper his own best tune;
And laugh that I could ever
Have striven thus to sever
The moonlight from the moon.

SONG

Tread softly as a cat
Uncoiling from the mat
In quest of prey;
For who treads soft goes far,
E'en to the Morning Star
And Milky Way.

But tread most softly when
You have to do with men
Of simple parts;
For, if truth were said,
All unawares you tread
Upon their hearts.

LUMBINI

I remember a pool of blue lotuses
Blooming at Lumbini near the dusty highroad,
And the miracle of those blue flowers rising
So purely from the black waters, told me
Far more of the birth of the Enlightened One
Than the broken Ashoka column, or ruined shrine.

PLATO'S REPLY[61]

'All dreams of the soul
End in a beautiful man's or woman's body.'
       W. B. YEATS

That is all very well ...
But the bodies of your beautiful man and woman
Must one day grow old –
Yea, though they had walked about all their lives
With limbs of gold.
One day they must perish and then the dead are
Most grey and cold –
But not so cold and grey as the dreams that have ended in them,
No, nor so old.

But if the beautiful man's or woman's body
End in a dream
Of Beauty Itself, the Shine behind the shadows
Of things that seem,
That perishing bodily beauty will the Eternal
Beauty redeem,
And keep it alive in the soul like a dream folded
Within a dream.

ANIMIST

I feel like going on my knees
To this old mountain and these trees.
Three or four thousand years ago
I could have worshipped them, I know.
But if one did so in this age
They'd lock him in a padded cage.
We've made the world look mean and small
And lost the wonder of it all.

MAITREYA

Lost in these yellowing Autumn woods, I see
A Buddha seated under every tree;
And each white peak, and each dark violet hill,
Seems a giant Buddha meditating still.
So poised this earth, so quiet its sky above,
They seem like Maitreya deep in thoughts of love.

RHYMED HAIKU

Autumn clouds, like snow
In Summer, drift the way
We all must go.

RHYMED HAIKU

Oh darkness is done
And snow-peaks catch crimson
The smile of the sun!

RHYMED HAIKU

How still the mists lie
Growing deeper till hills are
As blue as the sky!

RHYMED HAIKU

On the hillside wait
Clouds calm as my thoughts
And as intimate.

RHYMED HAIKU

Dawn brightening
Across the sky like the unfolding of
A sunbird's wing!

BUFFALOES BEING DRIVEN TO MARKET — 1952

We know when market-day is near,
For village folk to vend their store,
Because the blue-grey buffaloes
Are driven in the night before.

With long-lashed eyes, and massive horns
Low-curving from each patient head,
They shuffle sadly up the road,
Dusty, and lowing to be fed.

Their drivers, shouting from the rear,
Urge them with blows to left or right,
And, mindful of the broad red sun,
Make haste before the fall of night.

One evening, as I watched them pass,
My heart was heavy for their kind,
To see how slowly one great beast
Limped painfully along behind.

Slowly he moved, and slower yet,
Despite their whip and blood-stained goad,
Till, sagging at the knees, he dropped
On the sere grass beside the road.

He tossed his patient head; I saw
The deep blue eyes were glazed with pain.
Though shivering in a storm of blows
He could not rise and walk again.

And as the darkness fell, I mused
That simple folk who sell and buy
Could herd him to the butcher's shed,
Yet could not let him rest and die.

THE CHARCOAL-BURNERS

Once more the deep blue Winter skies
Dissolve in tenderest green;
Once more in purple shadow rise
The hills; once more is seen
Eve's first faint star; and lo, once more
The charcoal-burners pass my door.

First gnarled old men, then cheerful boys,
With young men in the pride
And blush of opening manhood's joys,
Plod up the mountain-side;
And after, sharing all they do,
Red-shawled, blue-skirted women too.

Up the long, winding mountain road,
With naked, sturdy limbs,
Each bears his black, dull-gleaming load,
Before the red light dims;
With broad, bowed backs, and labouring breath,
Like lost souls on the road to death.

The sweat-drops tell how far away
That world where fancy sees
The glooms wherein they heard all day
A noise of falling trees;
And saw, to charcoal slowly turning,
The beauty of the forest burning.

What tongue can tell, what happy flight
Of fancy e'er discover,
How many trees that loved the light
Were stricken from their lover;
How many forests filled with breath
Charred into hideousness and death.

Year after year, this mountain road
Remorseless will they tread,
Like death's own self, with ghastly load,
Till the forests are all dead;
Like man himself, that will not cease
Till he has ruined Nature's peace.

TIBETAN TRUMPETS

Knit with my heart these trumpets seem
That deeply sound from hill to hill;
Booming through mist so mournfully,
Holding their note of pain, until
With its reverberation loud
The sympathetic valleys fill.

Groaning their sorrows out, all night
Far off the giant trumpets play;
But the deep thunder of their grief
Resounds within my heart all day –
Type of the anguish of mankind
Rolling among life's hills for aye.

NO WORD

Some men can find no word for Love:
What Truth is, none could ever say.
But I, this day,

Though searching, for the beauty of
A bamboo by the breezes stirred
Can find no word.

'UP AND DOWN THE GRAVEL PATH...'[62]

Up and down the gravel path,
Between the flowering trees,
I've walked this Summer afternoon
To give my spirit ease.

I could not idly stand, nor sit
Upon the grassy ground,
For like a mill-wheel in my head
The thoughts flew round and round.

Oh thoughts of life and thoughts of death
Chased thoughts of love and pain
Like golden hawk and sable dove
Inside my reeling brain.

The withered hopes like wind-whirled leaves
Thick on my heart did come,
With dreads like shapes that dance for blood
About the sorcerer's drum.

So up and down the shadowy paths,
Between the moon-white trees,
Through pools of silver, I must walk
To give my spirit ease.

QUATRAIN

Walking along the mountain paths,
A pink-white cloud I saw appear
Floating athwart the trees – the first
Wild cherry-blossom of the year.

HIEROGLYPHICS

Sun, moon, the mountains and the plain,
The silvered ocean's ceaseless roll,
With all four seasons in their round,
Are hieroglyphics of the soul.

And that is why yon Evening Star
Can script the secret of my breast,
And hang, an unshed burning tear,
On the wan visage of the West.

'I THINK THERE LIVES MORE WISDOM…'

I think there lives more wisdom
In what the poets write
Than all the scribbling fingers
Of sages could indite,
With doubt and speculation
Troubling the starry night.

I think there shines more charity
From wretched broken hut
Or hovel than from churches
And sects where hearts are shut,
Whose rule and motto seems to be
'We must love our neighbours – but …'

Therefore a poet
And a poor man will I be,
Loving my neighbour as myself,
Of wealth and wisdom free;
And from sages, sects and churches,
Good Lord, deliver me.

SUMMER AFTERNOON

Now it is early summer, and the woods
Ring all day with the cuckoo's double cry;
The heat grows week by week, and from the blue
Intolerable heavens beats the sun
Fiercer and fiercer on the huge red flowers
That droop among the grasses; dragonflies
In their bright sapphire mail hang glitteringly
Upon the fountain's edge, four gauze wings poised
For instant flight. At peace amid the sights
And sounds of nature, with a drowsy cat
Limp on my knee, and an unheeded book
Of poems slipping down into my lap
Unread, I dream away the quiet hours.

THE POET'S EYE

Though veil on veil of gleaming blue
Translucence o'er the hills is furled,
The poet's eye sinks through and through
Deep as the beauty of the world;

Deep as the Truth all men desire
He plumbs, and then his vision sings
With lightning glance that sets afire
The poetry of common things.

MAN'S WAY

The red rose does not whisper
'What loveliness is mine!'
Nor the sun upon his azure tower
Cry out 'Behold, I shine!'
Yet some poor mortal women,
By passion crazed or worse,
Can flaunt a rag of beauty

O'er half the universe;
And men no whit the better
Think that if they but frown
A cloud will darken heaven
And the stars come raining down.
Even the ragged goose-girl
Preens as her bare feet pass
By her face's muddied image
In the rain-filled rut, her glass;
While the young wretch, her brother,
Leaps toward her with a gun
And a dead crow, shouting joyfully
'Oh look what I have done!'

'IN THE WOODS ARE MANY MORE'

Selling wild orchids at my door one day
A man said, 'In the woods are many more....
Deep in the gloom, high on the thickset trees,
Wild orchids hang like clouds of butterflies,
Golden and white, spotted with red and black,
As huge as birds, or tiny as a bee,
Wild orchids which no eye has ever seen
Save ours, who wander in these rich green glooms
All day throughout the year.' I bought his sprays,
Paid him, and bore them in; and as I went
My eyes by chance fell on a shelf of books, –
The Buddha's Teachings, – and thereafter glanced
Up to the Buddha's image as He smiled
Above them from the alcove. Strange it was
That, as my eyes from book to image passed,
Dwelling an instant on that calm, pure Face,
There, with the frail cold blossoms in my hands,
The words that man spoke at my door should ring
Through my stilled heart again and yet again
Like music – 'In the woods are many more....'

HAIKU

Water falls from stone
To mossy stone trickling
Down deep cool ravines.

HAIKU

White clouds on the hills
Linger a while, then vanish
In the blue distance.

THE SURVIVOR

The loose red earth is washed away,
At once the storm-swept hills are bare;
Gaunt trees fall crashing down the slopes,
And sodden leaves stick everywhere.

Day after day the rains drummed down,
Nor sturdiest growth could meet the shock,
Save one frail bush, with scarlet flowers,
Whose root had pierced the stubborn rock.

LINES

Men think that they have understood,
When, at some rose or butterfly
Which they have sighted in a wood,
They fling some gross latinity.
O empty heads, O hearts in folly old,
To dream the truth of things could thus be told!

MANIFESTO[63]

I'll write my poems for my friends,
For those who love me. Why to waste
Long hours in studying schools and trends,
For what would suit the public's taste?

These rocks shall be my publisher;
I'll raise a column in the sun,
And, like Ashoke, that faith aver,
Which made my heart's torn empire one.

Or else, when other Muse conceives,
I'll scatter, subtly Sibylline,
My love upon the forest leaves,
On every leaf one burning line.

AWAKENING

Often do I remember the huge untidy nests
Of peacocks on the Ganges' silver shore,
Built in the forks of gnarled and stunted trees
Among the red flowers of the oleander;
Often remember with what beauty streamed
The long tail feathers of the sitting bird
Over the edge, and almost to the ground;
Often remember all those moonlit nights,
When swifter than a dream the river fled,
Riddled with silver, through its ghostly banks,
While in the heaven of heavens above us marched
Bright squadrons of innumerable stars;
Often remember the coming of the dawn,
The first faint silver in the east, the glow
Of rose-gold light among the pale green trees,
The coolness, and the stir of things from sleep;
Often remember, through my dreams, that world
Of beauty shattered by a peacock's raucous cry.

A RAINY DAY IN THE MOUNTAINS

The rain has been falling all day; the maize-fields are sodden and brown;
The green lush growth of the garden is matted and beaten down;
The hills round their bare blue shoulders draw closer their mantles grey,
And the sun gleams through like a pearl, but so faintly it scarce seems day.

Yet the road that winds up from the valley is thronged with market-folk;
White bulls draw the creaking waggons, lurching beneath the yoke;
With wet brown limbs plod the coolies, bearing their loads from the plain,
While the women hurry behind them, red-shawled from the streaming rain.

I have watched all day at the window, while strange thoughts came and went
As I mused on the life of the mountains, wherewith mine own seems blent;
And I glimpsed through the rain-dark heavens a cloudless Autumn sky,
While the mists round the mountains' loins hid no secret from mine eye.

Deeper the life of the mountains, oh richer and grander far,
Than the huddled life of the cities, where the mushroom hovels are,
Where no change of tint in Autumn, no show of leaf in Spring,
Brightens the dusty wayside trees where bird ne'er hops to sing.

But the cheerless day is ending, and the rains have almost done;
Creeps with the lengthening shadows a redness round the sun;
With eve-gilt limbs, with baskets of charcoal, rice and corn,
In the shadow of the mountains plod on the mountain-born.

RECIPROCITY

The surest way of gaining is to give.
To learn a secret, tell one of your own.
How often lovers, wishing to find out
If the beloved loved or not, have said
'I love you', waiting what seemed endless minutes
To hear those three words echoed back again.
Loving means giving, just as dawn means day,
So that to say 'I love', means 'I will give',
And to find out if the beloved loves
Means to find out if he or she will give
What we desire to have. This subtle key
Unlocks full many a time life's fast-closed doors.
Poet or painter gazes at a flower,
Mountain or stream, or any living form,
Until he falls in love with it, and gains
Its heart by the surrender of his own, –
Till he can re-create, not what he saw,
But that which he experienced and became.
Giving his heart to Truth, the devotee
Wins in return the sacred heart of Truth,
And keeping nothing for himself, gains all.
Selfish and secretive can ne'er believe
The surest way of gaining is to give,
Nor learn life's secret, holding fast their own.

THE ABOMINABLE SNOWMAN

I

Where the ice glitters, where untrodden snows
Stretch soft and soundless, where a frore wind blows,
The Abominable Snowman comes and goes.

Oft the lone mountaineer, through a swarm
Of snowflakes whose white dance presages storm,
Has glimpsed the naked giant's fearful form.

While oft the hermit, solitary quite,
Has heard him howling all a Winter's night,
And tow'rd the monster winged a shaft of Light.

But whether these be tales or no, by day –
A thing of dread for all who pass that way,
Deep in the snow the giant Footprints splay.

II

Appear, as soon as newspapers are able
To send reporters, photos of the fable;
And hot words flow at many a breakfast-table.

Pundits in London, Paris and Berlin
Let loose at once a loud but learned din,
All arguing, not for Truth, but just to win.

'I'm sure there must have been a bear about!'
'Nonsense, a monkey's paw, without a doubt!'
'A human footprint by the wind splayed out!'

Pamphlets fly back and forth, as Doctor D.
Refutes Professor M., though all agree
A Snowman's footprint it could *never* be.

III
Yet still, despite a hundred learned Noes,
O'er shining glaciers, through unruffled snows,
The legendary Creature comes and goes.

But even if one day the truth came out
That it was ape or bear they'd fussed about
I should not think my faith had suffered rout.

Nor could I share the gleeful scholar's pride
That, thanks to Science, another myth had died,
And one more fact been neatly classified.

Rather than one of that all-knowing band
I'd be a Sherpa or Tibetan, and
Believe there are some things we *don't* understand.

1953 TRANSFORMATION

No fruit without the seed. Desire
Has flowered into a star tonight.
By subtle alchemies my fire
Turns heatless, and shines forth as light.

From link to link th' enchainment grows
That each to all and all to each
Doth bind, – the ordure to the rose;
Height mates with Depth, while thought to speech

Leaps as a lover to his love.
Oh fools who strive to separate
Below from the embraces of Above,

Wisdom from Beauty, if the seed's destroyed
Where are the flowers that ye would consecrate?
Ye know not the great mystery of the Void.

ARGOSIES

A solitary boy would sail his boat
All day in a green pool, where willows wept
Over the stony verge, and sadly trailed
Their slim green leaves along the water's face.
Only the bright-eyed ducks with blue-barred wings,
And small black waterfowl with scarlet eyes,
Saw him, as, racing half way round the pool,
With eager eyes he waited for his joy
To steer towards him from the other side.
Oh how like a white swan it seemed to cut
Through the clear water, tilting as the breeze
Leaned on the silver sails, until it dipped, –
So gracefully, – one white wing in the waves!
Now like a crescent moon its sharp prow cleaves
The cloudy shallows, where dead yellow leaves
And floating sticks impede its passage, and
It drifts into the small exultant hands
Outstretched towards it. With what ecstasy
Did that boy, more than twenty years ago,
Sail his white boat on that green pool! – Oh why?
Was to his infant soul obscurely given,
Beneath the brown shade of the willow trees,
Foreknowledge of those argosies which now
Loom white-winged o'er him from the deeps of life?

TAKING REFUGE IN THE BUDDHA
N'atthi me saraṇaṃ aññaṃ
Buddho me saraṇaṃ varaṃ

Not where the gardens blossom;
Not where the fountains rise
In plumes of trembling whiteness
To the blue of sunlit skies;
Not where the forests murmur;
Not where the rivers meet;
Not where the mountains ponder:
– My place is at Thy Feet.

Not where the spring Castalian
Spreads glimmering as it gropes
Through the ever-living laurels
That throng Parnassus' slopes;
Not where the Nine still follow
With dance and chorus sweet
In the footsteps of Apollo:
– My place is at Thy Feet.

Not where the armies muster;
Not where the trumpet calls
To the legions as they glitter
Beneath beleaguered walls;
Not where the vultures gather;
Not where the ravens eat;
Not where the nations wrangle:
– My place is at Thy Feet.

Not in the preacher's pulpit;
Not in the scholar's chair;
Not where the lawyer chambers
With lies and musty air;
Not on the throne of judgement;
Not in the scorner's seat;
Not at the merchant's counter:
– My place is at Thy Feet.

Not where the gaunt Cross rises;
Not where the Crescent shines
Like a drawn blade in the heavens;
Not where the Gopi pines;
Not where the organ thunders;
Not where the tom-toms beat;
Not where the conch is wailing:
– My place is at Thy Feet.

Not where the gold spire flashes
Against blue sun-drenched skies;
Not where the vestments dazzle;
Not where the prayers arise;
Not where the incense thickens;
Not where the priests repeat
Dead words they do not understand:
– My place is at Thy Feet.

Not in Nirvāṇa's stillness;
Not in Saṃsāra's flow;
Not in the heavens above us;
Not in the hells below;
Not in thought or word or action;
Not where mind and object meet:
– With Wisdom and Compassion
My place is at Thy Feet.

THE TREE OF WISDOM
A Poem for Wesak

All pleasures of all sense; the fickle mind's
Delight in idle thought; attachment strong
To child and wife, to pomp and luxury
And empire, dropped away like withered husks,
Till only a naked love for all mankind
Was left Him, as a heart within His heart.
This love He scattered seedlike on the rocks
Of penance, where the thorny cactus grew
Sere in the blistering sun; but all He reaped
In that harsh field was pain, while through a mist
As though of blood He saw around Him men
Whose arms, stretched motionless above their heads,
Were like the dead boughs of a withered tree
Blasted by lightning; others in the midst
Of four bright fires, the sun in heaven for fifth,
Squatting in filth and nakedness He saw;
While smeared with dust and ashes others crouched
Beastlike at roots of trees, or hung like bats
Head downward from the branches, or like dogs
Ravened on ordure, hoping thus (vain hope!)
To conquer heav'n, or stay their minds on peace.
Then darkness fell, and ringing in His ears
A voice came, like a peal of jangling bells
Clanging out doubts, and then a silence, till
After He knew not how long nothingness,
The trickle of warm milk between His lips
As the goat straddled, and the neatherd pressed
The new life drop by drop into His own,
So that the loveseed nestling in His heart
Swelled quickening. Then with joy He cast it down
Like a wise sower on the fertile soil
Of perfect meditation. All night long
He watched the germ burst and the young shoot climb
Up higher; the stem thicken; branches spread
More plenteously, twigs finelier, broad green leaves

Denser and darker; while the Wesak Moon
Climbed with the climbing tendrils till she stood
High in the heav'ns, and poured her silver light
Wave after wave upon the full-grown Tree
Of Wisdom, as it towered between the earth
And heavens in one white and dazzling sheet
Of radiance, glittering gem-like as it moved.
Thenceforward through a score of centuries,
That men beneath its far-flung shade might rest,
Unshakeably it stood. Love from its boughs
Dropped seedlike, and a family of Trees
Of Wisdom overshadowed half the world.
Then from the West moaned thunder, and a storm
Blackened the sky with clouds that, rolling thick
In the meridian, round its stately crown
Flung furious bolts as the bright levin-flash
In crescents and in crosses struck the Tree
Time and again, while the fanátic winds
Howled round the pillared trunk and, tugging, strove
To drag its ancient boughs down, or pluck out
Those roots that through a hundred thousand lives
Mined dragonwise, and coiled round mighty stones
Far in the depths of being. But the Tree
Firm as the ponderous axle of the world
Stood until morning, with its family
Of trees, though somewhat shorn of leaves, with here
A rotten branch down, there a sapling split,
Fronting the clear sky like a giant refreshed
By dreams of battle. Oh drop down again,
O seed of love, upon the storm-scarred earth,
Drop richly from those fruitful boughs, and plant
Fresh families more thick and tall and fair
Than she has known before, that all her graves
May turn to greenness, all her blood to beauty.
Plant every valley, every hillside slope
And bouldered mountain; plant the yellow sands;
Plant the five continents to their coasts, until
The seas are overarched, the ocean spanned

With many-pillared leafage, and the Trees
Of Wisdom, overshadowing all the world,
Spread wide and deep and cool their shade, that man
May rest beneath them, even as the Lord
Beneath His Tree on that first Wesak Morn
Rested, and knew that the long quest was done!

THE MODERN BARD

We cannot sing as Orpheus wist
To sing upon the hills of Thrace
When the beloved, serpent-kissed
To death, is snatched from our embrace.

Profounder hells than Orpheus knew
We've plumbed, and yet we cannot sing
Persephone and Dis so true,
So sweet, so wonderful a thing

As Orpheus sang in those dim halls,
By that still stream, with eager breath;
'Twixt our Inferno's brick-built walls
Love never triumphed over death.

And even when we've stumbled out,
Too sick for mirth, and have been torn
In pieces by the wild-beast rout
And man and music wildly borne

Down some swift river's flow, and flung
Headlong into the sounding sea,
Our lyre, though it had oft-times sung
Her name, calls not 'Eurydice!'

WINTER IN THE HILLS

The icy wind has planted
Fresh roses in your cheek;
Your voice rings clear and joyous
Through the cold air as we speak.

By day the sky is bluer,
By night the fire more red;
For coldness brings out colours
That heat could ne'er have bred.

Between the leafless branches
The landscape is ablaze
With green and gold and scarlet
All the short bright winter days.

When youth and beauty vanish,
And death impends above,
May age but make more vivid
The colours of our love.

LOOKING AT THE MOON ON A FROSTY NIGHT

The moon is cold and hard and small
And glitters like a crystal ball;
The trees are steeped in silver light: –
Ah, what a clear-cold winter's night!

THE CONQUEST OF MĀRA

Whether within his mind dark forces rolled
Wavelike along, and dashed their bitter spume
At his enlightened dawn-skies' blue and gold;
Or whether, like a bank of clouds that loom

On the horizon's verge, presaging storm,
Black Māra and his host embattled came
With many a fearful face and hideous form,
On monsters mounted, panoplied in flame,

I know not. Fact or symbol, all I know,
Or care to know, is that the arrowy showers,
The hard-flung spears and javelins of the foe,
Touching his halo's edge, were turned to flowers

That rained all night beneath the Bodhi Tree
As though in adoration, or as though
In homage to his súpreme victory....

Flowers of the earth or thought-flowers, all I know
Is that Compassion, sunlike, can transmute
Our hate not only into flowers, but fruit.

THE PIONEER

Since that his eyes were like two wells
Wherein black waters sparkle deep
They thought him well-nigh dead, and said
His spirit could no longer keep
Firm hold of its exhausted frame,
More than on burnt-up sticks a flame.

Later, his eyes were like two stars
Glimmering at eve through dewy air
(Sujáta's gift had wrought the change),

And then they murmured one so fair
Enlightenment could hardly gain
Through comfort, who had failed through pain.

But when his eyelids drooped, half closed
At dawn, on sun-surpassing eyes,
They knew whate'er they'd thought or said
Had been to him but as the cries
Of weak-eyed bats that flit about
At evening ere the moon is out.

For one whose undimmed eye sees Truth
Like sunlight on a distant hill
Mindful of that alone must fare,
Deaf and blind to all else, until
Dawns in his face, grief's long night spent,
The sun-smile of enlightenment.

SONNET

Oh Death himself was Orpheus' audience!
And Death's pale consort, on her ivory throne,
Could weep as though her heart was not a stone
As the song breathed into her buried sense
The fields of Enna and lost innocence,
And love lost, and the lyrist singing lone
Sadder and sweeter than the earth had known.
Rough beasts themselves were then his audience.

But we, tired lyrists of a tuneless age,
Soothe not the ear of Death in shadowy grot.
Death's consort sits unmoved the whole night long.
Uncharmed the red-pawed wolf and leopard rage.
Oh what to speak of Death! Life hears us not!
Or brutes, when men themselves are deaf to song!

SONNET

The thunders rolled beneath me, as I sate
On Truth's most high, cold mountain-peak alone,
Secure within the 'intellectual throne',
Ruling Thought's kingdom with Olympian state;
Open upon my knees the Book of Fate
Rattled its iron leaves madly, tempest-blown,
While, from the dim horizons of the known
I lifted up mine eyes to contemplate

The unknown Void beyond. Oh bright as dawn
The Heaven of Beauty shining there afar
I saw, and rose as wild with love and joy
As Zeus did, when his sleepless lids one morn
Saw far below him, like a fallen star,
The beauty of the fair Bithynian boy.

EPITAPH ON KRISHNA, PRINCESS IRENE'S SQUIRREL

Now he's gone, the best of squirrels,
Not ev'n his mistress can entice
His happy spirit to her shoulder
From the trees of Paradise.

ON A POLITICAL PROCESSION
Calcutta, 1953

Red-bannered hatred fills the streets
And flows from square to square,
Gathering as though in pools of blood
Around the rostrum, where
A speaker hoisted from the van
Upholds the Brotherhood of Man.

MADRIGAL

Red as roses blushing,
White as lilies paling,
Hot as Summer flushing,
Cold as Winter failing –
Love is like all weather,
Everything together.

Hoping and despairing,
Singing loud and sighing,
Smiles and frowns both wearing,
Living and yet dying –
In Love's bitter-sweet
All extremes do meet.

CERTAINTIES

The wisest doubt if Truth
Be true indeed;
But that a rose is beautiful
The world's agreed.

Whether we hold or not
Life ends in death,
That love's most bitter-sweet
Who questioneth?

Based not on dreams, but on
His certainty
Of beauty, love and pain
Man's life must be.

THE BODHISATTVA'S REPLY

What will you say to those
Whose lives spring up between
Custom and circumstance
As weeds between wet stones,
Whose lives corruptly flower
Warped from the beautiful,
Refuse and sediment
Their means of sustenance –
What will you say to them?

That woman, night after night,
Must sell her body for bread;
This boy with the well-oiled hair
And the innocence dead in his face
Must lubricate the obscene
Bodies of gross old men;
And both must be merry all day,
For thinking would make them mad –
What will you say to them?

Those dull-eyed men must tend
Machines till they become
Machines, or till they are
Cogs in the giant wheel
Of industry, producing
The clothes that they cannot wear
And the cellophaned luxury goods
They can never hope to buy –
What will you say to them?

Or these dim shadows which
Through the pale gold tropic dawn
From the outcaste village flit
Balancing on their heads
Baskets to bear away
Garbage and excrement,
Hugging the wall for fear
Of the scorn of their fellow men –
What will you say to them?

And wasted lives that litter
The streets of modern cities,
Souls like butt-ends tossed
In the gutter and trampled on,
Human refuse dumped
At the crossroads where civilization
And civilization meet
To breed the unbeautiful –
What will you say to them?

'I shall say nothing, but only
Fold in Compassion's arms
Their frailty till it becomes
Strong with my strength, their limbs
Bright with my beauty, their souls
With my wisdom luminous, or
Till I have become like them
A seed between wet stones
Of custom and circumstance.'

CALCUTTA

How can wracked soul and ruined body pass
Their days in this grey city, year by year?
Street after street without a blade of grass!
Face upon face and not a smile or tear!

IMMENSITIES

Round this boundless universe's
Unseen axle, night and day,
Roll in clouds the bright star-clusters
Billion trillion miles away –

Wheel the great galactic systems
Whose immensities appal;
But the Wisdom of the Buddha
Has plumbed and measured all.

Spinning round this dire becoming's
Nave of ignorance, desire
And hate, our lives whirl madly
Like sparks of crimson fire –

Scarlet rings of pain and anguish
That to gods and men befall;
But the Buddha's great Compassion
Has embraced and conquered all.

NAGARJUNIKONDA[64]

Lines written on hearing that, under a scheme for the irrigation of the area, the ancient Buddhist site of Nagarjunikonda, so intimately associated with the career of the greatest Mahāyāna sage, was threatened with submergence.

Where hills humped, there must be
The swirl and swish of the sea
We know. But oh must man
Inaugurate Nature's plan
Before the crumbling age
Confounds in dotard rage
Solid and liquid mass?
(Continents change and pass!)
With Titan force, need he
Stretch river into sea
And bury these green graves
Of faith, far under waves?
The gaunt-framed people grow
Spectrally thin: we know
That hunger's filled and fed
Not with carved stones, but bread.
Yet (not against thy voice,
Compassion, nor by choice)
Culture drops tears and pleads
For toppled shrines in weeds
Clad, and sad sculptured stone, –
Little she has to call her own, –
And to Pity cries for pity
On Nagárjun's city,
On the ruined roofs of the wise, where
Iron wall, gold stair
Flashed sheer in the sun. Oh let
Wisdom, Compassion's dam, be honoured yet,
And, like long buried seed,
In earth-womb stir, leap, breed,
Till branched o'er Deccan plain
Broods the Dragon Tree again.

1954 THE VASE OF MOONLIGHT

Your beauty, in repose, is like a vase
Of jasper or white jade with moonlight filled;
Your smiling is as though the moonlight spilled;
Your laugh, its shivering into a thousand stars.

A movement is as though the jewels within
Had fountained, or run sparkling like a stream;
Your sleeping is as though the heavenly gleam
Had found a soft white cloud to harbour in.

Your loving is as though the moonlight poured
In one bright stream from your vase into mine,
Whose earthen lip dare greet not crystal thine;
Your faithfulness is moonlight sealed and stored.

But melancholy makes you sapphirine,
O Vase of all my joys, and endless yearning
As though it were an evening sky is turning
Your moonlight into palest, purest green.

THE STREAM OF STARS

The stream of my desire no more
Rolls through the muddy fields of earth;
Between the azure banks of heaven
A stream of stars has come to birth.

No more on my soul's current float
Dead leaves from wind-dishevelled trees;
But swanlike, many a shining boat
Bends low before the heavenly breeze.

The fountains of my heart no more
Ooze slow into some stagnant place,
But in great tranquil rivers pour
Into the boundless sea of space.

NOCTURNE
Calcutta, 1954

Grey sleepers, wrapped in noisome rags,
Lay stretched out on the paving stones
As through the silence of the streets
We walked, and talked in quiet tones.

Against black walls belatedly
Old beggars crouched with rusty tins;
Rummaged the famished dogs and cats
Through overflowing garbage bins.

Sometimes a taxi, creeping past,
Purred to us of debauch's lair,
While blue and red the neon lights
Burned through the smoke-filled city air.

Our theme was friendship, beauty, art,…
And as we thrid those streets, despite
Their squalor, in the moon, all round
We saw the beauty of the night.

JOY IN FLIGHT

How like a bird it comes and goes,
This joy, this sudden rapt ascension
Where knowledge pure as nectar flows
Beyond all earthly apprehension;

How like an eagle, whose descent
At noon upon the sleepy fold
Is as though wrath Olympian sent
A thunderbolt new-fledged with gold;

How like a gull, whose lonely flight
Must span a thousand leagues of foam
And breaking billows infinite
Before it ends in rest and home;

How like – when thought and image fail
As clouds wind-scattered from the moon –
The glorious unseen nightingale
That sings in leafy woods of June!

THE GREAT WORK

With grey-green fir and blue-black pine communing,
With tulip-tree and smooth camellia, – where
The last dark red and first white rose are blooming,
I sit, reclining in my cane armchair.

Head propped on hand, from dawn to dusk the garden,
Through sparse leaves peering with a thousand eyes,
Beholds me as I watch the sunbeams harden
And eve drip coldly from the wintry skies.

Day after day, beside my friend the mountain
I sit, and as in dream hear close at hand
My neighbours, tall bamboo and bubbling fountain,
Talking in words that I half understand.

Not indolence or ennui, soul-destroyers,
Nor sickness convalescent, holds me here,
But the Great Work, which to all mere enjoyers
Of 'doing' must as idleness appear.

But if against the sun you ever lifted
Red wine or emerald water in a bowl,
You'll know, recalling how their dregs were sifted,
I clear the turbid liquid of my soul.

And since in those dark waters still is lying
Thick sediment uncleared, so many days
Musing I sit, till, slowly purifying,
Shine through them as through crystal the sun's rays.

LINES

Between the mountain-crest and valley hung
A rainbow fragment, yellow, red and blue,
The iridescent child of light and rain,
And as I saw it from the height above
It seemed a symbol of my life, which gleams
Half way between the heavens and the earth
Rich with the rose of friendship, blue of art,
And glorious yellow of religious lore –
A rainbow fragment that one moment shines
And then dissolves in natal light and rain,
Until, as I believe, a purer heaven
Sees its unbroken circle shine serene.

ELUSIVE BEAUTY[65]

Well might the Poet question
Goddess Beauty, if she keeps
Her high state in heavenly mansions
Or in the infernal deeps –
Well his heart, perplexed, grow doubtful
As he worships at her shrine
If the Power which overshadows
Be demoniac or divine.

Thousand-eyed, to see our sorrows,
Thousand-armed, for succouring grace,
The Lord of Boundless Mercy
Looks down on every place;
But Beauty's forms protean
Have hands and feet and eyes
From the carrion by the wayside
To the moon in cloudless skies.

At times she haunts the forest,
Dryad-like, with naked feet;
Sometimes stumps an old blind beggar
Down a modern city street;
We see her in our sorrows
No less bright than in our joys –
In the smile beatific of the Buddha,
And the mischievous faces of boys.

Elusive as the shadows
That on windy days we see
Racing up and down the smooth white bole
Of the eucalyptus tree,
Beauty flies, and we must follow
Till she grant at last her kiss,
Caring not, so that be given,
Be it to Heaven or the Abyss.

EPIGRAM

We who have seen men murdered,
We who have seen bombs fall,
Muse not that Beauty passes
But that she stays at all.

STANZAS

Here, through the deep dark valley,
There, o'er the snow-peaks high,
Flows the turquoise green of water,
Towers the turquoise blue of sky.

As the eye tracks, so the heart treks
Earth below and heaven above –
Plunges deep to seek out wisdom,
Soars on high in quest of love.

A CRUMB FROM THE SYMPOSIUM

Believe not what you have heard
That love is a blazing fire:
Desire's not always love,
True love is never desire.
A reveller reeling
From Plato's feast
Has cried to the Morning Star
High in the East:
Let the torch burn on:
We shall waken at morn
To loves colder and purer
Than snows or the dawn.

KALINGA[66]   1955

The third day of the slaughter saw a change;
The King no longer in his peacock tent
Cried 'Victory! Boundless now mine empire's range!'
He asked no longer how the death-roll went.

Head deep in hands, in that red dawn he sate
As stricken, and in fearful vision saw
The blackened land, the people's piteous fate,
Heaped slain, and all the ghastliness of war.

Lifting his eyes, grown sick of bloody sights,
And weary of the bloated face of Death,
He saw what gave him, after many nights
Of unquiet slumber, a more peaceful breath:

Instead of a red disc, it seemed there rolled
Across the heavens an eight-spoked Wheel of Gold.

DEFIANCE

Yet shall my soul burn upward like a fire.
Torment and sickness, penury and pain,
Shall be but as fresh fuel heaped amain
That makes the licking flame-tongues leap up higher.
Winged as an eagle shall my soul aspire
And, soaring sunlike in the sun's domain,
Scream loud defiance to the distant plain
Where creep the dull slow rivers of desire.

Or, if the flame *must* sink, my soul shall burn
In red denial underneath the white
Ash of the world, and warm the grating-bars;
Or else, an eagle wearied, it shall spurn
All but the iciest crag, and brood all night
With no companion save the wind and stars.

THE QUEST

He could not find it with his wife and child,
Nor yet beneath dark-fronded forest boughs
Where peaceful hermits grazed their placid cows
Round quiet hermitage in pastures mild;
Something they lacked, though living undefiled
By aught sublunar; bright their anchorite brows
With prescience wreathed, and yet, for all their vows,
That which He sought He found not in the wild.

Six years of penance till His eyes were dim,
And shrivelled skin clung round the brittle bone,
Wondering the Band of Five saw then befall:
He found it not with them, nor they with Him.
But when they left Him He fared on alone,
And in that loneliness He found the All.

QUATRAIN

Evening. Unstirred the western cloudlets lie
Like russet leaves in a blue lake of sky.
And in between them, silently and soon,
A gilded pinnace, glides the crescent moon.

SONNET

To Him Who on that night of sleeping flowers
Left father, mother, child, wife – everything,
And went forth from His Palace of the Spring,
Forth from the hushed zenána's inmost bowers, –
Wherein, delighting and delighted, hours
He'd passed while smooth musicians strummed the string
And sang, – into the moonlight wandering,
Be praise from men, and from the heavenly powers!

Praise, that He left the pleasantness of love,
And praise, that He renounced the path of pain;
Praise, for those nights in meditation spent
Beneath the Tree, and praise, all praise above,
That in compassion, for our bliss and gain,
He could give up His 'own' Enlightenment.

RHYMED HAIKU

After three months rain
In a million drops the sun
Shines out again.

1956 POSSIBILITIES

Our heart's a shapeless clay-lump
Whence by degrees we mould
Or Shiva's phallic emblem
Or Buddha bright with gold.

Our heart's a heap of tinder
Behind life's brazier-bars
Passion-consumed, or burning
With the ecstasy of the stars.

NĀLANDĀ REVISITED[67]

Think not, my friends, that piling stone on stone,
Or laying brick on brick, as now we must
In this degenerate age, shall from the dust
Raise up those glories which were overthrown
When, like autumnal floods, from icy zone
Islam rolled down. Oh do not too much trust
Arches that ruinate and gates that rust
To guard the Buddha's treasure for His own!

Within our minds must Nālandā arise
Before we draw up plans, or measure ground:
If the foundation on our thoughts we lay,
Calm meditation, contemplation wise,
Above mundane vicissitudes shall found
A Nālandā that cannot pass away.

QUATRAIN

I saw two men, who nailed upon a cross
A third, high on a hill, outside a town;
All three I knew: one wore a crown of thorns,
A Homburg one, and one a triple crown.

TO MAÑJUŚRĪ[68]

Lord of the Lotus, Flaming Sword, and Book,
Eternal Wisdom, Ever-Youthful One,
Dispeller of Illusion – as the sun
Packs off the clouds – with single radiant look, –
O Prince, whose pure compassion undertook
Freely, when Land-of-Snows was overrun
With evils, and the Good Law nigh undone,
Rebirth as him whose keen mind could not brook
Impurity or error, – yet once more
Descend! In this cold heart set up Thy state!
Give me Thy Lotus, spiritual rebirth;
Give me Thy Flaming Sword, that I may score
Vict'ry o'er those who darkly congregate
Against Thy Book, and drive them from the earth!

HOPE

Your sadness is my sadness, friend, and so
When yesterday I saw you, wan with grief,
I yearned to give some comfort or relief,
And thus it was, the reason of your woe,
Not merely curiously, I sought to know:
Your lofty tree of sorrows, leaf by leaf
You shed upon my breast, until in brief
Space you had covered it; naught else could grow.

What solace could I give? Yet, sipping tea
And darkly brooding o'er the future years
Half an hour later, – blessed with gleams of mirth
And friendship strengthened, – did we then not see
Shine through sun, rain, like Hope through smiles and tears,
The sev'n-hued rainbow spanning Heav'n and Earth?

THE VOICE OF SILENCE

Close, eyes; behold no more the rich array
Of forms and vivid colours. Touch, be still;
Grope not for lover's hand, or lips that will
Sting you awake to bliss by night or day.
Relish no more the scent of new-mown hay,
Or flowers, or incense, nostrils. Take your fill
Of tastes no more, O watery tongue, nor trill
Delicious notes in cadence grave or gay.

For when the senses and the sensual mind
Are laid asleep, and self itself suspended,
And naught is left to strive for or to seek,
Then, to the inmost spirit, thrice refined,
Thrice pure, before that trance sublime has ended,
With voice of thunder, will the Silence speak.

MEMORY

More than ten years ago, old Father Thames,
I saw your sluggish waters greyly glide
Washing th'Embankment on the northern side,
And on the southern lapping sodden stems
Of reeds with mud-encrusted diadems
Round crumbling steps, while up and down did ride
Trim launches, broad flat barges dignified
Piled high with huge, dull-gleaming sable gems.

More than ten years ago! Oh then it was,
Upon Westminster Bridge without a word
We stood, and saw below bright-glittering bars
Of moonlight on black water, – happy because
We were together, – and at midnight heard
How solemnly Big Ben spoke to the stars.

SONNET

Flowers, that turn their faces to the sun,
And mighty forest trees, which seem to rise,
In Autumn, like a music to the skies,
Majestically green when day is done;
Fountains that laugh in gardens, every one;
Snowpeaks, half way to Heaven, that despise
Even the rosy kisses of sunrise;
Fire, mist, white clouds, and exhalations dun, –
All these, with man's own works, – as Gothic spire
And steeple, poised and tapering minaret,
Domed stupas, ruined but majestic yet
Above tree-tops, – in universal choir
Sing out above our mortal fume and fret,
With pealing organ voice, 'O Man, aspire!'

SONNET

Work out the secret of your blood. The bright
Red drops into a ruby rosary string;
Tell on Desire's beads, importuning
With silk-smooth touch, the mantra of Delight;
Black is not always black, nor white aye white:
Yon snows, round whose purpúreal bases cling
The close-packed clouds, such colour-changes ring –
Now grey, now golden in the morning's light.

Dream not, therefore, that reddest need blush red
For ever, but as heavenliest nenuphar
From dunghill blooms, learn to distil, my son,
Wisdom divine from earth's rank lustihead,
Knowing that sunset shrouds the Evening Star,
And your life's secret and your blood's are one.

SONNET

Reading some books, you'd think the Buddha-Way,
As though macadamized, ran smooth and white,
Straight as an arrow, bill-boards left and right,
And that the yellow buses, thrice a day,
Whirled past the milestones, whose smug faces say,
'Nirvāṇa 15 miles.... By 10 tonight
You'll all be there, good people, and alight
Outside the Peace Hotel, where you're to stay.'

But those who read their own hearts, inly wise,
Know that the Way's a hacked path, roughly made
Through densest jungle, deep in the Unknown....
And that, though burn a thousand baleful eyes
Like death-lamps round, serene and unafraid,
Man through the hideous dark must plunge alone.

QUATRAIN

When Inspiration cracks the moulds of verse
The Poetry is not one whit the worse;
But when mere Theory, with hammer blows
Smashes – the result's not even prose.

STANZAS

From tone to tone of azure
The landscapes round me rise:
Blue-black are the valleys,
Ethereal blue the skies.

So may my love and passion,
That are darkness in the Abyss,
Be, in the heights of being,
All brilliance and bliss.

THE CULT OF THE YOUNG HERO[69]
Written after reading Stefan George

Do we not love the dawn, when first
Its faint streaks thread the eastern sky,
And snow peaks, greyly shadowed forth,
Flush rose and golden by and by?

Do we not love the new moon, when,
Like a young child, from cloudy bars
Released, it fingers wonderingly
The bright pure faces of the stars?

Then wherefore should we not, set free
From man's injurious hate and scorn,
Love, in the very eye of noon,

This boyish immaturity –
This beauty in its bud, its dawn,
And at the first phase of its moon?

LIFE AND DEATH
To J. E. C. and I. B. H.

Against a sky of purest turquoise rayed
The five symbolic hues, as from a sun,
While in the midst thereof sat, unafraid,
The Lord Chenrezi, the Compassionate One.

One pair of hands in taper fingers pressed
A lotus white and pearly rosary;
The other, palm to palm upon his breast,
Displayed the gesture of tranquillity.

Below, a ghastly skull, from which outcurving –
Black and obscene – two spiderish arms I saw,
With huge claw hands and talons vulturine,

Which, never from their evil purpose swerving,
A mangled human heart and cup of gore
Clutched, as the monstrous Female shrieked out 'Mine!'

TRIOLET

A sweet singing bird
In his summer array
This morning I heard
As he perched on the spray,
A sweet singing bird
With his little heart stirred
This fine morning in May –
A sweet singing bird
In his summer array.

QUATRAIN

Peach-bloom, each Springtide, fills my heart with grief
That the so beautiful should be so brief.
This year, more bright than bloom of peach *you* come,
And grief is now so deep that it is dumb.

QUATRAIN

What though so near upon the tree
The golden apples bob and dance?
Around them, like a dragon coiled,
Insuperable circumstance!

COUPLET

What though the mining's done, th' ore told?
While the vein lasted, it was gold.

A LIFE

With kingcups from the meadow
And bluebells from the wood
My boyish heart was mirthful
Before I understood
Aught evil or aught good.

At dawning adolescence,
As dreamer is by drums
I was startled by the odour
That from ancient gardens comes
Of starred chrysanthemums.

In pride of youth, unhindered,
I plucked whatever grows.
If my left hand clasped a lily
My right would fast enclose,
Set round with thorns, a rose.

Magnolia and hibiscus
In manhood showered like rain,
With orchid and datúra –
Flowers dealing bliss and bane
And madness to the brain.

All earthly blossoms scattered,
In middle and old age
With one white unfading lotus
Let me fare from stage to stage
Till ends my pilgrimage.

LEPCHA SONG

The Teesta in the Summer
From distant mystic lands
Winds like a vein of turquoise
Between her silver sands.

In the Rains, with splintered tree-trunks,
Foam, and forest creatures dead,
She hurtles tiger-tawny
Along her bouldered bed.

In Autumn, calm and queenly,
She descendeth statelily
From her castle in the mountains
To her palace by the sea.

When Winter comes, the garments
Wherein she sweeps arrayed
Flash malachite in sunshine,
Gleam amethyst in shade.

Her silver arms in Spring time
She coils, no cloud above,
Around the smoke-blue mountains
And sings to him I love.

VISITING THE TAJ MAHAL AT THE TIME OF THE
SUEZ CANAL CRISIS AND SEEING THE TOMBS OF THE
EMPEROR SHAH JAHAN AND MUMTAZ MAHAL

I passed the square and scripted gate
And saw the tombs with fluttering breath;
For all without was life and hate,
And all within was love and death.

STANZAS

If but the soil were richer
'Twould ask no gardener's art:
And lyric flowers would overspread
The greensward of my heart.

The odes would tower like cedars,
Your name bloom like the rose, –
If but the soil were richer
Nor strewn with rocks of prose.

SPRING – WINTER

The hills of the horizon
With snow are dappled round.
White blooms the sweet plum-blossom
Six foot above the ground.

As a bird in the blue ether
My joy is on the wing
'Twixt the purity of Winter
And the loveliness of Spring.

STUDY IN BLUE AND WHITE

Though depths of perfect azure
Invest the sun on high,
The hills, with haze and distance,
Show darker than the sky,

Save where, as though disrupting
The blueness of the real,
Shine in their absoluteness
The snows of the Ideal.

STANZAS

From pavilions of azure
Let us charge when night is done
And fight in golden armour
The battles of the sun.

From sable tents at midnight
Let us sally for a boon
And tilt, all silver-armoured,
In the love-lists of the moon.

QUATRAINS

Spring, in my boyhood it was understood,
Meant crystal streamlets full of bream and perch,
A mist of bluebells in a little wood,
And lambtails shivering on the silver birch.

Now, for my riper years, the meaning's swerved
To mountain rivers green as tourmalines,
And galaxies of waxen orchids curved
Against the ink-blue foliage of the pines.

SAPPHO[70]

Men plucked like flowers which pass,
Old nations reaped like corn,
Great cities scythed like grass –
Oh, not for these I mourn

Any more than for dreams that fade,
But I'm wild with grief to think
What deathless songs were made
Oblivion's meat and drink.

'MY SOUL BETWEEN THE FEELING AND THE THOUGHT...'

My soul between the feeling and the thought,
The known and the experienced, would I hold
Taut, as between the ridges of a lute
A wire of gold,

That when the Buddha-hands shall take me up,
And Wisdom hold, Compassion's plectrum bright
May strike, transcending thought and sense, one note
Of pure delight.

THE SANGHA

He wanted that His followers should be flames
And burn up to the Zenith. Now they are
Faint embers underneath a mound of ash,
Afraid of claiming kinship with a star.

THE SCHOLARS

Asked 'What is Buddhism?' off they go,
Consult the dictionaries, row on row,
Sanskrit, Tibetan, Pāli – German too,
As though it was the only thing to do,
Until we wish, in all sincerity,
A second Burning of the Books could be.
Have they no other word for sick souls full
Of doubt than 'Read my latest article'?
Off with your shoes! 'Tis holy ground! Depart!
Buddhism's in the life and in the heart.

QUATRAIN

What though with cloud the sky be grey,
The ocean wild and dark?
Tonight sleeps in the moonlit bay
My storm-bewildered bark.

QUATRAIN

Though sinks into the western hills
The sun through orange-amber bars,
In silence deep the moon fulfils
Her destined path among the stars.

TO ——

You remind me of whatever's made of gold –
Burmese pagodas, mediaeval rings,
Dragons that writhe on Anglo-Saxon helms,
And curious tomb-gear of Etruscan kings.

You remind me of whatever's like the sun,
Whatever's strong and shines, that burns and breeds –
Sunflower whose aureole of yellow flames
Hovers about a disc of bright black seeds.

QUATRAIN

Better, O Bull of Memphis, that we should
Have worshipped thee, or bowed to Roman Fate,
Than to that One hung on the Sacred Wood
Whose festering love fills half the world with hate.

STANZAS

Back to where the paths divided,
Shouldering past the empty tomb;
Twenty centuries elided,
Back into the Asian womb;

Back into the ancient darkness
Where the golden figures rise,
Peaceful hands and lips compassionate,
All wisdom in their half-closed eyes!

EPITAPH ON A 'POEM'

For Poetry, this 'poem' shows,
Your heartstrings are the only stuff;
Only for what's mere verse or prose
Mere grey matter is enough.

COUPLET HAIKU 1958

Above black pine-trees, on my homeward way,
An orange moonrise in a sky of grey.

IN PRAISE OF WATER

All living things should worship
The element that flows.
Was it not from The Waters
That life, at first, arose?

Sing, then, the holy dewfall,
The blessing from on high,
Which spangles earth's green tresses
With jewels of the sky.

The rains, when frogs in chorus
With croaking fill the night,
And peacocks in kings' gardens
Clap wings in their delight.

Sing, too, in all its splendour
Of sound and surge and foam
The sea which is leviathan's
Inviolable home.

Broad rivers that flow majestic,
Small streams that skip and race,
Record! Like their mother-waters
They seek the lowliest place.

Sing the fairest of all waters –
A mountain pool that lies
Unstirred, at peace reflecting
Calm moon and cloudless skies.

RETURN JOURNEY

Along the tempting byways
I wandered many a day,
But now my feet turn back into
The right, remembered way.

The bright forbidden thickets
No more my steps entice
Where baleful under blossoms
Lurks armed the cockatrice.

Winds the right path how many
A hot and dusty mile
I know not, only knowing
It never can beguile.

Though dense the frowning forests
That threat on either hand
The Buddha's path will lead me
To the Buddha's shining land.

LINES

These gods and goddesses that men have framed,
They help not much, for in the end we come
Back to an empty heart, a brain that aches,
And our two hands before us on our knees.

MEDITATION ON A FLAME

Twisting, writhing, leaping,
Low curtseying, ne'er the same,
Burns in its silver cresset,
Blue-eyed, a tawny flame.

Life from the air receiving,
Light to the world it gives;
No winds its pride extinguish:
Because it yields it lives.

Yet drop by drop, in darkness,
Consumeth that whereon
Its bright fantastic beauty
Must feed, or else begone.

For whether fire or water,
Earth, air, or flower or stone,
The seen lives from the Unseen,
The known from the Unknown.

And man, within whose bosom
Lurks the subtlest flame of all,
Must feed on The Undying
Or flicker, fade and fall –

Must feed on The Undying,
On that which has no name,
But which the Dark Sage calleth
'An Ever-Living Flame'.

THE YOUNG HILLS

Wonder it is to dwell at last
In hills without a human past,
Where not one building that we see
Before us, has outlived a tree.

In other prospects, hill or plain,
As stone men's histories remain
Centuries on centuries, making fast
Present to immemorial past.

But here, where man has newly made
His home, the human does not shade
Back into rocks and ferns and trees
By imperceptible degrees.

Abrupt transition! Naught between,
The subject meets his savage queen,
And man and Nature strive their best
To conquer, breast to naked breast.

And yet some comfort may be wrung
From this: as hills go, these are young,
Being born, for all their snow,
But fifty million years ago.

THE GUARDIAN WALL

With sweet compassionate faces,
Hands outstretched, humanity's friends,
Up to the golden Zenith
The Hierarchy ascends.

In glory on glory I see Them,
Helpers of all of us;
But the loveliest Bodhisattvas
Are the anonymous.

Lotus-seated, rainbow-circled
In the heaven of the Void,
They rear about the race a Wall
That may not be destroyed.

Its base is built of coral –
The blood that They have shed;
Its turrets sheerest diamond –
The life of purity led.

O Hierarchy Celestial,
O Tārā, from Thy throne,
Grant that in Thy Great Guardian Wall
My life may be one stone!

1959 RHYMED HAIKU

Old frog on the brink
Of the lotus pond jumped in –
Not stopping to think.

HAIKU

Visitors all day!
Morning mist, afternoon flowers –
And now the full moon.

QUATRAIN

The periwinkle flowers among the stones;
Where naught else lives, it grows –
A common hardy plant, scarce beautiful,
That shall outlast the rose.

SIDDHĀRTHA'S DREAM　　　　　　　　　　　　　　　1960
Mahāvastu[71]

From the four compass-points a green, a gold,
A red and a blue vulture, birds of prey,
Come swooping down; they kiss Thy sacred feet,
And fly all white away.

Bound by their several duties, warrior, priest,
Trader and serf, for refuge come to Thee,
Follow one Path, and, having followed, all
Become for ever free.

THE THREE MARKS

Impermanent, impermanent!
Whatever flowers must fade.
The world's most white perfection
In dust at last is laid.

Miserable, ah miserable!
Commixed with bale our bliss,
For pleasure's fanged and poisonous
As any viper's kiss.

Substanceless, oh substanceless!
A bubble or a star,
Like waves that dance on water
Nor things nor nothings are.

Wisely thus existence viewing
The Buddha's child shall be
From this world of flame and shadow
Into Boundless Light set free.

1961 THE BUDDHA[72]

Lean, strenuous, resolute, He passed His days
Trudging in dust-stained clouts the forest paths;
Stood as a beggar at the beggar's door
For alms, and more than kingly, spoke with kings.
Only when blue-black elephants of heaven
With bellowings filled the vast plains of the sky
Sat He aloof, and listened, heart at ease,
To the soft thunder of the rain on leaves.
Else was He as the sun unwearying
Full five-and-forty years, and as the sun
Shed upon all the beams of truth and peace.
This did He out of love for all that lives.

They carved Him out of sandal, chipped from stone
The Ever-moving, cast in rigid bronze
Him Who was Life itself, and made Him sit,
Hands idly folded, for a thousand years
Immobile in the incensed image-house;
They gilded Him till He was sick with gold.

And underneath the shadow of the shrine
They sauntered in their yellow silken robes,
Or – lolled replete on purple-cushioned thrones –
In sleepy stanzas droned His vigorous words
To gentle flutterings of jewelled fans....

Arise, O Lord, and with Thy dust-stained feet
Walk not the roads of India but the world!
Shake from the slumber of a thousand years
Thy dream-mazed fold! Burn as a Fire for men!

TIBETAN REFUGEE

You were my mother once, the Scriptures say,
A hundred or ten thousand lives ago,
And now with bloodstained feet you trudge the roads
Of India, exiled from your native land.
Driven, not exiled! The barbarian horde
That burned down temples, looted monasteries,
Tortured to death old holy lamas, they
That stood your husband up against a wall
And shot him, sent your brothers and your sons
To prison for a sullen look or word, –
Even they who on the holy citadel
Set their unholy flag, the flag of blood, –
They drove you forth with terror of the whip
And torment of the unfilled belly. You
Were working on the roads. Twelve hours a day
Breaking the stones, and you were seven months pregnant.
One night you slipped away. A month it took you
To reach the Indian border. On the way
Was born the baby strapped upon your back,
Born by the roadside. But you could not wait,
And feeble as you were pressed on and on
Through leech-infested jungle, dark and rain,
While all the time the dread of what might come
Behind you, drummed like madness in your heart.
Mother, you do not listen to your son!
Your eyes are dull and vacant, you do not hear
Your infant crying for your breast, nor see
Kind faces round you, hands outstretched to aid!
Above the clouds you see, as in a dream,
The golden roofs of the Potála gleam.

TO SHRIMATI SOPHIA WADIA IN HONOUR OF HER SIXTIETH BIRTHDAY[73]

Away with prosy greetings!
Today I cannot choose
But sing in verse the praise of one
Who is herself a Muse.

Full sixty glorious Summers
Have bloomed from sixty Springs
Since for their present mansion
She closed her heavenly wings.

As infant, girl and woman
Into gracious middle age
She has trod with step unfaltering
Truth's arduous pilgrimage.

Nor trod alone; beside her
Urging upward, to the end,
Strode the faithful Elder Brother,
The husband, master, friend.

With him she climbed, and gathered
Rare flowers beside the way –
Blossoms of love and beauty
That fade not night or day.

Though fixed her pilgrim vision
On the summit and the snow
Her mother's heart forgot not
Those who wandered, lost, below.

She lit and high uplifted
For them a ruddy flame
That blazed a path through darkness
And justified her name.

Now as the moon she shineth
In cloudless, starlit skies;
As Sarasvatī eloquent
And as Minerva wise.

Or like the sev'n-hued rainbow
That comes to glorious birth
From rain and sunshine – linking
High heaven and lowly earth.

To her all men are brothers,
All guests at Life's great feast;
She's her own United Nations,
A bridge 'twixt West and East.

However much we praise her
Still could we praise her more;
If all our words were diamonds
The gift were still too poor.

Oh sweet the Indian bulbul
That warbles through the night!
But only her own eloquence
Could tell her praise aright.

Hence on this day auspicious
We pray to her threescore
The gods may add – for *our* sakes –
Just forty-eight years more.

THREE COUPLET HAIKU

How bare and dead the branch! But look, again
Burst forth pink buds, as soon as touched by rain.

The red leaf falls upon the lake below.
Ah well, perhaps the water's lovelier so!

Though vigorously the high wind shakes the bough,
The unripe fruit sticks on to it, somehow.

POINTS OF VIEW

The politician on the platform
Is sleek, unctuous and smiling.
He is impeccably dressed
In the best silk handloom cloth
And wears a dazzling white Gandhi-cap.
His notes rustle crisply as he tells you
That your standard of living is going higher and higher.
What does it matter, man in the audience,
With the sunburned face and puzzled brow,
That your five hungry children
   Will have no food tonight?
The man behind the microphone
   Is always right.

THE PEOPLE

We are the people.
Round and round like dumb chained cattle we go
As though in the oil-mill,
But we must be silent, for we are the people.
Round and round we plod, while they squander
Untold millions of money on costly projects,
Building with sand instead of cement for us,
But for themselves with gold and silver and pearls.
If in the night of terror
Walls crumble, banks burst, waters roll down unleashed,
And we lose beneath the floods the little that was our all,
We must be silent, we must not say anything,
For we are the people.
We must hush our little boy in the night if he cries,
For their feelings might be hurt, thinking
We do not appreciate all they are doing for us.

1962 PLANTING THE BODHI TREE
Triyana Vardhana Vihara, Kalimpong, 18 June 2506

The morning sunshine saturates the heavenly blue as we
Beside our mountain hermitage plant firm the Bodhi Tree.

Oh not with turquoise-hafted trowel, nor yet with spade of gold,
We turn the warm and fragrant mould to plant our Bodhi Tree.

No streams of milk from silver pots, no sprinkled rare perfumes
From musk distilled, or crimson blooms, refresh our Bodhi Tree.

With Faith and Energy for hands, and Mindfulness for spade,
The soil of Meditation's glade we dig deep for our Bodhi Tree.

By day among the forest boughs the peacock preens a listless wing;
No frogs in deep-voiced chorus sing all night unto our Bodhi Tree.

With lightning in its dark blue breast if monsoon cloud appears,
What use? Oh blood and sweat and tears must water well our Bodhi Tree!

The heart-shaped leaves will twinkle out, huge boughs bespread, and then
May shelter multitudes of men beneath our towering Bodhi Tree.

And so, with joyous-solemn chant, this gold-blue morning, we
Beside our cliff-perched hermitage root fast the Bodhi Tree.

SPRING

The quick sap rises in the dry stalk;
On naked boughs the furled green buds appear;
Returning swallows beat about
The clay-built house they left last year.
Earth smiles, and like an almond tree
The Bodhichitta flowers in me.

WAITING IN THE CAR 1966

How beautiful is Berkeley Square!
Sunlit in the Spring air
Green leaves float round gnarled boles
Like young thoughts come to aged souls.

How beautiful is London now!
Pink bloom and white bloom along the bough
Sprinkle their odours on the morning airs
Between iron statues in green-swarded squares.

COUPLET HAIKU

Yellow in green, by woods we chance to pass,
The daffodils diversify the grass.

1967 STANZAS[74]

'Hammer your thoughts into a unity.'
This line once read
The sound came clangingly
Of golden hammers in my head
Beating and beating sheet on sheet
To make the figured foil complete.

Religion, friendship, art
Were hammered there
On the cyclopean anvils of my heart
Into an image bright and fair.
Under the strain the forge-floor split;
Nerveless the arms that fashioned it.

THE CRYSTAL ROSARY

Tenderly smiling, White Tārā
Sits on a mountain of green jade,
Telling through the ages the mantra of Great Compassion
On her crystal rosary of the tears of men.

POEMS FOR FOUR FRIENDS[75]

1. TO VEN. SOCHU SUZUKI

This bright Autumn morning
I have not yet opened my books.
The smoke of the incense stick
Still hangs motionless in the air.

2. TO MISS ———

Among the rich Autumn foliage
A delicate touch of green.
In the depths of the misty waters
The red blur of the rising sun.

3. TO STEPHEN

One would be far too many;
Ten is not nearly enough.
When the wind strips the last leaves
Oh the mossiness of the gnarled bough!

4. TO TERRY

The small blue monkey
Sits on the bough
With no companion
But the bright moon.

TEN VIGNETTES

I
Last year the lightning
Struck the mountain pine.
This year through the split trunk
Spills the Autumn moon.

II
On wind-tossed branches
Against blue sky
Chestnut leaves clinging
Like big yellow birds.

III
Careful! This morning
Down the temple steps
A thick brown carpet
Of sodden leaves.

IV
From the train window –
White gulls on the greensward
Neatly framed
By the white-painted goal-posts.

V
Lying on the bank
With their hair in the water
How beautiful they are,
The chopped-down willows!

VI
The multitudinous whisper
Of dead leaves
Hurrying along the pavement
To meet the Winter.

VII
White-winged for an instant
Against russet trees,
Flying inland for Winter
Seagulls scream.

VIII
To stand naked
In the Winter sunshine
They are not ashamed,
The strong brown trees.

IX
Alone in the fork
Of the frosted oak
The old grey squirrel
Cracks a Winter nut.

X
From a sky of unclouded
Blue, the sun shines
On flower-beds, statuary
And cigarette-ends.

AFTER MEDITATION

As the last gong-stroke dies away,
Shiver on shiver, into the deep silence,
Opening my eyes, I find myself
In a green-mossed underground cave
Overarching still waters whereon
White lotuses, half open, are peacefully smiling.

'FROM THE EVER-FAITHFUL PRESENT...'

From the ever-faithful Present
Turning wide, we run and play
With the will-o'-the-wisp, Tomorrow,
Or the ghost, Yesterday.

Reft from the living Moment
We dream of 'then' and 'now';
Through 'here' and 'there' we stumble,
Perplexed by 'why' and 'how'.

THE MARTYRDOM OF SAINT SEBASTIAN
After Sundry Old Masters

Three nails were enough for your Lord. But you
Hang with your Apollonian trunk and limbs
Stuck with a host of darts. One in your tender side,
One in your smoothly contoured breast, one in your belly,
One in the shoulder, one in the well-curved thigh,
One in the groin, one in the knee, the neck,
All neatly spaced, and at appropriate angles,
While from each deeply-buried shaft the blood
Steals down in thin red unassuming trickles.
Below you, aiming upwards at the tree
Whereon you are bound, the brutal-featured archers
Stand coats girt up, and feathers in their caps,
Giant forearms flexed, and sturdy legs apart.
But you, you do not notice. A faint smile
Curves your calm lips. Your face is half upturned.
Backed with blue sky, you seem to look, to listen,
For that which shall redeem your agony,
O Saint Sebastian of humanity.

'I WANT TO BREAK OUT...'

I want to break out,
Batter down the door,
Go tramping black heather all day
On the windy moor,
And at night, in hayloft, or under hedge, find
A companion suited to my mind.

I want to break through,
Shatter time and space,
Cut up the Void with a knife,
Pitch the stars from their place,
Nor shrink back when, lidded with darkness, the Eye
Of Reality opens and blinds me, blue as the sky.

THE MASK

For seven years a mask I wore,
Secure behind, and firm before;
A mask acceptable and neat,
As folk accustomed are to meet.
It went to school, it went to college,
A mask it was of wit and knowledge;
Older grown, it wined and dined,
Was mask superior, mask refined,
Mask prominent, mask most renowned,
Mask with a hundred masks around.
One day, it felt so hot and tight,
I took it off to say goodnight,
Shake hands, – I think I tried to smile
('Twas only for a little while).
They shrieked aloud with rage and pain
Until I put it on again.

CHINESE POEMS

I

For you in the North, the first Winter snow;
For me in the South, the last Autumn leaves.
Meeting not long ago, we were quickly parted.
Who knows when we shall meet again?
With filigree-work of frost bare branches glitter;
Raindrops on the window-pane make strange patterns.

II

Taking a sudden turn, the sunlit path
Is lost among the shadows of the dark old trees.
On the black leaves of the coarse wayside bushes
Frost gleams like silver in the faint light.

III

Façade after façade, along the Embankment,
In serried whiteness Corinthian pillars confront the moon.
Fluttering on tree after tree, beside the black water,
Ghostly leaves, bathed in cold lamplight, shine silver flowers.

IV. SIX POEMS WRITTEN IN RETREAT

1.

Beyond the deserted paddock, a dark wood;
Before our secluded hut, wet strips of green and brown.
Watching the incense burn in this quiet room
We have forgotten the passing of days and hours.

2.

The candle has long since guttered and died,
And in the darkness there is no sound but the slow click of wooden
    beads.
The Winter moon has long since risen and set
    And dawn waits for the sleepy crow of the first cock.

3.
A tangle of knotted branches on either side,
The lichened steps, deep in red leaves, wind to the brow of the hill.
The morning air is tinged with sadness, when we reflect
How short a path leads back into the dust of the world.

4.
A solitary figure, you pick your way
Among orange bracken and silver birches.
What thoughts are yours, I wonder,
Gazing up at the old pine-tree?

5.
Paths left behind, I lose myself
In the violet shadows of deep woods.
Idly gazing up at the old pine-tree,
No thought mars the tranquillity of my mind.

6.
Among dense trees, dimly lit,
Moisture drips from dank branches.
Deep in wet leaves, the muddy lane
Vanishes downhill into the white mist.

V. REMEMBERING THE RETREAT
At the wood's edge, a solitary hut;
Sharing my quiet room, a single friend.
Here on the table, two or three books of verse;
There on the shelf, half a dozen frost-blackened violets.
Hour after hour, we exchange only a few words;
Day after day, I polish a single poem.
Who would have thought it? A whole world of content
Found in these things!

VI
Heavy-winged, the last crow disappears
Over leafless tree-tops into amber light.
As dusk deepens, the solitary willow
Sees naked branches mirrored in chill water.

ORPHEUS IN THE UNDERWORLD

Suddenly he was there. The darkness glowed
With light, the hollow caves with music rang;
Frantic, to his lyre-music Orpheus sang.
Mortality had plumbed the weary road
Down into Hell, and Pluto's black abode,
Past Charon's creaking boat, past Cerberus' fang,
Down oozing tunnels where the blood-gouts hang,
Past Ixion's wheel, and Sisyphus's load.

Once there, what could he do? He could only sing
Blinded by tears, could only sob aloud
With grief, till after much heart-harrowing
By Pluto's grace he felt, but could not see,
His ravished but restored Eurydice
Floating behind him like a thin white cloud.

ST JEROME IN THE DESERT

Cavern or shed, in the one-candled gloom
We know not; through the black hole of the door
The desert, where red winds howl evermore:
Within, Christ's peace; without, impending doom.
Gigantically crouched in little room,
A lion against his feet upon the floor,
St Jérome sits, the dropping sands before,
The skull beside him where the shadows loom
Blacker and blacker. In a world of sin
The Empire changes hands, the Churches fight
Factious as dogs. By day the old man, stung,
Magnificently answers Augustine,
Then, dredging from the deep, night after night
Translates THE WORD into the vulgar tongue.

NEW   1969

I should like to speak
With a new voice, speak
Like Adam in the Garden, speak
Like the Rishis of old, announcing
In strong jubilant voices the Sun
Moon Stars Dawn Winds Fire
Storm and above all the god-given
Intoxicating ecstatic
Soma, speak
Like divine men celebrating
The divine cosmos with divine names.
I should like to speak
With a new voice, telling
The new things that I know, chanting
In incomparable rhythms
New things to new men, singing
The new horizon, the new vision
The new dawn, the new day.
I should like to use
New words, use
Words pristine, primeval, words
Pure and bright as snow-crystals, words
Resonant, expressive, creative,
Such as, breathed to music, built Ilion.
(The old words
Are too tired soiled stale lifeless.)
New words
Come to me from the stars
From your eyes from
Space
New words vibrant, radiant, able to utter
The new me, able
To build for new
Men a new world.

FOR THE RECORD

You wrote four letters, one
To your parents, one
To the girl who looked after you, one
To your accountant, and one
To your best friend
Me,
Sealed them neatly.
You wrote out
Two cheques in settlement of small
Debts,
Walked around
Here and there
Came in, went out
Two or three times
Returned my typewriter
(It was early morning,
I was in bed, asleep, did not hear you)
Felt a little uneasy,
Perhaps, for a minute or two
Parked your bus
Down at Kentish Town
In front of an old brick wall
Where it would not be in anybody's way
(After drawing the faded red
Curtains) bought a ticket
To somewhere, anywhere
Rode
Down the escalator
Stood
Heron-hunched in your old black duffle-coat
Hands thrust deep in pockets
Brooding, thinking,
Meditating,
Watched, waited
Anticipated
And when the train came

Heavily lumbering along the platform
Slowly gliding along the smooth shining rails
Suddenly threw yourself under, and in a moment
Found what you had been seeking
All your life.

WISH

I should like to live
In a room with four white walls
Live alone there with one
Flower.
Sunlight streaming in at the window
I would see
Pictures in the grain of my deal table
Hear
Poems in the flow of the traffic outside.

PETALS

Petals
Of the lilac, petals
From mauve and white plumes from
Orchard appleblossom foamy behind
Brick walls from
Gnarled grey branches green lofty
Crowns from
Manycandled chestnut, petals
Of hawthorn plum pear cherry rambling
Rose bushrose bougainvillea elder lime rowan, petals
Dropping on running water, on sunlit silent
Green scum, pink and white
Confetti on gleaming black car-roofs, petals
Borne over ancient chimneys, swept
Down dim avenues, falling
Like rain like seed like swansdown flying
Like spindrift against blue sky like whiteflock
Dawnbirds, petals
Tossed scattered whirling spiralling, littered
Down loamy furrows, sticking
To mudcaked boots, petals
Blowing into eyes hair hands, drifting
Over naked bodies of lovers, collecting
In crimson pools, in purple heaps, pink
Streams along country roads, rivers
Of petals to the horizon, rising
Tide of petals throughout the world flooding
Earth surging into the sky cloudburst
Apocalypse of petals Spring's
Manifesto of petals poet's
Signature of petals red
Petals.

SHELLS

Shells from the sea, shells
Opening red-lipped opening pearl –
Wombed nacre-mouthed, shells
With the curious names, hawkshead
Harp cone conch spider scorpion
Whiteconch milkconch primroseconch, rose
Murex, black murex, tigercowrie, red
Abalone, green turbo, foxhead
Silverlips, marlinespike, shells
Lying labelled in baskets, seaspoil sandspoil heaped
Among ties ashtrays teapots trinkets souvenirs (A Present
From Penzance) yet shells everlastingly
Whispering of the sea chanting
Sun wind sand foam celebrating
Distant oceandepths blue
Immensities, shells oh so marvellously
Specked spotted mottled blotched clouded
Grooved groined whorled pearled spiralled spiked
Spined clawed toothed, yet shells
Of rustpatch purple sandstone warmyellow
Cotswold, glinting Cornish
Granite, cathedrals
Manyarched manypillared, once
Storming heaven with stainedglass windows rubysapphire
Lights ladders apparitions, but now
Left high on the beach of the world, left
Waveless tideless lifeless, left
Decorous but deserted beautiful
But lost, shells of stone, dead shells.

MOTHER

Three weeks before he died
(That is, before he committed suicide)
Terry
Made a hollow pottery head
Blackbald hideous, huge
Aztec eyes staring
Sanpaku, great
Gaping mouth-hole lined
Sharklike with jagged teeth
Was going to
Paint the inside red
Before he died
(That is, before he committed suicide)
So that the red colour would show through
Eyeholes and mouth-holes
Like blood
He called it
Mother
Could just as well have called it
Woman
Or perhaps
Death

FOURTH METAMORPHOSIS

Too long have I been a camel
Ship of the Desert
Too long knelt to be laden
With other men's merchandise.

Too long have I been a lion
Lord of the Jungle
Too long fought
Paper-and-tinsel dragons

Too long have I been a child
Parent of the Future

Now it is time to be
Myself.

VARIATIONS ON A MERSEY SOUND I
for Adrian Henri

Tonight at noon
The pricetags will be taken off everything
Tonight at noon
Eros in Piccadilly will come to life[76]
Politicians and nuns walk naked in the streets
Neon signs will flash sayings of Zen Masters
And Her Majesty's Stationery Office
Will distribute ten million copies of Shakespeare's Sonnets
Printed in gold ink
On the best handmade paper.

Tonight at noon
Churches will be turned into pubs and art galleries
Stonehenge will be reopened and a red sun
Peer through the stones at whiterobed worshippers
Mistletoe will flourish on every oak
Oakgroves spring in everybody's backyard
Ten thousand Buddhas will hold up a forest of golden flowers
And the Sphinx tell the secret kept for five thousand years

All the radio networks of the world
Will broadcast Bach Beethoven Indian ragas and
Zen meditation music
Science fiction fantasies will all come true
People will break down walls everywhere and plant flowers
Muslim will embrace Jew in the streets of Jerusalem
Protestant and Catholic Irish pelt each other with flowers
All the clocks in the world will stop
Sun revolve round the earth, earth round the moon
Time will flow back to the beginning of things
First light shine on first waters
Agony will be one with ecstasy union with separation
And
You will tell me you love me
Tonight at noon

VARIATIONS ON A MERSEY SOUND II
for Roger McGough

You are the distance
Between man and Reality
Measured in pilgrim's footsteps

You are the distance
Between peace and war
Measured in broken promises

You are the distance
Between war and peace
Measured in unkept graves

You are the distance
Between life and death
Measured in drops of blood

You are the distance
Between galaxy and galaxy
Measured in blades of grass

You are the distance
Between the seed and the womb
Measured in lightyears

You are the distance
Between the ideal and the real
Measured in wings

You are the distance
Between love and hate
Measured in petty frustrations

You are the distance
Between Spring and Winter
Measured in falling leaves

You are the distance
Between prose and poetry
Measured in madman's laughs

You are the distance
Between last year and this year
Measured in lonely nights

You are the distance
Between Buddha and disciple
Measured in golden flowers

You are the distance
Between light and darkness
Measured in rainbows

You are the distance
Between death and rebirth
Measured in archetypal visions

HAIKU

Bank holiday –
Wet sunlit roads reflecting
A million cars.

THE TIME HAS COME...
for Lama Trungpa Rimpoche

The time has come
For us to lay aside the masks
Painted hieratic masks
The time has come
For us to hang up the gorgeous costumes in the greenroom cupboard
To leave the brilliantly lit stage
The applause
And to go home
Through deserted streets
To a quiet room
Up three flights of stairs
And to someone perhaps
With whom we can be
Ourselves

1970 LIFE IS KING

Hour after hour, day
After day we try
To grasp the Ungraspable, pinpoint
The Unpredictable. Flowers
Wither when touched, ice
Suddenly cracks beneath our feet. Vainly
We try to track birdflight through the sky trace
Dumb fish through deep water, try
To anticipate the earned smile the soft
Reward, even
Try to grasp our own lives. But Life
Slips through our fingers
Like snow. Life
Cannot belong to us. We
Belong to Life. Life
Is King.

DREAM

Nightrace of silver-white coach of ghostly
Sledge maybe chariot drawn
By white horses, nightrace
Through whitewinter landscape through frozen-
Fast-world. In the back, behind me, –
Arms slightly spread, rime-bright hair
Stiff on your shoulders, palms
Open, cold blue eyes staring, – you
Silverking deadking driving
Towards Spring towards Winter
Who knows.

CHAIRLIFT[77]
Rajgir, 1969

Up the side of the sacred mountain
Where the Buddha preached (said the traveller)
Runs a brand-new electric chairlift,
'Made in Japan'. People sit in it
Clasping oranges, bags of peanuts, and bottles
Of fizzy lemonade. Some of them
Look at the sacred mountain, others
Chatter and laugh; but all
Are glad to be able to tell their friends
That they have been to the top
Of the sacred mountain, seen the peak
Where two thousand five hundred years ago
Our Lord Shakyamuni the Buddha
Proclaimed to gods and men the White Lotus
Of the Good Law Sūtra. Oh yes, they certainly
Have had their money's worth.

MIRRORS

They are decidedly
Not the best, the Graeco-Roman Buddhas
From Gandhara, from Bactria, from even
Farther north-west, from even closer
To the heart of Central Asia, – not the best
From an artistic point of view.
Cheeks are too softly rounded, lips
Too sweetly smiling, and sometimes
They seem perched rather awkwardly
On their lotus-thrones (preferring
To sit on a chair, or stand),
As though golden-haired Apollo or
Swift-foot Hermes, or whoever else
May have been the shapely white original,
Was not quite accustomed
To his new position. Sometimes
They appear a trifle uncertain, not quite sure
Of their welcome in the world
Either among Hellenized Indians
Or Indianized Greeks. And yet
We should be grateful
To the Graeco-Roman Buddhas, even
Love them, representing
As they do the first
Shadowy reflection
Of the goldgleam of Enlightenment
In the mirrors of western man.

THE GREAT READER

Always a great reader
In bed,
Ever since I was a boy
I sat up late, hunched
Among the pillows, leaning
On my elbow in yellow light
Reading
Poetry romance philosophy magic.
Now
Decades later
Night after night, I read
The Book of You, turning
Page after illuminated
Page, dazzled
By the gold, lost
Among red and blue traceries,
Interlacing leaves
Flowers
Tendrils, vines,
Unicorns rampant, dragons, pink
And blue carpet-pages, gardens,
Fountains, faces, all the while
Desperately
Seeking to spell out the subtleties
Of a smile, the meaning
Of your life for mine
Maybe.

SCAPEGOAT

How did it feel
To be left alone in the desert
Loaded down with the sins
Of a whole people?

How did it feel
To have hanging round your neck
Dragging on your horns clogging
Your steps thousands of
Thefts murders fornications
Perjuries blasphemies –
Sins of a whole people
For a whole year?
How did it feel
To be weighed down by all that,
You just a black goat,
Comparatively small?

Vultures circling
Overhead, did you remember
Hands of the High Priest on your head, flash
Of the jewels on his breastplate, remember
The last shouts dying behind you
As you were left alone in the desert
Crushed beneath the weight of the sins
Of a whole people?

How did it feel?

Not so bad, I think,
As being left alone in the universe
With one's *own* guilt.

Mankind should be grateful
To goats.

AT THE BARBER'S

Talkative one morning, the Cypriot barber
Asked me what I did for a living.
'Write', I replied, not feeling
Particularly communicative. 'You write!
What do you write?' 'I write poetry.'

Ah, delight of the suspended scissors, exhilaration
Of the raised comb! 'You write
Poetry!'
      In depths of the mirror behind him
Athenian walls standing intact,
Long-haired warriors spared for great verses.

IN THE NEW FOREST
Summer 1969

Space, infinite space! Heather
Purple to the horizon, wind
Bending the stiff gorse, rippling
Beds of young fern.... By the roadside
Horses cropping the turf, foals
Straddling ungainly, manes wind-
Tossed across slim brown faces across
Pricked ears scared eyes.
      Over all
Blue sky blue sky blue sky....

Deep in the woods, lost
Among ancient trees, shining red
In sunlit spaces tall
Foxgloves....
      An oak
Marks the spot where William Rufus fell.

CRIMINALS

'The early Christians
Were criminals,' he said. 'They refused
To offer incense
To the Deified Roman Emperors, refused
To fight, insisted
On loving one another, loving
Everybody, even
The Emperor (but they wouldn't
Offer the incense). They were marked men.
Wanted by the police, watched
In the market-place, hunted in their own
Homes, on public holidays they were
Fished out of catacombs, flung
To the lions, tortured
Crucified. Now we call them
Saints, martyrs, venerate them
In churches, light candles
Before their images, kneel, pray, but then
All right-thinking respectable people
Held up hands in horror
At the name of Christian, then
They were just criminals,' he said
Reflectively,
Pulling on the joint and passing it
To the next man.

SANGHARAKSHITA'S VERSES OF ACKNOWLEDGEMENT 1971
Lines written on receiving from a member of the Western Buddhist Order the gift of his record collection, accompanied by some verses

Though one's food is not perfect
It is enough to maintain health and strength.

Though one's house is not perfect
It is enough to shelter the body.

Though one's job is not perfect
It is enough to make both ends meet.

Though one's wife is not perfect
She is enough to keep the home going.

Though one's children are not perfect
They are enough to continue the family name.

Though one's Morality is not perfect
It is enough to make meditation possible.

Though one's Meditation is not perfect
It is enough to support flashes of insight.

Though one's Insight is not perfect
It is enough to reveal the emptiness of mundane existence.

Though one's Guru is not perfect
He is enough to show one the Right Path.

Though one's fellow disciples are not perfect
They are enough to give moral support.

Though one's Generosity is not perfect
It is enough to loosen the bonds of attachment.

Though one's Patience is not perfect
It is enough to put up with having to live in the city.

Though one's Vigour is not perfect
It is enough for daily practice.

Though one's Wisdom is not perfect
It is enough not to be fooled by worldly things.

Though one's record-collection is not perfect
It is enough to make an acceptable offering.

Though one's verses are not perfect
They are enough to show one's sincerity.

Though one's letters are not perfect
They are enough for keeping in touch.

Though one's appearances are not perfect
They are enough for friendly recognition.

Though this acknowledgement is not perfect
It is enough to show deep appreciation.

EASTER RETREAT   1972

Páck your suitcase, cátch the train,
Eastertide has come again.
Now at last your way lies clear
From Waterloo to Haslemere.

Praise British Rail! How smoothly slide
The houses by on either side,
Until the train, now fairly gliding,
Runs through the primrose-tufted siding.

Typewriter, textbook, left behind,
To higher things you tune your mind,
Solaced, between the well-kept stations,
With tea and Góvinda's 'Foundations'.

At last! In carriage window framed
You hear the well-loved place proclaimed
In Saxon accent bold and clear
Along the platform, 'Haslemere!'

Free, down elm-shadowed lanes you wend,
Where British blackbirds call 'Attend!'
Making your way, with quiet elation,
To Keffolds, brown rice, and meditation.

1975 THE BALLAD OF JOURNEYMAN DEATH[78]

'Oh what do you want, you wandering man,
So far out in the wild?'
'I've come to help you build the house
To shelter your wife and child.'

'Oh why do you work so fast and sure,
And why is your line so true?'
'Oh it's many a house I've built before
For many a man like you.'

'Oh will you not stay for a bite to eat,
For the midday sun shines strong.'
'I'll eat my food in my own good time,
And that will not be long.'

'Oh why do you keep your head so low,
And your hat-brim over your face?'
'I would not frighten your wife and child,
For my visage lacketh grace.'

'Oh what will you take now the work is done,
And what is the wage you would borrow?'
'I'll take your wife and I'll take your child,
And I'll take yourself tomorrow.'

'Oh what is your name, you wandering man,
That can build a house in a day,
And will take the living for daily wage?'
'My name is Death, men say.'

FOUR GIFTS

I come to you with four gifts.
The first gift is a lotus-flower.
Do you understand?
My second gift is a golden net.
Can you recognize it?
My third gift is a shepherds' round-dance.
Do your feet know how to dance?
My fourth gift is a garden planted in a wilderness.
Could you work there?
I come to you with four gifts.
Dare you accept them?

SEQUENCE IN A STRANGE LAND[79]

I
Rusty pine-needles
Sprinkling the green-mossed top
Of an old boulder.

Spring buds,
Half-opened, shiver
In untimely snow.

Two or three buds
Are enough to show that Spring is here.
A few words
Are sufficient to say what the heart means.

I do not care at all
About writing any more poems.
Enough if I can say
How the heart bleeds and bleeds.

White wings flash, then nothing
But blue sky.

A long road,
An empty house,
And at the crossroads
Someone watching,
Someone waiting.

Mandalas
Need
Space.

A gift of violets
For the Buddha
And me!

In the front garden
Red tulips, yellow daffodils,
Stand tiptoe in sunshine
As it falls on the white
Walls where the green blinds
Have not yet been drawn.

Reading
Is not a Muse.

II
Green pine-trees, and in between
The white box-like shape
Of apartment houses.

The sun sets
Behind dark woods.
Clear voices carry
Over mirror-like water.

Past the eaves of the sauna
Swallows, newly arrived,
Darting, swerving.

Somehow, today
I think of the blue poppy
That grows in the Himalaya.

SONG OF THE WINDHORSE

I am the Windhorse!
I am the king of space, the master of infinity,
Traversing the universe
With flashing, fiery hooves!
On my strong back, on a saddle blazing with gems,
I bear through the world
The Three Flaming Jewels.

Once, long ago,
My galloping hooves were upheld
By the delicate hands of gods
As I bore through the night,
From home into homelessness,
A young prince of the Shakya clan.

With elephant, bull, and lion,
I stepped stately round the capital
Of Ashoka's column,
We four beasts bearing between us
The mighty eight-spoked Wheel
That through heaven and earth
Rolls irresistibly.

Nostrils breathing fire, I uphold,
Quadriform, the throne of the Jewel-Born Conqueror in the south.

I am the Windhorse!
White, like a shooting star,
I appear in the midst of the darkness of the world.
Sometimes I trot, sometimes gallop,
Sometimes stand stock-still in the midst of the heavens
So that all can see me in my glory.
My neck, proudly arched, is white as snow,
And my flanks gleam like mother-of-pearl.

Mane and tail are flowing gold,
And my harness of silver studded with turquoise.
My loud neighings, as I paw the clouds,
Echo and re-echo throughout the universe,
Waking those who sleep, putting to flight
The hosts of indolence, apathy, and despair.
Hearing the sound of my voice
Heroes regain their courage, warriors grasp the spears of keen thought
Against the day of intellectual battle,
Against the day of the great spiritual war
For Life, Consciousness and Vision, when the bow sings
And arrows of desire are loosed at immortal targets.

I am the Windhorse!
I am thought at its clearest,
Emotion at its noblest,
Energy at its most abundant.
I am Reverence. I am Friendliness. I am Joy.
I only among beasts
Am pure enough, strong enough, swift enough,
To bear on my back the Three Flaming Jewels.
The pride of the lion is not enough.
The strength of the bull is not enough.
The splendour of the peacock is not enough.

With what joy I sweep through the air,
Bearing age after age
My thrice-precious burden!
With what joy, with what ecstasy, I fulfil
The greatest of all destinies!

Plunging or soaring, I leave behind me
A rainbow track.

HOMAGE TO WILLIAM BLAKE[80]

My Spectre stands there white as snow;
Whate'er I ask, he answers 'No'.
Till I can melt him with my fire
He blocks the path of my desire.

My Emanation, weak and poor,
Lies outstretched upon the floor.
Till I can claim her for my own
Both of us must howl and groan.

Therefore will I, all I can,
Build up complete the Fourfold Man,
Head and heart, and loins fine,
And hands and feet, all made divine.

Banish single vision far!
With double vision ever war!
Fourfold vision night and day
Light and guide you on your way.

In that fourfold vision bright
See the whole world with delight.
Rock and stone, and flower and tree,
And bird and beast, are men like thee.

Men like thee, and women too,
Androgýnous, ever-new –
Divine Imaginations free
Exulting in Eternity.

MAY 1976

'Tis Chaucer's month, the merry month
Of May, when all day long
The earth is full of blossom,
And the sky of skylark-song; –

The Buddha's, when He broke at last
The chain of birth and death,
When the earth was called to witness
And the heavens held their breath.

1977   I. M., J. AND K.[81]

Los and Enitharmon wandered over the graves
Hand in hand, plucking now the nettle now the briar. The sun
Shone on their faces and their limbs were bright with sweat.
'Here let us rest,' said Enitharmon, 'here let us build our bower.
Let us forget the wars of Urthona and the strife of blood,
Forget the flames of inspiration and the terrors of intellect,
Forget Jerusalem, forget Albion and all our brethren, forget
The labours of the furnace and the loom, harp and song.
Let us be all in all to each other, you and I,
Here in a world apart, a Paradise, an Eden, and here
Let us live, drinking each other up, night and day.'

Long Los looked back on the fires of Golgonooza
Flaming against the stars, but at length
Lay down with his head in Enitharmon's lap. She smiled.

Ages passed. The giant forms, covered with snow,
Harden and petrify. The wind howls in the waste.

'EVERY DAY IS A GOOD DAY'[82]

'Every day is a good day': a thousand doors fly open.
'Every day is a good day': the sun and moon stand still.

The Blue Cliff rises high into the air;
Below it is wrapped in mist, above it is shrouded in cloud.
What use is a path up the sheer side,
If, however far you climb, you can never reach the top?

A hundred peaks behind, a hundred peaks before;
All at once, the Blue Cliff rises in the distance.
Birds disappear into the mist, monkeys' cries are lost in silence;
Darkness gathers, and there is still a long way to go.

THE SUNFLOWER'S FAREWELL   1978

Aloft on its tall stalk the sunflower hangs
As though half weary. Harvest long since reaped,
It sees beyond the ivied crumbling wall
Blue-vaulted stubble in faint sunlight steeped.

Aloft on its dry stalk the sunflower hangs
In silence: in the West, the round red sun.
The yellow petals, once its glory, wilt:
Its seed is ready and its work is done.

AUTUMN VIGNETTE

Leafless, the walnut's twisting branches spread
Against the glowing pink of evening skies.
Crossed by unweeded paths, and warm within
Its walls of brick, the kitchen garden lies.

Groundsel and rough grey nettle intermixed,
Cabbages yellow in depleted rows.
Ripening alone in its deserted house,
Through humid glass the red tomato glows.

Deep in the cobwebbed grasses underneath
Their parent boughs, the rancid apples hide.
His arms outflung, above the raspberry canes
The scarecrow leans, head fallen to one side.

PADMALOKA[83]

Three Summers and three Autumns have I seen,
And two white Winters, in this quiet spot,
And now the gold shines out among the green,
And reddest roses are remembered not.
For the third time are Winter's icy fingers
Stretched out – and yet the latest sunflower lingers.

Three Summers and three Autumns! In that time
I have made friends with walnut and with oak,
Have clasped the trunks of holly and of lime,
And cómmuned with them, though no words we spoke.
Watching black ants among the roots of grasses
I heard the wind sigh how our pleasure passes.

Russet and gold, the drifts of leaves are deep,
And the third Winter deep will be the snow;
But the trees mourn not, though no sap may leap,
For deeper still the gnarled roots thrust below.
In this quiet spot, girt by the reeds and rushes,
The soul roots deeper, and the spirit hushes.

Summer and Autumn, on the margined pond,
The waterlily's leaves are broad and green,
Soon to be yellowed, with the shrubs beyond,
And underneath a film of ice be seen.
But come first Spring, among her budding daughters
Red blooms the lily on the sunlit waters.

Dreaming and thinking as the Autumn ends,
I like the swallow must prepare for flight,
Must leave deep-rooted here my ancient friends
And go where night is day, and day is night.
Brief though my stay, I shall be thinking ever
Of this quiet spot, beside the sluggish river.

Thinking and dreaming, in this quiet spot,
Summer and Winter, I shall end my days,
Till like the rose I am remembered not,
And life has vanished with the sunset-rays.
Then, among silver lakes and golden mountains,
The new-born lotus smiles beside the crystal fountains.

THE GODS

One by one the Gods
Of the Underworld emerge
Into the light of day.

Some have raised arms. Some
Bear on their heads
Sun, Moon, horns,
A wide-open lotus flower.

Slowly, gravely, they move,
Emerging from the Underworld
With steady steps,
Walking in procession
Along the curved edge of the world.

Slowly, gravely, they walk,
Descending into the Underworld,
Into the darkness....

And we must follow.

LINES WRITTEN FOR THE DEDICATION OF THE SHRINE AND THE OPENING OF THE LONDON BUDDHIST CENTRE

    Flanked by the lotus red
    The Buddha's golden head
And golden body on the altar gleam.
    The white-robed worshippers
    And red-stoled servitors
In through the open doorway joyful stream.
A thousand days of labour done,
Glad faces, as they sit there, catch the evening sun.

    In through the windows wide
    The slanting sunbeams glide,
Setting on each bowed head a crown of flame,
    As from a thousand throats
    Chanted are sweetest notes
Praising the Buddha's, Dharma's, Sangha's name.
The sound of tinkling silver bells
And long-reverberant gongs the mighty chorus swells.

    On this triumphal day
    With gods and men we say:
Long by the Buddha may the lotus red
    Bloom and rebloom! Oh long
    May we uplift our song,
Bringing light to the blind, life to the dead!
From this gold Presence, day and night,
Long may there shine on all, undimmed, the Infinite Light!

THE PRIEST'S DREAM

Once more a virgin acolyte he stands
Beside the altar, reverent and demure.
He sees the flutter of white priestly hands:
His head is empty, though his faith is sure.

But now? Awake, slumped in his easy chair
He sees the scattered ash upon his knee,
His greasy cassock – rusty black, threadbare –
And yawns, and wonders if there's fish for tea.

TOO LATE

*'The new pope has decided that he will not be
crowned in the traditional manner.'*
NEWS ITEM

Moved by the spirit of the times, the heir
Of Gregory and Innocent puts by
The triple crown, the shoulder-lifted chair
Borne through the crowd, and comes to men more nigh,
Pastoral now and not pontifical
As when he trod the necks of princes all.

But what are these grey shapes that float athwart
The cúrtailed pomp? What makes the taper stir?
From racks in dungeons, stakes in public squares, –
From Béziers, Carcassonne, and Montségur, –
The victims of each cruel pontificate,
Long silenced, cry 'Alas! Too late! Too late!'

THE SIRENS

They sing with fairest looks and sweetest breath,
While all below is darkness, stench, and death.

BEFORE DAWN

Cut off from what I really think and feel,
The substance of my life becomes ideal.

A whited sepulchre, a plaster saint,
Is not much use, however bright its paint.

Dreaming, awake, I must do all I can
To join the inward and the outward man.

Death stares me in the face: I watch and pray.
So near the goal, and yet so far away!

HOPE 1979

By hope inspired, we make – though foiled
Again, and yet again –
A Pure Land out of a suffering world
And Angels out of men.

AFTER READING THE VIMALAKĪRTI-NIRDEŚA[84]

Mañjuśrī sits upon his throne of gold,
And Vimalakīrti on his straw mat.
The Bodhisattva has laid aside his flaming sword,
And the Elder has dismissed his attendants and dancing-girls.
So close are their two heads that they almost touch,
But what passes between them no one knows,
Only the golden throne melts, the straw mat disappears,
And the two forms are one, and more than one.

SONNET

Among the mighty mountains sojourning,
Years and decades went by as I beheld
Peak after peak at dawn or evening
Flushed with a golden glory that compelled
An ultimate homage as the day upwelled
Or night descended. Thrones of gods they seemed,
Those dazzling virgin snow-peaks – gods who dreamed
Immortal lives away, by time unknelled.

But now, as in a dream myself, I see
The bare and level fields stretch far away:
Nothing but light and space the scene affords.
Through th' green, a ground of lapis lazuli
Shines deepest blue, and hedges, brown and grey,
Turn to a net of glittering golden cords.

ALEXANDRINES PERHAPS[85]

'An ineffectual angel', unable to do
Anything very practical, or to follow through
Ideas to the end, – beautiful, soft in the brain, –
'Beating in the void his luminous wings in vain.'

That was Matthew Arnold's well known estimáte
Of Shelley the poet: a pitiful creature, but great.
One would have thought that Matthew, in front of Percy,
Would have fallen on his knees and begged for mercy.

But no, the critic, whether lover or hater,
Invariably trips over the creator.
Creators are stumbling-blocks and stones of offence
To those who are merely pickers up of pence.

Not that Matthew comes in the latter categóry:
He was a poet too – that's another story.
'Mind how you distribute your blessings and curses'
Is the moral of these Alexandrine verses.

(In Racine or Rimbaud, so supple and strong,
Alexandrines elastically bounding along
Are the delight of the French, both the rich and the poor,
But they're not yet acclimatized on England's shore.)

THE SCAPEGOAT
After Holman Hunt

Half hoof-deep in the salt-encrusted sands
Of the Dead Sea, he stops and hesitates
At last, perhaps because he understands –
Far from the rancid herd-loves and herd-hates –
What place it is his red eye contemplates
With head half turned. Beyond the bottle green
Of stagnant waters, mauve-pink hills serene
Border, and yellow sky commensurates.

Baffled but undismayed, his horned head bent,
And threads of tell-tale scarlet on his brow,
He halts before the staring countershape
Of last year's victim, with salt sludge half blent.
Green, mauve-pink, yellow glow intenser now
And throb insistent. *There is no escape.*

VERSES

My mind's a silver awning,
My heart a golden throne,
But none to sit beneath it,
Or rule from it alone.

My thought's a pearly chamber,
My love a crystal stair,
But none here to explore it,
Or to climb it there.

My joy's a dome of azure,
My bliss a glassy sea,
But none to make it echo,
Or ride the waves with me.

My life's a rainbow tower,
My death a diamond well,
But none to scale or fathom
In heaven or in hell.

HAIKU

Thrown on the white wall
Shadows of flowers
Have nothing to say.

RESURRECTION

Osiris is green in colour, dark green.

Long has the embalmed body lain in the tomb,
In the darkness and silence of the stone chamber
Where rows of maidens in black wigs
Walk with lotuses on their heads and lotuses in their cupped hands
For ever and ever round the walls.
Long has the black curled beard pointed at the ceiling, unchanging.
Long have the narrow feet pointed at the ceiling, unmoving.
Long have the fish-eyes stared at the ceiling, unwinking.
Long have the crossed arms grasped flail and sceptre, unyielding.

But now,
Something stirs in the quiet chamber,
Stirs in the darkness.
Shoots, tiny shoots,
Sprout the length of the embalmed body on the painted couch,
Sprouting through the bandages
Like green spears.

Osiris is risen.

GREENSTONE

High in the mountains, up creeks,
Between slopes densely tree-covered,
In the beds of ancient streams,
Stand the boulders.

Split them open,
And they are pure green –
Spinach green, apple green, and sea green.

The Maoris
Carved neck-amulets
And gleaming translucent fish-hooks
Out of the pure greenstone,
And polished batons
For great personages to hold
On ceremonial occasions.

Tourists
Can buy it made into ashtrays,
Lampstands, and little boxes.

What a pity!

EPIGRAM

What said you, *Short, swift swallow-flights of song?*
Mine like a little sparrow hops along.

THE REALMS OF EXISTENCE AS DEPICTED IN THE TIBETAN WHEEL OF LIFE

SIX SONNETS

1. The Realm of the Gods
The gods, throned in their radiant overworld,
Are loath to spare a thought for human care,
But drain the blissful nectar unaware
Of human labours to perdition hurled,
And human lives away in shipwreck whirled,
And human hearts abandoned to despair.
Smiling they sit, as ever young and fair,
With fingers round soft fingers tenderly curled.

But hark! the music of impermanence
From the White Buddha's transcendental lute
Swells in their ears. With garlands fading fast,
They wring their hands in hapless impotence.
The time has come for tasting other fruit
In other realms. Their glory ends at last.

2. The Realm of the Asuras
'The Tree! the Tree! the Wish-fulfilling Tree!
Tear down its branches! Bear its fruit away!
Fight off the gods, or else we'll lose the day!
Discharge your arrows! Bring up th'artillery!'
Thus shout the anti-gods, as desperately
They strive to conquer in the cosmic fray
With visages distorted, minds astray,
Mad for the prize of immortality.

Sudden amid them shines a fiery sword,
Held in the Verdant Buddha's powerful hand.
It blazes in those faces void of ruth,
Blinding their eyes. They fall back overawed.
Nothing the Sword of Wisdom can withstand.
The noblest warfare is to strive for truth.

3. The Realm of the Hungry Ghosts
With barrel-bellies, mouths like needle-eyes,
And necks as thin as neck of mountain crane,
They seek to feed on what becomes their bane.
Food turns to ordure, pus, or blood – or flies
Up in their face as flame that never dies.
They feed upon themselves, – arms, legs, – in vain.
They feed upon each other. Oh the pain,
Ravening on that which never satisfies!

Ah drops of mercy! Drops of rare content!
See, the Red Buddha dawns upon their night,
Sprinkling His Nectar from a golden vase –
The nectarous Message of Enlightenment.
There's no fulfilment in reflected light.
Man's treasure is laid up among the stars.

4. The Realm of the Beings in Hell
Horror and anguish! Madness and despair!
Weltering in floods of fire, or pinioned fast
In ice, they see a leprous sky o'ercast
With gouts of blood, and suffering everywhere.
One torment worst: amidst the stench and glare,
Within the crystal mirror of the past, –
Mirror of Judgement, – they behold, aghast,
How their own deeds of blood have brought them there.

Yet hope still springs, ev'n in the black abyss.
Purging with flame, with water purifying,
The Smoke-Grey Buddha makes the darkness bright,
Shining a silver cloud. He tells them this:
That from hell's depth there runs, the past defying,
A fearful, narrow pathway to the Light.

5. The Realm of the Animals
The lion, the horse, the elephant, the whale;
Bulls under yoke; rooks noisily debating;
Panthers at play, and goldfish coruscating;
Snake swallowing frog; thrush picking off the snail;
Bird, beast and fish, the female and the male, –
In flocks, in herds, in shoals and schools relating, –
Hunters and hunted, – eating, sleeping, mating, –
Something they lack. By wood, hill, stream, and dale,

The Dark Blue Buddha shows an open book,
Jewel-charactered on leaves of burnished gold.
Behold the treasure of communication, –
Treasure of knowledge, – ne'er to be forsook:
Deeds of great heroes, thoughts of sages old,
Bequeathed to man's remotest generation.

6. The Realm of Men
Grasping the plough, with horse or ox they till
The broad black earth, and having tilled they eat
(Man's honest labour makes his bread more sweet);
They ply the oar; they labour at the mill;
They sing, they dance, carousing with a will
Round festal bonfires; they build towns complete
With walls, towers, temples, markets where they meet;
They shrink from pain, they shrink from death, – until,

Rising in beauty, like the Morning Star,
The Saffron Buddha cries, 'Oh have no fear!
Go forth, O mortals! Open is the Door
Of Immortality! Go forth! Here are
The Goal, the Way, the Way-Declarer, – here
Are bowl, robes, ringed staff: you need nothing more.'

LOVELACE REVISITED[86]

My mind to me a kingdom is,
Was the gallant poet's song.
Our minds are democracies,
And that's what's wrong.

Every whim has a vote,
Every passion is free to speak.
Our lives are turned upside down,
With a change of government every week.

Sometimes the 'Prime Minister' pleads,
Sometimes tries to be strong,
But take it either way,
He – or she – doesn't last long.

The monarchical principle
Is badly needed, that's plain,
In the mind at least, if it
Is to be a kingdom again.

SNOW-WHITE REVISITED

Mirror, mirror on the wall,
Who is most beautiful of all?

'*You* are most beautiful,'
The mirror always replies,
Else he'd be smashed into pieces
For telling lies.

So he says his piece,
And stays intact.
We're easily flattered,
That's a fact.

We'd as lief hear the truth
As see a ghost.
Mirrors, mirrors on the wall,
Know this better than most.

Truth can appal.

AFTER RILKE[87]

The poet is the world's interpreter,
At least to his own self. He recreates
In his own heart the things he contemplates,
And brings them forth transformed from what they were
Into a beauty-truth that cannot err,
That cannot fade or die. Though dull ingrates
May mock, no vile disparagement abates
The benefits the poet's words confer.

A tree is not a tree, unless within
The poet's all-transmuting mind it grows
Refined, reborn, – by his own power redeemed
Into a truer life. The poet's kin
Are Memnon, Orpheus, Merlin. History shows
The best but live what once the poet dreamed.

THE STRICKEN GIANT

After the storm, the day dawns calm and fair,
With soft white cloudlets spread against the blue;
Hedgerows, reviving, sparkle with the dew:
Blown twigs, and pools of water, everywhere;
Fresh beauty crowns the broken branches bare,
And pale gold sunlight slowly filters through
The dripping woods; the elms their strength renew:
All things the general renovation share.

All things but one. Athwart the hoof-churned track,
The giant Form that for a thousand years
Sheltered the herds, in leafy ruin lies –
A tangled mass of branches gone to wrack.
As into their dark pit the daylight peers,
Its uptorn roots point helpless to the skies.

'BLAKE WALKED AMONG THE STONES OF FIRE...'[88]

Blake walked among the stones of fire,
And yet not scorched was he.
He sang a song of sixpence,
And songs of Eternity.

Blake danced upon the moony banks,
Yet did not lay him down.
He trod the stars beneath his feet,
And had the sun for crown.

Blake fought the intellectual fight
With burning bow and spear.
We'll need his likes in Albion
For many, many a year.

Rouse up, young men of Albion,
Blake calls you from the fire,
Gives you his fiery chariot
And arrows of desire.

Go forth, young men of Albion,
To harrow, forge, and plough,
And build *more* than Jerusalem
In Albion – *now*.

THE DREAM 1982

My heart was held within an Angel's hands.
He looked at it and said, 'It's brighter now,
But still it needs more cleaning.' Smiling then,
He bent and kissed it with serenest brow.

LINES COMPOSED ON RETREAT DURING A PERIOD OF SILENCE

O Sacred Silence, now at last
We let you softly enter in,
Suspending for your lovely sake
Th'unthinking laugh, the mindless din.

O Queen of Contemplation, deign
Within our walls an hour to dwell,
And let no foolish voice profane
Dare to break your holiest spell.

O Star-bedecked, O Full-moon-crowned,
Shed on our hearts your dew of grace;
Teach us the softness of your touch;
Show us the beauty of your face.

Eternal Finger on the lip
Of Being, make us truly blest.
O give us from the ceaseless noise
Of our own lives a little rest.

1983 REALITY TELEGRAMS[89]

Telegrams deal with matters
Of life and death. Mostly death.

Meet me in the usual place.
Something important has happened.

Have arrived in New Zealand
But have forgotten my socks.

Yesterday I saw the first
Aconite of the year.

I don't think I'm in love
But the symptoms are the same.

Have sold house at last. Don't know
What to do with the money.

Invest everything you've got
In the firm I told you about.

Illness serious. Patient
Not expected to recover.

Nothing happened last week.
Will write if any news.

Don't reply telegrams.
No reply needed.

Dreamed about you last night.
Hope everything all right.

Holiday ruined. Cheque books
And everything stolen.

Have met nice girl.
Getting married soon.

Please return book immediately.
Urgently needed.

I love you. I love you.
I love you. I love you.

Terrible accident. Leg
In plaster. Please write.

Leaving hospital Thursday.
Don't bother to meet.

Revolution over. Three
Hundred injured. Ten dead.

Car broken down. Stranded.
Won't be home tonight.

Have forgotten to send flowers
To funeral. Please send.

When you get this
Will be dead. Don't worry.

Arriving Tuesday. Make sure
Beds properly aired.

Congratulations on passing
Examinations. Delighted.

Have found wonderful island.
Drop everything. Come soon.

Zen Master arriving Monday.
Arrange lectures. Entrance free.

Have given everything to poor.
Still feel miserable.

Divorce made absolute.
Children staying with mother.

Page proofs despatched Saturday.
Please return immediately.

Coronation postponed.
King has had heart attack.

Poems not written in blood
Are best not written at all.

If blood not available
Tears may do.

Hospital urgently needs blood.
Donors apply immediately.

Hotels in Majorca fully booked.
Please suggest alternative.

Earthquake. Post Office refuses
To accept any more telegrams.

Reality has no answers.
If there are answers it isn't reality.

Angels wake us up when we're asleep,
Put us to sleep when we're awake.

Angels come to me in the night.
Angels are telegrams.

Telegrams are angels.

The more important the telegram,
The longer it takes to arrive.

Telegrams teach us
The meaning of words.

The greater the angel,
The less he has to say.

The wider the wings,
The taller the angel.

Writing a telegram
Is a liberal education.

The lowest angel
Speaks to the highest man.

The highest angel
Speaks to the lowest man.

A telegram is intelligible
Only to the recipient.

The higher the angel
The more languages he speaks
And the fewer words.

With angels
A word is a language.

Reality sends no telegrams.

Reality is telegrams.
Telegrams are reality.

ST FRANCIS AND THE BIRDS

St Francis in the Umbrian glades
Preached gospel to the birds;
The feathered songsters flocked around
And listened to his words.

Some on his shoulders and his arms
Alit, some on his head;
Whene'er he paused they chirped their joy
At what St Francis said.

Even the solitary owl
Showed his approval too;
He looked out from his hollow tree
And gave a loud 'Tu Whoo!'

For Francis, with a radiant face,
Declared there to them all
How God loved man, and man must love
All creatures great and small.

But now on Sunday afternoons
(Six hundred years have passed)
Come men with dogs and traps and guns
Those happy birds to blast.

They blast them here, they blast them there,
They blast them all around,
Until spent cartridges in heaps
Bestrow the darkening ground.

The cartridges are green and blue,
And yellow, white and red,
But far more beautiful the birds
That sang, and now are dead.

Oh holy Francis, in the height
Of heaven, where'er your place,
Tell me, does God on Sunday nights
Dare look you in the face?

TUSCANY 1983

Between the tree-clad hills the misty plain,
Beyond the misty plain the sea –
A silver-shining ribbon void of stain;
Above, the sky's immensity
Intensely blue, and at the zenith bluest,
As truth within the faithful heart is truest.

On the hill opposite an ancient town
Dreaming, compáct of houses white,
Red-roofed, green-shuttered, some half tumbling down,
With yellow clock-tower shining bright
In th' evening sun, and telling every hour
How time holds all things mortal in its power.

On *this* hill, deepening silence all the day
Inside the convent's crumbling walls;
Through the gloom slanting, many a golden ray
Lights dusty corridors and falls
On red uneven pavements where, long since,
Shuffled cowled monk, strolled courtier, and strode prince.

Below us, at the bottom of the hill,
Beneath black cypresses the dead
Are quiet in tombs, but we are quieter still
In cloisters long untenantéd,
Learning what to be and not to be
Between the olive harvest and the sea.

THE WONDERING HEART

What can it do, when friends avert
Their eyes, or choose to dwell apart?
What can it do when looks grow cold
That once with love shone bright as gold,
What can it do, the wounded heart?

What can it do, when fairest words
Are changed to foul by devilish art?
What can it do when praises turn
To bitter taunts that scar and burn,
What can it do, the weary heart?

What can it do, when in the midst
Of Truth's own household errors start?
What can it do when from the throne
Of Wisdom folly rules alone,
What can it do, the faithful heart?

What can it do, when all around
The fires of hatred leap and dart?
What can it do when smoke and ash
Await the final thunder-crash,
What can it do, the loving heart?

What can it do, when in the night
A thousand dismal shapes upstart?
What can it do when witches prance
Where shining angel-forms should dance,
What can it do, the wakeful heart?

What can it do, when there are none
To whom it may its griefs impart?
What can it do when on the land
And sea are none that understand,
What can it do, the lonely heart?

What can it do, when oracles
Are dumb, and silence fills the mart?
What can it do when no reply
Comes to it from the earth or sky,
What can it do, the wondering heart?

LINES TO JAYAPUSHPA ON HER RETURN TO MALAYSIA

Dear daughter of a tropic isle,
For twice twelve months your radiant smile
Has blessed our dreary London streets,
Whereon the rain remorseless beats,
And where the sun is rarely seen
Gilding grey roofs and treetops green.
You stayed with us to learn anew
The song that had enraptured you
In your green paradise, but which
Had fallen from its proper pitch,
And having learned, you sang as clear
And sweet as some who'd practised here
For many a month and many a year.
But now that your two years are flown,
When you have won all hearts, and grown
For radiant smiles and sweetest song
One of the dearest of our throng,
You must return to your own groves,
To brighter flowers, and warmer loves,
And sing that song again there which
Is dearest, at its proper pitch.
We will sing here, and singing we
Shall hear far off *your* melody
On moonlit summer nights – you ours
Seated among your tropic flowers.

LINES COMPOSED ON ACQUIRING 'THE WORKS OF SAMUEL JOHNSON, LL.D.', IN ELEVEN VOLUMES, MDCCLXXXVII

Three years in earth had Johnson slept,
Three years for him his friends had wept,
When from the presses of the town
That saw him risen to renown
And in meridian splendour glowing
(Though fear of death was ever growing),
Eleven volumes issued forth
To vindicate his lasting worth,
His learning, piety, and wit,
And wisdom, for most subjects fit,
By Hawkins' diligence compiled
And bound, and stamped, and gilt, and styled
The Works of Samuel Johnson. Grand
In their integrity they stand,
Thrice worthy of the library shelf
Of any man that loves himself
And letters, and humanity,
Even in nineteen eighty-three.
The first set forth the sage's life,
His outward and his inward strife,
His struggles and his victory –
'Lord, I commend myself to Thee!' –
Over himself. The other ten
Were traced by Johnson's vigorous pen.
(Remembering what the Decad meant
You'll own that ten's no accident.)
Heading them all, three volumes stand,
Lives of the Poets of the land
From Cowley down to studious Gray
And Lyttelton (unread today),
With lives of heroes, scholars' lives,
Where courage dares, and wit contrives.
Decisively he hands them down
The fadeless or the fading crown.

Ramblers and Adventurers follow,
And Idlers too, all far from hollow,
But giving us, in language dense,
Solid truth without pretence
Heightened to rare magnificence
By strong Imagination's aid:
Four volumes to be truly weighed
In none but giant scales – the treasure
Of 'Johnson on Shakespeare' for good measure,
Together with the mighty Plan
Of that on which, a lonely man,
For ten years long he dauntless wrought,
And slowly to completion brought,
Till *Johnson's Dictionary* stood
Foursquare, and trees became a wood.
Next, in one volume marshalled, we
The Statesman and the Traveller see –
And the Apologist of Tea;
The Thinker too, who through a crack
Spied Evil, shuddered, and drew back.
In the last volume of the set
Three well-known characters are met:
The Prince of Abissinia goes
To study men (from boredom's throes
Seeking release), but though long brooded
The *choice of life* is unconcluded;
Tragic Irene meets her fate,
Victim at once of love and hate,
And Theodore his Vision sees.
Thus in their various way do these
Teach us, both whales and little fishes,
The Vanity of Human Wishes.
Now in these dark uncivil days,
Where few indeed can justly praise,
These volumes in my hands I hold,
And though the binding and the gold
Are worn and faded, and the pages
Faintly stained with damp of ages,

In spite of type-face that distresses
The eye with unfamiliar esses,
Still Johnson's spirit shines as bright
As ever when he saw the light –
Indeed, *our* spirit's lack compounding,
Shines brighter for the gloom surrounding.
Therefore, – although we do not need
The remnants of that savage creed
Which clung to him as Nessus' robe
To Hercules, who'd borne the globe
With less unease, by Pallas aided, –
Because our intellect's degraded
To whim and fancy, and because
We need the strength of wholesome laws
To discipline our wayward hearts
In useful science, joyful arts,
These volumes on the noblest shelf
I place, a blessing to myself
And others, praying they may grant
What men today so badly want,
That bracing 'Clear your *mind* of cant.'

THREE RUBÁIYÁT

Seek not in gloomy charnel-grounds to see
The scattered remnants of the fair and free.
One crimson fallen petal of the rose
Shall read the lesson of mortality.

Sunk in the stream-bed where the hills begin
The wrinkled boulders are as black as sin.
Strike but one blow, and 'Open Sesame!' –
Chambers of glittering crystal lie within.

In Amitābha's paradise, we're told,
Bloom flowers of jade and crystal flecked with gold.
Could but one petal to the earth descend
To purchase it should all my goods be sold.

A WISH

Oh for a Persian garden,
Where perfect roses bloom!
Oh for a white pavilion!
Oh for a blue-tiled room!

Oh for an open window
Through which the birds can fly!
Oh for a young musician!
Oh for a golden sky!

Oh for a turquoise fountain!
Oh for a crystal rill!
And oh for a song in the evening
So sweet that time stands still!

YEMEN REVISITED

Flýing slower, flýing faster,
Birds through a ceiling of alabaster,
Gold against an azure sky,
Trace in bright calligraphy
On those rainbow-bordered pages
Lore sublime of ancient sages,
Wisdom-treasures of the heart
Distilled in words by subtlest art;
Words that through the alabaster
Make the listless heart beat faster,
Till like an enchanted thing
Anon it spreads its golden wing
And seeks to join the happy birds
That on the azure trace those words,
Truth to other eyes revealing
From behind that wondrous ceiling.

BHÁJÁ, 1983[90]

Behind, ascending by degrees,
The mountain-barriers stand,
And rocky spurs on either side
Enclose the quiet land,
Where fields on fields, now fawn now dun,
Lie basking in the evening sun.

Here Nature with unsparing hand
Gives man whate'er he needs;
She sends the swift torrential rain
That swells the planted seeds;
She clothes the earth in living green
And scatters sunshine o'er the scene.

But most of all she gives the peace
Within which we can find
The deeper peace she cannot give –
The peace of heart and mind:
The peace that monks in woods and caves
Have found before they fill their graves.

EPIGRAM ON MOLLY THE MEDIUM

Her skin is greasy, and her garments stink.
The medium is the message, don't you think?

POEMS ON PAINTINGS FROM THE 'GENIUS OF VENICE'   1984
EXHIBITION AT THE ROYAL ACADEMY[91]

I. PROLOGUE
With acknowledgements to A. E. Housman

Noblest of schools, the Royal today
Is hung with paintings grave and gay,
And rises mid the streets and mews
Clad in a thousand wondrous hues.

Now, of my threescore years and ten,
Sixty will not come again,
And take from seventy years three-score,
It only leaves me ten years more.

And since for seeing works of grace
Ten years is but a little space,
This morning I must go, it seems,
To see the Royal hung with dreams.

II. TOBIAS AND THE ANGEL
After the painting by Savoldo

He sits at ease upon the rocks,
The Angel with the outspread wings;
Loosely to limbs of noblest mould
His rose and silver vesture clings.

Watchful he sits, right arm half raised
In monitory gesture sweet,
While travel-worn the small grey dog
Sleeps darkling near his naked feet.

Caught by that gesture as he kneels
Tobias turns, as in a dream;
Knowing his destined hour is come
The great fish gapes from out the stream.

III. THE TEMPTATION OF ST ANTHONY
After the painting by Veronese

Again with hideous thud the club descends,
Wielded by naked devil's brawny arm,
As, sprawling on his back, the red-robed saint
Clutches the book that wards off ultimate harm.

Behind his grizzled head, her bosom bare
Save for light gauze, a female devil bland
And beautiful, bright hair in snaky wreaths,
Scratches with coal-black claws his upraised hand.

IV. SALOME
After the painting by Titian

1.
With looks demure, and tress that down her cheek
Straggles, enhancing every ripening charm,
She holds the Baptist's head upon a dish
And feels his hair upon her naked arm.

2.
Corpse-grey, a cupid flutters on the arch
That frames blue sky, and clouds touched by the sun.
Half hidden by her daughter's crimson sleeve,
Herodias broods upon the work she's done.

V. THE ADORATION OF THE MAGI
After the painting by Schiavone

Heretics roasted for the love of Christ
Can things inanimate indeed foresee?
Between the Magi and the holy Child
The giant pillar writhes in agony.

Fluttering above, a half-clad angel bears
Both crown and wreath on this tumultuous morn.
Oh turn him back! Oh bid the horsemen go!
Better that Mary's Son had ne'er been born.

VI. THE LION OF ST MARK[92]
After the painting by Carpaccio

Behold the Lion of St Mark!
His steps are on both land and sea;
Proudly he wears his eagle wings,
For power is his, and victory.

Opened before him is the Book
In which are written, black and bold,
Those words which to the Most Serene
Like thunder down the ages rolled.

Beneath his wings the galleons ride;
Before his face rise dome and tower,
Together with that sumptuous pile
In which three architectures flower.

In aureoled glory self-absorbed,
And fangs half-bared, he does not see
The beauty of the humble shrubs
That clothe with life the sandy lea;

He does not see the lowly weeds
That pave the ground, and still will pave,
When all the pomp of Venice lies
Beneath the green and gilded wave.

MINERVA'S REBUKE TO JEAN COCTEAU[93]

My wisdom cold? It was not cold
When amid flames I sprang to light
From Jove's cleft forehead fully armed,
A maiden goddess stern and bright.

It was not cold that day I strove
With blue-haired Neptune on the lea
For Athens of the Violet Crown,
And won her with my olive tree.

Ulysses, Perseus golden-haired,
And many a brother hero bold
Whom I had tutored in their dreams –
They did not find my wisdom cold.

Sleepless am I, nor do I need
The madness of the Bacchic throng
To trace the steps, or sound the note,
For my majestic dance and song.

Whether beneath the Eye of Day,
Or looked on by the Starry Seven,
Around I lead my votaries on
The everlasting roofs of heaven.

THREE EPITAPHS

1. FOR A PERSISTENT DEBTOR
For years I bilked my debts, and bilked with mirth,
But cannot bilk the last sad debt to earth.

2. FOR A LIBERTINE
I laughed at death with women, wine, and song;
But now death laughs at me, and *he* laughs long.

3. FOR A YOUNG CHILD
Short were my steps upon the earth, and few,
And yet they very quickly brought me here.

THE GOLDEN FLOWER

So love grew up between us like a flower,
Though neither made a sign, or breathed a word,
Content to watch it growing hour by hour,
And see its petals by the breezes stirred.

At length it grew to such a breadth and height
It stood there like a mighty forest tree,
With thousand glorious petals golden-bright,
And I could not see you, nor you see me.

And so the flower, for both, is all in all,
Though each is in the flower, the flower in each,
And each in each, for ever, past recall –
A mystery this, beyond the grasp of speech.

EIGHT TUSCAN HAIKU

In shine and shower,
Beside each other they stand –
The silver birches.

Pigeons in the elms –
They do not disturb him,
The old stone Buddha.

After last night's rain
In the grass of the hedgerows
Frail pink cyclamen.

The tortoise we saw
By the roadside this morning –
How far he had come!
(Had nothing to say)

Reeds tied up in a bundle
With a twist of straw –
How long will they stay together?

My pains are my own.
There is no one to share them with me.
Likewise my poems.

The bee takes the honey
From the flower, but does not know
What the flower really thinks.

My mother hasn't written to me
For a long time.
At eighty-seven one's fingers
Are stiffer than they used to be.

AFTER ABŪ SA'ĪD[94]

When shall a man from all his wants be freed
And break the chains of folly, hate, and greed?
Only when in his loving, longing heart
Subtly is sown the transcendental seed.

1986 THE BALLAD OF THE RETURN JOURNEY[95]

I walked across to the lecture hall,
The sun shone bright overhead.
Toby was standing outside the door;
'You're two minutes late,' he said.

Inside, the panelled room was full
Of ladies and gents so refined,
All talking about their previous births
And how it was all in the mind.

They talked so loud, and they talked so long,
That they never even heard
What I'd come five thousand miles to say –
No, not a single word.

For they only wanted to sit and gaze
At my yellow robe so exotic,
And watched the gradual growth of my hair
With a fascination neurotic.

When I spoke of the Way in practical terms
They thought it was frightfully sordid.
Toby put on his little black cap
And everyone applauded.

I. M., TARASHRI[96] 1988

Late in your life you found the Eightfold Way,
And having found it, trod it night and day; –
Trod it with Friends, whose praises you would sing
As loud as any songbird in the Spring.
Now you are gone; but only as a star,
Which, though extinct, sheds radiance from afar
To those who on this dark earth wandering are.

1989 NEIGHBOURS

We have interesting neighbours.
They live on the third floor
Of the block of flats opposite,
In a flat with three lace-curtained windows
And a corner balcony.
They are mother and son,
Or perhaps husband and wife
(One can't be sure of these things nowadays:
In fact one can't be sure of anything.)
The woman (as we call her) always appears on the balcony in
    déshabillé,
A cigarette dangling from the corner of her mouth.
Four times a day she cleans the windows,
Every now and then putting out on the balcony –
And almost immediately taking it in again –
A birdcage complete with small bird.
On what would appear to be festive occasions
She hangs out rags or minor items of washing
On a line stretched diagonally across the balcony from a convenient
    drainpipe.
The behaviour of the man (as we call him) is even more interesting.
Suddenly appearing on the balcony
He squares up to his reflection in the balcony window,
Thrusts out his chin,
Throws out his chest,
Flexes his muscles,
Turns this way and that,
Tosses his head –
All for his own benefit,
Unless the woman (as we call her)
Happens to be watching from the wings.
The whole performance is repeated half a dozen times
In quick succession,
Often several times a day
And with a variety of costumes.

Sometimes he appears on the balcony so suddenly,
And goes through his routine so quickly,
That the show is over almost before we realize it has begun.
But just as *we* see
Both his back *and* the reflection of his chest and face in the window,
Does *he*, I wonder, ever see
Not only his own reflection
But also, behind it,
The reflection of two pairs of eyes
Watching him from the building opposite?
Does *he*, I wonder, ever think
'We have interesting neighbours'?
Probably not.
Narcissus has no time for neighbours.

THE PEOPLE OF BETHNAL GREEN

The people of Bethnal Green are not beautiful,
Especially when looked at closely.
The women are overweight and loaded down
With shopping baskets and plastic bags.
Moreover they have peroxided hair
And fags dangling from slack, loose lips.
Even the young girls, who *should* be beautiful,
Are puffy and piggy, wear unsuitable clothes,
Walk on black trotters, and munch sweets and pastries
With slow-moving hippopotamus jaws.
The men, who are frequently alcoholic,
Have a wife on one arm and push a perambulator.
But some of the young men, every now and then,
Glance up at the pale blue sky
(Sometimes, of course, it is raining),
As though they had mislaid their destiny.

The people of Bethnal Green are not beautiful,
But some of them *could* be.

PARADISE LOST

Living in Paradise
Before the Fall
You'd soon get bored,
And with Eve most of all.

Her silly chatter
Would drive you mad,
Till you felt like doing
Something really bad.

When you had that feeling
The Devil would come along,
Twitching his tail
And singing a merry song.

The Devil and you
Would have long debates
About good and evil, etc.,
And you'd soon be mates.

The Devil and you
Would sit on your bums
Putting Paradise to rights
And you'd soon be chums.

Over pints of the best
You'd natter and natter.
Eve, out in Paradise,
Would simply grow fatter.

THE OAK AND THE IVY

The oak stands in the forest
Among his brother trees.
The weak and harmless ivy
Has crept up to his knees.

The oak stands in the forest
With green and golden crest.
The weak and harmless ivy
Has twined about his breast.

The oak stands in the forest
Upright still, but inly dead.
The weak and harmless ivy
Has covered up his head.

The oak lies in the forest
Dismembered and apart.
The weak and harmless ivy
Has pierced him to the heart.

1990 BETRAYAL

    What agonies await him now,
    The scourge, the nails, the thorn-crowned brow;
    But none to be compared with this –
    That treacherous, seeming-friendly kiss.

THERE IS A LAND MORE LOVELY   1991

There is a land more lovely
Than that which now we know,
A land of gold and jewels and light –
A land devoid of woe.

Glimpses of that land we get
In poem, painting, tune;
We see it in the lordly sun,
And in the gentle moon.

But most of all we see it
In the lives of saint and seer –
In lives wherein embodied truth
Shines brighter year by year.

KALIMPONG

The name of the place
Meant 'A Skull Capsized'.
Fourteen years I lived there,
But *my* skull never capsized.
I left as sane as when I arrived,
Unfortunately.

'A MAN WAS WALKING BEHIND ME...'

A man was walking behind me
Wrapped in a grey cloak. He was walking
Slowly, but somehow, imperceptibly,
He overtook me
And I saw it was Old Age.
'Hurry up!' he said, looking back at me
With a broad grin,
'Or you'll be late for your own death.'

'THE PAST IS IN THE MIND...'

The past is in the mind,
The future too.
Life is a dream, a cloud,
A drop of dew.

The present is – and isn't;
It comes but to depart.
Only Eternity
Can glut the heart.

AN OLD STORY

It was Lilith out of Eden,
Half woman and half snake.
She took his heart from Adam;
Her heart he could not take.

And thus do Lilith's daughters
With the sons of Adam live.
Sweet-smiling and cold-blooded
They take – but never give.

THE GREAT THINGS OF GUHYALOKA[97]
With acknowledgements to Thomas Hardy

Pine-scent is a great thing,
   A great thing to me,
Settling down on needles brown
   By Lion Rock mindfully,
And word and image summoning
   To aid my ecstasy:
O pine-scent is a great thing,
   A great thing to me.

Poetry is a great thing,
   A great thing to me,
With gas lamp lit and sonnets fit
   For night-long rhapsody;
And sleeping till the blackbird
   Trills sweet within the tree:
O poetry is a great thing,
   A great thing to me.

Friendship is, yea, a great thing,
   A great thing to me,
When, having borne a lot forlorn
   In patience, eagerly
A bright form breaks as though a-wing
   From out the greenery:
O friendship is, yes, a great thing,
   A great thing to me.

Will there be always great things,
   Great things to me?...
Will it befall that Voices call,
   'Soul, you are now set free':
What then? Pine-scents, impassioned song,
   Friendship, and its liberty,
Will always have been great things,
   Great things to me.

THE GURU OF DHARSENDO[98]

I rejoice in the merits
Of the Guru of Dharsendo;
I rejoice in his life
Of mindfulness and compassion.
I rejoice in his confident turning
Of the Wheel of the Immaculate Dharma,
And in his faultless wielding
Of the Diamond Sceptre of Wisdom.
I rejoice in his proclamation
To his disciples both young and old,
To his disciples both near and far,
Of the threefold inspiring message
To cherish the Doctrine, live united, and radiate love.
I rejoice in his practice
Of the Six Perfections:
In his practice of unfailing generosity:
In his practice of flawless Ethics and Manners;
In his practice of infinite forbearance;
In his practice of inexhaustible vigour;
In his practice of unshakeable concentration;
In his practice of profound and far-reaching Wisdom.
Humbly and heartily,
Gratefully and reverentially,
With body, speech, and mind,
I rejoice in the merits
Of the Guru of Dharsendo,
I rejoice in the merits
Of Dhardo Rimpoche.

MY SECRET GARDEN   1992

Blessed is my secret garden
With sunshine, rain, and snow;
The noisome weeds all flourish,
Sweet flowers they cannot grow.

Oh that some ancient gardener
Could scythe there for an hour,
So that one rose or lily
Had room to breathe and flower!

TIME AND ETERNITY

Stand still, O Time, that I may see,
Beyond your flow, Eternity;
Then flow again, that I may bring
Eternity within your ring,
And, bringing it, endow my days
With cause to wonder and to praise.

FOR P—— ON SOLITARY RETREAT

My friend has gone
To the Cymric shore,
Where the waves beat
And the winds roar.

My friend has gone
To a cabin on a green hill,
Where the white clouds drift past
And the peewits are shrill.

My friend has gone
Where, men's madness afar,
One can muse on the sunset
And the evening star.

My friend has gone
Where lonesome nights see
Time intersect
With eternity.

My friend has gone
Where white dawns bring
Dreams and visions
On angel wing.

My friend will come
From the Cymric shore
Refreshed, a flame burning
At the heart's core.

My friend will come
Like the heroes of old,
Victorious brow
Encircled with gold.

BIRDS AND THEIR GODS

1. BLACKBIRD

Trill trill trill goes the blackbird
At the cold blue edge of day,
Trill trill trill goes Apollo's bird
From the chimney pot across the way.

Perched above the roof tiles
Old oracles he quotes,
Pouring, in lingering moonlight,
His thoughtful, liquid notes.

Stationed at my window
I hear the darkling bird,
And wish that I could give the world
As divine a word.

2. SPARROW

Cheep cheep cheep goes the sparrow,
Pecking in the dirt for crumbs;
Cheep cheep cheep goes Aphrodité's bird,
Familiar of a thousand slums.

Black-bibbed and tawny-coated
He noisily debates,
As prompt in eaves and gutters
He quick-fire copulates.

No wonder that our forebears,
In palace or in shack,
Deemed sparrow pie a sovereign
Aphrodisiac.

3. RAVEN

Croak croak croak goes the raven
In London's fatal Tower;
Croak croak croak goes Woden's bird
In his flinty Thames-side bower.

Kings and queens has he witnessed
Coming and going in state;
Once, a princess sitting on a stone in the rain,
Just landed at Traitor's Gate.

The day that sees those grim walls
From his ghastly presence free,
That day brings on the Twilight
Of Britain's monarchy.

4. PEACOCK

Miao ... miao ... miao ... goes the peacock,
Lifting his golden crest;
Miao ... miao ... miao ... goes Hera's bird,
Ensconced in his low-built nest.

Bronze-winged and sapphire-bodied
He eats, nor eats in vain,
Snakes whose poisons make more brilliant
The colours of his train.

Eyes of mauve and violet,
Ringed with turquoise, purple, green,
On a ground of bronze and copper
That shimmers in between.

5. OWL

Tu-whit tu-whoo goes the owl,
Tawny or white or grey;
Tu-whit tu-whoo goes Athené's bird,
That shuns the light of day.

Perched in the breathing darkness
Above his pellet-mound,
Through the moonlit olive gardens
He sends his wavering sound.

Wise, vigilant, and fearsome,
He lives from age to age,
Staring with great round eyes
From Athens' coináge.

6. EAGLE

Kwark ... kwark ... goes the eagle,
Gazing into the sun;
Kwark ... kwark ... goes Zeus's bird,
His task nearly done.

Ganymede in his talons,
He heads for Olympus' height,
Where the deathless gods have their thrones
In the Titans' despite.

The boy of matchless beauty
Is lost to mortal ken,
Pouring the golden nectar
For the Father of gods and men.

MUCALINDA[99]

Bowing I stand
As I am in truth,
From snake transformed
To radiant youth.

Sev'n days and nights
My serpent form
Has sheltered him
From the raging storm.

Sev'n days and nights
About his frame
I've clasped my coils
As the buffets came.

Sev'n days and nights
Above his crown
I've spread my hoods
As the rain poured down.

Now the sky is clear,
The sun shines bright,
And the green earth glitters
In morning light.

Reverie ended,
He opens his eyes
And looks at the world
Sans surprise;

Looks at the world
With compassion for
Men locked in inner
And outer war;

Looks at a world
Where his task will be
To speak the word
That sets them free.

So bowing I stand
As I am in truth,
From snake king transformed
To radiant youth.

DIPTYCH

One wears a yellow robe,
Neat and freshly laundered;
One wears *his* black and orange stripes
Who once in jungle maundered.

One shows a bald pate,
Round and razor-levelled;
One shows an Afro style,
Spiky and dishevelled.

One has a gentle look,
Soft and reassuring;
One has a wrathful smile,
Fearsome yet alluring.

One chants the scriptures,
One beats a drum;
To one come the high gods,
To one the *demons* come.

These figures rise before us,
Both ancient and yet new.
So Western Buddhists, make your choice –
Or combine the two.

THE GODS

Gods in the gallery I behold –
All white, all marble, and all cold.

WORK AND PLAY[100]

'Work is the companion,'
The Sage of Weimar said;
But play is the lover
With whom we go to bed.

Play is the lover
From whose embrace there springs
A Helen medievalized,
A Euphorion with wings.

CONTRARIES

For you the restless ocean,
For me the rocky isle;
For you the fluid manner,
For me the chiselled style.

For you mercurial passion,
For me crystálline thought;
For you the blithe 'I want to',
For me the grave 'I ought'.

Meeting at the shoreline
Where stone is ground to sand
And foam sucked into shingle
We wander hand in hand.

THE NEOPLATONISTS[101]

Within the shadowy colonnade
The white-haired sages sit or stroll,
Discoursing on the highest good
And on the greatness of the Soul.

Gravely they speak, in accents mild,
With many a solemn pause between,
As if with inward eye they glimpsed
Beyond the seen, the vast Unseen.

The young men, seated on the steps
Below, drink in each quiet word;
They may not always understand,
And yet their hearts are strangely stirred.

About the temple roof there clings
A glory, while above the sun
There spin the holy Archetypes
In cosmic dance around the One.

MY PEARL

I dived and found a pearl, but when I brought
My pearl into the market-place I found
No one had eyes for treasures of that sort.
There were too many glass beads heaped around.

1993 PEOPLE LIKE THINGS LABELLED

People like things labelled. They want to know
If you are fish, flesh, fowl or good red herring.
In particular they want to know
If you are *bad* red herring. Thus it was
That they asked me if I was monk or layman (meaning
Really if I was chaste or unchaste). I pointed
Skyward, saying, 'The stars belong to the sky, but the names
"Orion", "Andromeda", "Great Bear", *they* belong to the earth.'
They replied, 'You are being evasive. We knew it all along.
You are *bad* red herring.' And they threw me
Back into the sea, where I swam
Happily with other bad red herrings. The loss was theirs.

YESTERDAY'S BLOSSOMS

Sing? This is not the time for singing. This
Is the time for reflection, the time
For seeing yesterday's blossoms
Mirrored in today's black waters.

THE TEACHER OF GODS AND MEN
Satthādevamanussānaṃ

His dreams were visions. In the night
He saw the lords of love and light,
And did to them, in song and story,
Reveal the Peace beyond the Glory.

His speech was music. All the day
He pointed out the Noble Way
To men who, wandering in the dark,
Had quite forgot their ancient Spark.

CRYSTAL BALL

Crystal ball, showing
Not the future but the past, showing
Snow peaks, showing
Blue sky, and in the sky
The smile of the Buddha.

MY LIFE

My life is a dance
In which every movement
Is planned yet
Spontaneous.

FOUR HAIKU

Seen through the fanlight
On my way to the bathroom,
A misty moon.

How many inkstains
On its chipped surface –
My old wooden desk.

What's all this talk
Of the ocean and its waves
As we drink our tea!

Midnight.
When the revellers have passed,
A deeper silence.

REMEMBERING THE POETRY READING

Read aloud,
all poems
are good poems.
Otherwise,
they lie dead on the page,
cold Adams
awaiting the touch
of the Divine
Finger.

EX LIBRIS

One day I must leave you, my old friends,
Silent upon your shelves in serried rows.

ZEN[102]

A golden flower held up, an answering smile –
Just that. No explanations! Words defile.

LONDON BRIDGE

London Bridge is falling down,
And falling every arch and tower;
And pointed brick and polished stone
Prove weaker than the tiniest flower –

Prove weaker than the tiniest flower
That through the rubble thrusts its head
When silence settles on the globe
And man with all his dreams is dead.

ON A CERTAIN AUTHOR

Myself into his book I hurled
Like Orpheus visiting the underworld.

TO P—— IN PRAGUE[103]

Defenestration was the word in Prague
Five hundred years ago or thereabouts –
A throwing of opponents out of windows.
First it was Catholics, then Protestants,
Came sailing through the Gothic émbrasures –
Arms and legs flailing, cloaks blown out behind –
To fall uninjured in the moat below.
More recently they've thrown the Marxists out,
This time not literally but metaphorically
(The Marxists, too, have landed on their feet).
Now *you* are there, there in Bohemian Prague,
Prague of Jan Hus and Good King Wenceslas,
Prague of the Emperors and Alchemists,
Prague of the dreams in stone and dreams in glass.
You see the Castle, see the Golem's haunts,
Stand on Charles Bridge, and watch the Vltava flow.
Perhaps you muse upon that century when
Defenestration was the word in Prague.
Perhaps, from those same Gothic windows gazing,
You tell yourself, there in Bohemian Prague,
'Open the windows of the heart and mind!
Throw out old passions, ancient prejudices!
Empty the Council Chamber of the Soul,
And there install, with all due ceremony,
The Emperor who turns the Wheel of Truth,
The Alchemist who transmutes our lead to gold!'

1994 'SURELY KING MARK WAS MAD...'[104]

Surely King Mark was mad,
And godly Arthur too,
Sending so graced a knight
On his behalf to woo,

Unless his soul divined
Some deeper, richer plan,
Whereby his future queen
Should have the better man.

Perhaps there *is* a destiny
That shapes our several ends,
Rough hew them how we will – or one
That makes divine amends

For human insufficiency....
And yet our lives we must
Rough hew as best we can or be
Accounted less than dust.

THE POETRY OF FRIENDSHIP[105]

The poetry of friendship
Is the poetry of tears –
Of the dreams across the distance,
The partings lasting years.

The poetry of friendship
Is the poetry of death,
From Callímachus to Milton
And Shelley's tuneful breath.

The poetry of friendship
Is the poetry of fate.
Friends rarely know how much they love
Until it is too late –

Too late for recognition,
Too late to speak the word
In which the heart discloses
How deeply it is stirred –

Too late for anything, when the Fury
Slits the other's thread in half,
Save to urn the long-cold ashes
And compose an epitaph.

1995 THE CALL OF THE FOREST

What does the forest whisper
With every wind-stirred leaf,
From many-centuried oak tree
To hour-old blossom-sheaf?
What does the forest whisper
When nightingales are dumb
And cícadas fall silent?
The forest whispers, 'Come'.

What does the forest whisper
In sunshine and in shade,
Down every moss-hung alley,
In each deer-haunted glade?
What does the forest whisper
When full or crescent moon
Steeps nodding crests in silver?
The forest whispers, 'Soon'.

What does the forest whisper
From depths primeval, where
A sound is lost in stillness
As clouds dissolve in air?
What does the forest whisper
When from the darkling bough
Drop one by one the dead leaves?
The forest whispers, 'Now'.

But the whisper's a dream-whisper,
For years on years have flown
Since oak and ash and holly
Could call the land their own.
The whisper's a dream-whisper,
For Cities of the Plain
Usurp the once-green kingdom
Of forests they have slain.

The whisper's a dream-whisper,
For 'forest' is a dream
Of days when Man through Nature
Had sense of a Supreme.
The whisper's a dream-whisper
Of a time when he could feel
In the pressure of the actual
The touch of the Ideal.

The whisper's a dream-whisper,
But dreams are of the Soul
And Soul itself a forest
Beyond the mind's control.
The whisper's a Soul-whisper,
That like a muffled drum
Calls, 'From your mind-built Cities,
O Man, to Freedom come!'

THE ANGEL IN THE HOUSE

I am the Angel in the House
I am the Angel
Virginia Woolf tried to strangle
But I'm still around
I wipe children's noses
Place a cool hand on hot foreheads
Make tea
Knit
Welcome tired husbands home from work
Et cetera
I like doing these things
And I guess I've as much right to exist
As any other kind of Angel
Especially the Female Writing Angel
Who despite having a private income
And a Room of Her Own
And a perfect husband
And two or three lovers
And her own publishing house
Goes and throws herself in the nearest river
(Silly woman)
So as I move about the House
Wings demurely folded
Skirts rustling
I sing this song to myself

    Virginia Woolf
    All teeth and pearls
    Was fond of men
    But fonder of girls

    Virginia wrote
    Pages and pages
    Thought she was heir
    Of all the ages

Though she was Leslie
Stephen's daughter
She ended up
In three feet of water

THREE PLUMES

I understand the blind old king who rode into battle
At the head of his troops, a knight on either side to guide him.
He did not wait for Death, but went bravely to meet him;
The three white plumes on his helmet danced in the sunlight.

1996 THE MINOR POETS

Shakespeare, Milton, Wordsworth, Coleridge
Are godlike spirits; we are men,
And cannot always brook their splendour –
The Minor Poets please us then.

The singers of the lesser vision,
Who never soar beyond our ken –
When we grow tired of greatness, they,
The Minor Poets, soothe us then.

Oppressed by fears, by doubts bewildered,
From Melancholia's cluttered den –
For all their charm, for all their solace,
The Minor Poets, we thank them then.

Faded bindings, dusty edges,
Words underscored by studious pen –
Rejoice to see them on the shelves,
And *praise* the Minor Poets then.

IN MEMORY OF ALLEN GINSBERG 1997

Best minds, he called us, of his generation,
And howled, at our destruction, through the night;
But some of us, thanks to a Word well spoken,
Survived, and deep in darkness saw a light.

Now, Allen, you are gone, best mind of all
For honesty in thought and word and deed,
And I salute you, though I cannot write
My name to every item of your creed.

But let me pluck a leaf from Cowley's book,
And separate the dogma from the dean
In some respects, give praise where praise is due,
And celebrate the *man* that you have been.

Lover of Blake and boys, to you was given
The rage that burns within the tyger's heart,
To you, likewise, the meekness of the lamb,
The victim's posture, but the hero's part.

You were no devil, though some thought you were,
No angel, either, but a star whose spears
Down on the floor of heaven long since were thrown
Gladly; and *earth* was watered by your tears.

God on his throne, if God above there be,
Has surely smiled to hear you sing and play
Your cymbals. Now, as by his side you sit,
He crowns you king of his eternal May.

TRANSMISSION

'Grain threshed and ready?'
'Ready, long ago.'
'Come then at midnight;
Don't let others know.'

Two heads together
In the Master's room.
Diamond words whispered:
A thousand flowers bloom.

THE POET

I have never regretted
Buying a book,
Though it left me no money
With which to hook
A woman, or spend
With a like-minded friend.

I have never regretted
Not being rich,
Though nights I had
To lie in the ditch
With a rose overhead
And mud for bed.

I have never regretted
Serving the Muse,
Though well she knew
I could not refuse
The heavenly chore,
Though at death's door.

THE DANCE OF DEATH

You dance with emperor, pope, and king,
With knight and dame of high degree;
You dance with youth, you dance with eld,
And one day you will dance with me.

You take for partner whom you please;
To choose is yours, and yours alone,
And one day I will surely find
Your bony hand within my own,

Your bony knee against my knee,
As whirling with you in the dance
My eyes behold, an inch away,
Your ghastly, grinning countenance.

But if I do not shrink from it,
And boldly look you through and through,
Your bony frame in dazzling light
Will be dissolved, and born anew.

Oh you a shining angel shape
Will be, and I, released from strife,
Will find the Dance of Death to be
The Revels of Eternal Life.

AFTER VISITING NEW ZEALAND

What I am left with
Now the long journey's been made?
A handful of memories
And a polished piece of jade.

REVENGE

Red were the leaves upon the beech
Between me and the setting sun,
But redder on the turf beneath
The heart's blood of my brother's son.

And that is why at break of day
The sun shall see upon my knife,
And on the castle steps, the blood
Of those who foully took his life.

O he was fair and *she* was fair,
Yet one was fairer, wealthier still,
And so the traitress and her man
Conspired my brother's son to kill.

In shadow of the castle wall
I wait to see the sun uprise,
My hand upon my knife, a mist
Of blood, red blood, before my eyes.

FROZEN TULIPS

Frozen tulips, mauve and green,
You have lost your heavenly sheen,
Transported, from I know not where,
To florists in the city square.

Perhaps, hermetically sealed,
You left by air the happy field
Where millions of you, rainbow-hued,
With scent and colour were imbued.

Now, stiffly in my vase you stand,
Petals unable to expand,
Your green to yellow slowly turning,
And mauve to black, as though from burning.

WHITE TĀRĀ

Appearing from the depth of heaven,
The white-robed goddess, calm and bright,
Sheds moon-like on this lower world
The blessing of her silver light.

Seven eyes she has, all open wide,
In face and forehead, hands and feet,
For she of Pure Awareness is
Embodiment and paraclete.

One hand, in teaching gesture raised,
Imparts a wisdom thrice-profound;
The other, open on her knee,
For endless giving is renowned.

A lotus at her shoulder grows,
Complete with flower, and bud, and fruit;
Her form is straight and still, for she
Is grounded on the Absolute.

'Awake! Arise!' she seems to say,
'Leave dreams, leave sloth, leave passions vile!'
Oh may we, seeing her, go forth
Encouraged by her perfect smile.

SPLENDOR SOLIS
After Omraam Mikhael Aivanhov[106]

Though ninety million miles away,
A ball of heat, and light, and song,
His gifts to us are infinite,
And yet we do him grievous wrong.

We say that he is dead, although
We live. Can life from death arise?
Oh hail him monarch of your hearts,
As sovereign of the azure skies!

That blaze of light unbearable,
That golden splendour, pure and whole,
That burning disc, that crimson orb,
Is temple to a living soul.

So worship him at dawn and dusk,
And noon; at midnight breathe a prayer.
Behind the curtain of the dark,
Oh he is there, oh he is there.

PADMASAMBHAVA

Riding a tiger
The Guru came,
Smile fierce and friendly,
Eyes aflame.

Riding a tiger
From coast to coast,
With his vajra he scattered
The demon host.

Guru, great Guru,
Dispel my sin;
Hurl back the demon
Hordes within;

Transform them to powers
That protect the Right –
Thou, the Thousand-armed,
Thou, the Infinite Light.

LETTER TO ĀNANDA[107]

Ānanda, thirty years ago
We walked abroad through sleet and snow
Along the Embankment, underneath
A freezing sky. Apollo's wreath
Was yours, Tiresias' fillets mine,
Though you from discontent divine,
Night after night, in coffee bars
Would grasp at novelistic stars
Beyond your early reach; while I,
Fresh from a cloudless Indian sky,
Down in my weekly catacomb
Strove hard to make a little room
In people's minds for faith and hope
Beyond the *Daily Mirror's* scope.
Now three decades and more are flown
And each has reaped as he has sown.
In Bristol you, these many days,
Are crowned with bright poetic bays
(Bays only seen of those, I grant,
Who've signed the Muses' covenant
In Churchill's 'blood, toil, tears and sweat'
Without repining or regret);
While I, in Birmingham, can see
Where once a seed was, now a tree
Beneath whose branches, widely spread,
Thousands are on ambrosia fed
Who once had only stones for bread
(An image from the Bible drawn
Yet common property, like corn).
But poet or prophet, lion or lamb,
In Bristol or in Birmingham,
We face a common destiny:
You're fifty, I am seventy-three,
And do not know how many times
Again we'll hear the ponderous chimes
Of old Big Ben (per courtesy

Of your once boss, the BBC)
Before we stand on Styx's shore
(Not that we really knew before),
There to wait till Charon yields
Us passage to the Elysian Fields;
Or ere (another speculation,
Or glorious imagination)
We somehow wake to find ourselves
On lotus-calices, like elves,
And as the petals open see
The wonders of Sukhāvati.
But whether to Elysium,
And heroes' company, we come,
Or whether join, with dance and song,
The noble Bodhisattva-throng,
To feel with them the Buddha's grace
And sense, beyond the Light, his face,
Beneath the jewel-trees, in the Happy Place,
Our time is short. Oh let us strive
To keep the precious link alive
With visits and with messages
From home or from beyond the seas;
And if sometimes we cannot meet
Be sure to keep our friendship sweet
With spices of the written word,
By which the heart is strangely stirred.
Donne's dictum down the ages rolls
Unchallenged: 'Letters mingle Souls.'

DONNE'S BELL[108]

Jack Donne he was a Roaring Boy
And loved a Southwark wench;
He loved the bottle, loved the Muse,
And dearly loved his friends;
For youth must learn, and so will burn
The candle at both ends.

Dean Donne he was a preacher,
Grandiloquent, severe;
In Paul's churchyard he wrenched his text
Twenty times a year;
For when you're old the blood runs cold
And soon you're on your bier.

When naked at the bar of heaven
John Donne for judgement stands,
Without his sword, without his plume,
Without his cap and bands,
He'll get from God a kindly nod
Because God understands.

He understands that man is clay
As well as breath of heaven,
And that the second's to the first
As one to six or seven,
And that to bake a human cake
There must be dough *and* leaven.

Though which is clay, which heavenly breath,
Men cannot always tell,
And therefore should be slow to think
A soul in heaven or hell.
Come weal or woe, we only know
'It tolls for *thee*,' that bell.

REVISED VERSION[109]
With Apologies to Philip Larkin

They bring you up, your mum and dad.
They don't know how to, but they do.
They buy you things they never had
And save some money, just for you.

For they were brought up in their turn
By folk in Oxfam hats and coats,
Who played at being soft or stern
With laughter bubbling in their throats.

Man hands on happiness to man.
It rises like a coastal shelf.
Get in as early as you can,
And have a lot of kids yourself.

EPIGRAMS

Barking dogs all round me
My footsteps try to clog;
But if I don't bark in reply
It's because I'm not a dog.

What have their contents told me,
These volumes old and stout?
Naked we came into the world
And naked will go out.

Academics in their ivory tower
Discuss Blake's worth, and estimate his power,
Careful, although his genius admiring,
To worship Urizen before retiring.

1998 GUHYALOKA: JULY 1998[110]

Back in the magic valley
I breathe the smoke-free air
And listen to the silence
Distilling everywhere.
Far from the roar of traffic,
Far from the frantic crowd,
I feel my soul expanding
With dreams not disallowed.

Back in the verdant valley
The pine trees lift their arms
As if in joyous welcome
To this refuge from all harms; –
To this refuge – or this respite –
From the venom-dripping tongue
And the shafts that fly in darkness
From a bow by malice strung.

Back in the fragrant valley,
Care-emancipate, alone,
I communicate in silence
With the giant shapes of stone –
Grey, ancient forms that tell me,
In the stillness, 'Time will cure.
Meanwhile, be calm, be silent;
The secret is: Endure.

'We endure the cold of winter,
We endure the summer's heat,
Clouds resting on our shoulders,
Trees crouching at our feet;
And even when the storm-gods
In furious cavalcade
Sweep through the darkening heavens
We are no whit dismayed.

'Yea, though the lightning flashes,
Yea, though the thunder rolls,
They cannot move our spirits,
They cannot shake our souls.
Earth-born, no god affrights us,
No younger power defeats;
Wrapped in eternal silence
We keep our ancient seats.'

Back in the secret valley,
I hear their soundless voice;
I hear their admonition;
I hear it, and rejoice.
Though the 'worldly winds' assail me,
Though friends my cause abjure,
Far from the magic valley
The word will be: Endure.

MOTHER GOOSE REVISITED
or Innocence and Experience

My Granny said that little girls
Were made of all things nice,
Making particular mention
Of sugar and of spice.

But as for little boys, she said,
It really was heart-breaking,
For frogs and snails and puppy-dogs' tails
All went into *their* making.

But since I was the kind of boy
Who loved the croaking race
I didn't mind what Granny said,
And so was in disgrace.

I had at home a pet green frog
That I loved tenderly,
And liked to think that frogs like him
Were really part of me.

While as for snails, I often wished
(And asked it in my prayers)
That *my* two eyes were mounted
On long thin stalks like theirs.

And puppy-dogs? Oh puppy-dogs,
So playful, cute, and small,
I'm sure my very dearest wish
Was to be one, tail and all.

But now I am a big boy
With lessons to repeat,
I've learned that sugar's poisonous,
Although it is so sweet,

While spices, taken in excess,
Are really rather dire;
Red chillies, in particular,
Can set your throat on fire.

So I wonder why my Granny,
As she stroked my golden curls,
Should have given me that nonsense
About little boys and girls.

TO C—

'Far lies Patroclus from his native plain!
He fell, and falling, wish'd my aid in vain.'
HOMER'S ILIAD

You and I, brother, we dreamt the same dream –
The dream of weightlessness:
To launch oneself into space; to step out
Into that which cannot be grasped;
To be borne aloft, as if in the palm of a hand –
Glorious, like a god of light.
But as we dream so we often fall.
We all fall, each in his own way.
They say that only saints are blessed with weightlessness.
Icarus, too, rising sunward,
Fell, and made the sea his home.
The sun that blinded him
Is the same sun we strove for.
So continue your ascent, my brother,
Into that which is ungraspable – sunward and skyward
Into heart-space, perhaps, even mind-space;
Let death be your foothold.
They say that only saints are blessed with weightlessness.

THE PILGRIM[111]

'Who is this, in pilgrim garments,
Who kneels before St Peter's throne?'
'Forgive my sins, O Holy Father,
For Venus' secrets I have known.

'Seventeen years upon her mountain
Did I serve the heathen dame,
Learned the arts by Church forbidden
And renounced the Christian name.'

'Not on earth and not in heaven
Can your sins forgiven be;
Sooner will this staff I carry
Bear blossoms like a living tree.'

The pilgrim has from Rome departed,
A third day rises cool and bright;
Pope Urban, waking, sees with wonder
His staff has blossomed in the night.

With news of sins by heaven forgiven
His messengers scour hill and plain;
The pilgrim's not in croft or castle,
Nor was Tannhäuser seen again.

LAMA GOVINDA IN CAPRI[112]
After seeing a reproduction of his painting Capri at Night

Capri at Night. A harmony
In brown and black, with here and there
An orange light that softly falls
On walls cylindrical and bare
Pierced by dark apertures like eyes
And mouths, but barren of replies.

Beyond, an alley, and an arch
That leads into a deeper gloom,
While high above, a yellow light
Shines faintly from an upper room
In which, perhaps, one sick or dying
On an uneasy bed is lying.

Artist and sage, whose poet soul
Served Truth and Beauty all your days,
Did you then have to wander, lost,
Through dark and labyrinthine ways,
Before at last could rise for you
The dome of Kailash, white against the blue?

1999 DANCING ROUND THE MAYPOLE

'Dance, children, dance,
Dance round the Maypole,
Lifting your feet
In time with the music!'

Thus spoke the teacher
In my happy schooldays,
Spoke in the playground
On May Day morning.

From the top of the Maypole
Hung marvellous streamers
Of many different colours,
All bright in the sunshine.

Each child seized the end
Of a streamer, and with it
Danced round the Maypole
In time with the music.

Fifteen or twenty
Happy London children
Dancing round the Maypole
On May Day morning!

Clockwise and anti-
Clockwise we danced
In our asphalted playground,
Backwards and forwards,

Weaving and un-
Weaving round the Maypole
Wonderful patterns
With our bright-coloured streamers.

And the tall old Maypole
Looked down benignly
On the dancing children,
Looked down and blessed us.

Fifty years later
No tall old Maypole,
No children dancing
On May Day morning.

No bright-coloured streamers,
No wonderful patterns.
In the empty playground
Only the asphalt.

THEN AND NOW

We waved our little Union Jacks,
And stood and sang God Save the King.
Now 'Empire' is a dirty word,
And loyalty a shameful thing.

Nelson and Drake are villains now,
We wish that they had never been,
Give the thumbs down to our history
And never sing God Save the Queen.

QUEENS PAST AND PRESENT

Elizabeth Tudor
Was frequently ruder
Than queens are today.
She boxed courtiers' ears,
Swore roundly at peers
And had plenty to say
For herself in English, French, Latin, Greek, Spanish, and Italian.
She could ride a stallion
As well as a man,
And flutter a jewelled fan
With the best of the saucy, aristocratic girls
Who arranged her red curls....
What a pity
That in London's city
Our Sovereign Lady today
Should be so polite, well mannered, and grey!

EAST IS EAST

East is East and West is West
And ever the twain shall meet.
Opposites belong to each other,
Like sour and sweet.

East is East and West is West
Each for himself discovers.
Love and hate are near akin,
Fratricidal, yet brothers.

POET AND MUSE[113]
After looking into a biography of Robert Graves

The poet has his Muse, the terrible White
Goddess who is the sole object
Of his adoration, and to whom
His whole life is consecrate. But naturally
The Muse has her attendants, her personal
Assistants, and there may even be
A Deputy Muse or two to whom,
When not in the mood, she from time to time
Delegates a portion of her authority, and all these
Divine and semi-divine ladies
Collaborate happily
(Or not so happily, as the case may be)
In the production
Of the poet's *oeuvre*, and in the completion
Of a learned treatise
In which he gives a comprehensive account
Of the religious-cum-anthropological-
Cum-sociological-cum-linguistic
Theory behind
His poetic practice.

THE DOUBLE ROOT

Poetry has a double root
In nursery rhyme and prophecy;
Mother Goose and Apollo
Are its twin progenitors.
But mother doesn't croon nursery rhymes any more,
And the poets are all in hiding.
English poetry's on its last legs,
Lost between pop lyric and Laura Riding.

THE WARNING VOICE

'Don't touch the red-hot pokers,'
Our kindly teacher said.
'They're sure to burn your fingers,
And you'll wish that you were dead.'

We stood and gazed upon them,
Inquisitive and scared,
For red and sulphur-yellow
Those red-hot pokers flared.

Beyond the purple pansies
And marigolds aglow,
Untouchable for ever
They stood in fiery row.

It was in the playground-garden;
We were very, very young,
And every word was gospel
That fell from teacher's tongue.

We are older now, and wiser;
The warning voice is spurned.
Life's reddest red-hot pokers
We touch – and are not burned.

GUHYALOKA, SEPTEMBER 1999

Drenched in silence, drenched in sunlight,
I survey the valley round,
Where the pines stand green and upright
And the grey dwarf oaks abound.
Between sheer cliffs of limestone
I muse the livelong day,
Wrapped in silence, wrapped in sunlight.
The world is far away.

Drenched in silence, drenched in moonlight,
I listen to the sound
Of the darkling owl's tu-whooing,
Hear the bat's wings hovering round.
With scent of pine for incense
I meditate and pray
Wrapped in silence, wrapped in moonlight.
The world is far away.

Drenched in silence, drenched in starlight,
With peace my thoughts are crowned
And I sense within this 'being'
A 'not-being' more profound.
No one – nothing – for companion
I sit till break of day
Wrapped in silence, wrapped in starlight.
The world is *far* away.

REMEMBERING ARTHADARSHIN[114]

The wooden hut stands empty amid the pine trees;
No one climbs up the slope to water my garden.
Owls hoot all night, but in the cold dawn
The sound of a voice chanting the Refuges is heard no more.

THE GREAT BURNING

The year will soon be at an end
And it is time to start sweeping up the fallen leaves,
Yellow, brown, and red leaves
From oak, beech, birch, and elm,
Time to start gathering them up into baskets
In readiness for the great burning.
Only the leaves of the holly are green
And have not fallen,
Glossy-green with – brilliant amidst them – red berries.

THE LISTENER

The poet listens for the inevitable word,
The word which from eternity has waited
To reveal itself to him.

Having heard it, he takes a diamond pen
And with tears of gratitude inscribes it
On a jade tablet upheld by angels.

THE ECONOMIC ARGUMENT   2000
The People of Denmark Reject the Euro 28 September 2000

'The economic argument
Is sure to win the day'
Said businessman to banker,
And who more wise than they?

Oh could they not remember
What long ago was said
By him they call their master:
'Man lives not just by bread'?

The bread may be well buttered
On both sides, but even so
In tones of proud defiance
The Viking breed shouts 'No!'

Oh may that shout be echoed
From Albion's doubtful shore,
And the businessmen and bankers
Rule over us no more!

JUSTICE AND PITY

I saw a woman, beautiful but blind,
Lying upon the ground in pools of blood
And asked her name. My name, she said, is Justice.
And who has given you these cruel wounds,
That thus your very lifeblood drains away?
Her name is Pity, Justice said, and died.

THREE ARTHURIAN POEMS

1. THE WHITE HAWTHORN
A Recollection of Burne-Jones' 'The Beguiling of Merlin'[115]

If it could speak, the white hawthorn,
What would it say?
Merlin and wily Vivian
Wandered this way.

If it could speak, the white hawthorn,
What could it tell?
Vivian wrested from Merlin
A mighty spell.

If it could speak, the white hawthorn,
What then the sound?
With the spell Vivian pent Merlin
Far under ground.

If it could speak, the white hawthorn,
What were the sighs?
Female beauty can overbear
Even the wise.

2. LOVE AND DUTY

Guinevere loved the King
Much less than she esteemed,
And so of gallant Lancelot
She dreamed and dreamed and dreamed.

One day the dream became so deep
That it was dream no more,
And she and gallant Lancelot
Stood on a lonely shore,

And standing on that lonely shore
They heard a dreadful sound,
A sound as of the Crack of Doom,
As split the Table Round;

And thus the lawless passion
Of Arthur's guilty queen
Broke up the goodliest fellowship
That e'er on earth was seen.

Let love and duty coincide,
Lest both of them be hurled
To ruin, and the Crack of Doom
Be heard around the world.

3. THE CELL OF GLASS

Merlin, in his cell of glass
Imprisoned, sees the centuries pass;
Sees the nations come and go
Like clouds in Autumn, fast or slow;
Sees cities rise and cities fall
Like flowers in Springtime, one and all.
Grieved or rejoicing, inly wracked,
He sees, and sees – but cannot act.

THE SIX ELEMENTS SPEAK

I am Earth.
I am rock, metal, and soil.
I am that which exists in you
As bone, muscle, and flesh,
But now I must go,
Leaving you light.
Now we must part.
Goodbye.

I am Water.
I am ocean, lake, rivers, and streams,
The rain that falls from clouds
And the dew on the petals of flowers.
I am that which exists in you
As blood, urine, sweat, saliva, and tears,
But now I must go,
Leaving you dry.
Now we must part.
Goodbye.

I am Fire.
I come from the Sun, travelling through space
To sleep in wood, flint, and steel.
I am that which exists in you
As bodily heat, the warmth of an embrace,
But now I must go,
Leaving you cold.
Now we must part.
Goodbye.

I am Air.
I am wind, breeze, and hurricane.
I am that which exists in you
As the breath in your nostrils, in your lungs,
The breath that gently comes, that gently goes,

But now I must go,
For the last time,
Leaving you empty.
Now we must part.
Goodbye.

I am Space.
I contain all,
From a grain of dust to a galaxy.
I am that which exists in you
As the space limited by the earth, water, fire, and air
That make up your physical being,
But now they have all gone
And I must go too,
Leaving you unlimited.
Now we must part.
Goodbye.

I am Consciousness.
Indefinable and indescribable.
I am that which exists in you
As sight, hearing, smell, taste, touch, and thought,
But now I must go
From the space no longer limited by your physical being
Leaving nothing of 'you'.
There is no one from whom to part,
So no goodbye.

Earth dissolves into Water,
Water dissolves into Fire,
Fire dissolves into Air,
Air dissolves into Space,
Space dissolves into Consciousness,
Consciousness dissolves into – ?
HŪṂ

IN KRAKOW

1. IN THE GREAT SQUARE

Love is of so delicate a nature, I said,
Quoting the old Indian poet,
That it cannot bear the burden of wisdom;
But you seemed not to understand.
Perhaps, in your case, love *can* bear the burden of wisdom.
We were sitting in the great square of Krakow,
Drinking tea, surrounded by our friends,
And listening to the gypsy musicians.
The musicians could understand
That love cannot bear the burden of wisdom.
Did not their ancestors come from India, long ago?

2. TO MICHAL, MY INTERPRETER[116]

In your apt mouth
My silver words are transmuted into gold;
In your young life
My frozen sap puts forth leaves and flowers.

3. ON THE BALCONY

Breakfast was on the balcony. The sparrows were there too,
Chirruping loudly, and flying in and out of the eaves.
Below, men were working in the fields. A cock crew.
'It's too early', someone said, 'for the storks.'

TO MY TEACHER, CHATTRUL SANGYE DORJE

You revealed to me the face of the Green Goddess
And spoke of the scholars of old.
I could only guess your meaning.

You showed me a handful of seed pearls
Taken from the ruins of a stupa.
I could only guess your meaning.

You sent me a ceremonial scarf,
White as the snows of Kanchenjunga.
I could only guess your meaning.

You sent me two packets of medicine,
Compounded from rare Himalayan herbs –
Medicine over which you had repeated thousands of mantras.
I could only guess your meaning.

Now you send me a thangka depicting
A white, naked ḍākinī.
She is smiling, and holds
A chopping-knife and skull-cup filled with golden nectar.
Once again, O inscrutable guru, I can only guess your meaning.

THE SILVER SPOON

On my birthday
You gave me a silver spoon with a bear handle.
'In Tibetan Buddhism,' I said,
'Silver is one of the three pure metals,
The others being copper and gold.'
Now, I use your spoon every day,
Stirring my tea with it,
Eating kiwi fruit with it,
Gripping the handle tightly
Because I cannot feel the touch of your hand.

TO MICHAL, WITH A PHOTOGRAPH

'Have it taken together with birch trees,' you said, referring
To the 'official' photograph that was to be sent to our friends in the
    Ukraine.
Like the Russians, the Ukrainians love the birch tree,
So here am I, leaning against the black and silver trunk
Of the old birch tree on which I looked out from my study window
    each morning, all those years ago.

I hope the Poles, too, love the birch tree
And that you will like this photo of your white-haired old friend.

I AM SITTING IN THE LATE AFTERNOON SUNSHINE…

I am sitting in the late afternoon sunshine,
An old man with tired bones and a heart empty of desires.
Nearby, a bird is singing in the trees,
And a puff of wind is soft against my cheek.
Soon the sun will be setting, and I wonder
If tonight I shall see the stars.

EPIGRAMS

Crows, in their collective spite,
Will peck to death a crow that's white.
We humans show as little sense
When forced to deal with *difference*.

The world continues on its crazy course;
Where love is needed, they resort to force.

We realize that war has snags
When men come home in body bags.

A cobra in a basket
Remains a cobra still,
Don't just suppress the kleśas;
With the sword of Wisdom, kill.

THE LURE OF DOMESTICITY
Another youthful hero bites the dust,
By dreams deluded, and consumed with lust.

In vain we flee before the King of Death;
We feel upon our necks his icy breath.

HAIKU

The grey clouds are my friends.
They visit me every evening
With messages from the West.

What is the wine you bring me, Cupbearer?
Ah, it is the bitter wine of separation.
But at the bottom of the cup
There is the taste of union.

Beauty such as yours
Is for seeing, not touching.
Perhaps not even for seeing
Except with closed eyes.

The ship sails on its way
Leaving behind a brilliant wake
On which the moon shines
Dazzlingly.

AN APOLOGY   2009

We live in the Age of Apologies. Here is an apology that is much more meaningful than many being made today.

Mankind owes a profound apology:
To the Birds, for having polluted the air through which they fly,
To the Ape and the Tiger, for having destroyed the forests in which they live,
To the Deer and the Bison, for ruthlessly hunting them almost to extinction,
To the Rivers and Streams, for poisoning them with chemicals,
To the Earth itself, for greedily pillaging its riches of silver and gold,
To the Ocean, for slaughtering the greatest of her children, the Whale, 'for scientific purposes',
To the Mountain Peaks, for defiling their virgin snows with our trash,
To the Moon, for rudely invading her sacred space,
To the Stars, for obscuring their brightness with the smoke of our cities,
To the Sun, for not gratefully acknowledging our dependence on his bounty,
To the truly great Men and Women of the past, for not honouring their memory as we should and for not walking in their footsteps.

WRITTEN AFTER HEARING A RADIO PROGRAMME ON DEMENTIA

My mind is a theatre
Where every kind of play
Is staged with lights and music
All night and half the day.

I myself am all the actors
In gold and red and blue,
Myself the fickle audience
Myself the critics too.

One day that mad theatre
Will show a red-nosed clown,
And mournful placards will announce
'Last performance. Closing Down.'

MR WIRELESS

Meet my best friend, Mr Wireless,
I've known him years and years.
We've laughed a lot together;
Together we've shed tears.

He wakes me in the morning
With news from round the world,
News of earthquakes and agreements,
Troop withdrawals, rockets hurled.

He talks to me of people,
Of lands both near and far,
Plays me tunes on the piano,
Or conducts an orchestra.

Yes, we grew up together,
And I remember yet
The days when Mr Wireless
Was Little Crystal Set.

Accumulators then he had,
And did in valves rejoice;
And I had to put on headphones
To hear his muffled voice.

Now I hear him very clearly,
He doesn't need to shout.
From sitting room to kitchen
He follows me about.

Meet my best friend, Mr Wireless.
The last sound I shall hear
Will be that well loved voice of his
Receding from my ear.

THE FAMILY REUNION

Full twenty years I stayed away.
My father grew thin; my mother grey;
And my young sister went astray.

Now, I see them in my dreams;
A mystic light about them gleams.
They have become my Muse's themes.

My mother and I in an orchard strolled.
Her looks were neither young nor old,
And she was wearing a gown of gold.

Apple blossom was overhead;
Sunlight on the green grass was shed.
At peace we walked, and no word was said.

In front of his cottage my father stood;
Before him a stream, behind him a wood.
He has lived his life as a true man should.

Black his hair as the fur of mole;
He beckoned me in to share a bowl,
And I saw that his withered arm was whole.

My sister had lived with a gypsy man
In a gaily painted caravan
Drawn by a horse. So the story ran.

Now she was dancing the 'Dying Swan'.
Snow white the plumage that she had on,
And joy from her every movement shone.

THE WIND

A wind was in my sails. It blew
Stronger and fiercer by the hour.
I do not know from whence it came,
Or why. I only knew its power.

Sometimes it dashed me on the rocks,
Sometimes it spun me round and round.
Sometimes I laughed aloud for joy,
Sometimes I felt a peace profound.

It drove me on, that manic wind,
When I was young. It drives me still
Now I am old. It lives in me,
Its breath my breath, its will my will.

THE BRAHMAS AND THE SAGES

The Brahmas sit on thrones of light
Immersed in meditation.
For them there is no day, no night,
No worldly perturbation.

Above the lesser gods they dwell,
Immaculate, sublime.
Their bliss no mortal tongue may tell;
They have no sense of time.

Age after age they sit, until
At last their life-span ends.
Each Brahma then, against his will,
To lower realms descends.

Some wake on earth, and find their light
Obscured by mortal clay,
Though still there struggles through that night
A faint celestial ray.

Beside it streams a second ray,
A glittering ray of gold
From Buddha's hand. It shows the way
To wonders manifold.

It points beyond the Brahma-realms
To realms of pure delight.
It points beyond the Brahma thrones,
To Light beyond their light.

'Nirvāṇa' it those sages call
Who dwell on Himalay.
It is their hope, their life, their all,
Their Way beyond the way.

Upright upon their seats of grass
They sit when death is near.
Released, their spirits slowly pass
Beyond, and disappear.

THE TWIN TOWERS

Proudly they stood, those towers, a monument
To money, and the power that money brings.
But hate was stronger. Now they lie in dust,
And impotent hands a mighty nation wrings.

THE BEGUILING OF MERLIN[117]
After the painting by Burne-Jones

From his own book of spells she chants, and lo
The charmed earth opens. Sadly, Merlin thinks
How vain is wisdom. The last sight he sees
Is Vivian's smile of triumph as he sinks.

TO MY FRIEND PARAMARTHA 2014

Blond, blue-eyed, and beautiful,
You swam into my sight,
Like a new planet suddenly
Emerging from the night,
And all at once my heart was filled
With measureless delight.
Delight in friendship, hitherto
Unknown, whose upward flight
Can bear the soul to realms beyond
This sorry human plight
And give it there a glimpse at least
Of treasures infinite,
Treasures of eternal life
At one with boundless light.

TO DEJI[118]

Blessed be the noble tree
That bore these plums so rare,
And blessings on the lady dear
Who sent to me a share.
May the tree live a hundred years
And may that lady too;
And may we all meet in Paradise
Where the sparkling jewel-trees grow
And see them shed their jewel-flowers
On the lapis ground below.

COUPLET

That you must feed the brain with facts, I see;
But mind you feed the soul with poetry.

TO PARAMARTHA IN LONDON

In a dream more like a vision
You with love regarded me.
But that love was also knowledge,
Not sentimentality.

Your face was radiant, smiling;
I could not but draw near
And face to face reciprocate
That love so clean and clear.

Whatever dreams may follow,
And wherever you may be,
I will not forget that dream in which,
You with love regarded me.

A FANTASY

From world to world, from star to star,
I travelled in my gilded car,
And in each one acquaintance made
With souls of every shape and shade,
But none so worthy of my mirth
As those on this ridiculous earth,
Who, seeking happiness to attain,
Will do the things that bring them pain,
And then in angry tones declare,
To God or gods, 'It isn't fair!'

I'll turn about my gilded car,
And travel to some distant star
Where friendship is the rule of life
And men can live without a wife,
And women live without a master.
Go, my chariot! Faster, faster!

THE HOLIDAY

In the morning, in the morning,
With bucket and with spade,
We ran down to the beach, the beach,
And there sand castles made.

In the afternoon, the afternoon,
We lay down in the sun
On bath towels, on bath towels,
Until the day was done.

In the evening, in the evening,
We drank our ginger beer
At the Rose and Crown, the Rose and Crown,
While parents gossiped near.

At midnight, at midnight,
We frolicked in the sea;
The moon was brighter, brighter,
Than ever moon could be.

We are dreaming, we are dreaming
Tucked safely in our beds;
The sea was far away, away
From our well pillowed heads.

In the morning, in the morning
We leap, and skip and run.
Another day, another day,
Another day's begun!

THE TWO RISKS

If you're 'not' a poet you run the risk
Of one day going mad.

If you 'are' a poet you run the risk
That your poems will be really bad.

THE BLUEBELL WOOD

We wandered in the bluebell wood
One day in mid-July
Between the trees, that azure flood
Was all we could descry.

Not now. July has come again,
The woods, the trees, are there,
But of that host of azure flowers
The ground between is bare.

What brought about the change, I know.
In droves there cyclists came
And tore those flowers up by the roots
Sans any sense of shame.

Long, slim, and white the roots hung down
Behind the cyclists' backs;
And many an azure head bestrewed
The cyclists' dusty tracks.

Without their roots, my father said,
They will not grow again.
Vandals are with us still, I fear,
In forest, field, and country lane.

SAY PADMALOKA

Say Padmaloka and there arises a vision
of a porch white-pillared, square windows on either side.

Say Padmaloka and there arises a vision
of ancient oak trees overspread with foliage.

Say Padmaloka and there arises a vision
of a lawn molehill-pitted with flower beds on its two outside edges
And a rose bed in the foreground, abloom in summer.

Say Padmaloka and there arises a vision
of a stretch of shady woodland,
The trees of which I planted thirty years ago,
Where come the small shy deer from the riverside sedges.

Say Padmaloka and there arises a vision
of a lily pond on whose edge there sits a small Buddha, gently smiling.

Say Padmaloka and there arises a vision
of a small inner courtyard in the middle of which there stands a stupa
With its threefold inscription: 'Cherish the Dharma, live united,
radiate love' –
The words of my teacher, the loving Dhardo Rimpoche,
Circumambulating the stupa.

THE COSMIC DREAMER

Supine he lies, the blue-complexioned god,
His head protected by the spread-out hood
Of Sesh, the Cosmic Snake. His eyes are closed,
While from his navel springs a lotus flower
Upon whose calyx sit, serene and grand,
The triune gods of birth, and life, and death –
Brahma, and Vishnu, and Maheshwara.
They are his dream, and all their works his dream.
Supine he lies, the blue-complexioned god,
Age after age until he dreams no more
And he alone exists, the undreamt dreamer,
Until he sleeps and dreams some other dream.

SHIVA AND THE LOVE GOD

Silent he sits, the white-complexioned god,
His brow effulgent with the crescent moon,
His three eyes closed, his vision all within.
Naked he sits, save that round neck and arm,
For ornament he wears the serpent race.
But lo, before him stands another shape,
Young, beautiful, seductive, delicate.
A bow he bears and arrows tipped with flowers.
But ere one flower-tipped arrow he can launch
At the god's heart, his terrible third eye
Darts forth a flame of fire that in a trice,
Burns up the archer and his comeliness.
Henceforth, the sages say, the god of love
Is known as 'Bodiless'. He goes everywhere
And none can see him or his flower-tipped darts,
And so he works his mischief as he will.

SALUTATION TO THE LADY FROM THE LAND OF SNOWS[119]

Salutation to the Lady from the Land of Snows,
who practises indefatigably the precepts of the guru.
Salutation to the Dolma of Battersea Park,
the palms of whose hands are stained with the henna of compassion.
Salutations to the partner of the immaculate Paramartha,
who is faithful to him as the moon is faithful to the earth, or the earth
    to the sun.
Salutation to the mistress of a million mantras,
who repeats constantly, by day and by night,
the names of Buddhas and Bodhisattvas innumerable.
Salutation to the true daughter of Padmasambhava,
who treads underfoot the demons of greed, hatred, and delusion.
Salutation to the maker of ten thousand offerings,
who keeps nothing for herself but gives everything away.
Salutation to the sister of Mandarava and Yeshe Tsogyal,
who in this degenerate world helps to keep the Dharma alive.

2016 UP AND DOWN THE GRAVEL PATH: AN UPDATE[120]

'Up and down the gravel path
Between the flowering trees,
I've walked this Summer afternoon
To give my spirit ease.'

But that was sixty years ago,
And now I walk instead
Between the duck-frequented pond
And roses white and red.

And as I walk I push before
The Roamer that I prize
Though not to give my spirit ease
But my body exercise.

So gaily up and down I go
Upon the crunchy gravel,
For that, at ninety years and more,
Is as far as I can travel.

PART II
LONGER POEMS

THE AWAKENING OF THE HEART

As children on a Summer's day   1949
In some bright upland meadow play,
And there with laughter tumble over
On every patch of purple clover,
And pluck in handfuls as they pass
The dewy flowers and fragrant grass,
And chase, with eager shouts and cries,
The lazy, painted butterflies,
Or, resting for a moment, see
The busy lives of ant and bee
With a child's curiosity –
So in my youth did I disport
In that lush wonderland of thought
Which blooms within the guardian walls
Of hushed and silent library halls,
And there from shelf to shelf did range
In eager quest of all of strange
And rich and rare and wonderful,
And terrible and beautiful,
That man, in any age or zone,
Had ever wrought, or felt, or known.

In that sweet meadow bloomed for me
The golden flower of poesy;
The violet of philosophy
That loves to hide itself in leaves,
Though from its breath the air receives
Of wondrous fragrance such a trace
None but would seek its hiding-place
Who'd breathed it in when passing by,
Did gaze on me with starry eye;
The babbling brook of history
Ran through that magic mead for me,
And in its dancing waves I saw,
In broken reflex, peace and war.

   The classic lore of Greece and Rome,
Entombed in many a ponderous tome,
With all the wisdom of the East
Which saintly sage or poet-priest
Mused in lone cave or solemn fane,
On frozen peak or burning plain,
And all good, beautiful and true
Runes of the Old World and the New,
Before me like a pageant passed
Of rich cloud, variable and vast,
Which on some splendid Summer eve
Of gold and silver light doth weave
A cloth to deck as though for feast
The purple chambers of the East.

   Oh, from the dewy Summer dawns,
Upon the sunlit upland lawns
Of thought which opens prospects wide,
Till breathless Summer eventide
Childlike I ran from flower to flower,
Nor passage felt of any hour,
But deemed the longest Summer day
Too brief for that sweet bookish play.

Though dazzling through the windows fell
The sunshine that I loved so well,
And set the page my hands did hold
Open, ablaze with burning gold,
Its beauty could not coax me from
That universe within a room,
Save with in hand, for quiet rehearse,
Some book of more than golden verse,
Or more than more than golden lines
Where poesy with wisdom twines
In double charm, as if a rose
Should sisterlike with jasmine close
And from a common archway fling
One heavenly scent, all-perfumíng.

Thus oft upon a Summer morn
On our close-cropped suburban lawn
Beneath a plum-tree's shadowing spray
For hours entranced I sat or lay,
On chair or rug, with cushioned head,
And converse held with poets dead;
Till, heat-oppressed, I sank at noon
Into a kind of waking swoon,
Wherein the sense of what I'd read,
And consciousness of heat o'erhead,
And coolness of the leafy shade,
In which, with hot lids closed, I stayed,
And murmurous sounds of bumble-bees,
And leafy whispers of the trees,
And street-sounds, faint at that noon hour,
And scent of many a garden flower,
And all which that rich morn had mused,
Were blended, subtly interfused,
Like dewdrops on a window-pane
When the sun smiles, or drops of rain
Conglobed upon a lily's stem
In one bright orb, and all of them
Blent with my trance, and did express

For one brief hour of timelessness
Its mood of utter blessedness.

   When golden Summer's green leaves burned
To thoughts of Autumn tint I turned;
And when they fluttered to the ground
Plunged into reverie profound,
And asked my books to solve for me
The riddle of mortality.

   How oft before the crackling blaze
Of well-lit fires on Winter days –
Log-fires whereon, at half-past three,
The cheerful kettle sang for tea –
Have I, ensconced in hearth-side seat,
With fireward-stretching legs and feet,
Dreamed all a drear December day
O'er some rare lyric of Cathay,
And felt its subtlety of art
Quicken the blood within my heart!

   A small, quiet chamber of my own,
Where I would read or muse alone,
Had I that youthful study-tide
Upon the house's garden side,
Whence I could watch the Summer dawn
Bedew the bloom-surrounded lawn,
And glimpse the white patch that discloses
My father busy with his roses;
But where, more oft, with loving looks,
I gazed upon my rows of books
(For every one that I could see
To me meant 'Open, Sesame!')
Until not merely days I thought,
But life itself, for learning short,
And yearned, with foolish boyish tears,
To study for a thousand years.

   Thus in the Spring-tide of my days
I trod entranced those meadowy ways
Whose beauty bloomed for such as me
In richly-volumed library,
And flitted there, with eager look,
From shelf to shelf, and book to book,
As in a Summer meadow sweet
A child will flash on dancing feet,
Minute by minute, hour by hour,
With laughter shrill from flower to flower.

   What time such youthful bookish sport,
And ardent quest, and burning thought,
Unfroze the fountain of my mind
I lived at home with parents kind,
And with us, like a loved relation,
Stayed leisure, nurse of contemplation;
And in our quiet suburban street
Passed time with dull and languid beat,
And at our table all the while
Did plenty like a mother smile;
And there was love, bright fount of youth,
And in the books about me truth,
Beauty and good – that triple tiar
Ideal humanity doth wear
On forward brow – and musings strange,
And pageants rich of seasons' change,
And dew-pearled dawn and starry night,
And Autumn moons all silver-white,
And many a joy we thought would stay,
And oh, so many a bookish day
My folly dreamed they ne'er would cease,
And, in the world we lived in – peace.

   But ah! as that rich month which shows
The gold leaf crops the Summer rose,
And as when cold-month's winds awaken

That leaf itself is twirled and taken,
So did those thousand bookish days,
And all life's quiet domestic ways,
And leisure, smiling plenty too,
And youth, and much of good and true
And beautiful, at one fierce stroke,
With peace itself, dissolve like smoke.

   Tearless I saw, one day of doom,
The bomb-struck rubble of my room,
Whose books, with many a muddy stain,
Exposed to sun and wind and rain,
Rolled, in that war-scarred wilderness,
With shreds of many a silken dress;
And calmly on the brick-strewn lawn,
Which was so trim but yester-morn,
With household things my father gave
Heaped up whatever I could save.

   Thereafter it was mine to roam
Without a friend, without a home,
For many a year, with unquiet breast,
Perplexed between the East and West;
But sometimes, too, the chance was mine,
'Neath desert palm or mountain pine,
In houses, tents and hermitages,
To con the runes of saints and sages,
And thus, for one short hour forget
All worldly fume and mortal fret,
And dream I roamed, exempt from pain,
Those magic meadows once again,
And ranged, as in my happy youth,
Those flowers of beauty, good and truth.

   As in some upland meadow play
Those children on a Summer's day,
Without a single thought of rest,
Till shadows, lengthening from the West,

By slow degrees enlarge their bound,
And evening darkens all the ground;
But then, when that bright day is done,
Stand breathless as the setting sun
To fling all fiery-faced doth seem
His blinding horizontal beam,
And do upon the sudden feel
A tiredness o'er their members steal,
That grows with star-rise still more deep,
Till all their being cries for sleep;
And as they leave that meadow sweet
With nodding heads and stumbling feet,
To trudge the long and weary road
Which winds through fields to their abode,
And drop, not caring now for play,
Their withered posies on the way,
And reach at last, as shades grow deep,
Their doorways more than half asleep;
And as, while being washed and fed
By patient hands, and put to bed,
From very tiredness tearful grown
They raise a fretful childish moan,
And feebly to their father cry
For the full moon in the sky,
Whose beams, with soft compassion shed
The casement through, a sheet do spread
Of dazzling silver o'er their bed –
So in youth's golden sunset days
I wearied of those meadowy ways
Which bloom within the guardian walls
Of hushed and silent library halls,
And there from shelf to shelf did range
Less eagerly for aught of strange
And rich and rare and wonderful,
And terrible and beautiful,
That man, in any age or zone,
Had ever wrought, or felt, or known.

With dubious fragrance bloomed for me
The golden flower of poesy;
The violet of philosophy,
That loves to hide itself in leaves,
Though from its breath the air receives
Of wondrous fragrance such a trace
None but had sought its hiding-place
Who'd breathed it in when passing by,
Did gaze on me with jaundiced eye;
The babbling brook of history
Ran no more through that mead for me,
And in my restless heart I saw
The deeper springs of peace and war.

   Then from my books with long-drawn sigh
Upward I looked with tear-dimmed eye,
And saw how darkly fell on me
The shadow of mortality;
And when at once through heart and head
A kind of aching tiredness spread,
I fancied that upon my breath
Was laid the icy hand of death;
And feeling their diminished glow
Knew that the fires of life burnt low.

   Oh, in those darkening sunset days,
Weary of meadowy youthful ways,
I learned, from tiredness almost dead,
Experience' flint-strewn path to tread,
Which winds through many lives a road
To Peace, the pilgrim's true abode;
And shed along that weary way
The relics of my bookish play,
Until at last with lighter load
And brisker step my path I strode,
And saw that night, much comforted,
The full moon shining overhead.

   Now in less bright and bookish days
I grope through all those devious ways
Which wind, unmapped by mortal art,
Within man's own mysterious heart,
And in the moonlight see unroll
The wondrous landscape of his soul,
Where all degrees of dark and bright
From lowest depth to loftiest height
Like tiers of shifting clouds are ranged,
And by the fitful moonlight changed
From shapes as though of meadows green,
With small brooks babbling in between,
And fields of poppied corn beside
Some quiet bulrushy riverside,
And woodlands where the sweet briar-rose
Above the bluebelled bracken grows,
To shapes as though of chasms deep
Wheredown the torrent waters leap,
And dreary wastes of desert sand
With blinding light on every hand,
And many a heavenward-soaring height
That wears a wreath of stars at night,
And many a fathomless abyss,
And many a plunging precipice
Whereon the eye naught growing sees
But thorns and thunder-blasted trees –
Yea, and to scenes for which our crude
Earth-scenes have no similitude,
Unless it were, at dawn of day,
The sunlit snows of Himalay.

   Not often do I care to see
The meadowy ways of library,
For every bloom, I know not how,
Seems half as fair and fragrant now,
And rarely, rarely, comes to me
The scent of golden poesy
Or love-of-wisdom's purple flower

With sweetness as of that far hour
When on their petals, bright as truth,
There shone the morning sun of youth.

 For in that meadow green I've found,
With pure white lilies bordered round,
A pool as smooth and still as glass,
Through whose clear, tranquil depths there pass
Reflected, all the day, a crowd
Of changeful shapes of Summer cloud;
And on whose moonlit face at night
Doth bloom with petals silver-bright
That deathless flower without a flaw,
The pure white lotus of the Law,
Which wafts, with all its heart unfurled,
Undreamed-of fragrance o'er the world.

 Oh, from those moonlit lotus beds
The sweetness of compassion spreads
From heart to heart, and bound to bound,
In peace and purity around;
And borne on many a votive breeze
Across the purple midnight seas
To far-off lands, at dawn distils
Its perfume o'er their streams and hills,
And drops together with the dew
Upon their flowery meadows too,
Till earth receives, in every part,
The sweetness of the lotus-heart,
And vaguely wonders whence is blown
That wondrous fragrance not her own.

 Bright shines the silver moonlight cool
Upon that lily-bordered pool,
And bright, supremely bright, unfold
On leaves as though of burnished gold
Those dazzling petals silver-bright
Which breathe their heart abroad tonight;

But brighter, brighter, brighter far,
From heavens sown thick with many a star,
Upon that mystic lotus-bed
The full moon shineth overhead.

   And as when all their meadowy play
At evening melts like mist away,
And they have trod that weary road
Which winds through fields to their abode,
Those tired and fretful children cry
For the full moon in the sky,
So, having seen how black, alas!
Death's shadow lengthened o'er the grass,
And from my Summer meadow fled
Experience' flint-strewn path to tread,
And seen from that white lotus-bloom
The fragrance of compassion fume,
Oh now, of all the flowers of earth
Grown weary, and the coil of birth
And death no more desiring, I
Dissolve in yearning tears and cry
For that full moon whose beams are sent
From wisdom's star-strewn firmament –
The Full Moon of Enlightenment.

   Nor ever shall I cease to cry
And stretch my arms towards the sky
Until that dazzling orb depart
From heaven, to shine within my heart,
And yet, though there its beauty reign,
Still in the heaven of heavens remain.
Then, only then, for me may cease
The well-nigh endless road to peace,
And all things be, life's journey ended,
In all-at-one-ment fused and blended,
And there at last, no more apart,
Awaken to the Buddha-Heart.

THE VEIL OF STARS

INTRODUCTION TO 'THE VEIL OF STARS'
by Lama Anagarika Govinda

The author of this slender volume is a Buddhist monk who has already made a name for himself as a poet and writer. He has made the Himalayas his home.

The rhythm of the hills, the sparkling realms of the eternal snow above the clouds and the dark valleys in their shadow, the world of gods and the world of man, the realm of stars and the flowery meadows, have been the godfathers of these pearls of poetic thought and feeling. I call them pearls not only because they are precious and luminous, but because each of them forms a complete unit in itself, though in the way they are strung together they reveal a still deeper meaning, that goes beyond that of the single unit. And in this respect they are like all things in Nature, nay, like all living beings, who, in their subtle connection and relationship to each other as well as to the Infinite, are imbued with a transparent and transcendent quality beyond space and time, in love and death, in desire and renunciation, in joy and suffering. But it needs the sensitivity of the poet and the ecstasy of vision, that springs from a life of contemplation and inner awareness, to express it.

It was the poet in Sangharakshita that led him to the religious life, and it was the path of renunciation that enabled him to see the world in a wider and truer perspective, which is the hallmark of genuine poetry.

Here the words of Novalis come to one's mind:

Poets and priests were one in the beginning, and only later times have separated them. The real poet, however, has always remained priest, just as the real priest has always remained poet.

The poet is ever true. He remains constant in the cycle of Nature. The philosopher changes within the eternal immutability. The eternally immutable can only be represented by that which is changeable, the eternally changeable only in the immutable, the completeness of the present moment.

Each of Sangharakshita's poetic aphorisms is such a complete moment, in which the eternal presence is mirrored, and in which everybody will rediscover his or her own intimate experience; because poetry is the art of saying in simple words what the average man feels most profoundly, without being able to express it, and of putting into the language of feeling what the philosopher tries to express in terms of reason without ever being able to realize it. It is the art of giving meaning even to the inconspicuous, apparently trivial things of life, so that they stand out as something new and fresh, as if they had never been seen or felt before. This is the secret of spontaneous vision, the heart of creative meditation.

It was this attitude which made the Buddha 'see' the whole significance of illness, old age, and death, when he met (or had the 'vision' of) a sick man, an old man, and a corpse – sights which the ordinary person may meet a thousand times without being stirred, without experiencing anything, without realizing their significance.

It was this same attitude which, life after life, caused the Bodhisattva to sacrifice himself for others, and finally even to sacrifice his own personal liberation when it was within his reach at the time of Buddha Dīpaṅkara, and take upon himself the burden of innumerable rebirths and untold sufferings, in order to attain perfect enlightenment for the good of all, for the benefit of the whole world.

It is this Bodhisattva Ideal that inspires every line of this book and the life of its author. Infinite tenderness for all that lives begins as the love between two human beings, with all their faults and shortcomings, in which desire and possessiveness lead to infinite suffering and disillusionment. But these sufferings themselves are the purifying flame in which the limitations and impurities of that love are consumed, until a greater love emerges from the ordeal.

Thus pain and suffering are not something merely negative, something from which we should shrink or run away, but something that has to be faced and overcome in the battle of life, and which, for the sake of others, we should take upon ourselves unflinchingly, just as the Buddha did in his long career as a Bodhisattva. 'I wish to be bread for those who are hungry, drink for those who are thirsty,' exclaims Śāntideva, who was as great a poet as he was a saint.

This ideal is nowadays conveniently forgotten by many of those who imagine themselves to be the keepers of the Buddha's word, though they have merely gone to sleep upon it, and who evade the real issues of life by sheltering behind cloistered walls and the armour of orthodoxy.

But a religion that is not strong enough to include the world, and love that is not great enough to go beyond the world, are not worthy of their name.

Love may or may not be bound up with desire, but it certainly cannot exist without an element of renunciation. Even what we call worldly love often proves stronger than life, stronger even than death. The greatest sacrifices that a human being is capable of, have been made for the sake of love, because love means to give up something of ourselves, and perfect love means the complete surrender of our 'self'.

Therefore the very soil from which grows the renunciation of a Buddha, is the soil of love, in all its *human* forms. I emphasize the word *human* because the Buddha's *maitrī* is not just a kind of cool or attenuated benevolence or well-meaning kindness; and his *karuṇā* is not a kind of condescending compassion, but an attitude which is born out of the intense realization of oneness, in which there is no room for the difference of 'I' and 'thou', 'self' and 'other'.

Like a mother, whose love for her child flows naturally and without any trace of moral or spiritual superiority, simply from the feeling of an inseparable inner relationship and essential oneness, so the Buddha's *maitrī* and *karuṇā* flow naturally from the all-embracing radiance of his mind and heart.

> The tear of the Bodhisattva's compassion flows through the world as love,
> Even as the austere snows of the Himalayas flow in rivers down into the green plains.

It is this spiritual background which gives to Sangharakshita's poetry its depth and emotional appeal. It rests on the inner parallelism between the most fundamental human emotions and the highest experiences on the path of liberation and enlightenment, the relationship between love and wisdom, the individual and the universal, the moods of Nature and the moods of the human heart. And this parallelism finds its expression in a juxtaposition of lines and a rhythmic flow of thoughts and words which can dispense with the outer embellishments of rhyme, because their inner relationship is strong enough to establish their harmony.

Sangharakshita's poetry reminds us of that of the Chinese Chan (Zen) School, in which this parallelism has been cultivated to the utmost perfection and simplicity, and in which the economy of words enhances their strength and significance. But this similarity is only natural. Sangharakshita's poetry flows from the same source and has grown into the same natural surroundings which inspired the Chinese Masters.

I cannot give any better illustration to characterize the form as well as the spirit of Sangharakshita's poetry than the following lines:

Reality is reflected in my heart as love, and this love of mine is in turn mirrored in the all-embracing bosom of Reality,
As though the moon lay reflected in the depths of the ocean, and the ocean in the calm clear heart of the moon.

Lama Anagarika Govinda
1954

ARGUMENT PREFIXED TO 'THE VEIL OF STARS'

The Lover is full of wonder at the coming of love, and feels that the transcendent beauty of the Beloved has opened for him a newer and higher world. Though ashamed to declare his love, he believes that the whole of Nature reveals it. But the Beloved shrinks from him, and in his despair the Lover feels that his passion has been frustrated. Yet it is impossible for him to forget the object of his adoration. He meets the Beloved every evening, but although a friendship does develop between them, it is not deep or close enough to satisfy the demands of the Lover, who is exasperated by the changeful moods of the Beloved and tortured by an outward proximity which only makes him feel more acutely their inner remoteness. Nevertheless he resolves to meet inconstancy with constancy, and increases his endeavours to win the Beloved's love. His mad pursuit brings him, however, no nearer to his goal, and his violent attempts to force a response from the Beloved meet only with rebuffs. In his despair he feels that even hatred would be preferable to such absolute indifference. All the joy of love now turns into pain. But from this pain he gradually learns of a higher love, and while reaffirming the eternity of his passion he resolves to accept the will of the Beloved in all things. A temporary separation teaches him that Love is above space no less than beyond time, and he begins to realize that it was the very impetuosity of his desire which had prevented its fulfilment. He begins to understand that spiritual Masters such as the Buddha deny satisfaction to desire, the lowest form of Love, only in order to grant it fulfilment in its highest form, Compassion. At this stage the Lover joyfully embraces the pain of Love, seeing in it a key not only to the mysteries of Art, but to the secrets of spiritual development. He retires for solace to the bosom of Nature, and under the influence of her peace purges his love of the dross of selfish desire. Yet far from imagining a duality between profane and sacred love, he sees that under the stress of experience desire naturally evolves into true Love, and Love into Compassion. Love destroys every thought of self, and the Lover feels the distinction of 'I' and 'Thou' fading away. Nothing in the universe is separate or independent, but as though in a mirror all reflect each, and each reflects all. With joy the Lover realizes that his own earthly love is only a faint reflection of the divine Compassion of the Bodhisattva. On the wings of this joy he rises to spiritual illumination, understanding the true nature of Love, and realizing that his own love, like all other things in the universe, is in turn reflected in the heart of Reality. Overflowing with gratitude to the Beloved for having revealed to him the Supreme Mystery of existence, he declares that after the recognition of the ultimate nature of Selfless Love there can be only Silence.

THE VEIL OF STARS
To Sachin

1950–53

I

The coming of love is mysterious as the flight of a bird from unknown lands,
Its going mysterious as the unseen tumult of the wind blowing we know not whither.

II

What is this mystery of love that has opened in my heart like a bud at midnight,
And sends its sweetness crying through the dark like the voice of one mad with desire?

III

Strange it is, strange indeed that, shooting up through the crevices of my heart,
Unfolds itself ever whiter and whiter the pale green lily of love.

IV

If the flower of love blooms not within the garden of my heart
With what shall I come in my hands to worship Thee, O Lord?

V

Bring flowers, bring lights, bring incense!
Oh fools, that do not know the holiness of love!

VI

I do not want to find out that you, my idol, have, like all other idols, feet of clay –
That is why my love has hidden your feet away beneath the heaped-up flowers of its worship.

VII

Not for your beauty alone do I love you, my love, though you are beautiful indeed;
But because, when in this life we met for the first time, a passion re-awakened within me that had slept for a thousand years.

VIII

I know not whether I love you because you are beautiful,
Or whether you seem beautiful because I love you.

IX

Strange is this love of mine, strange but beautiful, like the pale greenness of the Western sky before the coming of a night of a million stars.

X

My love is nothing but the image of your own beauty reflected back to you from the spotless mirror of my heart.

XI

The echo of the song you sing rings still within my heart,
And is woven into the melody of my life like the thread of gold that runs through the texture of all my dreams.

XII

The midnight darkness of my heart is full of thoughts of you,
As the grass of the riverside is with glow-worms or the sky with its millions of stars.

XIII

Why trouble to keep my love for you secret within my breast,
When it is blazoned across the sky in stars for all to see?

XIV

How can my heart bear to be ever dressing the perennial newness of its love in the rags of the same old words soiled and stained with a million usings?

XV
Like a melody so faint and delicate that it eludes the listening ear
The rhythm of my love ripples into nuances that slip through the fingers of expression.

XVI
I cannot speak my love: It is too delicate and fine for the coarse utterance of words.
Instead, let the shy young grass speak to you for me in tiny whispers,
Or let the stars at midnight breathe my love into your ear with their million silences.

XVII
Does not the moon speak to you in the night of the fullness of my love,
Or the stars unfold before you the unutterable height of its aspiration?

XVIII
The music of the stars is mine, and the melody o' the moon.
Oh do you not hear them singing to you in the silence of the night?

XIX
What matters it to me that a million lovers may sigh over my lines in days to come,
If today you know not that the red rose of love blooms for you among thorns in the garden of my heart!

XX
What use to be decked with the jewels of learning and pride
When at their terrible radiance the beloved cowers down in the dust with fear!

XXI
The earth seeks to prove her love for the sun
With the heavenly rhetoric of flowers.

XXII

When the flower shrank from the sun's love
The sun wished it was a flower.

XXIII

Bitter as death is it to me that you should clasp your hands together in reverence before me,
When I am longing for you to take my hands in your own with love.

XXIV

The rose-bud which I have kept in a glass of water beside my bed
Will reveal its inmost heart to me if I wait for a few short hours;
But the secret hoard of love's honey stored within your heart
Remains, alas! sealed away from me day after day!

XXV

I thought that I saw the golden fire of love burning within your heart,
But when I approached and tried to warm my hands at its flame
I found that it was only the red image of my own love reflected in the ice there.

XXVI

Mournfully flutter down from my heart poems for the death of love,
Even as the curled crisp petals fall in showers from the rose that is dead.

XXVII

One morning I awoke and found love cold within my heart, like a fledgling dead in the nest.

XXVIII

No, my love for you is not dead, but only so tired out with continual weeping that it has fallen asleep in the cradle of my heart.

XXIX

Sometimes, my love, I forget you for hours together.
But strange! when I think of you again I realize that the thought of you had somehow been nestling beside my heart all the time!

XXX

Now it is evening, and the thought of you rises in my heart like the
full moon in the sky.

XXXI

This is the early evening hour at which daily I wait and listen for the
music of your coming,
When all the unlovely happenings of the day are touched by your
presence into perfect beauty like the sudden blooming of a rose,
And when the yearnings unutterable of a million life-times seem to
find love's highest fulfilment in a few familiar words.

XXXII

I sit in a breathless agony of suspense in your presence,
As though upon a single flicker of your eyelid hung the destiny of a world.

XXXIII

Presses upon me heavier and heavier day by day
The unfathomable mystery of existence.

XXXIV

Though the little plant of our love seems not to grow, and though it
puts forth not even a single leaf or bud,
Yet I feel that the hidden roots of it are striking ever deeper and deeper
into the soft red soil of our hearts.

XXXV

The beauty of your face was the portal through which I passed into
the inner chamber of your heart's love.

XXXVI

Like a waterfall your young life leaps joyfully down the precipice of
existence in the midst of the rainbow spray of beauty.

XXXVII

You are elusive as a light wind playing among the leaves of Summer,
Or like the playful brightness of water that slips laughing away
between the clenched fingers of the hand.

XXXVIII
Though your moods are variable as the play of sunlight on shifting
    leaves,
Let my love be steadfast as the shining of the sun.

XXXIX
My love, that falls like moonlight upon the shifting leaves of you,
Flashes all the more brightly for your inconstancy.

XL
You can no more confine love within the limits of human hearts
Than you can catch the showering moonlight in cups of gold.

XLI
You are near to me, my love, near indeed.
You are standing close to my side, and I can feel your presence even
    though you are not touching me....
    But you are near to me only as the inaccessible stars are near to the
lonely hills, and stand beside me only as the full moon in the midnight
sky seems to stand beside a moonlit cloud.

XLII
Sometimes a few light words smilingly spoken
Seem to bring you nearer to me than the beatings of my own heart;
But the next instant, before my heart can respond to the ecstasy of
    your presence,
A word or glance has carried you far away from me
    Beyond the millionth star.

XLIII
Mine is not a love that can feed only upon the sweetness of replies,
For it nourishes its delicate life upon the bitterness of your silences day
    after day.

XLIV
Round and round in the ever-recurring starless night of frustration
The black flame of my love pursues your golden youth.

XLV
I hammer with bleeding fists on the cold stone wall of your indifference
Seeking in vain to break through into the inner citadel of a smile.

XLVI
Dashing against the black rocks of your indifference again and again,
The raging waves of the ocean of my love are shattered incessantly into a tingling agony of foam.

XLVII
Better bare-faced hatred and scorn
Than indifference hiding itself behind the grinning mask of conventional regard!

XLVIII
Your beauty is like the inaccessible beauty of the stars
Pitilessly smiling down on the tortured questionings of humanity.

XLIX
Your indifference strikes into my heart a deeper deadlier wound
Than the utmost skill of hatred could ever have devised.

L
Let the sharp nails of your cruelty tear and lacerate my heart if you will,
But slay me not, I pray you, with the ice-cold scimitar of your indifference!

LI
The same melody which flooded my heart with joy in the sunrise of union
Now breaks it with the agony of remembrance in the starless night of separation.

LII
My love is bewildered and lost in the wide heaven of your beauty,
Like the ghost of a cloud in the midst of the moonlit sky.

LIII
Fiercely I battled with cruel words against the invincible army of your silence
Until I had won from your eye the victory of a tear.

LIV
I have made a little crevice of pain in your heart
Hoping that a seed of my flowering love may fall and find lodgement therein.

LV
All over the restless ocean of my mind there flashes only the cold green agony of remembrance.

LVI
It grieved me that I did not recognize you when you passed me by in the dark,
For it felt like a warning that I will not be able to recognize you when we meet again in other lives.

LVII
This love of mine will pursue you long after I am dead,
Long after the frailty of your beauty has taken refuge with the dust,
Flowering into the long delayed fulfilment of its longing
From some other green bud on the tree of the multitude of our lives,
Finding you out and choosing you from the whole world again and again,
Even though you hide yourself on the other side of the universe
In the midst of millions of stars.

LVIII
Though unravelled and torn apart by the pitiless hands of Fate,
The threads of our destinies will be woven together again by the fingers of triumphant Love.

LIX
Even to part from you is sweet, if parting be your pleasure.

LX

The pain of your absence teaches me the difference between the clamorous demands of desire and the calm quiet acquiescence of perfect love.

LXI

Love is like ice and trickles away in tiny streamlets between the fingers of the hands that seek to grasp it too tightly.

LXII

It was desire that dashed from my hands the chalice that love raised to my lips.

LXIII

Siddhārtha dashed from the hands of Yashodhara the little earthen cup of his love,
Only that as Buddha He might lift to her lips the crystal chalice of His Compassion.

LXIV

Put your foot in the stirrup of Love if you wish to mount the steed of Wisdom.

LXV

He must pass beneath the arch of Pain who desires to enter into the shrine of Love.
He must enter into the shrine of Love who seeks to gaze upon the face of the image of Wisdom.

LXVI

The music of my life will come forth only when upon my heart-strings play the fingers of Love and Pain.

LXVII

Poesy comes to birth from the dark womb of Pain,
Where it was begotten of the fiery seed of Love.

LXVIII

So delicious is the pain of Love that it has persuaded me into the love of Pain.

LXIX

The pain of loving is surpassed only by the pain of not loving.

LXX

It was pain that bore to me in careful hands the bottomless cup of joy.

LXXI

The red wound made by the sunset of love has healed within my heart,
And in the darkness I see that the sky is full of stars.

LXXII

There is no wound man can give
That nature cannot heal.

LXXIII

Be like wax beneath the signet of green jade that Nature wears upon her hand,
And she will stamp deep upon your heart the secret emblem of her ineffable peace.

LXXIV

The silence and peace of the old hills sinks ever deeper and deeper into my heart,
Until it seems as though the clouds were resting on my shoulders and my head was crowned with stars.

LXXV

Sitting for hours and hours among the calm, quiet, kind old hills,
I feel that somewhere behind the veil of things there is a Friend;
Walking all day upon the soft green hillside grass,
I feel that I have touched with my lips the finger-tips of Reality.

LXXVI
What is it that these ancient hills are trying to speak out to me from the wordless depth of their silence?

LXXVII
Oh living, breathing Silence,
That integrates with the soundless music of its almighty harmony the harsh dissonance of mortal lives!

LXXVIII
Now the sunset glows red in the West, and the mountain with its two or three white clouds
Looks like an old man sitting beside the fire with his children in their night-gowns on his knee.

LXXIX
Night broods upon the hills like a great bird with downy purple wings outstretched
And bearing a crest of dazzling stars.

LXXX
The cherry-blossom shows like a blush on the dark blue cheek of the hills.

LXXXI
What is love but the rosy tinge at the edge of the white petal of the lotus of Compassion.

LXXXII
Remember that which shines in brightness above your head;
But do not forget that which lies folded in shadows beneath your feet.
The stems of the bamboo shoot upward into the sky;
But their leaves, like green fingers, point downward to the earth.

LXXXIII
My love for thee is not alien to the stars,
But whispers in my ear the secrets of the Void.

LXXXIV
Lamp-like, your beauty lights my path through the dark labyrinth of passion into the white simplicity of love.

LXXXV
Though housed in the shabby scabbard of desire
The blade of love is bright and keen enough to cut asunder the cords of self.

LXXXVI
All the tears of desire reflect only the agony of its own frustration,
But in a single tear-drop of compassion are mirrored all the sorrows and miseries of the world.

LXXXVII
Desire seeks to possess and dominate the lives of others,
Love simply to sacrifice its own.

LXXXVIII
Break up all thy worldly goods for fuel,
But keep, at all costs, the flame of love burning day and night in the house of thy life.

LXXXIX
All the riches accumulated by Desire are poverty indeed,
But in the beggary of Love that gives its all is a treasure inexhaustible.

XC
I crave not for the peripheral contact of lips,
But for the central and essential union of our hearts.

XCI
Man seeks to satisfy with a handful of glow-worms
His hunger unappeasable for the stars.

XCII
This love of mine is for you and not for you,
As the moonlight is for the cloud and not for the cloud.

XCIII

When Love has conducted you into the golden presence of his
    master Compassion he bows to the ground before him and departs.

XCIV

When the sun of passion has gone down dazzlingly behind the
    Western horizon of my heart,
The moon of love will arise starrily behind the Eastern horizon of my
    soul.

XCV

Time was when, at the sight of you, love ran through my veins like
    fire.
Now, when I behold your face, the moonlight of compassion universal
    floods my heart.

XCVI

What I thought was my love for you is, now I find, in reality
    compassion for all sentient beings.
Thinking to pick up a glow-worm from the grass, lo! I plucked down
    a galaxy of stars from the sky.

XCVII

Seeking for glow-worms in the long green grass of the bank
I have glimpsed the reflection of the stars trembling in the dark blue
    depths of the pool.

XCVIII

At first I thought that my love for you would bind me to the earth,
But now I find that it liberates me into the heaven of the spirit.

XCIX

The Evening Star of love becomes the Morning Star of the life spiritual.

C

I cannot believe that the best way of seeing the stars in the sky above
    one's head
Is by crushing the glow-worms in the grass beneath one's feet.

CI

Comes the flower more quickly by tearing up the roots of the plant whereon it blooms?
No, nor the pure white light of Compassion by extinguishing the flame of the dark red lamp of love.

CII

Love does not argue with Compassion within my heart,
Any more than the Summer flower, if it could speak, would try to refute the ripe red fruit of Autumn.

CIII

Shall I disdain to hold a glow-worm in my hand
Simply because a wreath of stars has been placed upon my head?

CIV

Better a glow-worm if it guides you along the homeward path,
Than a star that leads you astray.

CV

When the horizon is shrouded in darkness I cannot tell where end the glow-worms of earth and where begin the stars of heaven.

CVI

Love is like a pool of water at midnight,
Which shows to us the stars of heaven even though we look for them in the wrong direction.

CVII

Place it in the sunlight of Compassion and the hard green fruit of desire will ripen into the softness and sweetness of golden love.

CVIII

Desire for anyone flowers into love for someone
And at last bears fruit as compassion for everyone.

CIX

The tear of the Bodhisattva's compassion flows through the world as love,
Even as the austere snows of the Himalayas flow in rivers down into the green plains.

CX

It is the smile of the Bodhisattva that flashes upon me from the heart of the golden sunset,
And the flood of his Compassion that inundates my soul with streams of love.

CXI

Joy deepens and deepens within my heart until it opens into an infinite sky of Knowledge ablaze with stars.

CXII

Only fools think that love is something that happens between a man and a woman.
The wise know that it is love that makes the planets join hands together in their dance of joy about the sun.

CXIII

It is this great rhythm of joy that, having given birth to millions of stars in the sky,
Now pours down into my heart and ecstatically begets there the unending mystery of my love.

CXIV

What joy it is to realize that every atom of the universe is reflected in my heart, and that the love of my heart is mirrored in every atom of the universe!

CXV

The sorrows of the earth cast little shadows of darkness across the sunshine of my heart,
Even as the joy of my love is written in stars across the darkness of the sky.

CXVI
Reality is reflected in my heart as love, and this love of mine is in turn mirrored in the all-embracing bosom of Reality,
As though the moon lay reflected in the depths of the ocean, and the ocean in the calm clear heart of the moon.

CXVII
I know that even from the inmost depths of heaven I shall see your face shining out upon me above the utmost beauty of the stars.

CXVIII
The secret of love is love.

CXIX
Let the silence speak.

ON GLASTONBURY TOR

Dragons were slain here   1969
Ages ago. Dragons' blood
Soaked into the earth, stained
White chalk miles deep.
Now, westward looking at evening, all that we see
Is the dragon's back humped
Half out of the earth (a little path
Running along the spine) and a red sun
Staining the atmosphere, as we stand
On Glastonbury Tor.

   Arriving in the evening from Stonehenge
Long we gazed up at the great mound.
From over the hill's brow the grey tower
Loomed higher and higher as we climbed.

   Michael, Archangel of the Summit, were you defeated
When the elements raged, when the lightning
Struck? Were you unable to defend your own?
Giant spear broken, did you flee
Discomforted, your church in ruins, the tower alone
Erect, funnel now between heaven and earth, linking
What the swing of your sword
Had striven to keep apart, releasing

The old gods beliefs myths rituals
Religions, all that your bright feet
Would have trodden down forever?

   Cauldron unlidded long ago, the Tor
Still boils over. White mist from wet clay
Ascending, clockwise we climbed
From ledge to ledge, waded
Obliquely through the evening, swam
Through magical shapes, phantoms, mysteries
Thick as weeds in water, through
Voices from the past, visions
Of Arthur Merlin, Cup Lance, till at length
Emerging, the massive bulk of the tower,
Strong, foursquare, stood over us
Threatening protective.
                    Long we gazed
Over miles of green brown patchwork, into shimmering blue
Distance, gazed
Down into the West, into
Red gold pink grey
Sunset on cloud hill, gazed
From Avalon into the world, saw
In middle distance the dragon's blue
Bulk in fading red
Light, and nearer at hand
On spurs of the Tor,
Black against the last amber
Glow, solitary
Shapes.

   Squaring the tower and iron
Railing, and rounding
The railing a human flowergarland, forty
Pairs of hands joined, circling
Gravely on the dark hub of the tower, wheeling
Clockwise in the clear night, turning
In solemn solar dance, in cosmic

Ritual, churning
Energies out of the earth, energies
Out of the Tor, up through
The tower, moving
Silent ecstatic round
And round, slower
And slower, coming
At length to rest, hands
At sides, facing
Inward onto the four walls, breathing
Deeply, breathing
Inaudibly, standing
Immobile now
As the circled stones of Stonehenge.

   Flowercircle suddenly unfolding
Outward, a dark shape
Darts from the door. A voice
Through the strong young body speaks.
𝕬𝖓𝖆𝖗𝖆𝖐𝖆𝖙𝖎𝖞𝖆 𝖒𝖆𝖇𝖆𝖓𝖆
𝕶𝖆𝖙𝖆𝖓𝖆𝖒𝖆 𝖗𝖆𝖌𝖆𝖑𝖎𝖞𝖆𝖕𝖆𝖛𝖆.
Hieratic infallible voice, voice
Abysmal, daimoniacal, voice
Of Glastonbury, we do not comprehend
Your meaning, we can only listen
To the flawless metallic sounds
Streaming staccato into the night, shooting up
Through loins lungs breast belly throat, bronze
Hammering bronze, resonant
Bellbody vibrating, saying
Things we cannot understand
In a language we do not know. We can only
Admit incomprehension, confess
Defeat. There is now
No seer, no soothsayer, no reader of dreams, no
Interpreter of oracles to unravel
The dark sounds, to pursue
Through mazes the Merlinvoice, and yet

Now, more than ever before,
We understand or perish, learn
That language or die. Oh but what if
There were nothing to understand, nothing
To learn, what if we had simply
To accept incomprehension, accept defeat, accept
Collapse, disintegration, death, face
Dissolution of the mind, abdication of reason, erasure
Of what can be weighed numbered measured sensed known, face
Descent into Hell without hope of resurrection
On the third day. Are we prepared for this?

   Oh I would lie down in the dark, in the depths
Of the sea with my love, I would drift
Red weed in green water, sway
To and fro with the clock of the tides,
Sway as we swayed that night
On the Tor, at the foot of the tower,
In the mauveblue twilight, slowly
Languidly peacefully, forty
Bodies beeclustered together
Heaving, breathing as one.
Oh I would lie down with my love
And be at rest.
              Look look look!
Silently, suddenly appearing
Above the bent backs the bowed
Heads laid together, above the
Greenbrown patchwork humped dragonback red
Light, mysteriously emerging
From among the stars, bigger
Brighter than the stars, hovering
On the horizon, skimming
High above gold clouds black hills, three
Lamps three lights three eyes three
We know not what, one
Larger two smaller, all moving
In fastformation, in orangeoval flight

Triangular, steering toward the Tor
Through the mild blue night, darting
Fishlike to explore, eyeing
Approaching, investigating, visitors
From Mars or Venus perhaps, messengers
From outer space, heralds
Of transcendence, sparks flashing
Between terminals between
Here There, Known Unknown, Tor
Eternity, forces pulsing
Momently on the horizon, brilliant
Terrible a moment, focused
Urgently on the Tor, then
As though satisfied, reassured,
Veering disappearing
In deep blue depths indigo
Distance, leaving us
Dreamily swaying no longer, scattered
Round the tower base, clustered
In groups in halfgroups, talking
In whispers, some drifting
Down the slopes, hailing
With friendly voices vehicles
With dimmed lights parked far
Below.

   Night. Night. Night. Night. Night.
Within the tower within the funnel the grey
Space troglodytes we sat, refugees
From civilization from the world from
Ourselves perhaps, sat
On damp earth amid cold stone. Above
Skypatch glimmering blueluminous. Below
Cavernous gloom flickeringly
Onecandlelit, and in
The candlepatch we sitting
Circlewise against the rock, sitting
Silent at first, separate
At first, but eventually

Thawed relaxed related, sharing
Bread, sharing blankets, sharing
Ourselves....
           On the stroke of two,
Softly at first, then steadily,
Down came the rain, down
Through the dark, dropping
On recumbent bodies outflung
Hands arms, drenching
Hairtangles on improvised pillows, soaking
Icy into sleepingbags cold and clear
Into sleep into dreams soaking
Through manylayered illusion through
Life death space time, washing
Thought washing emotion washing
Perception, rendering
Consciousness diaphanous transparent
To existence to reality strains
Of unearthly music songsound
Approaching receding voices
Vibrations. We looking
Up through the tower see
Starpoints in the skypatch
Glittering intense see
Tower shooting upwards reaching
For infinity, walls
Expanding in all directions, dissolving
Collapsing
As
Swimming in space, spinning
On its own axis, us
And all things within it, cosmic
Dimensionless, the Tor
Soars.

THE CAVES OF BHÁJÁ

Often, now, I find myself											1985
Thinking of the Caves of Bhájá,
Thinking of the silent valley
Where they look down on the rice-fields.

Carved out of the living rock-face
In the Western Ghats, I see them,
Steeped in shadow in the morning,
Pierced by sunlight in the evening,
Cell and meeting-hall and stupa,
All so silent and deserted.

Once the yellow-robed and shaven-
Headed monks harmonious dwelt there.
Every day at dawn assembling
In the pillared meeting-hall
They would kneel before the stupa, –
Lofty stupa, hung with garlands, –
They would chant the Buddha's praises,
Chant the praises of the Dhamma,
And the Sangha's, deep-intoning.
Then, as starting with the eastern
Quarter, all the sky above them

Turned one living dome of azure,
And the sun in all his glory
Rose up from behind the mountains,
Some would to the distant village
Trudge for almsfood for the brethren,
Older monks would teach the younger,
And the younger serve the older.
Some again would ply the mallet
And the chisel, cutting deeper,
Deeper in the living rock-face,
Hollowing out another cavern,
Making little doors and windows,
Decorating shaft and lintel,
While their nimbler-fingered brethren
On palm-leaf with iron stylus
Copied ancient manuscripts
Or recorded oral teachings.
Others still, in neighbouring thickets
Spent the hours, so swiftly flying,
Plunged in deepest meditation.
Thus the day passed. Every evening
In the pillared hall assembling
They would kneel before the stupa, –
Lofty stupa, hung with garlands, –
They would chant the Buddha's praises,
And the praises of the Dhamma,
And the Sangha's, deep-intoning,
Till above the Caves of Bhájá
Rose the moon, and with its radiance
Turned the whole façade to silver.

Now the ruined cells are empty,
And the meeting-hall deserted.
Only buzzards can be seen there,
Circling high above the rock-face,
Or else bats, that in the evening
Flicker in and out like shadows.
Not a sound disturbs the silence,

Save when, once or twice a fortnight,
Bands of little, flower-like children
(Streaming from the local railway-
Station just around the ridge-end),
Marshalled by perspiring teachers,
Fill the place with furious babble.

From the steps of Dhammadeepa
We can see the Caves of Bhájá
High up on the rocky spur there,
Facing West across the rice-fields,
Grey in morning, gold in evening.
We can see the children racing
Back and forth along the terrace,
Dots of green and red and yellow;
We can even hear their babble,
Hear it thin and faint with distance
Like the hum of a mosquito.
For, within the silent valley,
With its back against the mountains
We have built a place of refuge.
Dhammadeepa – thus we call it,
'Light of Dhamma,' 'Dhamma-Island.'
On the solid rock we built it,
Built it well with stone and mortar,
Laid the red tiles on the rafters,
Painted it all white and azure.
Then we sunk a well beside it,
Planted trees and shrubs around it,
Laid out gardens, walks, and pathways,
Till our refuge was complete.

Twenty months ago I stayed there,
Stayed a while at Dhammadeepa,
Saw each day the Caves of Bhájá
High up on the rocky spur there,
Saw each day the buzzard circling,
Even heard the children's babble,

Heard it thin and faint with distance
Like the hum of a mosquito.
Then, one afternoon, I issued
Forth into the blazing sunshine,
And, with many friends about me,
Crossed the parched and empty rice-fields,
Climbed the steps cut in the rock-face
Flight by rough-hewn flight, until I
Stood within the Caves of Bhájá,
Stood within the meeting-hall where
Long ago the monks, assembling
In the morning and the evening,
Loud would chant the Buddha's praises,
And the praises of the Dhamma,
And the Sangha's, deep-intoning.

Often, now, I find myself
Thinking of the Caves of Bhájá
Thinking of the quiet valley
Where they look down on the rice-fields.

But it's not of mighty pillars
On their patient heads supporting
Rock-cut vaulting that I'm thinking,
Distant from the Caves of Bhájá,
Nor of that impassive stupa,
Lofty still, unhung with garlands.
No, not even of our refuge,
Dhammadeepa, am I thinking,
Not of the ten days I spent there,
Nor the friends who came to see me,
Nor the meeting that we held there,
When we raised the glorious banner,
Five-hued, of the Buddha's Teaching.
For, when now I find myself
Thinking of the Caves of Bhájá
It is always of our noble-

Hearted Maha Dhammaveera,
Our 'Great Hero of the Dhamma,'
Our old warrior, that I'm thinking.

'When I die,' he said, 'cremate me
Here within this quiet valley.
Build a stupa for my ashes –
No, not in the Caves of Bhájá
But beside our Dhammadeepa.'

Scarce a month ago he came there,
Came to lovely Dhammadeepa,
Came, as ever, friendly, cheerful,
Came, as ever, kindly, helpful,
Came on what – though no one knew it
Save himself – would be his last and
Best retreat at Dhammadeepa.
There, among his friends and brethren,
Day by day he grew more happy, –
Grew more radiant, – even as the
Moon, above the rock-face rising,
Night by night increased in splendour:
Happy kneeling in the shrine-room
Chanting loud the Buddha's praises,
And the praises of the Dhamma,
And the Sangha's, loud and fervent,
While the white wreaths of the incense
Curled above the small red roses,
Curled above the lighted candles;
Happy squatting in the sunshine
With his well-loved Dhamma-cronies;
Happy talking, joking, eating;
Happy washing clothes and dishes;
Happy when the time of silence,
On the whole retreat descending,
Brought refreshment; happy sitting
On his meditation cushion.

Thus it was that when the full-moon
Rose at last above the rock-face
Our Great Hero's heart was filled with
Happiness as she with splendour.
Long he sat there in the shrine-room,
Long he meditated; wrote a
Note and pinned it to his pillow:
'My own action this: none other's';
Then upon the gravelled terrace
Took a turn or two (I see him
Solitary in the moonlight!);
Took a turn or two, considering,
Making firm his resolution,
Weighing all things in the balance;
Saw the scale of life plunge downward
And the scale of death fly upward.
Yes, the time had come now: midnight.
Down he sat there in the moonlight,
Sat not far from Dhammadeepa;
Wringing wet his yellow robes were,
Wringing wet, but not with water;
Down he sat, serene and mindful;
Gazed across the quiet valley
Up to where the Caves of Bhájá
Shone like silver in the moonlight,
Gazed a while, his last look taking.
Seventy years and more he'd laboured,
Laboured for the good of others,
First as son and elder brother,
Then as husband and as father,
Finally as homeless-wandering
Dhamma-farer, ever cheerful,
Ever friendly, ever active.
Much he loved his Dhamma-brothers,
Much he loved to serve and help them,
But alas! his strength was waning
And the time was fast approaching
When he could no longer render

Joyful service to the Order
But himself have need of service.
'Better far this frame should perish
Than that I should be a burden
To my noble Dhamma-brothers.
Enough have they to do without me.'
Strong in this belief he'd come there,
Come to lovely Dhammadeepa
For his last and best retreat there.
Strong in this belief, and happy,
Quiet he sat now in the moonlight,
Sat not far from Dhammadeepa;
Smiled, and then, his robes igniting,
In a sudden blaze of splendour
Passed in glory from the world.

That is why I find myself
Thinking of the Caves of Bhájá
Thinking of the quiet valley
Where they look down on the rice-fields.

HERCULES AND THE BIRDS

1985

I

Pink and white upon the hillside
Down in Naples, stands the massive
Archaeological Museum.
Palm trees stand before its portals, –
Date palms, crowned with feathery branches, –
While all round it, never ceasing,
Roars and howls and shrieks the traffic.
Silent in the lofty galleries
Stand or sit the white Immortals,
With the Heroes and the Roman
Emperors, naked or be-toga'd –
Stand or sit in bronze and marble,
Sad remains of ancient greatness.
Some, alas, are headless, armless,
Some, alas, are cracked and broken,
Or disfigured by the vandal.
There, majestic, stands Athené,
But her hand is Victory-less;
There the wise and bright Apollo,
But his bow and lyre are broken
(Headless, buxom Aphrodité
Shameless shows a shapely bottom).

Yet, within those lofty galleries,
One, at least, stands whole and perfect,
Clean as from the sculptor's chisel;
One, at least, shows undiminished
All the living faith of Hellas.
He, the greatest of the Heroes,
He, the Herculés Farnése,
By the undelved earth protected
Centuries long, and resurrected
To the wondering gaze of mortals
At the height of the Renáissance
Stands there, looking down gigantic
On this modern world of pygmies.

II
Later, back at Il Convento,
At my desk before the window,
Taking up the picture postcard
That I bought in the Museum,
Long I gaze at the completeness
Of the Herculés Farnése.
Brawny thighs and massive torso,
Shoulders broader than a barn-door,
Small head, curly-haired, based solid
On a bull-like neck half hidden
By a beard that falls luxuriant
To a chest of amplest measure –
Thus I see him. He is leaning
On a club of knotted olive,
That head downwards he is resting
On a round and rugged boulder.
On the club is draped a lion-skin, –
Lion-skin many-folded, ample, –
While beneath the Hero's dangled
Left arm, with its hand half-curving,
Hangs the lion-head, jaws disparted.
Stern but gentle he is leaning
On his club of knotted olive,

Thoughtfully his brow inclining,
Resting from his mighty labours.
Simple and sublime he stands there,
Less than god, but more than mortal.
He has slain the lion Neméan,
Wears its pelt now for a garment.
He has slain the marsh-born Hydra,
Crushing with his club the monster's
Multiplying heads, and dipped his
Arrows in the poisonous blood-gouts.
He has caught alive the magic
Brazen-hoofed and golden-antlered
Cerynthéian Hind, the fleet one:
Over hill and dale he chased her
One whole year; then caught and bound her.
He has caught alive the monstrous
Erymánthian Boar, the fierce one;
Chained him, foaming, in a snow-drift.
He has cleansed the Áugean Stables,
Where three thousand head of cattle
Thirty years and more had sheltered;
Cleansed them in a day, diverting
Through their doors a mighty river.
He has chased away the Harpies,
Foul defilers of the banquet;
Chased away the noisome Bird-things,
Woman-headed, with his arrows.
He has caught alive the Cretan
Bull, the fiery-breathed, the white one;
Caught the Minotaur's begetter.
He has from the Thracian uplands
Stolen Diomedés' Horses;
Horses that their cruel master
Fed on human flesh each morning.
He has reft the Golden Girdle
From the breasts of Hippolyté,
But, alas! has slain the maiden
In her Amazonian fierceness.

He has sailed towards the sunset,
To an island in the Ocean
Where the Sphinx's monstrous father
And the progeny of Arés
Guard the Oxen of Gerýon:
With his club he overcame them
And possessed him of the cattle.
He has brought the Golden Apples
From the ever-blooming Garden, –
Golden apples, dragon-warded, –
While the white-robed maidens, singing,
Circled round the sacred branches.
He has into Hell descended,
Dragged the triple-headed Guardian
Of the Gates of Hell, protesting,
Up into the light of Heaven.
Many other mighty labours
He, unceasing, has accomplished;
Labours for the good of others
And himself to purify
From pollution of kin-murder:
(Driven mad by jealous Hera,
Queen of Heaven, he, unwitting,
Took the lives of sons and nephews).
All the monstrous births of Nature,
Misbegotten, slime-engendered,
He has wholly extirpated;
All their foully-nurtured children
He has either slain or shackled.
Tyrants from their thrones deposing,
Succouring the weak and helpless,
Law and justice like twin pillars
He has planted in the kingdoms.
Now, deep-brooding, he is resting,
Resting from his mighty labours –
He, the greatest of the Heroes,
He, the Herculés Farnése.
There, within those lofty galleries,

Leaning on his club of knotted
Olive draped with pelt Neméan,
He is standing, whole and perfect.
Laying down the picture postcard
That I bought in the Museum
Long I dream of his completeness.

III
Sudden, from beneath my window,
Comes a sound of shouting, barking.
Looking out, I see below me
Men and dogs from Fiats tumbling.
All the men are armed with rifles,
All are dressed in olive denim;
All upon their heads are wearing
Shooting-caps with little feathers,
While from bulging jacket pockets
Necks of bottles are protruding.
On the slope they stand consulting,
Loading rifles, slamming car doors,
Then with dogs behind them frisking
Scatter out across the hillside
As, above the dying hubbub,
From the church across the valley
Clangs the Sunday early Mass bell.
Soon, from deep within the foothills, –
Tuscan foothills, forest-mantled, –
We can hear the crack of rifles,
As the modern race of heroes
There pursue their weekend labours.
Later, on our walks we meet them
Skulking in the rock-strewn by-paths,
Crouching underneath the bushes,
With their rifles at the ready
And their fingers on the trigger.
Some are camouflaged with branches,
Some have decoy-birds in cages;
Others, from their hide-outs, blow on

Decoy-whistles, sweetly warbling
(Every now and then a bottle
Raising to their lips and swigging).
Year by year they come, remorseless,
In the pleasant Tuscan Autumn,
When the olive-fruits are gleaming
Black among the grey-green foliage,
And, beside the stony pathway,
Cyclamens, the pink and frail ones,
Push up through the rotting leafmould
And the withered leaves and grasses.
They have slain the chirping sparrows,
Slain the linnet and the whitethroat,
Slain the robin and the wagtail,
Slain the magpie and the pigeon,
Slain them in their tens of thousands,
Till within those ancient foothills, –
Tuscan foothills, forest-mantled,
Ever green, and aromatic, –
Rarely now are heard the songbirds
Fluting from the leafy branches;
Rarely, rarely, do we see them
Flitting to and fro like shadows
On the outskirts of the forest.
Yet, though year by year the hunters
Farther have to range and wider
(As the birds, their numbers dwindling,
Deeper shrink within the coverts),
Still, on pale blue Autumn mornings,
Off they go with dogs and rifles;
Still, on deep blue Autumn evenings,
Back they come with bulging game bags:
While, throughout the gold-blue Autumn
Day, from deep within the foothills,
Comes the hateful crack of rifles
As the modern race of heroes
Go about their weekend labours.

IV

Last night in a dream I saw him,
He, the greatest of the Heroes,
He, the Herculés Farnése,
Less than god, but more than mortal.
Like a solitary mountain
That, upon the far horizon,
In some long untrodden region
Looms above a barren landscape; –
Like a thundercloud that, swollen,
Rolls up from the heaving ocean
And, above the earth impending,
Threatens to discharge its burden; –
Like the smoke of a volcano,
That, in mighty volumes towering,
Spreads across the face of heaven,
While, within the parent crater,
Bubbles up the yellow lava; –
Like a forest fire that, raging,
Roars and crackles through the woodland,
Licking up the trees and bushes
With its tongues of gold and scarlet –
Thus I saw him. From his shoulders
Hung the skin of lion Neméan, –
Lion-skin many-folded, ample, –
With the mighty forepaws, knotted,
Crossed upon his naked bosom,
While above his head the massive
Lion-head, like a crested helmet
Resting, reared itself, triumphant.
Whirling high his club of knotted
Olive, that athwart the landscape
Cast a black and dreadful shadow,
He with giant step was striding
Ridge to ridge across the foothills.
As he went, he drove before him
All the men with dogs and rifles,
All the modern race of heroes:

Like a flock of sheep he drove them.
With his foot the weapons crushing,
With his hand the decoys freeing,
On he strode – the birds around him
Fluttering cloudlike, loudly singing.
Birds upon his head and shoulders,
Birds upon his beard and lion-skin;
Birds upon his club of knotted
Olive perching in their thousands –
On I saw him moving: – saw him
Pass from land to land, redressing
All the wrongs that on the weaker
By the stronger are inflicted,
And, within the souls of millions,
Sow the dragon seed of vengeance;
Saw him drive before him, headlong,
All the brood of fraud and rapine,
All the hosts of lust and violence,
All the forces of destruction;
Saw him crush the robot armies;
Saw him smash the hideous weapons;
Saw him from their sunless prisons
Free the victims of oppression;
Saw him cleanse the earth and ocean;
Saw him build anew the cities;
Saw him forge between the nations
Golden links of truth and friendship,
Ever-during. – *Thus* I saw him
Last night in my dream or vision,
He, the greatest of the Heroes,
He, the Herculés Farnése,
Bent on ever-nobler labours
For the good of others; – saw him –
Sun of Justice – in the heavens
Blazing; saw him golden, glorious,
Showering beams of blessing; – saw him
Show how strength, by love directed,
Shapes anew this world of mortals,

And, upon a nobler pattern,
Rears our heavenly-earthly city;
Till, from mortal to Immortal
Changing, after many labours
We, like him, to high Olympus
Raised, from Hébe's rosy fingers
Receive at last the cup ambrosial.

SHORT STORIES

PUBLICATION HISTORY

These six stories were written over a period of almost forty years and appear here in what I think must be roughly chronological order. I can't find any record of the circumstances in which they were written, but some of them have been published before in various editions. 'The Two Roses' (1952), 'The Artist's Dream' (1972), and 'The Parable of the Talking Buddha' (1971) were published by Ola Leaves in 1980. 'The Parable of the Talking Buddha' had previously appeared in the *FWBO Newsletter*, no. 14, in January 1972, and 'The Two Roses' and 'The Artist's Dream' were published in India as *Dhammamegha* pamphlets in 1988 and 1989. 'The White Lotus' and 'The Antique Dealer' appear not to have been published before and the manuscripts are undated, but from the style and (in the case of the latter) the autobiographical content, I would guess that 'The White Lotus' was written in India at around the same time as 'The Two Roses', and 'The Antique Dealer' was written in England in the 1970s. The last story, 'The Cave', was written in 1990 and read by Sangharakshita on the occasion of the twenty-third anniversary of the Western Buddhist Order, celebrated at Manchester Town Hall in April 1991. It hasn't been published before, as far as I know, but a film of Sangharakshita's reading of the story in Manchester is available from the Clear Vision Trust and a recording and a transcript are available through freebuddhistaudio.com.

Vidyadevi

THE TWO ROSES

The trees had been planted so closely together that the rays of the rising sun were unable to pierce the tangle of interlacing branches, and they grew so tall that it was more than an hour before he could climb up behind them and look down over their green nodding heads into the garden at their feet. The flowers enjoyed this hour more than any other of the whole hot June day, unless the hour at which the day slips into night, and the first stars show their timid faces in the blue sky, was more delightful to them still. At any rate, they laughed and talked together as the cool morning breezes played among their leaves, and rejoiced that their petals were still heavy with drops of icy dew.

Near a bent old magnolia tree, whose two or three huge purple flowers had opened their silver-lined petals, grew a rosebush, and on the highest red-clawed branch of the rosebush two white roses were blowing. They were not the big blowsy kind of blossom known as the cabbage rose, which indeed does look more like a powdered and rouged vegetable than a flower, but genuine aristocratic white roses, neither very big nor very small, and they were at that most delightful stage of a rose's life when it is neither a bud nor a full-grown flower.

The two blooms were, of course, sisters, and like most sisters they dearly loved a little early morning chat. Every day at this hour they gossiped about the tall guardian trees whose branches rose so lovingly and so protectingly above their heads, about what the little stream had murmured to the bamboos, and what the bamboos had whispered to the stream, about the birds that pecked the slowly ripening fruit, the bees that went gathering honey from flower to flower, and the yellow and blue butterflies that danced brightly along the garden paths. Then they talked about the coolness of the night, when the moon smiled down upon them and threw over the garden a mantle of silver, and about the dreadful burning heat of the day, when the fierce sun wrapped them in a cloak of gold.

But sometimes they remained quite silent, dreaming of the soft spring rain, and of all the days which had been before they budded from their mother's side. They dreamed, too, of the morning on which their sheaths had split, when for the first time they had peeped out, as through a half-opened window, and seen the blue sky, and the tall trees, and all the other flowers of the garden, and felt on their cheeks the coolness of the wind and the kiss of falling dew. They had wondered, then, why they had come to the garden at all, and whence, and what was beyond the trees. But their mother could not tell them, and the winds only sighed when they asked, and the gay butterflies hurried on with a laugh, so that in the midst of all their dreams they still wondered about the meaning of it all and the purpose of their lovely perfumed lives. And one day, while the two white roses dreamed and wondered in this manner on the topmost spray of the rosebush, they were plucked by two young girls, who bore them away in a wicker basket together with four or five of their dark red cousins, and many blue, yellow, and pink friends and acquaintances.

At first they were so astonished at this sudden, unexpected and rather painful change, that they lay there among the lilies, gladioluses and larkspurs without uttering a word. The other flowers were no less astonished than the two roses, and the whole fragrant party therefore remained absolutely silent until the wicker basket had been carried indoors and placed on a small round Kashmiri table of elaborately carved walnut.

After a few minutes had passed the flowers started nudging each other and whispering, and those who had been placed at the sides of the basket tried to peer through the gaps in the wickerwork in order to find out to what sort of garden they had been brought; for they had lived in a garden all their lives and were unable to imagine any other kind of place. The two young roses, having been plucked last of all, were at the top of the basket, and one of them could even raise her head just above the edge in order to take a quick look round. But she saw nothing which even slightly resembled a tree or a flower, and there was not a single blade of grass in the whole place. As she searched her brain for suitable words with which to describe the strange ungardenlike scene her sister whispered, 'Can you see anything, dear? What sort of a garden have we been brought to? Has the sun yet risen above the trees?'

Before the rose could reply, however, there had come a sound of quickly approaching footsteps, the basket had been turned upside down, and the flowers lightly shaken out into a heap on the smooth brown table top. As they opened their eyes after the soft shock of their fall, and looked up, what should they see bending over them but two strange flowers, one with pink petals and the other with white, but far bigger and infinitely more beautiful than any of the flowers they could remember having seen in the garden.

'Poor things,' said the white flower, as she carefully sorted the gladioluses from the other blossoms, 'How limp they have become! We must put them into vases quickly, Savitri, otherwise they will fade and die.' And already her nimble fingers were busy with the larkspurs.

'Where shall we put them all, Sujata?' asked the pink flower. 'We've gathered quite a lot this morning. It's weeks since we visited the old garden, and how quickly the flowers are blooming nowadays!'

'Especially the roses,' said Sujata, as she gathered the five dark red sisters into a bunch and gazed at them admiringly. 'We can put these in mother's room, she loves June roses. The gladioluses can go into that tall black vase on the dining-room table. There are some jugs in the kitchen which will do for the larkspurs and the other common flowers.'

The poor blue larkspurs blushed deep purple at these last words, but to be sure, had Sujata known that the flowers were listening eagerly to every word that was spoken she would never had said anything so unkind, for she was a compassionate-hearted girl who did not like to hurt the feelings of even the humblest of living things.

The two white roses, having been originally at the top of the basket, were now of course lying at the very bottom of the heap, and the girls did not find them until they had almost finished sorting and arranging the other flowers.

'Oh look!' cried Savitri, as she picked up the two last yellow lilies from the table. 'Here are the white roses we plucked near the magnolia tree! How lovely they are with the dew still fresh upon them! But where are we to keep them? The jugs and vases must all be full by now.'

'Let's have them for our own room, Savitri,' suggested her sister. 'We had forgotten that. One for you and one for me. We can put them in that little cracked glass on the mantelshelf.'

'I shall wear mine to the cinema tonight,' said Savitri promptly. 'There will be Clark Gable and Errol Flynn and….'

'Oh Savitri,' cried Sujata in dismay. 'Haven't you forgotten something? We have to keep the Eight Precepts today and visit the temple again in the evening – it's the full-moon day and –'

'Of course I haven't forgotten, silly,' was the reply, as the girl's protests were silenced with an affectionate hug. 'But don't you understand, it's the last day of the big film, and I simply couldn't miss it, could I? We can keep the Eight Precepts some other day, it doesn't make much difference.'

Sujata sighed. 'All right,' she said at last. 'You take your rose to the cinema. I shall give mine to the Buddha.'

The hours passed quickly for the two white roses, for the water was pleasantly cool about their stalks, and only an occasional shaft of sunlight fell faintly golden through the windows into the room, as for a moment the wind puffed the drawn curtains aside. Besides, there were many new and exciting things to look at, and no sooner had Savitri and Sujata left the room – for they were big girls, and had to help their mother prepare *dāna* for the monks who had been invited to take their meal at the house – than they began to exchange soft flowery whispers with each other.

'Just look at those huge white petals lying down there,' said the elder of the two, leaning over the rim of the glass and looking at the counterpanes which had been neatly spread over the girls' beds. 'I wonder what sort of a flower they could have fallen from.'

'Oh, and just see the moss,' whispered the younger rapturously, gazing at the little green carpet between the two beds. 'How soft and cool and green it looks, just like the moss on the bole of the old pine tree that used to stand behind us in the garden.'

In this pleasant fashion the two sisters beguiled the time, identifying, as they thought, the various objects in the room, but in fact making, as we all know, any number of queer mistakes. But it would be wrong of us to laugh at them, or to think that we are any better ourselves, for do we not behave in exactly the same manner all our lives?

Towards noon the room became rather warm, and the breezes that stirred the window-curtains no longer breathed so coolly on their cheeks. It is hardly to be wondered at that the two flowers, quite tired out by their strange and unlooked for adventures, should soon fall fast asleep and be dreaming they were back in the garden talking to each other in the cool morning shade of its tall guardian trees.

They must have slept soundly for several hours, for when they at last awoke the room was cooler and much less bright than it had been before, and they were no longer standing in the little cracked glass on the mantelshelf. The younger white rose was now pinned on Savitri's breast, where she gently rose and fell with the rhythm of the girl's breathing, while the elder lay on a small round brass tray so highly polished that she could see therein not only her own reflection but the reflections of the little oil lamp, the thin black sticks of incense, and the few other flowers by which she was surrounded as well. Savitri was speaking.

'We won't have to wait a single minute,' she said gaily. 'Auntie bought the tickets yesterday, so we can go straight to our seats as soon as we get there. I do hate waiting, Suji, the suspense is so awful. You keep wondering if the tickets are all sold and whether you will be able to get in or not. We can't all be patient souls like you. In fact,' she continued with a burst of laughter, 'sometimes I think that as far as cinemas are concerned you don't care in the least whether you ever get in or not, even apart from full-moon days.'

Sujata only smiled as she smoothed the folds of her clean white cotton sari.

'Well, goodbye, dear,' said her sister from the doorway. 'I won't be very late but you needn't wait up for me. You're sure to be tired after walking all that long way to the temple, and of course you won't be able to have any supper when you get back.'

'Goodbye,' replied Sujata quietly. 'I shall go to bed, but I won't sleep until you come.'

The white rose bobbed up and down on the pink dress as Savitri ran downstairs. So astonished was she at the suddenness of this new change that not until the little party had left the taxi and entered the cinema, and she once more felt herself rising and falling with the girl's breathing, was the poor flower able to collect her scattered wits and look about. It seemed already night, for the garden to which they had come was very dark, while not far away shone a luminous patch which she thought must be the moon. But it was not round and calm and bright like the moon she had seen only the night before, and neither did it smile sweetly down upon her, as the moon always did. Instead, it was in shape almost square, and the light that came from its blotched and changeful countenance darkened and brightened flickeringly every second. The rose thought that this unfamiliar garden must have its own strange moon, just as hers did. Perhaps every garden had its own moon, she reflected, just as it had its own trees and flowers, its own birds, butterflies, and bees. There was no doubt each had its own sounds, its own nocturnal voices. It had been so quiet in the dear old garden, and after saying goodnight to the gnarled magnolia tree she and her sister used to lie listening to the cicadas chirring softly in the grass, and the frogs croaking from their reedy pool. The stream and the bamboos used to talk to each other all night, but so quietly that when you had grown accustomed to the sound you no longer heard it. How different it was now! Here in this dreadful garden loud voices were talking, shouting, screaming, and terrible weird music, quite unlike the song of any bird she knew, continually sobbed and wailed and throbbed and crashed.

The hours passed slowly and uncomfortably for the poor bewildered rose, and it seemed that the air of that strange garden, instead of becoming gradually cooler, as it always did at night in her own green bower, was growing hotter and hotter every minute. The girl's bosom, too, was dreadfully warm, and the two or three drops of water that had clung to the little flower's stalk when she was taken from the mantel-shelf had evaporated long since. She began to feel sick and giddy from the continuous heaving up and down, and closing her eyes wished with all her heart that she had never left the shelter of her own garden, which assuredly would never have treated her so cruelly. Suddenly her white petals became limp, the waves of noise and heat engulfed and swallowed her, her head drooped to one side, and with a little sigh she lost consciousness.

At that very moment Sujata entered the temple, bearing in her hand the brass tray, whereon stood the lamp, with the incense lying on one side and the white rose on the other. They had become good friends on the way, and the lamp, who made the journey almost every morning, had pointed out to his two companions a number of interesting things as they went along. He had also explained to the little rose, who appeared very ignorant, the difference between a garden, a house, and a temple.

In this way the time had passed pleasantly enough, and the road, which was really quite long, had seemed short to the little white rose, who did not in the least mind being thought ignorant, and lay there looking up at the evening sky thinking she had never seen anything so beautiful, or felt so happy, in all her life.

Inside the temple it was cool and dim, and, in spite of the large numbers of people who were constantly coming and going, the place was quiet with that intense quietness which is far more than mere absence of sound. Chanting voices softly rose and fell, but they disturbed the ocean of that immense silence no more than the rising and falling of waves troubles the ever-tranquil depths of the central sea. Hardly had the first thrill of awe and delight subsided in the perfumed heart of the white rose than Sujata's lamp and stick of incense had been lit and offered, and she herself lifted gently from the tray and laid upon the shrine together with hundreds of other flowers.

She lay there with closed eyes, overwhelmed by the strong sweet smell of the flowers by which she was surrounded. Sujata was now chanting in a low quiet voice, and the white rose sighed happily and thought that if only she could fall asleep her dreams would surely be sweeter than any she had ever known before. But the hour of dreams had not yet come, for curiosity proved stronger than sleep, and before many minutes had passed she opened her eyes and looked wonderingly round. How many flowers there were, of every colour, how many burning lamps, and not very far away, how many people in white garments kneeling at prayer! Between the devotees and the shrine was squatting a group of yellow-robed monks, and the white rose thought that even the giant sunflowers of her own garden had never been so big or so bright as these. Strange white trees, incredibly straight and smooth, and apparently without leaves or branches, rose into the sky, where four or five small suns had appeared without warning and, what was even more extraordinary, hung there burning brightly but without heat. The walls were covered with paintings, in some of which were depicted tall green guardian trees like those that sheltered her own dear garden, and in her happiness she thought that in one dimly lighted corner she could even discern a bush with white roses growing all over it.

With so many new things to see and hear an hour passed like five minutes, and suddenly the little flower noticed that nearly all the people had departed. Sujata too was gone. One by one the suns went out, and the flickering light of two or three lamps on the shrine was all that remained. The echoes of the chanting had long since died away, and now a deep and awful silence reigned in the holy place.

She was looking up at the dark ceiling, where the feeble lamplight could not penetrate, when all at once a cool breeze sprang up outside and swept through the temple, extinguishing some of the lamps and disarranging all the flowers upon the shrine. The white rose shivered with delight as she felt his kiss on her pale cheek; but the breeze was mischievous, and after ruffling her petals and bending her head round towards the back of the shrine he blew out of the windows with a merry laugh, and started playing in and out of the trees that grew in the temple garden.

When the white rose again lifted her head she saw not far above her a huge pair of hands, one resting on the other, and suddenly the hush of the place entered her inmost soul. Breathlessly she watched the great fingers as they lay there in the flickering yellow light of the lamps, waiting for them to move; but though she waited for a long time they remained utterly motionless in the great lap, as though having been clasped once they had been clasped for ever. So the little flower looked above them, and what she saw seemed like the fulfilment of all her dreams, and she knew that all her life she had been unconsciously waiting only for this moment. The eyes of the great calm face were half closed, but in the dying flicker of the last remaining lamp she saw that they were looking down at her, and the beautifully moulded lips were curved into a smile. The rose thought that she had never seen anything so fair and wonderful as this, and as she lay among the other flowers looking up at the silent stone face a great peace, such as she had never known before, possessed her heart. Just then, the lamp went out, and suddenly the temple was plunged into darkness no less profound than the silence. But the white rose did not care, for those pure and tranquil features had remained so vividly impressed upon her soul that she could see them in her mind's eye long after they were no longer to be seen with the eyes of the body. She had perhaps remained thus all night, absorbed in blissful contemplation of the mental image of that face, but a vision even more splendid was yet to come. The full moon, which until that moment had been obscured by clouds, shone through the window, and the stone face was at once adazzle with silver light. The white rose looked from the Buddha's face to the full moon, and from the full moon to the Buddha's face, but although the full moon was beautiful, the Buddha's face was more beautiful still. So she remained awake all night, gazing and gazing at the half closed eyes and gently smiling lips, and as she gazed the Aspiration to Enlightenment rose up like a wave of music in the blissful silence of her heart, and when the stars set and the white dawn came the little flower breathed that mightiest of all prayers, which like a rainbow overarches the ages, which even the gods of the highest heaven dare not utter, – the prayer that for the deliverance of all sentient beings she too might one day become a Buddha.

It was when dawn came, too, that the sweeper found the first white rose on the taxi floor, where she had fallen the night before. She was neither white nor fragrant now, for she had been trampled on as the party left the car, and all that was left of her was a clot of evil-smelling brown petals, so that the man swept her into his tin with the dust, cigarette-ends and orange-peel without even a glance. But when some time later, the priest came to clear away the flowers that had been placed on the shrine the previous evening, the second white rose looked as fresh as though she had been plucked and laid there that very morning.

'It's a pity to throw her away with the other flowers,' he said, and he carried her to the bottom of the temple garden, and dropped her into a stream which ran through a grove of bamboos. For a moment the white rose spun round and round in a little eddy, then the stream picked her up and laughing carried her with it on its way.

THE WHITE LOTUS

It was dim and cool in the room after their hostess had stepped to the windows and pulled together the long, pale curtains. A raising of a slim white forearm, a tiny rainbow flash of rings in the sunlight, two or three sharp tugs, a heavy swishing sound like the rending of silk, and suddenly the great white sunbeams no longer fell with fierce brilliant slant through the windows halfway across the room.

She turned and faced her guests, looking down on them as they settled themselves in the armchairs, their eyes blinking in the unexpected twilight. Settled down like great fish, she thought, in the submarine coolness of the green-walled room, like fish easing themselves into the mud. Stick-in-the-muds. The men wallowing in their chairs like porpoises, the women perched on the edges of theirs like goldfish, like angelfish, perched in the midst of the stream, their transparent fins sensitive to every breath of water.

She paused a moment, then with three short steps reached the nearest empty seat. Her voice fell through the cool air, sprinklingly, like little drops of water, as she sat down.

'George, could I have a cigarette?'

The man beside her fumbled in his breast pocket, withdrew a thick, deeply dented case and, leaning heavily across the arm of the chair, went through the customary ritual.

Relaxing her limbs, she leaned against the hard leather upholstery, the thin blue smoke curling upwards into little spirals and rings above her.

For several minutes no one spoke. Luncheon had been rich and substantial and now, as the hottest hours of the hot summer's day were still heavy upon them, the centre of their beings sank downwards, the brain almost ceased to function, and the digestive organs assumed command of the dark battalions of the blood.

Presently Mary spoke. 'What was it you were saying about Harry, George?'

Her husband snorted. 'Bankrupt, that's what he'll be before much longer, bankrupt, and no wonder.'

'Is it really as bad as that?' she asked plaintively, with an uneasy glance at their hostess. After all, Jane was not only her friend but Harry's sister, and George ought not to sound quite so sure of himself, quite so positive. There were occasions when one could be sorrier to be right than wrong; but then, George had never been able to understand refinements of that kind.

A second series of rings floated up beside the first as Jane took the cigarette from her mouth and held it between her fingers for a moment, her wrist hanging limply over the chair-arm.

'Too soft,' George went on, blundering his way through his wife's feelings like a dog through a flowerbed. 'Too idealistic, yes, that's the word, idealistic. You've got to be hard to make your way in the world; it's each man for himself and the devil take the hindmost. There's no place for idealism. No place for sentiment. You've got to have common sense … like Jane here,' he continued hastily, abruptly conscious of his wife's warning eye and the restless tapping of Jane's white-shod foot. 'Now if Harry had only half of Jane's common sense, he wouldn't be where he is now, he wouldn't …'

His voice trailed off mumblingly, apologetically, into the silence, and his brown eyes looked up at Mary with that penitent, vaguely puzzled expression which crept into them whenever he felt he had offended her, but he knew not how or why. The clumsy compliment to Jane had only made his original tactlessness worse, as though a dog who had dug up some of his mistress's most cherished plants should offer her, in compensation for the damage done, the bone he had unearthed.

Mary shifted her position on the hard edge of the chair, like a rainbow-fish changing direction with the soft sweep of the current through the water.

'I think,' said Dr Castle in his quiet, incisive voice, from the other side of the room, 'that Harry's health has something to do with the matter. He's never been strong, you know, and I believe the strain and worry of the last few years have at last proved too much for him. After all,' he continued graciously, with an inclination of his head in George's direction, 'you of all people, Mr Smith, should be able to appreciate the tremendous strain of running a not inconsiderable business without previous experience. When Harry bought the concern it was in flourishing condition, agreed; but the people who sold it to him had been in the retail business for more than ten years, and in wholesale for approximately twenty-three, whereas Harry was an absolute novice.' He pursed his thin, dry little lips, the lips of a scientist, and went on firmly:

'In my opinion, his business has been ruined by lack of experience – if it is ruined; while long working hours, lack of recreation, and anxiety have contributed to the ruin of his health. And when health goes,' – he took off his spectacles and polished them energetically with his large white pocket handkerchief – 'then everything goes. Spirit is a form of matter, if there is such a thing as spirit, and mental health depends upon physical well-being. A man with a broken constitution can hardly be expected to pull his business together.... Something seriously wrong with the liver, I think,' he muttered half to himself in conclusion, replacing his spectacles on his nose and smoothing the grey hair above his right ear with an automatic gesture of his hand.

'If he would only take life a bit more easily,' said a high-toned voice from the depths of the sofa, 'then he wouldn't be in the mess he is. Why can't he go to parties and dances and enjoy himself? He'd work all the better for having some fun now and again.'

The speaker uncrossed her slim, satin legs and then recrossed them. They were all silent, knowing that the full-breasted young woman in bottle-green silk had been after Harry ever since his wife's death more than ten years before, ever since Molly had been left a motherless baby. Not that April liked babies, or even that she liked Harry overmuch; but he was not badly off and could give her what she considered the right kind of setting for the jewel of her youth and rather petulant brand of beauty. She lay there on the brown leather sofa like an emerald slipping from the mouth of a jeweller's wallet and thought unkind thoughts about Harry.

'But had he not given all his time to his business it would have failed years ago,' protested Jane's gentle voice.

'And if he had not given all his time to it then, he wouldn't be where he is now,' said George. 'Perhaps if he had his health he'd be able to grapple with his present difficulties. But no health, no business. And no business, no Harry.'

'No setting, no jewel,' thought April discontentedly. But aloud she said, 'If he doesn't play about a bit he can't work. What else can you expect?'

'It's a vicious circle,' said Dr Castle, removing his spectacles again and polishing them more vigorously still. 'Poor Harry's got into a vicious circle.'

They were all silent now, feeling that nothing remained to be said.

The curtains had turned from yellow to orange-gold while they were talking, and the folds that ran from top to bottom stood out in amber ridges.

For a moment longer, silence suffused the cool aquatic greenness of the room, and the smoky spirals of Jane's second cigarette rose lingeringly, thoughtfully, towards the ceiling, making a filmy grey-blue canopy above her head. April fingered the brooch on her bosom and felt the tautness of the material it held together. George's canine eyes sought his wife's as she perched on her chair's edge, her eyes fixed on Jane.

'Yes,' Dr Castle was repeating primly, 'A vicious circle. If Harry doesn't ...'

The door suddenly opened and before he could complete his sentence a child said, 'Oh, look, it's the first one of the year!'

Five heads automatically turned to look, and five pairs of eyes rested in mild astonishment on the little girl who stood framed in the open doorway. She wore a short white dress and white socks, and there was a big white bow in her dark hair. In one hand she held, as carefully as though it had been a star, a great white lotus bud, with the water still falling from the end of the thick green stem in slow quicksilvery drops.

They stared at her in wonder as she advanced into the room, her bright blue eyes glancing eagerly from face to face. 'I saw it only just now,' she breathed, 'in the pool at the bottom of the garden. I never knew it would come so quickly.' She spoke in dreamy, subdued tones, full of wonder and awe, and at the sound of the soft thrill in her voice the five adults somehow felt embarrassed.

'I had watched it ... oh, for days and days,' she murmured rapturously, scarcely conscious of the five faces that were looking down at her, one now smiling a little sadly, another puzzled, a third bored, the others wearing the same expression of mild astonishment as before.

One never knew what Molly would do or say next, they thought, as she took another step into the room. Her soul was full of a wonderfully calm exultation, a hushed delight too deep for words. It shone through her blue eyes until they appeared to have risen like two stars in the awestruck heaven of her face, seeming to grow in size even as they increased in lustre and intensity. She gazed at the white lotus bud as she had gazed when first she saw it growing half-hidden among the other buds and leaves, drinking in its perfect beauty, feeding and nourishing the inmost quick of her being on the great smooth bud, intensely white, with just a hint of ivory where one firm petal curved over another.

Oh, but it had been glorious standing there on the brink of the lotus-heaven, looking into its cool green-budding depths and seeing him there at last, the king-lotus, the white lotus, god of the blue waters! She could not remember how long she had stood there but at last, ankle-deep in the cool stream, she had plucked him reverently, oh so reverently, from his stem and held him, actually held him, in her hand. She could not remember for how long she had been holding the glorious flower. In the calm, deep joy which filled her whole being, as water soaks into a sponge, there was no change or variation by which she might measure the passing of time. Her joy was abiding, even as the blue summer sky, so that people and places, works and days, seemed like clouds idly drifting through. She had stood there at the brink of the fountain, the white wonder in her hand, until the flood of joy within her, rising, engulfed and overflowed her own being, and scarce knowing what she did she ran breathlessly into the house to share her treasure.

'Take it, Auntie,' she whispered to Jane, holding out her star.

Jane had been sitting upright in her chair but as the child spoke she drew back with a little hasty jerk. 'Why don't you put it in a vase?' she asked, with a curious tremor in her voice, as though not quite sure what it was she was talking about. 'You could take one of those nice red vases from my bedroom mantelpiece, dear, the ones with the yellow dragons on.' She did not withdraw the flower from the child's outstretched hand.

Molly turned to George. 'My, just look at that bloom!' he exclaimed. 'They must be at least five rupees a head in the bazaar just now. Where did you say you found it, Molly?'

The girl did not answer but stood there in the same dreamy rapture, holding the bud out to George, who bent forward gingerly and patted the almost luminous wax globe as though it was a very small, fragile dog.

'Here, Molly, give it to me,' April's shrill voice demanded shortly.

Gravely, reverently, the child surrendered the treasure into the emerald woman's outstretched hand, and in an instant April had wedged the stem behind her gold brooch, between her heavy pointed breasts, and was standing before the fireplace gazing at her vague reflection in the shadow-world of the mirror above. But the green sheath wherefrom the bud had burst that morning matched the colour of her dress, so that it appeared as though a third breast, a naked, white, pointed breast, was rising ludicrously from between the other two. Turning with a gesture of impatience, April tore the bud from her bosom and gave it to Dr Castle.

'A fine specimen, a very fine specimen indeed,' he said, his fingers turning the great white moon of a blossom round and round on its stalk. 'Do you know what it is called, Molly?'

'Yes, a lotus,' she said, uttering the word as though it comprehended everything that was holiest, rarest, and most beautiful.

The precise little doctor pretended to frown and clicked his tongue in disapproval. 'Lotus! Tut tut, that will never do. Its real designation, if I am not mistaken, is *Nelumbo nucifera*. It's a long time since I did any botany, all the same,...' His words broke off in another series of sharp little clicks. But the lotus bud had been taken from his hand, and now Molly stood with it in front of Mary.

'Don't you want it, Auntie Mary?'

She was not disappointed because no one seemed to be able to love the flower as she loved it, or to see its world of beauty as she saw it; but the two stars in her eyes had begun to set, and it seemed as though a wisp of cloud had trailed across the heaven of her face. Joy still filled her within, but the flood which had overflowed her own small heart, which had wanted to flow on and fill all other hearts as well, had trickled away into a desert and lost itself among the arid dunes of dry, burning sand. If only her Auntie Mary would understand!

'Don't you want it, Auntie Mary?' She repeated the question, looking eagerly up into the woman's still sadly smiling face. Mary wasn't her real aunt, but Molly always called her 'auntie' because she was Jane's friend and she loved her as much as though she had really been her aunt, perhaps even more.

Mary looked at the child, not knowing what to say. 'What do you want to do with it?' she asked doubtfully.

'Do?' said the child in surprise. 'I don't want to do anything with it.'

Suddenly Mary understood, and Molly knew that she understood. Mary's mind became utterly transparent, her heart suffused with an ultimate calm and bliss. She smiled joyously at the child, and joyously the child's eyes smiled back. For one timeless instant their hearts touched and were united, even as two white birds might meet on the wing in the blue sky.

'Why don't you show it to your father?' asked Mary, very gently.

The two stars had risen again, more intensely lustrous than ever, and Molly bore the white lotus bud from the room as though it was a lighted candle, a tall white candle that she was bearing to the rites of some solemn and mysterious altar whereof she was priestess, as indeed she was.

The five adults eased themselves back into their seats and the tension they had all felt while the child was in the room relaxed. Only Mary sat quite still, looking at the empty doorway. Suddenly she turned towards the window, where the curtains were now hanging darkly gold, almost brown.

'Isn't it time to pull the curtains back?' she asked Jane.

'Oh Lord, no,' her husband protested as Jane half rose. 'Let them be as they are for a bit. There's still a terrible glare outside.'

No one else spoke. Jane relapsed into her chair, April yawned, Dr Castle removed his spectacles again and tugged his handkerchief from its pocket. Mary sat very still, listening to the silence.

THE PARABLE OF THE TALKING BUDDHA

Once upon a time the people of a certain village built a temple. But they had no Buddha to sit in the temple and be worshipped. So they asked one of the village elders, who was a trader in rice and accustomed to dealing with the outside world, to order a Buddha for them on his next visit to the big city, where there was a place that made Buddhas.

Six months later the Buddha arrived in a bullock cart, wrapped in straw mats and none the worse for his journey. When the villagers saw him they were delighted. He really was beautiful. They had not been able to afford marble, but he was made of the best plaster-of-paris, and his curls were glossy black and his gently smiling lips bright red, while his robe shone with gold paint that looked just like real gold.

Without delay the villagers installed him in his temple, into which he fitted so perfectly that it seemed to have been built specially for him. Every day they brought flowers and incense and lighted candles, and every day they asked him to cure them when they were ill, or give them rain for the crops, or grant them relief from the pangs of childbirth, or for help in passing their examinations, or for success in love, and a hundred other things. Unlike some Buddhas of whom they had heard, he granted all their requests, so that on the whole they were very pleased with him. In the course of time, indeed, they became quite fond of him, and not a little proud, and used to tell people from other villages that he was a very good Buddha. Whenever they passed the temple, the door of which always stood open, they could see him sitting sedately within, on his beautiful lotus-throne, inhaling the incense fumes with half closed eyes, and it gave them a nice comfortable feeling to think that he was sitting there all the time, always available, and always ready to listen to their requests.

For his part, the Buddha became quite fond of the villagers, did whatever he could for them, and liked to see them happy.

One day, however, after an old lady had burned an unusually large bundle of incense under his nose, he could not help feeling just a little bit tired and stiff in the joints. 'I think I'll go for a little stroll,' he said to himself. 'The villagers won't mind.'

So very slowly and carefully he got down from his lotus-throne, crossed the threshold of the temple, and descended the steps to the road, taking good care not to let his golden robe trail in the dust. Ah! it was good to breathe the fresh air. He had never really liked the smell of incense, especially the cheap kind the villagers brought. And how beautiful the trees were! He could not help looking at them admiringly as he walked at a slow dignified pace along the road. The temple was situated on the outskirts of the village, and it was his intention to spend half an hour or so in the fields before returning to his duties.

Only a minute or two after his departure the old woman returned. She had forgotten her umbrella. To her astonishment she saw that the lotus-throne was empty. The Buddha was no longer there. Without waiting a moment, she rushed out of the temple shrieking aloud to all the other villagers that the Buddha had gone, that he had been stolen, that he had abandoned them, that the people of the next village had offered him a bigger temple, and a dozen other things.

On hearing her cries the women and children came to the doors of their huts, the men hurried back to the village from the fields, and the village elders hastily gathered beneath the spreading branches of the council-tree.

When the old woman had related her story, and told them how with her own eyes she had seen the Buddha stamping angrily out of the temple shouting, 'I've had enough of those damned villagers!' they decided to go in a body to the temple and see for themselves. Some believed her story, some did not. Others just did not know what to think.

Within a few minutes they had all surrounded the temple. The elders slowly and cautiously ascended the steps. The Buddha was nowhere to be seen. They looked in the cupboard where they kept the decorations that were put up every year on his birthday, they lifted up the cloth and looked under the offering-table, they even stared up into the hollow dome. But there was no trace of the Buddha.

Meanwhile, strange reports were circulating among the crowd outside. Someone had seen the Buddha resting under a tree. Someone had seen him strolling in the fields. Someone had seen him plucking a flower. Someone had seen him talking about Buddhism with a young man.

The last report in particular enraged quite a number of villagers. 'How can he be talking about Buddhism?' they demanded. 'Buddhas don't talk. They just sit and sniff incense and answer prayers. If he's talking about Buddhism he's not a real Buddha.'

'He's not a real Buddha!' repeated a portion of the crowd, who had never liked him, but had been afraid of saying so until now. 'Why, his robes aren't even made of real gold!'

'He's not a real Buddha!' shouted a villager who had once offered the Buddha some damaged fruit. 'Let's stop him coming back. We don't want a Buddha who can talk. It's uncanny.'

Some of the villagers accordingly proceeded to bar the temple door. As it had not been made to be closed, they had some difficulty, but eventually it was done, and great planks of wood nailed across. 'Let's get a new Buddha!' they shouted.

Many of the villagers were not satisfied with these high-handed proceedings, but they did not like to oppose the others by force. In their heart of hearts they did not think the Buddha had really left the temple, or he was tired of them, and neither did they mind him talking sometimes if he wanted to. So they decided to send two or three of the elders to tell him what had happened and offer to build him a new temple.

The elders found him sitting cross-legged underneath a tree, and could not help thinking that he looked more beautiful there than in the temple. When they told him what had happened he laughed and said, 'I know. A little bird told me. But I have been thinking.... I don't think I want to go back to the temple anyway. I've spent enough time there inhaling incense and listening to prayers. I don't even want you to build me a new temple. (The little bird told me about that too.) I like it out here in the fields. I like being able to see the blue sky and the trees, and being able to smell the flowers. But don't think I want to leave you,' he added quickly, seeing the tears gathering in their eyes. 'I really don't. So I'll tell you what you can do for me. Those who still love me can build me an ordinary hut – not a temple, but a hut. I shall live in the hut, and whenever I feel like it, I shall walk out into the fields and breathe the fresh air. And whenever you feel like it, you can come and see me, and we shall talk about Buddhism. You know, talking about Buddhism is much more interesting than offering incense and lighted candles – both for me and for you.'

So an understanding was reached. The villagers who still loved the Buddha built him a hut in a mango grove, halfway between the village and a nearby mountain. Every day, in the morning, he went out for a stroll through the countryside. Every day, in the evening, his friends came to see him. And as the light waned, and the stars came out, and the moon rose, they talked about Buddhism. Sometimes the villagers brought incense and lighted candles, just for old times' sake, but what the Buddha had said was true – talking about Buddhism was really far more interesting.

As for the other villagers, after a while they ordered a new Buddha and installed him in the temple. Actually, he had been rejected by the manufacturers as he was cracked right down the middle, but as they had got him cheap the other villagers did not mind. Though their prayers did not seem to be answered as often as before, he never moved from his lotus-throne, and he never spoke, and after all that was the main thing.

THE ARTIST'S DREAM

In the days when Henry VII sat on the throne of Charlemagne and Clement V in the Chair of St Peter, and when Dante Alighieri was discovering, in bitterness of soul, how steep was the path of one who trod another's stairs, there lived in Italy an Artist. Though not the greatest or most famous of his time, he had laboured diligently and well for many years, and in grey stone churches and red-tiled monasteries all over the peninsula murals and altarpieces testified to the skill of his hand.

One afternoon in early summer, when he had been working all through the heat of the day, he fell asleep, and while he slept he had a dream. The sky opened like the sudden drawing apart of curtains, and before him, as though depicted on a great wall, he saw a new heaven and a new earth. There, against a background of burnished gold, was God the Father on his throne, the Divine Son on his right hand and the Virgin Mother on his left, while all about them stood choir upon choir of angels with multicoloured wings. Below the steps of the throne were apostles, and saints, and martyrs with branches of palm, and below these a great company of the blessed. As the Artist looked he saw the angels that were nearest to the throne put to their lips trumpets of gold, and as they blew a loud blast the whole host cried, 'Holy, holy, holy!' So great was the sound, and of such unbearable intensity the joy it produced, that the Artist awoke. His brush was still in his hand, and it was night.

Some months later he received an invitation from the abbot of a large but impoverished monastery situated in a remote part of the land.

As soon as he saw the vast empty space that the abbot wanted him to paint he knew that here, and nowhere else, was the place where he would have to depict the new heaven and the new earth that he had seen in his dream. He also knew that this would be the last painting that he would do on earth.

For two years the Artist worked, but though he worked hard every day at the end of this time he had made very little progress. Scaffolding had to be erected, the surface of the wall cleaned and made ready, colours ordered. There had also been many arguments with the abbot about the cost of all the gold that would be required for the background of the work, for the latter, though a worthy and pious man who wanted the wall to look as rich and splendid as possible, doubted if the monastery would be able to raise the funds necessary to meet the Artist's demands. Moreover, the Artist himself was now growing old, and was unable to work as fast or for as long as he done in the days of his youth.

When five years had passed the Artist had completed only the top left hand corner of the wall, amounting to not more than a twentieth part of the whole undertaking. There had been many difficulties. The old abbot had died, and the monks had elected in his place a hard, austere man who thought that the wall would look better simply whitewashed and begrudged all the money that the monastery was having to spend on ultramarine and vermilion and gold. More unpleasant still, a few months earlier two local artists, angry that so important a commission had gone to a foreigner, had plotted against his life. Stealing one night into the great chapel where he worked, they had climbed up to the top of the scaffolding, sixty feet above the ground, and sawn through the plank on which, they knew, he would be standing next day. Only luck – or a special providence – had saved the Artist. As the plank gave way beneath him and he fell with a great cry the hem of his jerkin had somehow caught on a projection, so that instead of dashing his brains out on the flagstones below, as the rival painters had hoped, he remained suspended in mid-air until rescued by his assistants. Though uninjured, the Artist was badly shaken by this experience, and was unable to paint for several days.

Thinking it all over, and reflecting on the greatness of the work he had undertaken, and the shortness of the time that, he felt, remained to him, the Artist realized that it would be quite impossible for him to paint the whole wall single-handed. Depicting the face and hair of one angel was the work of weeks, and there were hundreds of angels. Obviously he would have to get help. But from where? All those who had been his fellow students were now dead, or had forsaken painting, or turned out only indifferent artists. After much thought he eventually decided he would teach and train two or three of the young men who ground his colours and prepared the surface of the wall for painting. They were good lads, and even though they might not have much talent, and perhaps would never be great artists, under his supervision they would undoubtedly be able to accomplish much useful work.

The very next day, therefore, he started putting his plan into operation. Elated by the prospect of becoming artists, the young men threw themselves into the work with a will and before long were able to help fill in some of the bigger patches of colour, where not much skill was required. For a while this arrangement worked quite well. Under the expert guidance they were receiving the young men grew more proficient in their work every day, and the Artist began to think that it might be possible for him to finish the painting of the entire wall before his death.

Nevertheless, when another year had gone by the Artist was forced to admit that despite the assistance he was now receiving the great work had not really made much progress. Since he had started teaching he had not been able to spend so much time painting as before. Moreover, hearing that he had opened a training school for artists all the young men of the locality had poured into the chapel and stood at the foot of the scaffolding begging to be taken on. Every one of these candidates the Artist had had to interview personally. Some of them he had accepted. Others – and these were the majority – he had turned away. All this had not only taken up time that should have been devoted to painting but been a serious drain on the Artist's energies. Still, it was over now, he reflected, and he had as fine a band of young assistants as any artist in the land. Once they had completed their training he would be free to devote all his time to painting, they would be able to help him, and the great work would at least make rapid progress towards completion. True, there had already been a few casualties. One of the young men, coming up onto the scaffolding a bit drunk, had overbalanced and fallen to his death on the flagstones below. Another had decamped with some of the gold dust that was being used for the background of the painting, while yet another, whom the Artist had considered a promising youth, as soon as he had received a few lessons had gone and set himself up in business as a painter of street signs. Still, on balance it had been worth it, he thought, and the time that had been lost in the course of the last year would surely be more than made up in the next.

During the months that followed it indeed did seem that the Artist's plan was succeeding and that what was now the one hope of his life would be fulfilled. Working more and more independently, the young men covered a larger and larger part of the wall with the first layer of pigment, while the Artist was able to devote an ever-increasing proportion of his time to his own more exacting task. Two or three of the more highly gifted young men, moreover, asked him what it was that he was painting on the wall, and to them he had the satisfaction of telling the story of his dream. Soon they were almost as eager as he was that the new heaven and the new earth that he had seen should be depicted on the chapel wall.

At this stage a serious disturbance occurred. Some of the young men had wives and sweethearts in the town, to whom they went home in the evening, or whom they saw on holy days. As the painting of the wall progressed, and the Artist's passion for the completion of the great work seized hold of them too, they got into the habit of sleeping in the chapel with the Artist so as to be able to get back to their painting as soon as it was light, without having to waste time travelling to and fro. Not only that. Sitting with the Artist at night, and sharing the simple food provided by the monastery, they listened to his tales of the great artists he had known and the fine paintings he had seen. They also got to know one another better. Before long most of them were thinking that there was no life on earth like the life of the artist, and nothing better than painting one's dreams on empty walls.

One day, when none of the young men had left the chapel for more than a month, and when the work was making really good progress, twenty or thirty women suddenly appeared at the foot of the scaffolding. Some were weeping, others shouting angrily. One, seeing a young man grinding colours at the foot of a ladder, seized him by the belt and tried to drag him away. The women were the wives and sweethearts of the Artist's assistants. They were tired of living on their own, they declared, and wanted the young men to go home with them. Several of the young men at once agreed, and walked off with their arms around the waist of wife or sweetheart as though they had already completely forgotten about painting. Others were undecided, and stood arguing with their women in corners before either going off with them or returning to their work. One young man, who frankly told his wife that he had never been so happy before, had his face badly scratched for his pains. Only two or three of the Artist's assistants remained undisturbed by the commotion. These were the same young men who had asked him what it was that he was painting. Ignoring the shouts and cries of the women, they quietly carried on with their work.

When the uproar had died down and the women had all gone away the Artist found that he had lost well over half his helpers. He also found that very little work had been done that day. Moreover, some of the young men who had argued with their women and decided to stay did not seem to be working with the same enthusiasm as before. Every now and then they would glance in the direction of the chapel door, half hoping and half fearing to see there the figure of wife or sweetheart. Indeed, when night came and the young men gathered round the Artist for the evening meal, two more of their number were found missing. Yet the Artist did not despair. If they all redoubled their efforts, he told those who were left, the great work could still be completed before he died.

A week later, however, there came another disturbance, even more serious than the first. This time it was not only the wives and sweethearts of the young men who appeared at the foot of the scaffolding but their mothers as well. Indeed, there were even a few aunts, sisters, and grandmothers in the crowd of angry, excited women who stood there brandishing their fists in the direction of the Artist and loudly demanding the restoration of their menfolk. Strange to relate, young men who had stoutly resisted the entreaties of wives and sweethearts left without a murmur as soon as they saw their mothers.

Seeing how angry and upset the women were, and realizing that in their fury they might tear down the scaffolding, the Artist decided to try pacifying them. Coming down a few stages, and standing on a plank only a few feet above their heads, he called out to them to listen to what he had to say. At first they refused, and so loud, indeed, was the chorus of 'husband-stealer!' and 'sweetheart-snatcher!' that greeted him that for some time he was quite unable to make himself heard. However, when the young men too came down, and shouted to the women to be quiet, order was eventually restored and the Artist enabled to speak. After telling the women about his dream of the new heaven and new earth, and explaining that he needed the young men's help in depicting it on the chapel wall, he assured them that the work would be finished within the next five years, and that he had no wish to keep the young men away from their homes any longer than was absolutely necessary – any longer, in fact, than they themselves wanted to stay. As for himself, he was now an old man. The one hope of his soul was to see the painting finished before he died. Would they not allow him to complete the work to which he had devoted himself for so many years and die in peace?

From the expression on the women's faces it was clear from the beginning that they did not understand a word of what he was saying. Some looked bewildered, others deeply suspicious. Even before he had finished there were murmurs of disapproval, and the words of his final appeal were hardly out of his mouth before there burst from the crowd at the foot of the scaffolding a perfect volley of abuse and protest. 'He's crazy!' shouted some. 'He wants to make our men crazy too!' 'Burn him at the stake with his own scaffolding!' shrieked others. 'He's a wizard! He's bewitched our boys!' In vain the Artist tried to explain that he was neither a madman nor a wizard but only a man who had had a dream and wanted to preserve it for the benefit of all mankind. Frantic with rage, some of the women started swarming up the scaffolding, while others, with blood-curdling shrieks and howls, lifted up their skirts and exposed themselves to the young men. Four or five of the latter, unable to resist so direct an appeal, jumped from the scaffolding into the midst of the women and were borne in triumph from the chapel, not without receiving a few loving scratches and bruises in the process. A few of those who were left on the scaffolding were so disgusted by the behaviour of the women, however, that they vowed never to go home again.

By this time the Artist was in serious danger. The women who had climbed up onto the scaffolding were tugging at the plank on which he stood while from below half a dozen others pelted him with mud. Some of the mud hit the Artist. The rest spattered the wall behind him, where the more expert of his assistants had already started work on the white robes of the blessed. Fortunately the monks, alarmed by the uproar in the chapel, had already sent for the town guard, and twenty armed men arrived before further damage could be done. After he had cleared the chapel of the half-demented women, the captain of the guard arrested the Artist for causing a breach of the peace and brought him before the magistrates.

What with explaining himself to the magistrates, who confined him to a dungeon for a week while they were deciding whether or not he was guilty, as well as cleaning up the wall where the young women had spattered it with mud, and getting together again the young men who still wanted to help him, it was a full month before the Artist could get back to work. But at last everything had been done, and he stood once again at the top of the scaffolding, his brush, loaded with gold, poised above the head of the Divine Son. Only six assistants were now left. Among them were the two most gifted of all the young men, and though he could no longer be sure of being able to finish the painting before his death he pressed on with his work as best he could, and both by word and example encouraged the others to do likewise. The week he had spent in the cold, wet dungeon had not improved his health. Every now and then his frame was racked by a hard, dry cough that seemed about to tear his lungs out, and sometimes, by the end of the day, he felt so weak and exhausted he was hardly able to stand.

When six years had passed yet another disturbance occurred. Compared with the disturbances of the previous year it was of a minor nature, but so few were the hands that were devoting themselves to the great work, and so slow the rate at which it was now progressing, that if anything it had a still more disruptive effect. Four of the young men still occasionally went home to their wives and sweethearts. One morning these women appeared in the chapel and respectfully saluting the Artist begged to be allowed to stay and help. The young men had told them all about the painting, they said, and they were anxious to do whatever they could to help bring it nearer to completion. Now the Artist had never had women assistants before, and at first he was extremely doubtful whether such an arrangement would work. However, the women seemed so sincere in their desire to be of assistance, and the young men so happy at the idea of having them around, and so confident they could be of use, that in the end they agreed to take them on.

For a week the arrangement worked quite well. The women soon learned to wash brushes and rinse out rags, and in the evenings, after supper, they carried the dirty wooden platters back to the monastery kitchen and replenished the jugs with wine. During the second week, however, the Artist noticed that the painting was making hardly any progress. The women spent all their time laughing and talking with the young men who, in consequence, did very little work. One of the women even snatched the brush from her lover's hand and with shrieks and giggles tried to finish painting the folds of the robe on which he had been working. Her efforts were not very successful, and to the accompaniment of much mirth, and many kisses, her lover wrested the brush from her hand and rubbed out what she had done. Eventually the Artist realized that the women had, in fact, no interest whatever in the painting of the wall and only wanted to be with the young men. At the end of the fourth week, having warned them about their behaviour several times, and received more than one impertinent reply, he told them that they would have to leave. Noses high in the air, skirts scornfully lifted, they at once swept out of the chapel. With them went three of the young men. 'If our women aren't good enough to help you in your work,' they told the Artist, 'then we aren't good enough either.'

Only three of the Artist's assistants now remained. Since there were so few hands working on the wall the rate of progress was so slow as to be almost imperceptible, and the Artist realized that unless a miracle occurred there was now no possibility of his being able to finish the painting before he died. Yet he carried on. Though it was winter, when the chapel was as cold as a tomb, and though his cough sometimes almost tore him apart, he still spent the greater part of the day on the scaffolding, frequently working by the light of a pine torch held by one of his assistants. At the end of the day he was usually so stiff, and so faint with cold, that he would have to be carried down to the ground.

When ten years had gone by only a quarter of the space had been covered with pigment, and the Artist knew that he would not live to see the new heaven and the new earth depicted on the chapel wall. Still, he had done his best and he was content. All that he now wanted to do was to make it possible for his assistants, and their assistants after them, to continue and if possible complete the great work that he had begun. Accordingly, though so weak that he had to be hoisted up onto the scaffolding by a sort of pulley, and so blind that he could hardly see, he somehow managed to finish drawing the outlines of the angels and the apostles, the saints and the martyrs, as well as every member of the company of the blessed, all of whom, he hoped, would one day be depicted on the wall in all the glory of golden aureoles, white robes, and multicoloured wings. As for the figures of God the

Father on his throne, the Divine Son, and the Virgin Mother, these were almost done, and only a few finishing touches remained to be given.

One freezing cold morning, when he saw the celestial faces on the wall through the white mist of his own breath, he was painfully putting the finishing touches to the aureole of the Divine Son when his sight suddenly seemed to clear, and he saw, to his astonishment, that the brush strokes he had been about to make had already been given. The aureole was complete. Thinking that his mind must have been wandering, and that he had finished painting the aureole without realizing it, he glanced along the wall to the bowed head of the Virgin Mother, intending to put the finishing touches to her aureole. But her aureole too was complete. Not another stroke was needed. Now convinced that he was thoroughly out of his mind, the Artist looked down the wall to the figures of the apostles, on whose aureoles he knew he had not even started working. But they were all complete. By this time the Artist was aware that he was no longer on the scaffolding but somewhere out in the middle of the chapel, opposite the spot where he had just been working, and that he was as it were suspended in mid-air. From his present position he had a perfect view of the entire chapel wall. To his amazement it was crowded with brilliantly coloured figures, all complete in every detail. There, against a background of gold, was God the Father on his throne, with the Divine Son on his right hand, and the Virgin Mother on his left, while all about them stood choir upon choir of angels with multicoloured wings – not one of which, he knew, he had had time to finish. Below the steps of the throne were apostles, and saints, and martyrs with branches of palm, and below these a great company of the blessed. It was all exactly as he had seen it in his dream.

He was still wondering who had finished the painting when he saw that God the Father was smiling at him, that the Divine Son was smiling at him, that the Virgin Mother was smiling at him. There were three smiles, and yet they were one smile, and he had never painted that smile. It was real! Then, as the angels that were nearest the throne put their golden trumpets to their lips, he saw that the company of the blessed had as it were overflowed from the wall and stood all around him – that the walls of the chapel had expanded to infinity. But it was only when the angels blew a great blast on their trumpets and he found himself shouting 'Holy, holy, holy!' with the rest, and when looking down he saw that he was robed in white and gold, that all at once in the midst of the intensity of his joy, he knew that he had died, and that the new heaven and the new earth were eternal, and himself for ever a part of them.

THE ANTIQUE DEALER

It was a small place, about two miles down the coast from the big holiday resort with the bleached stone promenade, the glittering amusement arcades, and the dipper with the trough-like seats, some red and some blue, dangling helplessly from the rim of the gaunt forty-foot wheel. Hardly anybody ever stopped there, though quite a lot of people passed through on their way into or out of the big holiday resort. Not that everybody who spent a week or a fortnight or a weekend at Great Barrow thought it worthwhile even to pass through Gormsby-on-Sea. A new metalled road connected the bigger place with the hinterland direct and whether going in or coming out most people, being in a hurry, took that.

Gormsby-on-Sea was therefore left pretty much to its own devices, even at the height of the holiday season. For all practical purposes it consisted of one long narrow street, usually called the High Street, which worked its way crookedly round the coast for about half a mile. Sometimes the street rose, sometimes it fell, and sometimes it suddenly disappeared round a corner. But however much it turned and twisted, it never quite succeeded in shaking off the load of houses that crouched on either side, heads bent together maliciously over the narrow width of the street. Some of the houses had once been shops, and some of the shops had once been houses. Others were so boarded up that it was difficult to tell what they might have been. There was a tobacconist's with a rack of fly-blown papers outside the door, a sort of general store with piles of dusty tins in the window and, past three or four grim, flat-featured house fronts, there was a barber's shop with curtains of white cheesecloth that looked as though they hadn't been washed in ages.

There was also an antique shop. It stood about halfway down the street, only two or three doors from the public house which, withdrawing itself from the smaller buildings on either side, presided gloomily over a small forecourt. The shopfront, which was dark without being of any particular colour, consisted of a single large window flanked on the left by a glass-panelled door. Above the window, barely decipherable against the dark woodwork, was the single word 'Antiques', in gothic letters that had once been gold and which, even now, glinted patchily in the sunlight.

One day in early summer someone did pass through Gormsby-on-Sea. Not only passed through it, but actually stopped. At about eleven in the morning, when the High Street was looking more desolate than ever, a small dust-covered four-seater that had once been a dark olive green rattled in from the south and, having come to a halt outside the public house, backed left into the deserted courtyard. Out of the car stepped a young man in his early twenties. For a moment he stood there, hand on the open door, his long fair hair, pale blue T-shirt and red bellbottom trousers making a vivid splash of colour against the whitewashed frontage of the public house. Then, seeing that the place was not yet open, he slammed the car door shut without bothering to wind up the windows and, taking in the High Street at a single alert, relaxed glance, started strolling back the way he had come. Outside the antique shop he paused. The window was full of bric-a-brac of various kinds. Much of it was only Victorian junk – flower-patterned washbasins, tapestry screens, a spindly-legged china cabinet or two, things made of spotted bamboo, stuffed birds under immortelles, pottery figurines, and the like. But here and there among the early and late Victoriana stood more exotic objects. Fat Chinese ginger jars, all blue and white, rubbed shoulders with solemn-faced clocks and sharp-spouted copper kettles with black wooden handles. Across a double row of bone-handled knives and forks lay a pair of wickedly curved Moorish daggers. In the right-hand corner of the window, on a kind of crimson hassock, sat a tarnished brass Laughing Buddha, only the protuberant belly of which still showed a dull gleam. Victorian or exotic, all the objects in the window were covered with a thin film of dust that imparted to them, different as they were, a curious unity of character, as though they were all thoughts in the same mind.

As the young man pushed open the door and entered the shop a bell tinkled dustily in the distance. The antique dealer, he reflected, would in all likelihood be able to tell him what he wanted to know as easily as the publican up the road. For several minutes no one came. The young man looked about him. At the back of the shop, against the wall, stood a full suit of armour, the stiff-jointed, erect figure somehow giving an eerie impression of being alive and dead at the same time, like the Ghost in *Hamlet*. On the wall itself hung two or three long-handled copper bed-warmers, a brass hunting horn, and sundry oil paintings, most of them crudely executed portraits of simpering Victorian misses with dogs and flowers.

The young man was still looking at these when he became aware that there was somebody else in the room. It was the antique dealer.

'Can I help you?' he asked mildly.

'Yes,' said the young man, with a smile that was half diffident and half eager, as though he was shy of asking yet confident that he would not be rebuffed. 'I don't want to buy anything. I just wondered if you could tell me the quickest way to Framlingham. I'm visiting some friends there, and I want to avoid going through Great Barrow if I can.'

'It's not easy to avoid Great Barrow,' said the antique dealer, looking at the young man. 'Most people don't want to avoid it anyway. But I think I can help you.' And he gave a few simple directions.

'Thanks,' said the young man, adding automatically, as he moved to the door, 'See you!'

'See you!' thought the antique dealer, as he watched the colourful figure pass the shop window on his way up the street. 'I shan't ever see you again.' All the same, he felt he would have liked to, even though he knew it was impossible.

But as it turned out he was wrong. He did see the young man again. That very night.

He was sitting by himself in the saloon of the Ship, the public house up the road, when he became aware of a splash of colour among the drab browns and greys at the bar. Even without looking round he knew it was the young man. Once again the gold and the pale blue and the red had appeared. The first time could have been an accident, but the second time.... Sitting there at the marble-topped table, fingers curved round the handle of a glass beer-mug, eyes absorbed by an intricate pattern of gold and black beer-rings, it was as though he heard, for the second time that day, a mysterious chord, a chord of vibrant colours, and hearing it he knew that he would be hearing it again – knew that even when he had heard it for the first time that morning, it had not been an accidental collocation of sounds, but the opening bars of a symphony which he had yet to hear to the end.

He wasn't surprised, therefore, when, a few minutes later, he found that the pale blue T-shirt was opposite him. The young man had recognized him, and sat down at his table. For several minutes neither of them spoke. The young man, indeed, seemed quite content not to say anything, and after the initial half-smile of recognition sat on there in friendly silence with his slowly diminishing beer and a thoughtful cigarette or two. The antique dealer, however, wanted to speak. What it was he wanted to say he did not know. But he wanted to say something. He wanted to say everything. In the end he said, 'So you're still here.'

'Yes,' said the young man, smiling, with a slight lift of the eyebrows that gave his face an extraordinarily open look. 'There's something wrong with my car. It wouldn't start this morning. I had to push it to the garage and leave it there.'

A long silence followed, a silence in which the antique dealer could hear a loud empathic tick as the pendulum of the clock behind the door swung to and fro in its coffin-shaped case with all the vigour of a beating heart – a silence which, for him, gradually assumed something of the quality of suspense. But before it had time to become unbearable the suspense was broken. Rising easily to his feet, the young man went up to the bar and, depositing his glass gently on the polished mahogany, ordered another pint of lager. The antique dealer had seen that his glass was empty, and for several minutes had been considering whether or not he should offer to buy him a drink. In the end he had decided against it. Beside that chord of flaming colours, so conventional a gesture of friendliness would have had the effect of a dissonance, as though the first movement of the symphony had been interrupted by a sudden scraping of chairs. Better that they remained in their separate identities, without overt gestures, and that whatever exchange might take place between them should be through a medium so subtle as to be almost imperceptible even to themselves.

He had barely had time to absorb this insight before the young man was back in his seat. The antique dealer saw at once that his mood had changed. From the way in which he settled his smooth brown arms on the cool marble and leaned forward over his beer it was clear that he was going to speak. On the other side of the table the antique dealer waited, pale and expectant in his dark suit. The tick of the clock seemed louder than ever, the swing of the pendulum so vigorous that it might shatter the sides of its case.

'How long have you lived here?' asked the young man at last, mildly turning on the antique dealer a gaze which, though perfectly clear and open, was at the same time curiously reserved.

'About eight years,' replied the other.

'And the antique shop, how long have you had that?'

'For about the same length of time. Previously I had one at Aimsbury, a market town about twelve miles from here. Then when I got married, my wife and I moved to this place.'

The young man appeared to ponder this information. Though it was he who had asked the questions, there was nothing in either tone or manner that suggested curiosity, certainly not curiosity of the personal sort. For all his friendliness, he was detached, impersonal, even neutral.

Presently he asked, 'Do you like antiques?'

The question sank into the antique dealer's soul like a stone into deep waters. 'Oh yes,' he responded eagerly, though not without a tremor of uncertainty. 'I've never really been interested in anything else – not for long, that is. It all started when I was quite a small boy. Every Sunday morning my father used to take me to see my grandmother. Her house was full of antiques, most of which had been collected by my grandfather, who had spent many years in Africa and the Far East. By the time of his death, which took place before I was born, the house was so crammed with antiques and curios of various kinds that according to my father it was more like a museum than a home. Even in the bedrooms there were cases of coins and minerals, not to speak of live shells (grandfather had been in the army for a time), while every inch of wall space was covered with swords, knives, grass skirts, Chinese painted scrolls, bamboo dart-throwers, and stuffed tropical fish. As I well know, my grandmother was a strong-minded woman, and her first act after my grandfather's death was to throw almost everything out of the house. She had loved her husband dearly, she told her two sons and her daughter, but she had no intention of spending the rest of her life dusting grass skirts. So out the antiques and curios went, especially the live shells, which my father, mortally afraid, carried in a suitcase to the nearest police station.'

The antique dealer paused, almost out of breath. It was a long time since he had spoken at such length to anyone, least of all about personal matters, but there was something in the young man's manner that encouraged communication, that made it easy for him to talk, to be himself. So after a glance at the other's still, attentive face he continued.

'Even though my grandmother had thrown away most of the things that Grandfather had collected, quite a few of them still remained, certainly enough to keep me happily occupied on my Sunday visits. There were Chinese cloisonné vases, blue as the sky, on which wonderful dragons disported themselves among clouds; there were strange bronze gods from India and tiny porcelain tear-bottles from Japan; there were wicked-looking Gurkha knives and Tibetan ritual bells. When I was older, my grandmother started giving me curios as presents. On my thirteenth birthday she gave me a chopstick-set in a silver-mounted ivory case, and one Christmas I found in the toe of my stocking a pair of silver opium pipes with mouthpieces of green jade. Seeing how fascinated I was by such things, my father not only started looking out for curios for me but introduced me to two or three antique shops in the City, where he worked. Soon all my pocket money was going on curios. I would save up for a Dutch tile, or a Chinese bowl, as other boys saved up for a new football or a cricket bat. To me money that was not spent on curios was money wasted. Curios were my whole life. Even when we went away to the seaside for our summer holiday I was more interested in looking in the windows of the second-hand shops than in playing games on the beach or going for a swim in the sea. Then came the war. After being evacuated with my school for a few months I returned to London in time to catch the tail end of the Blitz, worked in an office for two years, spending most of my wages on curios, and was conscripted. In the army there was not much scope for collecting curios, and I hated it. Towards the end of the war, however, my unit was posted to India, where I was soon combing the bazaars of Agra and Lahore in search of those beautiful things of hammered copper and brass, of carved ivory and sandalwood, which, much as they might be considered curios at home, were here familiar articles of everyday use.

Some of the things I bought I sent home to my father. Others I stowed away at the bottom of my kitbag. After returning to England and being demobilized, I was faced with the question of what I was going to do for a living. As I still had only one real interest in life the best thing for me to do, it seemed, was to combine business and pleasure and become an antique dealer. My father had just died, leaving me a few hundred pounds, and with this I bought a small antique shop in Aimsbury. Shortly afterwards my grandmother died too. As she left no will, what remained of Grandfather's collection passed to my uncle, who was something of a recluse and extremely tight-fisted. Though his interest in antiques was almost as great as my own, it was of a very different kind. To him things like cloisonné vases were little more than a good investment. They were a form of material wealth, of capital, whereas to me they were very much more than that. To me they were....'

The antique dealer broke off, his pale face suddenly fixed as he groped blindly for the words that would convey his meaning. Across the table, the young man continued to be steadily attentive. His blue-grey eyes, that were set a little close together in the smooth, rather large face, were bright with unspoken sympathy as he watched the struggles of the older man to express himself. But he made no attempt to supply the missing words. Eventually the antique dealer gave up.

'Never mind,' he said abruptly, with a movement of his hand across his brow, as if brushing away whole cobwebs of inadequate words. 'It's just that antiques have always meant a great deal to me, and after I had bought the shop they seemed to mean more than ever. For months at a time I hardly ever thought of anything else. Though Aimsbury was only a small place, well off the beaten track, I did quite well there. In fact in the course of the next ten or twelve years I became fairly well known, not only as a dealer but as an expert in several minor branches of the trade. People used to write to me from all over the Continent, even from America. Sometimes museums consulted me. My proudest moment was when I was asked to write a guide to antique collecting for a well-known series of do-it-yourself books. After that I did quite a lot of writing. There was a book on Victorian hall chairs, and a monograph on South Indian bronzes, besides a number of articles in the trade journals.... Then rather late in life I married. My wife didn't like Aimsbury. She wanted to live in the country, or by the sea. So we moved to this place. I've been here ever since.'

After the circumstantiality of the rest of the narration, the even flow of which had been checked only once, when the antique dealer had been unable to put into words what antiques meant to him, or had meant, the abrupt sentences into which he telescoped the events of the last eight years seemed to make a lame, even an impotent, conclusion. It was as though something was missing, or had been left out. What that something might be the young man did not know, but it was not unconnected, he thought, with the discrepancy between the successful, even distinguished, antiques business in Aimsbury, as portrayed by the antique dealer, and the shabby shop in the Gormsby-on-Sea High Street, with its clutter of dust-covered Victoriana in the window, as he had seen it himself that very morning. What had happened, then? Had the antique dealer lost his old passion for antiques? Had his marriage anything to do with it, or the move to Gormsby-on-Sea? Before he had time to ask, or even to think of asking, the clock behind the door was striking eleven, the landlord moving from table to table collecting the glasses and calling out 'Time, gentlemen!' in a peremptory, chief petty officer tone of voice, and the customers were already streaming, black and grey and brown, out of the door.

The young man rose to his feet, hitching his red bellbottoms as he did so. 'I shall have to find somewhere to stay the night,' he said, with the same smiling mixture of diffidence and eagerness as in the morning. 'My car won't be ready until midday tomorrow.'

The antique dealer rose too. He knew what he wanted to say in response to the other's remark, and he felt ashamed, even hurt, that he was unable to say it simply, straightforwardly, naturally, as he wanted to say it, and as he knew it ought to be said. But something prevented him. Something in his ancestry, in his upbringing, in the conditioning to which he had been subjected all his life, made it impossible for him to say to the young man, 'Come home with me,' made it impossible for him to do anything but accompany the gold and the pale blue and the red to the door and look on, helpless, as he heard the chord that had sounded so compellingly in his ears about to fade forever from his life.

At the door the young man paused, recollecting something. Behind the door, slumped underneath the clock, was a battered brown holdall. The young man bent down and picked it up. As he straightened himself, he turned his head, looking up full into the antique dealer's face as he did so with a smile of such disarming directness that the latter felt as though he had been transfixed by a sunbeam. Gentle but irresistible, the sunbeam passed right through him, uncovering what had long lain hidden, touching what had never been touched before, and enabling him to feel alive again in parts of himself that for years he had hardly known existed. All at once he felt able to say what he had wanted to say to the young man.

'You can spend the night at my place, if you like,' he said, tentative but not unconfident. 'There's a spare bedroom. It won't be any trouble.'

The young man quivered like a stringed instrument that has been touched. 'Can I?' he exclaimed, his blue-grey eyes sparkling with pleasure. 'That would be really great. Are you sure your wife won't mind?'

The antique dealer shook his head. 'No,' he said quietly, 'she won't mind.'

A few minutes later they were sitting in the small, overcrowded parlour behind the antique shop. They had come in the back way, through the tiny garden, and in the semi-darkness the young man had been able to make out the shapes of trees and flowers.

For some minutes neither of them spoke. There was no sound anywhere in the house, and without actually thinking about it the young man assumed that the antique dealer's wife had gone to bed. If he was in the habit of going out for a drink in the evening, it would be nothing unusual for her not to bother to wait up for him. At any rate, the place was as quiet as the grave – so quiet that there might well have been only the two of them on the premises. Indeed, what with the silence inside the house and the silence and darkness outside, it was as though the two of them were not only alone in the house but alone in the world, sole survivors of the general shipwreck of mankind.

What was there, then, for them to say? What could two survivors possibly have to say to each other, alone together in the silence, in the outside darkness? One could, of course, ask the other if he would like a cup of coffee, and the other could indicate his acceptance with a nod of the head and a swift upward smile, bright yet self-contained; but that was on the surface. Underneath the surface they were not in the kitchen at all but on a desert island, rocky and remote under the blue sky, where they could hear in the distance the dull crash-boom of the sea on the coral beaches, where they could see strange ornate trees, wreathed in huge red flowers, swaying in the wind, and where, alone together on the hot bare sand, the naked being of the one must interrogate the naked being of the other.

On the surface, the antique dealer put down his cup. 'Shall I show you your room?' he asked at length, solicitous, as somewhere in the depths of the shop a clock struck twelve, the thin silvery strokes piercing through layer on layer of dust.

'Yes, please,' said the young man, who despite three cups of coffee was already smothering his yawns. 'I'm more than ready for bed. What with driving from Glastonbury to London, and London to this place, and not being able to get the car to start, it's been quite a day for me.' He spoke simply, without self-pity, as though he regarded the whole business as a joke which he could appreciate even though the joke was at his expense.

Switching on the light in the hall, the antique dealer led the way upstairs. 'But your day hasn't ended too badly, I hope,' he said, as they reached the top.

The young man responded with a smile of pure complicity. 'Not at all badly,' he said, as their eyes met. For an instant they were alone together on the hot bare sand, with the sound of the sea in their ears, and the strange ornate trees wreathed in red blossom swaying before their eyes.

Halfway along the passage the antique dealer paused outside a door painted in the same nondescript colour as the front of the shop. 'Here you are,' he said, pushing it open and flicking on the light. 'This used to be my wife's room. She died of cancer about three years ago.'

For an instant the young man thought that he was mad, or dreaming, or the victim of some monstrous hoax. Stretched out on the bed, rigid, lay the body of a woman, tightly bound from head to foot in discoloured bandages. Surely the antique dealer could not have.... But the next instant he had seen the chequered blue and yellow of the mummy case leaning upright against the wall, and the antique dealer was saying, 'I'll move that off the bed. It can stay outside for tonight. Tomorrow I'll take it downstairs into the shop. There's room for it there now. No, it isn't very heavy. I can manage.'

Had the young man dreamed that night 'of witch, and demon, and large coffin-worm' it would not have been surprising; but he did not. After unrolling his primrose-coloured sleeping-bag and spreading it out on top of the bedclothes he sank at once into a deep, dreamless sleep. The next thing he knew was that pale shafts of sunlight were streaming in at the window, imparting to the fading greens and washed-out mauves of the room something of the opalescence of the rainbow, and that the antique dealer was standing over him with a cup of tea.

Rubbing his eyes, the young man sat up, the yellow hair falling in tangles over his bare shoulders as the upper part of his smooth, sun-browned body emerged from the yellow sheath of the sleeping-bag as though from a cocoon. 'Thanks,' he said, taking the proffered cup with a faintly apologetic smile. 'I'll get up as soon as I've had this.' Sleepy as he still was, he saw that a change had come over the antique dealer. Whether it was the early morning sunlight that fell across him from the window, or the fact that he was in his pyjamas, he looked a different man.

'That's all right,' returned the other, looking down at the young man as he pursed his lips over the hot tea. 'There's no hurry. Stay in bed as long as you like.'

It was in fact another hour before the young man appeared downstairs. Not finding the antique dealer in the parlour, he passed through the tiny kitchen and out of the back door into the garden, where the rich, profuse green of lilac trees was trapped between walls of sulphur-coloured brick. The antique dealer was standing over a flower-bed in the far corner. Hearing the young man's light step on the grass, he turned round.

'Come and have a look at my flowers,' he called out, in tones fuller and more cheerful than the other had yet heard from him. 'I seem to have had a bit more luck than usual with them this year.'

Sure enough, in the narrow bed at the foot of the wall, clumps of deep red salvias scattered their fire in all directions, while behind them, standing as though on tiptoe, pale blue delphiniums rose in frail columns against the horizontal courses of mottled brick. The salvias were the colour of the young man's red bellbottoms, the delphiniums the colour of his pale blue T-shirt.

For some minutes the two men stood in silence together, looking down at the thick masses of flowers and inhaling the rich warm smell of vegetation, both old and new, that came steaming up to them from the sun-hot earth. A single humble-bee, black with yellow bands, was buzzing heavily about the delphiniums, one of the frail columns bending dangerously as he came to rest on the ragged pale blue flowers. Presently the antique dealer turned to the young man.

'Do you know,' he exclaimed, 'I've only just now realized it, but I think that originally I was almost as fond of flowers as I was of antiques. It was simply that I didn't have time for them, especially after buying the shop – the one at Aimsbury, I mean. My wife was fond of flowers. In fact, she was fond of everything that lived and grew. She didn't care much for antiques. When we got married she wanted me to give up the antique business and go into market gardening. I suppose I could have done so, especially as she wanted to live in the country, but at that time I was still mad about antiques. As a compromise we decided to move to the seaside, to this place. Sometimes I think it was a mistake. If I had gone into market gardening, and we had lived in the country, perhaps it would have been better for her. Perhaps it would have been better for me. Perhaps …'

'So you're not so keen on antiques as you used to be,' suggested the young man quietly, beginning to understand.

'No,' admitted the other, almost guiltily. 'I don't think I am. Not that I've got anything against antiques, of course. It's simply that I don't seem to feel the same enthusiasm for them as before. A really fine Victorian hall chair, for example, picked up for next to nothing at a sale, would have sent me wild with delight a few years ago. Now I can appreciate it, I can see it's a fine piece of work, and so on, but that's about all there is to it. I don't *feel* anything.'

The expression with which he said this was almost desperate, like that of a man at the end of his tether. Yet at the same time it was possible to detect a note of relief in his voice, as though the fact of his having said it, of having at last openly admitted, to himself and another person, that antiques no longer meant as much to him as before, had not only freed him from something that had been burdening him for a long time but also left his way clear for the future. There was a long silence.

'Perhaps it's time you had a holiday from antiques, then,' said the young man at last.

'Perhaps it's time we had some breakfast,' retorted the other, with a change of subject so blatant that the young man, knowing he had been right, could not help smiling as they walked together across the lawn.

Inside the parlour it was dark and cool after the glare of the garden. 'Don't you usually have any luck with your flowers, then?' enquired the young man over his third slice of toast, reverting to the starting point of their conversation.

'No,' returned the other slowly. 'Not until this year, that is. My wife was awfully fond of the garden. Sometimes I think it was the only thing that kept her alive. It was she who planted the lilac trees, not long after we came here. Everything she touched seemed to grow. She really did have green fingers. I had very little to do with the garden. During her last illness I had to do a bit of watering, of course, but apart from that I hardly set foot in it from one year's end to the next. I was too busy with the antiques. Then after she died I got into the habit of sometimes spending a bit of time there. It was almost as though I felt she wanted me to. Then I started noticing that there were things to be done. Flower-beds needed weeding, or dead blooms needed picking off – things like that. Eventually I started putting in plants, and sowing seeds, just as she had done. Though I had never done anything like it before, I seemed to know instinctively what to do, probably because I had seen her doing it so often. At about the same time I started losing interest in antiques. It was almost as though the centre of gravity in my life was beginning to shift, from antiques to the garden. At first I felt terrible about it. It was as though I was not being true to myself, or as though I was suffering from some dreadful disease that was eating my life away bit by bit. Since I was now taking much less interest in it than before, the business started going downhill. I still made a living, but that was about all. For weeks on end I didn't even bother to dust the things in the shop. All my spare time was spent in the garden, and I was often in the garden when I ought to have been answering letters and going to sales. For a long time I felt quite guilty about this, but eventually the feeling wore off. What made me feel really bad was the fact that none of the plants I put in ever came to anything. As for the seeds, even if they did sprout, they very quickly withered and died. Spring or summer, it was always the same. Unlike my wife, I just didn't seem to have green fingers. But this year ...'

While the antique dealer was speaking the young man had given a swift glance, just one, at his watch. When the other finished, or when, for the second time since they had met, he came to a point where he was unable to put into words all that he felt, the young man rose to his feet. 'My car should be ready by now,' he remarked amiably. 'I'll go to the garage and have a look. See you!'

Before the antique dealer could reply, or even think of replying, he was gone. Though he made no response to what the other had been saying, there was nothing abrupt or discourteous about his departure, no lack of sympathy in his silence. Rather, it was as though his departure was itself the answer, as though he went on some mysterious errand of particular relevance to everything that the antique dealer had been telling him.

The antique dealer sensed this, but he could not be sure. He could not even be sure if the young man was coming back, or whether his casual-seeming 'See you!' had not been an expression both of thanks and farewell. He had hardly shifted the mummy and its yellow and blue case downstairs to the shop, however, when there was the sound of a car pulling up outside. Less than a minute later, he heard a light step coming through the kitchen and into the parlour. The young man's blond head appeared in the doorway.

'The car's ready,' he announced, with a faintly conspiratorial smile, as though something had been agreed between them.

There was a long pause. Even now the antique dealer could not be sure. 'So you're going,' he said at last, uncertain.

'Yes,' replied the young man, still smiling. Then he added, casually but with complete inevitability, 'Why don't you come with me? I'm only going to stay with friends. You'd be quite welcome.'

The antique dealer stood stock still, rigid as the mummy he had just deposited on the floor, or as the full suit of armour that stood bright and upright against the back wall. Once again, for an instant, he heard the sound of breakers on the seashore, saw the ornate trees wreathed in red blossom dancing in the wind.

'What do your friends do?' he asked at length, almost mechanically, like a man in a dream.

'They've got a market garden,' said the young man.

In less than ten minutes the antique dealer was ready. 'Look after this for me, will you?' he said, settling himself in the front seat and holding out a massive iron key: the key of the shop. 'I don't have any pockets in these trousers.'

The young man took the key and slowly pushed it down into the front pocket of his red bellbottoms. Then he started the car, and they were off.

Ten minutes later, after they had bypassed Great Barrow and were running along between flat green fields, the sunlit sweep of the road brought them to an ancient stone-built bridge humped over a river.

Slowing down the car, the young man drew the key from his pocket and with a swing of his bare arm flung it over the parapet.

'You won't be needing that,' he said, accelerating.

'I don't think I will,' said the other.

THE CAVE

The cave was situated in the middle of a sandstone ridge, three hundred feet above the rice fields and mango groves. It was a man-made cave. Just when a niche in the soft brown rock had been deepened and widened to form a cave no one knew, but it must have been hundreds of years ago. But at all events, for as long as even the oldest man in the village could remember, or remember his grandfather remembering, the cave had been occupied, especially during the rainy season. It had been occupied by a succession of holy men, either singly or less frequently in twos and threes. Some of the holy men who occupied the cave went naked, others wore yellow or white or red cotton garments, or even garments of bark. Most were shaven-headed, while those who were not shaven-headed generally had shoulder length hair, or wore their long braided locks piled high up in coils on their heads. The holy men passed their time in a variety of ways. Some meditated, some repeated the teachings they had heard, and some – those occupying the cave in twos and threes – engaged in discussion. There were even some holy men who did nothing at all, unless it were to watch the clouds moving across the sky, or listen to the shrill churring of the cicadas.

Sumana was shaven-headed, wore yellow garments and spent much of his time meditating, or at least trying to meditate. He had occupied the cave for nearly three years. Originally it had been his intention to occupy it only for the duration of the current rainy season. But having found staying in one place more conducive to meditation than wandering from village to village all the time, as he had been in the habit of doing, he had decided to stay in the cave indefinitely. Sumana was a follower of a famous if somewhat controversial teacher who had appeared in the middle country a few decades earlier. This teacher was generally known as the Buddha, or Enlightened one, though his Brahmin critics called him in derision the *muṇḍaka*, or shaven-headed one.

Strange to relate, Sumana had never actually met the Buddha, for though his wanderings had been quite extensive, he somehow had never managed to be in the same place at the same time as the Buddha, who was himself on the move for the greater part of the year. He had, however, been the personal disciple of a holy man who in his younger days had spent a whole rainy season in the company of the Enlightened one, and was never tired of singing his praises. Sumana had met the holy man six rainy seasons earlier, not long after the memorable day when, at the age of nineteen, he had left his father's mansion in search of something that would give greater meaning to his life. In the teaching of the Buddha as explained by the holy man he had found what he was looking for. With the holy man, therefore, Sumana had stayed, and the holy man, whose name was Aniruddha, shaved Sumana's head and clad him in yellow garments. He had also taught him how to meditate, as well as teaching him the poems and lists of doctrinal categories that summarized the Buddha's message, and had to be learned by heart. Then, when Sumana had been with him for two years, Aniruddha had told him that from now onwards he should wander from place to place. 'The water is pure that flows, the holy man is pure who goes,' he had said, quoting a jingle that was very popular with the followers of the Enlightened one.

So Sumana had gone, and had kept on going. For nine months he had wandered from village to mud-walled village, and from town to orchard-girt town, rarely spending more than a single night in the same place. Usually he started out quite early in the morning, well before the golden or crimson disc of the sun had risen above the horizon, and when the sky was still bright with stars. In the hot season he started out thus early in order to avoid having to travel during the middle part of the day when the heat could kill, while in the cold season he did so because he would be too cold by that time to sleep any longer, and needed to walk to get warm.

Some mornings found him making his way along the narrow embankments between the rice-fields. Others found him following a desultory track through the jungle, or even taking advantage of a stretch of royal highway where he might pass a string of bullock carts on their way to market, or be himself passed by a horse-drawn chariot. After walking for four or five hours, Sumana would generally come upon a village, or at least a cluster of huts, where he could beg his food. Some holy men were wont to bawl out, 'Give food!' on entering a village, but such was not the practice either of the Buddha himself or of those holy men who acknowledged him as their teacher and exemplar, and it was not Sumana's practice. He would go from house to house, at each house standing silently outside the door until a handful or two of rice was dropped into his bowl, or until it became obvious that he was not going to get anything. Occasionally he would be roughly told to go away. 'We want no bald-heads here!' an unfriendly Brahmin might exclaim. When his bowl was sufficiently full, Sumana would retire to a mango grove, or if there was no mango grove nearby, to the foot of the village banyan tree, or to a quiet corner of someone's veranda, or even to an empty cow shed, and there consume his one meal of the day, which in accordance with the practice of the Buddha and his holy men had to be finished by noon. His meal over, Sumana would rest for a while, after which he might meditate, or talk with any villagers who had gathered round until it was time for him to seek a lodging for the night.

In some villages, especially those in which the Buddha's name was already known and honoured, he would be asked to give an account of the teaching he professed to follow. Whenever that happened he would recite one of the poems, or one of the lists of doctrinal categories, that he had learned from Aniruddha, and then explain it line by line or item by item in his own words. Often he would illustrate a point by telling a story, for the villagers liked to hear stories, and Sumana himself enjoyed telling them. Occasionally questions would be forthcoming. Sumana would answer them, his answers would lead to further questions, and in this way there would develop a discussion that might last far into the night.

Not all Sumana's days had ended in this congenial fashion. More than once in the course of the nine months for which he had wandered, he had walked all day without coming upon a village or even a cluster of huts where he could beg his food. More than once therefore he had perforce slept on an empty stomach. On one dreadful occasion he had been lost in the jungle for three days and three nights together, and had had to live on fruits and berries. Nor had this been his only misadventure. One morning, as he picked his way among the boulders of a dried-up riverbed, he had been suddenly surrounded by five or six fierce-looking men armed with swords. The men had seized him, bound his hands and feet with a length of creeper, and deposited him behind a rock. From their conversation he gathered that they were worshippers of the Great Mother and were looking for a young man to sacrifice to her on the next new-moon day. Whether or not he himself was to be the sacrifice, Sumana never discovered. His captors having fallen asleep after emptying a pot of liquor, he had worked his hands free and untied his feet, and making a quick but quiet escape had carried on walking.

Thus, Sumana had certainly obeyed Aniruddha's instructions. He had gone, and he had kept on going. But to his dismay, Sumana had found that the second half of Aniruddha's jingle was not being fulfilled. The holy man had indeed gone, but he was not pure. Purity of course meant mental purity, and mental purity was achieved through meditation, in which the mind, freeing itself from attachment to earthly things, rose to a higher, more radiant state of consciousness wherein Truth could be directly perceived. Since wandering from place to place had the effect of weakening a holy man's attachment to earthly things, it made it easier for him to meditate, and easier therefore for him to achieve purity of mind. Such at least was the theory. In practice Sumana had not found matters quite so simple. Wandering from place to place might indeed have had the effect of weakening his attachment to earthly things, though he could not be absolutely sure of this. But it had also had the effect of making him restless and anxious, and restlessness and anxiety were he knew as much a hindrance to meditation (and therefore as much a hindrance to the achievement of mental purity) as was attachment to earthly things. He had tried to meditate twice a day, in the morning before setting out and in the evening before lying down to sleep. More often than not, however, he would be either too restless to be able to sit in the meditation posture for very long, or too worried about meeting with wild beasts, or not getting his daily dole of rice, to be able to collect his thoughts. Sometimes he would be simply too tired to meditate, either because cold or hunger or the hardness of the ground had prevented him from sleeping, or because he had been walking all day. After nine months he had therefore not been sorry when, the hot season being at an end and the rainy season about to begin, he was obliged to stop wandering from place to place at least for the time being, and could take up his abode in the cave.

He had found the cave by accident. He had entered the village towards the end of the afternoon when it was too late for him to beg his food. The villagers had been quite friendly and had not only given him a refreshing drink, but told him that if he cared to stay overnight they would be glad to provide him with food in the morning. He could stay at the cave, they added. By that time it was quite dark, so a boy was deputed to show him the way to the cave. Having crossed fields and forded streams, they had scrambled up to the ridge and Sumana had found himself inside the cave and trying in complete darkness to find a corner where he could sleep. In the morning he had crawled to the mouth of the cave and looked out. The sun was high in the blue sky and the earth flooded with golden light. Below him were the darkly wooded slopes of the hill, beyond the last of the slopes the brown and green patchwork of fields and groves, and beyond the patchwork, the grey roofs of the village, from which wisps of smoke rose straight into the clear air, while beyond the village, encircling everything and extending to the very horizon, was the vast expanse of the jungle, with here and there a hill showing ship-like above the sea of green. Sumana had been deeply moved by the sight. He had wanted to spend the whole day at the mouth of the cave simply gazing at the scene. He had wanted to gaze at it not just for one day, but every day; and then he had had an idea. The rainy season was about to begin, and for the three or four months of the rainy season holy men, including those who were followers of the Buddha, instead of wandering from place to place stayed in one spot. Why should he not spend the coming rainy season in the cave, provided the villagers had no objection, and provided of course he could beg his food at their doors each day? Fortunately for Sumana the villagers had had no objection at all. They had been overjoyed that there would again be a holy man staying in the cave. As the headman of the village put it, giving expression to the general sentiment, 'To have a holy man staying in the cave brings good luck to the village.'

Sumana had therefore taken up his abode in the cave and had spent the rainy season there. In fact he had now spent three rainy seasons in the cave, as well as three cold seasons and three hot seasons. For in the course of the first rainy season he had made an important discovery. He had discovered that he meditated better, and achieved mental purity more easily, when he stayed in one spot and did not wander from place to place. At the end of the rainy season he had therefore decided not to resume his wanderings, and nor had he resumed them since. He felt rather guilty about this, especially when the jingle that was so popular with the followers of the Enlightened one happened to come into his head. 'The holy man is pure who goes,' it would insist, 'The holy man is pure who goes.' At such moments, Sumana would be inclined to feel that he was not a real holy man. He would also wonder what Aniruddha would say if he knew that his erstwhile disciple was no longer wandering from place to place as directed. What the Buddha would say he dared not think.

During his first rainy season in the cave Sumana's movements had naturally been rather restricted, as they also were, though to a lesser extent, during the subsequent rainy seasons. The rains were notoriously heavy in that part of the world, and he ventured out each day only to make a quick dash down the slippery hillside and through the flooded fields to the village for food, sometimes sheltering beneath a broad green plantain leaf. The practice of storing up food from one day to the next was frowned upon by the more ascetic holy men, and Sumana tried to avoid doing this. During the other two seasons he was able to move about more freely and his activities tended to follow a definite pattern. Rising before dawn, he washed in water from a rock-hewn cistern beside the entrance to the cave, then sat on the ledge in front of the cave and meditated for two or three hours. At least he tried to meditate. Though no longer restless and anxious, he still found it difficult to sit in the meditation posture for very long, difficult to collect his thoughts, and even more difficult to rise to that higher, more radiant state of consciousness wherein Truth can be directly perceived. All the same, there occasionally were times when he really was able to meditate, when he really did achieve mental purity, and this being so, he felt less guilty about not wandering from place to place.

When he had finished meditating, Sumana relaxed his limbs, and sat for a while simply gazing at the sun-drenched prospect before him and allowing the silence, unbroken save for the occasional birdcall, to sink deep into his heart. To his surprise he sometimes experienced greater peace of mind at those moments than when he was actually meditating.

Next came what for his first year in the cave had been the most difficult part of Sumana's day, the taking of his morning bath. The taking of the bath itself presented no difficulty. Sumana took it in the sparkling waters of the stream that, having tumbled down through the rocks of the hill on which the ridge was situated, flowed through the fields and groves and on past the village to the jungle. What made the taking of his bath difficult was the fact that three or four girls from the village also took their morning bath in the stream, or at least started taking it there when they discovered Sumana was doing so. At first the girls kept well downstream, but then, growing bolder, they started moving a little further upstream with every day that passed until Sumana was not only hearing their every shriek and giggle, but also seeing far more of their persons than it was proper for a holy man to see, as was obviously their intention. Aniruddha having told him what to do in such circumstances, Sumana henceforth took his bath later and further upstream, but it was of no use. The girls also took their bath later and further upstream, and Sumana started finding it quite difficult not to look in their direction. Indeed, he was sometimes surprised to find his heart racing and the blood pounding in his ears as he made his way down to the stream. One day the oldest of the girls, having wriggled out of her clothes, swam up to Sumana as he stood waist-deep in the water, his back towards her and her companions, and playfully splashed him. Sumana simply gathered up his yellow garments and fled. Fortunately, an old man who was working in the fields saw the incident and must have spoken of it to the other villagers, for from the following day the girls took their bath almost within the shadow of the village, where their elders could keep an eye on them, and where they were out of Sumana's sight. The matter did not end there for Sumana, however. For many a night he was troubled by dreams in which a horde of naked women dragged him down into the water and seduced him, afterwards turning into hideous demons who mocked him for having broken his vows. It was months before the dreams faded completely, but fade they did, and from that time onwards the taking of his morning bath was no longer the most difficult part of Sumana's day but often, in the hot season especially, the easiest and most delightful.

From the stream, Sumana went straight to the village and there begged his food. On most days his bowl would be full after he had visited no more than six or seven houses, and as there were nearly three hundred houses in the village he did not need to visit any one house more than once or twice a year. Thus he was neither a burden to the village, nor likely to become dependent on, even attached to, particular families, faults of which the Buddha, according to Aniruddha, was constantly exhorting his holy men to beware. When the earthenware bowl in his hands had been filled, not just with rice but also with lentils and curry and sometimes with sweetmeats (for the handsome young holy man was quite popular with the housewives of the village, some of whom viewed in him in the light of a prospective son-in-law or brother-in-law), Sumana returned to the cave, sometimes following one route through the fields, sometimes another, always being careful not to frighten any snake or lizard that he might come across as it lay basking in the sun. Back in the darkness and coolness of the cave, he ate the food he had begged, eating as slowly and mindfully as he could, and trying to remember that he ate simply to sustain life as he strove to achieve mental purity and perceive Truth.

When he had finished eating, he washed his bowl with water from the cistern and put it in the sun to dry. He then took a short rest, it being axiomatic among the Buddha's holy men that after their one meal of the day, which naturally tended to be a heavy one, time was needed to allay what they called 'digestion fatigue'. Digestion fatigue having been allayed, Sumana spent the afternoon doing such things as mending his yellow garments, which were always catching on thorny branches and tearing, sweeping out the cave, and repeating aloud as many as he could remember of the poems and lists of doctrinal categories he had learned from Aniruddha. Twice a month, on the full-moon and new-moon days, he shaved hair and beard with the razor that together with three yellow garments, a belt, a water-strainer, an alms bowl, and a needle was one of the eight personal belongings permitted to those holy men who were followers of the Buddha. Towards evening he sat out on the ledge in front of the cave and gazed at the darkening landscape until it was time for him to meditate. When he opened his eyes, the sky would be ablaze with stars, and for an hour or more he would gaze at them as in their tens of thousands they flashed and glittered in the depths of space, or he would watch the moon rising, or mark a shooting star suddenly trail its fiery pennant across the face of the heavens.

Occasionally, when there was a moon, the more thoughtful of the village men would come and sit on the ledge with Sumana in the moonlight. For a while they would sit there together in silence as though unwilling to break with the sound of human voices the greater silence of nature by which they were surrounded. When he felt the silence between them had lasted long enough, Sumana would start reciting a poem or a list of doctrinal categories. At first he recited very softly, then more and more loudly. By the time he finished, his companions would have roused themselves as though from deep sleep, and he would start explaining the poem or list. Questions and answers followed, as well as a certain amount of discussion, just as on similar occasions during his wandering days, and as on these earlier occasions discussion might last far into the night. The only difference was that in the case of the discussion that took place on the ledge in front of the cave there was an element of continuity from session to session in as much as the same men tended to be present each time. Discussion could therefore go deeper. So deep did it sometimes go that there were nights when Sumana sat gazing at the stars, his mind full of thoughts, long after the others had left. There were thoughts about the universe, about the human condition, about death, about meditation and mental purity, about Truth. There were also thoughts about his present way of life, for although his meditation had improved, Sumana still felt guilty about staying in one spot, was still inclined to feel he was not a real holy man, and still wondered what Aniruddha, not to speak of the Buddha, would think of him. At times there were even thoughts he dared not acknowledge as his own, and which he therefore tended to push to the very back of his mind.

One windy morning shortly before the start of the rainy season, Sumana was begging his food in the village when he saw, a stone's throw ahead of him, another holy man evidently also begging his food. Wandering holy men were not an uncommon sight in the village and at first Sumana did not take much notice of the newcomer. In any case he was a little preoccupied that morning. There had been a discussion on the ledge in front of the cave the previous night, and thoughts from the discussion were still very much in his mind, especially thoughts about his present way of life. So much were they in his mind that he was not surprised to find after a few minutes that without realizing it he had come right up behind the other holy man, who must have slowed down. Like Sumana himself, the newcomer was shaven-headed and wore yellow garments, from which Sumana concluded that he was probably a follower of the Buddha. He did not ask him about this, however, for it was not the custom of the Buddha's holy men to speak when begging their food. After visiting a couple more houses, therefore, Sumana left the village and made for the cave. Half way up the hill he became aware that the other holy man was following him. Not that he was actually able to see him, but he could hear the stones rattling downhill from beneath somebody's feet and he knew that it was the other holy man. Sure enough, it was not long before the latter had come into view and was making his way along the ledge where Sumana was standing. As Sumana could now see, he was a little above average height and about the same age as Aniruddha, who was rather more than twice the age of Sumana himself. 'If you have no objection, friend,' said the stranger, speaking in a dialect with which Sumana was not wholly familiar but which he understood well enough, 'I shall take my meal here on this ledge with you.'

Naturally Sumana had no objection, and soon the two holy men were sitting side by side on the bare rock and working their way through the contents of their respective bowls, eating slowly and mindfully and of course in silence. When they had both finished, Sumana brought the other holy man water for washing his bowl, and offered him a bamboo toothpick. These small services the newcomer accepted in silence, but with a friendly smile. It was a smile that Sumana hoped meant conversation, for the young holy man very much wanted to talk to his unexpected visitor. He wanted to ask him who he was and where he came from, and why he had followed him to the cave and taken his meal with him there on the ledge. But friendly as the newcomer's smile was, it apparently did not mean conversation, at least not just then, for having made use of the toothpick Sumana had offered him, he stretched out his legs and closed his eyes with the evident intention of taking a short rest, presumably to allay digestion fatigue. Sumana therefore had to restrain his desire to talk, for among the Buddha's holy men, and Sumana was now convinced that the newcomer was one of these, it was not etiquette for a younger holy man to initiate conversation with an older one, much less still to ask him personal questions. He had to restrain his desire to talk for quite a long time. Having rested, the Elder, as Sumana mentally now called him, composed himself for meditation, and the young holy man felt obliged to follow suit. They meditated for what to Sumana seemed an age – that is, the Elder meditated, while Sumana tried with varying degrees of success to collect his thoughts and purify his mind. When the Elder at last uncrossed his legs and leaned back against the rock, as Sumana had done much earlier, the sky was more grey than blue, and the first stars had appeared. But even then, the Elder did not say anything. For an hour or more he sat gazing at the stars as Sumana himself had so often done. Only when the objects of his contemplation had filled the sky with their brightness and Sumana had begun to think that his visitor was about to depart as unaccountably as he had arrived did the Elder turn to the young holy man and speak.

'If you have no objection, friend,' he said, speaking in the same dialect as before, 'I shall spend the night with you in your cave.' Once again Sumana had no objection, adding this time that he would be glad of His Reverence's company, that the cave was spacious enough to accommodate five or six persons, that he himself had lived there alone for the last three years, that the cave was warm and dry, and free from bats and scorpions, and that there was always water in the cistern even if at times it might be less pure and less fresh than one could desire. To all this and much more of similar tenor the Elder replied with the same friendly smile with which he had acknowledged Sumana's services earlier on. But so warm was the smile and so full of understanding, as by the light of the stars Sumana could easily perceive, that the young holy man not only felt that his commonplace remarks had met with complete acceptance, but felt that the Elder, without actually saying anything, had responded to each one of them individually. When he lay down on his bed of leaves that night two feet away from the Elder it was therefore with a feeling that there had been conversation between them after all. Perhaps there had been, and there was much for him to look forward to the following day.

The following day was in fact a very happy one for Sumana. The Elder of course left his bed long before Sumana left his, but apart from that he and the young holy man did everything together. They meditated together, they took their bath in the stream together, they begged their food in the village together, Sumana walking a few paces behind the Elder as was proper, they returned to the cave together, they ate together, and they took a short rest together. After they had rested, however, the Elder seemed to be in a more communicative mood than he had been the previous day. With the same friendly smile that had already made such an impression on Sumana, he proceeded to recite one of the poems summarizing the Buddha's message, then nodded for Sumana to do likewise. In this way, with each of them in turn reciting a poem or list of doctrinal categories, they spent the greater part of the afternoon, pausing only when Sumana's stock of poems and lists was exhausted. The Elder then questioned Sumana about the meaning of some of the more difficult words and phrases, evidently in order to test his knowledge of the Buddha's teaching. So gentle and so sympathetic was the questioning that Sumana did not feel he was being questioned at all, much less still that he was being cross-examined, as he had sometimes felt when Aniruddha catechized him. Instead he felt stimulated and excited, even inspired, and replied to the questions with as much ease and freedom as if they were not coming from any external source but from the depths of his own being.

Nonetheless, he was conscious of a vague disquiet. Though most of the poems and lists the Elder had recited were already known to him, a few were not only quite unknown, but were somewhat at variance, he thought, with the Buddha's teaching. According to the Buddha's teaching, the spiritual life consisted mainly in the progressive elimination of negative mental states. The hitherto unknown poems and lists spoke of it as consisting mainly in the development of positive mental states. Were they perhaps an unauthorized addition to the Buddha's teaching, and if they were, what was their source? But before Sumana could question the Elder on these points, the latter had composed himself for meditation and the young holy man was obliged to wait.

Prior to their meditating, the Elder announced that providing Sumana had no objection he would be spending a few more days with him, a proposal to which Sumana at once joyfully assented. For the next few days, therefore, Sumana and the Elder continued to meditate, bathe, beg, eat, and rest together. They also continued to spend the greater part of the afternoon reciting poems and lists of doctrinal categories. Sumana of course had to repeat himself each time, and the Elder continued to test the young holy man's knowledge of the Buddha's teaching. The Elder also gave Sumana detailed explanations of some of the more abstruse and cryptic of the poems and lists, making everything so clear, and at the same time so interesting, that Sumana's confidence in his new companion grew like a bamboo in the rainy season, and he quite forgot about the questions he had wanted to ask.

One afternoon that confidence suffered a severe blow. The Elder having explained a poem on the subject of perceiving Truth with even more than his usual clarity, Sumana had felt moved to tell him how he had wandered from place to place for nine months, but having found that despite going he was not pure, he had taken up his abode in the cave one rainy season, and had now lived there for three years. He also told him that although he was meditating better and achieving mental purity more easily, he felt guilty about not leading a wandering life and sometimes doubted if he was a real holy man. To all this the Elder had replied, not without a gleam of amusement, 'Being a holy man has nothing to do with wandering from place to place, and nothing to do with not wandering from place to place.' Nothing to do with wandering from place to place! Sumana had been quite shocked by this apparent repudiation of the way of life enjoined upon him by Aniruddha, a way of life to which despite his long sojourn in the cave he still felt himself to be in principle committed. The questions he had wanted to ask and which he had forgotten came back to him with redoubled force, and for one dreadful moment he thought the Elder must be one of those renegade disciples who Aniruddha had once told him interpreted the Buddha's teaching according to their own whims and fancies, and in this way did a great deal of harm. But although Sumana's confidence in the Elder suffered a severe blow, the blow did not prove mortal. This was partly because the Elder went on to explain what being a holy man really meant, and partly because Sumana himself was in any case beginning to suspect that there was a good deal more to the Buddha's teaching than he had imagined, and that the Elder had spent in all probability more time with the Buddha than had Aniruddha. The young man's confidence in his new companion therefore soon recovered from the blow it had received, and once again grew like a bamboo in the rainy season. What was more, he found that when he and the Elder meditated together he was able to collect his thoughts and achieve mental purity more easily than ever before. He also found that he no longer felt guilty about not leading a wandering life.

By this time the clouds had begun to gather on the horizon, and the first faint rumblings of thunder could be heard. The rains were approaching. Sumana was therefore not surprised when on the morning after his fifth night in the cave the Elder announced that he would be leaving that day. The two of them had just finished meditating, and though they did not usually talk at this hour Sumana fervently hoped that on this occasion at least the friendly smile that had accompanied the Elder's announcement really did mean communication. During the short time that they had spent together the young holy man's confidence in his companion had not only grown like a bamboo in the rainy season, but had also, like the mythical seven-year bamboo, put forth a milk-white flower, the flower of affection. Now that they were about to part, perhaps forever, Sumana realized how much he had come to like the Elder. He liked him much more than he had ever liked Aniruddha, much more than ... but here Sumana's courage failed him. He became aware of thoughts he had hitherto not dared to acknowledge as his own, and which he had therefore tended to push to the very back of his mind. He also became aware that the Elder was looking at him, and in fact questioning him, but so gently and so sympathetically that once again he did not feel he was being questioned at all.

'Why was it, do you think, that even though you wandered far and wide for nine months you never actually met the Buddha?'

Sumana could of course have replied that it was because he had somehow never managed to be in the same place at the same time as the Buddha, who in any case was himself always on the move. But instead he told the truth.

'I suppose I never met the Buddha because I did not really want to meet him,' he said.

'But why did you not want to meet him?' persisted the Elder. 'Was he not your teacher's teacher, and was it not in his teaching that you had found what you were looking for when you left your father's mansion? Surely the Buddha of all the people in the world should have been the one you were most anxious to meet.'

Sumana was sorely perplexed by these questions. The Buddha was indeed Aniruddha's teacher, and it was indeed in the Buddha's teaching as explained by Aniruddha that he had found what he was looking for when he left his father's mansion. These were the facts and he could not deny them. He had no wish to deny them. Why then had he not wanted to meet the Buddha? Why, having been told to wander from place to place, had he not managed to find his way to the Buddha, fall at his feet and tell him how glad he was to have met with his teaching and how grateful he felt to him for discovering it and making it known to the world? Eventually, with the help of the Elder, help given he knew not how, the answer to the question emerged. It emerged from the very back of Sumana's mind, from that dark hinterland of consciousness to which it had been relegated during the time he had spent with Aniruddha and where it had remained hidden ever since.

'I didn't want to meet the Buddha,' he faltered, 'because I don't really like the Buddha.'

At last the shameful secret was out. Sumana more than half expected the Elder to be shocked and horrified, and would not have been really surprised if he had at once shaken the dust of the cave from his feet, leaving his erstwhile companion to his own sinful devices. But the friendly smile did not waver, and when the Elder spoke it was as gently and as sympathetically as before.

'But how can you say that you don't like the Buddha when you have never met him?' Sumana thought for a moment. Many memories came back to him. 'Well,' he said at last, 'I may not have met the Buddha, but I've heard quite a lot about him. Aniruddha was always singing his praises, as was indeed right and proper. He used to praise him for his wisdom, his mindfulness, his energy, his skill in debate. But most of all he used to praise him for his severity and strictness, especially his strictness. "The Buddha's so strict," he would exclaim admiringly, "that his disciples hardly dare breathe in his presence." As a result I developed a sort of dislike for the Buddha, even though it was in his teaching that I had found what I was looking for. I felt that if ever I met the Buddha he would be sure to criticize me. He would criticize me for getting up late, for not eating slowly and mindfully, for forgetting so many poems and lists, not to speak of criticizing me for not collecting my thoughts and purifying my mind. There was hardly anything for which he would not criticize me.'

'If he was here now,' he added with a wry smile, 'I expect he would criticize me for talking to you so much.'

'Do you really think he would?' asked the Elder, the words falling as softly and gently as dewdrops on the petal of a lotus flower.

But before Sumana could reply, there came the sound of stones rattling downhill from beneath somebody's feet, and soon another holy man could be seen scrambling up onto the far end of the ledge. The newcomer was shaven-headed, wore yellow garments and was of about the same age as the Elder, whom he indeed strikingly resembled. Having paused for a moment to get his breath, he advanced briskly towards Sumana and his companion, who were standing before the entrance to the cave. As Sumana was the nearer to him of the two, the newcomer did not at first see the other, but as he drew closer he caught sight of him over Sumana's shoulder and his wrinkled, kindly face at once lit up.

'There you are, Lord!' he exclaimed, with a hasty genuflection. 'The good people in the village told me I should find you here. It took me longer than I thought to deliver your messages and on the way I ...'

But Sumana heard no more, and neither did he hear what the Elder said in reply.

'Lord,' he repeated to himself in wonder. The newcomer had addressed the Elder as 'Lord'! Among the followers of the Buddha, only the Enlightened one himself was referred to or addressed in that way. What could it mean? Involuntarily he turned to the Elder, as if seeking an explanation. As he turned, the well-known form was suddenly transfigured by a brilliant golden light like a cloud at sunset. So brilliant was the light that Sumana closed his eyes, at the same time falling at the Buddha's feet with a great cry.

When he opened his eyes, there was no light other than that of the morning sun, and the Buddha and the newly arrived holy man were quietly chatting. 'Ānanda has been telling me,' said the Buddha, 'that according to local opinion the rain will be here in a day or two, and that he and I ought to be on our way. He also tells me that we don't have to beg our food today as the villagers are going to give us a special meal in the village hall. They've asked us to be there a little early, so perhaps we'd better go and take our bath straightaway.' The three of them accordingly made their way down to the stream, now no more than a trickle of silver over the white stones. As was their custom, the Buddha and Sumana took their bath in silence and without being in the least in a hurry. Ānanda, on the contrary, not only kept feeding bits of news to the Buddha, but seemed bent on completing his ablutions as quickly as possible. He had to go on ahead, he explained, catching up his bowl, in order to make sure that the villagers had made proper arrangements for the Buddha's reception.

It was very quiet after he had left. The only sound to be heard was that of the water gurgling over the stones. The Buddha and Sumana finished taking their bath, then followed after Ānanda, though at a more leisurely pace. They did not speak, but shortly before they reached the village the Buddha turned round and looked at Sumana with a smile that penetrated the young holy man's heart to its very depths.

'Do you still not like the Buddha?' the smile seemed to say. And deep in his heart Sumana could only reply, 'I like him very much. I think I like him even more than I liked the Elder.'

On their arrival at the village hall, the Buddha and Sumana found Ānanda helping to put the finishing touches to an elaborate arch of welcome. It was evident that he was already quite popular with the villagers. On catching sight of the Buddha, he dropped the piece of greenery he was holding, darted forward and, after making the Buddha pass beneath the arch round which were assembled the village elders, ushered him into the hall and to the seat of honour. The meal that followed was the best that Sumana had seen for a long time (not that a holy man was really supposed to notice such things), and members of the village's leading families not only served the Buddha and his two disciples with their own hands but, as etiquette required, continued to press further helpings upon them long after they had 'withdrawn the hand from the bowl', as the phrase went. During the meal Ānanda told Sumana that he had given the villagers a good scolding the previous day for not inviting the Buddha earlier, and for allowing him to beg his food from door to door like any ordinary holy man. They had protested that they had not known it was the Buddha. 'Not known it was the Buddha!' Ānanda had retorted. 'Surely you are able to know a Buddha when you see one!'

But the villagers were not so sure. Neither was Sumana. The special meal being over, members of the leading families brought water for the Buddha and his two disciples to wash their hands, and offered them toothpicks. The rest of the villagers were then admitted, and the Buddha recited verses of benediction and gave a short talk on the importance of leading an ethical life and practising generosity. On such occasions at least two or three people usually came forward at the end of the talk and asked the Buddha to accept them as his followers, but this time nobody came forward and after waiting a few minutes the Buddha rose to his feet, Ānanda and Sumana following suit. Clouds had now overspread half the sky, and Sumana realized with a pang that it was time for the Buddha and Ānanda to be on their way and for him to return to the cave. Already the more pious of the villagers were thronging round the Buddha and touching his feet in farewell.

Sumana allowed them to finish, then went and knelt before the Buddha, placing the palms of his hands on the ground and his head on the Enlightened one's feet. He kept his head there for some time, so overcome by emotion that he was unable to speak. When he at last stood up, Ānanda patted him on the back and whispered a few words of encouragement. The Buddha himself was silent. He remained silent for a long time. When he did speak, it was with the same friendly smile that Sumana knew and loved so well, and his words were at once an invitation and a command.

'Come, Sumana,' he said, 'you have stayed in the cave long enough. Ānanda knows a place where the three of us can spend the rainy season together. Others will perhaps join us there.'

When the Buddha and Ānanda left the village, Sumana therefore left with them. The villagers stood on either side of the dusty track to see them go. There were several whom Sumana recognized, among them the boy, now a boy no longer, who had shown him the way to the cave; the girls, now girls no longer, who for a while had made the taking of his morning bath the most difficult part of his day; and those thoughtful men who when there was a moon had sat with him in silence on the ledge until it was time for discussion. He would miss them as no doubt they, perhaps for different reasons, would miss him. At the same time, he was glad to have met the Buddha, glad to be leaving the village with him and Ānanda, glad that the three of them were stepping out together along the same dusty track. When they had gone four or five miles, there was a sudden rumbling of thunder directly overhead and a few big drops of rain fell. 'We must hurry,' said Ānanda. But Sumana was looking back at the ridge, now silhouetted against a rapidly darkening sky. A new phase of his life as a holy man was about to begin, and for a moment he stood lost in thought. Then, recollecting himself, he turned and caught up with the others, who had already quickened their pace. The cave was left vacant for the next holy man.

NOTES

(S) indicates a note supplied by the author. All other notes are written by the editor.

1 'My Relation to the Order', given on WBO (Western Buddhist Order) Day, 8 April 1990 to Order members celebrating the Order's 22nd birthday. The full text is found in *Complete Works*, vol. 2.
2 Since 2013 Adhisthana, in rural Herefordshire, has been the UK headquarters of the Triratna Buddhist Community. It includes a retreat and study centre and a large residential community and was Sangharakshita's home for the last six years of his life.
3 *Saṃyutta Nikāya* v.437; see Bhikkhu Bodhi (trans.), *The Connected Discourses of the Buddha*, Wisdom Publications, Boston 2000, pp. 1857–8; or F. L. Woodward (trans.), *The Book of the Kindred Sayings*, vol. v, Pali Text Society, London 1956, p. 370.
4 Sangharakshita, *A Survey of Buddhism, Complete Works*, vol. 1, p. 416.
5 *Mahāsaccaka Sutta, Majjhima Nikāya* 36 (i.246). See Bhikkhu Ñāṇamoli and Bhikkhu Bodhi (trans.), *The Middle Length Discourses of the Buddha*, Wisdom Publications, Boston 1995, p. 340; or I. B. Horner (trans.), *The Collection of the Middle Length Sayings*, vol. i, Pali Text Society, Oxford 1995, p. 301.
6 Sangharakshita, *Moving Against the Stream*, Windhorse Publications, Birmingham 2003, p. 212 (*Complete Works*, vol. 23).
7 Sangharakshita, *The Rainbow Road from Tooting Broadway*

to Kalimpong, *Complete Works* vol. 20, p. 36.
8 Sangharakshita, *The Rainbow Road from Tooting Broadway to Kalimpong, Complete Works* vol. 20, p. 100.
9 Sangharakshita, *In the Sign of the Golden Wheel*, Windhorse Publications, Birmingham 1996, p. 106 (*Complete Works*, vol. 22).
10 *Urthona*, issue 29, p. 46.
11 'A Complex Personality – a Note' (17–27 July 2017), in *Adhisthana Writings*. Towards the end of his life Sangharakshita wrote a number of short pieces which were made available at the time of writing on his website and in the Order newsletter *Shabda*. They will be found in *Complete Works*, vol. 26.
12 Lama Anagarika Govinda's Introduction to 'The Veil of Stars', p. 477.
13 Percy Bysshe Shelley, *A Defence of Poetry* (written in 1821).
14 'St Jerome Revisited', in Sangharakshita, *The Priceless Jewel*, Windhorse Publications, Glasgow 1993, p. 90 (*Complete Works*, vol. 26).
15 Shakespeare, *King John,* Act v, Scene vii, line 41.
16 Edwin Arnold, *The Light of Asia* (1879), book 3.
17 Sangharakshita, *Milarepa and the Art of Discipleship II*, *Complete Works*, vol. 19, p. 350.
18 All trace of this talk seems to have been lost. However, the poem 'Meditation' is discussed in the first of Sangharakshita's ten conversations with Saddhanandi; see p. 41.
19 *Phaedrus* 244a.
20 See D. T. Suzuki (trans.), *The Laṅkāvatāra Sūtra*, George Routledge, London 1932, pp. 124–5.
21 This is now the basis of the Sangharakshita Library at Adhisthana.
22 *Sutta Nipāta* 10.4.
23 Glenn Hoddle was manager of England's national football team 1996–1999.
24 'I am certain of nothing but of the holiness of the Heart's affections and the truth of Imagination.' John Keats, in a letter to Benjamin Bailey, 22 November 1817.
25 Exodus 3: 1–5, Authorized Version.
26 *Dhammapada* 348, Sangharakshita's translation.
27 These memoirs were published as *Moving Against the Stream* (*Complete Works*, vol. 23).
28 *The Religion of Art* was first published in 1973 by the Arya Maitreya Mandala in a book celebrating the 75th birthday of Lama Anagarika Govinda. It is included in *Complete Works*, vol. 26.
29 *Dhammapada* 354.
30 See chapter 1 of the *Śūraṅgama Sūtra* in Dwight Goddard (ed.) *A Buddhist Bible*, Beacon Press, Boston 1970, p. 112: 'The first thing that impressed me were the thirty-two marks of excellency in the Lord's

personality. They appeared to me so fine, as tender and brilliant, and transparent as a crystal.'

31 Clothes in the world certainly have no scent in themselves, but if a man permeates them with perfumes, then they come to have a scent. It is just the same with the case we are speaking of. The pure state of Suchness certainly has no defilement, but if it is permeated by ignorance, then the marks of defilement appear on it. The defiled state of ignorance is indeed devoid of any purifying force, but if it is permeated by Suchness, then it will come to have a purifying influence.

Aśvaghoṣa, *The Awakening of Faith in the Mahāyāna*, trans. Yoshiko S. Hakeda, Columbia University Press, New York 1967, p. 56.

32 From *Travel Letters*, Windhorse Publications, Glasgow 1985, pp. 173–4 (*Complete Works*, vol. 24).

33 The poem was written at the Raipur Ashram; see *The Rainbow Road from Tooting Broadway to Kalimpong*, *Complete Works* vol. 20, p. 217.

34 Herman Melville, *Moby Dick*, chapter 87.

35 For Sangharakshita's account of his visit to Delphi, see *Moving Against the Stream*, Windhorse Publications, Birmingham 2003, pp. 237ff. (*Complete Works*, vol. 23).

36 Stephen Spender, 'The Truly Great', published in *Collected Poems 1928–1953*.

37 For Sangharakshita's account of this, see his memoir *Moving Against the Stream*, Windhorse Publications, Birmingham 2003, p. 388 (*Complete Works*, vol. 23).

38 This story is told in the *Kakacūpama Sutta*, *Majjhima Nikāya* (i.125–6); see Bhikkhu Ñāṇamoli and Bhikkhu Bodhi (trans.), *The Middle Length Discourses of the Buddha*, Wisdom Publications, Boston 1995, pp. 219–20; or I. B. Horner (trans.), *The Collection of the Middle Length Sayings*, vol. i, Pali Text Society, London 1967, p. 162.

39 This was a saying of Richard of St Victor, a medieval Scottish philosopher and theologian who was the prior of the Abbey of St Victor in Paris in the twelfth century.

40 Gandhi often reflected on ends and means and the connection between them; for example, he once wrote (*Hind Swaraj*, 1952),

> The means may be likened to a seed, the end to a tree, and there is just the same inviolable connection between the means and the end as there is between the seed and the tree.

41 Matthew Arnold, *Empedocles on Etna*, act 1, scene 2, line 237.

42 For Sangharakshita's initial realizations about Sangharakshita I and Sangharakshita II, see his memoir *The Rainbow Road from Tooting Broadway to Kalimpong, Complete Works* vol. 20, pp. 449–52.

43 'The Time Has Come' – see page 321.

44 The story of this event (which took place in Los Angeles) is told in Michael Schumacher, *Dharma Lion: a critical biography of Allen Ginsberg*, St Martin's Press, London 1992, p. 242.

45 For a little about Sangharakshita's connection with Ginsberg, see 'With Allen Ginsberg in Kalimpong', in Sangharakshita, *The Priceless Jewel*, Windhorse Publications, Glasgow 1993, pp. 215–8 (*Complete Works*, vol. 22); and Sangharakshita's poem, 'In Memory of Allen Ginsberg', in this volume, p. 411.

46 Sangharakshita learned these communication exercises in the early sixties from Muriel Payne, an English educationalist working in India who had found that teachers, generally speaking, taught very poorly and came to the conclusion that this was because they were not able to communicate, either with their pupils or with one another. She therefore devised a series of communication exercises. Sangharakshita gathered a couple of dozen friends and arranged for Miss Payne to conduct a series of workshops, at which she taught these exercises, which Sangharakshita was convinced brought one to a level of communication way beyond that which normally exists between people. 'During those exercises I experienced communication as I had never done before, especially when I did the exercises with her.' Each person says, turn by turn, a banal phrase such as, 'Do birds fly?' In Sangharakshita's experience, 'Through a verbal exchange that does not have any objective meaning you experience the other person as though there is, one might almost say, a merging of your two beings – it is very like that experience of the angels merging that Raphael describes in *Paradise Lost*.' Some years later, when leading FWBO retreats, Sangharakshita introduced these exercises and they proved very successful. (Condensed from a conversation between Sangharakshita, Mahamati, and Subhuti in 2009.)

47 Edward Burne-Jones was a British Pre-Raphaelite painter who painted *The Beguiling of Merlin* in the 1870s. The painting is in the collection of the Lady Lever Art Gallery at Port Sunlight.

48 Matthew 6:21.

49 This conversation is recounted in the *Mahāparinibbāna Sutta*,

50 *Dīgha Nikāya* (ii.101); see M. Walshe (trans.), *The Long Discourses of the Buddha*, Wisdom Publications, Boston 1995, p. 245; or T. W. Rhys Davids (trans.), *Dialogues of the Buddha*, part 2, Pali Text Society, London 1971, p. 107.

50 Sangharakshita, *In the Sign of the Golden Wheel*, Windhorse Publications, Birmingham 1996, p. 35 (*Complete Works*, vol. 22).

51 *Saṃyutta Nikāya* v.437 (56.31); see Bhikkhu Bodhi (trans.), *The Connected Discourses of the Buddha*, Wisdom Publications, Boston 2000, pp. 1857–8; or F. L. Woodward (trans.), *The Book of the Kindred Sayings*, vol. v, Pali Text Society, London 1956, p. 370.

52 The last of the eight qualities of the great ocean described by the Buddha in *Udāna* 5.5 (*Uposatha Sutta*) is that it is 'the abode of vast creatures'.

53 Proverbs 29:18

54 Written after studying the writings of Arthur Avalon (Sir John Woodroffe) on the Hindu Tantra, as well as his translations of Sanskrit and Bengali Tantric texts (S).

55 Some of the imagery of the poem derives from Sinhalese classical poetry (S).

56 *Dhammapada* 175. Some sources give *haṃsādiccapatha yanti* here, which means the same thing.

57 Verse 5. The three worlds are the *kāmaloka* or world of sensuous experience, the *rūpaloka* or world of (archetypal) form, and the *arūpaloka* or formless world; and the three bodies are the corresponding aspects/levels of our total (phenomenal) being, through which we have access to these worlds (S).

58 Clare Cameron, editor of the *Middle Way*, was a friend of Sangharakshita and a mentor and guide in his early development as a poet. As editor of the journal she was not averse to making improvements to submissions when she saw fit and rewrote the second stanza of 'Buddhaṃ Saraṇaṃ Gacchāmi'. Many years later Sangharakshita still recalled clearly the lines he originally wrote. Thus the poem as it appears here is as he originally intended it.

59 Verse 1. The asses were in fact mules (S).

60 William Spencer Bagdatopoulos (1888–1965) was a painter and commercial artist known for his depictions of people and monuments in the East.

61 From W. B. Yeats' poem 'The Phases of the Moon', published in his 1919 collection *The Wild Swans at Coole*.

62 In his 1823 essay 'My First Acquaintance with Poets', the essayist William Hazlitt quoted Coleridge as saying of the poet William Wordsworth that 'Wordsworth always wrote (if he could) walking up and

down a straight gravel walk, or in some spot where the continuity of his verse met with no collateral interruption'.

63 Verse 2. The emperor Aśoka (in the poem the name is a dysllable) inscribed his edicts on columns and rocks in many parts of India. In some of these he testifies to his faith in the Buddha and his teaching (S).

64 'The greatest Mahāyāna sage' is Nāgārjuna. A *nāga* is a serpent or dragon, the *arjuna* a kind of tree; hence 'dragon tree' in the last line of the poem (S).

65 Verse 1. The poet is Baudelaire, who in his 'Hymne à la beauté' (*Les Fleurs du Mal* 22) asks 'Viens-tu du ciel profond ou sors-tu de l'abîme, / O Beauté?' (S).

66 Verse 1. The King is Aśoka, who on seeing the horrors wrought by his conquest of Kalinga abandoned violence for non-violence. 'Peacock tent' because the peacock was the emblem of the Maurya or Peacock Dynasty to which he belonged. I imagine the tent to have been emblazoned with peacocks or to have displayed a peacock banner (S).

67 Nālandā was a great Buddhist monastery and university in the ancient kingdom of Magadha (modern-day Bihar) which flourished from the fifth century CE until the early thirteenth century, when it was destroyed by Muslim invaders. Its ruins can still be visited and a modern university has recently been established nearby.

68 Lines 8 and 9. 'Him whose keen mind could not brook / Impurity or error' refers to the Tibetan reformer Tsongkhapa (S).

69 Stefan George (1868–1933) was a German symbolist poet and translator.

70 Sappho was a poet of ancient Greece (c.630–c.570 BCE). She lived on the island of Lesbos and wrote a great deal of poetry, though only a fraction of it survives today.

71 J. J. Jones (trans.), *Mahāvastu*, vol. ii, Luzac, London 1952, pp. 131–2 (*Mahāvastu* ii.137).

72 Line 5. The 'blue-black elephants of heaven' are the storm clouds. The image is traditional in Sanskrit poetry (S).

73 Last verse. 48+60 = 108, which according to Indian tradition is an auspicious number (S).

74 These words were written by the Irish poet W. B. Yeats in an article published in the *Irish Statesman* (23 August 1919):

> One day when I was twenty-three or twenty-four this sentence seemed to form in my head, without my willing it, much as sentences form when we are half-asleep: 'Hammer your thoughts into unity.' For days I could think of nothing else, and for years I tested all I did by that sentence.

75 2. To Miss——. Miss—— was Ven. Sochu Suzuki's charming young Japanese companion; hence 'a delicate touch of green' and 'the red blur of the rising sun' (S).

76 Although the statue in London's Piccadilly is popularly known as Eros, it was intended by its sculptor Alfred Gilbert to be the brother of Eros, Anteros, who represents (in Gilbert's words) 'reflective and mature love, as opposed to Eros or Cupid, the frivolous tyrant'. The fountain was erected in Piccadilly in 1892–3 to celebrate the philanthropist Anthony Ashley Cooper, seventh Earl of Shaftesbury.

77 The chairlift continues to take visitors up and down the hill called Vulture's Peak, near Rajgir in northern India, where the historical Buddha is said to have taught, and the mythical scene of the teaching of the *Saddharma Puṇḍarīka Sūtra* by the archetypal Buddha. It is also possible for the pilgrim to walk up the hill!

78 Prompted by a painting in the Academy Gallery, Helsinki (S).

79 The strange land is Finland (S).

80 Part of the mythology devised by the English poet and painter William Blake (1757–1827) was the 'fourfold vision', as evoked in his works *The Four Zoas* and in the prophetic book *Jerusalem*:

> I see the Four-fold Man, The Humanity in deadly sleep And its fallen Emanation, the Spectre and its cruel Shadow.

81 Los and Enitharmon are two of the characters in William Blake's self-devised mythology, and among the places in his imagined world are those mentioned in this poem: Urthona, Jerusalem, Albion, and Golgonooza.

82 'Every day is a good day' is a phrase from Case 6 of the Zen classic *The Blue Cliff Record*.

83 Verse 5. The poem was written on the eve of a visit to the Antipodes, where – from the standpoint of England – 'night is day, and day is night.' (S)

84 The *Vimalakīrti-nirdeśa* is a Mahāyāna text whose main protagonists are the layman bodhisattva Vimalakīrti and the archetypal bodhisattva Mañjuśrī.

85 The poet and critic Matthew Arnold described Percy Bysshe Shelley as 'a beautiful and ineffectual angel, beating in the void his luminous wings in vain' in an essay on Byron in his 1888 collection *Essays in Criticism*.

86 The title suggests that the reference is to a poem by the seventeenth-century Royalist poet Richard Lovelace, but 'My mind to me a kingdom is' is in fact the first line of a poem by the sixteenth-century English poet Sir Edward Dyer.

87 Rainer Maria Rilke (1875–1926) was a Bohemian-

	Austrian mystical poet. Among his best-known works are *Duino Elegies* and *Sonnets to Orpheus*; this poem seems to recall the latter.	93	A French writer and film maker, Jean Cocteau's 1959 film *Le Testament d'Orphée* features Minerva.
88	Among the works of English poet and painter William Blake (1757–1827), *Jerusalem*, from one of the plates of his poem *Milton*, is one of the best-known; this poem recalls it.	94	Abū-Saʿīd Abul-Khayr was a Persian Sufi mystic and poet of the eighth–ninth century CE.
		95	'Toby' is the late T. Christmas Humphreys, Q. C., Founder-President of the Buddhist Society and judge of the High Court (S).
89	These poems 'came' to me one night when I couldn't sleep, in the course of about an hour. I do not know whether they can really be called poems. Perhaps they are Allen Ginsberg's 'first thoughts'. Whether they are 'best thoughts' is another matter. Anyway, I give them just as they came (S).	96	Tarashri was a member of the Western Buddhist Order (as it was still called when she belonged to it) and died in 1988. She lived in Norfolk.
		97	Guhyaloka is a men's retreat centre in Spain where Sangharakshita used to go on solitary retreat. The reference is to Thomas Hardy's poem 'Great Things', published in 1917.
90	The reference is to a retreat centre run by the Triratna Buddhist Order in Maharashtra, India.		
91	The acknowledgement is to the English twentieth-century poet A. E. Housman because the form of the poem echoes a poem from Housman's collection *A Shropshire Lad*, whose first two lines are	98	The Guru of Dharsendo was Dhardo Rimpoche, Sangharakshita's teacher and friend.
		99	According to Buddhist legend (*Udāna* 2.1) Mucalinda was a great snake who spread out his hood to shelter the Buddha during a storm after his Enlightenment, and, as the poem suggests, was transformed into a youth.

> Loveliest of trees, the cherry now
> Is hung with bloom along the bough.

92	*Verse 3*. The 'sumptuous pile' is the Doge's Palace and the 'three architectures' are (according to Ruskin) the Romanesque, the Gothic, and the Saracenic (S).	100	The Sage of Weimar is Goethe. Helen and Euphorion (Byron) appear in *Faust*, Part Two (S).
		101	Neoplatonism is a term used to describe a succession of philosophers in the Platonic tradition from the third to the sixth century CE, beginning

with the Egyptian Plotinus. Sangharakshita was deeply interested in Neoplatonism.

102 The reference is to the traditional story that Zen began when the Buddha held up a golden flower and his disciple Mahākāśyapa understood what he meant.

103 The Defenestrations of Prague were the occasions when first the 'Protestant' Hussites (1419) and then the Catholics threw their opponents out of the windows of the Town Hall (S).

104 The reference is to two Arthurian kings who sent other men courting on their behalf. King Mark of Cornwall sent his nephew Tristan to woo Isolde, but (through a love potion), it was Tristan and Isolde who became lovers. And according to one version of the story, King Arthur himself sent Sir Lancelot to meet Guinevere and bring her to Camelot, but Guinevere mistook Lancelot for Arthur and fell in love with him.

The third verse of the poem is a reference to Shakespeare's lines in Hamlet (Act V, Scene ii):

> There's a divinity that shapes our ends,
> Rough-hew them how we will.

105 *Verse 5.* The Fury is Atropos, the Fate who in Greek mythology cuts the thread of a man's life (S).

106 Ananda was one of the first people to be ordained within the Western Buddhist Order (later the Triratna Buddhist Order) in 1968. A fellow poet, he and Sangharakshita were friends throughout the years. The last line of the poem, 'Letters mingle souls' comes from a poem, 'To Sir Henry Wotton', by the seventeenth-century poet John Donne.

107 Omraam Mikhaël Aïvanhov (1900–86) was a Bulgarian philosopher and mystic. Sangharakshita's reference here suggests that the poem was perhaps written in response to a reading of Aïvanhov's work *The Splendour of Tiphareth: the Yoga of the Sun.*

108 John Donne (1572–1631) was an ardent love poet in his younger years, but he was later, as Dean of St Paul's Cathedral, the writer of the Holy Sonnets. The last line of the poem refers to Donne's most famous words, the passage from a sermon which begins 'No man is an island' and ends 'Never send to know for whom the bell tolls. It tolls for thee.'

109 This is a pastiche of Philip Larkin's infamous poem 'This Be the Verse', first published in 1971.

110 Guhyaloka, 'the secret valley', is a men's retreat centre in the Spanish mountains near Alicante. It was founded in 1986 and Sangharakshita spent much time there.

111 The poem is about the German legend of Tannhäuser, also the subject of Wagner's opera.

112 Lama Govinda was a German Buddhist scholar and writer whom Sangharakshita met and became friends with in the Himalayan town of Kalimpong, the two in particular sharing a belief in the important place of art in the spiritual life. Lama Govinda lived in Capri in the 1920s and it was there that he first came across Buddhism. The 'dome of Kailash' of the last line of the poem is Mount Kailash, the sacred Tibetan mountain around which pilgrims circumambulate and where Lama Govinda spent some time.

113 *The White Goddess*, an exploration of poetic myth, is one of the best-known works of the poet and writer Robert Graves (1895–1985).

114 Arthadarshin was a member of the Western Buddhist Order who died of heart failure in 1999 while on retreat at Guhyaloka.

115 Edward Burne-Jones was a British Pre-Raphaelite painter who painted *The Beguiling of Merlin* in the 1870s. The painting is in the collection of the Lady Lever Art Gallery at Port Sunlight.

116 Michal, the Interpreter, was ordained by Sangharakshita in 2004 and given the name Nityabandhu.

117 Edward Burne-Jones was a British Pre-Raphaelite painter who painted *The Beguiling of Merlin* in the 1870s. The painting is in the collection of the Lady Lever Art Gallery at Port Sunlight.

118 This poem is dedicated to Deji, the Tibetan partner of Sangharakshita's friend Paramartha.

119 This is another poem about Deji.

120 This is a reference to Sangharakshita's 1952 poem 'Up and Down the Gravel Path...'

INDEX OF FIRST LINES

A cobra in a basket 445
A golden flower held up, an answering smile – 404
A man was walking behind me 390
A solitary boy would sail his boat 249
A solitary figure, you pick your way 311
A sweet singing bird 281
A tangle of knotted branches on either side 311
A wind was in my sails. It blew 450
Above black pine-trees, on my homeward way 289
Above me broods 175
Across the vastness of the sky 176
After the storm, the day dawns calm and fair 359
After three months rain 273
Again with hideous thud the club descends 376
Against a sky of purest turquoise rayed 280
All dreams of the soul 232
All living things should worship 289
All pleasures of all sense; the fickle mind's 252
Aloft on its tall stalk the sunflower hangs 343
Aloft the many-petalled lotus rears 181
Alone in the fork 307

Along the tempting byways 290
Always a great reader 327
Among all branched things, I for beauty choose 217
Among dense trees, dimly lit 311
Among the mighty mountains sojourning 349
Among the rich Autumn foliage 305
'An ineffectual angel', unable to do 350
Ānanda, thirty years ago 420
Another youthful hero bites the dust 445
Appearing from the depth of heaven 417
As bellows roar, and red coals glow 221
As children on a Summer's day 463
As the last gong-stroke dies away 307
Asked 'What is Buddhism?' off they go 286
At the wood's edge, a solitary hut 311
Athens, the olive and grey eyes 155
Autumn clouds, like snow 234
Away with prosy greetings! 298

Back in the magic valley 424
Back to where the paths divided 288
Bank holiday – 323
Barking dogs all round me 423
Beauty such as yours 446
Because I could not muse apart 220

Before me through the evening air 198
Behind, ascending by degrees 374
Behold the Clouded Dragon – 172
Behold the Lion of St Mark! 377
Believe not what you have heard 270
Below in the deep 219
Best minds, he called us, of his generation 413
Better, O Bull of Memphis, that we should 287
Between the mountain-crest and valley hung 268
Between the tree-clad hills the misty plain 367
Beyond the deserted paddock, a dark wood; 310
Blake walked among the stones of fire 360
Blessed be the noble tree 453
Blessed is my secret garden 393
Blond, blue-eyed, and beautiful 453
Bowing I stand 398
Brain says, Beauty will perish 230
Breakfast was on the balcony 442
Build thou upon thy spirit's mountainous height 197
By hope inspired, we make – though foiled 349

Capri at Night. A harmony 429
Careful! This morning 306
Cavern or shed, in the one-candled gloom 312
Cheep cheep cheep goes the sparrow 395
Close, eyes; behold no more the rich array 276
Compassion is far more than emotion 215
Croak croak croak goes the raven 396
Crows, in their collective spite 445
Crystal ball, showing 403
Cut off from what I really think and feel 348

'Dance, children, dance 430
Dawn brightening 234
Dear daughter of a tropic isle 369
Defenestration was the word in Prague 405

Do we not love the dawn, when first 279
'Don't touch the red-hot pokers' 434
Dragons were slain here 499
Drenched in silence, drenched in sunlight 435

East is East and West is West 432
Elizabeth Tudor 432
Evening. Unstirred the western cloudlets lie 272
'Every day is a good day' 342

Façade after façade, along the Embankment 310
Fall, Rain, upon the dry and thirsty land 156
Field-freshening rain 214
Flanked by the lotus red 346
Flowers, that turn their faces to the sun 277
Flying slower, flying faster 373
For Poetry, this 'poem' shows 288
For seven years a mask I wore 309
For the Boundless, the Unlimited, the Infinite I long 229
For years I bilked my debts, and bilked with mirth 379
For you in the North, the first Winter snow; 310
For you the restless ocean 400
Forgive me if I have stained 230
From a sky of unclouded 307
From his own book of spells she chants 452
From pavilions of azure 285
From the ever-faithful Present 308
From the four compass-points a green, a gold 295
From the train window – 306
From the unlocked cage of my heart 163
From tone to tone of azure 278
From world to world, from star to star 454
Frozen tulips, mauve and green 416
Full twenty years I stayed away 449

Gods in the gallery I behold 400
Golden in laughing sunlight 218

598 / INDEX OF FIRST LINES

'Grain threshed and ready?' 414
Grasping the plough, with horse or ox they till 356
Grey sleepers, wrapped in noisome rags 265
Guinevere loved the King 438

Half hoof-deep in the salt-encrusted sands 350
'Hammer your thoughts into a unity' 304
Hardly in words these lips can tell 204
'Have it taken together with birch trees' 444
He could not find it with his wife and child 272
He sits at ease upon the rocks 375
He wanted that His followers should be flames 286
Heavy-winged, the last crow disappears 311
Her skin is greasy, and her garments stink 374
Here on the river-brink I sit 211
Here perpetual incense burns 167
Here, through the deep dark valley 270
Here, where the Goatherd's banyan-tree 210
Heretics roasted for the love of Christ 376
High in the mountains, up creeks 353
His dreams were visions. In the night 402
Horror and anguish! Madness and despair! 355
Hour after hour, day 324
How bare and dead the branch! 300
How beautiful is Berkeley Square! 303
How can I scorn the beggar's lot 207
How can wracked soul and ruined body pass 262
How did it feel 328
How like a bird it comes and goes 266
How still the mists lie 234
How sweet is love's austerity 223
How sweet it is, how sweet again 177

I am Earth 440
I am sitting in the late afternoon sunshine 444
I am the Angel in the House 410
I am the Windhorse! 338
I come to you with four gifts 335
I did not seek, and so I found 165
I dived and found a pearl, but when I brought 401
I do not want to see this world of Thine 159
I feel like going on my knees 233
I have found you, India 212
I have never regretted 414
I laughed at death with women, wine, and song 379
I listened all day for the knock of the Stranger 184
I'll write my poems for my friends 243
I passed the square and scripted gate 283
I questioned, in my greener age 231
I rejoice in the merits 392
I remember a pool of blue lotuses 232
I saw a woman, beautiful but blind 437
I saw His shining footprints 187
I saw one misty morning 222
I saw two men, who nailed upon a cross 274
I should like to live 315
I should like to speak 313
I think there lives more wisdom 239
I understand the blind old king 411
I walked across to the lecture hall 382
I want to break out 309
I will not read the scriptures 186
If but the soil were richer 284
If it could speak, the white hawthorn 438
If thirst for truth doth like a fire 193
If you're 'not' a poet you run the risk 456
Impermanent, impermanent! 295
In a dream more like a vision 454
In Amitābha's paradise, we're told 372
In shine and shower 380
In the dim green stillness of the pool 225

In the midnight of the dense ignorance
　of the world　202
In the morning, in the morning　455
In the saffron robe of yearning　213
In vain we flee before the King of
　Death　445
In your apt mouth　442
It is not love that seeks to bind　223
It was Lilith out of Eden　390
It was the season after rain　170

Jack Donne he was a Roaring
　Boy　422

Knit with my heart these trumpets
　seem　237
Kwark kwark goes the eagle　397

Last year the lightning　306
Late in your life you found the
　Eightfold Way　383
Leafless, the walnut's twisting
　branches spread　343
Lean, strenuous, resolute, He passed
　His days　296
Let my life burn like incense　219
Living in Paradise　386
London Bridge is falling down　404
Lord, from my shadows do I flee　164
Lord of the black locks, lord of thy
　handmaid　178
Lord of the Lotus, Flaming Sword,
　and Book　275
Los and Enitharmon wandered over
　the graves　342
Lost in these yellowing Autumn
　woods, I see　233
Love finds no fulfilment　221
Love is of so delicate a nature, I
　said　442
Love springs into the Bodhisattva's
　eyes　156
Lying on the bank　306

Mañjuśrī sits upon his throne of
　gold　349
Mankind owes a profound
　apology　447
Many were the friends who sought
　with eager hands　226
Meet my best friend, Mr Wireless　448

Men plucked like flowers which
　pass　285
Men think that they have
　understood　242
Merlin, in his cell of glass　439
Miao miao miao goes the
　peacock　396
Mirror, mirror on the wall　358
Mock me not, O Rose, that I am
　hidden　229
More than ten years ago, old Father
　Thames　276
Mountains bathed in mist　211
Moved by the spirit of the times, the
　heir　347
My friend has gone　394
My Granny said that little girls　426
My heart was held within an Angel's
　hands　361
My heart-wick now is charred with
　sin　215
My life is a dance　403
My mind is a theatre　447
My mind to me a kingdom is　357
My mind's a silver awning　351
My soul between the feeling and the
　thought　286
My Spectre stands there white as
　snow　340
My wisdom cold? It was not cold　378
Myself into his book I hurled　405

Nightrace of silver-white coach of
　ghostly　324
No fruit without the seed. Desire　248
Noblest of schools, the Royal
　today　375
Not where the gardens blossom　250
Now he's gone, the best of
　squirrels　258
Now it is early summer, and the
　woods　240

O great golden image!　158
O limpid river in the evening air　157
O Sacred Silence, now at last　361
Often do I remember the huge untidy
　nests　243
Often, now, I find myself　505
Oh darkness is done　234

Oh Death himself was Orpheus' audience! 257
Oh for a Persian garden 373
'Oh what do you want, you wandering man 334
Old frog on the brink 294
On my birthday 444
On the blue hill-side 217
On the hillside wait 234
On wind-tossed branches 306
Once more a virgin acolyte he stands 347
Once more the deep blue Winter skies 236
One by one the Gods 345
One day I must leave you, my old friends 404
One need, and one need only 210
One wears a yellow robe 399
One white wave of snow 219
One would be far too many 305
Osiris is green in colour, dark green 352
Our heart's a shapeless clay-lump 274
Out of the sunset with the Evening Star 200
Outstretched upon the sandy ground 206

Páck your suitcase, cátch the train 333
Paths left behind, I lose myself 311
Peach-bloom, each Springtide, fills my heart with grief 281
People like things labelled. They want to know 402
Petals 316
Pine-scent is a great thing 391
Pink and white upon the hillside 512
Poetry has a double root 433
Proudly they stood, those towers, a monument 452

Read aloud 404
Reading some books, you'd think the Buddha-Way 278
Red as roses blushing 259
Red were the leaves upon the beech 416
Red-bannered hatred fills the streets 258
Riding a tiger 419

Roll forth, O Conquering Wheel 169
Roll on, roll on for ever 226
Round this boundless universe's 262
Rusty pine-needles 336

Salutation to the Lady from the Land of Snows 459
Say Padmaloka and there arises a vision 457
Seeing this world, this hapless world 214
Seek not in gloomy charnel-grounds to see 372
Seen through the fanlight 403
Selling wild orchids at my door one day 241
Shakespeare, Milton, Wordsworth, Coleridge 412
Shells from the sea, shells 317
Short were my steps upon the earth, and few 379
Silent he sits, the white-complexioned god 458
Since that auspicious Full-Moon Day 188
Since that his eyes were like two wells 256
Sing? This is not the time for singing 402
So love grew up between us like a flower 379
Some men can find no word for Love 237
Space, infinite space! Heather 329
Spring, in my boyhood it was understood 285
St Francis in the Umbrian glades 366
Stand still, O Time, that I may see 393
Suddenly he was there. The darkness glowed 312
Sun, moon, the mountains and the plain 239
Sunk in the stream-bed where the hills begin 372
Supine he lies, the blue-complexioned god 458
Surely King Mark was mad 406
Swanlike, upon the Sun-Path let me soar 182

Taking a sudden turn, the sunlit path 310
Talkative one morning, the Cypriot barber 329
Telegrams deal with matters 362
Tenderly smiling, White Tārā 304
That is all very well... 232
That you must feed the brain with facts, I see 453
The ashes of all my heartaches 222
The Brahmas sit on thrones of light 451
The candle has long since guttered and died 310
The coming of love is mysterious as the flight of a bird 483
The dim sun sinks to rest 181
'The early Christians 330
'The economic argument 437
The gardener crops his rose-tree's hundred buds 219
The gods, throned in their radiant overworld 354
The grey clouds are my friends 446
The hills of the horizon 284
The icy wind has planted 255
The lion, the horse, the elephant, the whale 356
The loose red earth is washed away 242
The Lotus blooms tonight 208
The moon is cold and hard and small 255
The morning sunshine saturates the heavenly blue 302
The multitudinous whisper 306
The name of the place 389
The noise of day is hushed at last 167
The oak stands in the forest 387
The past is in the mind 390
The people of Bethnal Green are not beautiful 385
The periwinkle flowers among the stones 294
The poet has his Muse 433
The poet is the world's interpreter 359
The poet listens for the inevitable word 436
The poetry of friendship 407
The politician on the platform 300
The quick sap rises in the dry stalk 302

The rain has been falling all day 244
The red leaf falls upon the lake below 300
The red rose does not whisper 240
The ship sails on its way 446
The small blue monkey 305
The stream of my desire no more 264
The surest way of gaining is to give 245
The swiftest, sweetest pen could ne'er indite 184
The Teesta in the Summer 283
The third day of the slaughter saw a change 271
The thunders rolled beneath me, as I sate 258
The time has come 323
The Tree! the Tree! the Wish-fulfilling Tree! 354
The wisest doubt if Truth 259
The wooden hut stands empty amid the pine trees 435
The world continues on its crazy course 445
The world is full of falling leaves 221
The year will soon be at an end 436
There is a land more lovely 389
There wends a long procession 209
These gods and goddesses that men have framed 290
They are decidedly 326
They bring you up, your mum and dad 423
They sing with fairest looks and sweetest breath 348
Thine is the outward action 166
Think not, my friends, that piling stone on stone 274
This bright Autumn morning 305
Those who have hid themselves on heights of snow 183
Thou art not dead, nor dost Thou even sleep 196
Though depths of perfect azure 284
Though ninety million miles away 418
Though one's food is not perfect 331
Though rained thy kisses on His hand 228
Though sinks into the western hills 287

Though veil on veil of gleaming blue 240
Though vigorously the high wind shakes the bough 300
Three nails were enough for your Lord. But you 308
Three Summers and three Autumns have I seen 344
Three weeks before he died 318
Three years in earth had Johnson slept 370
Thrown on the white wall 352
Tired of the crimson curtain 194
'Tis Chaucer's month, the merry month 341
To Him Who on that night of sleeping flowers 273
To stand naked 307
Tonight at noon 320
Too long have I been a camel 319
Tread softly as a cat 231
Trill trill trill goes the blackbird 395
Truth is not truth, unless to men it is 203
Tu-whit tu-whoo goes the owl 397
Turn away from the world, weary pilgrim 195
Twisting, writhing, leaping 291

Up and down the gravel path 238
'Up and down the gravel path 460
Up the side of the sacred mountain 325

Visitors all day! 294

Walking along the mountain paths 238
Water falls from stone 242
Water from the thawed-out snow 164
We are the People 301
We cannot sing as Orpheus wist 254
We cry that we are weak although 185
We have interesting neighbours 384
We know when market-day is near 235
We realize that war has snags 445
We walked where thick green bamboo groves 224
We wandered in the bluebell wood 456

We waved our little Union Jacks 431
We who have seen men murdered 270
Well might the Poet question 269
What a fantastic creature is the poet 228
What agonies await him now 388
What can it do, when friends avert 368
What does the forest whisper 408
What I am left with 415
What is the wine you bring me, Cupbearer? 446
What said you, *Short, swift swallow-flights of song?* 353
What though so near upon the tree 281
What though the mining's done, th' ore told? 281
What though with cloud the sky be grey 287
What thoughts are present to Thy mind 173
What will you say to those 260
When Inspiration cracks the moulds of verse 278
When shall a man from all his wants be freed 381
Whén the latency of thought 162
When the pearls of morning 160
When Truth and Good like phantoms fade 168
Whence come these asses, brazen-belled 216
Where green and purple strips of earth 174
Where hills humped, there must be 263
Where the ice glitters, where untrodden snows 246
Whether within his mind dark forces rolled 256
White clouds on the hills 242
White mist drifts down the valley dim 218
White-winged for an instant 307
'Who is this, in pilgrim garments 428
With barrel-bellies, mouths like needle-eyes 355
With grey-green fir and blue-black pine communing 267

INDEX OF FIRST LINES / 603

With kingcups from the meadow 282
With looks demure, and tress that
   down her cheek 376
With slender rosy stem 224
With sweet compassionate faces 293
'With your holy vows 192
Within the shadowy colonnade 401
Wonder it is to dwell at last 292
'Work is the companion' 400
Work out the secret of your blood.
   The bright 277

Yellow in green, by woods we chance
   to pass 303
Yet shall my soul burn upward like a
   fire 271

You and I, brother, we dreamt the
   same dream 427
You are the distance 321
You dance with emperor, pope, and
   king 415
You remind me of whatever's made of
   gold – 287
You revealed to me the face of the
   Green Goddess 443
You were my mother once, the
   Scriptures say 297
You wrote four letters, one 314
Your beauty, in repose, is like a
   vase 264
Your sadness is my sadness, friend,
   and so 275

INDEX OF SUBJECTS, THEMES, AND REFERENCES

This index covers the commentarial elements of this volume and also includes the subjects and themes of the poems, to help the reader to locate specific poems and trace themes throughout the collection. Subjects and themes are presented in order of page number (or the page number at the start of a sequence), so they follow roughly the chronological order of the collection as a whole.

abominable snowman 246–7
Abū Sa'īd 381, 594n
action: vitality in 20; while maintaining stillness 47–8; inability to act 439
Adam: in the garden lii–liv, 313; in *Paradise Lost* 19; and Lilith 390; poems as cold Adams 404
Adam's Peak 27
Adhisthana 587n
adultery 104–5
aesthetic appreciation 55–6, 538–9
aestheticism 28–9
air element xxx–xxxi, 440–1
Aivanhov, Omraam Mikhael 418, 595n
Akong Rimpoche 92
alchemy xxvii, 405
alms collection 204–5; metaphor for spiritual quest 213
aloneness: not easy to follow the spiritual path on one's own 34; of the Buddha 257; no companion save the wind and stars 271; Man through the hideous dark must plunge alone 278; wish to live alone 315; without a friend, without a home 468
See also loneliness
Ambedkar, Dr B. R. xxv, 9, 123–5; bodhisattva-like 129
Amitābha lviii, 372
Ānanda (the Buddha's disciple) 31, 160–1
Ananda (Stephen Parr, member of the Triratna Buddhist Order) 305, 310–11, 420–1, 595n
androgyny 340
angels: making 349; heart held by 361; telegrams 364; characteristics 365; Tobias and 375; in the House 410–1; and the poet 436; depicted in a fresco 544, 546
anger 215

animals: cruelty towards 54, 235; treating kindly 58, 366; in the Wheel of Life 356
See also individual names
animism xlii, 233, 418
Anteros 593
Anthony, St 376
Antinous 258
anxiety: anxious thoughts 166, 167; hindrance to meditation 572
ape 447
Aphrodite 395, 512
Apollo 250, 326, 395, 420, 512
apology 51, 447
appreciation 332
Arahants 189
argument 'just to win' 246
Arnold, Edwin, *The Light of Asia* lvi–lvii
Arnold, Matthew 83, 350
art: appreciation of 140; critique of Buddha images 326; Royal Academy exhibition 375–7
Arthadarshin 435, 596n
artist 110, 245, 544–53
Arthur, King 97–110, 406, 438–9, 500, 595n; Round Table 99–100, 107, 439
Ashoka 232, 243, 271, 338, 405, 592n
aspiration: taking Refuge in the Buddha xxxvii; and Shelley xlvii; like an eagle's flight 27; unreal 78; feeble 168; may my heart unfold 181; aspiring wing 182; like mountains 218; expressed by nature and architecture 277; 'O Man, to Freedom come!' 409; to Enlightenment 532
Athene 397, 512
Atropos 407, 595n
authenticity: taking off the mask xxviii, 88–96, 309, 323; through meditation 91; of Allen Ginsberg 93, 413; as an Order member 94–5; being oneself 319; a plaster saint is not much use 348
autumn, *see* seasons
Avalokiteśvara 269; *See also* Chenrezi
Avalon 500
Avalon, Arthur 591n
awakening 417
Awakening of Faith in the Mahāyāna 32, 589n

Bagdatopulos, W. S. 228, 591n
bamboos: beauty of 217; no word to describe 237; in a garden 524, 529
Baudelaire, Charles: *Fleurs du Mal* 73, 117, 269, 592n
beauty: is truth, truth beauty xxxiv; your beauty, in repose, is like a vase xlii, 264; of the Buddha 31; Neoplatonic 46; of nature 54, 236, 243, 359; without ethics 110; warped 118; of the Dharma 143; looking at something fair 163; of Chenrezi 164; rose and nightingale at night 167; can soothe when neither Reason nor Goodness can 168; of the monk Siddhārtha saw 180; Realm of 182; 'I will fill my life with beauty' 186; of Indian village 212; of bamboos 217, 237; fashioning use to beauty's ends 221; of orchids 222; without form 223; forgotten 228; stained by desire 230; impermanence of 230, 232, 270; Eternal (Plato) 232; of the Void 258; agreement 259; of the beloved 264, 446, 484, 489, 494; despite squalor 265; Goddess – demoniac or divine? 269; of the young 279; of a person 287; of a flame 291; of London 303; of silence 361; unseen by a self-absorbed saint 377; lack of 385; created by the presence of the beloved 487; of a lotus 537–8
bees 54, 178, 241, 380, 463, 465, 502, 525
beggars: in India 115, 265; 'How can I scorn the beggar's lot?' 207; Beauty as 269; the Buddha as 296; the beggary of love 494
See also alms
Bhaja: retreat centre 374, 508; caves 505–11
Bible: as cultural heritage 18–19, 420; 'Where your treasure is, there will your heart be also' 103; 'Where there is no vision the people perish' 144; symbol of garden 146
birch 285, 311, 380, 436, 444
birds: singing 281; and Saint Francis 366; hunted 366–7, 516–7;

606 / INDEX OF SUBJECTS, THEMES, AND REFERENCES

happy 373; and their gods 395–7;
apology to 447; Hercules and
512–20
See also individual names
bison 53, 447
blackbird lx, 333, 391, 395
Blake, William: influence on
Sangharakshita xlvi, lvi; and
symbolism of stars 78; homage
to 340; Fourfold Man 340;
Golgonooza 342; Los and
Enitharmon 342, 593n; walked
among the stones of fire 360; and
Allen Ginsberg 413; academics
discuss 423; Urizen 423; fourfold
vision 593n; Jerusalem 594n
blindness: to the starriness of things
185; Beauty an old blind beggar
269; blinding Reality 309; light to
the blind 346; blind old king 411;
Justice 437; of the artist 551
bliss: changeless lvii; monstrous
thought of 162; the Buddha an
Immensity of 173; finding 183;
borne within the heart 184; of
non-desire 189; of almsfood 209;
Nirvāṇa's 220; of touching thee
223; passion transformed to 278;
commixed with bale 295; a glassy
sea 351; of the Brahmas 451;
blissful contemplation 531; heart
suffused with 539
bluebells 285, 456, 471
boat: symbolism of xlviii–xlix, 249,
264; rowing to the Lotus of
Compassion 208; storm-bewildered
bark 287
See also ship
Bodh Gaya, see Buddha Gaya
bodhi tree: Tree of Wisdom 253; the
Buddha beneath 256; planting 302
bodhicitta xli, 302, 532
bodhisattva xxv–xxvi, 111–29; ideal
43–4, 113, 207, 220, 478; how a
bodhisattva thinks and acts 127–8;
compassion of 127, 157, 260–1;
love of 156; altruism of 220;
hierarchy 293; sacrifice of 478;
smile of 497
body witness 12–15
Bombay 9, 89, 114–15, 119

books: about Buddhism xxxix, 133,
241, 276, 241; burning 10–11,
286; their dust blown away by
music 170; 'crazed by close-printed
volumes' 194; learning more from
bamboos 217; unheeded 240; of
Mañjuśrī 275; 'I have not yet
opened my books' 305; on retreat
311; of You 327; in the Wheel of
Life 356; return 363; of ancient
sages 373; of St Mark 377; as
friends 404; what have they taught
me? 423
Brahma 458
Brahmas 451
breath: mindfulness of breathing
45–6; of the universe 162; the air
element 440–1
brotherhood: universal 207; of man
258
the Buddha: anniversary 5; footprints
27, 187; historical 30; in one's
heart 33; emulating 57; the guest
87; serving 124; eternal 135; at
the heart of the world 159; going
for alms 160–1; the Buddha's heart
173, 196, 210; Enlightenment
of 173, 184, 252–4, 256–7, 272,
341; parable of the plough 174–5;
request for teaching 181; compared
to a swan 182; Great Physician
190; word of 193; voice 196; 'the
light he saw I could not see' 198–9;
attraction to 199; compassion
202, 214, 398; Going for Refuge
to 209, 250–1; vision of humanity
like lotuses 210; longing for
226–7; birth at Lumbini 232; love
252, 296, 479; and Māra 256;
smile 257, 403; first five disciples
272; teachers 272; praise of 273;
followers 286; energy 296; like the
sun 296; and disciple 322, 569–86;
teaching on Vulture's Peak 325;
devotion to 346; in the Wheel of
Life 354–6; and Mucalinda 398–9;
teacher of gods and men 402;
shower of the way 451; thirty-two
marks 588n
See also Siddhārtha
Buddha Day, see Wesak

INDEX OF SUBJECTS, THEMES, AND REFERENCES / 607

Buddha Gaya 209, 210
Buddha images: destruction of 32;
  in the alcove 130, 241; devotion
  before 158, 173; at Kusinara 196;
  made the Ever-moving Buddha rigid
  296; Graeco-Roman 326; in the
  temple 531; talking 540–3
Buddhism: What is it? 16–17; western
  18–20, 28, 326, 382, 399; in the
  heart 20, 286; conventions 31–2;
  monastic/lay split 90; always more
  to understand 133; driven out of
  India 253, 274; different forms of
  399; talk about 524–3
Buddhist scriptures 11, 26, 76
  See also names of scriptures
buffaloes xxv, 235
bulbul 299
Burne-Jones, Edward 101, 452, 590n,
  596n
Burns, Robert lvi

Calcutta 132, 258, 262, 265
Callimachus 407
Cameron, Clare 87, 591n
Capri 429
caste system 117, 124, 261
cat 231, 240
Cathars 347
challenge: to accept incomprehension
  xxix, 502; of the four gifts 147
charcoal burners 236–7
charities 52
Charon 312, 421
chastity 162, 402
Chattrul Sangye Dorje xxix, 443
Chen, Yogi 23
Chenrezi 164–5, 280
cherry-blossom 238, 493
chestnut 306
childhood, *see* Sangharakshita
China 189, 191
Christianity: heritage 18–20; popes
  90, 347, 428, 544; lack of charity
  239; the gaunt Cross 251; Jesus
  274, 287, 376–7, 388, 437; early
  Christians 330; persecution of
  heretics 347, 376; priest 347;
  Tobias and the angel 375
  See also Bible; individual saints
chrysanthemums 282

cinema 212, 527, 528–9
cities 73, 126, 155, 186, 244, 261,
  262; of the Plain 408
clouds: Shelley's 'The Cloud' l, lvii;
  nations come and go like 99,
  439; Clouded Dragon 172; white
  continents of cloud 176; of strife
  193; aspiring through clouds
  and sunlight 218; of compassion
  219; drift the way we all must go
  234; calm as my thoughts 234;
  will darken heaven 241; wind-
  scattered 266; Illusion dispelled
  like clouds 275; 'What though
  with cloud the sky be grey?' 287;
  life is 390; my friends 446; in
  the landscape of the soul 471;
  moonlit 488; love bewildered like
  the ghost of a cloud 489; resting
  on my shoulders 492; moonlight
  and 494
Cocteau, Jean 378, 594n
Coleridge, Samuel Taylor xlvi, 135,
  412, 591–2n
comfort zone 76–7
commerce 437, 535–6
communication: between root and
  rose 72; preparation for 86;
  exercises 94–5, 590n; conventional
  conversation 96; gentle 231;
  on friendship, beauty, art 265;
  treasure of 356
compassion: for everyone xxvi–vii;
  fragrance of xl, 202, 208, 214,
  472–3; of the bodhisattva 112–13,
  127, 157, 260–1, 482, 497; an
  essential part of spiritual life 116;
  Siddhārtha's 180; of the Buddha
  202, 214, 398, 479; lotus of 208;
  birth of 210; the unseen flower
  215; lamp of 215; perfume of the
  void 219; and wisdom 251, 286;
  transforms hatred 256; of White
  Tārā 304; begins with love between
  two people 478; and love 493,
  495–6
complacency 354
concealment 89–90
conditioned, transformation of 73–4
confession 95
confidence 142; lack of 143, 185, 211

consciousness: expansion of 162–3;
    element 441
consumer society 122–3, 186, 260,
    416
contentment 186, 311, 355
convention 309
Cooper, Anthony Ashley 593
courage 95, 339
craving 32–3
creativity 35, 135, 245
crocus 221
crow 445
cruelty: to animals 54, 235, 447;
    capacity for 117; to Tibetans 297;
    to victims of Pontificate 347; to
    birds 366, 517; of the lover 489
crystal ball 403
cuckoo 240
cultural heritage 18–20; 27–8
curios 558–60
cyclamen 380, 517
cynicism 57

daffodil 303, 337
ḍākinī 443
Dalits 44, 52, 58, 114–15, 119,
    123–4, 261
dāna 114, 139; giving alms to the
    Buddha 160–1
    See also gifts
dance: symbolism of 145; life as 403;
    Maypole dancing 430–1
Dante Alighieri 544
dawn: Rock of 176; golden-white
    187; dawning of a light more
    glorious than the sun's 189; first
    rays 207; dews of 222; a great
    golden bird 227; a sunbird's wing
    234; coming of 243; means day
    245; of Enlightenment 256, 257;
    tropic 261; loves colder than 270;
    love of 279; the new dawn the new
    day 313; before dawn 348; sun
    worship at 418; Summer 464, 466
death: awareness of li, 470, 473;
    ship of liv; contemplating lvii;
    and purification lviii; afterlife
    lviii–lix, 421; acceptance of lix,
    502; character in *Paradise Lost*
    19; spiritual 43; intervention
    of 77; breaking bonds of 175;

the Third Sight 180; birth and
    217, 341, 473; Wheel of 226;
    thoughts of 238; and Orpheus
    254, 257; the end? 259; Ashoka
    and 271; and Chenrezi 280;
    the Underworld 312, 345; of
    Terry Delamere 318; and rebirth
    322; Journeyman 334; Sirens
    348; 'stares me in the face' 348;
    a diamond well 351; fear of
    356, 370, 445; laughter of 379;
    epitaphs 379, 407; being late for
    390; and friendship 407; king
    riding out to meet 411; Dance
    of 415; can life from death
    arise? 418; the tolling bell 422;
    foothold 427; King of 445; god
    of 458; love stronger than 479;
    of Maha Dhammaveera 510–11
Deathless 180, 183, 191, 196, 291
deer 447
defilements, *see kleśas*
Deji 453, 459, 596n
Delamere, Terry xxviii, 65, 89, 305,
    314–15, 318
delight: footprints of 29–30, 187;
    in the Dharma (*dhammarati*) 30;
    spurning in meditation 41–2, 167;
    in moonlight 163; the Buddha's
    173; Siddhārtha renounces 179,
    273; false 181; in the Things
    That Are 195; in idle thought
    252; mantra of 277; one note of
    pure delight 286; of the suspended
    scissors 329; see the whole world
    with 340; realms of 451; in
    friendship 453; in devotion 531;
    too deep for words 537
dementia 447
demons 269, 399, 419, 535, 579, 591
desire: cessation of 176, 264, 381;
    for truth (*dharmachanda*) 193,
    213, 226–7, 229, 473, 494; for
    being 194; and compassion 215;
    for the inaccessible 222; fierce
    223, 225; staining beauty 230;
    transformation of 248, 481–2; in
    the Wheel of Life, 262; and love
    270, 491, 494, 496; defiance of
    271; tell on desire's beads 277; of
    hungry ghosts 355; the blithe 'I

want to!' 400; no more for birth and death 473
destiny 385, 406, 420, 490
devil: in the Palace of Art 110; attacks a saint 376; in Paradise 386
devotion: at the feet of the Buddha 158, 250–1; at Kusinara 196–7; the devotee gives his heart to Truth 245; to the Three Jewels 346, 505–6, 508
Dhammadeepa 507–8, 509–11
Dhammapada 22, 30, 133, 182
Dhardo Rimpoche 92, 114, 392, 457, 594n
the Dharma: as many Dharma teachings as leaves in the forest xxxviii, 131; *akāliko* (timeless) 31; hostility to 32; always more to learn 133, 136; feeling you've understood something 136; interconnectedness of 142–3; rain of 156; Wheel 169, 191, 271, 338, 392, 405; Trumpet of the Law 190; taught by the Buddha's followers 197
Diamond Sūtra 26
dictionaries 6–9, 286, 371
Dis 254
disciples 5, 13, 131, 322, 331, 570, 581, 583
dissatisfaction 146–7
doctrine follower 12–15
dogs 252, 375, 423, 426
domestic life 146, 445, 468
Donne, John 421, 422, 595n
doubt: sick souls full of 15–16, 286; 158; frogs of 193; because of imperfections 209; and speculation 239; the Buddha-to-be loses his 252; if Truth be true 259; of the poet 269; bewildered by 412
dove 163, 209
dragon 172, 287, 499
Drake, Francis 431
dreams: the dust of a hundred dreams xxxviii, 222; you tread on my dreams xlvii; of family 60–70, 449; take at face value 64–5; of Guinevere 98, 101, 104–5, 438; land of 164; the world an empty dream 195; lone garden of 227; of Yashodhara 228; grown grey with dreaming 230; of the soul 232; of Beauty 232, 243; not dreams but certainty 259; Siddhārtha's 295; dream-mazed fold 296; of 'then' and 'now' 308; of a nightrace 324; priest's 347; 'Dreaming, awake, I must do all I can' 348; of the Pure Land 349; 'The best but live what once the poet dreamed' 359; of an angel 361; Minerva in 378; life is a dream 390; the Buddha's were visions 402; man with all his dreams 404; dream-whisper 408–9; leave dreams 417; not disallowed 424; of weightlessness 427; deluded 445; of Paramartha 454; of the cosmic dreamer 458; texture of 484; of Hercules 518–20; of the artist 544
duty: and love 110, 438; the grave 'I ought' 400
Dyer, Sir Edward 593

eagle 162, 266, 271, 397
earth: the bodhisattva leaves 156; the sky seems strange to 158; the Wheel of Dharma conquers 169; praise to patient 177; bloodstained centuries 188; the City of the Law 191; peace 192, 210; fragrance of compassion fills 214; another 226; roots hidden in 229; fierce fiery centre 229; poised 233; muddy fields of 264; rank lustihead 277; smiles 302; sun revolve around 320; called to witness 341; this dark earth 383; names belong to 402; element 440; apology to 447; ridiculous 454
See also world
economics 437
ego 81, 83
See also self
elements, six, *see* six elements
elephant 54, 296, 338, 356, 592n
Eliot, T. S. 61, 146
Elizabeth I 432
Elizabeth II 432
elm 333, 359, 380, 436
emotions 106, 480
encouragement 417

endurance 220, 424–5
energy: bringing into harmony with ideal 102–3; harnessing 136; divine 172; of the Buddha 296; not perfect but enough 332; of the Windhorse 339
Engels, Friedrich, *The Condition of the Working Class in England* 121
enjoyment, *see* pleasure
Enlightenment: symbolized by the moon 29, 176, 202, 473; Enlightened mind symbolized by perfume 32; how does it come from the *kleśas*? 73; aiming for in this lifetime 136; feeling near to and far from 136; of the Buddha 173, 184, 252–4, 256–7
environment: apology to 50–9, 447; saving the planet 57–8; Buddhists should speak out to protect 59; destruction of 236–7, 263, 404, 408, 456
See also nature
eternity: unending vistas 195; exulting in 340; Blake's songs of 360; can glut the heart 390; time and 393, 394; the word which from eternity has waited to reveal itself 436; of passion 481
ethics 110, 142, 146, 331, 392
Euphorion 400
Eurydice 254, 312
Eve 386
evil: flowers of (Baudelaire) 73, 117; the word used in the puja 75; potential in all of us 75–6; shouldn't be afraid to use the word 117–18; social 118; the evil one (Māra) 143; spied 371; talking with the Devil about 386
evolution 56, 140
existentialists 116–17
exploitation 115, 301

faith: confidence in what one is doing 33; something you have to maintain 42; an integral part of the spiritual life 47; conviction of potential for Enlightenment 136; unfailing 182; lack of – 'We cry that we are weak' 185; faithful heart 197, 367, 368; 'which made my heart's torn empire one' 243; taking Refuge in the Buddha 250–1; hand of Faith 302; making room for 420
See also devotion
faith follower 12–15
faithfulness: moonlight sealed and stored 264; faithful as the moon to the earth 459; through many lives 490
family 65, 72–3
fear: of the surrounding darkness xxxix, 278; of the stranger 80, 184; something wanted but also feared 81, 84–5; the mundane fears the Transcendental 82; prayer not to fear destruction 165; of death 179, 370; of the forest 180; the Buddha's freedom from 181; of the shadow one has oneself made 185; stalking the world 190; don't fear Māra 197; no fear of the Buddha 198; have no fear! 356; oppressed by fears 412
fearlessness: serene and unafraid xxxix, 278; following the Buddha fearlessly 33; dare you accept the four gifts? 147, 335; not shrink back from the Eye of Reality 309; no fear of Death 415; Chenrezi unafraid 280
Female 280
feminists 119
fidelity, *see* faithfulness
Finland 4, 336–7
fire: the burning bush 18; the stars on fire for the rose's beauty 71, 229; in a clothing factory 122; recoiling from the world as the burnt hand from the fire 176; of lust 189; thirst for truth like a fire 193; of compassion 215; fire-drops on my heart 220; anguish red as 225; of the heart's desire 229; fury of 230; setting afire the poetry of common things 240; turns heatless 248; lives whirl like sparks 262; don't believe that love is a blazing fire 270; soul burns upward 271; meditation on a flame 291; Burn as a Fire for men!

296; Windhorse breathes 338; of Golgonooza 342; of Hell 355; Blake walked among the stones of fire 360; of hatred 368; element 440; of the love god 458; of life burnt low 470; love like fire 486, 495; Hercules like a forest fire 518

five spiritual faculties 302

flattery 358

flight: the coming of love as mysterious as the flight of a bird from unknown lands xxvii, 483; the upward flight of friendship xxxv, 453; the swallow preparing for flight lviii, 344; unwearied 182; swallows through the skies 221; love's flight among the stars 229; joy in 266; we try to track birdflight through the sky 324; swallow-flights of song 353

flowers: of compassion xl; symbol of culture 27–8, 187; heart unfolding like 181; compassion, the unseen flower 215; many were the flowers that blossomed around me 226; Māra's arrows turned to 256; living alone with one flower 315; petals 316; golden 320, 322, 379, 404, 464; shadows of flowers 352; what the flower really thinks 380; cannot grow in my secret garden 393; yesterday's blossoms 402; and the love of the sun 485–6; in the antique dealer's garden 564–5

See also individual names

forests: as many Dharma teachings as leaves in the forest xxxviii, 131; call of xlii, 408–9; destruction of 50, 52, 58, 236–7, 447; orchids growing in 131; symbol of deeper experience 136–7; fear-haunted 180; the forest vast of the Void 181; peace of 195; my love upon the forest leaves 243; beauty haunts 269; sing out 'Aspire!' 277; frowning 290; of golden flowers 320; New Forest 329; the oak stands in 387; of Tuscany 516–7

forgiveness: we did our best according to our understanding at the time 74; 'Forgive me if I have stained your beauty with my desire' 230; sins by heaven forgiven 428

fountain: joy's xxxiv, 163; in the Pure Land lviii, 345; waters that end where they began 162; in palace gardens 178; not where the fountains rise 250; of my heart 264; talking 267; laughing 277; turquoise 373; of my mind 467; the brink of 537

Four Noble Truths 11, 133, 188, 196

Four Sights, *see* Siddhārtha

foxgloves 329

fragrance: of compassion xxxx, 202, 208, 214, 473; bittersweet of love 221; of philosophy 464, 470; of the Law 472

See also perfume

Francis, Saint 366–7

freedom: *śamatha-vipaśyanā* leading to 44; living and talking freely 95; goal of spiritual path 114, 295; lack of 116; existentialist view of 116–17; *dāna* a free gift 139; set the world free 169, 399; poet like a freed songbird 192; longing to be free 196; the freed swan 201; Love free as the air 203; setting free beings in hell 220; set free from hate 279; sense of freedom going on retreat 333; of Divine Imaginations 340; every passion free to speak 357; freedom from wants 381; liberty of friendship 391; 'O Man, to freedom come!' 409

friendship: when friends avert their eyes xxxv, 368; spiritual 33, 34, 74, 140; romantic 106; with the Buddha 226–7, 492; 'Let us be friends' 230; the rose of friendship 268; comforting a friend 275; search for a companion 309; 'a great thing' 391; a friend goes away 394; contraries 400; poetry of 407; keeping friendship sweet 421; birthday gift 444; delight in 453; the rule of life 454; golden links of 519; the Buddha's golden flower 595n

frog 289, 426, 529

frustration 221, 321, 481, 488–9, 494

Gandhi, M. K. 83, 589n
Ganges, River 160, 188, 190, 243
Ganymede 397
gardens 145–6, 156, 219, 227, 228, 267, 335, 373, 483, 524–6, 529, 564–6; secret 393
generosity 245, 331, 417, 459
George, Stefan 279, 592n
gifts 138–48, 335, 336
Ginsberg, Allen liii, lvi, 93, 413, 590n, 594n
Glastonbury Tor xxix, xxxvi, 499–504
glow-worms 484, 494, 495–6
Gnosticism 87
goal 83–4, 164
goat 328, 350–1
God 18, 19, 163, 366–7, 413, 422
gods and goddesses: Greek 20, 266, 397; of the mountains 55, 349; 'They help not much' 290; of the Underworld 345; of the Wheel of Life 354; in the gallery 400; the White Goddess 433; Brahmas 451; old 500
  See also individual names
Goethe, J. W. 400, 594n
Going for Refuge xxxvii–viii, 20, 29, 63, 119, 175, 209, 250–1
Going Forth, see Siddhārtha
gold: pillaging the earth for 50, 447; golden net 142–3; inspiring 143; golden lotus 202, 208; Wheel of 271; golden apples 281, 515; 'You remind me of whatever's made of gold' 287; silver words transmuted into 442; nectar 443; thread of 484
goldfish 225
Golgonooza 342
Goodness 168
Govinda, Lama Anagarika 333, 429, 477–80, 596n
gratitude 69, 331–2, 412, 436, 482
Graves, Robert 433, 596n
great men and women 447
Greece, ancient 512–3; Delphi 55; Bull of Memphis 287; Sirens 348
  See also individual figures

greed 215, 381
grief 168, 281
Guhyaloka 391, 424–5, 435, 594n
guilt 98, 328, 439, 581
Guinevere 101–2, 105–6, 438–9, 595n
gull 266
Gunn, Thom xl
guru 331
gypsies 69, 442, 449

Hafez 26
happiness: happy family 65; happy childhood 69; of the people who gave alms to the Buddha 161; because of being together 276; the Happy Place 421; Man hands on happiness to man 423; through seeking, find pain 454
Hardy, Thomas lx, 391
harmony 59
hatred: clearing away thorns of 32–3; sleeps in a den of darkness 169; tidal wave of 189; born in the hearts of men 190; heart-wick glows with 215; transformed by compassion 256; of political protest 258; at the heart of the world 262; at the time of the Suez crisis 283; caused by religious division 287; the distance between love and hate 321; chains of 381; love and hate near akin 432
healing: powers 43, 167; Nature heals the wound of love 492
heart: bleeds and bleeds xxx, 336; the holiness of the heart's affections xxxiv, 17; ice of the heart broken xxxiv, 163; empty xxxv, 290; a mother's heart xxxvi, 207, 298; the wondering heart xxxvii, 368; stilled heart xxxviii, 130, 195, 241; the ashes of all my heartaches xxxviii, 222; those who read their own hearts xxxix, 278; the Buddha's xxxix, 173, 196, 210, 252, 296; awakening xliv, li, 463–73; treading upon xlvii, 231; horizon of 1, 495; Buddhism in 20, 256; distinction between heart and life 20; removing weeds and thorns from 32; the Buddha found in 32–

3, 159, 187; turns to meditation 41–2; where your heart is 102; we *are* our heart 103; in the Dharma 103; enchanted 151; 'going after mine own heart' 158; systole and diastole 162–3; unlocked cage 163; weary 168, 209; heartstrings 171; recoiling from the world 176; of compassion 180; unfolding like a flower 181; the Buddha sitting on the lotus of 181; bears a mite of bliss 184; incense of 186; moonlight of 189; on fire with lust 189; questing 193, 204, 270; faithful 197, 367; as citadel 197; a lamp 215; aspiring 218; of the bodhisattva 220; pain of being reshaped 221; of Reality 223; lonely 224; contorts 225; ashes kindled 227; like a bird in song 229; a sickly rose raised in 230; refusal to accept rational thinking 230; anguish resounding in 237; sects where hearts are shut 239; torn empire 243; the artist surrenders 245; the devotee gives his heart to Truth 245; fountains of 264; the poet's heart perplexed 269; a lump of clay to be fashioned 274; cold 275; mangled 280; filled with grief 281; greensward 284; for poetry your heartstrings are the only stuff 288; anvils of 304; a few words sufficient to express 336; golden throne 351; held within an Angel's hands 361; what can it do? 368–9; wayward 372; words that make the listless heart beat faster 373; peace of 374; the transcendental seed sown in 381; Eternity can glut 390; 'Open the windows of the heart!' 405; tyger's 413; empty of desires 444; filled with delight in friendship 453; restless 470; mystery 471; compassion spreads from heart to heart 472; a garden 483, 485; mirror of 484; darkness of 484; cradle of 486; red soil of 487; love cannot be confined within 488; wounded 489, 492; union of 494; Love and Compassion within 495; joy within 497; every atom of the universe reflected in 497; Reality reflected in 498

Hebe 520

heights and depths 229, 248, 270, 278

Helen 400

Hell: sorrows of 216; the bodhisattva liberates beings in 220; and the Wheel of Life 226, 355; the hells below 251; Orpheus in 254, 312; should be slow to condemn a soul to 422; Hercules and Cerberus 515

helping: you need spirituality to really help 116; bringing the garden of the sangha into existence 146–7; bodhisattvas 293; the 'help' of Death 334; to keep the Dharma alive 459; Maha Dhammaveera 510

Henri, Adrian 320

Hera 396, 515

Herbert, George 80

Hercules: no literal belief in 20; the robe of Nessus 372; in the Naples Museum 512–3; labours 514–15; as bodhisattva 519–20

Hermes 326

hermits 106, 212, 246, 272

heroes: Hercules 20, 513; great lives 56–7; modern 57; young 279; Greek 378; my friend like a hero 394; Allen Ginsberg as hero 413; bites the dust 445; Maha Dhammaveera 509

hibiscus 160

hierarchy, spiritual 136–7, 293

Hoddle, Glenn 16–17, 588n

holidays 455

holly 436

Holman Hunt, William 350

Homer's *Iliad* 19, 427

honesty 68, 356, 413; with oneself 94

hope: for the Dalits 58, 124; for the future of the planet 58–9; of the world 180; despair not 197; approach to begging alms 204; white hopes are winging 209; withered 238; helping a friend to find 275; inspired by 349; in hell

355; making a little room for hope 420
horses 324, 329, 338, 356, 514
   See also Windhorse
Housman, A. E. xlvii, 375, 594n
Huineng (in 'Transmission') 414
human life: the arising of the *bodhicitta* the most important event in xli; potential for spiritual development lvi, 29, 140; dark times 30; does harm to the planet 51, 53–4, 58; highest product of evolution 56; refuse 112, 126, 261; dehumanized 122; barren fields of 193; only of value if it seeks for Truth 203; in the Wheel of Life 356; Vanity of Human Wishes 371; end of human life on Earth 404; to bake a human cake 422; forced to deal with difference 445; plight 453; forms of love 479; tortured questionings of 489; in deadly sleep 593n
Humphreys, Christmas ('Toby') 382, 594n
hungry ghosts 355

Icarus 427
ideal: in principle devoted to, but in practice attracted to something else 102; serving 140–1; snows of 284; distance between ideal and real 321; touch of 409
idleness 267
ignorance: soil of 32; innocence of 120; teach me, being ignorant 181; purple flowers of 193; of the world 202, 262; chains of folly 381
Ilion 313
illusion: Dispeller of 257; many-layered 504; queer mistakes 527
imagination: stimulated by cultural heritage 19, 99; loss of 54; beyond 144; Divine 340; strong 371; truth of 588n
immortality: brink of 162; Draft of 193; *Asuras* battle for prize of 354; Door of 356
imperfections 209, 331–2
impermanence: acceptance of lvi; meditation on lviii; contrasted with the eternal Buddha 135; taught by nature 195, 221, 242, 372; rational acceptance of 230; of beauty 230, 232, 281; like snow in Summer 234; as *lakṣaṇa* 295; music of 354; 404
   See also transience
India: Sangharakshita's first experience of 115; prostitution 119; village 212–3; Taj Mahal 283
   See also individual places; Dalits
indifference: of scholars 16; of beloved 481, 489
indirect methods 140
individual: illusoriness of individuality 45; true 95; tension with sangha 108; influence of 128, 129
individualism: in the Order 63; in the West 105; destructive of spiritual fellowship 108
industry and industrialization 121–2, 186, 260
infinity: the Buddha in 173; reflection of 175; the Windhorse the master of 338
innocence: emotional xlv; lost 111, 120, 257, 260; two sorts of 120; and experience 426
insubstantiality 295, 324
integration: of different interests 102, 110; my heart's torn empire one 243; Fourfold Man 340
interconnectedness: universal brotherhood xxxvi; of the Dharma 142–3; all with all are one 176; each to all and all to each doth bind 248; of all living beings 477; nothing in the universe is separate or independent 482
intuition: when writing poetry 39; of the Sage 172
Islam 251, 274
Itylus 194
ivy 387

Japan 189, 191
Jayapushpa 369
Jerome, Saint 312
Jerusalem 360
Jesus, *see* Christianity
jewel in the garment 207

Jewel-Tower 213
Johnson, Dr Samuel 370–2; dictionary 5, 371
joy: fountain xxxiv, 163; Wesak 184; transfiguring life with 186; on seeing the Heaven of Beauty 258; comes and goes 266; on the wing 284; of the Windhorse 339; laughed aloud for joy 450; we thought would stay 467; on realizing that earthly love is a reflection of compassion 482; bottomless cup of 492; deepens and deepens 497; of a child 537–8
judgement: the throne of 250; Mirror of 355; we should be slow to judge 422
justice: blind 437; law and 515; Sun of 519

Kailash, Mount, *see* mountains
Kakacūpama Sutta 589n
Kālī 76
Kālidāsa 26
Kalimpong xxvii, 131, 134, 302, 389
Kāmadeva 458
karma 226, 355
Keats, John xxxiv, lv, 17, 25
kindness: to animals 58, 200–1, 206–7; encourages growth 140; of the poor 204, 239; to a Tibetan refugee 297; to living things 526
kingcups 282
Kipling, Rudyard xlvii
kleśas (defilements) 73, 75–6, 136, 445
Krakow 442
Kusinara 196

lakṣaṇas 295
Lancelot 105–6, 438–9, 595n
lark 163, 194, 229, 341
Larkin, Philip 423, 595n
Lawrence, D. H. liv
learning: forget 165; what to be and not to be 367; of Dr Johnson 370; what if there were nothing to learn? 502
See also scholars
Li Bai 26

library, Order 12, 132
life: distinguished from heart 20; great lives 56–7; irruption of a higher dimension in 87; what are we to do with our lives? 113; unfathomable 133; as teacher 203; conquered when we yield to it 217; as furnace 221; shaping 221, 406; deeps of 249; is king 324; a rainbow tower 351; ordinary 362–5, 384–5
See also human life
light: consciousness of man expands like 162; borrowed 163; of Chenrezi 164–5; lamplight and starlight and moonlight 179; Light beyond light 181; stand athwart the Light 185; a Light more glorious than the sun's 189; the path of 196; Strongholds of 197; the light the Buddha saw 199; of compassion 215, 496; clear serene 230; trees that loved the light 236; heat of desire turned to 248; neon 265; of a flame 291; Boundless 295, 453; first 320; lightyears 321; and darkness 322; of day 345; Infinite 346; no fulfilment in reflected light 355; pathway to from Hell 355; a land of jewels and light 389; deep in darkness saw a light 413; death dissolved in dazzling light 415; silver light of White Tārā 417; Padmasambhava, Infinite Light 419; a god of light 427; mystic 449; thrones of 451
See also sun, moon, stars
lightning: intuitions like 172; fitful 206; piercing through the veiled heart of Reality 223; the poet's lightning glance 240; practitioners of austerities as though struck by 252; struck the mountain pine 306
Lilith 390
lily lvii–viii, 221, 282, 393, 344, 483
lion 377, 513–4, 518
literalness 136, 144
lokuttara 144
London: Thames 53; in wartime 155, 468; Westminster Bridge

276; Berkeley Square 303; the
Embankment 310; Buddhist Centre
346; Bethnal Green 384–5; Tower
of 396; Bridge 404
loneliness 224, 322, 368
See also aloneness
longing: for the divine xxvi; to go
upon the Solar Path 182; for the
inaccessible 222; for the Buddha
226–7; for the infinite 229; endless
yearning 264
Lord of the Rings, The 100
lotus: of the Pure Land lviii, 345,
421; gift of a lotus flower 138,
335; as symbol of spiritual
development 139–40; of Chenrezi
165, 280; of my heart 181; of the
Buddha's compassion 202, 208; the
Buddha's vision 210; at Lumbini
232; of Mañjuśrī 275; one white
unfading 282; pond 294; vision
after meditation 307; 'Long may it
bloom!' 346; of White Tārā 417;
of the cosmic dreamer 458; white
lotus 472–3, 533–9
love: mystery of xxvii, 483–98; pain
of xxxv, 481–2, 486–91; mirrored
in Reality 1, 498; deserving 103;
romantic 106, 223, 224, 255, 264,
281, 283, 284; and duty 110,
438–9; of the bodhisattva 156;
unfolds its petals 162; stronger
than steel 169; and wisdom 173,
270, 491; of Siddhārtha and
Yashodhara 178–9; in the hearts
of men 190; the Buddha's 200–2,
252, 296; equal for all 203; the
world's need for 210; bittersweet
221, 258; thwarted 221; austerity
of 223; sublimation 223; secret
225, 498; among the stars 229;
folly of 230; 'I love' means 'I will
give' 245; of the Void 258; like
moonlight 264; difference from
desire 270, 491; transformation
of 278; of youthful beauty 279;
and death 283; and hate 321, 432;
of early Christians for everyone
330; I love you 363; grew up
between us like a flower 379;
delicacy of 442, 485; and force

445; knowledge, not sentimentality
454; love god, mischief of 458;
and surrender of self 479; higher
481; destroys thought of self 482;
and compassion 482, 493, 495–6;
holiness of 483; like a melody 485;
steadfast as the shining of the sun
488; inaccessibility of beloved 488;
ungraspable 491; dance of the
planets 497
Lovelace, Richard 357, 593n
Lumbini 232

Maha Dhammaveera 509–11
Mahāsaccaka Sutta 587n
Mahāvastu 295
Mahāyāna *sūtras* 11
Maheshvara 458
Maitreya/Metteyya 189, 322
Malory, Thomas 99
mandala 336
Mandarava 459
Mañjughoṣa/Mañjuśrī 56, 275, 349,
593n
Māra 143, 169, 191, 197; conquest
of 256
Mark, King 406, 595n
Mark, Saint 377
marriage 81, 102
Marxism 124, 405
McGough, Roger 321
meditation: tranquillity xxxiv; the
heart turns to 41–8, 167; how
important is meditation? 44;
śamatha 44; *vipaśyanā* 44, 46–7;
mindfulness of breathing 45–6;
connection with relationships 48;
system 48; fear of the unknown 81;
and becoming more authentic 91;
benefits everybody 141; calm 274;
on a flame 291; vision after 307;
restlessness and anxiety 572; just
sitting 574
Memnon 359
Merlin 100, 359, 438, 439, 452, 500,
501
Michael, St 499
Michal 442
Milarepa 28
Milton, John 25, 407, 412; *Paradise
Lost* xlv, 19

mind: purified 33; nature of 104;
  work on like tending a garden
  219; rational 230, 242, 288; a
  silver awning 351; kingdom or
  democracy? 357, 405; clear your
  mind of cant 372; a theatre 447
mindfulness 143, 576
mindfulness of breathing, see
  meditation
Minerva 299, 378
mirror: my face in the mirror is
  strange to me 158; naked branches
  mirrored 311; the goldgleam of
  Enlightenment in the mirrors of
  western man 326; at the barber's
  329; mirror-like water 337; of
  Judgement in hell 355; Mirror,
  mirror, on the wall 358; yesterday's
  blossoms mirrored in today's
  black waters 402; eternal presence
  mirrored 478; love mirrored in
  Reality 480, 498; compassion
  mirrors the sorrows of the world
  494; love mirrored in every atom
  of the universe 497
Moby Dick 53
Molly the medium 374
monastic life 141
moon: visit of xlii, 294; full moon as
  symbol of Enlightenment 29, 176,
  202, 473; the moon how bright!
  163; Chenrezi's light like the moon
  on flowers 164; of Beauty 168;
  silver moonlight 170; the calm of
  the Buddha's face like the full moon
  173; white like a bride 184; Wesak
  191, 253; swan like the moon of
  Autumn 201; at midnight, when
  the moon is full 208; crescent 211,
  272; sever the moonlight from the
  moon 231; love like moonlight
  264; new 279; her destined path
  287; orange moonrise 289; Winter
  moon 255, 310; misty moon 403;
  shines on the wake of the ship 446;
  brighter, brighter 455; comforting
  moon 470; moonlit lotus beds
  472–3; reflected in the ocean 480,
  498; speaks of love 485; you can't
  catch moonlight in cups of gold
  488; and the Buddha's face 513–2

Morris, William 102
mortality: meditation on lv, 470, 473;
  riddle of 466
Mother Goose 426–7, 433
mountains: apology to 50, 447;
  sacred 55; Kanchenjunga 55, 219,
  267; mystery of 211; aspiring 218;
  piled up inky blue 224; mountain
  people 244; hills without a human
  past 292; thrones of gods 349;
  Kailash 429, 596n
Mucalinda 398–9, 594n
Mumbai, see Bombay
Muse: a poem directly from xli;
  madness that comes from 4; what
  does it mean to have one? 65;
  when other Muse conceives 243;
  one who is herself a Muse 298;
  Reading is not a Muse 337; serving
  the Muse 414; the Muses' covenant
  420; John Donne loved the Muse
  422; the White Goddess 433
music: the wandering singer 170–1;
  of life 226, 491; Tibetan trumpets
  237; the soul like a lute 286;
  Bach, Beethoven, Indian ragas
  and Zen meditation music 320;
  of impermanence 354; a song in
  the evening 373; listening to the
  wireless 448; of the stars 485
mystery: of the coming of love
  xxvii; world of mysteries xlix,
  175; of the Dharma 133; of the
  universe, and of people 133; of the
  Clouded Dragon 172; of universal
  brotherhood 207; of the truth of
  things 242; some things we *don't*
  understand 247; of the Void 248;
  of love 379; of Chattrul Sangye
  Dorje 443; of existence 487

Nāgārjuna 263, 592n
Nagarjunikonda 263
Nālanda 274
Naples 512
Narcissus 385
nature: beauty of 54, 243; loss of
  feeling for the natural world 54–5;
  learning from 157, 217; book of
  186; peace of 222, 240; destroyed
  236; hieroglyphics of the soul

239; attempts to classify 242; expressive of aspiration 277; man's relationship with 292; greenstone 353; giver of peace 374; a sense of the Supreme 409; reveals love 481; healer 492
See also animals, birds, environment, flowers
Nelson, Horatio 431
Neoplatonism 46, 82, 85, 401, 594–5n
New Forest 329
New Zealand 344, 353, 362, 415
newness lii–liii, 313, 455
Nietzsche, Friedrich 144
nightingale 158, 167, 194, 266
Nirvāṇa: Nirvāṇa's stillness xxxvii, 251; smug milestones to xxxix, 278; Nirvāṇa's night 157; won once more 191; the Ocean of 195; and the bodhisattva ideal 220; Nirvāṇa's peace 226; the hope of Sages 451
non-desire 189
non-self xli, 165, 195, 351
non-violence 116
not-being 435
Novalis 477–8

oak 307, 320, 329, 344, 387, 408, 435, 436, 457
ocean: primeval 82; qualities of 137, 591n; of Nirvāṇa 195; wild and dark 287; oceandepths blue 317; and its waves 403; apology to 447; the moon reflected in 480, 498
See also sea
old age: autumn years lv–lvi; looking back at one's life 22; First Sight 179; bodies must one day grow old 232; may age make love more vivid 255; stiff fingers 380; Old Age in a grey cloak 390; how long is left? 420; when you're old the blood runs cold 422; the wind in my sails 450
opposites 400, 432, 468
orchids xxxviii, 130, 131, 134–5, 137, 222, 224, 241, 282, 285
Order members, *see* Triratna
Orlovsky, Peter 93

Orpheus 254, 257, 312, 359, 405
Osiris 352
owl 366, 397, 435

Padmaloka liv–lix, 344–5, 457
Padmasambhava xxix, 419, 459
Pāli grammar 9–10
Pallis, Marco 132–3
palm 512
Paradise 258, 342, 386
See also Pure Land
Paramartha 394, 405, 453, 454, 459
parents 62, 65, 72, 77, 106, 423, 467; gratitude towards 69
passions: sun of xlx, 495; spurned 41–2, 167; of Guinevere 98, 105, 108, 439; treading underfoot 183; vile 188, 417; passion-consumed 274; darkness in the Abyss 278; free to speak 375; mercurial 400; throw out 405; frustrated 481; reawakened 484; dark labyrinth 494
path: the Way's a hacked path xxxix, 278; following the footprints of delight 24, 187; following through all the vicissitudes of life 29; not easy to follow alone 34; and goal 83; harnessing one's energies to practising 136; first weak steps 184; of truth 203; life's long street 213; leads to the Buddha's shining land 290; the Noble Way 402
patriotism 431
Patroclus 427
peace: Buddhists stand for 59, 189; within 166; of the Buddha 173, 198–9; the Law that leads to Peace most radiant 181; on knowing that the world is an empty dream 195; of nature 222, 240, 374; break down walls and plant flowers 320; the distance between peace and war 321; a peace profound 450; dissolved with the coming of war 467–8; a great peace 531
peacock 243, 289, 302, 396
pearl 401, 443, 477
perfections, six 392
perfume: of the flower of compassion xxxx, 214, 472; the Enlightened

mind leaves a trace of itself in the unenlightened mind 32, 589n; of red hibiscus 160; the perfumed way 161; and the pleasures of night 178; of incense 197; of the Void 219; no sprinkled rare perfumes 302
See also fragrance
periwinkle 294
persecution 32, 347
Persephone 254
philosophy: and the doctrine follower 13, 144; personal 17; the Dharma is not just a grey system of philosophy 143; reading 327; violet of 464, 470, 471; the philosopher changes 478
pilgrim: faith follower 12; sun-scorched 193; weary 195; at Kusinara 196; pledged to Truth 203; life as pilgrimage 282; Truth's arduous pilgrimage 298; footsteps 321; Tannhäuser 428
pine 289, 311, 391, 424, 435
pity 178, 220, 263, 437
Plato l, 4, 46, 232, 270
play: in the garden of the sangha 148; with Tomorrow and Yesterday 308; the lover 400; dancing round the Maypole 430–1; my mind is a theatre 417; children on a Summer's day 463, 468, 473; you are like the playful brightness of water 487
pleasure: transience of lvi, 344; giving up worldly 31, 157, 178–9, 252; of dancing 145; of work 145; dangerous 295; unsatisfying 213
Pluto 312
poet: poetic inspiration 'a kind of madness' 4; cannot be a true ascetic? 192; first sight of beauty 212; a fantastic creature 228; the truest Sage 231; poet's eye 240; falls in love with the subject 245; modern 254, 257; and critic 350; the world's interpreter 359; minor 412; no regrets 414; 'listens for the inevitable word' 436; risks of being and not being a poet 456; and priests 478
See also Muse

poetry: experience of akin to our experience of the Dharma 26–7; mediator between 'real' and 'Ideal' 36; has more wisdom than the writings of sages 239; of common things 240; contrast between Inspiration and Theory 278; and prose 284, 322; must come from the heart 288; 'in the flow of traffic' 315; alexandrines 350; benefit of 359; written in blood 364; 'a great thing' 391; reading aloud 404; of friendship 407; the 'heavenly chore' 414; roots of 433; scholarly approach to 433; feeder of the soul 453; seeing the world in a wider and truer perspective 477; the art of 478; born of love and pain 491
See also Sangharakshita
politics: engaging with 125–6; influence through 129; forging the chains of faction 166; the game of 186; a political procession 258; the Suez Crisis 283; the man behind the microphone 300; squandering millions on costly projects 301
popes, see Christianity
poppy 337
positive group 141
potential, spiritual: we have to be convinced we have it 136; the latency of thought 162; potencies deep 175; secret wings 185; shaping our heart into a Buddha 274
poverty: in big cities 126, 265; the kindness of the poor 204, 239; holiest 205; the jewel in the garment 207; giving to the poor 364
Prague 405, 595n
praise: to the rain 177; of water 289; to Shrimati Sophia Wadia 298–9; singing the praises of friends 383; cause to wonder and to praise 393; the Minor Poets 412
See also rejoicing in merits
Pre-Raphaelites xlviii, 99, 121–2, 590n, 596n
precepts 116, 119–20

prejudice 445
preparation, spiritual 79–87, 184
pretence 120–1, 220
pride: don't forget humble beginnings 74; to curb the flame-fierce pride of youth 204; longing to thrust pride into the dust 205; 'Oh look what I have done!' 241
priests 212, 251, 328, 347, 464, 478
prose: Sangharakshita's li, lx; mere Theory smashes poetry into 278; rocks of 284; for prose mere grey matter is enough; 288; the distance between prose and poetry 322
prostitution 118–20, 260
puja: faith type enjoys 12; the word evil in 75; welcoming the guest 87; opening the London Buddhist Centre 346
Pure Land: and Shelley lviii–lix; the new-born lotus 345; as in a dream 349; Amitābha's paradise 372; a land more lovely 389; the Happy Place 421; where the sparkling jewel-trees grow 453
purification: the purified mind 33; ethical preparation 80, 86; 'I clear the turbid liquid of my soul' 267; purifying beings in hell 355
purity: symbolized by the lotus lvii; pristine of snow 164; steps towards 184; of the rose 229; of winter 284; life of 293; mental 572, 574

radio 113, 448
rain: of the Dharma 156; falls on the fields 162; as on roses falls the rain 167; the season after 170; praise to 177; sheltering from 206; of the Buddha's compassion 214; day after day 242; a rainy day in the mountains 244; three months 273; the Buddha listens to 296; burst forth pink buds, as soon as touched by rain 300; at Glastonbury 504
rainbow: over ledges 164; rainbow-tinted plumes 185; rainbowed radiance of compassion 215; fragment 268; like Hope 275; link between heaven and earth 299; the distance between light and darkness 322; a rainbow track 339; a rainbow tower 351
Rajgir 325
Ratnasambhava 338
raven 250, 396
reading: advice on books on Buddhism; 11; quality of 11–12; not a Muse 337
See also Sangharakshita
reality: love and l, 480, 482, 498; in the form of external circumstances 77; relative and absolute 142; the Things that Are 195; passion pierces through to the veiled heart of 223; Eye of 309; the distance between man and Reality 321; telegrams 362–5; touching 492
reason: dies in giving birth to ecstasy 82; reason's lamp grows dim and faint 168; the philosopher's expression in terms of 478; abdication of 502
rebellion 309
rebirth: symbolized by spring lvii, 29; in the Pure Land lviii, 345, 421, 453; of the bodhisattva 128, 478; and death 227, 322; of Mañjuśrī 275
See also spiritual rebirth
receptivity 83–5, 217
reciprocity 245
red-hot pokers 434
reflection: about the nature of beauty 46; musing 84; need time for 91; the Great Work 267; contemplation wise 274; a pool reflecting the moon 289; yesterday's blossoms mirrored in today's black waters 402; of Reality 482, 498; of beauty 484; compassion mirrors the sorrows of the world 494; the stars reflected in a pool 495; the universe reflected in the heart 497
rejoicing in merits: Jayapushpa 369; Tarashri 383; Dhardo Rimpoche 392; Allen Ginsberg 413; Paramartha 453; Deji 453, 459
See also praise
relationship: between inner experience and what you do with your life 48;

between root and flower 73, 229;
all-consuming 342; between love
and wisdom 480
religions, history of: the cross 274;
better to have worshipped the Bull
of Memphis 287; where the paths
divided 288; persecution 347,
376–7; defenestration in Prague
405
renunciation: 183, 194, 195, 252,
477, 481–2
retreat: solitary 311, 394; Haslemere
333; silence during 361; Tuscany
367; Bhaja 374, 507; Guhyaloka
391, 424–5, 435
revenge 416
reverence: places where people feel
it 55; for great men and women
56–7; for the beggar 207; the
Windhorse 339; of the altar boy
347; for Dhardo Rimpoche 392;
bitter as death 486; for a lotus 537
See also praise, rejoicing in merits
Richard of St Victor 589n
Riding, Laura 433
rights and duties 63
Rilke, Rainer Maria 359, 593–4n
rites and rituals as ends in themselves
540–3
rivers: limpid river in the evening
air 157; of the Buddha's speech
193; on the river-brink 211; like a
silver thread 218; jade-green 222;
tranquil 264; dull slow rivers of
desire 271; green as tourmalines
285; that flow majestic 289;
sluggish 344; water element 440;
apology to 447; snows of the
Himalayas flow in 497; cleansing
of Augean Stables 514
See also individual names
rose: reddest roses are remembered
not lv; the root speaks 71–8, 229;
as on roses falls the rain 167; of
the Buddha's compassion 214; only
one day the Summer rose 221; the
White Rose white with morning
dew 226; the red rose does not
whisper 240; set round with thorns
282; one crimson fallen petal 372;
room to breathe and flower 393;

the rosebud will reveal its heart
486; the two roses 524–32
Rossetti, Christina xlvi
Rossetti, Dante Gabriel xlvi, 25
Royal Academy 375–7

sacred: moon xlii, 50, 54, 447; sense
of the 55; dust of the poor 205;
heart of Truth 245; Wood 287;
feet 295; mountain 325, 596n;
Silence 361; love 482; branches
515
sādhana 43
sadness: of an empty heart xxxv,
290; of the Buddha xxxviii, 178;
heartache 222, 290; of a friend 275
sages: the Clouded Dragon 172; the
sweetest Poet 231; poetry has
more wisdom than 239; of Weimar
(Goethe) 400; and Brahmas 451–2
Salome 376
saṃsāra: wilderness 146; the vortex
of existence 194; turn away from
the world 195; flow 251; world
of flame and shadow 295; this
ridiculous earth 454
sangha: like mountaineering in a team
34; leading 107–8; destroyed by
individualism 108; must be based
on a common understanding of
the Dharma 108–9; creating 109;
creators of a garden 146; afraid of
claiming kinship with a star 286
Sangharakshita:
childhood and adolescence: family
60–70, 380, 449, 467; happy
69; sailing a boat 249; mirthful
282; spring 285; dancing round
the Maypole 430–1; don't touch
the red-hot pokers 434; holiday
455; reading 463–7; experience
of nature 465–6; wartime 468;
discovery of Buddhism 472–3
in India: teachers 23, 64, 92, 132,
392, 443, 457; telling parents
he was staying 62; arriving 115;
wandering days 115, 468; teaching
prostitutes 119–20; contact
with Dr Ambedkar and the New
Buddhists 125, 128; Kalimpong
131–5, 302; going for alms 204–5;

memories of past life in Tibet? 216–17

return to England: how parents had changed 62–3; drug-taking 81–2; period of wearing robes and long hair 90–1, 402; public life 91–2; personal life 92; presentation of the Dharma 109; sabbatical 139, 147; giving a lecture 382; bad red herring 402; founding of Triratna 420

old age: more past than future 22; all earthly blossoms scattered 282; frozen sap puts forth leaves and flowers 442; tired bones and a heart empty of desires 444; listening to the wireless 448; walking with a Roamer 460

death: funeral xxiv, xxx–xxxi, lv

characteristics and experiences: suffering xxxvii, 225, 380, 490; intuition 39; meditation 42–3, 44–6; devotion 47; dreams 61, 64–5, 424, 449; spiritual life 84, 115–16, 393; misunderstandings of 86; social conscience 125; 400; in love 276, 481–96; aspirations 282, 473; Bodhicitta 302, 473; authenticity 319; desires 373; dutifulness 400; disregarded 401; judgements of 402; life a dance 403; awareness of mortality 470, 473; response to the Dharma 472–3; no more desire for birth and death 473

reading: poetry xliv–xlv, lix–lx, 25, 73, 391, 465–6; Western literature compared to Mahāyāna *sūtras* lix; translations 26; led to the spiritual life 26, 477; Dharma books 132–3; the great reader 327; 'Myself into his book I hurled' 405; in childhood and adolescence 463–7, 469–70; effect of 466; to solve the riddle of mortality 466; disillusionment with 470–2

writing poetry: 'I do not care at all about writing any more poems' xxx; a 'spiritual autobiography' xxxiii; literary influences xliv–lx; comment on other poets xlvi; shift from poetry to prose li;

understanding one's own poems 23–4; autobiographical 25; the whole world was a poem 35–6; natural state in teenage years 36; intuition 39; a poem that came very smoothly 42; connection with meditation 46; spontaneous or worked on 47; experience of writing 49; criticized 86; spontaneous 100–1; 'for those who love me' 243; what I do for a living 329; no one to share them with me 380

Śāntideva 479
Sappho 285, 592n
Sarasvati 299
Savoldo, Girolamo 375
scapegoat 328, 350–1
Schiavone, Andrea 376
scholars xxxiii, 4–21, 246–7, 286, 423, 433
Scott, Paul 110
sea: whales in 53; our goal 164; tumult of 172; the Buddha's Sea of Peace 173; of light 176; the word of the Buddha, pure from snow to sea 193; emerald 201–202; a tower by the sea 213; islands in a spectral sea 218; overarched 253; swirl and swish of 263; boundless sea of space 264; leviathan's home 289; shells 317; Dead Sea 350; bliss a glassy sea 351; between the olive harvest and the sea 367; they threw me back into the sea 402; Icarus made the sea his home 427; holiday beside 455

See also ocean

seasons 162, 195, 229, 234, 239, 244, 283, 344–5, 439; autumn lv, 221, 277, 305, 306, 310, 343, 436, 466, 517; spring lvii, 162, 221, 281, 284, 285, 302, 303, 336, 341; summer 162, 219, 221, 238, 240, 281, 460, 464–5; winter lvii, 236, 246, 255, 284, 306–7, 310, 466

Sebastian, Saint 308

secret: of the universe 165; sought by sages 183; secret wings 185; love 225, 484, 486; of the oneness of *saṃsāra* and Nirvāṇa 226; of my breast 239; to learn a secret, tell one of your own 245; of your blood 277; secret garden 393; Venus' 428; secret valley, *see* Guhyaloka

self: reduced to a pinpoint 47; concealment of 89–90; 'trying to be ourselves' 93–4; abnegation 140; 'our separate selves shall cease' 166, 479; low couch of 214; not there 215; all thought of 'I' and 'mine' 219; suspended 276; being oneself 319, 323, 559; being and not-being 435; surrendered through perfect love 479

self-centredness 240–1

self-knowledge 74, 76, 91, 95, 103

selfishness 117, 220, 245, 482

senses, withdrawal from 276

separation: from people we love 117; who knows when we shall meet again? 310; union and 320; bitter wine of 446; starless night of 489

service 40, 44, 124, 140–1

Shakespeare, William 25, 412

Shelley, P. B. xl, xlv, xlvii–xlviii, l, lvii, lviii, 25, 151, 350, 407

shells 317

ship: of Death liv; of the Desert 319; sails on its way 446

See also boat

Shiva 274, 458

Shrimati Sophia Wadia 298–9

sickness: suffering of 117; Second Sight 179; mankind needs the Great Physician 190

Siddhārtha: Four Sights 178–80, 478; Going Forth 180, 273, 338, 491; and the wounded swan 200–202; austerities 252, 256–7, 272; given sustenance after austerities 252, 256; teachers 272; dream 295

silence: on retreat xxxv, 361, 367, 435; enduring in xxxvii; poetry emerging out of 35; no word to say before the Buddha 158; of the heart 167; Central Silence 172; voice of 276, 498; deeper 403; of the forest 408; after recognizing the ultimate nature of Selfless Love 482; living, breathing 493; of the temple 530–1; sinking deep into 574

silver birch, *see* birch

simplicity 80, 315

Siṃsapā Sutta xxxviii, 131–2

sin 164, 190, 209, 328, 419

six elements xxx–xxxi, 291, 440–1

snail 426

snake: pleasure likened to viper's bite 295; eaten by peacock 396; Mucalinda 398; cobra 445; Sesh 458

snow: words bright as snow-crystals lii, 313; deep lvii, 344; defiling virgin snows 50, 54, 447; swallows born of 157; pristine purity 164; simple-sublime 180; snowy heights 183; waters pure from snow to sea 193; sunlight on 199; adazzle with the snowfall 203; Tibet, Land of Snows 216, 275, 459; bamboos in 217; white wave of 219; footprints of starlings in 221; melting 230; in Summer 234; Abominable Snowman 246–7; loves colder and purer than 270; peaks halfway to Heaven 277; hills dappled with 284; of the Ideal 284; first Winter snow 310; life slips through our fingers like snow 324; untimely 336; snow-peaks thrones of gods 349; of Kanchenjunga 443; eternal 477; austere 479, 497

Snow White 358

soul: holy ground xxxiv, 17; Neoplatonic Soul 82, 85, 401; alms for 213; dark green depths 225; nature hieroglyphics of 239; purifying 267; between the feeling and the thought 286; a forest 409; fed by poetry 453

space: Glastonbury Tor 'swimming in' xxix, 504; element xxxi, 441; shatter time and space xxxv, 309; sacred xlii, 50, 54–5, 447; new words from lii, 313; needed to grow 140; the Buddha hid by veils of Time and Space 159; breaking the bonds of time and space 175; sea of 264; infinite space! 329; mandalas need 336; Windhorse,

king of space 338; launching
   oneself into 427; Love is above 481
sparrow 353, 395, 442
Spender, Stephen 57
Spirit, in Neoplatonism 85
spiritual bypassing 74-5
spiritual death 43, 82, 165
spiritual life: appreciating our
   early efforts 74; routine of 77;
   preparation 83; myth or legend in
   100; putting your heart into 102-3;
   acting with compassion an essential
   part of 116;
spiritual rebirth 29, 43, 275, 415
spontaneity 294, 403
spring, see seasons
squirrel 258, 307
starling 221
stars: apology to 55, 447; represent
   spiritual ideals in Sangharakshita's
   poetry 78; flickering 170; Morning
   Star 176, 201, 270, 356, 495; the
   starriness of things 185; like doves
   198; fragrance of compassion
   coming to meet you beneath 208;
   immensities of galactic systems
   262; ecstasy of 274; Evening Star
   277, 394, 495; bright pure faces
   279; kinship with 286; the moon's
   destined path among 287; sheds
   radiance from afar 383; names
   402; music of 485; a crest of
   dazzling 493
stillness: Nirvāṇa's xxxvii, 251;
   experience of 47-8; of a bow 166;
   of the temple at Kusinara 196; of
   the sky 206; dim green stillness of
   the pool 225; of the forest 408; of
   Guhyaloka 424
Stonehenge 320, 499
Stranger 86-7, 184
struggle: long storm and xxxix, 222;
   to meditate 44-5; to live without
   a mask 93; to be faithful 105; to
   understand 173; Dr Johnson's 370;
   to find words 560
subject/object 36
Suez crisis 283
suffering: the wounded heart xxxvii;
   physical and emotional 117; the
   first three sights 180; floods of
   sorrow 190; ; to be faced 203,
   479; anguish of mankind 237;
   as lakṣaṇa 295; of beings in hell
   355; of hungry ghosts 355; of love
   487-91
suicide 65, 314-5, 510-11
Sujata 256
summer, see seasons
sun: worshippers 55-6; our debt
   to 56; the Wheel of the Dharma
   like 169; path 182; beats fiercely
   240; after rain 273; Mañjuśrī
   275; worship 418; striving for, like
   Icarus 427; love 485-6
sunbird 234
sunflower lvi, 287, 343, 344
sunset: vision in meditation 43;
   watery gold 181; a flood of beauty
   198; shadows of the tired sun 211;
   all flecked with gold 224; shrouds
   the Evening Star 277; orange-
   amber bars 287; and the sunflower
   343; musing on 394; glows red
   in the West 493; Hercules sailed
   towards 515
supra-personal force xli, 450
Śūraṅgama Sūtra 31, 143, 588n
Sūtra of Wei Lang 26
Sutta Nipāta 15
Suzuki, Ven. Sochu 305
swallow 157, 164, 221, 302, 337,
   344, 353
swan xlviii, lv, 249, 264; flight of as
   metaphor for spiritual quest 182-3;
   tended by Siddhārtha 200-2
Swinburne, Algernon xlvi
sword 165, 275, 499; of wisdom 349,
   354, 445

Tagore, Rabindranath xxviii, l
Taj Mahal 283
Tannhäuser 428, 595n
Taoist 165
Tārā 293; White 304, 417; Green
   443
Tarashri 383, 594n
Teesta, River 283
temptation 281, 290, 434
tenderness xxxvi, 478; like that of a
   mother 207, 298, 479
Tennyson, Alfred Lord xlvi, 99, 106, 110

Thames, River 53, 276, 396
thoughts: inability to communicate
   6; first thoughts not always best
   thoughts 7, 594n; leaving behind
   all worldly 42; the bodhisattva's
   156; arising 162; anxious 166,
   167; thunders 172; what are
   the Buddha's? 173; night 176;
   Wesak 188–91; sickly 193; heart-
   thoughts 205; pruning budding
   thoughts 219; oozy 225; Maitreya
   deep in thoughts of love 233;
   calm 234; flew round and round
   238; strange 244; intellectual
   throne 258; building Nālanda
   on a foundation of thoughts 274;
   young thoughts come to aged souls
   303; hammer into a unity 304,
   592n; 'What thoughts are yours?'
   311; of sages 356; crowned with
   peace 435; of you 484; mind full
   of 577; not daring to acknowledge
   577, 582–3
Threefold Way 197
Tibet: travellers from 215–16; Land
   of Snows 216, 275, 459; trumpets
   237; Tibetan refugee 297; Potala
   297; Lama Govinda in 429
tiger 413, 419, 447
time: measuring by the seasons lv;
   the beginning of things, before
   time 82; what's the best use of our
   time? 113; and space 175; past
   and present 308, 390; breaking
   through time and space 309; will
   flow back to the beginning of things
   320; power of 367; and eternity
   393, 394; short 421; will cure 424;
   gods have no sense of 451
Tiresias 420
Titans 354, 397
Titian 376
Tobias 376
Tolstoy, Leo 104
tortoise 380
tramp 186
Transcendental: the mundane fears
   82; having a glimpse of 144; lute
   354; seed 381
transformation: of love xxvii; of the
   conditioned 73–4; what we are
   trying to transform 74; infinite 181;
   of desire 248; the poet transforms
   the world 359; of Mucalinda 398–
   9, 594n; of demons 419
transience lvi, 182, 221
   See also impermanence
trees: celebration of lvi; destruction
   of 236–7; falling 236, 242, 359,
   408; of wisdom, planting 253–4;
   in different seasons 306–7; dark
   old 310; communicating with 344;
   as seen by poet 359; call of the
   forest 408–9: sweeping leaves 436;
   planted at Padmaloka 457; in the
   garden 524
   See also individual names, bodhi
   tree, forest
Triratna Buddhist Order and
   community: consequences of
   commitment to the Three Jewels
   63; and family life 63; shouldn't
   be too comfortable 77; kesa
   91; being authentic as an Order
   member; 94; not perfect 94;
   chapter 95; and the Round Table
   99–100, 107; project of 103;
   headship of 107–8; College of
   Public Preceptors 108, 109; social
   conscience 125; working together
   harmoniously 128; centres,
   purpose of 141; preparing for
   ordination 144; a dance 145;
   Mitraship 146; metaphor of a
   garden 146, 148; from seed to tree
   420
Tristan, Sir 406
Trungpa, Chögyam xxviii, 92, 323
truth: beauty is truth, truth beauty
   xxxiv; literal 19; a whole world of
   new truths 46; naked 93; speaking
   116; living 156; fading 168; quest
   of 185; to Truth alone submit
   186; sublime 188; foundation 191;
   thirst for 193; must be proclaimed
   through living, breathing lips 197;
   banner 197; only truth if a path
   that guides 203; striving for 203,
   354; pledged to 203; winning 204,
   245; what it is, none could ever say
   237, 242; the Truth all men desire

240; giving the heart to Truth 245; like sunlight on a distant hill 257; cold mountain-peak 258; questioned 259; the Buddha shed upon all the beams of truth 296; arduous pilgrimage 298; striving for 354; we don't want to hear 358; a beauty-truth that cannot err 359; within the faithful heart 367; errors in the household of Truth 368; revealing 373; embodied 389; Wheel of 405; serving Truth and Beauty 429; in books 467; bright as 472; golden links of 519; of Imagination (Keats) 588n
See also Four Noble Truths
Tsongkhapa 275, 592
tulips 337, 416
Tuscany: Il Convento 367, 380, 513; hunters 516-7
twin towers 452

understanding, intellectual: mistaking names for knowledge 242, 538; there are some things we *don't* understand 247; 'intellectual throne' 258; brain fed with facts 453
unfathomable: everything is 133; mystery of existence 487
ungraspable: Life 324; stepping out into 427; love 491
universe: mystery of 133; breath of 162; secret of 165; worships the Dharma 169; birth and dissolution of 227; the Buddha's knowledge of 262; within a room 465; interconnectedness of 482; every atom of reflected in the heart 497

values 57
vanity 240-1
vegetarianism 58
Venice 377
views, no need for abuse on account of 17
Vimalakīrti 349, 593n
violence 58, 241, 519, 592n; abstaining from 116
violets 311, 336, 464

Vishnu 458
vision: making something come into being 104-5; need for strong vision 143; acquainting ourselves with other people's vision 144; seeing as the Buddha sees 159; the Buddha's heights of 193; of the poet 240; the spiritual war for 339; fourfold 340; glimpses 389; arising of 531-2
visualization 43
Vivian 438, 452
Vltava, River 405
Void, the: forest vast of 181; perfume of 219; mystery of 248; beauty of 258
vulture 250, 295
Vulture's Peak 325, 593n

war: bloodstained centuries 188-90; atom bomb 228; wonder that Beauty stays in a violent world 270: Kalinga 271; the distance between peace and war 321; for truth 354; inner and outer 398; body bags 445
wasteland 146
water: from the thawed-out snow 164; of the Buddha's words 193; praise of 289; red leaf on the lake 300; element 440
See also rivers, ocean, sea
waterfall 242
Wesak (Buddha Day) 173, 184, 188-91, 252-4
whales 51, 53, 447
Wheel of Life 226, 354-6
white calf 206-7
White Lotus Sūtra 325
White Tārā, *see* Tārā
Whitman, Walt liii, lvii
wilderness: of the world 146; of words 194
will 221, 450
William Rufus 329
willow 211, 306, 311
wind: in my sails xli, 450, air element 440
See also worldly winds
Windhorse 337-8
winter, *see* seasons
wisdom: three levels of 14-15; and love 173, 270, 491; and compassion

251, 286; let it be honoured 263;
wisely existence viewing 295; not
being fooled by worldly things 332;
sword of 349, 354, 445; cold 378;
of White Tārā 417
withdrawal: from worldly thoughts
and passions 42; and service 44;
recoiling from the world as the
burnt hand from the fire 176; from
the senses 276
See also renunciation
Woden 396
wonders: the wondering heart xxxvi,
368; the moon as an object of
wonder 54; of Going for Refuge
209; we've lost the wonder of it
all 233; the song of Orpheus 254;
to dwell in hills without a human
past 292; cause to wonder and to
praise 393; manifold 451;
wonderland of thought 463;
wondrous fragrance 472; wonder
at the coming of love 481
Woolf, Virginia 410–1
words: consulting the dictionary
7–9; out of silence 36; in jest
165; Wilderness of 194; false 203;
finding no words 237; translation
312; pristine 313; soiled 313,
484; sufficient to say what the
heart means 336; of angels
365; wisdom distilled in words
by subtlest art 373; divine, of
blackbird song 395; of the Buddha
399, 402; defile 404; revealed to
the poet 436; cruel 490; unknown
501–2; inadequate 560
Wordsworth, William xlv, xlvi, 412
work: spiritual 83–4; dehumanizing
111–12, 122–3, 260–1; pleasurable
145; the peasant's labour 177; the
sullen millions languish 186; of the
charcoal-burners 236; the Great
Work 267; round and round like
dumb chained cattle we go 301; is
the companion 400
world: refugees from xxxvi, 503;
hapless xxxx, 214; of mysteries
and magnitudes xlix, 175; build
for new men a new world liii, 313;
the Mahāyāna *sūtras* transport

one to other worlds 11; Graeco-
Roman 20; being attracted by
the Dharma rather than repelled
by the world 31; a poem 36; of
pain 41, 43–4, 167; turning away
from 42, 195; ascent into a more
colourful world 43; of new truths
46; taking meditation out into
48; apology to 51; feeling for
the natural world 54; raising our
voices in protest against damage to
the world 58–9; born into because
of *kleśas* 75; idea that we have
come from some other world 87;
problems 125; beyond the world
(*lokuttara*) 144; wilderness 146;
the Buddha's abodes in a million
worlds 158; seeing the world
through the Buddha's eyes 159;
conquering new worlds 162; ten
thousand million 176; the hope
of 180; myriad 182; tumult 183,
227; seeing as dark or bright 185;
the reign of love in 190; an empty
dream 195; sick of 196; dense
ignorance of 202; sad 208; forlorn
210; has one need – boundless love
210; lost 214; stumbling from
this world to the stars 215; world-
oblivious ecstasy 220; transience
of 221; harsh 225; we've made the
world look mean and small 233;
beauty of 240, 243; white ash of
271; of flame and shadow 295; the
dust of 311; see the whole world
bright 340; suffering 349; the poet
is the world's interpreter 359; the
Buddha looks at the world with
compassion 398; naked we come
into 423; far away 435; continues
on its crazy course 445; news 448;
degenerate 459; the Bodhisattva's
compassion flows through the
world 479, 497
See also earth
worldly winds 368, 425
wrathful 399, 419

Yashodhara 180–2, 228, 491
Yeats, W. B. xlvii, xlix, liii–liv, lv,
232, 304, 592n

Yeshe Tsogyal 459

Zen: The bigger the heap of clay, the bigger the Buddha 73; the golden flower 320, 322, 404, 595n; Blue Cliff 342; Zen Master arriving Monday 363; 'Grain threshed and ready?' 414; poetry 480

Zeus 258, 397

INDEX OF TITLES

A Crumb From the Symposium 270
A Fantasy 454
A Life 282
'A Man was Walking Behind
   Me...' 390
A Rainy Day in the Mountains 244
A Wish 373
'Above Me Broods...' 175
Advent 79, 184
After Abú Sa'íd 381
After Meditation 307
After Reading the Vimalakirti-
   Nirdesha 349
After Rilke 359
After Visiting New Zealand 415
Alexandrines Perhaps 350
Animist 233
An Apology 50, 447
An Old Story 390
Argosies 249
Aspiration 181
At the Barber's 329
Autumn Vignette 343
Awakening 243

Bamboo Orchids 224
Bamboos 217
Before an Image of the Buddha 158
Before an Image of the Buddha 173
Before Dawn 348
Betrayal 388

Bhájá, 1983 374
Birds and Their Gods 395
'Blake Walked Among the Stones of
   Fire...' 360
Buddham Saranam Gacchami 209
Buffaloes Being Driven to Market 235

Calcutta 262
Certainties 259
Chairlift 325
Chinese Poems 310
Contraries 400
Criminals 330
Crystal Ball 403

Dana Parami 160
Dancing Round the Maypole 430
Defiance 271
Diptych 399
Donne's Bell 422
Dream 324

East is East 432
Easter Retreat 333
Eight Tuscan Haiku 380
Elusive Beauty 269
Epigram on Molly the Medium 374
Epitaph on a 'Poem' 288
Epitaph on Krishna, Princess Irene's
   Squirrel 258

'Every day is a good day' 342
Ex Libris 404

For P—— on Solitary Retreat 394
For the Record 314
'Forgive Me if I Have Stained...' 230
Four Gifts 138, 335
Four Haiku 403
Fourth Metamorphosis 319
'From the Ever-Faithful
  Present...' 308
Frozen Tulips 416
Frustration 221

Goldfish 225
Greenstone 353
Guhyaloka, July 1998 424
Guhyaloka, September 1999 435

Hercules and the Birds 512
Hieroglyphics 239
Himalayan Sages 183
Homage to William Blake 340
Hope 275
Hope 349

I am sitting in the late afternoon
  sunshine 444
I. M., J. and K. 342
I. M., Tarashri 383
'I Think There Lives More
  Wisdom...' 239
'I Want to Break Out...' 309
Immensities 262
In Krakow 442
In Memory of Allen Ginsberg 413
In Praise of Water 289
In the New Forest 329
'In the Woods are Many More' 130, 241
Inaccessible 222
Invocation 214
'It is not Love that Seeks to
  Bind...' 223

Jewels 526
Joy in Flight 266
Justice and Pity 437

Kalimpong 389
Kalinga 271
Kanchenjunga 219

Lama Govinda in Capri 429
Lepcha Song 283
Letter to Ānanda 420
Life and Death 280
Life is King 324
Life's Furnace 221
Lines Composed on Acquiring
  'The Works of Samuel Johnson,
  LL.D.', in Eleven Volumes,
  MDCCLXXXVII 370
Lines Composed on Retreat During a
  Period of Silence 361
Lines to Jayapushpa on Her Return to
  Malaysia 369
Lines Written for the Dedication of
  the Shrine and the Opening of the
  London Buddhist Centre 346
London Bridge 404
London in Wartime 155
Longing 229
Looking at the Moon on a Frosty
  Night 255
Love's Austerity 223
Lovelace Revisited 357
Lumbini 232

Madrigal 259
Maitreya 233
Man's Way 240
Manifesto 243
'Many Were The Friends...' 226
May 341
Meditation 41, 167
Meditation on a Flame 291
Memory 276
Messengers from Tibet 216
Minerva's Rebuke to Jean
  Cocteau 378
Mirrors 326
Mother 318
Mother Goose Revisited 426
Mountains 218
Mr Wireless 448
Mucalinda 398
Music at Night 167
My Life 403
My Pearl 401
My Secret Garden 393
'My Soul Between the Feeling and the
  Thought...' 286

Nagarjunikonda 263
Nālanda Revisited 274
Neighbours 384
New 313
Night Thoughts 176
No Word 237
Nocturne 265

On a Certain Author 405
On a Political Procession 258
On Glastonbury Tor 499
On the Brink 211
Orpheus in the Underworld 312

Padmaloka 344
Padmasambhava 419
Paradise Lost 386
Peace 195
People Like Things Labelled 402
Petals 316
Planting the Bodhi Tree 302
Plato's Reply 232
Poems for Four Friends 305
Poems on Paintings From the 'Genius of Venice' Exhibition at the Royal Academy 375
Poet and Muse 433
Points of View 300
Possibilities 274

Queens Past and Present 432

Rain 177
Reality Telegrams 362
Reciprocity 245
Remembering Arthadarshin 435
Remembering the Poetry Reading 404
Resurrection 352
Return Journey 290
Revenge 416
Revised Version 423
Ruba'i 156

Salutation to the Lady from the Land of Snows 459
Sangharakshita's Verses of Acknowledgement 331
Sappho 285
Say Padmaloka 457
Scapegoat 328
Secret Wings 185

Sequence in a Strange Land 336
Shells 317
Shiva and the Love God 458
Siddhartha's Dream 295
Snow-White Revisited 358
Song 231
Song of the Windhorse 338
Splendor Solis 418
Spring 302
Spring – Winter 284
Sri Pada 187
St Francis and the Birds 366
St Jerome in the Desert 312
Study in Blue and White 284
Summer Afternoon 240
'Surely King Mark was Mad...' 406
Systole and Diastole 162

Taking Refuge in the Buddha 250
Ten Vignettes 306
Tendai 207
The Abominable Snowman 246
The Alms of Compassion 213
The Angel in the House 410
'The Ashes of all my Heartaches...' 222
The Awakening of the Heart 463
The Ballad of Journeyman Death 334
The Ballad of the Return Journey 382
The Beguiling of Merlin 452
The Birthplace of Compassion 210
The Bluebell Wood 456
The Bodhisattva 220
The Bodhisattva's Reply 111, 260
The Brahmas and the Sages 451
The Buddha 296
The Call of the Forest 408
The Caves of Bhájá 505
The Charcoal-Burners 236
The Citadel 197
The Clouded Dragon 172
The Conquest of Māra 256
The Cosmic Dreamer 458
The Crystal Rosary 304
The Cult of the Young Hero 279
The Dance of Death 415
The Double Root 433
The Dream 361
The Economic Argument 437
The Evening Walk 224
The Ever-Beating Heart 159

The Face of Silence 198
The Family Reunion 60, 449
The Four Sights 178
The Fragrance of Compassion 214
The Gardener 219
The Gods 345
The Gods 400
The Golden Flower 379
The Great Burning 436
The Great Reader 327
The Great Things of Guhyaloka 391
The Great Work 267
The Guardian Wall 293
The Guru of Dharsendo 392
The Holiday 455
The Heart's No 230
The Lamp of Compassion 215
The Listener 436
The Lord of Compassion 202
The Lotus of Compassion 208
The Martyrdom of Saint Sebastian 308
The Mask 88, 309
The Message of the Bowl 204
The Minor Poets 412
The Modern Bard 254
The Moon of Beauty 168
The Neoplatonists 401
The Oak and the Ivy 387
The Only Way 210
The Parable of the Plough 174
'The Past is in the Mind...' 390
The People 301
The People of Bethnal Green 385
The Pilgrim 428
The Pioneer 256
The Poet 414
The Poet's Eye 240
The Poet's Reply 192
The Poetry of Friendship 407
The Priest's Dream 347
The Quest 272
The Rain of Dharma 156
The Realms of Existence as Depicted in the Tibetan Wheel of Life 354
The River 157
The Root Speaks 71, 229
The Sangha 286
The Scapegoat 350
The Scholars 286
The Secret 226
The Silver Spoon 444

The Sirens 348
The Six Elements Speak 440
The Stream of Stars 264
The Stricken Giant 359
The Sun-Path 182
The Sunflower's Farewell 343
The Survivor 242
The Taoist Teacher 165
The Teacher of Gods and Men 402
The Three Marks 295
The Time Has Come... 323
The Tramp 186
The Tree of Wisdom 252
The Twin Towers 452
The Two Risks 456
The Unseen Flower 215
The Vase of Moonlight 264
The Veil of Stars 483
The Voice of Silence 276
The Wandering Singer 170
The Warning Voice 434
The Wheel of Dharma 169
The White Calf 206
The Wind 450
The Wondering Heart 368
The Word of the Buddha 193
The Wounded Swan 200
The Young Hills 292
Then and Now 431
There is a Land More Lovely 389
Three Arthurian Poems 97, 438
Three Couplet Haiku 300
Three Epitaphs 379
Three Plumes 411
Three Rubáiyát 372
Tibetan Refugee 297
Tibetan Trumpets 237
Time and Eternity 393
'Tired of the Crimson Curtain...' 194
To —— 287
To a Political Friend 166
To C— 427
To Chenrezi 164
To Deji 453
To Mañjuśri 275
To Michal, with a photograph 444
To my friend Paramartha 453
To My Teacher, Chattrul Sangye Dorje 443
To P—— in Prague 405

To Paramartha in London 454
To Shrimati Sophia Wadia in Honour of her Sixtieth Birthday 298
To the Recumbent Buddha 196
Too Late 347
Transformation 248
Transience 221
Transmission 414
Triolet 281
Truth, Love, Life and Man 203
Tuscany 1983 367

'Up and Down the Gravel Path…' 238
Up and Down the Gravel Path: an Update 460

Variations on a Mersey Sound i 320
Variations on a Mersey Sound ii 321
Village India 212
Visiting the Taj Mahal at the Time of the Suez Canal Crisis and Seeing the Tombs of the Emperor Shah Jahan and Mumtaz Mahal 283

Waiting in the Car 303
'Water From the Thawed-Out Snow…' 164
Wesak Joy 184
Wesak Thoughts 188
'White Mist Drifts Down the Valley Dim…' 218
White Tārā 417
Winter in the Hills 255
Wish 315
Work and Play 400
Written after Hearing a Radio Programme on Dementia 447

Yashodhara 228
Yemen Revisited 373
Yesterday's Blossoms 402

Zen 404

A GUIDE TO THE COMPLETE WORKS OF SANGHARAKSHITA

Gathered together in these twenty-seven volumes are talks and stories, commentaries on the Buddhist scriptures, poems, memoirs, reviews, and other writings. The genres are many, and the subject matter covered is wide, but it all has – its whole purpose is to convey – that taste of freedom which the Buddha declared to be the hallmark of his Dharma. Another traditional description of the Buddha's Dharma is that it is *ehipassiko*, 'come and see'. Sangharakshita calls to us, his readers, to come and see how the Dharma can fundamentally change the way we see things, change the way we live for the better, and change the society we belong to, wherever in the world we live.

Sangharakshita's very first published piece, *The Unity of Buddhism* (found in volume 7 of this collection), appeared in 1944 when he was eighteen years old, and it introduced themes that continued to resound throughout his work: the basis of Buddhist ethics, the compassion of the bodhisattva, and the transcendental unity of Buddhism. Over the course of the following seven decades not only did numerous other works flow from his pen; he gave hundreds of talks (some now lost). In gathering all we could find of this vast output, we have sought to arrange it in a way that brings a sense of coherence, communicating something essential about Sangharakshita, his life and teaching. Recalling the three 'baskets' among which an early tradition divided the Buddha's teachings, we have divided Sangharakshita's creative output into six 'baskets' or groups: foundation texts; works originating in India; teachings originally given in the West; commentaries on the Buddhist scriptures; personal writings; and poetry, aphorisms, and works on the arts. The 27th volume, a concordance, brings together all the terms and themes of the whole collection. If you want to find a particular story or teaching, look at a traditional term from different points of view or in different contexts, or track down one of the thousands of canonical references to be found in these volumes, the concordance will be your guide.

1. FOUNDATION

What is the foundation of a Buddhist life? How do we understand and then follow the Buddha's path of Ethics, Meditation, and Wisdom? What is really meant by 'Going for Refuge to the Three Jewels', described by Sangharakshita as the essential act of a Buddhist life? And what is the Bodhisattva ideal, which he has called 'one of the sublimest ideals mankind has ever seen'? In the 'Foundation' group you will find teachings on all these themes. It includes the author's *magnum opus, A Survey of Buddhism*, a collection of teachings on *The Purpose and Practice of Buddhist Meditation*, and the anthology, *The Essential Sangharakshita*, an eminently helpful distillation of the entire corpus.

2. INDIA

From 1950 to 1964 Sangharakshita, based in Kalimpong in the eastern Himalayas, poured his energy into trying to revive Buddhism in the land of its birth and to revitalize and bring reform to the existing Asian Buddhist world. The articles and book reviews from this period are gathered in volumes 7 and 8, as well as his biographical sketch of the great Sinhalese Dharmaduta, Anagārika Dharmapala. In 1954 Sangharakshita took on the editing of the *Maha Bodhi*, a journal for which he wrote a monthly editorial, and which, under his editorship, published the work of many of the leading Buddhist writers of the time. It was also during these years in India that a vital connection was forged with Dr B. R. Ambedkar, renowned Indian statesman and leader of the Buddhist mass conversion of 1956. Sangharakshita became closely involved with the new Buddhists and, after Dr Ambedkar's untimely death, visited them regularly on extensive teaching tours.

From 1979, when an Indian wing of the Triratna Buddhist Community was founded (then known as TBMSG), Sangharakshita returned several times to undertake further teaching tours. The talks from these tours are collected in volumes 9 and 10 along with a unique work on Ambedkar and his life which draws out the significance of his conversion to Buddhism.

3. THE WEST

Sangharakshita founded the Triratna Buddhist Community (then called the Friends of the Western Buddhist Order) on 6 April 1967. On 7 April the following year he performed the first ordinations of men and women within the Triratna Buddhist Order (then the Western Buddhist Order). At that time Buddhism was not widely known in the West and for the following two decades or so he taught intensively, finding new ways to communicate the ancient truths of Buddhism, drawing on the whole Buddhist tradition to do so, as well as making connections with what was best in existing Western culture. Sometimes his sword flashed as he critiqued ideas and views inimical to the Dharma. It is these teachings and writings that are gathered together in this third group.

4. COMMENTARY

Throughout Sangharakshita's works are threaded references to the Buddhist canon of literature – Pāli, Mahāyāna, and Vajrayāna – from which he drew his inspiration. In the early days of the new movement he often taught by means of seminars in which, prompted by the questions of his students, he sought to pass on the inspiration and wisdom of the Buddhist tradition. Each seminar was based around a different text, the seminars were recorded and transcribed, and in due course many of the transcriptions were edited and turned into books, all carefully checked by Sangharakshita. The commentaries compiled in this way constitute the fourth group. In some ways this is the heart of the collection. Sangharakshita often told the story of how it was that, reading two *sūtras* at the age of sixteen or seventeen, he realized that he was a Buddhist, and he has never tired of showing others how they too could see and realize the value of the '*sūtra*-treasure'.

5. MEMOIRS

Who is Sangharakshita? What sort of life did he live? Whom did he meet? What did he feel? Why did he found a new Buddhist movement? In these volumes of memoirs and letters Sangharakshita shares with his readers much about himself and his life as he himself has experienced it, giving us a sense of its breadth and depth, humour and pathos.

6. POETRY, APHORISMS, AND THE ARTS

Sangharakshita describes reading *Paradise Lost* at the age of twelve as one of the greatest poetic experiences of his life. His realization of the value of the higher arts to spiritual development is one of his distinctive contributions to our understanding of what Buddhist life is, and he has expressed it in a number of essays and articles. Throughout his life he has written poetry which he says can be regarded as a kind of spiritual autobiography. It is here, perhaps, that we come closest to the heart of Sangharakshita. He has also written a few short stories and composed some startling aphorisms. Through book reviews he has engaged with the experiences, ideas, and opinions of modern writers. All these are collected in this sixth group.

In the preface to *A Survey of Buddhism* (volume 1 in this collection), Sangharakshita wrote of his approach to the Buddha's teachings:

> Why did the Buddha (or Nāgārjuna, or Buddhaghosa) teach this particular doctrine? What bearing does it have on the spiritual life? How does it help the individual Buddhist actually to follow the spiritual path?... I found myself asking such questions again and again, for only in this way, I found, could I make sense – spiritual sense – of Buddhism.

Although this collection contains so many words, they are all intent, directly or indirectly, on these same questions. And all these words are not in the end about their writer, but about his great subject, the Buddha and his teaching, and about you, the reader, for whose benefit they are solely intended. These pages are full of the reverence that Sangharakshita has always felt, which is expressed in an early poem, 'Taking Refuge in the Buddha', whose refrain is 'My place is at thy feet'. He has devoted his life to communicating the Buddha's Dharma in its depth and in its breadth, to men and women from all backgrounds and walks of life, from all countries, of all races, of all ages. These collected works are the fruit of that devotion.

We are very pleased to be able to include some previously unpublished work in this collection, but most of what appears in these volumes has been published before. We have made very few changes, though we have added extra notes where we thought they would be useful. We have had the pleasure of researching the notes in the Sangharakshita Library at 'Adhisthana', Triratna's centre in Herefordshire, UK, which houses his own collection of books. It has been of great value to be able to search among the very copies of the *suttas*, *sūtras* and commentaries that have provided the basis of his teachings over the last seventy years.

The publication of these volumes owes much to the work of transcribers, editors, indexers, designers, and publishers over many years – those who brought out the original editions of many of the works included here, and those who have contributed in all sorts of ways to this *Complete Works* project, including all those who contributed to funds given in celebration of Sangharakshita's ninetieth birthday in August 2015, and to a further outpouring of generosity after Sangharakshita's death in October 2018. All these donors have made the publication of this series possible, and we are very grateful. Many thanks to everyone who has helped; may the merit gained in our acting thus go to the alleviation of the suffering of all beings.

Vidyadevi and Kalyanaprabha
Editors

THE COMPLETE WORKS OF SANGHARAKSHITA

I FOUNDATION

VOLUME 1 A SURVEY OF BUDDHISM / THE BUDDHA'S NOBLE EIGHTFOLD PATH
A Survey of Buddhism
The Buddha's Noble Eightfold Path

2 THE THREE JEWELS I
The Three Jewels
The Meaning of Conversion in Buddhism
Going for Refuge
The Ten Pillars of Buddhism
The History of My Going for Refuge
My Relation to the Order
Extending the Hand of Fellowship
Forty-Three Years Ago
Was the Buddha a Bhikkhu?

3 THE THREE JEWELS II
Who is the Buddha?
What is the Dharma?
What is the Sangha?

4 THE BODHISATTVA IDEAL
The Bodhisattva Ideal
The Endlessly Fascinating Cry (seminar)
The Bodhisattva Principle

5 THE PURPOSE AND PRACTICE OF BUDDHIST MEDITATION
The Purpose and Practice of Buddhist Meditation

6 THE ESSENTIAL SANGHARAKSHITA
The Essential Sangharakshita

II INDIA

7 CROSSING THE STREAM: INDIA WRITINGS I
Early Writings 1944–1954
Crossing the Stream
Buddhism in the Modern World:
  Cultural and Political Implications
The Meaning of Orthodoxy in Buddhism
Buddhism in India Today
Ordination and Initiation in the Three Yānas
A Bird's Eye View of Indian Buddhism

VOLUME 8 BEATING THE DHARMA DRUM: INDIA WRITINGS II
Anagarika Dharmapala and Other 'Maha Bodhi' Writings
Dharmapala: The Spiritual Dimension
Beating the Drum: 'Maha Bodhi' Editorials

9 DR AMBEDKAR AND THE REVIVAL OF BUDDHISM I
Ambedkar and Buddhism
Lecture Tour in India, December 1981–March 1982

10 DR AMBEDKAR AND THE REVIVAL OF BUDDHISM II
Lecture Tours in India 1979 & 1983–1992
Other Edited Lectures and Seminar Material

III THE WEST

11 A NEW BUDDHIST MOVEMENT I
Ritual and Devotion in Buddhism
The Buddha's Victory
The Taste of Freedom
Buddha Mind
Human Enlightenment
New Currents in Western Buddhism
Buddhism for Today – and Tomorrow
Buddhism and the West
Aspects of Buddhist Morality
Buddhism, World Peace, and Nuclear War
Dialogue between Buddhism and Christianity
Buddhism and Blasphemy
Buddhism and the Bishop of Woolwich
Buddhism and the New Reformation
Great Buddhists of the Twentieth Century
Articles and Interviews

12 A NEW BUDDHIST MOVEMENT II
Previously unpublished talks

13 EASTERN AND WESTERN TRADITIONS
Tibetan Buddhism
Creative Symbols of Tantric Buddhism
The Essence of Zen
The FWBO and 'Protestant Buddhism'
From Genesis to the Diamond Sūtra

IV COMMENTARY

VOLUME 14   THE ETERNAL LEGACY / WISDOM BEYOND WORDS
The Eternal Legacy
The Glory of the Literary World
Wisdom Beyond Words

15   PĀLI CANON TEACHINGS AND TRANSLATIONS
Dhammapada (translation)
Karaṇīyamettā Sutta (translation)
Living with Kindness
Living with Awareness
Maṅgala Sutta (translation)
Auspicious Signs (seminar)
Salutation to the Three Jewels (translation)
The Threefold Refuge (seminar)
Further Pāli Sutta Commentaries

16   MAHĀYĀNA MYTHS AND STORIES
The Drama of Cosmic Enlightenment
The Priceless Jewel (talk)
Transforming Self and World
The Inconceivable Emancipation

17   WISDOM TEACHINGS OF THE MAHĀYĀNA
Know Your Mind
Living Ethically
Living Wisely
The Way to Wisdom (seminar)

18   MILAREPA AND THE ART OF DISCIPLESHIP I
The Yogi's Joy
The Shepherd's Search for Mind
Rechungpa's Journey to Enlightenment

19   MILAREPA AND THE ART OF DISCIPLESHIP II
Rechungpa's Journey to Enlightenment, continued

V MEMOIRS

20   THE RAINBOW ROAD FROM TOOTING BROADWAY TO KALIMPONG
The Rainbow Road from Tooting Broadway to Kalimpong

VOLUME	21	FACING MOUNT KANCHENJUNGA

               Facing Mount Kanchenjunga
               Dear Dinoo: Letters to a Friend

     22   IN THE SIGN OF THE GOLDEN WHEEL
               In the Sign of the Golden Wheel
               Precious Teachers
               With Allen Ginsberg in Kalimpong (essay)

     23   MOVING AGAINST THE STREAM
               Moving Against the Stream
               1970: A Retrospect

     24   THROUGH BUDDHIST EYES
               Travel Letters
               Through Buddhist Eyes

               VI POETRY AND THE ARTS

     25   POEMS AND SHORT STORIES
               Complete Poems 1941–1994
               Other Poems
               Short Stories

     26   APHORISMS AND THE ARTS
               Peace is a Fire
               A Stream of Stars
               The Religion of Art
               In the Realm of the Lotus
               The Journey to Il Convento
               St Jerome Revisited
               A Note on the Burial of Count Orgaz
               Criticism East and West
               Alternative Traditions
               The Artist's Dream and other Parables
               A Moseley Miscellany
               Adhisthana Writings
               Urthona Articles and Interviews

     27   CONCORDANCE AND APPENDICES

WINDHORSE PUBLICATIONS

Windhorse Publications is a Buddhist charitable company based in the UK. We produce books of high quality that are accessible and relevant to all those interested in Buddhism, at whatever level of interest and commitment. We are the main publisher of Sangharakshita, the founder of the Triratna Buddhist Order and Community. Our books draw on the whole range of the Buddhist tradition, including translations of traditional texts, commentaries, books that make links with contemporary culture and ways of life, biographies of Buddhists, and works on meditation.

To subscribe to the *Complete Works of Sangharakshita*, please go to: windhorsepublications.com/sangharakshita-complete-works/

THE TRIRATNA BUDDHIST COMMUNITY

Windhorse Publications is a part of the Triratna Buddhist Community, an international movement with centres in Europe, India, North and South America and Australasia. At these centres, members of the Triratna Buddhist Order offer classes in meditation and Buddhism. Activities of the Triratna Community also include retreat centres, residential spiritual communities, ethical Right Livelihood businesses, and the Karuna Trust, a UK fundraising charity that supports social welfare projects in the slums and villages of India.

Through these and other activities, Triratna is developing a unique approach to Buddhism, not simply as a philosophy and a set of techniques, but as a creatively directed way of life for all people living in the conditions of the modern world.

For more information please visit thebuddhistcentre.com